Red Star Down

ALSO BY D. B. JOHN

FICTION

Flight from Berlin
Star of the North

NON-FICTION

The Girl with Seven Names, co-written with Hyeonseo Lee

RED STAR DOWN

D. B. John

HARVILL

1 3 5 7 9 10 8 6 4 2

Harvill, an imprint of Vintage, is part of the
Penguin Random House group of companies

Vintage, Penguin Random House UK, One Embassy Gardens,
8 Viaduct Gardens, London SW11 7BW

penguin.co.uk/vintage
global.penguinrandomhouse.com

First published by Harvill in 2025

Copyright © D. B. John 2025

The moral right of the author has been asserted

This is a work of fiction. In some cases, real life figures appear but their actions and conversations are often fictionalised and are the products of the author's imagination.

Penguin Random House values and supports copyright. Copyright fuels creativity, encourages diverse voices, promotes freedom of expression and supports a vibrant culture. Thank you for purchasing an authorised edition of this book and for respecting intellectual property laws by not reproducing, scanning or distributing any part of it by any means without permission. You are supporting authors and enabling Penguin Random House to continue to publish books for everyone. No part of this book may be used or reproduced in any manner for the purpose of training artificial intelligence technologies or systems. In accordance with Article 4(3) of the DSM Directive 2019/790, Penguin Random House expressly reserves this work from the text and data mining exception.

Typeset in 10.75/15.75pt Scala Pro by Six Red Marbles UK, Thetford, Norfolk
Printed and bound in Great Britain by Clays Ltd, Elcograf S.p.A.

The authorised representative in the EEA is Penguin Random House Ireland,
Morrison Chambers, 32 Nassau Street, Dublin D02 YH68

A CIP catalogue record for this book is available from the British Library

HB ISBN 9781787301801
TPB ISBN 9781787301818

Penguin Random House is committed to a sustainable future
for our business, our readers and our planet. This book is made
from Forest Stewardship Council® certified paper.

For my grandfather,
D. Maldwyn James

This is a historical novel loosely set in the tumultuous months between Donald Trump's inauguration as president of the United States in 2017 and his bizarre summits with Kim Jong-un and Vladimir Putin the following year.

Excerpt from Glossary of Intelligence Terms and Definitions

CLASSIFIED

CIA Directorate of Operations

SEED-BEARING PROGRAM:

1. Originally (1970s—90s): a long-term North Korean conspiracy to abduct hundreds of randomly selected foreign nationals, mostly from remote beaches in Japan and South Korea, and compel them to become covert overseas operatives for the North Korean state.
2. More recently (1990s—2011): a long-term North Korean conspiracy to train the abduction victims' children, who were born and raised in North Korea, as covert overseas operatives for the North Korean state.

The Program was controlled by Section 915 of the Organization and Guidance Department of the North Korean Workers' Party, reporting directly to Kim Jong-il until his death in 2011. Now considered terminated.
[entry updated: 2012/05/04]

Prologue

Barrikadnaya Street
Moscow
January 2017

The moment he'd learned he would be in the studio audience, sitting just meters from the president *on live television,* Lyosha had found concentration almost impossible. For the next two days he'd gone through the motions of showing up for his law lectures at university, had taken no notes, and had recalled nothing of them afterward. His dissertation work, so engrossing and urgent two days ago, now seemed trivial and irrelevant.

One minute he was feeling such exhilaration that he could hardly breathe. The next he was almost hysterical with fear. His hockey training helped. He could calm his nerves by staying behind for solo practice at the CSKA Arena, doing sets of two-hundred-meter ice sprints, and four-hundred-meter laps around the rink. This left him physically wrecked but so buzzing with adrenaline that he couldn't sleep, so he'd get up and drink three shots of vodka in quick succession. That, too, helped. He wasn't much of a drinker and felt the effect strongly.

The organizers of *Direct Line with Vladimir Putin* had called Lyosha within hours of him registering his interest on the show's website. A woman from the production team named Polina had wanted to know a few things about him, his background, his opinions, his plans for the future. He'd tried to sound sunny and eager and humble all at once and had told her that the question he'd really, really like to ask the president was this: "What can be done to encourage talented youths like myself to make our careers in Russia and not be lured abroad by the false promises and hypocrisy of the West?"

Lyosha had agonized over this question. On the one hand it was an easy patriotic softball; on the other it carried a whiff of subversion because it was asking the president to admit what most people knew: that any graduate with half a brain was tempted to leg it to the West. But the woman on the end of the line had brightened at once. "That's a great question, Lyosha," she'd said. "We'll call you back." He'd guessed that the FSB, the internal police, were running a check to make sure he wasn't on a database as a dissident or an extremist, and he did worry that he'd been caught on camera at one of the massive student protests he'd attended where he'd chanted "PUTIN IS A THIEF!" along with thousands of others. But to his surprise Polina had called him back. She'd double-checked his question by repeating it slowly back to him and asking him to confirm it. He knew they were making sure that nothing caught the show's star by surprise, or, most terrifying for them, embarrassed him.

The next morning, he'd received the invitation by email.

Bozhe pomogi mne. God help me. This is it.

For a while he sat smoking in the window of his tiny shared apartment with its view onto twelve lanes of unmoving traffic. He watched the gilded spire of the Hotel Ukraina catch fire in the first rays of dawn, acutely aware of his good fortune in life. To have a privileged education, good health, loving parents . . . even if he was estranged from his father these days.

So why was he so dissatisfied? More than that. Why was he always feeling such outrage?

As if in answer to this last question, two traffic cops Lyosha recognized appeared in the street below—the goons who offered *protection* to the small businesses in the neighborhood. They'd emerged from the Azeri minimart with a bag of fresh pastries that Lyosha knew they'd been given for free, and they'd just ignored the Bentley coupé that was parked in the bus stop.

There it was again. His anger had kindled and flared, and he was instantly reminded of the final meeting with his father, Dmitry, last summer in that grotesque new dacha. They'd had such a violent row that they hadn't spoken to each other since.

Lyosha was angry for so many reasons, but the core reason, he knew—the reactor fueling it all—was the disgust and disappointment he felt with his father. He wasn't even sure anymore what Dmitry did for a career. Some kind of diplomat. One of those coveted state sinecures with a modest official salary and sweeping opportunities for graft. Lyosha felt hot with shame even thinking about him.

The sun's rays fanned brightly for a moment from behind a bank of gray cloud, then dimmed, and the gleaming spire of the Hotel Ukraina turned to dull metal. His anger died down, and his mind filled with a cool singularity of purpose.

He'd fooled the organizers of *Direct Line* into sending him an invitation. He'd committed himself. No turning back now. This time next month, he would be sitting in a studio audience facing the president of the Russian Federation.

And he was going to ask the president a question—a *real* question.

CIA Headquarters
Langley, Virginia

"Shall we talk about your sister?" the woman said softly.

Jenna sighed inwardly, even though she knew this was coming.

The origin story. The saga she was condemned to retell. She also knew very well that they were not here to discuss her sister.

"What was it like? Growing up with an identical twin?"

The woman's hair was an ash white that matched the décor of her office, which was devoid of any files or personal clutter. She was regarding Jenna in the way an expert art historian might do when judging the authenticity of a painting—from a distance, but seeing beneath the brushstrokes, searching for neuroses, unconscious intent—madness, even—in order to assess her mental and emotional state.

Hanging in the air between them was the question of whether Jenna remained fit for active service. This annual assessment always set her nerves jangling. She was midway through a productive tour in Malaysia, tracking the secret procurement networks for missile parts that ended up in North Korea. But she was all too aware that some folks on the seventh floor thought she should never have been sent back into the field.

Hence the subatomic level of these questions today.

"It's hard to describe to anyone who isn't an identical twin," Jenna said, patiently. "We thought the same thoughts, finished each other's sentences; we read each other's minds and moods, shared identical tastes in everything—food, music, boys, humor. We were two people but one person. If one of us stubbed a toe, both of us felt the pain. Until we were eighteen, there was nothing that me and Soo-min did apart. Everyone in our neighborhood knew us. We were the twins with an African American dad in the army and a Korean mom from Seoul . . ."

"Do you want to talk about the day she vanished?"

Jenna drew a long breath and cautioned herself to tell it straight, without emotion.

"It was just after our eighteenth birthday, in June 1998. Our gap year. First time in our lives that we'd been separated. I took a job on Capitol Hill. Soo-min went to Seoul, South Korea. She'd been there about a month when it happened, and I kinda knew straight away, before the police had even called our parents. I *felt* it. Call it some genetic force if you like, some juju that binds identical twins. I just knew—and I knew it was bad. Soo-min had disappeared from a remote beach where she'd gone for a picnic with a new boyfriend. The local police found their possessions—return ferry tickets, library IDs, wallets, clothing—abandoned in the dunes. They figured that the two had drowned by accident while swimming, and their bodies had been lost to the currents."

The woman nodded slowly and allowed a prudent pause.

"So, after Soo-min disappeared—and we're talking about your twin, one half of your own self—it must have felt like a kind of death for you."

"Yes. Some part of me did die," Jenna said carefully. "It wasn't a normal bereavement. More like a serious life-changing injury."

The woman shook her head gently. "And you believed she was dead for, how long was it? Twelve years?"

"Twelve and a half years."

"Must have been a heck of a shock for you when you learned that she was still alive."

Had it been a shock? She had not known the truth, and yet, she'd had a gathering awareness of the truth, like floodwater slowly rising behind a crumbling dam.

"Soo-min wasn't the only one," Jenna said. "Over the years, hundreds of people had been snatched from beaches in Japan and South Korea. All vanished without trace. It was increasingly clear to me who was abducting them. And it so happened that I knew quite a lot about the culprit. It was the reason the Agency recruited me. The reason I joined."

The woman continued to watch her, giving time for each answer to set and solidify.

"And the evening you extracted her. Tell me about that."

Jenna knew that this woman was familiar with every detail in the files—the debriefs, the polys, all the internal disagreements over whether to dismiss her or award her a medal. But she was getting Jenna to describe the events so that she could study her reaction for any signs of avoidance or deflection. Jenna felt like an actor reaching for the lines of a play she had performed many times.

"I found her on board a private train that had stopped near the border between northern China and North Korea. It all happened very quickly and in a situation of extreme confusion. I started a fire on board. I overpowered the guards. As the train started to move, I grabbed Soo-min's hand and we jumped from the door. Then I drove like hell to the US consulate in Shenyang."

Jenna's memories of that evening were fragmentary. Even now, she had to concentrate all her effort into assembling the scattered, flashing scenes into some kind of chronology.

She described the luxurious interior of the train, the silver Kalashnikovs of the North Korean guards. She vividly remembered the moment she had set eyes on Soo-min, who was dressed in a shimmering pale-blue *hanbok* dress, as if she were some kind of courtesan, and the expression on her face, which was softly made up and stiff with terror . . . She remembered how the sunset had cast a crimson light over the frozen rocky landscape, the border region . . . And the blaze she had started on board, the way the flames had licked swiftly upward over walls of the compartment; the curtains combusting brightly; the white, toxic smoke. She remembered opening fire on the guards. She clearly remembered clutching Soo-min's hand as they jumped together and landed in a snow drift . . . She retained a brief movie-clip memory of the train rolling onward, receding into the dusk, trailing smoke and flame . . . She remembered cupping her hands to Soo-min's face and kissing her—her beloved twin, her sister who in twelve and a half years had undergone a transformation almost as extreme as her own . . .

"Someone died in that 'confusing scene,' as you call it." In the carpeted stillness of the room every consonant of the woman's voice was flinchingly clear. "Are you avoiding talking about that?"

"Several guards died. I opened fire on them with an AKSU."

"I'm talking about the seventy-year-old man who died."

Jenna held the woman's gaze. From somewhere outside the window, across the acres of parking lot, she could hear the insistent bleat of a car alarm.

"The person you're referring to was a sick man," she said evenly. "He'd recently had a stroke and was being treated for heart disease. Yes, the shock of the fire and the smoke may have stopped his heart or given him another stroke. We don't know the precise cause of death."

"And now, five years on, that evening comes back to you often? You relive that experience?"

Jenna saw the trap. *Denying is lying.*

"I think about it often. Naturally I do. It was one of the most significant events of my life."

"And how do you feel about that man's death?"

Jenna didn't blink. "Utter indifference. No, that's not true. I felt satisfaction at his death."

The woman looked down at a pen on her desk and touched it with her finger, adjusting its position by a millimeter.

"Satisfaction and . . . a feeling of vengeance? For what was done to your sister?"

Another trap, and she was alarmed to see how close she was to falling into it. "Not vengeance, ma'am. I serve my country, not my ego."

The woman moved the pen another millimeter.

"It didn't disturb you that you'd caused the death of that person, of all people?"

"No."

"Are you going to say his name?"

Jenna's face remained impassive, but anxiety fluttered briefly in her belly like a trapped bird. She inhaled slowly through her nostrils.

"Kim Jong-il."

Once again, the woman peered into her, through her.

"It doesn't worry you at all? Tracking down North Korean agents in Malaysia? They know who you are, don't they?"

"My dip cover is solid. It's worked for me for three years without incident. The North Koreans don't know I'm in Malaysia."

The woman's eyebrows arched wryly. And then, Jenna might have been mistaken, but her tone seemed to change. There was a trace of respect in it.

"Let's hope it stays that way."

Marshall's Beach
San Francisco

"Group photo!" the red-haired girl said suddenly. To Stephen's horror her phone was out on a selfie stick. Her four friends squeezed in close for the picture, with Stephen wedged between them. It happened so fast that he stood rooted to the spot like a rabbit-in-the-headlights fool.

Now there's a photo of me.

The red-haired girl examined the shot she'd just taken. Then the damned stick was out again. "One more."

Stephen tore himself away from the group. "Good to meet you guys," he said quickly, and walked across the sand without looking back, his eyes watering in the brightness glittering off the ocean. He felt destabilized, deranged by dread.

How did I let that happen?

In moments like that, he thought, moments of real danger for him, his reality seemed to fall apart. Panic and paralysis took over. Straight thinking became impossible.

Any second now that red-haired girl would post the photo to her feed.

My image . . . My location. Online for anyone to see.

It was a Sunday afternoon, and such a mild, sunny day for the time of year, almost too warm for coats, that he'd risked a solitary walk along the beach toward the Golden Gate Bridge, thinking himself anonymous among the crowds of strolling families. He'd been watching the small white clippers and catamarans out in the bay, noting how the ocean merged hazily into a sky marbled by contrails.

He hadn't seen the group approaching until they were almost in front of him. They were five high-school students like himself, one of whom he knew, and in the moment of recognition he'd felt a sharp jolt of alarm. A split-second weakening of his spinal column. It was too late for him to turn away. They'd stopped to talk to him, curious to meet him. He'd found the red-haired girl pushy: *You live in the Bay Area? Which school are you at? How do you know Kyle?* And then: *Group photo!*

His personal safety: all gone up in pixels.

For two hours after that he wandered the grid of the city streets, aimless, starting to feel hungry and tired but unwilling, yet, to go home and report this fresh disaster to his guardians. Eventually, toward evening, he found himself sitting on a stone bench outside the park on Telegraph Hill.

The sky was darkening to a deep violet, the color of a bruise beneath a fingernail, and the lights of San Francisco Bay were starting to sparkle and dance. The air had become much cooler, making him shiver. He pulled up the hood of his shapeless old coat, hoping to dematerialize in the shadows and half-tones of the streetlamps.

Stephen was sixteen years old, turning seventeen next week. He'd arrived in San Francisco only six months ago. His previous home had been in Chicago, but he'd skipped town after someone in the small community of defectors had started asking questions about him. Before Chicago he'd lived in Wisconsin, but from there, too, he'd fled in a hurry after a stranger had come looking for him at school.

It amazed him to think that there'd been a time when he hadn't taken the danger seriously, not even after his great uncle had been murdered in horrific circumstances three years ago. But that, he now knew, had been the start of it, because soon afterward they came looking for him. Stephen didn't know if he was next on the killers' list, or next but one, or next but two. The hunt was on, and if they found him, he was dead.

He did not believe in the supernatural, but this *felt* supernatural, what was happening to him. Something malefic and ancestral, like a curse in a folktale. A nightmare he couldn't hide from or outrun, and yet he'd only survived this long by hiding and running.

If they saw that photo of him taken today, they would pick up his trail. They would head straight here.

He crouched forward on the bench and lowered his face into his hands. Now he'd have to drop out of school again and lie low until he figured out what to do.

He felt a great isolation descend upon him.

His guardians no longer had the strength to keep running. They were good people, his foster parents. They'd protected him for long enough. He would be eighteen next year. A man. Wherever he went next, he would go alone. But where? The West Coast felt like the edge of the map for him, the end of the road.

Out in the bay, a vast oil tanker sounded its horn as it passed beneath the Golden Gate Bridge. There was something festive about it, the way its deck was lit up like a carnival float.

If only he could slip aboard, cross the ocean, and hide beyond the sunset.

But nowhere in the world had a refuge for him. Besides, he had no valid passport, no money, no connections. He had nothing but his name, and it was a name he could never, ever use.

PART ONE
Malaysia

I'm always moving. I'm moving in both directions.

Donald J. Trump
2017

1

Datai Beach
Langkawi, Malaysia
Wednesday evening, mid-February

Jenna had dressed more carefully than usual. She'd styled her hair in a chignon, which gave her a glamor she didn't ordinarily possess. The pearls she'd chosen glowed luxuriously in the soft lights surrounding the mirror, and the black evening dress was of a silk so light it felt like a breeze against her skin. A glossy, plum-red lipstick completed the look. She tried adjusting the dress to make it a little more revealing but decided that was going too far. She wasn't here to seduce the guy. A dab of perfume on her wrists and she was ready. She stood to take a final, appraising look at herself, and felt another ripple of nerves. PANDA had a weakness for women, and this evening, when PANDA walked into her trap, she would use everything in her power to get him to talk.

Behind her, reflected in the mirror, was a marble-topped dressing table on which she'd placed a compact Beretta 8000, her preferred firearm; a pepper spray concealed inside a mascara tube; four bricks of cash shrink-wrapped in plastic; and a burner phone.

It was the sight of the phone that released another wriggle of anxiety in her.

She stepped outside and started to focus her thoughts. A hardwood veranda surrounded the suite. The hotel's guest rooms were in fact small, secluded villas that could only be reached by stone paths or wooden bridges. Each had a spacious modern living room and a private pool. Jenna's looked down onto a narrow, sandy cove that opened into the calm waters of the Malacca Strait, with views on both sides of dense rainforest and green volcanic hills. The evening air, though still heavy with moisture, was much fresher. Towering, electric-lined clouds were turning purple as the sun dipped into the sea.

An hour ago, she'd gone through the ritual she practiced before each op: her core strength crunches, a sequence of yoga stretches, and her meditation, in which she'd tried to synchronize her breathing with the slow, hypnotic rhythm of the surf. The calm she was feeling now—deep, alert, operational calm—had almost eluded her. She'd had to use all her tricks for tidying away troubling thoughts.

Not for the first time, she'd noticed how her tension and her fear tended to manifest themselves in a sense of guilt. She would catch herself wondering what on earth she was doing with her life. She was thirty-six, turning thirty-seven. Why was she chasing lowlifes when her sister was in a psych ward on the other side of the world and her widowed mom was at home alone in Annandale? But then maturer thoughts, calmer and more rehearsed, would remind her that she could never simply quit and go home; that she was working to make a dangerous world safer, wasn't she? That by doing her duty she was protecting those she loved, and everything else she held dear.

Hers was not a normal job. Its responsibilities were of a different order, and she took them seriously.

The last of the sun was bathing the veranda in a vermillion light. Dusk fell quickly in the islands. The trees were coming alive with the cries of nocturnal birds.

A small blue light lit up on her encrypted Motorola. The clunky radio was more secure than a cellphone, especially if signal channels on the island were being monitored. The message told her that PANDA's flight had landed. Her support team on the island was in place. In a minute or two they would have eyes on him.

She went back inside and slipped the cash and the mascara tube into her handbag, then checked the Beretta and racked the slide.

But as she reached for the burner phone, she again caught sight of herself in the mirror. And for one skull-tingling instant she saw not her own reflection in the glass, but that of her sister. Opaque, admonishing, partly in shadow. Suffering. Crazy.

Today was the anniversary of an event that only seemed to shine brighter with the passing of the years. They had been sixteen years old and competing in the Virginia junior league taekwondo championships. After a series of games that had electrified the crowd—tornados of lightning-fast spin kicks and hand-strikes—the twins had found themselves competing against each other in the final game. Their skills were equally matched, but only one of them could win the trophy and it went to Soo-min. The event had made the local TV news. For a brief period, they had been celebrities in Annandale. They were invited onto chat shows. Restaurants let them dine for free. People asked for their autographs in the street.

That day turned out to be the high-water mark of their lives, the meridian.

Many years later, after Soo-min had been found alive in North Korea and brought home, Jenna had made an effort to mark that day, to memorialize it. Wherever she was in the world, she'd call her sister on its anniversary, hoping to remind her how alive they'd both felt back then, when the world had been theirs for the taking, when they'd never been happier or more confident in themselves, when they'd been full of hopes for the future. But Soo-min had never given any sign that she even remembered it.

Virginia was twelve hours behind Malaysia . . . A call was not *impossible*. She had already figured out a way to reach the hospital, discreetly, if she absolutely needed to, without anyone knowing it was her . . .

No—crazy even to entertain it. A private phone call was just the kind of flap that could blow the op apart.

The Motorola lit up again. The team now had eyes on PANDA.

She breathed in and breathed out and counted slowly to ten. In this business, she could not be distracted. There were no mistakes. Make one, and you're cooked.

Along the stone path, small, waist-high lamps illuminated spirals of flying insects. Lizards darted silently out of her way. After a few yards, the path forked to the right and she glimpsed her destination through the trees: another guest villa, its lights golden in the gathering night. The leaves of a colocasia plant cast umbrella-sized shadows across the path. Jenna slowed her pace, then stopped and listened. She could hear the creaking of the coconut palms, the crepitation of bugs in the undergrowth, a scampering of long-tailed macaques on the villa's roof, and then: a car pulling in on the gravel lane.

PANDA had arrived.

The sound of a car's trunk opening and closing. A driver being tipped. Luggage being wheeled to the villa's door. Jenna couldn't see him from where she was positioned, but she could picture him very well: wraparound shades, short of breath, desperate for some aircon and a cigarette, taking off his baseball cap to wipe the moisture from his head, which was almost completely bald. For a high-rolling gambler and playboy, he made a good job of looking like a bum. He was a pudgy, unshaven teddy bear of a man. CIA cryptonyms were generated at random by an algorithm, which on this rare occasion had produced one that was bang on the money.

The doorbell rang.

What state of mind was he in? Excited, nervous, perhaps, at the prospect of a night in an expensive resort with his new girlfriend, but also edgy and on his guard because of his fear, which had grown acute in recent months, that he might be assassinated.

She heard the front door open and May Ling's voice raised in a delighted shriek of welcome.

Jenna moved closer, finding a spot of deep shade beneath the veranda. Inside, PANDA was speaking in Korean, talking about his flight as May Ling helped him off with his jacket and shoes.

Moments later the veranda creaked, and she caught an aroma of cigar smoke, which was mellow and not unpleasant. A gentle wreath of it floated into the night air. PANDA was almost directly above her. Music played softly on the villa's sound system, something lazy with double bass and solo trumpet.

"Sure you don't want to go out?" he said.

"No, it's beautiful here," May Ling said from inside. "I've ordered dinner." A cork popped.

PANDA went back inside, murmured something and chuckled. May Ling laughed again. Glasses clinked.

Months of work and patience had gone into bringing him to this moment, in this place, far from the watching eyes in Macau...

The doorbell rang again, and the catering staff entered with a rattling of wine coolers and plates. May Ling ushered them into the dining room while PANDA paced the veranda, puffing on his cigar, belching softly from the champagne bubbles. The catering staff left.

"Dinner in five minutes," May Ling called.

That was the signal.

Jenna circled the villa to the dining-room side, taking care to avoid the crunch of fallen acacia leaves, and climbed the steps to the veranda where May Ling, wearing a slim-fitting blue satin cheongsam, was waiting for her. She slid open the glass doors. Jenna slipped off her heels, stepped inside without a sound, and together they lowered the blinds around the room.

Neither exchanged a word.

Jenna was struck by how lovely May Ling looked. It was no surprise that PANDA had fallen for her. It was she who had done the fieldwork for this op, getting herself noticed by him one evening at the Ritz-Carlton Bar in Macau and accepting a drink from him—no easy feat considering how suspicious he was of any new faces; it was she who had suggested a late bite at a place that just happened to be his favorite sushi joint. Their second date had been his suggestion, and so were the trips out of town, away from his wife and children. Over the three months May Ling had been dating him, taking care not to rush or force a thing, not to press or push or ask too many questions, she had gained PANDA's confidence. For so young a case officer it was a remarkable achievement. But then, it was just as remarkable that an out-of-shape, forty-six-year-old family man had believed that a woman half his age was in love with him. Gradually, his desire for her had overcome his paranoia, which was careless. PANDA had good reasons to be paranoid.

May Ling nodded to her, then left the room to fetch her guest.

The room had a chill edge from the aircon. It was decorated in a rich-world version of the local style, with rattan chairs and dark hardwood walls, which made the lighting amber-colored and welcoming. Dinner was a sushi banquet for two, Jenna saw, exquisitely laid, with colorful dragon rolls and red sashimi, and a table display of tropical flowers. An array of crystal glasses for water and wine, and small, saucer-like cups for soju surrounded the plates.

"I hope you're hungry," May Ling said to him in the next room. The dining-room door opened. Jenna heard PANDA approach. "Hungry for you," he murmured.

And into my net swims the fish.

He entered the room and saw Jenna standing behind a chair. His eyes bulged in surprise. "Who the fuck are you?"

2

15th Street, NW
Washington, DC
Wednesday morning

The rooftop bar-restaurant of the W Hotel was not Eric Rahn's first choice of venue for a thirtieth birthday breakfast. However, he did need to stay close to the White House, plus it was expensive, and he would let the others pay. In the mirrored elevator he inspected his complexion, which was clear and looked excellent. His teeth were white and unstained. He was wearing a dark, single-breasted Brooks Brothers suit and handmade English shoes by Church's—black, polished to a high shine, a detail the Boss liked.

"Looks, looks, it's all about looks," he murmured, brushing lint from his sleeve without taking his eyes from his reflection. *How many staffers would still be with us if they'd respected that primary law!* He was suited up and ready to MAGA.

Eric was a Korean American of average height. He worked out regularly (CrossFit, free weights, boxercise); he allowed twenty minutes each morning for his exfoliation and moisturizing routine, and longer in the evening for his charcoal mineral face mask; he was careful about diet and sleep so that his constitution was robust enough to indulge in the occasional all-nighter with vodka and cocaine. His hair was moussed and combed straight back, and his cheeks dimpled when he smiled, an attribute that made him—he couldn't deny it—quite extraordinarily handsome. Last month's *GQ* magazine had featured his face on the cover with the banner "Trump's New Korea Move." He'd had it framed and mounted on the wall above his bed.

The maître d' was performing an unctuous welcome when the elevator doors opened. "How are we this morning, Mr. Rahn?"

"We are in excellent health, Sidney."

"Your guests are seated."

Then, Eric was led across the top floor toward the restaurant. Mirrors, mirrors everywhere. He was noticing again how nicely his hair had been cut (two hundred dollars at Delaunay's, plus tip), when his phone rang.

"Yes, professor. What is it?"

"Mr. Rahn, I received your talking points."

"And?"

Professor Maclean was at a loss for words. "Well, I . . . I can't say *this* on national TV!"

Eric screwed his eyes shut and tried to dredge up a few microparticles of patience. "Sure you can. Everything in those points is true . . . in a general sense. It needs to be said, and you're going to say it."

"*None* of it is true, Mr. Rahn. This gives a *completely* false picture of our strategic position, and that's going to be very damaging to our relationship with South Korea, a key ally. I'm not doing this."

Eric could see the restaurant ahead of him, sparkling and refulgent in the morning sun. His guests were turning in their seats to face him, smiling, waving. He hung back for a moment, turned his head away, and lowered his voice to a murderous whisper.

"Listen to me, you pompous crook. Stick to the damned script. Because if you don't, professor, I'm sure the Princeton board of trustees will be *very* interested to know about those highly lucrative, highly fucking illegal consultant's fees you've been paid by a

Chinese military tech firm. The president will be interested, too. He takes treason very personally."

"*Treason?* Mr. Rahn, I reject that accusation. If you persist in—"

"You're on air in ten minutes," he said, and hung up.

He approached the table, beaming, his palms raised in a gesture of modesty and gratitude.

"Happy birthday!" they called in a tuneless unison, with a smatter of genteel clapping.

"Don't get up," he said, once they were all on their feet. The men shook his hand; the women air-kissed his cheek.

"Nice haircut," Hunter said.

"I should hope so, Hunt. Cost four hundred bucks."

He'd booked a corner table for 8 a.m. From here he could keep an eye on the TV behind the bar. He'd double-checked the lineups on *Morning Joe, Good Morning America,* and *CBS This Morning* to make sure there'd be sufficient adulation and praise to keep the Boss in the residence until about ten thirty, before he'd descend, mood simmering, his agenda for the day taking shape. (That was the moment it was important to catch him, before he started crowd-sourcing opinions from bodyguards, catering staff, anyone who was nearby.)

A moment of panic had grabbed Eric in the taxi when he'd realized he'd slept through the Boss's 3 a.m. tweeting hour, but a quick roll through his feed—Crooked Hillary ... VERY low IQ person ... Dumbest guy in Congress ... Witch Hunt ... Greatest Presidency ever!!!—had put his mind at ease. The Boss was riled up, touchy, irritable—fertile conditions for Eric's scheme to succeed.

Fox & Friends was on the TV. He'd engineered an eight fifteen slot for Professor Maclean, his stooge. All that two-faced crapweasel needed to do was stick to the points Eric had given him. If all went to plan, the professor's words would detonate the IEDs Eric had been quietly planting in the Boss's mind for weeks. A cheap trick, but really effective. Trump would hear his innermost thoughts getting the thumbs-up from the morning talk show crowd, and BOOM! Hours later he was signing executive orders in front of the cameras. But Eric knew the risks. The Boss's moods were mercurial, protean, dangerous. Nothing was guaranteed.

"Your master's in the Dark Tower this week, isn't he?" Anne said, presenting him with a birthday card. "While the cat's away . . ."

"No, he's here," Eric said, glancing toward the White House, which from this vantage seemed a curiously modest building. Anne followed his gaze. When the Boss was out of town a calm descended on DC's political class, but when he was in residence they felt the gravity of his power, the strain of orbiting too close to the sun. Eric had a sudden image of the Boss right now: in a white bathrobe, his doll's hands knocking out a tweet, pausing over which words to capitalize, hitting send, then marveling as TV screens changed in real time all around the globe. BREAKING NEWS . . .

All of them had ordered some ridiculous green smoothie, which was now arriving in tall glasses.

"Nobody joining me in a toast?" Eric said, taking a seat with his back to the epic panorama of the National Mall and the Washington Monument, the angle he figured would work best for his Instagram. "Glass of champagne?"

Eric called the waiter, a young guy who was catwalk handsome, and ordered a bottle of Dom Pérignon, the most expensive, even though he wasn't intending to drink any of it. "And take this away? This is Evian, which is still. I'd like San Pellegrino, which is sparkling. And I *specifically* requested a waiter without tattoos." A silence fell across the table. They were all staring at him, entertained. He turned his head to them. "What?"

"Are you going to order any food, sport?" Tim said. "I have a senate judiciary committee at ten."

There were eight of them for breakfast. Eric wouldn't call them friends—he had no friends—but they were fellow players, enablers, in whom he recognized . . . a kindred inhumanity? A moral blindness? A belief in nothing at all?

Champagne flutes were set down, a cork popped. He leaned back in his seat, arched his fingers, and closed his eyes for a moment, letting the sweet venom of the chatter around the table wash pleasurably over him, soothe him, distract him from the dark, euphoric thoughts that were forming and expanding inside his head. He had no one he could really talk to, no one to appreciate his secret, hidden goddamn genius. It was enough to drive a man crazy.

"Oh, did I trigger your libtard anxieties, snowflake?"

"You can't polish a turd."

"Sure, Marcia, but we can sprinkle glitter on one, can't we . . . ?"

"Don't write it on a napkin, idiot. Anything in writing is discoverable . . ."

"Oh, shut up, Alex. It's very clear the governor wants to introduce sharia law and full communism, and that's what we're telling the voters . . ."

"Reality is a heartless bitch . . ."

". . . All the qualities we admire most in our president-for-life. Dignity, scholarship, humility, and a strong impulse control . . ."

Eric had joined in the snickering, though he didn't find it funny. His fake reactions to everything came so naturally to him that no one ever seemed to notice. But he felt oddly affronted by the last remark.

"Actually, Tim, Trump can be a good listener, as long as you avoid his triggers."

"Let me guess: migrants, golf, hookers, and *Cheeina*."

The table erupted in laughter.

Eric twirled the stem of his glass, musing on why this had touched a nerve, made him defensive.

His breakfast was placed in front of him, and suddenly, from the corner of his eye, he saw Professor Maclean appear on screen behind the bar, a balding, soundless, talking head, mouth opening and closing with the scripted points Eric had fed him. A power-coiffed female interviewer nodded gravely and asked the next question. Brief cut to a satellite shot of the Korean peninsula, then an aerial view of Camp Humphreys, the vast US Army base in Seoul, home to 28,500 US troops (33,000 if you included support staff).

A few hundred yards away in the White House, Eric pictured the Boss turning up the volume.

"So, you're the president's ideas guy now," Alex said with his mouth full.

"Special Assistant for East Asia," Eric said, with a conscious effort not to look at the screen.

"Great profile on you in *GQ*," Alex went on. "'Trump's New Korea Move.' Eric, I knew he'd pick you." Alex pursed his lips and mimicked the president's voice. "*Call Central Casting. I need a Korean dude who looks good on camera.*" Alex put his fork down and started shaking with silent laughter at this pathetic slur. "Oh, come on, man."

Eric stopped eating and smiled thinly, fantasizing about Alex's head exploding, imagining the projection of cranial debris before it hit the windows and tablecloth, the lumps of gore and brain matter, the shattered fragments of hair-covered bone. The screams.

"I'm Korean American, Alex," he said acidly. "I've lived here since I was eighteen."

Marcia, who kept her iPhone on a very loud notification setting, was the first to be alerted. "Oh, my *God*," she murmured, raising her hand to her mouth.

Marcia looked up at Eric with alarm in her eyes. The others instantly had their phones out, including Eric, who glanced first at his watch.

That didn't take long . . .

They'd all read the tweets and were watching him in stunned silence now, waiting for his reaction. Eric continued to stare at his phone, taking extreme care not to move a single muscle in his face.

Donald J. Trump @realdonaldtrump
How much is South Korea paying the U.S. for protection against North Korea???? NOTHING!

Donald J. Trump @realdonaldtrump
I can't believe we are not asking South Korea for anything. They make a fortune on us while we spend a fortune defending them—how stupid!

He breathed in and stood to face the window, his back to the others, as if deep in contemplation of a crisis.

The sun had risen, and the lightsaber of the Washington Monument was cutting its path into high blue skies. It was going to be a beautiful day. He was floating on clouds of unimagined power.

A birthday to remember.

He turned back to his guests, his face a study of resolution and concern, and took a moment to dab solemnly at his lips with his napkin.

"Thanks for breakfast. I gotta get to work."

"Better hurry, sport," Hunter called after him. "Sounds like he's about to leave South Korea defenseless."

3

Datai Beach
Langkawi, Malaysia

Jenna answered PANDA in Korean. "I'm a friend of May Ling's." She smiled, wanting to show she meant no harm. "Please don't be alarmed."

PANDA turned to May Ling. "What's going on? Who's she?"

"A friend." May Ling's grave tone must have sounded new to PANDA.

"This is a setup?"

May Ling leaned against the door, hands behind her back, barring his exit.

He was staring at Jenna now, trapped, and she saw in his face not just fear and alarm but hot, flushing humiliation. He had shaved and changed into a white linen jacket and a pressed pale-blue shirt. He'd lost weight. He'd dispensed with the gold chains and the bling. She felt sorry for him. For the effort he had made, for his being tricked.

"I'm here to make a proposal," she said. "I assure you it will be of interest to you."

"What fucking proposal?" He was almost shouting. "I don't know who you are—" But the instant his words were out, a dawning remembrance spread across his face. His voice dropped. "Wait . . . I remember you . . . The American lady who speaks Korean . . . I do know you. I never forget a face."

"The Casino Lisboa, three months ago," she said.

That had been the first time she'd observed him, laughing like a little boy as he'd raked in his chips in the glittering private members' lounge. He'd even raised his glass to her. "Red or black?" he'd said. "Red, of course," Jenna had said, to knowing laughter from the spectators. The wheel spun, and he'd won again.

He continued to stare, and then he let out an astonished huff, as if he'd been duped in a most extraordinary scam.

"You're CIA? Or South Korean Intelligence?"

A small silence ensued, as if to acknowledge that they were through to the next stage of a delicate game.

Jenna softened her voice further. "I work for the United States government in an intelligence capacity. I'd like a few minutes alone with you. Shall we sit down?"

PANDA's eyes drifted to some spot outside the room. "How could I have been so stupid?"

Sweat was spreading through his shirt like areas of deep water on an ocean chart.

May Ling poured him a cup of soju and served it Korean style, with one hand on her heart. He accepted it in a trance. Then he knocked the spirit back and pulled out a handkerchief to wipe the sweat from his face.

"I'm . . . going to leave now." He made a fluttering motion with his hands. "I can't talk to you."

"You've been talking to us for months."

He turned to May Ling, a terrible look of betrayal on his face, and May Ling, lowering her eyes, withdrew from the room and closed the door behind her, her role over.

Something inside PANDA seemed to crumple. His breathing became ragged and wheezy. He patted his jacket pockets and took out an asthma inhaler.

Jenna remained calm. "No one knows I'm here. No one knows we're having this conversation."

PANDA gave a mirthless laugh. "They will know."

"I understand your fear. Sometimes it feels like our families can read our minds, doesn't it? Family ties are so strong that we'll do anything they ask, however badly they treat us."

He peered at her then with a perplexed intensity, as if trying to empty the cupboards of his memory to recall the time and place he'd met her, as if it had been years ago. On that evening she'd seen him in Macau, betting big on roulette and ordering whiskey by the bottle, he'd been surrounded by women from the moneyed, international set. She was surprised he'd remembered her at all.

"You have a son in Macau," she said gently. "You have his safety to think of. Yong-won is, what, twenty-one now? He must be thinking of a career . . ."

"Stop. I'm not giving you anything." His voice held a weak note of defiance, but a condemned look had come over his face.

"Are you sure?" Jenna said, "Because I think I can offer what you desire most."

"Oh." A bitter cynicism, a weariness came over him. "And what's that?"

"A way out."

Outside, a breeze picked up, making the papaya trees rustle and sway. Further off, waves thundered in the cove.

Slowly he gave an incredulous shake of his head. "If you're asking me to be a Yankee snitch . . ."

"I wouldn't put it that way, but I don't think you have much choice," she said, not unkindly. "You're in a bad corner. Help us, and we can arrange safe passage for you and your son, and asylum in the United States."

"My son . . ." he whispered, as if seeing something precious slip from his grasp.

She spoke very carefully now. "Your firstborn and heir is in as much danger as you are. Do this for Yong-won, if not for yourself."

PANDA said nothing as her words sank in. He just stared at the uneaten banquet for two.

"Perhaps this will help you decide . . ." She opened her handbag and took out the four bricks of cash containing thirty thousand dollars in each. "One hundred and twenty thousand dollars—just a first, small offering to mark the beginning of our collaboration . . . and in acknowledgment of the intelligence *you have already* given us."

PANDA glared at the bricks of money, his eyes puckering.

"This is bullshit. I know how this works. You've got nothing." He let out a jittery laugh. "Sorry, lady, I'm not playing. Fool me once . . ." He glanced in the direction May Ling had gone. "Now, excuse me. Your meeting's over." He got up and moved toward the door.

"You've fallen out of favor," Jenna said coolly. "Your younger half-brother, whom you've never met, cut you off financially when he became the head of the Family. At best, he considers you an embarrassment. At worst, a dynastic threat to his rule."

PANDA went very still. His back was toward her, his hand on the door handle.

"You remain alive only so long as your half-brother desires it, and we both know what he's capable of. He had your uncle executed by anti-aircraft guns and his body fed to dogs. You fear your days are numbered. That's why you've been dashing around trying to make yourself useful to him, laundering millions of dollars of his money through your online gambling sites in Macau, carrying cash and diamonds for him all over Asia, and setting up Family meetings with corrupt politicians and bank presidents. But the truth is that your half-brother doesn't want you alive. And now that your uncle's dead there's no one left in the Family who can protect you. You have a wife and children to support, and you've got no money left to pay for bodyguards. Correct so far?"

PANDA turned back to her, and she saw a face she'd seen many times in these situations: the desperate, hunted look of someone realizing that nowhere was safe, there was no one to trust, and no option left but to talk to her.

She kept her voice neutral, businesslike. "You carry an ancient Nokia that can't be used to track your location. You've had your back tattooed with coiling dragons and koi carp, which you believe will protect you and ward off danger. The letter you wrote to your half-brother last month—*Please don't kill us. We have nowhere to hide*—was ignored."

PANDA's face had turned the off-white color of candlewax. "What do you want?"

Jenna put her hands on the table. "I want to know *everything* you've been doing for your half-brother. The money-laundering scams, the ransomware attacks, the secret procurement networks for the missiles that North Korea is aiming at America's West Coast."

4

The White House
Washington, DC

When Eric arrived at the White House the Boss's tweets were on every network. The place seemed empty; so many staff positions remained unfilled. He was hurrying toward his tiny cubicle next to the Press Office, when he heard his name called in a stage whisper. From the half-open door of the Roosevelt Room the White House press secretary was beckoning him in with an urgent flick of his finger.

"*In here.*"

The man was porridge-pale and perspiring, and wearing, oh my God, a *light-colored* suit that can't have cost more than two hundred dollars. He ushered Eric inside and closed the door.

"What's this?" Eric said. "A conspiracy?"

"You saw the tweets?"

At the far end of the room, standing in front of the grand fireplace and its mantel clock, a huddle of men was speaking in hushed voices—the defense secretary in uniform, ribboned and decorated; the secretary of state, silver-haired and towering, struggling to keep his Texan tones below a whisper; the chief of staff, on tiptoes, whose diminutive stature—a butt of the Boss's wonderful humor—surely meant that he wasn't long for the job; and, the only one of the men who turned to look as Eric approached, casting him a cool, appraising stare: the Son-in-Law, aloof, detached, entitled, like a Medici princess.

All of them had dark rings under their eyes, disoriented by their exposure to the president's rages, humiliated by his name-calling and falsetto-voiced mimicry. Donald Trump had made insomniacs of everyone who worked here. Eric imagined them waking in a sweat in the small hours, wondering if the president had fired them by tweet at 3 a.m., or launched a thermonuclear strike against Iran, or Venezuela, or Belgium, or picked some playground spat that had redirected the global news cycle toward total nonsense.

"Kim Jong-un just tested another new ICBM," the secretary of defense was saying, chin wattles shaking. "Now is *not* the time to pull our forces from that region."

"Isn't this exactly the time?" the chief of staff said, lamely. "I mean, to make a deal! Get the South Koreans to pay us for their protection?"

"We're not running a fucking protection racket," the secretary of state huffed. "The South Koreans give us ultrasensitive intelligence on the North. They're our allies. We need them. Thirty-eight minutes!" He said, jabbing his finger at the chief of staff. "That's how long it'll take a North Korean missile to reach Los Angeles."

"What do *you* think, Eric?" The Son-in-Law's smile was faint and mocking, his face as smooth as a waxed fruit. "You're the president's new . . . pet."

"Gentlemen," Eric said, giving them a smile that he hoped conveyed reassurance. "Allow me to try, if you would. Give me a minute alone with the president. Let's see if we can't walk him back from this . . . terrible mistake."

"If he won't listen to me . . ." The secretary of defense turned his blue eyes on Eric like laser sights finding their mark. ". . . why would he listen to a goddamn intern?"

Eric absorbed the slight with a rueful nod, sensing the mood, and faltered delicately before rallying. "Perhaps, sir, he might listen if it comes from a Korean," he said with a note of hurt pride. "In my experience of him, he'll agree to most things if he can call it a win."

"He's in a frenzy today," the press secretary said, visibly shrinking into the cheap suit. "Batshit crazy. I mean, talking-to-portraits-on-the-walls crazy."

"It's good for him to vent some anger," Eric said, reasonably. "It soothes him, helps him stabilize his emotions." He looked at these men, seeing himself through their eyes. Reflective, resolute, modest. "I'll make sure nothing's drafted for him to sign."

The secretary of state, exhausted, closed his eyes and pinched the bridge of his nose. "He may have already dictated something . . ."

Eric had anticipated everything. His patent sincerity was speaking for him. "If he has, sir, then, frankly, I'll remove it. With nothing on his desk, it might be days, weeks, before he remembers it again."

The tension in the room eased. Even the secretary of defense was regarding him thoughtfully.

Worms, mice, all of them, Eric thought. Pathetic. In the weeks since the inauguration, it had given him intense pleasure to see these men being stripped of their dignity and reputations by the president. Supporting cast, that's all they were. And still they presumed to counsel him when their only role was to praise. They served the man, not the office. When would they see it?

The Son-in-Law's princess lips had curled upward in an amused disdain.

"Nice suit, Eric," he said.

Eric inclined his head at the compliment and imagined popping the Son-in-Law's eye with a meat cleaver, seeing the ocular fluid spilling out like egg yolk.

"I'm at the end of my rope with the president." The secretary of state was raising his voice to a treasonous volume. "He's a fucking moron! Without our troops in South Korea, South Korea is exposed to a North Korean invasion. Why are we explaining this to him again? This isn't some lose-lose business gamble. He has the understanding of a fifth grader."

"You're right, sir." Eric's eyes shone with reason. "Our presence in the region keeps us safe. And South Korea is an ally we can't afford to lose, a democracy in a region of the world where we really need one. Our troops are there to prevent World War Three."

They fell silent for a moment, each wondering how on earth they'd got here.

"He may have cooled down by now," the press secretary said gloomily.

"Good luck," the Son-in-Law whispered.

Eric turned to leave, feeling cats' claws on his back.

He headed quickly toward the Oval Office, past the landscapes of Yosemite, past the portrait of Reagan smiling his darned-if-I-know smile. In the personal secretary's office, he asked for a few minutes alone with the president.

"Talk of the devil. He just asked for you." She winked at him and picked up her desk phone. "Mr. President—Eric Rahn is here." She replaced the handset. Eric shuddered with awe and apprehension.

"How's the weather?" he asked. Code for the Boss's mood.

"Changeable." She gave him the heartening smile she bestowed on those entering the lions' arena.

"Madeleine . . ." Eric took out his phone and emailed her a document. "Would you run off a couple of copies of this letter and bring them in?"

Eric opened the door and found himself alone in the Oval Office. The Resolute desk was bare apart from the telephones. Light from the rose garden filled the room, casting a lustrous sheen onto the new gold-brocade curtains, the gilt-edged rosewood, the new carpet rug encircled by a giant imperial laurel wreath. The leonine glow of the Trump Era. He stood still, feeling his heart rate rise, his breath fluttering. Churchill's bronze eyes scowled at him. George Washington peeped sideways at him from the wall. Eric shook his head in silent wonder. He was *in the room*. What fusion of destiny, cunning, and sheer will had brought him to this moment, in the most powerful locus on earth?

From the adjoining dining room, he became aware of sports commentary and an aroma of hotdogs, and he guessed that the president was in there watching the golf tournament. Eric gave a discreet cough. The TV fell silent.

And suddenly he was in the great man's presence. Trump was moving toward him, towering and dynamic, radiating the energy of a much younger man. His hand was outstretched. He clasped Eric's hand warmly.

"Eric, help me out, will you?" Sunlight blazed from his golden mane, the rich croissant of his hair. It gilded and burnished his tan. His teeth were reality-TV white. "That bunch of losers ambush you out there?"

"Yes, sir, they did."

5

Datai Beach
Langkawi, Malaysia

PANDA returned to the table and sat down very slowly, as if he'd aged thirty years. His hands were trembling as he poured himself another cup of soju. A good sign, Jenna decided. His breathing had become constricted again. He took another gasp from the inhaler.

This man looks utterly defeated, she thought. And although she loathed the Family, and everything it had done, she had to admit that she found it hard to dislike PANDA. Unlike the others, he was all too human. He had grown up the anointed heir to a hereditary Marxist dynasty. The night he'd turned eight years old they'd dressed him in a miniature uniform and the sky had lit up with a massive display of fireworks spelling "Happy Birthday Comrade General!" As a teenage boy, he'd stood behind his father as he took the salute before thousands of troops parading in massed ranks. The palaces, the power, were all destined to be his. But his drinking and his womanizing had gotten him into trouble with his father, and his total lack of interest in the Family's blood feuds had caused him to be sidelined. The final straw had been the Disneyland scandal in 2001. PANDA had been arrested at Tokyo's Narita International Airport for traveling to Japan on a forged Dominican Republic passport using the Chinese alias Pang Xiong ("Fat Bear").

He'd said he'd wanted to take his family to Tokyo Disneyland. The incident caused such a scorching embarrassment to the Family that his father canceled a state visit to China that year. PANDA was officially disinherited and banished in disgrace. His father's third son, the youngest, was granted the title Great Successor.

PANDA was a lost prince, she thought. And his exile to Macau had come at a price. There were always strings, always powerful ties to the Family. No one ever truly escaped North Korea.

He pinched his eyes, looking exhausted suddenly. "You can ask, but I may not tell."

Without taking her eyes off him, Jenna slid her hand into her handbag for the tablet issued to her by the CIA's Directorate of Science and Technology, and touched record.

6

White House
Washington, DC

President Trump used both hands to smooth back the lacquered wings of his hair. A few long strands trailed loose, waving like solar flares in the sunlight. He began to pace the room.

"I'm getting punched. I gotta punch back. I'm getting a royal fuck job by my so-called team . . ."

He was restless, agitated, but Eric could see that the heat had gone out of him for now, calmed by the golf.

"We're upside down on this South Korea thing. The generals don't understand business. All they want to do is protect everybody—and we're paying for it. Twenty-eight thousand troops. Three-point-five *billion* dollars a year to defend South Korea with *our troops*? I don't know why they're there. Let's bring 'em home."

Eric did not need to feign his expression. His gaze was true, his voice pure of heart.

"I agree, sir. Let's bring 'em home."

"Three-point-five billion dollars a year! How's that win-win? That's win-*lose. We're* losing!"

"The South Koreans are playing us for suckers, sir. It's very unfair."

"Very unfair," The president paused behind the desk, taking note of Eric's suit and shoes, his haircut. "You'd look good on TV."

Eric smiled and looked down, the heat rising to his face in what might have been a blush. The knowledge that he lacked any ability to feel empathy or pity gave him a heightened awareness of those emotions he *could* feel. And here, in the presence of this man, he was conscious of something wholly new starting to stir. He felt . . . humbled, vulnerable; he felt a *connection*, in a deeply human sense. It wasn't merely respect, which he always felt for those with power. This was something warmer, akin to adulation.

A squeak of leather sounded as the president lowered his backside into the executive seat.

"We'd be rich if we weren't so stupid. These countries, they've been shaking us down for years . . ."

The president was in full-flow monologue, like a guy in a bar talking at the TV, and Eric was mesmerized by it. He had only to listen, only to please, because he had come to understand something very important about this man: no one could touch the Boss in a battle of wills, but the man's grudges and vanity could put a clever operator in the driver's seat. He could be led by hands unseen. And now that the moment had come, Eric hadn't needed to say a thing.

"Okay, let's do this. I wanna see a draft. I wanna sign."

"Already done, sir."

Right on cue, Madeleine glided into the room with the document Eric had prepared, a curt letter addressed to the South Korean president, informing him, in a mere four lines, that the continued presence of 28,500 US ground forces on the Korean peninsula was no longer in the United States' national interest, and was incurring a cost it was no longer willing to shoulder. It was crude and magnificently undiplomatic.

"This is great," Trump chuckled, reading it. "This is what I want."

"It's a bold move, sir . . ." Eric said, his voice becoming silky and confiding. "And it frees you up to make a peace deal with North Korea."

Eric was holding out a Sharpie pen. All the man had to do was sign.

"Peace deal, huh . . . one for the history books." The president's smile was pure pleasure. "Kim Jong-un, he's a smart cookie."

"He is smart, sir."

The president took the Sharpie, uncapped it, and held it in his tiny white fist, which hovered for a moment over the document.

Eric wasn't breathing now. Seconds ticked away and to his dismay he saw the germ of an idea take root in the president's mind.

"You know what? Let's get the press in here this afternoon. I wanna sign this in front of the cameras. It'll send a strong message."

Eric's face clouded; his smile faltered. "Good idea, sir. Maximum impact."

He knew at once that he'd lost. The moment had gone. There was nothing he could say. And he knew there was no way in hell that letter would survive on the president's desk until the afternoon. One of the bottom-feeders would remove it.

The door opened. Madeleine's head reappeared. "Sir, Mr. Lavrov and Mr. Kislyak are here."

"Okay. Thank you, Eric. VERY good work. Really great." He patted Eric's shoulder and followed him out to the secretary's office.

Waiting for the president were two large, heavy-set men in dark suits: the Russian foreign minister, Sergey Lavrov, and the Russian ambassador to the United States, Sergey Kislyak, Vladimir Putin's two most senior diplomats. Trump greeted them like old chums.

Standing behind the Russians was a photographer who was not from the White House press pool. The man raised his lens. Lavrov turned to him and muttered a few words in Russian.

A Russian photographer in the Oval Office?

Trump grinned for the camera and gave him both thumbs up, then led the men into the Oval Office.

"I'm facing great pressure because of Russia," he was saying to them. "Great pressure. But I'm taking care of it . . ."

Following them into the meeting was the national security advisor, straight-backed, bald as an egg, face flushing hot with shame and embarrassment. He met Eric's eyes, casting a seal of silence upon him.

And on the heels of the national security advisor came one more person Eric had not seen before. A slender woman with a striking, Hellenic profile. Her hair was dark and silken and tied back in a French braid, and she wore a somber navy skirt suit. There was something distinctly un-American about her style. She was European perhaps, or Persian. In the door to the Oval Office, the national security advisor turned to her.

"Wait outside, Sofia. I'll call you in if I need you."

She nodded, her face expressionless, took a seat next to Madeleine's desk, and crossed her legs.

Eric continued to stare at her. She was pointedly not meeting his eye. She was young, in her mid-twenties, and carrying a briefing folder.

"I guess neither of us is important enough for that meeting, huh?" Eric said, his face all charm and dimples.

Her green eyes turned coolly in his direction. She did not smile.

"I'm Eric Rahn, special advisor to the president for East Asia." He offered his hand.

Reluctantly, she dropped her fingers into his palm. "Sofia Ali. Assistant to the national security advisor."

"First time in the White House?"

He could see she wanted to end this conversation. "Yes."

She betrayed no hint of the reverence and excitement Eric himself had felt when he'd first entered these rooms. A chill, off-limits vibe was coming from her, a palpable disdain for him that he found very alluring. She wore no makeup or jewelry, and her attire was simple—a failed attempt at plainness, perhaps.

"Does the national security advisor often bring you to meetings at this level?"

She drew a slow breath to indicate that this was her final answer. "No." She stared straight ahead. "Only when he needs a Russian speaker."

7

Datai Beach
Langkawi, Malaysia

"Let's start with your online gambling businesses in Macau," Jenna said. "That's a smart racket you're running. High cash flow from across the globe. Makes it easy to spread illegal funds around and dilute suspicious activity. And they're all fronts for your half-brother. You're using the gambling sites to pay for things that the Kim regime can't be seen paying for. The prizes you distribute are not all random—there's a pattern to some of them, isn't there? I'm interested in one in particular: a regular fixed-sum monthly payout to someone with the username 'juche888.'"

PANDA looked sharply at her, suddenly alert. Then, conscious that she was reading his body language, he made an unconvincing show of ignorance.

"Thousands of gamblers use the site. I don't know who they are. Why are you interested in that one?"

"Because juche888 is withdrawing his 'prize money' in the United States. That's not a player on a winning streak. Who are they? What are they being paid for?"

PANDA peered at her again, his eyes narrowing. The mention of juche888 seemed to have shaken loose some related memory in him. She could almost see it floating up through his mind, about to break the surface.

He said, "You're speaking Korean in the dialect of the North . . ."

Years ago, when she had been a junior professor at Georgetown, Jenna had spent three months in Jilin Province, China, near the border of North Korea, perfecting her grasp of North Korean dialect.

"You say we met in the Casino Lisboa," he said slowly, his mind working. "But I think I know you from before . . ."

"There was no 'before.' "

His eyes opened wide as it came to him. "I know you from Pyongyang!" He snapped his fingers. "You were in the compound. My father used to take me there. That was, God, *years* ago. Half Korean. Half African American. You were one of the Section 915 girls."

Jenna's blood froze.

What the hell . . .

He sat back, his nostrils flaring triumphantly as if he'd laid down a winning hand at poker. "Told you. I never forget a face."

PANDA had recognized Soo-min's face in hers. *PANDA had met her sister in that compound?* Section 915 was the Seed-Bearing Program.

"What happened to you?" he said with a sour chuckle. "They just let you go or something? And then you joined the fucking CIA?"

Jenna's thoughts had scattered like frightened fish. "Wasn't me," she murmured.

Her reaction puzzled him. "Well, if it wasn't you, it was someone who looked just like you."

The synaptic shock of realizing that PANDA had mistaken her for her twin sister was in danger of allowing another, critically important, realization to slip from her grasp. She chased after it through the clouds of confusion in her brain until she'd caught it by its tail.

And suddenly the crude progression of PANDA's thoughts was laid bare for her.

She said, "I asked you about a username called juche888, and next thing I know you're mentioning Section 915: the Seed-Bearing Program. What made you think of that? Is juche888 connected to the Seed-Bearing Program?"

PANDA's face slammed shut like a prison door. "Don't know what you mean."

Jenna's thoughts, so clear a minute ago, were faltering and disappearing like a distant ship's lantern in a storm.

"The Seed-Bearing Program ended . . ." she said, almost in argument with herself. Her mind was still reeling. *She* had ended it, five years ago. Twenty-two North Korean operatives had been arrested in the US and deported.

"Well, who knows?" he said tetchily. His skin was starting to blotch from the alcohol. "Maybe one of them slipped through your CIA fingers."

She had the sense of losing her composure, and she couldn't hide it.

"Who is juche888?"

"I don't know." PANDA had a hint of satisfaction in his voice now, a sense that something had turned in his favor. "But why are you asking me? You were one of them, weren't you? I don't know what your game is, lady, but you spent years in that compound. What was it called? Paekhwawon?"

"Humor me, please. Give me something to identify—"

A sound at the door—a quick double knock—yanked her attention back into the room. May Ling had spotted movement outside. They had agreed that if she detected the smallest anomaly, even if it turned out to be nothing, they would abort, night over. Jenna stood.

She said, "Take the money. You're my asset now."

"But—"

She left by the sliding doors and walked quickly back toward her own villa. Her mind was a disaster area. Roof collapsing, fires blazing, voices screaming.

There's an active Seed-Bearing Program operative in the US.

She had no secure comms on the island. She would have to alert Headquarters the moment she got back to Kuala Lumpur tomorrow morning.

Whoever juche888 was, he or she must have been in the States for years by now. Long enough to have graduated from college, possibly obtain citizenship, and started a career . . . where? Wall Street? Big tech? Air traffic control? Capitol Hill?

They might already be in position to do massive damage . . .

And this person was receiving monthly funds via PANDA's gambling app . . . an app that could also be used to transmit orders and receive reports. They would simply log on as a player, unnoticed among the thousands of daily gamblers on the site . . .

She slowed her pace as she considered this, the simple genius of it.

Then she stood still and stared at the stone path winding dimly ahead of her between the trees. All around her the orchestra of the night chirruped rhythmically. Bats squeaked and dipped between the palms.

She was suddenly wretched and overwhelmed by what had really upset her: the tremendous rush of grief she felt for her sister, for all that she had suffered, for everything they had done to her.

Years ago, neighbors in Annandale had gotten them mixed up all the time. "Which one are you?" they'd say. Being mistaken for Soo-min had been a regular part of Jenna's growing up.

But no one had made that mistake in a very long time. To hear PANDA making it, of all people, had been horrible, astonishing, uncanny. PANDA had been disinherited in 2001 and exiled in 2003. It had never crossed her mind that he might once have been privy to a state secret like the Seed-Bearing Program—that he may have met Soo-min in North Korea.

And she knew then, as surely as she knew anything, that she was about to risk the whole op and call her sister, just to hear her voice, just to tell her that she loved her, and because it was Trophy Day, the one day she always called, wherever she was.

8

The White House
Washington, DC

Eric walked back to his office deep in thought.

He'd come close, *so* close. The Boss had wanted to sign—the Boss loved signing things!—but when the moment came, vanity had distracted him.

I wanna sign this in front of the cameras . . .

Eric replayed the encounter in his head until he'd convinced himself that it had simply been bad luck. He cautioned himself to keep his nerve. Another chance would come soon. He'd make damn sure that letter found its way back to the Boss's desk.

And yet, something about what had just happened was niggling Eric, and he couldn't put his finger on it. The Boss had an almost supernatural feel for people's secret motivations and vulnerabilities . . . had he sensed he was being played? Or was it something to do with those two senior Russians, breezing in there with their *own* photographer . . . ? That was weird. Or was it that strange ice queen, Sofia Ali, who was from everywhere and nowhere? Something off about her, too.

Eric made a right past the vice president's office, and along the corridor of small offices occupied by the toadies, the schemers, and the leakers. An air of mania and desperation pervaded the place.

Every staffer he passed was yelling into their phones or whispering in groups, all of them pulling their hair out trying to navigate the extreme chaos field of the Trump White House.

"I did *not hear* that. For the record, I'm removing myself from this conversation . . . No, don't you dare put it in an email . . ."

"Yeah, her—get rid of her. The president said she looks like a refrigerator in a wig . . ."

"When you speak to him, open with positive feedback. Praise something he's done . . ."

"You took fucking *notes*? You've gotta shred 'em! . . . No, no—he'll pardon you."

Eric slipped into his office and closed the door.

Quickly, he swiped his phone and logged onto the gambling app.

Welcome back, juche888!

Then he proceeded gingerly through the long sequence of memorized passwords, with letters and symbols that had to be pressed simultaneously, until he'd accessed the encrypted secret messaging portal.

He typed out a brief contact report to Center describing his meeting in the Oval Office and expressing his confidence that another chance to present the letter for Trump's signature would come again soon, possibly as early as tomorrow.

To his surprise he received a near-instant response that caught him just as he was about to log off. Not a word of praise or thanks or encouragement from Center. Just a blunt demand for confirmation that he would be meeting GINKGO today.

GINKGO?

Eric threw back his head and bared his teeth in a silent scream of pent-up anger, exasperation, and hostility at the world. He wanted to smash his phone to tiny shards and smithereens with the heel of his shoe. Had they no appreciation for how fucking BUSY he was?

Didn't they understand that people in this country were expected to do REAL WORK! He had ZERO time to go chasing wild geese and lost causes. He had—

Then it came to him. Why they'd asked. He'd been so preoccupied with his plot this morning that the significance of today's date had completely slipped his mind.

Trophy Day. A red-letter day in the Williams twins' calendar.

The violence of his thoughts subsided with the suddenness of a tropical storm. He sent another message through the portal to confirm that he was heading out to visit GINKGO right now. Again, he received a response within seconds: Center was on standby to hack and disable the hospital's CCTV for the duration of his visit.

Eric leapt from his chair and grabbed his coat. He rushed past the secretaries, telling them to hold his calls: he was heading to an urgent off-site meeting that had only just been scheduled. He would be back in two hours.

The chances of getting a result were low, he knew. He'd visited GINKGO several times over the last five years, and not once had she cooperated, not once had she given him so much as a clue. None of his lies had worked on her, except to keep her quiet.

Silent, crazy, disloyal bitch.

But today—"Trophy Day"—was the day GINKGO always received a call from Most Wanted Person Number One. Perhaps he'd even be there at her bedside when the call came through.

GINKGO, the name of a nut. Hard to crack.

No one from North Korea had ever spelled it out for Eric, but in his heart he knew. You'd think there was nothing more important in the world to the Family in Pyongyang than the withdrawal of all US troops from the Korean Peninsula. It would leave South Korea vulnerable, powerless to resist the Great Successor's loving embrace. The reunification of Korea, through war if necessary, was the foundational creed of the regime Eric served. There was, however, one deeply classified and acutely sensitive matter that held an even higher priority for the Family: the elimination of Most Wanted Person Number One, CIA operations officer Jenna Williams. Nothing mattered more to them than the avenging of the crime she had committed, a crime so unpardonable, so horrifying in its magnitude, that it disgusted Eric, outraged him, made his blood seethe and white spittle appear at the edges of his lips whenever he thought about it, even now, five years on.

"Well, Soo-min," he murmured as he slammed the door of his Audi and fastened the safety belt. "Let's see if you give us Jenna this time."

9

Hay-Adams Hotel
Washington, DC
Wednesday morning

It was mid-morning by the time Dmitry Stepanovich Kuznetsov checked into his hotel. He hadn't traveled far—just a short flight from LaGuardia—but he was already exhausted. He'd gone straight from the airport to the Russian embassy on Wisconsin Avenue, where Ambassador Kislyak and Foreign Minister Lavrov had wanted to discuss strategy with him prior to their meeting with Trump in the White House this morning. (It had been decided that they should encourage the president to bloviate freely and without interruption, because the last time he had done so in the company of Russian diplomats he had blithely scattered a debris field of rich intelligence nuggets for the Kremlin to follow up and analyze.)

"Mr. Kuznetsov, welcome back." The desk manager gave Dmitry a smile that brightened to a very high watt. "Your reservation is for the presidential suite. We hope you enjoy your stay."

The man's familiar tone suggested that he knew who Dmitry was.

Well, his name was no secret. And there were plenty of images of him online—attending diplomatic parties, trade fairs, gallery openings, black-tie galas at the Met. Photographers sometimes singled him out. He was handsome in a bygone-era kind of way. In his late fifties, but in his prime—tall, dapper, with fine steel-gray hair, side-parted, and eyes of an unusual gas-flame blue. To a casual observer he might have been an actor famous in France, or an architect of iconic buildings. If anyone googled him, they'd know that he was a diplomat attached to the Russian Federation's UN mission on 67th Street, New York. Less well known, but much more significant, was the fact that he was also a colonel in the SVR, Russia's foreign intelligence service, and the most senior SVR officer stationed in North America.

Once he was alone in his room, Dmitry put the chain on the door and, from long habit, inspected the lamps and electrical sockets for hidden cameras and mics, even though he knew that surveillance tech these days was virtually undetectable. They could hide a lens in a pinhead, a microphone in a business card just half a millimeter thick.

The suite, reserved for two nights, had too much velvet and gilt for his tastes. But the bed was luxuriously soft, and once he'd kicked off his shoes and lain down on it, he knew he'd have difficulty getting up again. Perhaps he had time for a nap.

Just thinking about his schedule for the next forty-eight hours gave him a feeling of deathly fatigue. Midday today: back to the embassy for a debrief with Lavrov and Kislyak following their Oval Office meeting. This afternoon: a defense seminar at the State Department with his American UN counterparts. This evening: a UNICEF concert at the John F. Kennedy Center with all the usual DC grandees and their spouses in attendance, which meant that he'd have to mingle and network at the cocktail reception afterward. Not until he got back to the hotel late tonight, by which time he'd be practically brain dead, would he have time to write up the intelligence report that Putin would be expecting after today's Oval Office meeting.

Putin.

He'd just remembered that tomorrow morning every network in Russia would be airing *Direct Line with Vladimir Putin*, the president's live annual TV phone-in, a stage-managed extravaganza that went on for an epic *four hours*. He'd have to make time to watch at least *some* of it when he woke up in case the great man announced any surprise shifts in policy toward the United States which Dmitry might be called upon to explain to the US congressmen he was meeting tomorrow. (Five Russia-friendly good old boys, who seemed to parrot anything the Kremlin said, had invited him to lunch at the National Republican Club.)

He rubbed his eyes and groaned. He would have no time to himself until tomorrow night, and then, well. There'd be no chance of sleep, because he would be slipping out of the hotel at about midnight for a rendezvous in Rock Creek Park. And it would be dangerous, very dangerous. He would need all his wits about him, all his senses on hyperalert, because he was meeting secretly with the CIA and because Washington was crawling with Russian agents. They were already watching him, of course; they routinely kept an eye on their own, especially an SVR officer of his rank. They were probably watching him right now in this room. But if he could evade them for a few hours tomorrow night, and get to his meeting unseen, then the intel would be delivered. It would be out of his hands and his conscience clear . . . He simply had to make it through the next forty-eight hours. Then Friday morning, back to New York.

He curled up on the bed and tried to nap. Only the restless thrumming of his heart was preventing the full onset of sleep. He had long learned what it meant never to relax, to be always alert. He knew the extremes of loneliness and self-pity, the sudden aching desire for his wife, for the company of his dear son, who was no longer talking to him, for anything to take away the stress in his life. Lately he'd been starting to feel his age. His nerves were shredded. He'd been passing secrets to the Americans for three years and he didn't think he could do it for much longer. The fear of being caught was now ever-present and inescapable, like a tumor, like a gathering darkness.

And Dmitry was under no illusion about his fate if he was caught.

Years ago, when he'd first joined the SVR, he'd been shown a short film. It had been compulsory viewing for all new SVR recruits. Even now, as he closed his eyes and tried to nap, that grainy black-and-white footage projected onto the walls of his mind like a nightmare. It had shown a man gagged and tied with wires to a steel stretcher. He was being wheeled toward what looked like a heavy, cast-iron hatch door. The man was frantic; his body was straining so hard that tendons in his arms and legs were tearing. But the wires didn't give. The hatch opened to reveal a blazing furnace. The man screamed for his life. Then, with one quick shove . . . in he went.

An image that, once seen, was never forgotten. But that was the point.

This is the fate of an SVR officer who betrays our secrets.

If he was caught, things would happen quickly. There'd be no trial.

10

Psychiatric Wing, Mount Vernon Hospital
Arlington, Virginia

The ward was quiet. Smells of coffee and institutional omelets lingered in the air. Most inmates were still dosed up and dozing. Muffled laughter from a morning talk show emanated from behind the closed doors of the patients' lounge.

Eric paused to check his hair in the reflective glass of the security guard's office, then composed his face into its most sympathetic expression.

The nurse behind the desk was a portly young man with a gold ear stud and a name tag that said ADAM.

"I'm here to visit Soo-min," Eric said. "Is now a good time?"

Eric barely registered the man's eyes melting from professional distance into something more adoring. It was a reaction he got on a regular basis.

"Uh, Soo-min's only taking visits from her mom, sir."

"She'll want to see me, I'm sure. I'm an old, old friend."

"Oh, you're the gentleman who called the director's office. You wanted to surprise her?"

Center had thought of everything. Eric turned on his *GQ* magazine smile. "How is she?"

"A little brighter this week. Can you wait here a moment? I'll see if she's awake."

Eric watched the nurse, Adam, go to a door at the end of a short corridor and knock gently. "Soo-min? Susie?" He opened it ajar and put his head inside.

A ping sounded on the desk and Eric noticed Adam's iPhone light up with a Grindr notification.

The nurse beckoned to him.

"Loooook . . ." He was speaking into the room as if to a child. "Here's someone to cheer you up." He turned to Eric and in a whisper said, "Go in. She's just waking up."

"Thanks, Adam. I'll only be a minute. I don't wish to tire her."

Eric entered and closed the door softly behind him.

The room was very dim, with only the clouded morning light filtering through the gaps in the curtains. Soo-min lay with her forearm across her eyes, her chest rising and falling rhythmically, slowly emerging from a deep pharma sleep.

Standing there in shadow, his dark coat draped over his shoulders and his hands in black leather gloves, he imagined himself a vampire eyeing some maidenly artery.

No TV. No phone. Nothing to disturb or upset the patient.

"Mom?" Soo-min's voice was thick with sleep.

Eric sat down carefully on the edge of the bed and removed his gloves. Gently he took hold of her hand, which was cool and perspiring.

He spoke in Korean. "No, Soo-min. It's me."

Soo-min's eyes shot open.

Her hand flew from his as if she'd been scalded. "You!" Even in the room's twilight Eric could see her eyes were lit with fear and hatred. "You!"

"Hush, come on," he said. "I'm sorry the sight of me upsets you."

"Leave me alone," she gasped. She started kicking at him under the sheets. "Get out. *Get out!*" Her long black hair had fallen over half her face, like she was some apparition in a horror movie. Eric wanted to laugh.

"Calm down, for God's sake."

"You're a *bastard* . . . you're the devil . . ."

Eric could feel his patience ebbing. "You know why I'm here. It's a very simple deal, Soo-min." His voice rose over her cries. "My offer still stands, but this is the last time I'll make it."

"No!" She began to cry. "The answer's no." And now she really screamed. *"Get out!"*

Eric glanced toward the door, fearing that the nurse could hear. Then he got up and clamped his hand hard over Soo-min's mouth. She bucked and writhed beneath him.

"Listen to me," he said, bringing his face close to hers, "I'll *tell* you where your son is . . . I'll even give you his cellphone number. Right now, if you like." Soo-min's dark eyes glittered with hate. She was struggling to break his grip, but it was a vise over her mouth. He grabbed her other arm and pinioned it to the bed, feeling his strength from those hours in the gym. "It's a simple trade, Soo-min. You'll be reunited with him in no time. Mother and son. *Mother and son . . .*" She stopped fighting and went still. "Now, I'm going to take my hand away. Promise me you won't scream?" Slowly Eric removed his hand. Her face was full of terror and wild defiance, an animal in a trap. "You hate me, I get it," he said neutrally. "But I'm the only one who understands you. Your mom, your psychiatrist—they don't know what it was like, do they? It's a secret you share with me. Push me away all you want. But we can end this—" He gestured around the hospital room with his eyes. "These breakdowns you keep having, the medication—it's killing you, isn't it? But when you see your son again, you'll recover. I know you will. You know it, too." He paused, giving her a smile that he knew looked genuine. "All you have to do . . . is give me Jenna."

Soo-min's voice was wan and trembling. "So you can kill her? You're crazy if you think I'll ever do that."

"Kill her?" Eric said innocently. "No, we want her to stand trial. She's got to face justice, Soo-min." His voice dropped to a solemn whisper. "Your sister committed a heinous crime. The worst imaginable. We can't forget what she did, Soo-min. Ever. You understand that, don't you?"

"I don't know where she is ... I really don't." Soo-min's face creased as bitter, desperate tears began to flow. "Just please, please give me back my son."

Eric was struck by how strongly the accent of the North came out when she spoke Korean. He had worked hard, so hard, to rid himself of all trace of that accent. He reached over and brushed away her hair to get a better look at her face.

"I believe you. I don't think you do know where Jenna is ... but she *communicates* with you, doesn't she? And on a special day like today, 'Trophy Day' ..."

Soo-min gave a tight, quick shake of her head.

"How does she make contact? Some secret phone she's given you?"

Soo-min's lips remained compressed together.

"He's a young man now, you know, just turned seventeen. Your son, Ha-jun – he doesn't call himself that, of course – he's a nice-looking kid. He's applying to colleges later this year. Imagine how curious he is about his mother. How happy he'd be to know that you're here, in the United States. Don't deny him that bond, Soo-min. No mother should do that to her son." His voice softened further. "Just tell me how to find Jenna. And this will all be over. You'll never see me again."

For a few seconds they held each other's gaze, and Eric thought he saw a resolution, a decision taking shape behind her eyes.

That's it, he thought. *Give her up. Unburden yourself ...*

After an interminable pause, she spoke. Eric leaned his ear closer to her face.

"Again, please?"

Very faintly, her voice pure air: *"Go fuck yourself."*

Eric closed his eyes and sighed. For a moment he was lost in his own private labyrinth, musing on his severely impaired capacity to feel empathy, for her, for anyone. Occasionally he could note, with a curious detachment, when he had been feeling rage, or greed, or disgust, which were his dominant emotions, and he was certainly aware of the fizzing black rage that was gathering like a halo around his head right now. He wished he had orders to kill this woman, which he could do easily with his thumbs pressed to her windpipe, or with a fork from a breakfast tray plunged into her heart. It might even have given him a fleeting enjoyment, light up the void inside him just for a moment. Instead, with a very determined effort to contain his disordered self, he managed a consoling smile.

"Disappointing, Soo-min." He pulled his gloves back on, flexing his fingers as he did so. "I think your son can kiss goodbye to that college place. And citizenship." He stood up from the bed. "He'll spend the rest of his life picking dog shit off sidewalks. If he's lucky." He paused before he opened the door to leave. "If you ever open your mouth about me, or anything we've talked about, your son dies. I'll kill him with my own hands."

He closed the door gently behind him.

The nurse, Adam, was hovering at the reception desk. Eric gave him another flash of that grin that dimpled his cheeks. He lowered his voice to a confidential murmur.

"Tell me, Adam, has Soo-min's sister visited?"

"Soo-min's sister?"

"Yes, Soo-min has an identical twin sister—Jee-min, known as Jenna. She didn't mention her?"

"No, I don't think so . . . sorry."

"Well, if Jenna ever happens to show up here—you'd recognize her at once—perhaps you'd do me a real favor, as one boy to another, and let me know? Soo-min doesn't like to worry her. Jenna and I, well . . . I'd really like to discuss a care plan for Soo-min. But . . ." He winked at Adam. ". . . let's keep it between us? I know Soo-min gets a little paranoid sometimes. Probably best if she doesn't know."

Adam took the card Eric had placed on the desk.

As Eric was turning to leave, he heard Adam's iPhone ring. He stopped in his tracks and looked down at the lit-up screen. *No Caller ID.*

Adam offered him an apologetic smile and then picked up. "Hello? . . . Yes . . . Who's this? . . . How did you get . . . No, that's OK . . . I don't mind at all . . . Yes, she's awake . . ."

"A call for Soo-min?" Eric said, his voice a whisper.

Nodding, Adam clutched the phone to his chest and excused himself.

"Just one second . . ."

It was only his instinct, his sixth sense, but Eric knew. *It was her.* Jenna Williams. Right there on the line. In the palm of a nurse's hand. The opportunity, the *temptation*, to grab that phone and say something to her, the woman his country had spent years trying to find, was tremendous.

Was this faggot covering for her?

No . . . The guy was a dupe. Jenna wouldn't risk the hospital switchboard—with calls recorded and monitored for training purposes—so she'd gotten hold of a private number.

Eric watched Adam take the phone into Soo-min's room. Through the open door he saw him hand it to her in bed, and then, as if they had both sensed his lingering malignance, they turned to see him staring at them.

Seconds later, when Adam had closed Soo-min's door and returned to the desk, without the phone, he seemed puzzled to see Eric still there.

Eric rearranged his face into a bashful smile with a hint of a come-on. "I, uh . . . I was wondering . . . would you like to get a coffee with me sometime?"

The nurse gave a sudden laugh to conceal his embarrassment. "Oh!" Then he glanced about to make sure no one was nearby. "Um . . . Sure! I don't know your name."

"I'm Eric." He shook Adam's hand and gave its palm a soft stroke. Adam's cheeks reddened quickly but his eyes, Eric noticed, had become dull with desire. Eric could almost read his thoughts as if they were written on flashcards.

What're you into Eric?

Oh, I'm just a dom-top Daddy who's gonna bust your big candy-ass.

"Put your number in my phone, if you like," Eric said smoothly. "And I'll give you a call."

Adam tapped his number into Eric's phone and handed it back to him. "I'll look forward to that . . . *Eric.*"

Eric turned away just in time to hide a gag of revulsion.

Four minutes later, sealed inside his Audi in the hospital parking lot, Eric logged back into the encryption tool concealed inside the gambling app. His fingers trembled with excitement. He mistyped some of the passwords in the sequence, swore out loud, and had to start again. Then he sent the nurse's phone number to a colleague of his in the Reconnaissance General Bureau, North Korea's foreign intelligence agency. He added a high-priority message requesting the tracing of the most recent number that had called the nurse's phone, about five minutes ago, and the caller's call location coordinates.

Thrumming with anticipation and nervous energy, he turned the key in the ignition, and the powerful engine engaged softly.

Dear, dear GINKGO. He'd been lying to her, of course. He had no idea where her son was. But she believed the lie, and that was all that mattered.

But where was Soo-min's son?

Eric wished he knew the answer to that question because finding Ha-jun was one of his principal mission objectives. Center still insisted that the kid was in America, but Eric wasn't sure about that anymore. He'd been searching for this kid, on and off, for years now. His investigations had gotten nowhere, meaning that he had the monthly humiliation of reporting his lack of progress to Pyongyang. It wasn't fair. He had no one to help him search, and *no time for shit like that* . . .

Once again, he found himself bitterly wondering who the hell this kid was. What was so special about him? *Something* special, if he was this hard to find. Perhaps there was a clue locked inside Soo-min's mind, that sunken wreck of secrets. Perhaps he could twist it out of her one day.

He was in the fast-flowing traffic heading back to DC when he received a response from the Reconnaissance General Bureau. Not the text message he'd expected, but a phone call, from the intelligence officer in person, via the encrypted app.

The voice was faint, with a strong North Korean accent. He had to put it on speakerphone.

"Who's this caller you've asked me to trace?"

"A person of interest," Eric said, curtly. He was damned if he was going to share any credit with this guy. "Just tell me where the call originated."

"Malaysia, according to the network's hidden logs and switch routes. The Datai Beach Hotel in Langkawi, to be precise. The area's all rainforest and there's only one nearby call tower. But here's the thing . . . You won't believe who else is in the same location right now. We track him every time he leaves Macau. Your 'person of interest' must be there to meet him."

"Who?"

When Eric heard the name, he thought he'd misheard the man and asked for it to be repeated. Then he was so stunned that he lost all concentration, only jolting his focus back to the road when he heard the wheels rumble against the solid white lines of the shoulder.

He saw a sign for an upcoming gas station. He hadn't a moment to lose. Minutes later he pulled in, turned off the engine, and made the phone call of his life, this time to a Korean People's Army colonel with diplomatic cover working out of the United Nations Secretariat Building in New York—the contact he was only to call in the direst emergency.

"Why are you calling this number?" was the man's greeting.

Eric apologized and told him it couldn't wait. His visit to GINKGO had hit the motherlode! In a few brief words he relayed his discovery, but no words could convey the magnitude of it.

Eric pictured the man sitting up. His tone changed completely. "We'll take it from here," he said, and ended the call.

For a few moments Eric sat still, breathing deeply, still calm.

He, Eric Rahn, had not only located Most Wanted Person Number One Jenna Williams; he had uncovered a major conspiracy. A betrayal inside the Family. High treason.

The half-brother is talking to the CIA.

As he left the gas station, he began drumming his fingers on the steering wheel, chanting a war song he remembered singing long ago, on the other side of the world, by a campfire beneath the stars, in the beautiful, forested hills of his homeland. And with a small effort, like slipping his feet into a pair of well-worn shoes, his old accent, the accent of the North, came back to him. Suddenly he was whooping and laughing like a banshee, high on the intoxicating thrill of power.

We've found you, Jenna, we've found you! We will darken the sky with your ashes.

11

Datai Beach
Langkawi, Malaysia
Thursday morning

Jenna slipped her Beretta, passport, burner phone, and the Motorola into her shoulder bag, and called May Ling to say she was going to stretch her legs before the journey back. They had a quarter hour before their ride to the airport arrived. The support team had confirmed that PANDA had already left the island. He would be landing in Kuala Lumpur International any minute now and would transfer to an 11:50 Air Asia flight to Macau.

On the steps leading down to the cove, light was falling in long fingers from the canopy of trees; far off, white clouds rolled like cotton bales across a sky of clear, unstained blue. In a more relaxed frame of mind, she might have found joy in such beauty, but she had barely slept. She was too disturbed by last night's events to enjoy it.

PANDA had given off all the right signals—fear, weakness, desperation. May Ling had been reeling him in for months. She'd elicited all the information Jenna had needed to make a successful pitch—and he'd talked. She was pretty sure he'd meet her again and agree to work for the CIA.

And yet she felt she'd lost all control over the interview.

Because PANDA had revealed something wholly unexpected. Something he might *never* have mentioned if it hadn't been for a simple case of mistaken identity.

"You were in the compound. My father used to take me there. That was, God, years ago . . . Half Korean. Half African American. You were one of the Section 915 girls."

The moment she'd realized he was talking about her own sister she had become defenseless, utterly exposed.

The Seed-Bearing Program.

The cove was deserted, and the sand deep and cool at the edge of the surf. Distracted, she let the clear water rinse over her toes. The sun was still low in the sky, but the sand was already giving off a blinding glare. She put on her sunglasses and began to walk.

Last night she'd gone against all her tradecraft, all her caution, to call Soo-min.

The nurse had answered the phone. Then she'd heard the phone being handed to Soo-min, followed by panicky hyperventilation—presumably coming from Soo-min—and then the line had gone dead.

Her sister had hung up on her. Immediately and without a word.

Jenna was accustomed to the silent treatment. Even during the worst of these breakdowns, she usually found the words to reach her sister somehow, to connect with her. She would persist and keep talking until she had cut a path through the tangles of anxiety and paranoia and found the small, sunny clearing where Soo-min was still Soo-min—the embattled place inside her sister's head where her original self took refuge and could still smile.

But she'd never been hung up on like that before.

And that wasn't the only thing that had unsettled Jenna about that call: just after she'd spoken to the nurse, she could have sworn she'd heard someone whispering . . .

After that, she had lain awake for a long time, worrying, listening to the wind thrashing in the trees, thinking she should take leave to visit Soo-min now, in the next few days. It was hours before she had drifted off into a clammy sleep plagued by bad dreams.

Seagulls swooped and cried. The water was a patchwork of light and dark, turquoise and ultramarine. About a hundred yards out, a dozen windsurfers were steering their boards between bright red buoys.

Now and then she thought she heard a buzzing sound, moving in and out of the wind. She shielded her eyes against the sun and spotted, high in the air above the windsurfers, a drone filming them: a hexacopter, one of the large commercial types used for TV sports events.

Jenna's pace was slow, meditative, her mind full of Soo-min.

It had been five years since Soo-min had come home—or rather, since she had physically come home. Her mind, Jenna sensed, had never truly left North Korea, and maybe never would. Weeks sometimes went by without her speaking a word. Medication, psychiatric counseling, periods of hospitalization—nothing had helped.

There might have been one person with the power to restore her sister's sanity, but Jenna had not thought seriously about him for a long time.

In North Korea, Soo-min had given birth to a son. His name, she had said, was Ha-jun, and he had been taken from her when he was eight years old. For reasons that she had never been able or willing to explain, Soo-min was convinced that Ha-jun had been sent abroad and was living in the United States. That had seemed utterly delusional to Jenna. Why would North Korea send a boy of only eight years old anywhere, least of all to the Main Enemy, the United States? An eight-year-old couldn't be a spy, and he was too old to be adopted. Where at first Soo-min's desperation to find him had been all-consuming, it had later become despairing and agonizing as her mental state deteriorated.

So, for Soo-min's sake, Jenna had given the search her best shot. She had turned to her old CIA mentor Charles Fisk for help in finding Ha-jun. Fisk had called in favors from the FBI. For six months after Soo-min's return, Jenna had had the resources of the federal government engaged in the search for Ha-jun. But with no photo of him, and nothing to go on but a name and a birthdate, every line of investigation had drawn a blank. The Red Cross, the UN Commission for Refugees, immigration services, adoption agencies, foster care homes, Korean community databases—no one had heard of him. Schools, church organizations, police records, social media. Nothing.

After that, Jenna had hired one private investigator after another. But after three fruitless years, she was more convinced than ever that Ha-jun was not in the United States and that he had never in fact left North Korea—although she'd not dared say this to Soo-min. Ha-jun had become a mythic figure to Jenna, a child lost in time. The dead, she thought, could be mourned, wept over, laid to rest. But a missing person, as she herself knew only too well, was a phantom, a source of terrible anguish that could blight an entire lifetime. Soo-min's state of mind was dependent on a son who was *never going to be found*. This was too much for Jenna to deal with. Her own twin became someone she found it hard to be around. And the deep, tidal guilt she felt about this manifested itself in pre- dictable ways: an obsessive commitment to her work, nightmares, an unwillingness to make close friends or seek intimacy ...

She glanced at her watch. She'd wandered further along the cove than she'd meant to, and now turned and retraced her footsteps in the sand. The only sounds were the soft washing of the waves, the gulls' cries, and the bumblebee hum of the drone, which was still there, high above the windsurfers.

As she climbed the steps back to the hotel her thoughts finally circled back to PANDA. The man she'd seen last night was a dead man walking. But he was her asset now, and she would protect him. The recontact with him would need to be soon, within days. Some- where secure. Macau was too risky. The Chinese and the North

Koreans had eyes all over him in China. She would have to insist that he come back to Malaysia for their next meeting. In the meantime, she would request an exfil plan for PANDA and his son.

Her brain was whirring like a program she couldn't disable, calculating risk, probing for danger, reviewing data.

She had reached the terrace where the enormous kidney-shaped pool stretched out like a lagoon. A honeymooning couple waved to another couple across the row of sun loungers, but otherwise she could see that most of the hotel's guests were still at breakfast.

As she passed the restaurant, she saw that people were turning in their seats to watch the enormous flatscreen mounted above the buffet table. She followed their gaze to the TV.

For one innocent moment she thought it was news of another terrorist attack, but then a shot of PANDA's face filled the screen, a terrible old flash photo of him looking fat and blanched and stubbly—and the realization struck her like a kick to the stomach.

She ran to the window and cupped her hand to the glass. The breaking news ticker was inching along the bottom of the screen ... HAS DIED AT KUALA LUMPUR INTERNATIONAL AIRPORT. THE VICTIM IS THE HALF-BROTHER OF NORTH KOREAN LEADER KIM JONG-UN ...

Without a second glance, she walked quickly away, up the stairs that led to the lobby, heart pounding hard, her training kicking in. The op was blown. She had to get out of Malaysia—fast.

She started to tap out a message to May Ling as she walked, but May Ling beat her to it.

PAPAYA—their codeword for *ABORT—RETURN TO STATION.*

Her passport was on her, that was good, she was leaving this instant, crossing the hotel lobby, receiving the hospitality smiles from the desk staff. Then she was through the main doors and passing the taxi rank outside in the garden forecourt.

Not a taxi in sight. Just a couple of teens seated on scooters, smoking, both with spiky hair, checkered short-sleeve shirts, no crash helmets. They turned to look at her. Jenna moved directly toward them. In that momentum borne of urgency and need, the teen nearest to her seemed to anticipate her.

"Airport?"

Jenna pulled a handful of twenty-ringgit notes from her bag, which the boy took and stuffed into his shirt pocket, trying not to smile.

"Ferry," she said.

Suddenly she heard the buzz of that drone again, much closer. She turned to look but saw nothing between the tall palms lining the hotel's driveway.

She took out the Beretta and pushed it into her belt.

Seconds later she had her arms around the boy as the scooter sped away up the gravel road, banging and tripping over the ruts, the small engine whining like a lawnmower's. It was almost too rough for tires. They were racing along a track that ran parallel with the edge of the coast, beneath neat rows of planted palms.

The road was empty but for a few barefoot locals in sarongs carrying huge sacks on their backs.

Everything was unfolding in a rush. That sense of coming unstuck in space and time.

PANDA was assassinated. They must have had eyes on him for days, every damned place he went, including on this island . . .

The boy slowed to avoid a series of potholes left by the rainy season.

Instinct made her glance over her shoulder.

The drone was ten meters away and level with her head. Its cameras were pointing right at her. Before she could warn the boy, it accelerated toward her like a demonic hornet, blades screaming, red lights flashing. She pulled the Beretta from her belt and turned her body to aim, arm extended, feeling the gun's heft in her palm.

Lock the wrist. Press the trigger.

The scooter bounced. She squeezed twice, firing two distinct *pops* barely heard over the noise of the engine. Her aim was wide. The drone was almost in her face.

Jenna yanked the left handlebar and pitched the scooter hard into a grassy ditch.

The impact threw the boy clear as the explosion bucked the earth and warped the air. The last thing she remembered was the thudding of rocks landing all around her, and drone engine fragments raining from the sky, setting fire to a palm tree.

12

Beecher Street
Washington, DC
Wednesday evening

Word of the hit on Jenna had had a curious effect on Eric. His first reaction was one of soaring triumph and glee. He'd punched the air and hit the ceiling of his car. He'd shouted "Yes, yes, *yessss!*" The euphoria of vengeance had coursed through his nervous system like a mighty electric charge.

It's done! And I caused it. I am Justice and I am Death.

It was his contact in the Reconnaissance General Bureau, the North Korean intelligence officer who'd traced Jenna's call to Langkawi, who'd told him. The man had congratulated him warmly: the intel he had provided had been noted "in the highest circles."

Praise indeed . . .

He'd wanted to celebrate, snort a line of coke as long as his arm, book a girl, anything to release the anarchic exuberance that was condensed inside him and ready to burst.

But over the course of the night, those feelings had given way to a strangely contemplative mood, and he'd found himself sitting up for hours in his unlit apartment, thinking, listening to the rain and the wash of passing traffic, watching the shifting, subaqueous glow from the streetlamps as water streaked down the windows.

He was an agent in the heart of the White House. He had destroyed Most Wanted Person Number One Jenna Williams. He was on the cusp of persuading the president of the United States to pull all US forces from the Korean peninsula. Against the odds, his mission was bearing spectacular fruit—real-world results, tangible and quantifiable. He was succeeding far beyond Pyongyang's expectations . . .

But success was bringing home to him an uneasy, oppressive realization: that Center would expect more from him now, much more. And its demands would have no regard for the crushing workload and long hours of his day job, or for the capricious, malevolent moods of the president, who could turn on him at any time . . .

More than anything he was worried that Center would order him to renew the search for Soo-min's son, even though he had reported all his efforts in full. Surely, they could see that no more could be done . . . Nowhere was there a record of Ha-jun. There wasn't even a recent photo of him. In the only photo Eric had seen the kid had been eight years old.

Eric never questioned orders, but he wished he understood Center's fixation with this target. Why this kid? *Because he's Jenna Williams's nephew?* And why, why was it falling to him to deal with? Why not the network of spies and informers he knew operated among the North Korean defectors in the US?

If the task was so secret that it had been entrusted to him alone, he wondered what would happen to him if he did actually find Ha-jun and discover what this secret was . . .

One by one, fresh anxieties began to hatch and slither through his gut like newborn eels, so that by the time he went to bed they'd all coiled in the base of his stomach.

That night, perhaps because seeing Soo-min had reminded him of it, he dreamed of home.

Paekhwawon nestling in its soft green hills, so iconic of Korea. Paekhwawon, where deer roamed the woodland trails and the early morning skies were so clear and epic that he could see the towers of the capital, Pyongyang, shining in the distance.

Eric's earliest memories were of Paekhwawon. He may even have been born there, but he didn't know for sure. He'd never known his parents, did not even know their names. He assumed that all the children there understood that they were orphans, because they'd been given orphans' names (after the 114 martyrs of the eternal revolution), but they'd also been given Western names. And he had loved the heroic and manly sound of his own: Eric.

Paekhwawon was a walled compound secluded in a narrow wooded valley. It comprised male and female dorms, a block of classrooms, sports fields, a parade ground. It was nothing special to look at and yet there was nowhere else like it in the world. Security was tight; visitors were rare; outings were few and only under strictly controlled conditions.

The instructors had never missed a chance to remind them of their good fortune. *Other children don't have what you have,* they'd said. *Other children won't learn what you're learning.* It was true. Paekhwawon had good food, excellent teachers, modern facilities.

From infancy the children were schooled intensively in languages, math, and sciences, because all of them were destined to enter the best universities of the Main Enemy, America. That had been drummed into them from the start, to create an expectation that they'd excel. The afternoons were taken up by physical training. This could be very harsh and often went on till after dark, by which time they were filthy, hungry, and bleeding. Children who couldn't handle it were taken away in a truck at night and not seen again.

Once, when he'd been eleven or twelve years old, he remembered howling in distress because he'd had a nightmare. A young female helper—one of the foreign-born slaves who lived in the compound—had tried to comfort him and shush him, but the noise he'd made had woken the entire dorm. For the rest of that night, he was made to kneel on a ridged washboard, which had split the skin of his knees. In the morning, he'd had to stand in front of the class, offer self-criticism, and vow to do better. The young slave who'd tried to comfort him had been Soo-min. Director Pak had slapped her hard across the face for that and she'd spent three days locked in the standing cell.

Forbid empathy. Empathy engenders weakness.

Discipline at Paekhwawon was brutal. The smallest infraction of the rules would get him a ferocious beating with bamboo sticks. Snitching was encouraged; cruelty was rewarded; food was often withheld. The children grew up watchful and mean.

Trust no one.

To survive, they had to let go of any affection, playfulness, or emotional bond. They had to become more dangerous than anyone they feared.

Never show fear. Never yield an advantage.

To complain or show weakness was unthinkable.

Weakness is vulnerability. Vulnerability is fatal.

Eric had not been without love, however. None of them had. Love had shone upon them from the eyes of the portraits in every room; it had watched over them from great bronze statues that had towered over the parade ground. It was a love they believed in with fervor; a love they would defend with their lives. And on rare occasions—miraculous days they would remember forever—that love would become incarnate. Hundreds of bodyguards in black suits would descend on Paekhwawon. The children would wait in long lines on the parade ground until a gleaming black bulletproof Mercedes-Benz sedan with motorcycle escorts would roll through the gates, followed by the armored vehicles of Section One of the Guard Command, and the Dear Leader, Kim Jong-il himself, would step from the car. The god-king would walk among them, offer them small gifts from his own hand, tousle their hair, and embrace them.

In his senior year, Eric was schooled in weapons-handing and martial arts; he took courses on the culture and politics of the Main Enemy. He studied relentlessly.

This is what it takes. This is how you commit yourself if you want to succeed.

Senior year students wore Western clothes and ate Western food. They spoke American English fluently and were taught in English. At some stage, Eric had started to think in English. That didn't change the fact that they were Koreans, of course. Koreans born and bred—they never had any doubts about that. It *was* curious, though, because they knew that they were unlike any other Koreans. For one thing, they were at Paekhwawon. Also, a few of them didn't *look* like ethnic Koreans. They were of dual heritage.

Their commissions were awarded on a soft, bright morning in May. The parade ground was a field of flying red banners. In a solemn ceremony they stood to attention in uniform, sharp as a blade, facing the two bronze statues. No photographs were taken.

"Your great mission is beginning," Director Pak had told them. "Remember your training and you will succeed. You are the hammers of the Revolution. You are Korean steel, forged in righteousness. You are the bearers of the flag before the rank. The Enemy is a dotard, and weak. You will turn his boasts to ashes in his mouth! Who can defeat you?"

"NONE!"

Director Pak raised his fist: "Glory to the People's Army Patriotic Martyrs!"

"GLORY TO KOREA!"

Then they sang the "Song of General Kim Jong-il" and Eric's tears, along with everyone else's, flowed freely. After that, their morale was tremendous. At sunset they lit a fire on the riverbank and celebrated with a feast of grilled galbi and white rice. Director

Pak permitted them bottles of beer and soju. They raised their glasses in toast after toast.

"*To comrades! To glory! To death!*"

Later, the boys, quite drunk, cast off their uniforms and jumped naked into the river, singing.

"*We hate the weakling, hate the old,*
We hate the lame and dim
We love the strong, we love the bold,
We love the fire in youthful limb."

They were young and breathing in the air of the world! They were filled with animal spirits. What a feeling—to have so little road behind you, and so much ahead. They had been through blood and hunger and fire. A single individual was of no significance, but together they were cells in a mighty organism, the beating heart of a socialist warrior state.

He remembered lying on the grass that evening, feeling a wave of pure joy roll up through his body. Above him, shooting stars scratched brief trails of light. Fireflies blinked their golden glow on and off to a secret rhythm. The air was fragrant with pine resin.

He remembered thinking: *This is the end and the beginning. The world will change, and the change is us.*

Their documents were handed to them by officers of the Party's Organization and Guidance Department. These had been issued by North Korea's friends in the world—Iran, Malaysia, Russia, Syria, Venezuela, and China—allies whose security services were willing to do favors for Pyongyang: favors such as issuing valid passports and valid birth certificates. Uniquely, however, Eric's passport was South Korean, and valid. He had no idea how it had been procured, which made him wonder if his parents, whoever they were, might both have been from the South. Since the Korean he spoke in the North was audibly different from that spoken in the South and could arouse suspicion if he took the SAT examinations in Seoul, it was arranged for him to sit the tests in Shenyang, China, along with hundreds of Chinese students hoping to study in America.

To the US immigration officer at JFK who'd scanned his passport, checked his college offer letter, and asked some perfunctory questions, Eric had been an aspiring eighteen-year-old South Korean with an outstanding SAT score and a valid student visa. Nothing in his documents had aroused suspicion. Background checks, profiling, biometric data had nothing on him.

His goal, the goal of all of them, was to graduate, obtain a green card, and begin the route to citizenship. They would start careers in big tech, the federal government, energy and telecoms corporations, big pharma, Wall Street. And then, one day, maybe years into the future, the order would be given, and they would flash-crash the markets, disable the internet, cripple the power grid, mislead Congress. They would install malware in airplanes and nuclear submarines, foment mass social unrest, interfere with election rolls . . . America was an unstable and dysfunctional society, Director Pak had told them. When the shit started hitting the fan, and with no obvious enemy or motive behind the attacks, Americans would turn violently on one another, and their government would collapse. By the time the Yankees figured out what was happening, it would be too late. The graduates of the Seed-Bearing Program were not spies, as such. They were destroyers, saboteurs whose hatred for America had been kindled at birth and burned bright and fierce inside them.

And Eric had been light-headed with hatred. It had fueled him like heat from radioactive waste. It had driven him to work so hard to assimilate with the enemy that he had *become* a Yankee. He had toiled his way through Harvard and the godawful Kennedy School of Government so that he could *speak* like them, *think* like them, *look* like them, even though, in his secret heart, he knew that he was as different from them as human was to cockroach.

In his first few weeks living on an American college campus, his new freedoms had disorientated him, confused him. He'd become drunk with freedom. No one was monitoring him. No one was molding his thoughts or censuring his behavior; no was telling him what to wear, or when to sleep, or not to have sex, or not to drink.

Vigilance is essential, he cautioned himself. *Even the most disciplined mind can become careless.*

But very soon, that discipline had started to loosen and slip. There were no boundaries to contain him now. He experimented with sex, alcohol, cocaine. He was free to give full expression to his true self, and his true self, he realized, liked to get drunk and high, very much enjoyed sex with women, liked to indulge an unbounded ego, a talent for manipulation, a capacity to charm, a readiness to ignore rules and flout decorum.

An utter inability to feel empathy, he discovered, was a damned fucking superpower. Without empathy, there was no limit on what a human could do. No qualm or sympathy was there to inhibit him or give him pause. In fact, in place of empathy he experienced a new and altogether unexpected emotion: an exhilarating, righteous joy. It gave him *pleasure* to humiliate and degrade. It gave him *satisfaction* to see his rivals undermined and defeated. (Later, he would come to recognize remarkably similar impulses in the Boss. It was perhaps the reason Eric felt such a strong and uncanny affinity for him.)

But then: the disaster.

All twenty-two other members of his Paekhwawon year were betrayed and arrested within weeks of arrival after one of them, detained at immigration at Dulles before she'd even set foot in the country, had been deceived by the CIA into revealing the identities of the others, one by one. Only by a mighty stroke of luck had she realized the deception before Eric's identity was disclosed.

His burgeoning independence evaporated. He was the only one left. All the chips were on him. Center was counting on him. He felt the twitching of the chain, the heavy yoke of expectation. The eye of the Family was watching him from the East.

If Eric needed any reminder of the power and reach of Pyongyang, he awoke the next morning to some astonishing news. He'd been checking to see if there was any chatter online about the hit on Langkawi, even though he knew the CIA would have wiped it immediately if there was. There'd be no sign that Jenna Williams was ever on that island.

But there had been an assassination.

Reports of it were breaking sensationally across all his feeds. It was on every news channel in the world. The biggest story of the week.

The traitor half-brother was dead.

Details were still scant, but the murder had been captured on CCTV and fingers were already pointing at Pyongyang. It looked as if a professional hit had been carried out in the departure hall of Kuala Lumpur International Airport. The suspected murder weapon was a nerve agent...

This took a minute to sink in. *A murder inside the Family?*

Eric lowered the phone in a daze and slumped onto his sofa, his bathrobe flapping open. For a few stampeding seconds he wondered if he had caused this, too. That by finding Jenna's location he had exposed the half-brother's treachery, bringing death on the wind like a medieval plague.

On his commute into work, he thought hard about this.

The killing at Kuala Lumpur Airport had all the marks of a complex operation. It would have involved multiple agents who would have rehearsed and coordinated carefully. And the nerve agent— that would have required specialist containment and handling. The whole thing must have been *months* in the planning, so no... he couldn't have had any role in it. The half-brother's death had already been ordained, and the order could only have come from the top, from the Family, or rather, from the Leader in person. The Great Successor himself.

His own flesh and blood, murdered in public. On camera.

And with that scene vivid in his mind Eric trembled before the terrifying reality of the Family. He knew then, deep in his gut, that he was powerless. He was nothing but a vassal, a helot bonded for life to the Great Successor's will. No one was untouchable or beyond reach. Anyone, of whatever rank or status or value, even blood relatives, could be killed by a mere word.

When Eric arrived in the West Wing, he had a strange, faraway feeling, as if he were exhibiting signs of early dementia, or, like a cartoon character, had been hit very hard on the head. He made no response to the greetings of the passing staffers. By the time he was alone at his desk he could feel the millstone of his worries resettling itself heavily around his neck.

13

Langkawi
Malaysia

When Jenna came to after the crash, her ears were ringing like a note from the rim of a glass. Her cheek was pressed hard into rough earth. A tornado of gritty dust swirled around her, mixed with smoke from dry grass that had caught fire. She was on her side in the ditch, one leg wedged painfully beneath the scooter. Its rear wheel was racing, the fiberglass body blasted away, the engine exposed, still sputtering noisily, pumping out hot, noxious fumes. She could hardly see a damned thing. The boy was lying on his stomach a few yards away, naked from the waist up. She had most of his shirt in her hands. With an immense effort she reached out and turned off the engine. In the silence that followed she could hear the boy moaning. It was several minutes before she could heave herself free of the wreckage and get herself up onto one elbow.

"Hey," she called to him.

He got slowly onto all fours, then turned his small face to her with a thousand-yard stare in his eyes.

"Wait."

Before she could stop him, he had scrambled out of the ditch and disappeared.

She was choking and dizzy. Her head felt as if it had been hit by a lead pipe. Her jaw hurt, her arms and bare legs were striped with bleeding cuts.

Could she hear a phone ringing or was that the tinnitus? On the second attempt she managed to stand upright and the ground swayed beneath her. Her vision was blurred. She listened hard, then heard it again, faint, some meters away. She staggered toward it like a drunk, and found it in the grass, covered in earth: her burner phone. She had never been so relieved to hear May Ling's voice.

The next few hours passed in a blur. The whooshing roar of a helicopter's downdraft. The ambulance transfer to a private hospital in Kuala Lumpur.

The gash on her left thigh where she'd hit the ground was cleaned and dressed; the deep cut in her elbow stitched; the injury to her head examined. By the time May Ling arrived to check on her she was ready to discharge herself against the protests of the doctors. "You're in shock. You may be concussed," one of them said, trying to restrain her.

I'll take my chances.

Right now, she was in more danger from assassination than concussion, and she was a sitting duck in a hospital.

She limped away supported by May Ling. Her left leg went electric with pain.

May Ling looked shaken. "Jenna—what happened?"

"Drone," she breathed, wincing.

They exited the hospital into a wall of heat and humidity. May Ling helped her into the car and fastened the safety belt for her. Then they edged into the noise of the city's evening traffic crossing the Klang River.

Jenna stared out of the passenger window, her forehead resting against the glass, cool in the aircon. The stalagmites of the Petronas Towers dominated the city skyline with their peppermint-white glow. By day she thought them rather monstrous, but by night they appeared majestic, sacred.

May Ling glanced anxiously at her. "Jenna? Still with me?"

"Mm."

The car slowed as it approached the gates of the US embassy on Jalan Tun Razak. The mother of all headaches was brewing right behind her eyes, and her injuries were starting to pulse uncomfortably as the painkillers wore off. She began to realize that she was in a worse condition than she'd thought.

Passes were shown. The gate slid open sideways. The car glided into the embassy compound, leaving the traffic and the noise behind. She heard the clack-clacking of lawn sprinklers, and birdsong.

Sanctuary. No one could kill her here.

But how the hell had they found her?

CIA Station Kuala Lumpur was housed inside the US embassy near the Royal Selangor Golf Club. It was a three-story, walled compound with red-tiled roofs and surrounding gardens dotted with palms. A McMansion that might almost be mistaken for the golf clubhouse.

Jenna had been living in a small apartment in the Bangsar district of the city, but returning there was out of the question now. A guest suite had been prepared for her and someone had taken the trouble of laying out a selection of clothes that were clean and ironed but looked like they'd been salvaged from a yard sale.

She locked the door, swallowed a handful of painkillers, and picked up the suite's secure phone. The one voice she needed to hear right now was Charles Fisk's. Fisk, her old CIA mentor, her rock, her anchor. The one who was always there for her when she was in danger of a meltdown. She had to tell him what had happened. She needed to let him know that she was all right.

She started punching in the number, but then a thought gave her pause.

What had, in fact, happened?

There was an obvious explanation for how the North Koreans had found her: that they'd had rings of surveillance around PANDA on Langkawi, a crack team monitoring his every move—from the moment he landed till the moment they assassinated him this morning. They'd have seen everything he did, everyone he'd met, including his meeting with her.

Send in the drone. Bam. Twofers.

But there was another, much more unsettling explanation: that they'd traced her via her private phone call to that nurse at the Mount Vernon Hospital in Alexandria . . .

Slowly she replaced the phone handset.

Why was that possibility nibbling so keenly at her brain?

No one could have known that call was from her. No one could have known whose number she was even going to call. She'd identified the nurse on duty from the hospital's staff rota and she'd swiped the guy's cell number from a residents' association group chat.

A memory unfurled in the back of her mind.

That whisper she'd heard after the nurse had answered the phone.

A call for Soo-min?

Someone else had been present when she'd called. Someone, evidently, who knew Soo-min. Could just have been another member of staff . . .

Except that Soo-min had hung up on her in a clear panic.

Immediately and without saying a word.

Had someone been there with Soo-min? Someone who had been *expecting the call?*

The realization landed suddenly, shockingly, as if she'd been doused in iced water.

Oh, my dear God. She covered her face with her hands.

She had exhibited a *pattern*. A cardinal error in tradecraft. An annual call on a particular date—"Trophy Day"—could have been noticed, predicted, anticipated. How long had they known that she always called on that date? How many times had they visited Soo-min, hoping to intercept it?

Had they threatened her? Was that the reason she never talked?

Jenna was breathing so hard that she became feather-headed and faint. Yet she could not sit down or stand still.

She had placed her own sister in danger.

She drank shakingly from a bottle of mineral water, then held her breath and exhaled slowly—one, two, three, four—until her pulse began to slow.

Despite the strobing pain in her leg, she'd been circling restlessly about the room, but now another thought made her stop in her tracks.

The burner phone . . . It was still in her pocket.

She retrieved it. Three percent battery. The last number called was the nurse's. Once again, her pulse began to gallop.

Panic was in full control of her now. Clear thinking was impossible.

Before she knew what she was doing she had pressed call.

It rang once. Twice. A third time.

"Hello?"

"Ohhh, heyyy, this is Alice again?" she said, her voice trilling upward in the same pleading whine she'd used yesterday. "We spoke yesterday? I asked you if I could speak to Soo-min? I'm really sorry to bother you again."

She could hear a background roar of traffic and a baby crying. She guessed he was on public transportation.

"Yeah, I remember. I'm not in the hospital right now. I'm just heading into my shift."

"So, I hope this doesn't sound weird, but did anyone visit Soo-min yesterday? She seemed upset about something. There's, like, an ex-boyfriend who turns up out of the blue sometimes? I'm just worried that someone bothered her."

A brief, mistrustful pause on the line. "An ex-*boyfriend*?"

"Or anyone . . . ?"

Another loaded pause. She sensed an evasion coming. "No," he said, cautiously. "No ex-boyfriend visited Soo-min."

"Oh. OK. It's just, like, I thought I heard someone else there when I called—"

"That was just the guy I'm dating," he said primly. "He stopped by the desk. Listen, I, uh, don't think you should call my private number again, OK? It's kinda inappropriate."

Two tones stuttered in her ear. He'd hung up.

A good ops officer, Fisk had once told her, can detect lies and evasions immediately because they understand, at an elemental level, the urge to conceal the truth, with all its grammar and complex structures. She had no idea why that nurse had avoided answering her question. But she had zero doubt about her next course of action.

The tone rang and rang before it was answered.

"Oh, finally," Han said after the phone had been passed to her. "Well, it's nice of you to remember your mother."

In faraway Annandale, Jenna could hear a clink of teacups on saucers, and the chatter of elderly Korean ladies.

"Omma, no time to chat now, I just need you to—"

"Why are you calling me on Mrs. Choi's phone? You've got my number!" Then she muttered something inaudible, her hand over the phone. Presumably to Mrs. Choi.

"Omma, listen, I need you to bring Soo-min home—today."

"Soo-min's in the hospital."

"Yes, I know. Please go get her today until I can find another place for her."

Han went quiet then, and Jenna sensed the fear and befuddlement that came over her mother whenever Jenna couldn't explain. As far as Han was concerned Jenna worked for the US embassy's Trade Section under diplomatic cover, but she'd long guessed that wasn't the whole picture. She also knew that on no account, *ever*, was she to ask questions.

"Fetch her . . . today? She's not well."

"Today. I mean *now*," Jenna said, straining hard to keep the impatience out of her voice. "In the car, Omma. It's important."

"Oh . . ." Her mother sounded dubious, worried.

Jenna hung up before her mother could ask anything else while Mrs. Choi was sitting there, all ears.

Finally, she lay down on the bed and massaged her eyes with her knuckles, feeling too leaden with exhaustion to move. Every joint and muscle in her body seemed to be staging a sit-in protest. The whole day was catching up to her in an almighty wave.

PANDA, her new asset, murdered at the airport; a drone that almost torched her alive on a dirt road in Langkawi; her sister menaced by a person unknown in a place where she should be safe, a *secure ward* . . .

She opened her eyes. At least she could keep an eye on her mom's house in real time. A few years ago, she'd had security cameras installed around the house's exterior, which she could monitor from a phone. If anyone came looking for Soo-min at the house, she would know. And the house was the only place for Soo-min right now. She was too fragile mentally to be taken to another unfamiliar location. She wouldn't cope.

A soft knock sounded at the door.

"Jenna? Everything all right?" May Ling's voice. "Norman Rhodes is asking if you're well enough to see him in his office."

Damn, damn, no. "Tell him I need to lie down for a few hours?"

Norman Rhodes was chief of Station and the last person in the world Jenna wanted to face right now. She would deal with him tomorrow. By then, she might have figured out how she was going to explain such a catastrophic, career-ending fuck-up—why she'd put a target on her own back. Why she'd made an unauthorized private call during a covert op.

But right now, somehow, incredibly, she was going to have to store the wreckage of what had just happened in a separate compartment of her mind and come back to it later.

Because she had to get off this bed and head into Station, even if it meant sneaking past Rhodes's office door without him seeing her. She had to alert Headquarters to the fact that they had an active North Korean Seed-Bearing Program operative on their hands.

14

The White House
Washington, DC
Same day

Eric had come in early to catch up with the backlog of calls and emails that had accumulated while he'd been at the hospital yesterday. It was only when he saw the morning's *Washington Post* on his desk that he suddenly remembered the two Russians he'd seen in the Oval Office yesterday morning. There'd been nothing on the wires about their visit, which was why he'd forgotten about them. And now that he'd flicked through the *Post*, he saw there was nothing about it in print either.

Strange.

It had been almost twenty-four hours since he'd witnessed Sergey Lavrov and Sergey Kislyak meet with Trump. Press hadn't covered it.

Very strange.

He pulled up the president's schedule for yesterday: Kislyak had been in the calendar for a meet-and-greet, but there was no mention of Lavrov, and Lavrov was by far the more powerful and significant of the two . . .

Eric's instinct for conspiracy stirred and came sharply to life.

The media doesn't know about it.

And then, before he'd even had a chance to sip his coffee, the story hit the networks like a firestorm.

TASS, the Russian state news agency, had just posted its own photos of the meeting: Trump greeting Kislyak and Lavrov as if they were reality TV contestants; the two Russians looking menacing and lugubrious, like mafia undertakers. The pictures had been taken by the Russians' own photographer—the man Eric had seen with Lavrov.

Twitter went haywire.

Eric's phone was buzzing off the desk. Dozens of incoming messages from White House aides. *What's happening? Anyone?*

Lavrov had just given a presser in which he'd praised the Trump administration for being "businesslike" and for "wanting to make deals..."

Doubts and intrigues began spreading through Eric's mind like rumors of war.

He turned to the window, his tiny view of lawn and parking lot, and thought quickly. The Russians were exploiting the new diplomatic reality. Why be rebuffed by the State Department and the security services when they can go direct to the Boss? And the Boss had welcomed them... not as pariahs but as honored equals. The Russians wanted to make deals! Of course they did. Deals had nothing to do with values, feelings, the law. Deals were struck through personal connections, quid pro quos, unofficial contacts, secret meetings. Trump was the only one here who grasped this. Deals were *transactional*! And the Russians had much to offer. Personal enrichment, the silencing of critics, the secret to holding onto office for life—*those* were the ruling realities of power. The Boss knew that, too, and the Russians knew he knew it.

Once again, Eric felt a cult-like reverence for the Boss...

And suddenly his imagination was lighting up like a flight console.

The Boss didn't need a fucking State Department. He needed a work-around, a point man! A go-between to open doors!

He jumped to his feet, wanting to pace. He was tremendously agitated suddenly, plagued by a fear of being outclassed, of opportunities missed.

He pummeled his scalp with his knuckles; he rubbed his face and vigorously scratched the back of his neck; he opened his wallet to see if he had a Xanax, but instead he found white powder in a thin rime along the edge of his Amex, and packed like snow into the indentations of his card number. He licked the card and rubbed the coke onto his gums, breathing like a wild beast.

A soft knock on his door and a staffer's head appeared. "Hey Eric, just circling back to you about—"

She caught the psychotic light in his eyes, closed the door, and vanished.

He got a grip on himself and turned again to the window. This was ridiculous. He had something that his competition—the Russians—didn't have: he had *proximity, daily access*. The Boss *listened* to him, *liked* him.

So why, all of a sudden, did he have a feeling that the Russians were playing a more ambitious game than his own? They'd breezed in here for a secret meeting with the Boss . . . *because they knew they could*.

And with the clarity of prophecy, he saw that an enormous window of opportunity was about to be missed if he didn't act.

He'd been too modest in his aims. He had been conspiring to manipulate a man who needed no manipulating. Because with this president the unimaginable was possible. The unthinkable was normal.

And as his ego rallied and returned in force, an idea ignited inside his mind. Small at first, but dense and potent, like a dwarf star. Within seconds it was blazing so brightly it was consuming him, and he knew at once it was the greatest idea he'd ever had, something no one in the world would believe possible. An undreamed-of gambit, a game-changer. A chance to make history, *change* history. And best of all, a way to pre-empt the very real and mounting pressure that he knew was coming his way from Center.

Only under this president was such an idea conceivable. Every one of the Boss's predecessors in that office would have flat-out dismissed it.

He sat back down, his body tingling with destiny as the idea took on a life of its own. Already his surging ambition was turning to practicalities, to the *how* and *when*.

He would start by leaking stories to the press. American public opinion would need to be prepared. He would put feelers out to those spineless lackeys, the South Koreans. He would fan the flames of gossip and rumor around the Son-in-Law, the Boss's family ambassador, to make sure the role didn't fall to the eunuch. He would test the waters in Beijing and Tokyo . . .

And if he pulled it off?

The headlines would write themselves.

TRUMP MEETS KIM IN HISTORIC SUMMIT

TRUMP AWARDED NOBEL PEACE PRIZE

TIME MAGAZINE MAN OF THE YEAR: KIM JONG-UN

His mind whirled with the vertigo of greatness. And for a few heady minutes, he forgot he was a vassal, a slave indentured for life. He was once again the secret mover of life's events. He was the gloved, invisible hand.

15

CIA Station, US Embassy
Kuala Lumpur, Malaysia
Same day

Jenna was about to slip quietly out of the suite when she caught a sideways view of herself in the mirror and let out a gasp. The reflection confronting her was a wild woman, a bag-and-pushcart lady in blood-stained tatters, her hair a rat's nest trailing matted tails to her shoulders. She was not a vain person, but she felt her inner little girl burst into tears. Quickly, she washed her face in the bathroom sink, brushed the knots out of her hair as best she could, and changed into the charity clothes—faded bell-bottom jeans from the '90s, a Gap cornflower linen blouse, white sneakers.

Moments later she was moving through the corridors of the main building. She punched in the keypad code to enter the floor that housed Station. The security door clicked open, and she entered a room with gray carpet on the floor and up the walls, an acoustic-shielded enclosure impervious to electronic eavesdropping. As she passed along the narrow aisle of modular desks and workstations, the few colleagues still working looked up at her with concerned faces. She smiled and assured them she was fine.

Her desk was in the corner next to a small window of shatterproof glass. She turned on her computer and entered the sequence of passwords. Her face was bathed in the pale glow of the screen and her fingers crouched over the keys for a moment. Then she tapped out the cable in one continuous stream.

1. Developmental meeting with PANDA productive.
2. C/o believes PANDA has been funding an active operative of the SEED-BEARING PROGRAM via Macau-based online gambling app.
3. Ref operative has been accessing app from US and withdrawing "winnings" in US.
4. Further to incident today at KLI2, c/o recommends urgent exfil plan for PANDA's son, who is in clear and imminent danger of assassination.

Protocol dictated that Chief of Station Norman Rhodes approve the cable first, but Rhodes was about to fire her anyway. She'd been targeted by an enemy; her cover was blown; her tour in Malaysia was most definitely over.

She hit send. Moments later she sent a second cable attaching the recording of her interview with PANDA.

Then she leaned back in her chair and slowly exhaled a mix of breath, nerves, and tension. For a few moments the adrenaline pumping through her had an analgesic effect on her injuries and she almost forgot she was in pain.

A hair-raising thought occurred to her then, making her go dead still, as if she'd just noticed an enormous spider on the wall above her pillow.

What if this Seed-Bearing Program operative was the same person who had been at the hospital yesterday? What if this person was *known* to Soo-min?

The cramped room of Station felt insanely claustrophobic suddenly. She was overcome by an intense perturbation—a desire to get out of there and fly home, to be at Soo-min's side, to be her personal bodyguard, if necessary, until the danger had passed.

She dropped her face into her hands and dug her nails hard into her scalp.

What had happened to their lives? They should never have been separated. Soo-min should never have been on that beach . . .

The dismal orchestra of Should-Neverland had started up all over again.

A small flag appeared in the top right of her screen. Her cable to Headquarters had been acknowledged.

But by now Jenna was far away. For the thousandth time, she was replaying the scenes of that day as she had imagined them—through her twin's eyes. The sun's rays slanting across the soft, glowing sand. The picnic. Then, sometime around sundown: masked men emerging from the shadows of the dunes. Screams, a violent struggle, ropes, zip-cuffs, chloroform, syringes loaded with sedatives. A waiting dinghy.

Back then, she hadn't known that North Korea had been abducting random foreigners from beaches since the 1970s. She wouldn't find out about that until years later. The program had been a project of PANDA's father, Kim Jong-il, a dictator whose rather droll appearance—a kind of chubby North Korean Elvis impersonator—belied a sadistic personality and a psychopath's will to dominate and control. Over the years, there were hundreds, maybe thousands, of victims—some Westerners, but mainly South Koreans and Japanese. A special unit of commandos drugged and gagged them on the sand, then spirited them away in vessels disguised as fishing boats. The next day the victims awoke, shivering and seasick, in North Korea. Jenna could picture their horror as they grasped the reality of where they were.

But their nightmare was only beginning. Kim Jong-il imprisoned them for years in top-secret walled compounds known as "Invitation-only Zones." Their families had no idea what had happened to them, and many were given up for dead. A few were put to work teaching language skills to North Korea's spies. The rest were subjected to psychological experiments—all kinds of tortures that were alternately subtle and violent. The idea was to brainwash them and send them home as spies for North Korea. In the early days, this was known as the Localization Program.

The experiments failed. Even the youngest of the victims had such strong memories of home that they resisted all attempts at "re-education."

But you had to hand it to Kim Jong-il. He wasn't a quitter.

He persisted, and the program evolved. He decided that the prisoners should be made to produce children, because children were vulnerable to emotional manipulation and ideological indoctrination. The children, not the prisoners, would become the future operatives. They would be raised in a new, specialized school to prepare them for entry into the universities of North Korea's Main Enemy, the United States. The project was renamed the Seed-Bearing Program. The school was called Paekhwawon.

By the late nineties—about the time that Soo-min and her boyfriend were abducted—Kim had introduced a further twist. He set up a secret unit called Section 915 which targeted foreigners who were visiting North Korea on business or as part of a tour—specifically: men who had white, brown, or black skin. The target would find himself assigned a beautiful North Korean guide who seemed to find him irresistibly handsome. If all went to plan, a quiet romance would flower between them. Nothing sexual happened until the target's final night in the country, when the woman would knock on his door at the Yanggakdo International Hotel in Pyongyang, saying that if they were never to see each other again they could at least share a few hours of intimacy. But these beautiful operatives had a single aim: to become impregnated by the target. The result of Section 915's operations was a group of Seed-Bearing Program children who were North Korean born and bred, but who *looked foreign*.

Soo-min was a Westerner of dual heritage—half African American, half Korean. To North Korean eyes, she looked foreign. Her value to the Program must have been immediately obvious to her abductors. Jenna could just imagine the excited radio exchanges with the naval base at Mayangdo. Messages passed up the chain of command. The commendations. The promotions.

For about a year, Soo-min and her boyfriend were held in a gloomy compound that housed a number of Japanese victims kidnapped years earlier. The two were forced to marry. Soon afterward, Soo-min became pregnant and gave birth to Ha-jun.

Ha-jun . . . a baby born into shadow.

Perhaps that's why Soo-min gave him a name that meant long, glorious summer—so that the warmth of the sun would find him, even in that place. Many times, Jenna had fantasized about meeting this boy, her nephew, her own flesh and blood. He appeared to her on the periphery of her dreams sometimes, but he had no face, and he dissolved the moment she turned her mind's eye on him.

How Soo-min had protected Ha-jun in Paekhwawon, Jenna did not know. But Jenna had always believed that her sister had, somehow, protected him; that she had stopped him from becoming a monster. That might even explain why he had been taken away from her when he was eight. If he'd failed to exhibit the killer instincts required of him in that school, a decision may have been made to dispose of him, leaving Soo-min grieving for a son who had been "sent abroad."

Soo-min had spent years living among those children. The most she had ever talked about her experience was during the tumultuous days that followed her rescue—nothing coherent, just fragments uttered in unguarded moments, like phrases of a melody that would stop abruptly the moment it had your attention.

And Jenna knew then with the certainty of intuition that Soo-min *did* know the lone Seed-Bearing Program operative at large in the US. She would have watched this person grow up, seen them become what they became.

Jenna could simply ask her, of course, but it would be futile.

The door to that part of her sister's mind was protected by powerful magic. She had never opened it for Jenna, nor for the specialist CIA interrogators trained in debriefing subjects with PTSD, nor for her psychiatrist, not even for their mom.

Another flag appeared in the top right of her screen. A cable from Headquarters on the restricted-handing channel.

1. Reference SEED-BEARING PROGRAM cable received. Awaiting full ops report from c/o. Please advise time of Station debrief so that Hqs can join.
2. Hqs prepared for defector processing and resettlement once PANDA's son is located and is in US hands. Son has been encrypted DIAMOND.

Jenna logged off. She exited the cluttered space of the Station, and scurried past Rhodes's office. She could hear him talking loudly on a conference call, working late as usual, and had the sinking feeling that he'd spotted her. She picked up her phone from the locker in the office outside and saw that she'd received a brief message from her mother saying that she'd done as Jenna had asked. Soo-min had just been collected from the Mount Vernon Hospital. They were in the car and about to drive home.

Five thousand miles away in Virginia, Jenna knew that her twin had sensed her relief. She had felt it on the invisible genetic skein that connected them, and she imagined her sister's voice, quiet and soft inside her head, saying, "And you, Jenna? Are you safe?"

She began hobbling painfully back toward the suite, pausing frequently just to breathe, one hand against the wall for balance, noting the thin undertow of dread that had begun flowing beneath her relief as she asked herself the same thing.

Are you safe?

The question seemed to land on the shore of her own future, which was a sudden vision of immense red skies cracked open to reveal the dark throne of the Family, and beneath it: a flat, black body of water that stretched on and on, cold and forever, with nowhere to hide.

They will never stop hunting you. Never.

She had a memory just then of Kim Jong-il on board that train. The dictator had been picking at morsels of smoked squid and gingko nut with his silver chopsticks and sipping watered-down red wine from a crystal glass. His small fingers were as pale as grubs, she recalled. He kept patting them to his chest. He'd just told her that his doctors had warned him about his heart.

They know you watched him die.

Once more she had to pause and lean against the wall and breathe. By the time she reached her room she was exhausted and feeling decidedly unwell. She lay down on the bed on her side and stared at the room's secure phone, next to her on the table. The trauma of the day's events, the maelstrom of emotions she had experienced over the last few hours had created the momentum inside her for a confession.

She should do it now. Get it over with.

Fisk answered his phone before it had even rung once.

"Jesus Christ, Jenna. Are you all right? I heard you got smoked on Langkawi—"

"Someone got to Soo-min at the Mount Vernon Hospital yesterday. That's how they found me."

She sensed the gears of his understanding stop and undergo a rapid shift. "Soo-min?"

"My mom's just taken her home."

"Is she safe?"

"I'm not sure. But I can monitor the house in real time from my phone."

Another beat as he took this in. "I'm on it. I know a couple of retired ops officers living in Annandale. I'll get them to put a twenty-four-hour watch on the house and report anything suspicious to you."

"Thank you, Charles, thank you."

"*Who* got to her?"

Jenna took a breath. Time to face the music. "Someone who knew I was going to call her yesterday."

A long pause crackled down the line, punctuated by clicks as the call pinged between routers and cell towers, connected across continents and oceans.

"Trophy Day?" he said simply.

"I fucked up, Charles. I endangered Soo-min. And I risked the op."

Then he surprised her again. "Never mind the op. No officer truly matures until they've fucked up at least once, big time. Who would have known you were going to call, apart from Soo-min?"

"Maybe the very same operative who was the subject of my cable."

His capacious mind processed this. "A hostile foreign agent on US soil is a matter for the FBI, not us . . ."

"I know, Charles. But I'm asking you to keep this in house for now. The hospital's CCTV would be a start. The nurse on duty at the time was a guy called Adam Tan. It was his phone I called . . ."

After the call ended, she turned on the TV and showered. When she emerged, trailing a scent of lilies from the guest shampoo, PANDA's face was on the screen.

She grabbed the remote and turned up the volume.

On Sky News a forensic video analyst was explaining the grainy airport security cam footage, scene by scene.

PANDA was shown highlighted in a bright halo, so that the viewer could see him moving through the crowded terminal building carrying a small backpack.

He was looking up at the departures screen, then he turned

toward the self-service kiosks to check in for his 11:50 Air Asia flight to Macau.

So far, so normal.

Suddenly, also highlighted, moving quickly between the throngs of travelers with luggage, a young woman could be seen creeping up behind him. Quickly, she put her hands over his eyes, in the way people do for a lark, to say, "Guess who!"

PANDA spun around and yelled something; the woman ran off. He dropped his bag and wiped his eyes with his sleeve.

Just as he did so, a *second* woman ran up behind him, and *she did the same thing*—she covered his eyes with her hands and smeared something over his nose and mouth. PANDA thrashed his head and broke free from her.

The attack took just three seconds. No one nearby even noticed.

The footage cut to another camera: a security guard was escorting PANDA to the airport's small clinic. His feet were starting to drag as he walked. He was still visible through the clinic's glass wall when his body jerked violently. He collapsed onto a plastic chair in a seizure. Slumped unconscious, his pot belly was exposed. Medics rushed to him.

Something—vomit, blood—was pooling in his mouth. The footage ended.

Jenna flipped the channel. A toxicologist from Imperial College London was saying: ". . . if I must hazard a guess, I'd say the toxin used was a munitions-grade nerve agent. VX, for example, contracts the muscles of the heart and lungs and causes suffocation. It's an agonizing death . . ."

Jenna muted the volume and stared into endless dimensions of nothing.

No one deserves to die like that.

She got into bed and tried to rest, but the footage had shocked her. Soon, she'd sat back up and was flipping channels again.

Within hours of the assassination, the global news media had gone crazy. The Malaysian authorities had not officially confirmed the real identity of "Kim Chol,"—the name on the four North Korean passports the police had found inside PANDA's backpack, along with the bricks of cash, the hundred and twenty thousand dollars she had given him on Langkawi—but by now the whole world knew who he was:

Kim Jong-nam, elder half-brother of North Korea's Supreme Leader, Kim Jong-un.

What kind of a person makes a member of his own family die in agony, on video, in public?

Her headache was starting up again like an engine and the skin around her wounds was starting to itch and stretch. Pressure was building in her stomach; she was feeling nauseous.

This was the world she had chosen for herself. Deception, betrayal, blackmail. Spies, nerve agents, gruesome assassinations.

No one had forced her. She had chosen it freely.

When she logged into the security cameras surrounding the house in Annandale and saw her mom's car parked in the drive, her vision shimmered and the lights in the room acquired blurry coronas. There were the geranium pots on either side of the front door. There was the imitation celadon vase on the living-room windowsill. It was just after midday back home, the sky overcast and threatening rain. The backyard was covered in fallen leaves and branches. Nothing but a lone cat in the side alley.

Jenna wiped away her tears and logged off. For several minutes she just stared at the ceiling.

The suite was dark now, except for the soundless TV illuminating the room. With one eye open she read the subtitles.

And then, another sensational development started gliding across the news ticker. She unmuted the sound.

PANDA's assassins had been arrested.

Two young women in hijabs were behind the bars of a police cell, facing flashing cameras, crying. The two who had smeared the toxin on his face. They were not trained killers, it turned out, but migrant workers down on their luck. They said they'd been promised a hundred bucks to take part in a YouTube prank. Studio commentators were abuzz with this new twist. How had they smeared a deadly nerve agent with their bare hands and not been killed themselves?

Jenna continued watching for some time, twirling her hair, thinking.

The North Koreans didn't usually assassinate with nerve agents. It wasn't their weapon of choice. In fact, it wasn't an expertise she'd known they possessed. One thing was clear: this attack was sophisticated. It had involved a banned chemical weapon; it had used multiple actors, including dupes; it had taken place on foreign soil, and in full public view. And neither of the assassins had been harmed. That suggested that they had each been given separate compounds of the nerve agent, which only became lethal when *mixed together on the skin of the victim's face* . . . a tricky thing known as a binary weapon.

Why did she have an uneasy feeling that some other state actor—one with deep knowledge of such arts—had shown the North Koreans how to do this?

It struck her then how similar this method was to those in Russia's playbook.

16

Ostankino Television Center
Moscow
Thursday morning

Lyosha rode the metro to Channel One's studio at the Ostankino Television Center, arriving a full two hours early, as instructed, to stand in line next to a loading bay at the back of the studio complex. The line of audience guests was being patrolled by black-clad security, radios emitting bursts of static, and two smiling women with iPads who checked everyone's IDs and invitations against a list and asked them if they'd memorized the question each of them hoped to ask the president, if selected.

Calmly he showed them his invitation and ID. Yes, he'd memorized his question.

What can be done to encourage talented youths like myself to make our careers in Russia and not be lured abroad by the false promises and hypocrisy of the West?

With a Zen-like discipline that surprised even him, Lyosha had emptied his mind of thought. It was as if his body was on autopilot, a moving bundle of reflexes. He knew that if he paused for one second to ask himself what the hell he was doing, his hands would start trembling; his bowels would loosen; his knees would buckle.

A few single, teasing snowflakes floated like goose down. It was searing cold. He zipped his puffer jacket up to his chin, tucked his long, dark-blond hair behind his ears, and pulled his black beanie down low. Along the line, his fellow guests were laughing and chatting animatedly, and every single one of them, he saw, was young, about his own age, twenty-one.

Direct Line was an annual ritual, like the Easter Divine Liturgy, in which the president took questions by telephone, text, email, and satellite video link from across Russia's eleven time zones, his image beamed live over one-eighth of the inhabited world. For a marathon four hours, with scarcely a toilet break, the tsar of all the Russias would commune with his flock. He'd hear them all, housewives and war veterans, beggars and billionaires, all screened in advance, their questions honeyed with gratitude and praise.

But this studio audience—the people who would be seen surrounding the great man—were all youths . . .

And Lyosha saw right then that his question had struck a chord.

The president wished to pronounce some wisdom on the worrying matter of graduates deserting the motherland for the godless, pro-gay West. So today the nation would see him seated among golden Russian youths. He was their father. He was counting on them, for the greater glory of Russia. And, although nearly seventy years old, he was, in his own way, a youth himself, ageless, his face as smooth and timeless as the Christ child in an icon.

Lyosha could imagine how the youth issue might be troubling the president. To the nation's young, he wasn't simply their past and their present. He was their future, forever and ever, world without end. As it was, so it ever shall be: *Putin*.

If his hunch was right . . . *Putin was expecting his question*. There was every chance he'd be handed the studio mic. He felt a sudden flapping of nerves in his chest. His palms began sweating despite the cryonic temperature.

A sudden energy, an excited susurration, passed along the line of guests. They were going in! Two security guards patted him down, then two FSB men patted him down again, then he passed through a metal detector, then an X-ray machine, and entered the studio auditorium from the rear, which was smaller than he had imagined. The audience faced a glossy white semicircular panel with two chairs on either side for the show's hosts, and one in the center, larger and slightly raised, for the president. The studio backdrop was electric blue. Two enormous LED screens for live video feeds were running pre-broadcast tests; a complicated array of television cameras pointed toward the panel and toward the audience.

The auditorium filled quickly. Many in the audience were wearing hooded sports tops with RUSSIA emblazoned across the back, or scarves in the white, blue and red tricolor flag. They looked like the type of pro-Kremlin youths who yelled abuse at foreign diplomats and harassed reporters—the kind of people he avoided and would have nothing to do with, and now they were surrounding him on all sides. Why on earth had he been invited?

Because of my question.

He was feeling suddenly friendless and very alone. His gaze returned to the curved white panel with its three empty chairs. Its echo of the Holy Trinity was no accident.

A flurry of activity was taking place on the set. Cameras were lighting up, mics, acoustics, were tested. An armed security guard removed the glass and the bottle of mineral water set out for the president and replaced them with a glass and water bottle from a special case.

More lights came on, making the panel a luxurious, brilliant white. The show's two hosts entered, a man and a woman who took their seats on either side of the panel. The woman, an austere-looking blonde in a dark-pink blouse with white collar and radio mic, and matching dark-pink lipstick, sat up straight, ready to speak to camera. A makeup girl dashed over and quickly powdered away a nervous shine with a feathery brush, then the music began, the green applause sign lit up, and they were on air.

"Hello everybody! Welcome to the sixteenth annual *Direct Line*. We've received a record *two million* questions so far, and remember, we'll be answering your calls on the number shown at the bottom of your screen . . ."

Lyosha felt the audience's anticipation like static in the air. The next thing he knew the woman was standing up, arm stretched out toward the wing.

"Please welcome President Vladimir Vladimirovich PUTIN!"

Before she'd even finished, the audience had risen to their feet and an ovation like the sea rolled through the auditorium, a cresting wave of excitement and applause.

Lyosha clapped along nervously, feeling like an impostor. A traitor.

In he strode. The famous figure was both very familiar and utterly strange, as if Lyosha had never seen him before. Ridiculously ordinary and yet totally weird-looking in a way he couldn't have described. Perhaps power—not a normal politician's power, but *absolute* power—had this effect on a person, and on people's perception of him. Of course, Lyosha recognized very well the awkward, gangsterish strut with one elbow sticking out, the somber suit of the manager-in-chief, the personification of competence, stability. Putin nodded to the audience with a small, almost shy, smile. The short pepper-and-salt hair was neat and combed over. The icy gray eyes were as tiny as currants.

He shook hands with both hosts and took his seat.

A hush fell, and the first question, by live video link, got the show off to a strong start. Lyosha recognized the stage-managed nostalgia for the Soviet style. Rows of uniformed naval cadets in Sevastopol wished to thank the president for a mascot dog—and to thank him for Crimea! The audience applauded generously. Could they please know when they would get their promised sports facility? The president smiled. Such a cute dog! "Very soon," was his answer. They were followed by a large group of women from a fish processing plant in Irkutsk, who wished to plead for workplace childcare facilities. Putin scribbled down a note, and it was done! Next, three headscarved babushkas in some closed-down, empty-vodka-bottle town wished to inform him kindly that their pensions hadn't been paid in months. "My apologies, ladies," he said. "They will be paid at once, and I ask the chairman of the national pension fund to call me in person this evening with an explanation for his failure."

On it went. The callers marveled at the facts and solutions at his fingertips. "Thank you, Mr. President!" The people were being permitted to address a divinity. He could reach down with his hand and solve any mortal problem; he was a sacred figure from a realm far above politics. One moment he was promising a new children's swimming pool; the next he was conjuring up trillions of rubles for a new cosmodrome.

The audience was loving it, especially the moments when he turned prophet against Russia's enemies. "The West is dying because it has turned its back on the traditional family," he stated, as if it were a demographic fact. The two hosts on either side of him murmured their agreement, heads nodding vigorously. "In tolerating everyone's freedom of identity, sexuality, political views, and what have you, the West accepts the equality of good and evil . . ." The applause began to roll again. "Russia is strong because Russia has rediscovered its soul!" The cheer was a rousing wall of sound. A camera was panning across the audience.

Lyosha was amazed that educated people his own age would fall for this *bullshit*. Once again, he felt his anger stirring, the heat rising to his head. He glanced at the ecstatic faces on either side of him, surrendering to this man's every word, and he was struck by an insight.

With surrender comes liberation.

Putin sat back in his chair, his mouth stern but with a self-satisfied look playing about his eyes, which shone with a divine complacency. He was connecting them all to something deeply Russian, something mystical. Even Lyosha was impressed. The leader must be seen to answer everything. The leader is the state, which is almighty, omniscient, and will never perish. The leader must defend the state's power, even if it means the people suffer.

But just as Lyosha was thinking this, he began, from this moment of the show onward, almost imperceptibly at first, to notice a shift in the president's mood.

The great man had said what he'd wanted to say. Now he was growing bored.

Almost an hour had gone by, and his answers were getting shorter, less informative. The facts were all in his head, but, oh, there were so many of them. *Direct Line* wasn't for the benefit of ordinary Russians, after all. It was all for him, the star, to make him seem all-knowing and omnipotent, and it was starting to tire him.

Lyosha began to watch and listen to him intently. He was sure he could hear Putin's irritation and scorn seeping into the listless tone of his answers, like bad odors concealed by a superficial wipe of disinfectant. This annual circus had become a penance for him, Lyosha realized, a gift he couldn't return. Mothers concerned about contaminated baby powder, teenagers wanting to be anti-pedophile vigilantes, teachers, army conscripts, engineers, Orthodox priests, mayors—they were just props and supporting characters. He didn't need them anymore.

Lyosha wondered if he was the only one in the audience noticing this.

Putin poured himself a glass of water and listened without enthusiasm to Yelena from Murmansk. Should her husband Boris let her have a dog? ("Yes.") To an eight-year-old boy in Russian-liberated Donetsk. Should he, President Putin, be cloned for future generations? ("No.") To Yuri, a farmer in Primorsky Krai, wondering if his cows should wear Chinese-made GPS trackers ("I don't know").

Lyosha sensed from this man's increasingly monotonal, are-we-done-yet hubris that there were vast areas of vital human concern he couldn't give a bird's shit about—especially jobs and hospitals, about which there'd been a dozen questions already. Why should he? When he was the richest man on earth, when he had the elite Clinical Hospital of the Presidential Administration at his personal disposal, just in case he got a runny nose.

Toward the end of the second hour, Putin visibly perked up, just for a few moments. A video call-in from the workers of Uralvagonzavod, a factory in Omsk that manufactured tanks, had nominated the foreman to address the president. "Vladimir Vladimirovich, when we were having a hard time, you gave us stability. We want to say something about those student protests in the capital. If the police don't know how to do their jobs, my lads and I are prepared to come and sort out those do-nothings for you. Just say the word."

That takes the biscuit, Lyosha thought.

Putin was beaming. "Come on over," he said with a wave of his arm, to laughter and applause.

Lyosha stared straight ahead of him. He was beyond angry, and if he didn't get a grip on himself, it would be seen on camera. The whole country was afflicted by a vicious cancer. It was eating into Russia's vital organs, its lifeblood. The country was disintegrating, and the rot was coming from this man. It explained everything—the criminal courts with a ninety-nine percent conviction rate, the billionaire tax clerks, the abysmal roads, the dying villages, the alcoholism. Lyosha knew things did not have to be this way. Other countries allowed voices and differences. Other countries weren't dying root and branch from theft. Here, the graft started with the guy who unloaded the truck at his local minimart and went all the way up to the president in person.

Corruption is not a defect of the system. It IS the system.

Putin didn't just steal money. He stole votes, normal government services, people's dignity.

Calm down, Lyosha. Bozhe moy, *calm down.*

He was being gripped once more by that terror of losing control. *Breathe in, breathe out. Breathe in, breathe out.*

It took him a few moments to notice that the people sitting nearest to him had turned to look at him. In fact, one of the floor cameras was now pointing right at him.

". . . we have a lot of young people in the audience today," the woman host was saying. Then he saw his own face looking haunted and pale on the two giant LED screens. "Let's have a question from one of them. Alexei Kuznetsov, please."

Lyosha sat bolt upright, as if a string had yanked him up by the crown of his head. A studio assistant was passing him the mic. Its red light was on. His hand began to tremble violently. He felt weightless. He was floating in empty space. The studio lights were distant but bright suns blinding him. Everyone around him became out of focus, a blur, except for the president, who appeared pin-sharp and in high definition.

Slowly Putin's cold gray eyes turned upon him with a look of surly disinterest.

Lyosha's arms had turned to straw. He managed to reach into his jacket pocket and pull out the torn page of notebook on which he'd written his question, his *real* question. He'd been so frightened of his mind going blank that he'd taken the precaution of writing it down.

The seconds ticked by. The audience waited.

He held the paper shakingly, and raised the mic, which was slipping in his sweat-soaked grip.

"Hello, Mr. President . . ."

He sensed the words he wanted to say struggling to flee in terror. When he finally started to speak, his voice sounded odd, as if it were on a tape recording.

"I was born on Victory Day, twenty-one years ago. My grandfather was decorated after the Battle of Kursk and is buried in the

Kremlin walls. I love my country. But sometimes I feel ashamed of it. Nearly every week I have to pay a bribe, even for the most basic service, like seeing a doctor, or booking a train ticket. Will you agree with me that a life paying bribes is a life of humiliation?"

His voice had trembled, but it had held.

Time seemed to slow down. Now that he'd got to the end of it and he'd put his question to the bribetaker-in-chief, the tsar of all corruptions, he felt strangely serene. He'd committed himself, and nothing more could be done. When he looked up, he met Vladimir Vladimirovich's laser-cold stare with a feeling of peace.

Putin's retort was in fact instant and sharp.

"You read your question. Did you write it yourself, or did someone put you up to it?"

So, it had taken Lyosha's question to do it. The mask fell off. All this man's cynicism and contempt were on naked display. The audience's eyes turned back to Lyosha, electrified.

Lyosha wanted to marvel at his own daring, but the feeling of calm was filling him with a warm sense of well-being. A huge smile spread across his face, and across the two huge screens.

He shrugged. Wasn't it obvious? "Life prepared me for this question."

Then something happened which neither he nor surely the president expected.

The audience laughed.

The sass of this guy. What a smart-ass! But it's true, who isn't sick of paying bribes? Someone patted Lyosha on the shoulder.

Putin's instincts made an instant course correction. He forced a smile in a way that made his small head look like a lump of dough, ready for the oven.

"Good lad." The president cleared his throat, his smile angry and frozen while he waited for the laughter to die down. Then he spoke in his terse, KGB report-speak. "The country's judges, not the president, are in control of sentencing corrupt officials." He added a vague remark about corruption being an issue that all countries faced, and grudgingly acknowledged that more needed to be done.

It was a shifty, unconfident answer. And in the audience's reaction—a less enthusiastic, more muted applause this time—there was the palpable sense that it was the president, not Lyosha, who had seemed flat-footed and embarrassed, and that Lyosha's unblinking question and his genuine, disarming smile in the face of despotic power had, if only for a moment, caused a crack to open between Putin and the youth.

17

US Consulate
Kuala Lumpur, Malaysia
Friday morning

Jenna braced herself for the debrief with Norman Rhodes. Strangely, she was feeling almost exuberant—no doubt an irrational mood swing brought on by her injuries. She had, after all, survived an encounter with death, an exhilarating experience in itself. At any rate, she didn't get the usual heart-sink sensation when she saw Rhodes waiting for her in the sensitive compartmented information facility, the SCIF.

Rhodes was scowling crossly at a laptop screen and didn't even acknowledge her, a posture she took to be the intentional signaling of a vile mood. He was short and barrel-chested with a ginger Marlboro Man mustache and a baldness that gleamed salmon-pink under the strip lights. She knew that he resented her because she was well regarded at Langley and because his own career as a case officer had been a disaster. But she was also aware that he possessed a Machiavellian competence when it came to the politics of Headquarters. He had his eye on a big departmental job in DC next year, and the last thing he wanted was blame for an op that had gone sideways. She was quite sure that he was about to throw her under the bus.

"All right," he said, closing the laptop. "We'd better start. Langley's just joined."

Honestly, I'm fine, Norman, but thanks for your concern.

Two wall-mounted screens lit up and the head of Asian Ops Desk and the CIC for Asia Division appeared via live video link.

The SCIF was a secure, too-intimate room-within-a-room, like a refrigerated meat locker. Jenna was seated less than a meter from Rhodes, which would have been a severe trial for her even on a good day. This time, it was like being trapped in a box with an enraged baboon. By now, of course, he'd seen the cable she'd sent to Headquarters without his sign-off.

Still without looking at her, he said, "Would you like to start by telling us, Jenna, why you disregarded *basic* cable protocol by—"

"Okay, Norman," one of the heads on the screens said, holding up a hand. "I'm sure you can deal with that in Station. Jenna, take us through what happened on Langkawi."

Rhodes's face darkened to a deep brick color. "It was a total fucking shit show," he said.

Calmly, addressing the screens and speaking in clear, complete sentences, Jenna recounted every detail of the op to recruit PANDA as an asset: the preparation, reconnaissance, and countersurveillance measures she'd undertaken prior to PANDA's arrival on the island; her conversation with PANDA, including her impression of his state of mind; the surprise turn the interview had taken when she'd asked him about the identity of juche888, one of the usernames receiving regular "winnings" from his gambling app. It was the mention of juche888, she said, that made PANDA refer to the Seed-Bearing Program and led her to conclude that juche888 was in fact a North Korean Seed-Bearing Program operative.

"Why did you think that? He didn't *mention* the Seed-Bearing Program," one of the heads said.

"He didn't, but as you heard on the recording, that was the moment that he suddenly recalled where he thought he'd seen me before, in the Paekhwawon Compound in Pyongyang. He said: 'You were one of the Section 915 girls.'"

"He mistook you for your twin . . ."

". . . who spent twelve and a half years in the Seed-Bearing Program. Yes, sir."

The heads in Langley were thoughtful. Jenna's extraction of her own sister from North Korea was the stuff of legend among the seniors in the Agency, but Rhodes was in the dark. This had all gone over his head. He looked from the screens to Jenna, confused, like a boxer between rounds.

"Guys," he said, incredulously, "this was a straight-up developmental meeting with a potential asset. It was in a secluded location where hostile cover should have been easy to spot. Perhaps she needs a refresher course in basic—"

"Yep, got it, Norman," one of the heads said, irritably. "I guess that is our next point, Jenna. They found you. How?"

The moment of danger was upon her, like a spotlight finding a soloist on a darkened stage. She was going to tell the truth, but not all of it. Her private phone call to Soo-min, she had decided, was best left on the cutting-room floor. Besides, she had already confessed it to Fisk.

She said, "We weren't to know that Pyongyang was in the final stages of a complex operation to assassinate PANDA at Kuala Lumpur Airport the next morning. They knew every detail of his travel itinerary. They would have had eyes all over him in the days leading up to the murder. They must have seen that he was meeting me."

"Strange that you didn't detect their presence," one of the heads said.

Rhodes's shoulders slumped helplessly. "Strange my ass. It was incompetence!"

One of them said, "You think they bumped off PANDA for talking to us?"

"Might have been a factor, sir, but it wasn't the main one. They killed him because he was a threat to Kim Jong-un's legitimacy. Which is why I also believe that PANDA's son, now encrypted as DIAMOND, is the next target."

For two hours the heads in Langley asked detailed, probing questions to test the veracity of everything she'd told them. Rhodes stayed quiet during all this, smoldering. But as it began to dawn on him that Langley's interest in this Seed-Bearing Program signified a major piece of intel, and that Jenna had discovered it, he decided upon an outrageous change of tack. By the end of the debrief, he was referring to the op as one that "exhibited sound teamwork based on the ops plan I myself authorized."

Jenna didn't give a damn. Her final question to the chiefs was to ask whether Langley understood the urgency of locating and exfiltrating DIAMOND before he was hit.

"Already found him," one of the heads said. "Picked him up in Macau Airport yesterday. The kid was trying to board a plane to the Netherlands, but the Chinese wouldn't let him through the gate. We got him out secretly via Taipei."

"Is he okay?"

"You can judge for yourself. He's arriving at about 1 a.m. your time."

"DIAMOND is coming here?"

"Until we get a new identity and passport for him, yes. His mother and sister are with him."

Rhodes's anger returned quickly to the boil. "Well, that's just fucking dandy. Thanks for warning me, guys. Thanks for—"

"Back up a second," Jenna said. "You're bringing DIAMOND to Kuala Lumpur, the scene of his father's murder?"

"There's some serious shit going down between Malaysia and Pyongyang. The Malaysian authorities want a DNA sample to prove that the corpse is who they think it is before they kick up a massive diplomatic stink about a banned chemical weapon being used in their goddamned national airport. The kid's agreed to provide the sample. Also, he wants to identify the body."

18

Barrikadnaya Street
Moscow
Thursday afternoon

Lyosha opened his apartment door to thumping bass beats and boozy warmth—a student party in full swing. A raucous cheer went up when he entered. An ovation. When had all this started? His roommates had invited friends over and they seemed pretty wasted already. One of them started chanting "Lyo-sha! Lyo-sha!" and others joined in.

His best friend, Anya, screamed when she saw him and pushed her way through the bodies to hug him and give him a vodka-wet kiss. He was used to her startling changes of appearance, but he almost didn't recognize her. She'd dyed her hair electric blue and was dressed like a street urchin from a Dostoyevsky novel, with suspenders, thermal shirt, and ankle boots.

"Lyosha, *urrah*!" she cried, raising a bottle as if she were about to throw it at a tank.

It took him another few moments to understand that they were all here to celebrate his star turn on *Direct Line*.

In the tiny galley kitchen, he was mobbed. Students bear-hugged him and shook his hand. The music was so loud they had to shout straight into his earhole. A small *stopka* glass was pushed into his palm. Anya sloshed vodka into it, the cheap Karkov brand, and they raised a toast to him.

"To Lyosha!" she yelled. "Our YouTube star!"

"YouTube?" he said, smiling stupidly.

Anya pulled his head toward her and licked his ear, which turned him crimson with embarrassment. "You haven't seen?"

A fourteen-second clip of his exchange with President Putin, including the studio audience's laughter, was going viral, clocking up hundreds of views by the second. It was also spreading across VKontakte, Telegram, and Facebook like a pollen-rich breeze. Comments and likes were pouring in from every region of Russia.

Lyosha was shocked. He'd gone to that studio out of desperation, a feeling that whatever he did would be futile, a lone voice lost in four hours of praise. It was simply something he'd had to do for his own sake. It had never occurred to him that he'd have any kind of impact. He felt a sudden swell of anxiety.

"Aw, isn't he cute when he's worried?" Anya said, to more laughter from everyone. Her foghorn voice was the only one that carried easily over the noise.

Lyosha knocked back the vodka, winced as it scorched his throat, then held his glass out for another. The stuff was like turpentine. His belly caught fire, but then the burning died down and moments later the world began to seem a less cynical place.

"You stuck it to that wicked old thief!" Anya shouted.

"I did, didn't I?" Lyosha shouted back, and they both suddenly found this extremely funny.

An hour or so later he went unsteadily downstairs to buy more beers from the Azeri minimart and when he returned, someone had turned off the music in the apartment and plugged a phone into the speakers, with the volume turned up loud enough for the whole building—and the twelve lanes of traffic outside—to hear the clip.

"*You read your question. Did you write it yourself or did someone put you up to it?*"

A pause of four seconds followed.

"*Life prepared me for this question.*"

The studio audience laughed at his audacity. His friends laughed because they were drunk. Everyone was laughing. Laughing at Putin.

Another tendril of unease uncoiled in his stomach and groped its way through the vodka. For as long as he could remember, his father had warned him always to keep his head down, never get into trouble, and never do anything to draw the state's attention because the state was capricious and its repression had no logic.

Well, he and his father had parted ways. Permanently. He was free from his father's laws. Independent. Liberated.

To hell with him.

19

Hay-Adams Hotel
Washington, DC
Thursday morning

Dmitry Stepanovich Kuznetsov was already awake when the bedside phone rang with his 5 a.m. wake-up call. He'd slept, even by his reduced standards, very badly, awoken several times by his pounding heart. For the hundredth time, he tried to reassure himself that there was probably a simple, mundane explanation, that his imagination was spinning out of control.

Yesterday, he'd been due to return to the Russian embassy on Wisconsin Avenue for a midday debriefing with Ambassador Kislyak and Foreign Minister Lavrov immediately after their meeting with Trump in the Oval Office. He needed to know what Trump had talked about in case anything of intelligence value had been imparted. But just as he'd been about to set off to the embassy some functionary had called to tell him that the debriefing had been canceled.

"Canceled, why?"

"Scheduling issues."

"Well, is it being rescheduled?"

"I have no further information, sir."

The debriefing had not been rescheduled. Nor, ominously, had there been any call from Lavrov or Kislyak, both of whom he'd known personally for years, to apologize or explain. It had taken a tremendous effort of will for Dmitry to gather and calm his frightened herds of thoughts.

If the game was up for him, if, somehow, he'd been caught, then this, he knew, was one of the early signs—the sudden unavailability of colleagues, a silence.

He'd spent the rest of the day in a kind of hollowed-out limbo and had no idea how he'd gotten through it. His body and his voice had been on cruise control during the afternoon's defense seminar, to which he'd made no worthwhile contribution; he'd sat in a state of paralyzed unraveling for the evening's UNICEF concert, from which he'd made an unseemly dash afterward to avoid the dignitaries he'd been expected to meet and greet. When he'd finally arrived back in his room last night, he'd poured himself a cognac from the minibar and again tried to think, think.

Lavrov and Kislyak were extremely busy men. There were any number of reasons why they may have canceled. Perhaps the meeting with Trump had overrun. Perhaps Putin, impatient as always, had spoken to Lavrov and Kislyak by phone straight after the meeting. Maybe that was it. Dmitry's involvement simply hadn't been required.

But there were other worrying signs. The inbox of his encrypted email was almost empty of new mail. He was still being copied into reports, but it was low-level stuff.

They know.

Another icy trickle of fear passed through him and froze solid in the base of his stomach.

The rendezvous with his CIA contact in Rock Creek Park tonight was out of the question now. What had already seemed an extremely dangerous act now looked suicidal. He knew that SVR officers who fell under suspicion of passing secrets to the enemy were sometimes allowed to carry on as normal for days, even weeks, unaware that they were being watched around the clock for the moment when they could be caught red-handed.

And suddenly the reality of the danger he was in became as clear to him as a child's drawing. They didn't even need to catch him in the act of meeting the CIA in Rock Creek Park. He'd be caught red-handed if they searched this room.

Everything he'd intended to deliver to the CIA tonight was on a memory card concealed inside a gold cufflink—dozens of highly classified, compartmentalized intelligence files that he'd downloaded, at insane personal risk, from the restricted server of the SVR *rezidentura* in New York.

A weird calm came over him then, the kind of reconciled peace he imagined the terminally ill felt when told that they only had a few days left to live. His panic and anxiety subsided. In the bathroom, he turned on the lights surrounding the mirror, and slowly, methodically, began to shave. With surprising composure, he considered whether the moment had come for him to defect. He was in Washington, after all. He simply had to walk out of this hotel and present himself at the FBI Headquarters on Pennsylvania Avenue, a mere few blocks away. It would create a massive diplomatic scandal, with repercussions that could last years . . . but he'd have a new identity, a new life in the West. How would his wife and son take the news? Would they understand?

These thoughts had the effect of restoring some sense of perspective. He reminded himself that there was still a chance that he'd misread the signs, that he'd simply suffered a bout of paranoia, and—God knows—that was an occupational hazard.

For the time being, he decided, the most important thing was to act normally. Do nothing that they may interpret as panicky, irrational, suspicious. He got dressed and left the suite.

The hotel's corridors were silent and empty, the rooms still slumbering behind closed doors. In the Lafayette dining room he was told he was too early for breakfast: the breakfast bar opened at six.

So he returned to the suite, wrapped himself up in his coat, scarf, and gloves, rode the elevator down to the lobby, and went outside for a morning stroll.

This was his opportunity—to know for sure. Because if he genuinely had been caught, there'd be a bubble of watchers around him by now.

It was still dark outside, and the air so cold that his breath turned to plumes of white vapor. Pedestrians were few and traffic at this hour was sparse. Any tails, however professional, should be easy for him to detect.

Lafayette Square was deserted except for a pair of noisy street-cleaning machines. Dmitry took his time, walked along East Executive Avenue, past the White House, and down as far as the Ellipse with its wide-open view of the Washington Monument, which was floodlit like a moon rocket ready for liftoff. The first airplanes of the day, wing lights winking, were making their descent to Dulles. The city was only just starting to stir. Up on the Hill, the Capitol was a lemony gold in the floodlights. It was a most surreal feeling, he thought, walking alone amid the monumental grandeur of the American capital. Only Moscow emanated a comparable statement of power.

Whenever Dmitry was being followed, he'd feel an invisible string connecting him to his watcher. After all his years as an intelligence officer, he'd developed a hyperacuity for it, a subsense. And depending on the distance, he'd feel the string slacken or tighten. When it was tight, and he turned to look, that was when he'd see a certain figure jolt or stiffen or turn away. If he had watchers now, then he was forcing them to reveal themselves. He was drawing them into the flat, open space of the Ellipse. But he detected nothing. None of the solitary dog walkers or joggers braving the cold roused his suspicions.

No one was following him.

Satisfied, he returned to the hotel, feeling a sense of normality beginning to reestablish itself inside him. He'd simply been paranoid. Imagining things again. Just as he was re-entering the suite, his phone buzzed with a message. It was from his deputy in the *rezidentura*. That, too, was reassuring. Normal communications were continuing. The message asked if he was watching *Direct Line*, which was airing live in Russia right now, and added, *I think you'd better watch it.*

He'd been intending to watch it anyway before his lunch with the congressmen today. What fresh outrage had Putin uttered this time?

First things first. He picked up the bedside phone to order breakfast and coffee from room service. It was barely light outside. He left curtains drawn against prying eyes and the room lights off. Then, with another exhausted sigh, he turned on his laptop and began watching the recorded broadcast of *Direct Line with Vladimir Putin* from the beginning.

Putin's dismal voice filled the room. "*The United States doesn't need allies but vassals. Russia cannot exist in this system of relations* . . ."

He turned down the volume and went to splash cold water on his face. In the bathroom, by some acoustic effect of the marble, Putin's voice sounded clearer and more resonant, even with the door closed. Only the toilet flush drowned it out momentarily.

"*We don't consider anyone our enemy. And we don't recommend that anyone consider Russia to be an enemy* . . ."

He got back onto the bed and tried to rub the soreness out of his eyes. He was struggling to keep his attention on the president's words. A schoolgirl in Magnitogorsk was asking if he was the richest man in Russia.

"*No. That's such garbage. Where did you read that? They picked it out of their noses and smeared it on their newspapers* . . ."

The handpicked studio audience was applauding his every remark. Dmitry laced his fingers behind his head and stared at the ceiling, thinking that if Putin hadn't been accepted into the

KGB all those years ago he'd have had a career as a taxi driver. This uncharitable thought, he knew, was born of his fear of Putin. The terrible thing about Vladimir Vladimirovich was that if you made a mistake with him, it was like mishandling a grenade—it was the last mistake of your career. Putin never listened to excuses.

"No. There are no Russian troops in eastern Ukraine. That is another Western lie . . ."

Where was his breakfast? He needed that coffee.

"It is well known that the Americans like to be licked in a certain place . . ."

Audience laughter.

Direct Line was droning on interminably. Questions from pensioners; questions from veterans. Dmitry felt his eyelids sagging. He'd had so little sleep, and, somehow, he was going to have to make it through a long, tedious lunch at the National Republican Club.

"We have a lot of young people in the audience today. Let's have a question from one of them . . ."

The laptop screen was giving him a headache. Perhaps he had some Aspirins in his washbag . . .

"Hello, Mr. President . . ."

Some distant part of his brain must have stayed alert to what was happening on the screen while the rest of his mind had wandered, because he realized, very suddenly and with quite a sickening shock, that the voice now asking the president a question was a voice he knew extremely well.

Dmitry sat straight up. He turned up the volume. He scrambled to find his glasses.

No, no, no, no.

The TV camera had zoomed in on the face of his own son.

His own son had been handed the studio mic. His own son's hand was shaking quite violently.

"*I was born on Victory Day, twenty-one years ago. My grandfather was decorated after the Battle of Kursk and is buried in the Kremlin walls. I love my country. But sometimes I feel ashamed of it . . ."*

Dmitry was electrified, paralyzed, as if he were a split second away from crashing a car at high speed and could do nothing to avoid it.

". . . Nearly every week I have to pay a bribe, even for the most basic service, like seeing a doctor, or booking a train ticket. Will you agree with me that a life paying bribes is a life of humiliation?"

Dmitry forgot the room and the comfortable bed; he forgot about his paranoia earlier and his terror of being caught. He forgot about everything else in the world. His entire being was focused on what was happening on the screen. He was too thunderstruck to move. Two worlds that were never meant to meet were colliding before his eyes, one public, one private.

Now President Putin was speaking to his own son on national television.

"You read your question. Did you write it yourself or did someone put you up to it?"

Dmitry slapped his own face to make sure he wasn't asleep; that this wasn't some lucid nightmare.

"Life prepared me for this question."

A short pause followed, as if a punchline had been delivered and the penny was about to drop, and then the audience reacted.

And to Dmitry's astoundment and horror, he heard a few small, tentative exclamations of merriment, followed by a more emboldened collective laugh, and a smattering of applause.

Applause for his son.

Dmitry had to pause the footage.

He was hearing in his head a garbled, strangely joyous, jabber of terror and exhilaration, of accusation, fear, and anger. Anger that his own son, Lyosha, had just taken it upon himself to humiliate a vengeful, humorless dictator on *live television*. Happy—astounded—at Lyosha's bravery, his audacity. Furious, incandescent, at Lyosha's naivety, his folly, his failure to see the consequences.

"Holy Mother, Lyosha. What have you done?"

Dmitry skipped backward to watch the clip again, and again.

Lyosha's question had clearly excited viewers, because the text messages that had been running across the bottom of the screen throughout the show suddenly took on a most impertinent tone, catching the censors off guard.

Putin, when are you going to go off and retire? ... Three terms of the presidency are enough! ... The whole of Russia thinks you've sat on "the throne" too long ...

He was so possessed by what was happening on the screen that he barely heard the knock on the door, or a woman entering the room and saying, "Room service." He only vaguely heard her say, "Sir, do you mind if I turn on some lights?" He was hardly aware of the bedside lamps and the dining-room lamps coming on.

Only once the door had closed and he smelled the coffee did he fully register that room service had been and gone, and that a coffee pot and an arrangement of fruit and fresh pastries had been delivered to the dining table on the opposite side of the room.

Coffee ... yes. He'd wanted ... coffee.

His concentration had become strangely slippery and unfocused. For a moment he put it down to extreme tiredness, but no—there was a fog seeping across his brain, and the room was blurring and dancing before his eyes, as if he were drunk. He wasn't imagining it. Suddenly, he was also feeling very sick.

He got up from the bed and tried to steady himself, but something was wrong with his balance, as if the room was adrift on a heavy swell.

Before he could reach the table, he stopped, swaying and breathless in the center of the room. He couldn't take another step. His limbs had become weirdly leaden and feeble. And the light from the lamps, soft and golden a moment ago now seemed harsh and blinding. It was hurting his eyes. His heartbeat, too, was rising—not the ever-present flutter of anxiety, but something worse, something morbid, critical. His legs folded under him and he collapsed to the floor with a heavy thump.

He was on his back now, and he was frightened. A sinister feeling of discomfort was beginning to manifest between his shoulder blades. He was sweating profusely, and the scent was strange, chemical, unnatural.

The next thing he knew, his chest was firing jolts of hot pain through his nervous system. The realization of what was happening struck him with the force of revelation.

He lunged for the hotel phone on the bedside table, missed it, and knocked the lamp over with a crash. Then an almighty convulsion in his chest arched his back clear off the floor. His jaw clenched; his eyes bulged in disbelief.

After his heart had stopped, his brain remained dimly conscious for almost a minute, long enough for him to hear the door open again softly and men quietly enter the suite, whispering to each other in Russian.

Three last words crossed Dmitry's mind before he died.

Seed-Bearing Program.

20

US Consulate
Kuala Lumpur, Malaysia

Since it was now very much in Rhodes's interest to add his name to Jenna's ops report, he needed her to explain the Seed-Bearing Program to him, who DIAMOND was, and why the North Korean state wanted to murder a twenty-one-year-old. This was why, at their next meeting in his office after lunch, he proffered a box of Krispy Kremes, which was out of character with his legendary cheapness, and apologized to her for his ill humor at the debrief earlier, which was out of character with his legendary spite.

Then he leaned back in his chair and affected a tolerant, professorial air, as if he was about to hear a paper from a sub-par student. He disliked having anything explained to him, least of all by a woman. He waited in vain to be amazed, and then, out of the blue, he was amazed.

"North Korea *breeds spies* . . . ?"

But before his eyes had a chance to refocus on the room, Jenna had taken a page from her pad and was drawing the Kim dynasty's family tree.

"Kim Jong-il had three sons. PANDA was the eldest; Kim Jong-un was the youngest. Of the three, only Kim Jong-un showed the qualities his father deemed worthy of an heir—ruthlessness, cruelty, a cunning ambition. But when his father died in 2011, Kim Jong-un was only twenty-eight and his reign far from secure. He was surrounded by a powerful old guard who had been close to his father, and he had two older brothers with stronger claims to the succession. The middle brother, Jong-chul, whom the father dismissed as effeminate, is safely under guard in North Korea and poses no threat. But the elder brother, Jong-nam—PANDA—was living in exile in the relative freedom of Macau and under China's protection."

"PANDA was a drunk, a loser. I can't see how that fat fuck was any threat."

Jenna smiled patiently. "Look at it this way. If Beijing had ever decided that a change of leader was needed in neighboring North Korea, well, they had a replacement right up their sleeve. PANDA may have been hopeless for the job, but he was the real deal—first son of the Dear Leader Kim Jong-il, first grandson of the Great Leader Kim Il-sung, a descendent of the sacred revolutionary bloodline of Mount Paektu. In other words, a leader-in-waiting whom the North Korean people and military would accept as legitimate."

Rhodes's pupils were wobbling as he took this in. "Right, yes . . ."

"But even after murdering his own brother, Kim Jong-un will not sleep easy. He's produced no male children, and PANDA has a living, twenty-one-year-old son named Yong-won—DIAMOND. I follow him on Instagram. Nice kid; horrible family, but he can't help that. His own uncle, Kim Jong-un, has now murdered or neutralized every threat inside the Family, bar one—him. DIAMOND is the dynasty's sole remaining rightful heir. If we spirit him to safety in the US, then we, too, will have a North Korean leader-in-waiting, should we ever need him."

"Hm," Rhodes said after a lengthy pause. He was making a show of frowning with his head to one side, as if reserving judgment on her opinion. "That's an interesting take. Thanks." Then he drew a slow breath, got up, and sat with folded arms on the corner of his desk, facing her. "There's something else we need to talk about," he said ominously. "I think you know what I'm going to say, don't you?" He sounded like a highway cop who'd pulled her over.

Skip to the end, Norman.

"You're too hot for us, Jenna. Your dip cover's blown. You're a shit magnet. Now that they know who you are you'll place your assets here in danger. I'm going to recommend that your tour in Malaysia be curtailed."

Jenna said nothing, but regarded him mildly, wondering if he knew his staff called him Oompa-Loompa.

"Take a few days to recover, but in the meantime . . . I'll talk to Langley about your follow-on assignment."

She was feeling a mighty urge to end this face-to-face with a very purple flourish. Instead, she got up and said, "I understand. It's been an education to serve in your station, Norman. You're unlike any other chief I've worked with."

The mustache bristled into a smile, but his eyes were alert to mockery. "That's nice of you to say."

She left his office and closed the door, raising a casual middle finger in his direction as she walked away. A short-of-tour expulsion submitted by a chief of Station was the kind of black mark that landed you a basement job in records. Weirdly, she wasn't feeling that upset, perhaps because she was now preoccupied and intrigued by the imminent arrival of DIAMOND with his mother and sister in tow.

She had an uneasy premonition about this visitor, that his coming here was ill-fated, somehow. She was not a superstitious person, but she couldn't help noting that two members of his family, *the* Family—PANDA on Langkawi and Kim Jong-il on board that train five years ago—had died very soon after meeting her.

By the time she got back to the suite, she'd already put Rhodes to the back of her mind. It was the Family she was thinking about, specifically DIAMOND's uncle in Pyongyang.

Kim Jong-un...

Capricious like his father, Kim Jong-il. Wily, gluttonous, basketball-crazy, impulsive, secretive, brutal. How much he'd changed since his debut in front of the world's cameras little more than five years ago, when he'd appeared nervous and very young as he'd walked alongside his father's funeral cortège in a snowstorm— a black Lincoln sedan bearing a vast portrait of the Dear Leader's smiling face. She remembered thinking that he must have been freaked out by the crowds. That unearthly sound. Hundreds of thousands of citizens had prostrated themselves on the snow, wailing like the spirits of the dead. But now those same crowds were fueling his narcissism and glorifying him. How quickly he'd grown in aggression and confidence.

Everyone had underestimated Kim Jong-un . . . *She* had underestimated him.

When his Uncle Jang became too powerful, Kim had him shot. When an elderly general dozed off while Kim was speaking, he was shot. When Kim chose a wife—a beautiful former singer—all her fellow musicians were shot, and all recordings of her singing destroyed. She could have no past before Kim. Every word he spoke was noted down and became law. Every grain of rice he ate was inspected for imperfections. Absolute, untrammeled power—*what it must do to the brain*. The enormous dopamine rush. Power without check or limit. Pure, unadulterated power, and Kim Jong-un had been mainlining it for years now. How could anyone give that up? Any threat to it, however small or imaginary, he'd crush without thought or mercy. She wondered how he'd react—who he'd blame and have shot—when he found out that PANDA's son had slipped through his fingers . . .

She tried to nap in the suite while she awaited DIAMOND's arrival, but she was too wired with anticipation to rest, too keyed-up with curiosity.

By 2 a.m. they still hadn't arrived. The ambassador had arranged sandwiches for them in his office, but he'd given up waiting and had gone to bed, so Jenna went to the office alone and settled onto the comfortable divan beneath the window.

Her eyelids were starting to droop and close when the door was opened by one of the Diplomatic Security officers.

Standing behind him was a bespectacled youth with spiky hair and a large rucksack on his back. He was accompanied by a bewildered older woman whom Jenna guessed was his mother, and a young girl with a pink Hello Kitty hoodie that she presumed was his sister. They looked like survivors of a shipwreck—vacant-eyed and exhausted, too warmly dressed for the humidity of Kuala Lumpur.

"Hey," Jenna said, flustered, getting up and brushing hair from her face. "Welcome. I'm Jenna." She bowed to them.

Yong-won's face was nervous and very pale, but in it she discerned PANDA as he must have appeared in his youth. Slim, handsome, still holding dreams for the future. Vulnerable.

Yong-won said nothing.

"I'm so sorry about your father," she said in Korean.

"You knew him?"

Jenna smiled. "I knew him."

Yong-won stared at her without comprehension, and on an impulse Jenna stepped toward him and gave him that most un-Korean of things—a hug.

His arms stayed stiffly at his side. "What's going to happen to us?" he murmured.

She took a step back and addressed the family. "Well, someone will talk to you about that tomorrow, but you mustn't worry. You're safe here."

She saw sadness and sufferance in Yong-won's eyes, as if something he'd long dreaded had come to pass, and he had accepted it. He looked like a student from anywhere—geeky glasses, two gold studs in one ear. Nike trainers. And yet his predicament was a very ancient one. That of an heir whose uncle had seized the throne.

"Will we go to America?"

Jenna hesitated. "If that's where you'd like to go."

She wished she could promise him that he was now free to live any kind of life he chose, but the bleak reality was that he would always be looking over his shoulder. Nowhere in the world would be truly safe for him.

She was about to offer them refreshments when the Diplomatic Security officer reappeared.

"Ma'am. Call for you on the secure line in conference room one."

"Oh. Lucky I'm still awake," she said, and made her excuses to the visitors.

Who on earth was calling her at this hour?

She followed the officer out of the ambassador's office. He said, "Actually, they told me to wake you up immediately if you were asleep."

Jenna entered the conference room feeling a faint chill of foreboding. She picked up the phone. It was Fisk.

The deep voice spoke across a gulf of darkness. "Sorry, Jenna, I know it's kinda late."

"What's happened?"

"Listen, if you're well enough to fly, there are people on the seventh floor who want to see you as soon as possible."

"What?"

"Tickets for the next flight are in your inbox. I'll send a car to meet you at Dulles. It'll bring you straight to Headquarters. I'll wait for you in the Original Building lobby and take you up there myself."

Alarm bells went off all over her brain. Her first thought was that Rhodes had been spreading poison about her at Headquarters.

"What people?"

"Russia House."

Something's gotten mixed up here.

"Sorry, Charles. You just said Russia House?"

"Yes." Another oceanic pause. "Your debrief today caused quite a stir, Jenna."

Her eyes widened in the dim room. "Okay. Now I'm confused. Can you give me a heads up?"

Somehow, she could sense he wasn't smiling. "You'd better hear it from them first. Then we'll talk. Have a good flight."

The tone went dead.

She replaced the handset. *What the hell . . . ?*

His voice had held way too much behind it for comfort. His tone locked out all expression.

She peered down at the embassy gardens, now crisscrossed by glowing amber shards from the security lights.

Russia House was a kind of secret agency inside a secret agency, with its own distinct culture and identity. She knew little about it, except that it almost never shared its intel. Its location inside Headquarters was sealed off from the other divisions.

Her debrief had caused a stir . . . in Russia House?

21

Washington, DC
Thursday evening

Fate must have been paying special heed to Eric's ambitions and desires, because just as he was about to leave the West Wing and head home at the end of the day, another drama unfolded that convinced him that his fortunes were flowing in a very positive direction.

The Boss had been hosting the Japanese prime minister and his wife at Mar-a-Lago. In what was meant to be a relaxed couple of days of male bonding, the two leaders had spent the afternoon playing golf.

Half an hour ago, they had been joined by the first ladies in their finery and had sat down to dinner on the resort's candlelit terrace, surrounded by a hundred or so wealthy private members who were dining in the club restaurant.

The hors d'oeuvres had just been served; a crooner was singing to live piano music; the private members, who had risen from their chairs to applaud the leaders when they had entered, had felt no inhibition in holding up their phones to take photos of the august party at the center table. The setting was perfect for the kind of evening the Boss loved—a golden display of power and extreme wealth, glamor and informality, all of it shared instantly on social media. He was at the center of attention; he was among friends and admirers who loved him.

And then the evening was abruptly and spectacularly upended.

It was all captured on camera phone. The Boss's happy table talk was interrupted by a security official whispering urgently into his ear.

Just minutes ago, he was informed, North Korea had tested a powerful, solid-fuel Pukguksong-2 intermediate-range ballistic missile, which was at this moment flying over the Sea of Japan.

The timing—just as the heads of the United States and Japan were sitting down to a jolly evening of back-slapping bromance and bullshit compliments—was almost comically deliberate. The missile launch had been supervised by Kim Jong-un in person, it seemed. North Korea's Central News Agency had already released photos of the Great Successor being congratulated hysterically by some gruesome old generals in uniform.

In Mar-a-Lago, the Japanese prime minister was visibly outraged and shocked.

The dinner table then morphed chaotically into a security conference, with an out-of-his-depth-looking Boss scrambling to read incoming reports under the lights of his aides' cellphones (any of which, Eric knew, could be easily hacked and converted into spy cameras). In fact, the whole incident happened in full view of Mar-a-Lago's private diners who were live-streaming it to Facebook and Twitter. Within seconds, the Boss was being mocked and excoriated online for not immediately repairing to a secure, private room to handle the crisis.

But why would he do that? Eric mused, as he watched it all unfold on his laptop screen. This was theater. This was great TV.

He pictured the missile, still blazing its arc over the Sea of Japan.

It was a kind of calling card, he thought. A test. A gauntlet thrown down. This was the first security crisis of the Boss's administration. Kim Jong-un had publicly provoked him. How would the Boss react? The way he always reacted.

I'm getting punched. I gotta punch back.

He'd square up, of course. Shower his opponent in humiliating insults. Threaten him with thermonuclear Armageddon.

But the Boss's psyche was no deep mystery to Eric. The missile test was a crude demonstration of violence of the kind the Boss admired. The kind of machismo, rule-breaking, norm-destroying thing he'd do himself. Anyone capable of that was someone he'd want in his club—someone he'd far rather hang out with than the dreary Japanese prime minister and his silent wife.

22

Barrikadnaya Street
Moscow
Friday morning

Lyosha's mouth tasted bilious and rank from the vodka. His body was poisoned from alcohol and his head was gonging with pain.

He opened his eyes blearily, warily. Light filtering through the dirty windows revealed the detritus of a humdinger of a party. It had spilled into every room of the apartment. Outside, the rumble of the twelve lanes of traffic was as constant as a river after rain. The plosive sound of a soft snore, emanating from just inches away, startled him, and he turned to see Anya passed out next to him on his bed, fully clothed, blue hair splayed over the pillow like a mermaid's.

For a few brief seconds his mental picture of the last twelve hours was all confusion, his memories muddled and scattered by the party. But he was most definitely aware that somewhere, lurking in the befuddlement, was an awful truth he had to face.

And then, with a sudden cold clarity, he remembered. He reached for his phone, which he'd turned off and hidden under the bed last night, worried that his father might try to call him.

For a few more minutes he procrastinated, closed his eyes, rode the pulsing waves of pain in his head. But there was nothing for it: he had to man up. He turned on the phone.

His first feeling was one of relief. He'd received dozens of messages from school and college friends congratulating him for the clip of *Direct Line* . . .

But the relief was followed, more slowly, by unease.

There hadn't been a word from his mother or his father.

Surely, they'd seen the YouTube clip. Or if they hadn't, friends and colleagues would have told them by now. His father would be mad. Lyosha knew that, and could understand if he hadn't wanted to call—after all, they'd washed their hands of each other—but he thought his mother might have called, to tell him that she was proud, or worried, or disappointed, or something.

He lay still for a minute thinking about this, pondering the terrible power of silence.

When he'd gone to bed last night, the fourteen-second clip of his exchange with President Putin had attracted about ninety thousand views on YouTube alone. Now he checked again, and what he saw made him half jump out of bed, then fall straight back onto the mattress as the raw yolk of his brain resettled queasily inside his skull.

The clip was now racking up tens of thousands of views per hour.

"When I saw you stand up to the tsar," said one early comment, "you gave me hope that Russia can change . . ." But then, very quickly, like a sewer pipe bursting, the feed had been flooded by hate and abuse. "You are a traitor who shames Russia. I hope you die in PAIN!"

Any lingering elation from last night was dispelled instantly by thoughts that were sober and frightening: that this question to the president on *Direct Line* was already having consequences, for himself, for his family. He had humiliated Putin, and therefore he had also humiliated his father.

And just as he was thinking this, his mother called.

Lyosha flinched, and instinctively, childishly, covered his eyes with his hand. Then he took a long breath, holding it in as if he were about to go underwater, and answered it.

"Mama."

"Oh, Lyosha..."

"You saw me on TV?"

"What?... No." She sounded strange, as if she was panting and struggling for air, and he realized she was crying.

"Mama, what's wrong?"

It was several seconds before she could speak again. "Your father's dead."

PART TWO
Russia House

... and this high seat your Heaven
Ill fenc'd for Heaven to keep out such a foe
As now is entered ...

John Milton
Paradise Lost, Book IV

23

CIA Headquarters
Langley, Virginia
Sunday morning

After nearly twenty-four hours of travel, Jenna arrived at Washington Dulles International. A driver was waiting for her in arrivals and escorted her through an underground airport parking lot to a gleaming black Lincoln Navigator with government plates. Moments later they were on the freeway in driving rain, the unrolling road awash with spray. The sky was the color of pencil lead.

She felt as if she was being conveyed into the eye of a storm, and swirling inside it were unanswered questions to do with Soo-min, with juche888, and with Russia House.

This last mystery, at least, was about to be revealed to her.

Fisk was waiting for her, as promised, in the Original Headquarters Building lobby. He exhaled with relief when he saw her, as if he'd been counting down the minutes until she arrived. In the pale northern-hemisphere light she saw that his thick, crinkled hair had completed its fade from silver to white, like a new glacier. His face had grown heavier, craggier, making the bulbous, prominent nose seem even larger. But the beautiful plangent voice—that hadn't changed.

He gave her a perfunctory embrace. "How many of your nine lives have you used now?"

"This is definitely my ninth."

She wanted to ask him straight away whether he'd managed to swipe the hospital's CCTV, whether anyone had spoken to that nurse, if there'd been any leads on juche888.

But Fisk was already guiding her briskly toward the security turnstiles and the escalators, his mind casting ahead to the meeting.

"Charles, what's going on?"

"Might be nothing," he said quietly. "Or it might be the end of all we hold dear." He turned his head and winked sadly at her, and she knew at once it was grim. "Usual CIA predicament."

She had an odd premonition just then—that however familiar her surroundings appeared now she was about to enter a new reality. Kuala Lumpur already seemed far behind her. Whatever she was walking into now she was glad she had Fisk at her side.

"There was a time," he said, keeping his voice low, "when Russia House was the Agency's nerve center, the engine room." They had crossed the building's gray-marble lobby with its vast inlaid seal and were standing on a deserted ascending escalator. An enormous Stars and Stripes hung from the rafters. "But in the heady years after the Cold War, it was sidelined, its budget cut. The guys you're about to meet never lost faith. They have deep knowledge and long memories. They were the only ones warning us. That whatever changed on the surface—the smiling G8s, the reset buttons, Medvedev and Obama sharing burgers and fries like a pair of regular joes—deep down, nothing had changed. They were right. Russia's resentment of us, it never went away."

They turned into a windowless maze. No personnel in sight, but an atmosphere of intense concentration seemed to emanate from behind closed doors. Large signs in red capitals read RESTRICTED

ACCESS. They were in the inner sanctum of Counterintelligence Center, Russia Division.

Fisk's voice fell to a whisper. "They are the guardians of the flame."

He held his pass to the scanner and punched in another code; a heavy door unsealed with a hiss and opened inwards.

Jenna was shown into a space that reminded her of a college senior common room. Its walls offered no view onto the outside, but it was sunny and bright from large skylights. An enormous, faded map of the old USSR with all its vassal states dominated one wall, framed behind glass like an heirloom. She noticed the map before she noticed the people in the room. A woman and two men were seated in a close trio at the far end of an elongated table, which was marked by scuffs and ancient coffee stains.

No one got up. Fisk showed Jenna to a seat at the opposite end, facing them. And then, disconcertingly, he took a chair behind her, at the back of the room.

A willowy woman seated between the two men spoke.

"Welcome back, Jenna. This may look like a deposition, but it's really just a friendly talk. I'm Mira Kowalski."

Jenna's eyes popped wide in astonishment. Years ago, during her training, that name, Mira Kowalski, had been cited many times in examples of legendary tradecraft. Jenna had assumed she was long dead, if she had existed at all. This was the woman who had built networks of sources and assets during the Cold War by posing as a Polish academic authority on Marxism-Leninism. She had been a regular Communist Party delegate to the Kremlin Palace of Congresses, and had used her access to recruit chauffeurs, spurned mistresses, chefs, typists, archivists, and fellow party members, while all the time operating under conditions of extreme danger and regular hostile surveillance.

"Can we offer you something? Coffee? Cookie? No?"

Her voice was so soft it left almost no prints at all, perhaps the faintest trace of Central Europe. She smiled weakly. She had unkempt, shoulder-length auburn hair that displayed a good inch of gray root. A cameo brooch fastened the collar of her blouse, over which she wore a heavy dark-green knitted cardigan. Her eyes were a lovely honey color, and slightly hooded.

To her right was a heavy, jowly man wearing a polka-dotted tie; to Mira's left was a spry gentleman with a trim gray goatee that made him resemble some Soviet-era maestro. Neither was introduced. All three appeared to be in their late seventies.

"Thanks for dashing here at such short notice," Mira said. "We know what happened on Langkawi, Jenna. We know you're still recovering from injuries. But after Fisk alerted us to your cable, we decided to listen in on your debriefing in Kuala Lumpur on Friday—yes, sorry, we should have announced ourselves. The point is: we realized you needed to be here, not there . . ." She paused, something occurring to her. "Who was that *awful* little man? Reeds? Rudes?"

"Norman Rhodes, ma'am. Chief of Station."

"He was a piece of work. He curtailed your tour, I take it?"

"Yes, ma'am."

"Good," the polka-dotted-tie man said. "Means you're all ours."

Jenna was very much warming to these people already, but her puzzlement was only deepening.

"So," Mira said, opening a file in front of her, "we have a North Korean Seed-Bearing Program operative active in the United States."

"I believe so, yes. I think my source was funding this person via his online gambling sites."

"And your source was the asset codenamed PANDA, who is no longer with us and can't tell us more."

"Correct."

"You were the officer, weren't you, Jenna, who uncovered the North Korean Seed-Bearing Program in 2011."

"I was."

"Remind us, please. How many operatives were involved?"

"Twenty-two. I believed we'd caught all of them, but clearly, I was mistaken. One got away."

"And how were they caught?"

"That's the scary part, ma'am—only by pure chance. One of them was a nineteen-year-old woman arriving on a Malaysian passport. The immigration officer at Dulles became suspicious of her and alerted Homeland Security. She was detained at the airport, where I questioned her."

Mira ran her finger down a page. "Ah yes, I've got it here. A nineteen-year-old Malaysian national named . . ." She put on the reading glasses that hung around her neck. "Mabel Louise Yeo. And what was suspicious about Ms. Yeo?"

"The immigration officer happened to be of Malaysian descent. She questioned Ms. Yeo in Malay, but Ms. Yeo could not speak Malay. It also became clear that she'd never lived in Malaysia, despite stating that her home address was in Kuala Lumpur. She was not Malaysian at all."

Jenna glanced over her shoulder at Fisk, thinking he'd say something to back her up, but he remained as still as a boulder in the back of the room.

"Where was she from?" Mira said.

"North Korea."

Jenna sensed everyone's concentration sharpen to a fine point.

"What made you so sure?"

"Because she spoke to me in Korean, in the dialect of the North."

"She blew her own cover?" Polka-Dot Tie said, surprised. "Just like that?"

"No. She thought she recognized me—as someone she trusted. Someone she'd known for years at the Paekhwawon Compound in Pyongyang, where the Seed-Bearing Program was based."

There was a pause as the trio in front of her joined the dots. If they knew about her role in uncovering the Seed-Bearing Program, then they certainly knew about Soo-min's twelve and a half years in North Korea.

"Ms. Yeo mistook you for your twin?"

"Yes. It's not as crazy as it sounds. Believe me, it used to happen all the time. I hadn't planned to impersonate my twin. The deception simply happened the moment I walked into that airport detention cell and the girl threw her arms around me. I used the advantage to elicit the identities of the others from her, which she divulged over several hours alone with me."

"And where were they? The others."

"On various university campuses around the country. All of them were recent arrivals. We arrested them before they'd done any damage."

Their eyes were locked on Jenna now. "And their documents. They were false?"

"No. Valid, clean passports from Iran, Russia, Syria, Venezuela, Malaysia, China. Valid student visas. But all of those individuals were from North Korea."

She sensed that the answer she had just given had confirmed a highly troubling issue for them.

"What action was taken regarding those arrested?"

Jenna shrugged. "We knew they were North Koreans only because of secret intelligence. We could never use that in a prosecution. Their documents were valid. No crimes had been committed. We could only deport them to their countries of origin, according to their passports, and bar any right of re-entry. None of them contested the deportations."

"And what action was taken regarding Ms. Yeo?"

"None." Jenna could feel herself slipping into that dissociative state that protected her from memories exactly like this one. "She died in airport detention before any decision was made."

"Died how?"

"Suicide."

A chill settled over the room. A silence for the dead.

"So, at least one North Korean Seed-Bearing Program operative is still unaccounted for . . ." Mira was watching Jenna thoughtfully, her pencil tapping the file. "One who may have attained a position of influence by now."

"It's possible."

Gray Beard sat up, as if he'd just been activated by Bluetooth. "And we only caught them because of a *fluke*, a blind stroke of luck at the airport?" He was looking past Jenna at Fisk. "We'll need more than luck if we're gonna catch these new fuckers."

"That's why Jenna's here, Bill," Fisk said calmly from the back of the room. "To help us figure something out."

"Uh . . ." Jenna looked from one to the other. "Who are we talking about?"

"I was in the White House yesterday," Gray Beard muttered, his head wobbling. "Place is teeming with young special advisors with Oval Office access. Jesus Christ." He put his elbows on the table and rubbed his temples with bony fingers. "Young people, naturalized citizens, bedded in long-term, they'll pass any background check . . ."

The room lapsed into thought again. Throughout all this, Jenna had been poised on the edge of her chair anticipating the moment of enlightenment, the explanation for why she had been flown urgently from Asia to meet these Cold War spooks whose field of expertise—Russia—she knew nothing about. But every remark spoken led her further into the dark.

Mira, too, seemed momentarily detained in some troubled place of her own.

"Jenna, we've brought you here today because you know more about the Seed-Bearing Program than anyone else." She put down her pencil carefully and stared at it. "Apart, perhaps, from your sister."

A buzz of alarm shot through Jenna like an electric shock.

"My sister was debriefed when she was brought back here from North Korea in December 2011. She's been in and out of psych wards for the last five years. You're not going near her."

All eyes continued to watch her, reassessing her.

Polka-Dot Tie sat back in his chair and spread his hands on the table. "Jenna, you should know that you have admirers in this room. The facts of how you recovered your sister from North Korea are legendary in the Agency. We know what it cost you."

Mira was regarding her with a clear-eyed mix of admiration and ruthlessness.

"Don't worry. No one will approach your sister. It's just unfortunate that we don't have more first-hand knowledge of the program, given the scale of the threat we're facing now."

Jenna could bear it no longer. "What threat?"

Mira glanced at the men either side of her, who gave an almost imperceptible nod.

"While you were in the air, we bumped your security clearance up a level. And for reasons that will become obvious we're keeping the club on this one extremely small." She paused, girding herself. "A few weeks ago, we received intelligence about a very similar program that has been developed in Russia."

Jenna kept her face blank. Two words flashed up behind her eyes, like title cards in an old silent movie.

~ *We're Fucked* ~

"Russia has been training spies in a remote base east of Moscow that is registered as an engineering college," Mira went on. "Or I should say, *raising* spies. The graduates hold valid passports from other countries, which they use to obtain valid student visas to study here; their names are real, not fake, and may not be Russian names; they're westernized, speak English, and give no reason at all to be suspected of any ties to Russia. Most of these 'students' were born outside Russia, but they have at least one Russian parent.

They enter the college as children and graduate at twenty-one. Does this sound . . . familiar?"

The three in front of her were studying her reaction, but her face was an empty grave. These wise ones had been holding onto a tiny thread of hope, she realized—that this was bad intel, or misinformation designed to make America paranoid, tear itself apart hunting for non-existent spies. But in their hearts, they knew it was true. She'd seen the doom in their faces the moment she'd entered the room. They were familiar with the old-school sleeper agents (the "illegals"), married couples with murky accents who spent decades not drawing attention to themselves in American suburbs. What they weren't ready for was the next evolution in espionage. The bedded-in young people with clean documents who had been indoctrinated since junior school, people who were hardwired with hatred for America and knew that their mission to destroy it would take decades of patience and work.

Jenna said, "Do you trust your source?"

"We do," Mira said. "He is—*was*—an agent of ours inside the SVR, Russia's foreign intelligence service. He operated out of the Russian consulate in New York. Codename OPUS."

"And OPUS can't identify these operatives before they get here?"

Polka-Dot Tie exhaled and folded his arms behind his head. "They're already here," he said with a brittle lightness. "We don't know when they came. We don't know how many. We don't know who they are."

In the stillness of the room, in the most secure, secret building in the country, the five of them seemed strangely exposed.

"It gets worse, I'm afraid," Mira said. "OPUS was our only source for this intel. On Thursday, he was found dead in his room at the Hay-Adams here in DC. The Russians are calling his death a tragedy, a great loss, he was fifty-seven, overworked, et cetera. They're requesting custody of the body for burial in Moscow with full military honors. The medical examiner said he'd suffered a massive heart attack. There'll be a post-mortem, but the toxin may be difficult to identify by now."

"You're saying the Russians killed him?"

"We know they killed him," Fisk said. "He'd ordered breakfast from room service. The waitress who took it up to him also suffered a heart attack after she left his room. Luckily, she survived."

"My God," Jenna murmured. "Something they inhaled?"

Fisk got up from his invigilator's chair at the back of the room and joined them at the table. "A nerve agent smeared on the bulbs of the bedside lamps. When the lights came on the heat turned it to gas. Classic FSB job."

Another poisoning . . .

"By the time the FBI got there," Mira said, "his laptop, phone, and possessions had disappeared. The intel he was about to give us was big—big enough for them to murder him professionally, at very short notice, just a block from the White House. If they hadn't got him, we would now be in possession of the identities and locations of every Russian Seed-Bearing Program operative in the United States."

They fell quiet again, allowing a moment for Jenna to absorb the scale of this disaster.

She said, "Why was he in DC? Why didn't he just give us this intel in New York?"

"More bad luck," Mira said, simply. "OPUS's FBI handler in New York was away on honeymoon. So when OPUS sent us an emergency signal to meet we responded immediately. He said he could come to DC. We arranged a rendezvous in Rock Creek Park. He wanted to give the intel to me in person. Said he wouldn't trust anyone else." Her tone softened further, and an almost holy light came into her eyes. "OPUS had been passing secrets to us for three years. Not chickenfeed, but blockbuster stuff. Russian national-security level information. Classified, compartmentalized material from inside the SVR. His work took great courage. We will miss him."

"Unfortunately . . ." Polka-Dot Tie made an arch with the tips of his fingers. ". . . you can see now that his death leaves us with nothing to go on. We have a threat, and we don't even know where to look."

By some process at work in the room, Jenna sensed that everyone around the table had become a close ally. Through the skylights she saw that the rain had passed, but the shadows in the room had started to deepen, turning the vast, faded map of the USSR the color of tea.

"Your thoughts, Jenna," Fisk said.

Her eyes were lost on some point in the middle of the table.

"I'm wondering if Russia set up this program with North Korean help and expertise . . ."

"That's occurred to us."

"And I'm wondering what the North Koreans got in return."

The complicated art of assassination by nerve agent?

Mira said, "We'll get you an office of your own in Headquarters, away from Russia Division, so that no one here knows we've brought you into this. In the meantime, we're giving you access to OPUS's agent file. All the intel we have on this is in there."

"How did they know?" Jenna said suddenly. "How did the Russians find out that OPUS was working for us?"

The three before her stiffened.

"We're not sure yet . . ." Mira's next words were cautious. "OPUS was an experienced intelligence officer. He may have slipped up. But we think it's more likely that the Russians caught him the old-fashioned way."

"He was betrayed?"

The temperature in the room dropped.

"OPUS was codeword-classified," Fisk said. "His work for us was known only to those in this room, his FBI handler in New York, the national security advisor, and the president."

Jenna opened her mouth to speak and closed it.

Mira read her mind. "The CIA's discovery of a Russian Seed-Bearing Program was an item in the president's daily brief on Wednesday. I'm reluctant to speculate at this point, and it goes no further than this room, but we cannot discount the possibility that President Trump revealed classified information in his Oval Office meeting with Russian Foreign Minister Lavrov and Ambassador Kislyak."

24

Victory Palace Apartments
Moskva Embankment, Moscow
Same week

A subdued, lachrymose atmosphere pervaded Lyosha's parents' apartment. Lyosha's mother, Marina, looked stunned and diminished. She was staring into space from the corner of the sofa as various cousins and aunts crept about on tiptoe, arranging the lilies that had been arriving by the carload, or shuffling silently between kitchen and living room with plates of unwanted refreshments. The dining-room chairs had been placed with their backs to the walls, which gave the room the atmosphere of a vigil.

Occasionally Marina would gaze fiercely at the silver-framed photograph of Dmitry on the sideboard, in which he was smiling and in uniform, and then she'd start sobbing again, and Lyosha could not keep his own tears back either. He put an arm around her thin shoulders and with his free hand wiped the tears from his cheeks. He had no adequate words to say to her. Aunt Olga glided slowly into the room carrying a rattling tray of tiny glasses of vodka and set it down on the coffee table.

"He was fifty-seven," Marina whispered. "Fifty-seven..."

"Here, Mama," Lyosha said, unable to keep his voice from choking. "Have a small sip. Look, I'm having one. Anya's having one."

Anya had come to offer him her support. She was dressed more demurely now in a loose black sailor suit with a horizontally striped *telnyashka* undershirt, as if she'd stepped ashore from the battleship *Potemkin*. She was acting as a discreet majordomo, opening the door to the flower deliveries, directing visitors into the living room in a single file, allowing each of them a solemn moment to convey their condolences to Marina, before gently ushering them to a seat.

Marina gasped suddenly and her tears began rolling again like condensation down a window. She shook her head in amazement.

"Try to eat something, Mama," Lyosha said.

Marina looked at him helplessly, like someone who had forgotten her own name, and he saw how old she had become. She was a slight woman, with neat, dyed blond hair, and although she always took care of her appearance and wore good clothes, she had eschewed the cosmetic excesses of a wealthy wife. She worked for a living too, running her own psychotherapy practice near the Old Arbat, a profession that was still quite novel in Russia. Lyosha was deeply concerned about her, however. There had been occasions in her past when she had disappeared into a kind of internal exile of the mind, a deep resignation, which had been a common phenomenon in Soviet times. People hadn't been able to stomach the regime's lies, but open dissent had been too dangerous, so they had retreated inward, and spoke nothing of their true thoughts and feelings. Lyosha could see how that might have been comforting in times when the state turned against the people, which in Russia was as inevitable as winter. He was afraid that unless he could keep her tethered to present reality, one such period of exile was about to begin.

The doorbell rang again.

The hallway was now filling with colleagues of his father's, some of them in uniform, all of them talking in muffled voices about banalities and practicalities, even giving the occasional stifled laugh of awkwardness as Anya took their coats. Lyosha thought he heard someone mention *Direct Line*. Of course, everyone here would know about that ... Lyosha had almost forgotten about it until just then. What did that matter now?

The family was in a state of limbo until Dmitry's body was returned to Moscow and no one knew when that would be. Lyosha could hear Anya informing the visitors of this as they arrived, and he was grateful to her. It spared him and Marina the pain of being repeatedly asked.

Lyosha stared at the silver-framed photograph of his father smiling and felt a sudden, massive incomprehension of his loss. It reared out of nowhere like a rogue wave. He gulped, and was once more fighting back tears.

He'd always been close to his mother, but he'd resented his father. Why was that?

Even before they'd fallen out, Lyosha seldom saw much of Dmitry. He was almost always abroad, and when he returned, at New Year, or Easter, or for a vacation in summer, Lyosha found him as remote and unavailable as when he was simply not there at all. The two of them had never found that easy common ground. Dmitry would comment on the length of Lyosha's hair, which now fell in dark-blond curls to his shoulders, or on the small black stud in his ear ("Makes you look like a drug addict"), or on the shapelessness of his clothes, or on his lanky height, which was a perpetual surprise to Dmitry. Lyosha put it down to the fact that Dmitry had grown up in a time when people were told what to think. They thought women had no place in politics and gay people were sick and in need of a cure. They got their news from Channel One and *Sixty Minutes*. It was a generation of gloomy, paranoid people, haunted by memories of purges and gulags and forests full of mass graves. Lyosha's generation was free from all that, and Dmitry was jealous of it.

And yet, Lyosha had grown up without any grievance at all.

His upbringing had been loving. He had enough self-awareness to know that he was a decent person of average abilities. True, he'd got into MGU—Moscow State University, the best school in Russia—but that was because he'd been playing ice hockey since he was four and had a talent for saving goals, not because of his grades.

It was Anya who'd changed him, Anya who'd opened his eyes and ignited a fire inside him.

He'd met her at a dorm party. She wrote blogs about how everything was broken, from the economy to park benches. She organized groups on Telegram in support of the opposition. She'd posted a TikTok of herself lip-synching an outrageous Pussy Riot song called "Putin Pissed Himself." She was funny and rude; she questioned everything. And she had the loudest voice Lyosha had heard in his life. "Why do you need a phone?" he'd said to her, the first time they'd met. "Just open a window and your mother'll hear you in Nizhny Novgorod."

It was Anya who'd told him that the Moscow mayor's office had granted planning permission for the building of luxury houses on protected land in the Khimki Forest. That had really shocked him. He'd spent the summers of his childhood in that forest, picking mushrooms with his grandmother. It was ancient and mystical. To desecrate something so primal, so deeply Russian, for billionaires' homes? The idea of it was criminal, unthinkable.

"If you feel that strongly," she'd said, blowing a plume of cigarette smoke over his head, "you're coming on the demonstration."

The two of them had joined the hundred or so Muscovites who had turned up at the forest to protest, and Lyosha had been surprised to see not militants with banners, but pensioners, office workers, an Orthodox priest, youth hiking groups, elderly communists. Normal people. They'd set off along the trail, chatting and laughing in the patterned light beneath the oak trees. The laughter stopped when they reached the development site and they saw the raw amber stumps of felled trees, some of them a thousand years old, the logs already cut and stacked, and the bulldozers, and the line of loutish men in plain clothes: the private security guards of the development company. The logging had begun in secret, at night. As their eyes took in the carnage, Lyosha sensed a collective breaking of hearts.

Just days later, a huge demonstration took place in Pushkin Square. The crowd was angry and fired up by what was happening in the Khimki Forest. Anya led Lyosha to the front, squeezing her way through, holding his hand so as not to lose him in the scrimmage of bodies, until they were at the barrier erected in front of the platform where speakers with megaphones were calling on the mayor to halt the destruction of the trees.

But the crowd, as Anya knew, was angry about so much more than trees.

Before Lyosha could stop her, she tipped back her head, filled her lungs, and in an air-cracking decibel, cried:

"RUSSIA WITHOUT PUTIN!"

Ten thousand mouths opened and repeated the chant in a great battle cry.

"RUSSIA WITHOUT PUTIN!"

Fists punched the air. An instant kinetic force spread through the multitudes of people as they lost their fear of the police. The crush of bodies pushing from behind almost lifted the two of them off their feet, forcing them forward so that they had to carry the barrier itself toward the lines of FSB men. Lyosha and Anya found themselves bumping up against armor and riot shields.

"RUSSIA WITHOUT PUTIN!"

Before Lyosha knew what was happening, before he'd even heard a word of a speech, he was zip-cuffed, hands behind his back, and frog-marched between two FSB men toward a padded wagon with his head forced downward in a stress position. An hour later he was standing in a crowded, unventilated cell where no one spoke. Fear rose from people's bodies in a sharp, animal odor, rank in the summer heat.

At some point he heard Anya's voice outside in the corridor. "Cocksuckers!" she screamed. Everyone in the building must have heard her. "It's cocksuckers like you who are destroying Russia!"

Anya had figured out this technique over the course of five arrests. The first few times she'd tried to reason with her captors. Then one time she'd really lost her temper and discovered that yelling right back was much more effective. Russian men did not expect women to shout back at them. If she used their own language, and hurled it in their faces, it worked even better. They did not put her in the cell.

That day, so many people were arrested in Pushkin Square that the police didn't even bother booking them or taking their names. Lyosha was released after three hours.

He found Anya at their rendezvous near the Lubyanka, and they quickly decided they needed a drink. In a tacky tourist bar just off Tverskaya they ordered six shots of some sticky liquor that the barman set aflame, then they knocked them back one by one. The adrenaline was still singing in Lyosha's ears. He couldn't stop laughing. *Cocksuckers!* They emerged into the bright summer night trailing a haze of fumes that smelled like nail varnish remover. He was heady from a mix of alcohol, relief, righteous indignation, and the euphoric high of a narrow escape.

The Pushkin Square demonstration might have been the end of his activism had it not been for another incident soon afterward, one much closer to home.

He'd spent the rest of that summer at the *baza*, the hockey training camp in the forests northeast of the city, being put through grueling off-ice fitness training. When he returned to Moscow just before the end of the summer vacation, he visited his parents.

Lyosha had not lived with his parents for three years. It wasn't until he saw their new apartment on the Moskva Embankment, in a tower called Victory Palace, which was designed in the neo-Stalinist style—that unique Moscow blend of menace and glitz—that he understood that his parents had taken a significant step up in the world.

The apartment itself was all marble and gilt and recessed lighting, a city pied-à-terre for the super-rich. Lyosha hated the place. The *elitny* showiness of it! It made him feel displaced, uneasy, resentful. The residents, his mother told him, were mostly Kremlin officials and their families, which made Lyosha think that the apartment might be a perk of his father's job, like a company car. His parents were modest people. They'd never lived ostentatiously.

It was during a rather tense lunch at this new apartment, with its dramatic views of the river and the domes of Christ the Savior, that his mother had let slip the news about the new dacha.

"Your father's bought a lovely place off the plan. We'll spend next summer there if it's finished in time."

Lyosha wasn't sure how he knew. Some suspicion, some spiking new cynicism, perhaps, but he just knew.

"New dacha . . . ? Don't tell me it's in the Khimki Forest."

A terrible scene ensued, a violent, bridge-burning row with Dmitry, both of them yelling across each other, with Marina helplessly trying to referee. Lyosha was outraged, but almost worse than that was the plunging disappointment he felt with his father.

The unaffordable apartment, the billionaire's dacha—it was hard evidence that Dmitry had been gorging on dirty money, taking kickbacks, creaming off public funds.

"You're a bedbug!" Lyosha shouted. "Like all the others!"

Dmitry had chosen the regime over his own conscience, and now the regime was rewarding him!

Dmitry yelled the words "ungrateful" and "self-righteous," and told him he was "full of insufferable pretension."

During a pause in the shouting, they heard themselves panting for breath. Dmitry's eyes were locked on Lyosha's, and in that moment, father and son knew they were seeing themselves in the other.

"This," Lyosha said, his voice shaking and ill-controlled, gesturing with a swing of his arm to the Italian furnishings. "This isn't privilege. It's THEFT!"

Lyosha had never seen his father truly explode with anger until now.

He grabbed Lyosha's arms and slammed him hard against the wall.

In the brief, intense struggle a painting was knocked off the wall, a vase toppled and smashed.

Marina screamed, "Stop it!"

Although in his fifties, Dmitry was an athletic man, and strong.

"*You* . . ." he whispered in a fury, just millimeters from Lyosha's face, ". . . have . . . *no idea* . . . what I do. You have . . ." And then his voice died, as if someone had signaled a warning to him, as if there was something he was tremendously tempted to say to his son but couldn't.

"What, Papa?" Lyosha said coldly. "What do you do?"

Moments later, as Lyosha left the apartment and slammed the door, he'd distinctly heard his mother saying, "You say you have nothing in common with him. You're both exactly the same!"

Lyosha did not speak at all to his father for some eight months, after that. The two of them would meet one more time—at the dacha in the Khimki Forest. It had been a last chance for them to reconcile, Lyosha thought sadly, but the encounter had descended into another horrible row. That was in summer last year.

And now they would never meet again.

Lyosha knew that he would regret for the rest of his life the way he'd behaved toward his father. Knowing that he'd died believing that his only son resented him was turning Lyosha's bereavement and heartbreak into an unbearable physical pain.

25

Nashville, Tennessee
Saturday afternoon

Donald J. Trump @realDonaldTrump
North Korea has just launched another missile. Does this guy have anything better to do with his life?

The arena was a vast sea of red trucker's caps, MAGA T-shirts, and swaying Stars and Stripes. The air was charged. The crowd had been primed for outrage, feeding from the crackle of violence and fun. Twelve thousand camera phones were turned on the Boss. He was majestic, Eric thought, warming to his theme, enjoying himself. He was radiating a dazzling brass halo of power.

"This is a state I truly love . . ." The applause avalanched from all sides. "I'm here because I wanna be among my friends . . . and I wanna be among *the people*."

"*U-S-A! U-S-A!*"

The president spoke for about an hour. In the anarchic, revolutionary days that had followed the inauguration, no one in the White House had a clue what they were supposed to be doing. No one could think straight or get any work done while the Boss was in residence. It had been an idea of genius to send him off on a "victory tour."

Eric could smell the crowd—the cheesy corn snacks; the hot breath of thousands of loud, pissed-off voices, engorged by resentment.

He was sitting to the rear of the podium, some distance behind the president, alongside a dozen White House aides; a gathering of the Boss's cronies and fixers; and a few members of the Imperial Family. The First Lady, looking immaculate and glacial, was an enigma as usual. She hadn't wished to stand too close to her husband's supporters. She bore that air of distant feline inscrutability she adopted whenever she knew that her husband was about to lob a rhetorical turd.

The Boss raised his hand in his signature gesture, pressing thumb and forefinger together, and it was as if he held the whole world in his palm.

"We can't have madmen out there shooting rockets all over the place . . . And by the way, folks, L'il Rocket Man should have been handled a long time ago . . ." The audience whistled and jeered. "We're going to do it because we really have no choice. I wanna tell you something . . . And I'm sure he's listening 'cause he watches every word and I guarantee one thing . . . he's watching us like he's never watched before . . ."

A cheer spread across the arena. The crowd was eating it up with a spoon. This is what they had come for. The full-fat, high-caffeine sugar rush that nobody but the Boss could supply.

Li'l Rocket Man.

An American president's words were live ammunition. Eric had foreseen very well the effect such a dishonorable nickname would have on its target. A truly heretical thought had crossed his mind when he'd first heard it: that the Great Successor might be afraid of the Boss, that he had not yet appreciated that this firehose of testosterone was merely the Boss's way of sizing up of an opponent that he admired.

This missile test had come at a most serendipitous moment,

because it had opened the way toward a momentous possibility—a once-in-a-lifetime opportunity to elevate the Great Successor, to glorify the era of his rule, so that the Sun of Korea, the Highest Incarnation of Revolutionary Comradeship, could bestride the world's stage as the American president's equal and friend.

The rally had gone well, Eric thought, except for the moment when the president had misread "future" as "furniture." Within an hour they were headed back to the airbase in a convoy of black Suburbans and taking their seats on Air Force One for the return to Washington. The moment the president was on board, everything revved up at once and the wall of noise was tremendous.

The plane took off at a dizzying tangent, and once it had reached cruising altitude, the passengers started unfastening their safety belts. Eric looked at them. What a D-list assemblage of misfit toys made up the president's court. A former golf caddy, a reality TV contestant, a mafia-family fixer, a sleazeball campaign consultant with Kremlin ties. None of them could run a car wash let alone an office of the White House. But then, he supposed, a truly great man *had* to surround himself with dross. No other stars could be allowed near the sun.

Eric was seated next to the Son-in-Law. Mercifully, they were spared from having to engage in any chitchat by the approach of a bodyguard from the president's Secret Service detail.

The Son-in-Law made that Mona Lisa face again. "Excuse me, Eric. I think the president wishes to see me."

But the Secret Service man was leaning to Eric's ear.

"Mr. Rahn, the president is asking for you."

Eric gave the Son-in-Law a commiserating smile—*That's put you in your box, ladyboy*—and rose from his seat.

He smoothed his tie and calmly followed the Secret Service man through the giant aircraft, past the senior staff meeting room with conference table and enormous table lamps, the dining room, and up the stairs to the president's private lounge.

More Secret Service agents with radio earphones opened the doors onto a comfortable, deep-carpeted area with cream leather sofas and an enormous presidential seal mounted on a mahogany cabin wall.

A couple of aides were briefing the president, who didn't seem to be listening.

He was settled into a club chair with his back toward Eric, his head leaning to one side, his hair a soft, cotton-candy pancake. He was watching a news report of the rally on a giant flatscreen. The empty wrappers of his favorite candy bar, Three Musketeers, littered a plate in front of him.

Eric stopped in the door and lowered his head. "Mr. President."

Trump beckoned him to sit, without taking his eyes off the screen.

"Went well, huh."

"Really well, sir. Best rally yet."

Already he wanted to kick himself. The Boss demanded servitude, but at the same time was contemptuous of it. Groveling was weak, weak, weak.

"Give us the room, please."

The aides left, and Eric was alone with the president.

Trump turned off the TV and smoothed his hair absentmindedly. He seemed preoccupied, distracted. Eric had never sat quite so close to him before. The marmalade spray-tan could have been applied by a five-year-old. The rings around the eyes looked like powdered donuts. The eyebrows were furry, like two small paws pointing upward.

"I was first in class at Wharton, an Ivy League University," the president said vaguely. "I'm very smart. I have a very high IQ. You know I offered five million dollars to charity if Obama released his college grades? Obama was a terrible student. How the fuck did that guy get into Columbia and Harvard Law School? Where are his college transcripts?"

Eric could think of no response to this surprise stream of consciousness, but it took no psychologist to figure out that the Boss was feeling insecure about his ability to handle the crisis in hand, and out of his depth. His next remark confirmed it.

"This North Korea thing. I've just been on a call with the South Korean president and the Japanese prime minister . . . It's complicated."

Eric saw a small opening. Gently, he said, "Kim Jong-un, sir. I think you've got him on the run."

Trump picked up a tall glass of Diet Coke and rattled the ice.

"You can never show weakness," he said, looking out of the window. "You've *gotta* project strength. If he thinks *he* can fuck *me*, he'll try. If he thinks *I* might fuck *him*, he won't."

Eric's neck was pulsing. He might never get a better moment than this. "Maybe it's time—"

A muffled sound of a toilet flush, and the First Lady emerged from the president's private bathroom. The Boss made no acknowledgment of her, and she glided to the exit in silence, casting Eric a glance of botoxed chilliness.

He continued in a lower voice. "Maybe it's time to think about looking him in the eye."

Trump merely shrugged. "Sure, I'd be happy to meet him. Sit down with him over a hamburger. Not some fucking waste-of-money state banquet like we give to all those other countries that rip us off. I'll know within one minute whether L'il Rocket Man wants to deal. He plays the game. I play the game . . ."

Eric felt a buoyant rush of hope.

"We need a total rethink on North Korea, sir. A summit with Kim Jong-un would *transform* world opinion of your presidency. Taking on the world's most volatile situation and reversing it? It's a PR no-brainer. A major historical event. Think Nixon in China. If you can't disarm him, sir, no one can. Proclaim victory and declare peace."

And now for the kicker . . .

"The Nobel Peace Prize will be yours."

The co-pilot, uniformed and ribboned, was standing over them. "Mr. President, we're landing in ten minutes."

"Can I get another Coke?"

Eric, worried that the Boss's mind was already wandering, said quickly, "I can put feelers out to the South Koreans and the Japanese. Get them onboard first. You can leave the boring stuff to me, sir."

But he needn't have worried. He saw that the magical words *Nobel Peace Prize* had landed. He knew that look on the president's face. The way he cocked his head to the side, the way he seemed to inflate and glow the moment something of great value and prestige was dangled in front of him, something that was rightfully his and no one else's.

"You think he wants to meet me?"

"You've got his respect, sir. Yes, I'd say he's ready to meet."

Trump pursed his lips into an oval pout. "OK. Make it happen."

Eric descended the steps to the lower deck. A great symphony orchestra was playing inside him, a feeling that there was nothing in the world he couldn't achieve.

Just like that, the Boss's personal campaign to demonize and humiliate Kim Jong-un had been tossed aside!

Make it happen. Make it happen. YES, he would make it happen. He would—

Female laughter was coming from the direction of the president's private cabins in the nose of the plane, and the unmistakable Slavic tones of the First Lady's voice. She was speaking to another woman, with whom she was clearly on friendly terms . . . Suddenly the cabin door opened, and Sofia Ali emerged, still smiling from the conversation. She was dressed in a slim-fitting navy suit with large gold buttons. Her dark hair was down, so that it fell about her shoulders.

"Hello again," Eric said.

Sofia Ali regarded him coolly, the smile in her eyes fading to a look of faint aversion and suspicion.

And in that moment Eric had a most distinct perception—that game had just recognized game.

"I'm Eric? We met outside the Oval Office."

"Yes, I remember."

"What are you doing on board?"

The woman's gaze held him in its winter-green beam. "Do you keep tabs on everyone, Eric?"

"I thought you worked for the national security advisor, that's all."

"He's on board, in case you hadn't noticed. Excuse me, please? I need to take my seat. We're landing."

Eric continued to stare at her as she walked past him, breathing in her perfume, which was musky and strong.

Muslim name . . . European vibe . . . hostile demeanor . . . Russian speaker . . . ?

Well, well. Who are you, Sofia Ali? Who are you really?

It was late by the time they landed at Andrews Air Force Base in suburban DC. There weren't enough waiting government cars to collect everyone, so Eric was obliged to make his own way home, something that would usually have put him in a savage mood. He was exhausted from the long day, and hungry, and yet . . . he was feeling elated, blessed. That conversation with the Boss had yielded more than he could ever have wished for. He was convinced that his life was uniquely favored by Fortune.

As he was riding home in the backseat of an Uber his phone rang and he saw that the name displayed was ADAM. *Who?* He answered it.

"Hey, Eric . . ."

The voice was high and glassy, the tone hesitant and carrying an expectation of recognition.

"Uh . . . Sorry, buddy. Remind me who you are?"

A nervous titter. "It's Adam, silly. From the Mount Vernon Hospital? You gave me your card. And I put my number in your phone . . ."

Oh, *him*. In a normal frame of mind Eric would have hung up instantly, but his irrepressible good humor had brought with it an exceedingly rare feeling of generosity.

"Of course. Adam. How you doing? How's Soo-min?"

"Oh, she left on Thursday. Her mom came to take her."

"She left?" Eric said, puzzled. "I thought she was, like, a permanent inmate . . ."

"Yeah, it was unexpected."

A slight discord entered Eric's harmonious mood. A faint, minor key.

"Why did she leave?"

"*Well* . . ." And Eric could hear in the nurse's voice the warmth of a revving motor, a desire to gossip. "Some woman called. Said she was worried that Soo-min was being harassed by an ex-boyfriend. I guess that was the reason. Of course, I told her no ex-boyfriend had visited, 'cause that wouldn't include you, you dark horse." Another nervous giggle.

"What woman?"

"Uh, she said her name was . . . Alice? I think?"

"Alice?"

"Same woman who called the day before—while you were there, in fact."

"What?" Eric's came out in a falsetto. "You're certain it was Jenn— You're certain it was the *same woman* who called when I was there?"

"Yeah, I'm pretty sure. Why? D'you know her?"

Eric felt as if he'd just been tossed into an abyss and was freefalling into black, empty space. The world around him had gone dark and cold. The beautiful harmony had morphed into something nightmarish, atonal.

Adam was prattling again.

"So, when are we going for coffee? I've been telling all my friends about you—"

Eric hung up.

He lowered the car's rear window slightly, needing a flow of cool air. He was afraid that he was about to vomit. His chest was filling up with something hard and solid, like quick-setting concrete.

Most Wanted Person Number One Jenna Williams: *not dead*.

Not dead and suspicious.

Not dead and had already figured out how she'd been traced . . .

By the time he got home to his apartment on Beecher Street he saw with a terrorized clarity the jeopardy he was in. His exposure. For several minutes he was almost hysterical with panic. He had the helpless feeling of being surrounded on all sides by a large, invisible dragnet that was about to close on him slowly, and then suddenly. Time was trickling away from him like grains of sand through an hourglass.

And who would save him? Not the Boss, not the Great Successor. No one.

He crushed up a Xanax on the glass coffee table and snorted it through a rolled-up dollar bill. He poured himself a large whiskey and swigged a generous mouthful.

No one. Only he could save himself.

After half an hour of circling the living room, biting his fingernails until they leaked blood, he felt the sedative begin to blanket his brain like a soft eiderdown, and the whiskey working its confidence-restoring magic. Then he sat down and attempted a thorough, methodological setting-out of his situation. Slowly, his panicked perspectives reformed, and a level sanity returned.

No one was going to identify him.

Because he was absolutely certain that Soo-min would stay silent. She would say nothing that might endanger the life of her dear lost son, wherever he was.

He simply needed to tie up the one loose end.

Now that the solution had presented itself, he felt himself back on terra firma. His mind could turn to the practicalities, which further calmed him, restored his sense of order, and he realized that he was anticipating the task almost with relish.

It was close to midnight when he retrieved one of the charged burner phones he kept locked in the glove compartment of his car.

"Adam, it's Eric. I'm so sorry. My phone was on one percent. I'm calling from my other phone."

"I thought you'd hung up on me," Adam said in a boyish voice.

"Of *course* not." Eric gave an offended, mortified laugh. "Listen, you free in the morning? How about breakfast? I can come to you. We can meet somewhere quiet."

26

Annandale, Virginia
Sunday afternoon

The rows of clapboard houses looked especially forlorn on a damp, blustery February afternoon. The street had gone into a decline in the years Jenna had been away. Driveways were potholed and overgrown with uncut hedges. Trashcans, junk, kids' trampolines littered the yards.

The retired ops officers keeping an eye on the house from the street—Fisk had said they were glad to help out, amused to relive old times for a few days—had reported nothing out of the ordinary. No one had been here looking for Soo-min.

But still, Jenna didn't want her visit to be noticed by anyone.

She did not approach the house from the driveway but via the long backyard, scaling over the fence, agile as a puma, and onto a lawn thick with moldering leaves. The house appeared lifeless. She couldn't see the car, and guessed her mom had gone grocery shopping. She crept toward the back door, keeping close to the fence and the trees to avoid the eyes of the neighbors, then used her latchkey to enter the house without a sound.

In the kitchen she stood still for a moment, listening to the susurrating refrigerator, the hot-water pipes softly ticking. The place had barely changed since she was a teenager. The tidiness of a normal, orderly life. The residual aroma of baking and fresh laundry. The hum of the dishwasher. It made her feel wistful and sad.

She remembered which stairs creaked.

The carpet smelled new, but the same old tourist paintings hung on the landing—the temples around Seoul in the four seasons of the year. The upstairs doors were closed, the rooms silent as sepulchers.

Slowly, she turned the door handle to Soo-min's room, the bedroom they'd both shared as kids. The curtains were drawn and once her eyes had adjusted to the gloom, she froze in fright.

Her sister's face was turned toward her.

Soo-min was lying on her side in bed and staring straight at her, eyes wide and glittering.

Jenna rushed to her, gathered her up in her arms, sheets and pillows and all, and pressed her cheek to hers.

Soo-min's voice was almost inaudible. "This is a dream."

"No," Jenna said, her voice already choked. "Not a dream." Her eyes started swimming with tears. "I've come to say hello."

Soo-min breathed a sigh that might almost have been a laugh.

She could feel the thinness of her sister's arms. She touched the drawn boniness of her face, stroked her long hair, which still had the frowsy smell of hospital, and kissed her on the cheek. It was an effort to keep her voice to a whisper. An effort to speak without falling apart.

"I'm so happy to see you." She felt as if she were holding and comforting her own reflection, which had somehow become lost, damaged, sick.

Jenna parted the curtain an inch to allow a sliver of wintry light to fall across her sister's face. Her smile was an enigma, faint and full of secrets. Her pupils were huge and black, and dulled from medication. The bedside table was a small city of pill bottles.

"You've come home," Soo-min murmured. Her voice was dreamy, absent, but it carried a soft note of joy.

"I was so worried about you," Jenna said, clasping her sister's hand and holding it to her own heart. "Were you worried about me?"

"No," Soo-min whispered, with the faintest echo of her old mischief. She was so frail that her breaths were coming in shallow huffs. "I always know when you're OK." She gestured vaguely with a finger pointed toward her temple.

Soo-min's senses were deadened by drugs, Jenna thought, and she was glad of it. She could not bear the thought of her sister knowing that she, Jenna, had almost become a debris field of scattered body parts on a dirt road in Langkawi.

"Where's Mom?"

"Church."

Jenna allowed a long pause to open between them. All her instincts were urging her not to rush her question, not to ask it even, but she couldn't help herself.

"Did . . . someone come to the hospital to ask about me? Someone from North Korea?"

The shadows of the room seemed to stir, become alert. She could hear the beating of both their hearts, the blood singing in their veins.

"Soo-min?"

Soo-min's voice was small, breakably soft. "No."

"No one at all?"

Another long pause, and the air between them seemed to acquire a faintly repelling magnetism.

"No one came . . . Only Mom."

And then her sister's eyes closed. She turned her head into the pillow and went still.

She was shutting down again, Jenna knew. The channel that had opened between them for a few moments began to close the moment Jenna had asked her question. Soo-min had fallen straight back to sleep.

Jenna gazed at her sister's face in profile. She was feeling the loss and grief of a parting, as if Soo-min were a spirit whose visitation had ended, and she had returned to a dimension beyond reach. Then she lay down on the bed next to her and held her in her arms as she slept.

Finally, she again kissed her sister on the cheek and left the room, so leaden in heart that she barely had the strength to move or lift one foot in front of the other. She had thought of waiting in the living room until her mom returned, but she was in no state to face her mother right now.

Outside, she sobbed bitterly and without restraint. She felt overwhelmed by sadness and distress. The darkness that Soo-min was carrying inside her like a tumor was slowly killing her, killing them both. She inhaled and exhaled, filling her lungs with great mouthfuls of air.

By the time she'd walked back to her car, which she'd parked more than a mile away, she'd cried herself out. She sat for a while in the driver's seat, taking ahold of herself, allowing her pragmatism to regain control.

No one had visited her at the hospital, she'd said. No one but Mom.

But Jenna had seen her sister's jaw clench. She'd felt her body stiffen, seen her pupils contract and look away. Soo-min had not told her the truth, had not wanted to tell her—her own twin—the truth.

There was only one cause in Soo-min's life that was as close to her heart as Jenna. One cause so important to her that she'd be willing to lie, even to her sister. And that cause was her son.

That delusion again. But delusion or not, Soo-min *believed* that Ha-jun was alive and in America, so someone could be using that as leverage against her.

If Fisk had discovered what had happened at the hospital, she was about to find out. He had invited her to dinner in Alexandria this evening.

27

US Embassy
Kuala Lumpur, Malaysia
Monday morning

PANDA's son, Yong-won, had now been inside the American embassy for two days, and his biggest fear was that his mother and sister might watch the TV news channels while his back was turned.

It had been less than a week since his father had been murdered at the airport and the lurid revelations were still coming thick and fast. His mother had barely eaten in days, and his sister, who was eleven years old, seemed to have regressed into a world of preschool cartoons. He didn't think either of them could handle any more horror.

And Yong-won desperately wanted to shield them from the latest development, which was why he'd confiscated the TV remote and had been monitoring what they watched.

On the afternoon after his arrival in Kuala Lumpur the Malaysian police had taken him to identify the body of his father at the Putrajaya Hospital morgue. They'd made him don a hazmat suit with respirator mask and goggles and he was warned that he could not touch the body or even go within two meters of it. The rubber sheet had been lowered only for a couple of seconds, and Yong-won had witnessed a sight that he would never be able to unsee. His father's corpse was not serene in death. The muscles of his face, grotesquely contorted by the nerve agent, had frozen his final expression of agony. The eyes remained open; the skin appeared gray and waxy under the fluorescent lights.

When he returned to the embassy, sickened and shaken, he told his mother and sister only that his father had found peace and was now at rest.

Yong-won had performed his last filial rite. He had identified the body as that of his father, Kim Jong-nam, and the DNA sample he'd provided would prove it, which meant that North Korea could no longer insist that the dead man was a random citizen called "Kim Chol", the alias on his father's North Korean passports.

As if the visit to the morgue hadn't disturbed him enough, what happened next turned his grief into a blowtorch of hatred for the regime in Pyongyang.

The same night, masked North Korean agents had been caught trying to break into the morgue to steal his father's corpse before the autopsy was carried out and the cause of death confirmed.

On the evening news, a spokesman for the Malaysian prime minister, visibly angry, had announced before banks of microphones and flashing cameras that the government was responding to this outrage by expelling North Korea's ambassador to Malaysia, a weasel-faced apparatchik named Choe Ryong-hae. They had given him until midday today to pack his bags and leave the country.

Yong-won understood that his family's situation in the embassy was temporary. They were in transit. Just for a few days, the Americans had said, until plans had been made for their security and onward journey. And Yong-won could not wait to leave. Here, every fucking chat show was talking about his father. Every celebrity had some dumb opinion, every comedian had a joke, every two-bit politician had a new conspiracy to air. None of them had known his dad.

The Americans had been kind to the three of them, making sure they had anything they wanted—clothes, toiletries, books, even Yong-won's favorite video game, *Counter-Strike*. The embassy's kitchen had whipped up their favorite meals. But the food didn't taste the same. At home in Macau, his father had enjoyed playing the chef at family dinners . . .

Grief kept hitting him in raw, stinging waves. He'd lost his appetite.

The embassy's security officer had strongly advised Yong-won to erase himself online and had shown him how to do it thoroughly. The only safe way was to cut off the digital trail and go dark. By the end of the day, his email accounts, WeChat, Instagram, YouTube, Apple ID, had all been wiped and canned. He and his mother had ditched their phones. They felt as if they were about to enter a witness protection program. New names, new faraway home.

The ambassador broached this matter in his office by asking Yong-won about his plans for the future.

"I've talked it over with my mom and sister. We want to go to France."

"France?" The ambassador frowned and drummed his fingers on the desk.

"I've been accepted by the Sciences Po in Paris. I want to finish my studies."

The man nodded gravely, taking this in. "Son, France won't be as safe for you as the United States. You won't have protection there unless we make some arrangement with our allies in Paris . . ."

But Yong-won's mind was made up. He had fond memories of vacations in Europe, from the days when his father had plenty of money and could travel without fear for his life. The days before the Great Successor. He did not want to abandon his studies. And his mother, who spoke no English, did not wish to go to America.

Arrangements with Paris were duly made.

A minivan with diplomatic plates was sent from the French

embassy on Jalan Tun Razak to collect Yong-won, his mother, and sister. They would be under the protection of the French authorities while visas and travel documents for Paris were processed.

A storm had been slowly brewing overnight. The heat and humidity had been so high that Yong-won's clothes would be soaked through with perspiration if he ventured into the embassy gardens, even for a few minutes. Clouds and pollution strained the light, so that the disk of the sun appeared dim and sulfurous. Now and then, from far off, he'd hear the artillery boom of thunder, which reverberated through the ground like a small earth tremor. The palm trees trembled very slightly, even though there was no wind at all.

A junior French diplomat who introduced himself as Yves Laffite had come to escort them to French diplomatic territory. He was a young man, earnest and talkative, and was acquainted with the American ambassador and his wife from the diplomatic circuit. The ambassador and his staff shook the hands of each of them in turn; the ambassador's wife embraced them and wished them all the luck in the world as they quickly climbed into the minivan. Yong-won sat in the middle row next to Monsieur Lafitte; his mother and sister sat in the backseat. A security guard sat next to the driver in the front. The Americans waved them off from the doors of the embassy, not wishing to venture too far from the aircon, and Yong-won waved back at them, with a mix of feelings: sadness and gratitude; relief and foreboding.

They were moving on. Their new life in the West was about to begin.

The morning rush-hour traffic was frenzied and fast-flowing, as if everyone was trying to get to work before the heavens emptied and the streets flooded.

The minivan's driver, like many of the staff employed by foreign embassies, was a Malaysian local. So, too, Yong-won noticed, was the security guard seated next to him in the passenger seat. A Malaysian police escort followed them by motorcycle.

Monsieur Lafitte seemed anxious to put them at their ease, speaking rapidly in fluent, accented English, which Yong-won translated for his mother. He was a small slim fellow, with thinning blond hair, and he was wearing a cream linen suit that carried a faint reek of cigarettes. He seemed nervous himself, excited even, unable to keep his hands still, thrilled to have a minor role in such a sensational international *cause célèbre*.

The vehicle's aircon was ferocious. The glands in Yong-won's throat started to throb and dry. In the backseat of the car, Yong-won's sister and mother chatted about the cuisine they would eat in Paris, the sights they would see, the things they would buy, but he could tell that they, too, were as nervy as Monsieur Lafitte.

A very loud crack of thunder, from almost directly overhead, silenced them all for a minute and made the atmosphere inside the vehicle skittish and uneasy.

Yong-won had seated himself in the middle row so that he could keep his eyes on the road ahead and on the mirrors. It was only a ten-minute drive to the French embassy. He asked Monsieur Lafitte if the Satnav could be turned on so that he could see the minivan's location on screen. After a brief exchange with the driver in Malay, it was established that the Satnav was not working.

The car sped smoothly along the underpasses and overpasses of downtown Kuala Lumpur. Yellow flame trees, luxury brand boutiques, a giant advertisement for an iPhone flashed by.

Yong-won checked behind. The police motorcycle escort was following at a steady distance of about six meters, not allowing any other vehicles to cut in.

By Yong-won's estimation, they were about halfway to their destination, when, without warning, the driver hit the gas and accelerated straight through a red light, flipped the indicator to turn right, and took the exit for Jalan U Thant, another major thoroughfare. Horns blared. The screeching swerve sent them all lurching sideways in their seats. They had to grab the minivan's overhead handles.

Monsieur Lafitte turned to the two in the front seats, alarmed, shooting questions at them in Malay.

Neither driver nor guard turned their heads. One of them uttered something curt.

"What's happening?" Yong-won said.

"Ah, I don't know," Monsieur Lafitte said, with a high shrug. "He said it's quicker this way. Less traffic." He looked rattled.

"The French embassy's on Jalan Tun Razak," Yong-won said, leaning forward in his seat. "Same road as the US embassy. We're going the wrong way."

Monsieur Lafitte fumbled for his phone and pressed call. He was starting to sweat horribly, Yong-won saw, despite the aircon. A damp, yellowish rim was forming around the collar of his shirt.

But before Monsieur Lafitte could get through to the French embassy, the signal died. The car had shot down a narrow one-way tunnel. The orange lights above them barcode-scanned across the windshield. Massive ventilators hung from the roof. Yong-won turned to look at the road behind.

"We lost the escort."

The car picked up speed, its engine roar condensed and amplified by the tunnel.

"*Merde*," Monsieur Lafitte breathed. A drop of perspiration was gathering at the tip of his nose.

They emerged from the tunnel. The car swerved right again into a leafy residential neighborhood. Monsieur Lafitte was shouting urgently to the men in the front seats. Neither replied.

The signal was back. He tried his phone again. It was answered. He started speaking in rapid, panicky French. Fear and alarm were spreading through the minivan like smoke from an engine fire. Drops of rain had begun hitting the windshield in heavy, irregular splashes.

The opulent buildings were set far back from the road behind tall white walls and frangipani trees. The car was moving way too fast for a built-up area.

"Where are we going?" Yong-won's voice was thin with panic.

His mother and sister sat wide-eyed and tense on the backseat.

"Embassy. Here," The Malaysian driver said in English. "You've arrived."

Yong-won and Monsieur Lafitte were speaking across each other.

"This is not—"

"WHICH embassy? Hey!"

The car dropped a gear, slowing only slightly as it approached a tall, barred security gate that opened inward. Sentries waved them through. In front of them was the portico of a large white concrete building—part home, part office—with walls stained by mold and humidity and pillars painted a dirty yellow. The front lawn was dominated by an enormous satellite dish.

Monsieur Lafitte was yelling: *"Ah, non, non, non—"*

The car continued at speed into a vehicle yard at the building's rear; another barred gate rolled shut behind them. The vehicle came to a handbrake stop that sent up a hail of gravel. Security lights came on, blinding them.

The driver stepped out and unlocked the door next to Monsieur Lafitte.

The Frenchman unfolded his thin legs from the minivan. He was pale and trembling and holding up his hands as if he was about to be taken prisoner.

A voice from behind them spoke to him in English. "You. Go. Run!"

Monsieur Lafitte wavered for a moment, panting, then disappeared without looking back. Yong-won turned to see his cream pants scissoring at a sprint toward the gates.

Waiting for them in the building's rear door was a man whose features Yong-won couldn't make out, but when he stepped into the light, he saw a steely, bespectacled figure wearing a black Mao suit. Yong-won recognized him from the cable news—Choe Ryong-hae, the diplomat who was being expelled from the country today. The North Korean ambassador to Malaysia. Thunder drum-rolled again and cracked. Rain was coming down in a quickening tempo now, turning to rods of silver in the light of the lamps, but the full deluge was still a minute or two from breaking.

If this is a bad dream, please let me wake up.

The car had moved too fast for him to notice any crest or signage outside next to the gates, but he knew now where he was.

A simple security operation to transport three defectors from the American embassy to the French embassy had been leaked, infiltrated, sabotaged. The minivan had been carjacked by its own Malaysian driver and security guard. Both had been working for the North Koreans.

"What's happening?" Yong-won's mother gasped behind him.

His mother and sister remained stiff with fright in the backseat. He could hear his own heart rattling and threatening to come loose in his chest.

"Stay calm, Omma," he said, a tremor in his voice.

The ambassador approached the vehicle and indicated for the guards to open the doors. The minivan's interior lights came on.

"Welcome," he said. "I am Choe Ryong-hae. You are among your own people now."

"We are under the protection of the embassy of France," Yong-won said with a bravery he was not feeling.

"I'm afraid not. This is the diplomatic territory of the Democratic People's Republic of Korea."

Yong-won turned to his mother and sister. "They can't bring us here. It's against international law." But even as he said these words they turned to dust in his mouth. North Korea was outside international law. There were no laws here. "Let's get out of the car. We're walking out of here. They cannot stop us."

Slowly they got out of the minivan and into the static, sultry air.

"Open the gates," Yong-won said, shielding his eyes against the glare of the lights.

He began walking backward, taking his mother and sister with him, holding them by their hands, their feet sliding on gravel. "We're leaving . . . Open the gates."

The ambassador gave a signal with his hand. The guards rushed forward and grabbed Yong-won's mother and sister from either side of him.

His sister screamed, an awful baby's scream. His mother yelped, "Oh no, oh no." A violent tussle ensued, confused in the glare of the lights. Yong-won tried to pull one of the men away from his sister. An order was shouted. Yong-won was shoved back hard by a hand to his chest, and the men physically lifted his mother and sister and carried them inside.

Yong-won was now panting and alone, flailing, like a man who'd been in a fist fight with an enemy he couldn't see. He could hear the blood roaring in his ears like the flow of a mighty river. The breath in his lungs was a forest fire.

The ambassador watched him for a moment, then disappeared back inside the building and closed the door.

Yong-won was alone in front of the gates, alone and made sightless by the lights. All around him, heavy raindrops were hitting the gravel like arrows.

Another figure entered the yard, one he couldn't see at all behind the glare, but whose steady tread he could hear on the gravel. Then he heard the click of a safety catch and a short, loaded pause as his executioner took aim.

A sudden gust of wind made the trees thrash wildly, and finally the deluge broke, coming down in a great roar that blanketed out any other sound.

He did not run, or yell, or plead. He remained rooted to the spot, unable to move.

His whole life, he understood then, had been leading up to this moment, in this place, blinded by light, cleansed by rain.

Yong-won's final thought was of his father making him promise always to be kind to his sister because she was a good soul and not everyone in the Family was good.

The bullet struck him in the heart. The sound of his body crumpling to the ground was lost in the hissing and splashing of the rain.

28

Alexandria, Virginia

Charles Fisk lived in an elegant, federal-era townhouse in Alexandria, not far from the Potomac. Three stories, windows with small panes of rippled glass flanked by slatted white shutters. A short flight of steps led up to an arched front door. He'd been standing in the window waiting for Jenna. It was one of those clear, crisp nights when the sky faded from blood-orange to sapphire, and the air held a vague promise of spring.

"A magical evening, isn't it?" he said on the doorstep, looking at the sky.

This was something she loved about Fisk—he always noticed the beauty in the world, even when it was all going to shit.

Inside, an aroma of something wonderful was emanating from the kitchen.

As he was hanging up her coat in the hall, he said, "The Mount Vernon Hospital's CCTV was offline on the morning you tried calling Soo-min. If anyone visited her that day—if someone was with her when you called—there's no video record of it."

"Offline?"

"May not be suspicious. In my experience, institutions like hospitals, schools, prisons have dated, poorly maintained camera systems that are seldom useful when needed."

"What about the nurse? Adam Tan."

Fisk paused before turning to her. "Adam Tan didn't show up for his shift today. His co-workers haven't heard from him, and he's not answering his phone. They said it's unlike him . . . Yeah, I know," he said, when he caught the look on her face. "I've sent one of our retired ops officers to Fairfax to see if he's at home. Let's wait before we jump to conclusions . . . Did you get anything out of Soo-min?"

"She said no one visited her."

"You believe her?"

"No," Jenna said quietly.

Fisk exhaled thoughtfully, his hands on his hips. She knew they were both thinking the same thing. *Compromised witness. No video. No nurse. No evidence.* Either there was an innocent explanation for all of it . . . or someone had been actively and cleverly covering their tracks.

"Come through to the living room," he said. "I think we could both use a drink."

She followed him through a pilastered corridor spotlit with American landscapes. The house was enormous.

He showed her into a cavernous room of tall bookcases with library steps. A grandfather clock marked time, deep and soft, in the corner, and the furniture, all dark, rich hardwoods, looked like valuable Americana. He noticed her admiring it. "Settee's a Sheraton. Dining table's a Hepplewhite." One wall was devoted to memorabilia: diplomas, prizes, photographs of Fisk with the great and the good. She took in Fisk with Bill Clinton, with George W. Bush, with Barack Obama. Tony Blair and Angela Merkel. And in one unsmiling picture he was at a black-tie reception shaking hands with the Russian president, who looked bloodless and goblinlike in the camera flash.

"Keep meaning to take those down," he said. "My late wife liked them. Helped her to remember why I was never at home."

Jenna settled into a leather armchair and accepted a glass of wine. The glass was a tall-stemmed, large-bowled type favored by sommeliers. Not for the first time, she considered how Fisk personified all that was civilized and good in the world, all that was fine and true. But once he was seated, she could see that he'd lost some of his usual equanimity.

"Until we know more," he said, "there's little we can do. Soo-min's out of harm's way, and you, I trust, are keeping a very low profile."

Jenna shook her head vaguely. "The real Jenna Williams has barely existed for years."

"With luck, Pyongyang thinks you're dead."

They sat in silence for a while, listening to the *memento mori* ticking of the clock, contemplating the future, marveling at what had become of their lives. For the time being, a veil had been drawn over whatever had happened at that hospital.

Fisk said, "OPUS's body was handed over to the Russians today. Funeral is in Moscow next week. As far as the media's concerned OPUS died of a heart attack. It barely made page eight of the *Post*." He pinched the bridge of his nose, looking tired, troubled. "It's a full-blown intelligence disaster, Jenna—for us and the Kremlin. We lost our star agent. The Russians found they had a traitor at the top of the SVR. Russian state media is feigning grief, of course. Giving OPUS a burial with full honors. They'll never admit to a humiliation this big . . ." He took a thoughtful sip of his wine. "To be honest with you, the guy was lucky."

"Lucky to be murdered by a nerve agent?"

"He died quickly. They were forced to kill him in a hurry before he could spill the beans." Fisk put down the wineglass and stared at it. "Normally, they like to take their time with traitors, get creative." His large, heavy face was lost in its jowls as some memory played behind his eyes.

Jenna had not known OPUS, did not know what he looked like. She knew nothing yet of his story, or what had motivated him to spy for America, but she knew that his decision to do so had been an act of great bravery, bright enough to light a whole lifetime.

"I'd like to have met him," she said.

Fisk smiled sadly. "He was a legend. I knew him only by his deeds, but Mira knew him quite well. She's devastated." He sighed. "Get a chance to read his files?"

"I start tomorrow. There's a lot of them."

He left the room and returned with a plate of warmed blini and some caviar in a silver dish. They raised their glasses.

"We should be toasting with vodka," he said, "but I find it ruins the palate. To OPUS."

"To OPUS."

After a pause in which they again were lost in their own thoughts, she said, "Do you think the president really betrayed him to the Russians?"

Even as she said it, it sounded astonishing to her that she, an American and a patriot, was even asking the question of the commander-in-chief.

Fisk's face clouded. He took his time before answering and spoke his next words with care.

"Let us hope it wasn't ... deliberate. But Trump does like to boast how 'in the know' he is, and he's been grossly negligent with classified intelligence before. It's almost like he doesn't realize he's speaking to representatives of a hostile power. Doesn't *see* them as an adversary ... or just doesn't care." He ran his fingers through his crinkled white hair and let out a sigh. "We live in interesting times."

"I hardly recognize the country I've come back to," she said, staring into the fireplace. "It's just so ... *angry*. And the anger's found its voice."

"Trump is a vessel for people's grievances, their fear of change. I think they've been waiting for this man for a long time. He simply gauged the mood and fueled it. That's his real talent. The man himself is just a mob orator. A Borscht Belt comedian. But as a symptom of what's out there in the backwoods? He's a forest fire no one can stop." Fisk turned to the fading light outside the window. "And he's doing everything Russia's always dreamed of doing but has never had the reach for: he undermines European unity, undermines NATO, and to hell with the rules-based international order..."

Dinner was a veal Orloff, a dish mentioned in the great Russian novels, Fisk said. Braised loin of veal, thinly sliced, with layers of cheese, fried mushrooms, and onions, and covered in a béchamel sauce, browned to golden under the grill. It was delicious. She knew nothing at all about Russian cuisine.

She said, "The Russian Seed-Bearing Program, Charles. How does it work? I don't believe Putin would stoop to kidnapping foreigners from beaches."

"We've been trying to figure it out," Fisk said between mouthfuls. "The most plausible scenario goes something like this: male Russian agent is sent to work abroad as a contractor in, let's say, Syria. He has a child with a local woman. Man returns to Russia but sends funds to support the child. When the child reaches junior school age, he or she is invited to enroll in a private school in Moscow. Child vanishes into Russia and is never seen again. That would give you a genuine foreign national who is Russian raised. Then, after years of indoctrination and God-knows-what, this child, now a young adult, spends a year or so at some international school in France or Finland or Singapore. Then applies to study here. To all appearances our fanatical Russian spook is a Syrian national who speaks several languages—no different from thousands of smart kids from all over the world applying to college in the US every year."

"The untraceable spy..." Jenna murmured.

"And if Russia can do it, it doesn't bear thinking who'll do it next."

They ate in silence for a moment, neither of them wanting to contemplate the nightmare of a Chinese Seed-Bearing Program.

"We should have seen it coming," he said, dabbing his mouth with a napkin. "The old-school Russian sleepers received years of training in Moscow to pass as Americans, and they were a joke. Creepy accents, mysterious backgrounds, stolen birth certificates, disillusionment. They never fitted in here. They didn't learn a damn thing. The *next* generation of spies was more promising. Real-name Russians living openly here as socialites, investors, policy experts . . ." He got up to pour more wine for them both. "They were good at identifying targets—the people with power and access. But after a bunch of them were busted in 2010, that game was up for the Russians. Anyone meeting a Russian nowadays would wonder if they're a spook . . .

"But a *Seed-Bearing Program*?" He returned to his seat, shaking his head again, almost in admiration. "That has the huge advantage of scale—they can train, what, fifty spies for the cost of one? Real names, real foreign passports, but Russians born and raised, and taught to hate us since they were children." Fisk twirled the stem of his glass. "That would take foresight. The Russians have always played a long game."

"My history's hazy, Charles. If the Russians have Seed-Bearing operatives here now, then this program must have been set up, what, in the nineties? Wasn't Russia a basket case back then? A collapsed economy? Social chaos? Why would it invest in such a thing when it looked like Russia was about to join the Western world?"

"Incredible, isn't it?" he muttered. "Until you remember *who* became the director of the Russian Federal Security Service in 1998. Someone with a long vision for Russia as a great power, and boundless reserves of resentment toward us . . ."

"Vladimir Putin."

A draft of night air swept down the chimney and out of the fireplace, making Jenna shudder.

"Let's have our coffee in the study," Fisk said. "It's warmer."

In the comfortable, cluttered study another large landscape hung over the mantelpiece, but this one was Russian, not American—a nineteenth-century view of distant church domes surrounded by birch forests and an evening sky of feathered, peach-colored clouds. In the foreground, a rickety wooden bridge crossed a slow, reflecting river.

"*Evening Bells*, it's called," he said. "I had it shipped over here in case I had to bug out of Moscow in a hurry."

They gazed at it for a moment. The painting had a deep, meditative effect, and she had a sense then of how Russia could obsess those drawn to it, to its vastness, its mystery, and that Fisk, like many before him, had become hooked.

"Russia isn't just another country," he said quietly, "it's another world . . . where the laws of human nature are different. Superficially Western, but at its heart wild, Asian. There's something almost self-destructive in falling for its allure . . ." His voice drifted off, his eyes on some distant steppe. "Five thousand miles of forest, tundra, and desert. As close to limitless as we can imagine . . ."

They drank coffee and reminisced until they heard the clock in the living room strike ten.

"I'm on an early flight to Moscow in the morning," Fisk said. Jenna got up and thanked him for dinner.

In the hall, as he was fetching her coat, he asked where she was staying in DC. When she mentioned the temporary housing near Langley, he said, "Stay here. As a guest in my house. The place will be empty for months. It's yours."

"Are you sure? That's very kind of—"

A phone began ringing upstairs in the study. Not a normal ringing, but a low cicada-like sound that made them both turn their heads in its direction.

"Your secure line," she said. "You'd better take it."

She kissed him quickly on the cheek and left.

A few minutes later, as she was driving back toward Langley, Fisk called her. She put it on speaker.

"Hey. Did I leave something behind?" she said.

"That was Headquarters on the line. Some very bad news, I'm afraid. PANDA's son was abducted by the North Koreans while he was in transit to the French embassy in Kuala Lumpur."

"*What?*"

Neither of them could speak for a moment. Then Fisk said bitterly, "He did it. He finally fucking did it. Kim Jong-un just eliminated the last remaining rightful heir."

29

The Monocle Restaurant
Washington, DC
Monday afternoon

Eric was early for his table at Monocle, an old politico's hangout on D Street near the House. He usually made it a rule not to drink at lunchtime, but he ordered a vodka tonic to gulp down quickly before his guest arrived. He was feeling oddly dissociated and flat, as if he were suffering a comedown after cocaine, except that what he'd experienced yesterday had been a high no drug in the world could have given him.

It had been too easy, really, a gift on a plate.

The nurse, Adam, waiting for him in the parking lot of Katie's Coffee House just off the Georgetown Pike, as arranged. Eric inviting him to hop into his car. ("It's such a nice morning, isn't it? Thought it would never stop raining. We've got time for a stroll along the river, if your shift isn't until eleven . . .") The dripping trees, the birdsong, the smell of earth. The crude steps of gravel and plank leading down to the river, which was swollen and rapid after the rain. Adam prattling. Eric encouraging the prattle ("No, it suits you. You're never too old for highlights."). A good-natured jostle over who should go down the steps first. (Eric: "Be my guest. Careful, it might be slippery.")

No one about. Just the fish and the birds. And then—

A violent neck crank applied from behind. Fast and with great force, right to left.

The guy flopped heavily down the steps like a sack of laundry. Neck broken. No blood. Didn't utter a squeak.

An awful, tragic accident. And no one to admire his work.

But, oh, the power. The raging, burning light.

For a few moments the void inside Eric had lit up with the brightness of a double supernova. He'd felt ecstasy, he'd touched the face of God. The adrenaline rush was so pure, so intense, that he'd almost forgotten to retrieve the phone, warm from the body, which he then rolled over the bank and into the torrents with scarcely a splash.

Be our guest, be our guest . . .

He'd driven home humming a Disney tune. He'd showered and felt himself baptized. He'd gotten dressed in a state of grace. For the rest of the day he was aglow with power, illuminated from within like some demonic apostle.

Then this morning he'd awoken with an even deeper sense of emptiness than before.

"Mr. Rahn—your guest."

"Mm? Oh."

Eric stood up, buttoned his jacket, and extended his hand. His lunch guest was Song Sok-ho, a senior defense attaché from the South Korean embassy in DC, a man considerably older than Eric. He was thin and dapper with a genial, approachable face that belied a steely reputation for realpolitik.

"This is nice," Song said, glancing about, and waving to someone at the corner table, a congressman with a napkin tucked into his shirt. "Have you ordered?"

"I can recommend the entrecôte with herb French fries," Eric said, turning on his *GQ* smile. "The squid ceviche is also very good."

Song glanced at his watch. "I don't have long, I'm afraid." With barely a glance at the menu, he ordered a simple risotto.

All this cuisine and he orders a fucking plate of rice . . .

Then Song placed his hands on the table, looking at Eric with an expectant smile. The clock was ticking.

Eric hadn't planned to broach his dynamite subject until the end of what he'd hoped would be a relaxed lunch, but now, under time pressure from Song, he was mentally scrambling to condense his remarks. The lunch was a softening-up exercise, even though the outcome was not in doubt. The South Koreans would have no choice in the matter.

The waiter offered Song a complimentary aperitif (Eric's idea). Song waved it away.

They'd exhausted the pleasantries already, leaving Eric feeling he was coming to his subject cold. So he broached it—gently, in a sideways approach, but as he began to speak, he wondered if these points he'd spent so long crafting and redrafting, about world peace and the harmony of nations, were sounding faintly moronic. No matter.

Song frowned, listening carefully, and a wiliness came into his eyes.

The food arrived.

Song ignored the plate and continued to watch Eric. With some tact, he said, "If I am correctly understanding the direction of your remarks . . . perhaps we should speak in Korean?" He raised his eyebrows slightly to signal that anyone might be listening.

This was a turn in the conversation Eric had wanted to avoid at all costs. He had worked hard to eradicate all trace of his accent, the accent of the North, but he did not feel a hundred percent confident he could imitate a South Korean accent. The tiniest wrong tone or inflection might betray him. But before he could demur, Song had already switched to Korean.

"The security situation on the Korean peninsula is not optimal at present for a more, ah, direct intervention by the president of the United States, if that is indeed what you are proposing . . ."

Eric's armpits became heated and moist. He tried to conceal his discomfiture by taking a sip of water. Then he collected himself and smiled. Taking care to use the most polite and honorific Korean registers due a man so much his senior, he said, "The North's continued testing of long-range ballistic missiles is, of course, a cause of deep concern to this administration. However, the situation has reached an impasse. Respectfully, the belief here is that a breakthrough might only be possible by means of a personal meeting between . . ."

Eric faltered. Song was staring at him with a kind of whimsical puzzlement.

"That's very interesting," Song said.

"I'm . . . encouraged that you think so."

"No, I mean your accent."

Eric felt the blood rushing to his face.

"My accent?"

"Yes! I can't place it at all. May I ask where in Korea you grew up?"

Eric wanted to kick this man off his chair with such force he'd be sent crashing into diners behind him, legs in the air, plates breaking, soup flying.

Lowering his voice he said, "I . . . am . . . er . . . from Gangwon Province, a small fishing village you won't have heard of . . ."

"Are you? My father and grandfather were from the coast in Gangwon. They had that lovely sing-song way of speaking in those parts. No, yours has an echo of something stronger, from somewhere nearer the border perhaps . . ."

Eric regarded him as he would a fish in a tank, one he was selecting to gut with a small filleting knife and fry for his dinner. What would the Boss do in this situation? It was obvious, really.

"I wanted to say to you that President Trump wishes to meet

face to face with Kim Jong-un." Eric had addressed Song in Korean without any honorific form, but rather the register used for children, or for people at the lowest end of the social scale. His tone was so deliberately offensive that he could see Song's ears turn red. "If you stand in his way, he'll withdraw the 28,500 US ground forces protecting South Korea from North Korean attack. Then Korea will reunify. Just not in a way you'll like."

Song was stunned for a few seconds, then his face acquired the kind of expression one might have when painfully passing a kidney stone. Without another word to Eric, he got up, asked for his coat, and scuttled out of the restaurant.

Outside, Eric could see him making an immediate phone call.

Eric whispered after him in North Korean dialect. *"Yeah, push that up your ass."*

Then he went straight to the washroom, locked himself into a stall, and sat on the seat. He needed to file an urgent contact report on his meeting with Song. Pyongyang had to know at once that the South Koreans were now in the loop and that they had just been informed that they were in no position to object.

But once he was through the passwords to the encrypted portal, he found a message waiting for him. He opened it, and a collapsing feeling of doom came over him.

URGENT. Report to Center in person.

Advise soonest date of travel.

His head dropped back against the tiles. His whole life was unraveling.

He was being ordered back to Pyongyang?

30

**CIA Original Headquarters Building
Langley, Virginia
Monday morning**

In the curious senior common room with the enormous map of Russia, the mood around the table was collegiate and urgent, with none of the intimidating hierarchy of the day before. Jenna faced the same three seniors—Mira: wise, sweet, and heroically tired, looking like a harassed grandmother in her blouse and cardigan, and the two men, who, this time, were introduced. The heavy, jowly man who'd worn a polka-dotted tie was Warren Allen, the deputy director of Counterintelligence Division Russia. He looked as if the inside of his skin had been afflicted by an itchy rash that he was trying his hardest not to scratch. The spry man with the goatee, who resembled a kind of elderly Lenin, was Bill Cheney, chief of Central Eurasia/Russian Ops Desk.

Mira's coffee, which she took Russian-style—tar black, heavy on the sugar, and served in a short glass—gave off a charred aroma.

"After our meeting yesterday, Jenna, we requested authorization from the president to hunt for hostile foreign operatives inside the United States . . ."

"We can do that?" Jenna said, surprised.

"Section 503 of the National Security Act 1947 and Section 6 of the CIA Act 1949," Bill Cheney said, wiping his glasses with his tie. "They're seldom invoked, but if you ask me—"

"We kept the request vague and non-specific," Mira said, gently putting a hand on Cheney's arm, "to avoid triggering the president's sensitivities about Russia, which is a touchy subject with him, and to avoid furnishing him with any further specifics about the Seed-Bearing Program that he might be tempted to reveal to the Russians"

"All right," Jenna said slowly.

"Let's start with what we know," Warren Allen said. "None of these operatives were born in the US. All of them will be younger than thirty. That narrows things down less than you might think. In the federal government alone we've got tens of thousands of junior employees, and many departments have a policy of testing them with real responsibility, including the handling of classified intelligence."

"Our first priority is the staff around the president," Mira said. "There are currently . . ." She glanced down at the file in front of her. "Three hundred and ninety-six people working daily in the White House. As to their files, we made an interagency request to the White House Office of Security, the Office of Personnel Management, and the Presidential Personnel Office. This needs delicate handling. I suggest you start combing through the security-clearance background checks for all White House aides starting with their SSB1 forms and polygraphs."

Warren Allen shifted his considerable heft in his seat and succumbed to a vigorous scratch of his neck. "The vetting in this administration is in chaos, frankly. The president's burning through staff faster than I shit jalapenos, and the vetting can't keep up. Even worse, the PPO is packed with the relatives and cronies of the very people they're supposed to be vetting. In the meantime, any ticking time-bomb could walk into the Oval Office without an escort and—"

"All right, Warren." Mira's cool eyes fixed on Jenna. "We've no time to waste. The first batch of files on each individual vetted so far is now in a secure vault in the basement. Get yourself down there. See if you can find any anomalies in their backgrounds that could be cover for time spent in Russia or North Korea." She took a sip of the cold coffee and winced. "After that, familiarize yourself with the OPUS agent files."

Jenna took this as a dismissal. Just before she reached the door, she turned. "Just curious. How did OPUS usually deliver his intel?"

"From memory. OPUS had a formidable recall."

"And what if his list of Russian Seed-Bearing Program operatives was more than a few dozen names? What if it was hundreds?"

Warren Allen scratched again, at his wrists this time. "It's possible he was going to give us the intel electronically. We equipped him with gear to download material from restricted SVR servers in the Russian mission, if he absolutely had to . . ."

"What kind of gear?"

"Memory card concealed inside a cufflink," Bill Cheney said. His bony fingers fluttered. "I know what you're thinking, but they beat us to it. The assassins removed everything from the Hay-Adams before we got there. Laptop, cufflinks, glasses, phone, toiletries, everything. The only thing they left us were his suits and his goddamn socks."

Jenna thought about this. "Is there a chance they won't realize they're in possession of the gear?"

"These are Russians, Jenna, not Italians," Mira said, gathering up her file. "They'll take everything apart."

Nothing in the secure basement reading room could be copied or removed. Any notes Jenna made had to remain in the room. No personal electronic devices were allowed; no liquids were allowed. She had to stand in the corridor to drink the sour, superheated black coffee from the vending machine. Three archivists wearing gloves carried in the boxes of files and turned on a special monitor for her to view the material stored on a restricted server. Soundproofed walls deadened the room so completely that she could hear her eyes blinking.

She dealt first with the security-clearance vetting files from the WHSO and the PPO. So far, none of the vetted individuals working inside the White House was born outside of the US, with the exception of the First Lady, who was born in Novo Mesto in the communist former Yugoslavia in 1970. But, at forty-seven years old, the First Lady could be safely discounted from the search.

While Jenna waited for the next boxes to arrive, she turned to the eight volumes of agent books for OPUS, which she spread out before her on the table. No sooner had she started reading them than she experienced a violent time warp. Almost the next thing she knew it was six thirty in the evening and the archivists were returning to remove the boxes. Her stomach was rumbling. She'd forgotten to eat lunch.

She had come to the files knowing only the bare bones: OPUS was an SVR officer with UN diplomatic cover operating out of the Russian consulate in New York. He had been an FBI super-agent for more than three years, supplying the team in Federal Plaza with a steady stream of secrets until he was murdered at the Hay-Adams by assassins unknown, probably his fellow Russians.

In the first file, she found a passport photo of him, and his real name: Dmitry Stepanovich Kuznetsov. Born in Moscow in 1959.

She studied the photo for several minutes. She wasn't sure what she'd been expecting—some nondescript spook, perhaps. Someone so faceless he'd vanish when stood in front of wallpaper. But the good looks were a surprise. The man gazing back was masculine and distinguished. Deep, soulful eyes that were a shade of Arctic blue. A strong jaw. Fine, steel-gray hair, side-parted. Like a cosmonaut commemorated on a stamp, she thought.

The next photo, taken the day after he'd arrived in New York City in 2013, was an FBI surveillance shot. Most of the early files, in fact, were FBI reports. (The Bureau, not the CIA, was responsible for watching the activities of Russian spooks on American soil.) He'd been snapped while stopping to look at a display of menswear in the window of a department store on Fifth Avenue. His face, partly obscured by sunglasses and the upturned collar of his raincoat, was reflected in the glass. How much had changed since the Cold War, and how little . . . He was using the window's reflection to scan the street for telltale signs of watchers.

She turned the page and began reading the flimsy blue surveillance sheets—where he'd had lunch, the time he'd left work, the names of people he'd met during his day.

An FBI special agent named Daniel S. Hirsch had quickly noticed that although OPUS was accredited as second secretary at the Russian mission to the United Nations, he spent very little time at the mission on 67th Street. He preferred to work in the leafier surroundings of the Russian Consulate on East 91st Street, close to Central Park, and used his lunchtimes and evenings to network. He seemed to have no regular duties; he came and went as he pleased, but he had frequent private meetings with the *rezident*, the Russian UN ambassador. Hirsch suspected that OPUS's accredited role was cover for something much more interesting, and he was right.

OPUS was an *operupolnomochenny*, an operations officer with the rank of lieutenant colonel in the SVR, Russia's foreign intelligence agency.

The FBI in Federal Plaza assigned a twelve-man team to watch him closely at work and at leisure. Queries in different hands were scribbled in the margins of reports, pertaining to his habits, health, possible vices, clues to his state of mind.

By this point, Jenna was intrigued. How had the Feebs managed to turn him?

The developmental reports described OPUS living quite openly in Manhattan, seldom spending his evenings at the Russians' dingy residential compound on West 255th Street in Riverdale in the Bronx, where the diplomats and their families maintained the old Soviet habit of keeping an eye on each other. FBI watchers reported his solo dining at *Times*-approved restaurants, drinks at East Village bars that offered live jazz, weekend jaunts to upstate classical music festivals. He was a familiar face on the diplomatic circuit, though he always kept to the periphery of drinks receptions, an observer rather than a performer, never seeking the spotlight. Guests who met him were impressed by this mild-mannered Russian who spoke English exceedingly well, with just a trace of an accent. He dressed carefully, always wore tailored shirts with double cuffs; he was courteous and agreeable; he drank little. The files reported numerous conversations he'd had—about the latest Franzen or last season's *Lohengrin* at the Met. None of the usual Russian gripes that surfaced after a few drinks: the hypocrisy of the West, the treachery of NATO.

The FBI could see that OPUS was enjoying life in New York, but that was no reason to assume that he'd be willing to betray secrets to the United States. Rather, it was this otherness about him, a distinct sense that he didn't belong to his own tribe, that prompted the FBI to court him, slowly at first, probing for the elusive *hook*—that intriguing, hidden aspect in all of us that just might, if exploited cleverly, reel us in, tip us into doing the unthinkable.

But for all their efforts, the FBI detected nothing they could work with in OPUS. He was a geographical bachelor, yet he behaved himself with women and alcohol; he was solitary but not lonely, betrayed no outward signs of narcissism, disappointment, or resentment, nor any taste for a lifestyle beyond his pay grade. He presented no opening for blackmail, persuasion, or pressure, let alone that most potent of inducements, flattery.

Twice the FBI went right ahead and pitched him, just to see if he'd turn—one time over coffee in a quiet SoHo diner; once while he was jogging a Sunday-morning circuit of Central Park. OPUS declined both approaches with a firm negative, while making it clear that he took no offense at all. But that, too, was interesting. To be the target of an unwanted pitch was a grave dishonor for any Russian spook. They would have to report it to Moscow and would forever after trail the suspicious whiff of compromised goods. OPUS had not taken the pass, but he'd also given a signal, a kind of emotional brush contact.

I am not an enemy.

The FBI in New York asked the CIA in Langley for intel on this man, whatever they could dig up.

What the CIA gleaned from its own moles inside Russian intelligence revealed a career as remarkable as anyone could have in Russia. OPUS was the son of a legendary World War II tank commander decorated after the Battle of Kursk. Son followed father into the army's General Staff Academy. In the mid-eighties he saw action with a Spetsnaz unit fighting in Afghanistan and was awarded the Red Star for bravery. After that he'd enrolled in the elite Red Banner Institute in Moscow and began a career in the diplomatic corps (in reality, almost certainly the First Directorate of the KGB), he rose up the ranks in a series of swift promotions. OPUS proved skilled or ruthless enough to survive the purges that followed the collapse of the Soviet Union, eventually attaining a senior rank in the SVR. He was undoubtedly a very good spy, because he was sent on plum postings to London, Brussels, and Berlin, before being awarded the prize job in New York, reserved for only the most loyal. It was clear that OPUS enjoyed the trust and confidence of those in the very highest circles of the Putin regime and had worked hard to earn it. To cap it all, he was a personal friend of Vadim Ivanovich Giorgadze.

Even Jenna, who'd never had any past dealings with Russia Division, had heard that name. Giorgadze was notorious. He was Putin's most ruthless spy-catcher.

A photo dated 2010 showed the two of them, OPUS and

Giorgadze, in their shirtsleeves enjoying a beer at a barbecue thrown by Vladimir Putin at Novo Ogaryevo, the president's palatial dacha outside Moscow.

She moved the photograph closer to the reading lamp. OPUS appeared tanned and affable, but Giorgadze's face was one she hoped never to meet in an interrogation cell. Violence seemed to crackle about him like static. He was brutish, and strongly built. Large, strangler's hands. Bald head. Long pointed nose that protruded over a heavy mustache. Distinctly arched eyebrows, like Stalin's. He reminded her of some malevolent creature from a folk tale. And he was OPUS's old comrade from the Afghan War, a personal friend . . .

The FBI ended the courtship. Surveillance on OPUS was downgraded to routine only.

But then, in February 2014, the month Putin was hosting the Winter Olympic Games in Sochi, the FBI field office on Federal Plaza received a hand-delivered envelope containing a short note and a flash drive. It was addressed to *Daniel S. Hirsch, Special Agent in Charge, Counterintelligence, Federal Bureau of Investigations, twenty-sixth floor.* The note was in the file:

Dear Mr. Hirsch:
My position is branch chief of the SVR in New York. I believe you know who I am. I wish to volunteer my services to the United States. In token of my sincerity and good faith I enclose material that I presume is of interest. I await your response.
    Sincerely yours

The most senior SVR officer in North America! Jenna could just imagine the excitement on the twenty-sixth floor of Federal Plaza. They must have been cracking open the beers. OPUS occupied a position of stupendous access. He was responsible for all offensive Russian intelligence operations on American soil.

Headquarters in Washington was informed; the national security advisor was briefed. Inevitably, doubts were raised in dozens of memos from DC. What was his motivation? This was all very sudden. Was it a provocation? A Russian dirty trick?

But the intelligence on the flash drive checked out. FBI heads must have been shaken in wonder. Before their eyes was a long list of American citizens and organizations that had been co-opted by Russia. Most were what Lenin would have called *useful idiots*—congressmen with Russian business links, professors given lucrative airtime on RT, K Street lobbyists who didn't dig too deeply into their clients' post-Soviet careers. Others were unwitting dupes—shock jocks, 9/11 conspiracy theorists, a staggering range of anti-globalist, pro-life, environmentalist, neo-Nazi, Christian, and gender and race protest groups, some of them violently opposed to each other, all of them secretly funded by the Kremlin to create omnidirectional outrage. But of most interest of all to the FBI, the list revealed a small handful of outright traitors: low-level American intelligence and diplomatic personnel betraying secrets for cash.

Jenna stopped reading as she took this in.

Hauls of that value were rare in intelligence work. Very rare. An ops officer could spend decades figuring out dull scraps of data and never see a windfall like this. Mira Kowalski was right. This was no chicken feed. It was sensational. What on earth made him do it?

People usually betray their country for one of five reasons: money, ideology, compromise, ego, revenge.

The reason given in the FBI report was credible if uninformative.
SUBJECT CITES FAMILY REASONS FOR BEING DEEPLY DISILLUSIONED WITH PUTIN REGIME, WHICH HE BELIEVES IS CRIMINAL.

What family reasons?

Already it seemed to her that this man was everything the regime he served was not—honorable, cultured, decent, honest, fair. Jenna fetched another scalding coffee from the vending machine and started pacing the corridor to stretch her legs, listening to the hum of the ventilation system.

What had happened to him in 2014? What had the regime done to offend him?

The first face-to-face between OPUS and Special Agent Daniel Hirsch had taken place in Green-Wood Cemetery in Brooklyn at night. After that, they met roughly once a month in different locations—Central Park Zoo, Christopher Street Pier, Macy's department store. Every time, OPUS arrived black, even with Hirsch's guys trying to tail him. He was a pro, Hirsch noted, with real street skills. OPUS agreed, reluctantly, to accept payment for the risks he was taking. She knew this mattered to the FBI—money created an obligation between agent and handler, and greed was easy to understand. An escrow account was opened. OPUS signed a secrecy agreement and passed an FBI polygraph. As far as the FBI was concerned, he was now "boxed." No more questions were asked about motive.

At each meeting, OPUS would brief Hirsch on whatever was happening that month—American targets being courted by Russian sleeper agents; Russian plans to manipulate the UN Human Rights Council; news stories on *Morning Joe* that had been cooked up in a troll factory in Saint Petersburg; which oligarch was in favor in the Kremlin and who was under a cloud; the shrinking number of confidants surrounding Putin, and Putin's growing paranoia and sense of himself as a student and maker of history—"significantly delusional" was how OPUS described him. Each meeting generated multiple highly graded intelligence reports.

Jenna was astounded by the volume of material this man could relay from memory, pages of it.

Within weeks, the FBI was ready to take the relationship to the next level. Because the meetings had to be short—ten minutes was pushing it—Dan Hirsch arranged a safe house in a small newbuild apartment on the Upper East Side, not far from the UN Headquarters, where OPUS's debriefs could be less hurried, and in an atmosphere more convivial for Hirsch to get to know his remarkable new agent.

Mira Kowalski attended the first safe-house meeting, and she was a regular monthly presence thereafter. She was someone OPUS would have gotten to know well and would have trusted enough to meet in DC when he had intel that was too hot to wait for the monthly rendezvous.

Over the summer of 2016, things got very interesting.

Jenna was two-thirds the way through the files when she saw the name Donald J. Trump.

DHS: *OK. Recording now.* [Muffled noises. Paper shuffling.] *This is the sixteenth joint counterintelligence debrief with Dmitry Stepanovich Kuznetsov. We are presently in Safehouse 17. It is the twenty-ninth of August at 1:30 p.m. I refer to draft cable 27013 for Mr. Kuznetsov's previous statement regarding Kremlin interference in the current US election campaign. Interviewing officers present: Daniel S. Hirsch, FBI Counterintelligence, and Mira Kowalski, CIC Russia Division.* [Sound of repeated sneezing]. *You OK?*

MK: *Sorry, it's these damn horse chestnuts. I'm going to close the window.*

OPUS: [Voice inaudible]

DHS: *A little closer, please, Dmitry.*

OPUS: [Sound of furniture moving] *I said, Kremlin talking points from RT and Radio Sputnik are turning up word for word in Trump's stump speeches. You're dealing with a massive Russian influence offensive, Dan. The US is a wide-open door for this mischief. It's personal, too. Putin loathes Secretary Clinton. She seems to personify every grudge and grievance he*

> holds against America . . . A certain kind of man will always find ways to blame a woman.

DSH: [Laughter] *Donald Trump is not going to win the election.*

OPUS: *You're sure about that?* [Unknown sounds. Seven seconds of silence.]

Two days after the election:

DSH: [Long intake of breath.] *The FBI just learned that Russia has interfered in the voting process itself, digitally attacking the voter rolls in twenty-one states.*

OPUS: [Sound of furniture shifting. Long silence.] *I think you may have a problem with the president elect.*

By November 2016, OPUS had become the US's hottest Russian asset. The intel he was delivering to Hirsch was now on such a scale that it was beyond even his abilities to memorize. In one hair-raising incident, OPUS had inserted a thumb drive into a restricted *rezidentura* server, downloaded highly classified SVR files, and had walked casually through a security scanner to the exit with the thumb drive in his pocket. He'd obtained hundreds of decrypted SVR flash cables between New York and Moscow.

Hirsch described his next meeting with OPUS as "emotional" and "frank." He'd warned OPUS never to take a risk like that again.

After some argument between Langley and Federal Plaza, documented in dozens of memos, the CIA's Directorate of Science and Technology issued OPUS with spy gear: a pair of gold cufflinks that concealed a memory card. One of the cufflinks could be inserted into a rigged thumb drive of exactly the type used inside the Russian mission, and which OPUS could carry on his person. The genius of it was that if he was caught with the thumb drive, there would be nothing incriminating on it: everything was stored on the cufflink's memory card, which he wore on his shirt. Normally, spy gear trebled the risk for an agent, but Mira had insisted: OPUS was a trained professional. He could handle it.

Magnified photos of the cufflinks showed two flat disks of gold about 2mm thick and emblazoned with the tsarist double-headed eagle. The swivel bar was made of solid gold. A patina effect gave them a distressed, antiquated look. The user manual explained that they were a replica of a pre-1917 set treasured by Russian émigrés.

Jenna was amazed by them. She'd seen subminiature cameras concealed inside the frames of glasses and a mic hidden in the pendant of a necklace. But nothing like this.

In the final file she followed the chain of events that ended in OPUS's death.

Only three weeks ago, OPUS had been summoned to the SVR headquarters at Yasenevo outside Moscow for "consultations." He knew that his secret could destroy his life if discovered. A double life meant walking a tightrope, one that could end in a heartbeat if he made a slip. Any day could be his last. She could well imagine his relief when he walked into a full conference room, rather than into an empty room with thugs waiting behind the doors.

In that room, OPUS received the news that changed everything. In Hirsch's report:

OPUS has this morning returned to NYC from Yasenevo. OPUS reports that he is being promoted to head of Directorate S (illegals program worldwide). He is to return to Russia on a permanent basis from next month and has been ordered to wrap up his affairs in NYC.

Given the high significance of this promotion, DSH recommends urgent formulation of:

> 1. Plan to run agent-in-place in Moscow.
> 2. Provisional exfiltration plan.

A flurry of cables flew back and forth between Langley and Federal Plaza. This was the holy grail of Western intelligence. OPUS's promotion meant that he would be supplying secrets from *inside the regime*.

> In attendance at the Yasenevo meeting:
>
> 1. Sergey Naryshkin, a long-time crony of Putin's from St. Petersburg, now director of the SVR.
> 2. Vadim Giorgadze, SVR director of operations, who has known OPUS well since the Soviet Afghan campaign in the 1980s.
>
> Immediately after the meeting, OPUS was invited to sit for an SVR polygraph test.

So, they pulled a surprise poly on him . . . Strapped him in and attached sensors to his heart before he had a chance to think of an excuse to get out of it.

And yet, she already had enough of an impression of this man to know that if anyone could have survived it, he could. She pictured him, giving yes/no answers to the interrogator as the machine seismographed his pulse and blood pressure: urbane, calm, but his mind churning with terror. The sheer psychological stress he must have felt—not to betray any inward sign of guilt in front of two ruthless professionals with a nose for traitors. Controlling his heartbeat, his sweat glands, the tension in his muscles.

That must have taken real nerve. There were techniques for fooling poly tests, though she knew no one who had mastered them successfully. It involved controlled breathing and an ability to access a deep, inner stillness that no question could ripple or disturb.

> At a follow-up meeting in Yasenevo two days later, again with Naryshkin and Giorgadze, OPUS's promotion was confirmed.
>
> OPUS reports that he was then initiated into a compartmentalized covert operation known as the SEED-BEARING PROGRAM.
>
> OPUS understands that this is a highly classified aspect of the illegals program. It is based in a complex registered as an engineering college located in Krasnogorsk, twelve miles outside Moscow. OPUS expressed surprise that Center had been running a parallel illegals program without his knowledge.
>
> Before he departed Moscow, OPUS's appointment was made official in a closed ceremony in the Andreyevsky Hall of the Grand Kremlin Palace, where he was awarded an additional star and promoted to colonel.

OPUS had a video of the ceremony taken on someone's phone, which he'd given to Hirsch. Jenna accessed the secure server to view it.

In the golden splendor of the hall, Vladimir Putin himself presented the oblong felt box to OPUS and kissed his cheeks three times. The president, a diminutive man, had to rise up on his toes for each kiss. Whatever was going through OPUS's mind at that moment, it was masked by a stiff, rictal smile and a fixed stare. Behind Putin was a banner emblazoned with the globe and eagle emblem of the SVR. The president then gave a short address.

"I wish to pay tribute to the legendary unit of Directorate S and its roll call of heroes . . ."

Putin was reading out names from the illegals' hall of fame.

"It is no accident that the motto of the illegals is 'without the right to glory but for the glory of the nation . . .'"

In a room full of spies and uniforms he comes alive, she thought. The frosty gray eyes light up.

"*Other states have spies, but Russia has illegals. I can tell you from the heart that they are needed now more than ever . . .*"

Applause broke across his words.

"*I wish to thank you all for preserving their traditions . . .*"

The audience rose to their feet.

"*I wish you good health, good luck, and new victories for the greater glory of Russia!*"

More applause. A male-voice cry of "*Urrah!*"

What a strange, strange creature Putin is, she thought. His twenty-year metamorphosis was remarkable—from a spook so undistinguished you'd never remember you had stood next to him in an elevator, to this, the highest incarnation of the Russian state, a perfect amalgam of absolute tsar, Stalinist general secretary, and modern sound-bite politician, beaming with Botox and power.

> *OPUS reports that the SEED-BEARING PROGRAM comprises a new breed of illegals numbering in the hundreds; within a decade, many thousands. They possess valid, clean passports from a multitude of different countries; they are of many different ethnicities and speak the language of their passports fluently. Significantly, they are all of them raised in Russia. Background checks, biometric data, profiling will have nothing on them. They use their real names, and they are exactly who they say they are. All of them come first as university students on study visas, find work after graduation, then aim to embark upon prestigious careers—specifically in government, tech, finance—that will put them into positions of influence. They will look, speak, dress, and behave like young adults from anywhere in the Western world and will be no different from the thousands of young foreigners who come to the US every year to study. OPUS understands that the first wave arrived here some years ago and will*

have graduated by now. OPUS stresses that these are not spies in the conventional sense, but saboteurs. Their mission is to wreak havoc.

OPUS: *You'll never find them. No one will check to see if a Pedro Mendez Castillo from Colombia might have grown up in a suburb outside of Moscow . . . They're attempting nothing less than a civilizational game-changer, Dan. A final victory.*

DSH: *Can you ID them?*

OPUS: *[Unknown sounds. Sighing] I am now the de facto controller of all illegals including the Seed-Bearing operatives in the United States. If I can access the restricted SVR servers from the Russian mission here, yes. I can ID them.*

DSH: *How soon?*

OPUS: *Maybe tomorrow.*

DSH: *[Unknown sounds. Hesitation]*

OPUS: *Yes, I know, I haven't forgotten. Do not let Putin ruin your honeymoon, Dan, my dear friend. I wish you every happiness. If I can obtain the intel, I'll signal Mira.*

After this meeting with Hirsch—their last—bad timing and ill fortune had done a real number on OPUS.

The following day, the Seed-Bearing Program was mentioned for the first time in the president's daily brief. A few hours later, President Trump met with Foreign Minister Lavrov and Ambassador Kislyak in the Oval Office.

OPUS must have accessed the restricted SVR servers at the *rezidentura* in New York. Since the list of Seed-Bearing operatives numbered in the hundreds, he must have downloaded it to the cufflink-memory-card. *He was literally wearing the list on his sleeve.* In Hirsch's absence, he sent an emergency signal to Langley to arrange a meeting with Mira Kowalski, booked a room at the Hay-Adams, and flew to DC using his meeting with Lavrov and Kislyak as cover.

The final pages of the file were hard to view.

Police photographs of the crime scene at the Hay-Adams. OPUS, fully clothed, dead on his back on the floor, blue eyes bulging in surprise. His room-service breakfast and coffee cold and untouched.

A list from the DC metropolitan police itemized all personal possessions recovered from the room: three shirts; two suits, two pairs of brogues, wash bag, phone charger, glasses, laptop charger, carry-on luggage, underwear, socks.

But no laptop, no phone, no watch . . . no cufflinks. His assassins had taken them.

She turned again to the magnified photos of the cufflinks.

They'll take everything apart, Mira had said.

But this spy gear had no detachable parts. The memory card was embedded in a disk of solid gold . . .

Reading the OPUS files took up all of Jenna's time for the rest of the week. On Friday evening, when the secure reading room closed and Jenna was crossing the endless color-coded parking lots toward her car, a thought came to her. Not as a sudden revelation but on tiptoe, like a latecomer to a movie, edging her way down the rows in the dark.

OPUS's funeral was in Moscow tomorrow.

Suddenly she wanted to know the precise nature of the "family reasons" that had driven OPUS to turn.

31

The White House
Washington, DC
Thursday afternoon

On Thursday Eric was late for the daily afternoon meeting in the West Wing.

About twenty people were listening to the chief strategist, who had just squiggled the word *SHITZONE* on the whiteboard. He stopped talking when he saw Eric. "You OK, buddy? You're kinda pale." Twenty faces turned toward him.

Eric smiled soulfully at everyone in the room, even the chief strategist, whom he normally couldn't bear to look at. The man's face was such a grotesque, join-the-dots arrangement of moles, pimples, and weeping sores that it made him want to retch.

"Guys, unfortunately my mother's been in a traffic accident in Hong Kong. She's on life support."

Gasps from around the table. "Oh, *Eric*, oh my *God* . . ."

"If it's OK with you, I need to be with her . . . in case . . ." He broke off, fighting a sudden lump in his throat. ". . . she doesn't make it."

"Of *course*," they said, stricken. "*Oh*."

He would not be available over the weekend, he said, as one of the staffers rose and awkwardly tried to hug him, but he'd be back on Tuesday. "The president comes first."

The chief strategist raised a lazy fist. "MAGA."

All week Eric had been in a trance, weak-kneed and scatterbrained as he'd contemplated the awful summons back to Pyongyang. A childish idea had come to him that if he just sat quietly in his cubbyhole office for long enough and did nothing, all his terrors would lose interest in him and leave him alone. But Center had gone ahead and had arranged a travel plan that would get him to Pyongyang in secret, without arousing suspicion, and that was no straightforward matter. By the time he returned to DC next week—assuming Center didn't arrest him or shoot him—he would have taken *eight separate flights*. He had no need to fake anxiety for an imaginary mother—he had no mother!—because he was feeling a very genuine and acute anxiety for himself.

Of all the disaster scenarios he'd imagined over his years in America, a sudden recall to Pyongyang had never been one of them.

Your mission is for life, they'd told him. *You will dwell among the Main Enemy. You'll be buried in Yankee soil. You will never come back.*

But he was indeed going back, and now he found himself so paralyzed with fright that the most familiar sounds—a telephone ringing, a knock at his office door—sent his heart lurching into his mouth and his throat squeezing so tight that he could barely breathe.

He'd tried to calm himself. Wasn't he about to pull off a piece of global-historic theater? *A meeting between the world's two most famous men!* Of *course* Pyongyang would want to question him before any commitments were made. They'd need his strategic input, his secret knowledge. He had the access codes to Donald Trump's innermost thoughts. He *shaped* those thoughts. He had scoped the depths of the man's ignorance and had plenished it with ideas. They'd want to congratulate him! He had more than fulfilled his mission already, hadn't he?

After he'd excused himself from the meeting, Eric spent the next hour notifying the departments and arranging cover. The president had left for Mar-a-Lago already, thank God, but news of the "traffic accident in Hong Kong" had already spread through the West Wing, and to Eric's intense agitation, faces kept appearing in his office door, oozing sympathy and concern, asking if he needed anything. Someone to talk to? Compassionate leave? Every one of them lingered to tell him some turgid trauma story of their own and assured him he'd get through it—as if he could give a rat's fuck.

At 6 p.m. he left for the airport, taking only a small carry-on case, and boarded an American Airlines flight to JFK, where he transferred to an overnight Cathay Pacific Boeing 777 for the sixteen-hour flight to Hong Kong.

On the long flight over Hudson Bay and the Arctic he found he couldn't stomach eating any airline food, but he drank one whiskey soda after another, his head pressed to a cabin window flecked with ice crystals, staring at the aurora and the cold, cruel stars. Nothing could quell the black dread growing inside him. His mind was running riot, like a frenzied dog scurrying from one pungent corner to another. No matter how hard he tried, he couldn't shake the feeling that he was flying to his doom.

One scenario in particular made him almost manic with fear: that he would be arrested upon arrival in Pyongyang.

Paranoid? Maybe. But in North Korea paranoia was an essential survival tool. Every North Korean understood very well that the loyalty demanded of every citizen counted for shit. The Leader's terror was random, capricious, omnipresent. No one was safe. Rank afforded no protection, neither did connections, or success. Eric thought glumly of Kim Jong-un's murdered half-brother, prostrate in an airport clinic, pot belly exposed, pants soiled, mouth full of blood. The horror of it. The indignity.

For several minutes, he'd been unconsciously scrunching his

empty plastic cup in his fist until it had become a flower of sharp ribbons. Slowly he plucked away one serrated piece of it and began sawing it across the back of his hand, calmly, without the slumbering passengers noticing, until he drew thick drops of blood. A ruby bracelet.

By the time the plane landed at Hong Kong International in the very early hours of Saturday morning he was wild-eyed and delirious from lack of sleep. He took a cab to the Central district of the city, where he'd made a reservation for two nights at the Mandarin Oriental.

At the reception desk of the vast lobby he checked in and asked if anything had been left for him. The sleepy receptionist went to look, and—yes, sir—there was a FedEx parcel.

He swatted away the hovering bellboy and carried the parcel into the elevator himself, balancing it on top of his wheeled luggage.

His room, on the twentieth floor, offered a sweeping view of Victoria Harbor; Kowloon in the distance was a tight forest of towers sparkling with light, even at this hour. He wished he could enjoy this for a few hours. Curl up and sleep. Order a drink. Order a girl. But the terror inside him was a merciless engine. He could not rest.

Inside the parcel he found an envelope containing fifteen thousand yuan in new notes; a North Korean passport (with his photo) in the name Oh Chae-won; a Workers' Party membership card with up-to-date stamps; and a North Korean ID passbook stating that he was a permanent resident of Pyongyang. Beneath the envelope was a sealed freezer bag containing two sets of clothing and shoes and a new, fully charged Chinese Xiaomi smartphone—the internet-blocking model used in North Korea.

He stashed his US passport in the room's safe box along with his US phone, wallet, and watch, and threw the clothes he was wearing into the closet.

At 6 a.m., he left the hotel as Oh Chae-won, wearing a loose-fitting black Mao suit, and carrying a single overnight bag. He took a cab back to the airport and used the North Korean passport to check in for the three-and-a-half hour Dragonair flight to Beijing Capital International. There, he had barely half an hour transfer time before he boarded an Air Koryo Tu-204 for one of the two daily flights from Beijing to the Democratic People's Republic of Korea.

The moment he was seated inside the ancient Tupolev, with its reek of latrines and aviation fuel, and its beautiful stewardesses in their red uniforms, smiling their distant, unavailable smiles, he knew he was heading back for real.

The smell was nauseating. The synthetic fabric of the Mao suit was cheap and uncomfortable. He glanced about. His fellow passengers were all men and all of them were wearing variations of the same Mao suit, some gray, some navy. In the tunic pocket he'd found a pin of the Great Leader's smiling face, worn by all adult North Koreans over their hearts, and attached it shakingly to his chest.

Eric's stress was now at the level where his leg was in constant spasm and his spine had dissolved. A stewardess offered him wheat tea. He asked for a bottle of soju, but even after downing a twenty-proof drink his mind remained a caged animal.

An hour and forty-five minutes later, the crew announced the plane's descent to Pyongyang International Airport.

International, what a joke. He wanted to laugh maniacally. *No one comes here.*

Drifts of white vapor slipped over the aircraft's wing, then it cleared the clouds, and he had a sudden steep-angle view of brown, barren earth and endless, ghostly hills stretching far into the horizon. Far below, an ox dragged a farm cart across a boulder-strewn field, making long shadows in the afternoon light. He saw a sprawling army encampment. Hundreds of parked military jeeps. Rows and rows of dark-green pitched tents. By now he was sweating pure alcohol; his undershirt was drenched and icy.

Why was he being called back by the motherland? Hadn't he

always been loyal? Hadn't he dedicated his life to his country? He was only eighteen when he'd left. Why would a mother devour him now when he was thirty?

If he had failed, he would confess. He would trust in the Leader's mercy.

He'd been too quick to claim the glory for the drone strike on Jenna Williams, he saw that. He'd been vain, conceited, and this filled him with a morbid shame.

Oh, my dear ancestors.

The plane landed bumpily on the potholed runway. He descended the steps and followed the other passengers in single file toward a new terminal building, feeling his breath turn to frost and his bowels to water. The air was searing cold and smelled of coal smoke. A deep stillness pervaded the place, made unearthly by the slanting spring light and the silence. No jets roared overhead. There was no traffic, no birdsong. He felt no nostalgia, only a black foreboding.

He passed through border control under the eyes of surly border police, and through to the sparse arrivals hall with its near-empty flights display board. WELCOME TO PYONGYANG—CAPITAL OF THE REVOLUTION! He glanced about stupidly. No one was waiting for him. Not knowing what to do, he continued in an exhausted shuffle toward the exit, wheeling his case. Suddenly, the hairs on the back of his neck prickled.

Two stony-faced men in long uniform coats had appeared from nowhere and were either side of him.

"Keep walking," one of them said. "Car's outside."

Oh, God, no. No, no, no.

Outside, he saw a gleaming black Mercedes-Benz S-Class with darkened windows. One of the men held the rear door open for him, then got into the front, and handed Eric a bottle of mineral water. The other drove. The seats smelled of new leather. The car's audio was on low, playing some tinkling Korean zither music.

Eric's mind scrambled to process the signals, the details. The men's uniforms were vaguely familiar to him. Olive Green, blue collar insignia with gold pip, gold epaulettes.

Not police. Not Ministry of State Security. Not army . . .

Supreme Guard Command.

Eric's fears, coiled tightly inside him, suddenly sprang apart and electrified him. Now he was wishing he hadn't drunk so much on the flight.

After about ten minutes the car turned off the empty highway to Pyongyang and onto a single-lane unmarked road that wound northwest through bare hills denuded of all trees.

Another hour or so and the terrain became noticeably more fertile. The fields were not given over to crops, but had been allowed to grow wild with grasses and tree saplings. A few early wildflowers had bloomed colorfully between the retreating snow drifts. They passed a half-frozen, clear-water stream and woods of oak trees that must have appeared beautiful in summer. He'd seen no people for miles. The sun, now low in the sky, bathed everything in a deep, golden light, which only heightened the dreamlike feeling of the journey.

One of the men spoke into a two-way radio. Moments later they approached a military checkpoint with a striped barrier lowered between sentry boxes. Twelve helmeted soldiers of the KPA. The barrier was raised. A mile further on they arrived at a massive security gate with guard houses of reinforced concrete and coiled barbwire fencing, this one manned by troops with silver-plated Kalashnikovs and high, polished boots. The car window was lowered. Eric's face was inspected. Documents were checked. A paper signed. A salute given. The gates opened.

And then they were driving through the most beautiful park Eric had seen in his life. Cherry blossoms lined the driveway, ready to release drifts of floating pink petals in spring, Korean red pines towered into the clear spring sky, persimmon trees were laden with flame-orange fruits, ripened by the frost. They passed a pond covered in lotus flowers, and lawns with ornamental boulders. It was like a vision of Korea from a dream, an idealized, unreal place. The car was humming along at a respectful crawl.

"What is this place?" he murmured.

The driver met his eyes in the mirror. "Ryongsong Residence."

They were approaching a large, low, modern compound of pale stone and glass. This, too, seemed unreal, like an architect's watercolor. The fading blue sky added to the effect. The place was completely hidden by the surrounding hills. Ornate flower beds lined the drive. To his left was a fountain casting a rainbowed spray. They circled the house and turned down a stone ramp to an underground tunnel walled with white marble. It was wide enough for two cars. The vehicle stopped in a subterranean reception area. In front of them were two massive rosewood doors inlaid with gold-filigreed lotus flowers.

More guards with silver Kalashnikovs. A phone call was made. The doors were opened. Eric was ushered out of the car. He felt seedy and ragged from so much travel, jet-lagged, and dissociated from reality.

The men escorted him to a glass elevator which carried them up one floor to a vast high-beamed hallway of ash and elm. Everything—sofas, table, lamps, fireplace—was huge and stately. Floor-to-ceiling windows gave views of green in every direction, the splendid grounds and trees, now shadowed and glistening in the sunset.

He was told to remove his shoes, and was shown into a rather spartan room, lit theatrically by dying light outside. The door closed and he was alone. It looked like some kind of audience chamber. Enormous armchairs with white-lace antimacassars lined the walls. A low dais stood at one end, with three gilded chairs like thrones. Next to one of the chairs was a coffee table with a heavy glass ashtray and one stubbed-out cigarette. A smell of tobacco smoke hung faintly in the air. Above the chairs were the Father–Son portraits of the Great Leader and the Dear Leader watching him from the wall. The only other object in the room, bizarrely, in the middle of the floor, was an orange basketball. Eric picked it up. It was signed in black Sharpie pen. *Dennis Rodman.*

Eric paced the room for a while until even his feelings of dread were overcome by exhaustion. Finally, he sat in an armchair near the window. No one had turned any lights on. The room was in a twilight of its own.

Ryongsong Residence.

He'd never heard of it, but it was not hard to guess whose home this was. He waited. An hour went by, then another, and the room became dark. Outside, the grounds and trees had been hidden by the night, although a faint pink-gold light lingered in the sky. His frayed nerves began to settle. He needed the bathroom. His eyes were beginning to droop, and his neck slacken, causing his head to drop repeatedly forward onto his chest. He was in a losing struggle to stay awake.

He was awoken by bright overhead lights being turned on and a sharp clapping of two hands. An officer in the uniform of the Guard Command was looking sternly at him and gave an impatient signal for him to stand. Outside, floodlights illuminated the park.

Eric stood in the center of the room and faced the dais. He had an urgent need to pee now. His bladder, which he'd been trying to ignore before he fell asleep, was screaming *full*.

The door opened. Footsteps were approaching from the hall.

Eric bowed low, a fully ninety-degree bow, so he could not see who had entered the room. The guard left and closed the door, and Eric was alone with whoever was now standing in front of him.

"Oh Chae-won." A woman's voice, high and clear. "Or Eric Rahn, as I should call you now. I believe the last time we met we were both ten years old."

Eric unbent himself to an upright position and found himself facing a very slight, very gaunt woman whose complexion was the color of white emulsion. Her face was almost skeletal, making her eyes large and dark, but there was a faint sweetness about her lips. Her black hair, long and lank, was pushed back behind her ears, which protruded somewhat, and she wore the somber garb of a functionary: black skirt suit, white blouse, flat black shoes. Had it not been for the pin of the Great Leader's smiling face on her lapel she could have been an office worker from anywhere in the world. If he had met this woman as a child, he did not recognize her now.

Her face hardened. "I am Kim Yo-jong. Sister of Kim Jong-un."

She extended a small cool hand.

Eric clasped it in both his hands and fell to his knees. "Most Respected Comrade." Overcome, and unable to stop himself he began to weep. "I am not worthy to enter your house."

32

CIA Headquarters
Langley, Virginia
Saturday morning

"Of course, I asked OPUS the same question. Why turn? Why now?"

In the small office allocated to her by Russia Division, in an elephants' graveyard area of the Original Headquarters Building, Jenna faced Special Agent Daniel S. Hirsch on an early morning secure video teleconference call.

A cool intellect regarded her from behind wire-frame glasses. Hirsch was clean-shaven but with an incipient beard so dark it made his skin almost blue.

"Must have been a hell of a surprise," she ventured. "When he turned."

Hirsch shrugged. "The Russkies are complicated souls. Why do any of them betray their country? In the Cold War it was ideology. In the gold rush of the nineties, it was money, but there were always deeper reasons: grudges, ego, family. And it was never the ones you expected to turn who did. Not the embittered officers who drank, but often the high-flyers like OPUS . . ."

"What was his answer?" Jenna said, "Why did he turn?"

"He said, 'personal family reasons,' and I left it at that."

"He must have wanted something in return."

"That was my next question. Was he out to feather his nest? A retirement condo in Palm Beach? Expensive chemo for a sick kid? His answer: 'To rid Russia of Vladimir Vladimirovich Putin.' His words."

That, at least, is credible.

"Want me to be honest with you, Jenna?"

No, Dan, I'd like you to bullshit me.

"I knew right off the bat that this guy was genuine. When he sent that note to us, he crossed into a zone of no return, without any hope of mercy if he was caught. It's a big step for a spook, and I wasn't going to diminish it by questioning his integrity, or his courage."

True, who can read a human heart? "So, this was February 2014 . . ."

"Yeah, it was a busy month in Russia. Putin had just staged the Winter Olympics in Sochi with the whole world watching. Even before the closing ceremony, he was annexing Crimea. At the same time, he was passing a bunch of repressive new laws. Laws to protect the church, laws controlling foreign organizations . . ."

"Laws against 'homosexual propaganda' . . ." Jenna said.

Hirsch shot her a quizzical look. "Funny you should say that. OPUS mentioned LGBT rights in Russia a couple of times."

"In what context?"

"Said he hated the way Putin spoke about gay people as if they're dangerous but also subhuman. He said Europe has heard that kind of talk before, and it ended in Auschwitz. That surprised me, I guess. His views, I mean. Russian men are usually very conservative on such matters."

"Why do you think he mentioned it?"

Hirsch blew out his cheeks. "Who knows? Perhaps he had a family member who's gay."

That struck Jenna as significant. If OPUS had felt forced to choose between the regime and someone close to him, clearly he had chosen . . .

"He never mentioned family?"

"Nope. He kept his family life private. I'd have done the same."

You and me both . . .

"I'll miss him," Hirsch went on. "I was *pissed* when he got hit. Can't understand how they caught him. A spook that good doesn't make a slip. You guys think we have a mole?"

Jenna kept her expression neutral. *You have no idea, Dan.*

She said: "The funeral's today, right?"

"About to watch it on RT."

Jenna ended the call and turned on the TV in her office to watch the live footage.

RT, Russia's foreign language service, was a curious channel that mixed good journalism with disinformation and crass propaganda. Yesterday it had broadcast a short biopic about OPUS's life entitled "Soldier, Diplomat, Hero," to a background of stirring anthems from the Red Army Chorus. The funeral service had taken place in a small Orthodox chapel near the Kremlin, but the main televised spectacle was the burial at the Novodevichy Cemetery.

"*. . . is being buried with full military honors. Colonel Dmitry Stepanovich Kuznetsov, recipient of the Red Star for bravery, a veteran of the Afghan War, a distinguished diplomat respected by European heads of state, was a hero of the Russian Federation. Dmitry Peskov, spokesman for President Putin, said: 'We have lost one of Russia's true greats. A man we honor today for his selfless service and deep patriotism . . .*"

Jeez, they were going to town on the cover-up.

She was surprised by the numbers of mourners, hundreds of them. Putin wasn't there, but was represented, the commentary said, by the Minister for Foreign Affairs, Sergey Lavrov.

The burial plot was a modest one surrounded by fir trees, lodged in between austere Soviet grandees whose busts looked down upon the graves. A bright, cold afternoon in Moscow. Deep shade among the firs, speckled light on white stone.

Old Spetsnaz comrades, she guessed from their medals, Duma representatives in black ties, fellow intelligence officers, diplomats. The British ambassador. The German ambassador. All laid wreaths of white lilies and roses.

The coffin, draped in the Russian tricolor, was carried by pallbearers in dress uniform who followed an Orthodox priest swinging a thurible on chains. Prayers sung at the graveside as the coffin was lowered. Clouds of incense.

And the family: a slow-moving group of seven desolate people dressed in black.

One by one they cast earth onto the coffin, then stood to one side.

And there, next to the veiled woman she presumed to be OPUS's wife, was a tall young man of about twenty, looking pale and distraught. His hair was dark blond and tied back in a ponytail. He seemed ill at ease in a shirt and tie and polished black shoes. She was struck by how strongly he resembled OPUS, a younger version of him, the man OPUS must have been at that age. Soulful eyes that were a remarkable mineral blue, strong jaw, full lips. OPUS's son? One arm was around his mother, consoling her.

Lavrov, surrounded by bodyguards, put in a hasty moment of contemplation at the graveside, then offered his condolences to the wife, but he ostentatiously ignored the son, Jenna noticed.

And then another figure, bareheaded and burly, appeared behind Lavrov wearing a long black coat with a turned-up collar. She could see him only from behind, but she guessed instantly who it was. Some people bring the sunlight wherever they go, she thought. Others bring a chill. Vadim Giorgadze. The spy-catcher.

The two men, Lavrov and Giorgadze, must have known that OPUS had betrayed them. This cynical show of mourning was a counterintelligence sham. A grotesque piece of theater designed to shield the public from the knowledge that a hero of the Russian Federation had stabbed little Putin in the back.

Giorgadze's back remained toward the cameras. She saw him say a few words to the widow before he turned to the young man, leaned into his ear, and spoke to him for what seemed like two minutes, occasionally jabbing a black-gloved finger at the young man's chest.

Jenna could not see his face, but she could see the young man's. To say that his expression was one of aversion would have been an understatement. He grew paler, his mouth fixed into a tight grimace. He appeared appalled, frightened, his body tensed for a fight-or-flight moment in which he might have shoved Giorgadze backward into the open grave.

Giorgadze departed, and the young man stared ahead, his eyes watering and wild. He crossed his hands solemnly in front of him, mindful of the cameras on him, as if he were trying to hold himself together.

And there, in the late afternoon sunlight as he crossed his hands, Jenna saw something flash gold on the cuff of his shirt.

33

Novodevichy Cemetery
Moscow
Saturday afternoon

Lyosha felt hollowed out, detached from reality. Everything that was happening right now was so unreal to him that he thought he might be dreaming and would wake up in his bed at any moment. He had one arm around his mother, whose thin body he could feel trembling. She looked up at him, and he pulled her toward him and kissed her veiled forehead.

He knew she was holding back a tsunami of loss and incomprehension, which would break again later and engulf her when they got home, but for now he could only marvel at her dignity. She thanked each mourner, one by one, for coming.

"That's so kind of you to say. Dmitry would be deeply touched..."

Lyosha kept thinking of the last time he'd seen his father. The horrible row they'd had. The bridges burned; the earth scorched. They'd said things that could never be unsaid, things they could never take back. Now there was no chance to say sorry. All he could do was hope that his father had found it in his heart to forgive him and that his soul was at peace.

Love, he thought. *We always remember it at the end.*

He looked up. The sky was a harsh, clear blue with high cirrus clouds. Suddenly his nostrils flared, and his lip was trembling.

The mourners, dozens of old army comrades and diplomats—men his father had fought with and worked with—dutifully paid their respects and shook his hand. The fucking news cameras were pointing right at him, making him wonder if they were more interested in him than in his father.

It had been just over a week since Lyosha's appearance on *Direct Line with Vladimir Putin*. The YouTube clip of his exchange with the president had now been viewed 11.2 million times. Strangers had started recognizing him in the street. "Hey, YouTube guy!" someone had yelled in his local minimart. Two young Chechens, both drunk, had blocked his way in the dairy aisle. One of them had tried to grab his sleeve. He almost pushed the guy onto a display of cheeses. They were recording the whole thing on their phones. "Aw, don't be an asshole!" He'd left the store in a panicky run, hearing vulpine whoops behind him. "That was him! That's the guy!"

Two days later, when he'd shown his face at MGU for his law lecture, students in the locker corridor had turned to watch him pass, smiling at him and snickering, or holding up their fingers in a peace sign, and saying, *"Life prepared me for this question,"* as if he were the butt of some national joke. It had made him so self-conscious that he had started walking oddly, in small, stiff steps with his eyes fixed ahead. And later that week, when the ice hockey team filed out of the rink toward the locker rooms, Coach Golubev had pulled him aside and told him that it might be an idea for him to keep a low profile, "until things blow over," which made Lyosha think he was being dropped from the team. He hadn't been to a training session since.

The mourners parted to clear a path for Foreign Minister Lavrov and his bodyguards. The man's face was as heavy and dull as a bag of flour. Lyosha detected no compassion in his eyes, or in his voice when he spoke some brisk homily to Mama. The man was a nothing. A husk containing a void. One of the ring-wraiths who surrounded Putin.

Lavrov ignored Lyosha and left. As the bodyguards departed, Lyosha felt a dark chill, as if a freezer door had been opened. Vadim Giorgadze was approaching, smiling venomously, his high, arched eyebrows giving him a look of knowing irony.

"Marina Vladimirovna, my deepest sympathies." The voice was whispery and sibilant, part rasp, part hiss, like the sound of snakes in a burial chamber. "Dmitry was a true patriot. His loss will be keenly felt by us all."

"Thank you, Vadim Ivanovich," Lyosha's mother murmured, visibly recoiling from the man's hand.

Giorgadze was a family acquaintance, a powerful *silovik* who had known the president in Saint Petersburg, one of the self-enriched ex-KGB men who ran the country—someone Lyosha might have forgotten like a bad dream had it not been for the arresting phenomenon of his voice. A mujahideen sniper's bullet had split the man's larynx in Afghanistan, turning his speech to a contortion of whispers. Lyosha knew that he held some senior rank in the SVR. He also knew—had known since he was a boy, in the way children always knew such things—that the grown-ups were afraid of him.

Lyosha's mother glanced at her son from beneath her veil. He did not need to see her eyes.

Get this man away from me.

"If there's anything I can do," Giorgadze breathed, still smiling, "you know you can call me anytime."

"Of course."

"And you, young man," he said, turning to Lyosha. "Our YouTube star!" Giorgadze was now just inches from Lyosha's face, so close that Lyosha could see the gray hairs in his nostrils, smell the sweetish odor of vodka on his breath. His eyes had a deadness in them, Lyosha thought, like the rank water at the bottom of a pond. "Are you pleased with yourself?"

"Sir?"

Giorgadze leaned in closer so that the writhing, thin-air voice would not be carried away by the breeze. "Your little prank on live TV," he whispered. The words were soft, but Lyosha felt real heat from the man's face and a small fusillade of his spittle. "You thought that was clever? Eh?" He moved even closer so that his long arrowhead nose was almost touching Lyosha's ear. "Eh?"

Lyosha felt his toes curl and his buttocks clench. Suddenly he was sweating uncontrollably. "I asked the president a fair question about—"

"Listen to me, pretty boy, you ungrateful little cunt. The only reason you weren't thrown in fifteen-day detention is because of your FAMILY NAME." Giorgadze withdrew a step to glare at him full beam, and nodded slowly, pointing a finger at Lyosha's face. "We're watching you now, you piece of shit, we're watching you. If I hear so much as a *murmur* of dissent from you, if your face *ever* shows up among those do-nothings in a demonstration, if you utter even a *word* against our president—a *man like that!*—you'll end your days *sucking cocks for kopecks in Lefortovo! Do you understand me?*"

Giorgadze moved on to offer his condolences to Lyosha's cousins, but he cast one last smoldering glance back at him.

We're watching you.

As they left the cemetery, seated in the backseat of a funeral car, his mother squeezed his hand. "Lyosha, my love . . . that man. What did he say to you?"

They spotted Anya waiting for them at the gates of the cemetery. She was smoking, headphones on, her head bopping to a silent beat. She'd braided her blue hair and was dressed like a pop star in heeled boots and a black velvet coat trimmed with white faux fur. She hadn't wanted to attend the burial. "Too many bastards there who want to arrest me." She blew a plume of smoke at the sky, tossed the cigarette, and got into the car.

While Anya and his mother chatted with that exuberant relief that rises up, spontaneously, in people after a funeral ("We were so lucky with the weather! The sun came out for Dmitry"), Lyosha could feel himself sliding closer and closer to a depression. It was almost a physical pull, as if he were skating in slow, decreasing circles around a hole in a frozen lake.

When they arrived home Marina pulled off her veil and opened a bottle of Sémillon. The sun had moved into the west, trailing dark, ragged clouds tipped with flame. The city's lights were coming on. Down below on the river, a party barge chugged past, sending up beams of colored lasers.

She sat in the pool of light over the dining table, her head in her hands. When she looked up, exhausted, Lyosha thought she'd aged years. "There's potato salad in the refrigerator . . ." she said vaguely.

Suddenly the loneliness in the apartment became insufferable.

He said, "I'm going to change out of this suit."

Anya followed him into his bedroom and lay on his bed. He could see her in the mirror, watching him undress, taking in the contours of his legs, the smoothness of his skin.

"Take your eyes off my butt."

"Why are you sooo sexy . . . ?" she murmured.

Lyosha gave a sad smile as he pulled on a pair of clean white Calvin Klein briefs. He'd never felt less sexy in his life.

He threw his shirt onto the heap of clothes next to his bed. She picked it up and pressed it to her nose, breathing in his scent. Then she noticed the heavy cufflinks and removed them. She examined them and weighed them in her hand.

"These are solid gold."

Lyosha sprayed antiperspirant across his chest and zipped up his jeans.

"The Foreign Ministry returned them with Papa's things."

34

Ryongsong Residence
North Korea

Kim Yo-Jong sat at the edge of one of the chairs on the dais. Her posture was graceful and upright, like a queen's. Ominously, she did not invite Eric to sit. Her voice was high and cold.

"I wish to ask you about the situation in the White House. We are hearing rumors from our spies in Seoul that the Yankee enemy wishes to treat with us."

"Respected Comrade," Eric said, lowering his head. "I can humbly confirm that those rumors are true."

Ignore the bladder. I have stamina.

"Why?" she said, gazing down upon him. "Why would the jackal who insults my brother at every public opportunity wish to meet with him? To insult him again? This is not to be borne. My brother is extremely angry."

Eric closed his eyes for a second, mentally turning off the flashing red light of his bladder, and focused his thoughts.

"The Yankee president is alarmed by the rapid progress of our nuclear capability. He views the situation as a contest of wills. Leader versus leader. Man versus man. However, it is a bluff. In private he has spoken warmly of our Great Successor, your brother. President Trump is an uncomplicated man. His public insults are a means of establishing an opening position favorable to a deal. It is a technique he learned from his many years of performing in TV entertainment shows. In America this strategy is termed 'bullshitting.'"

"Bull-shitt-ing?"

"We have no equivalent word in Korean. It means to mislead with words and behavior that are intentionally lacking in candor. It is an art of deception."

"*Bull-shitt-ing.*" She pronounced the alien word carefully, turning it over on her tongue, committing it to memory.

"It is also my strong impression that this *bullshitting* is a cover for feelings of envy that President Trump harbors toward our Great Successor."

Eric risked a glance at Kim Yo-Jong.

Her eyes widened. "Are you making fun of me? This man has been most offensive and disrespectful. He called my brother a crafty biscuit!"

Eric flushed red and gave a pained smile. "Not true, Respected Comrade; he said '*smart cookie.*' It is an expression of admiration for a superior person."

"Admiration? How do you mean? Look at me."

Eric looked up, feeling a twinge of pain in his neck from the abject position he'd been in. "As the Great Successor has said, President Trump is a mentally deranged dotard. He is ashamed of his own low intellect compared with what he perceives as the shining genius of our beloved Leader's. He envies the Great Successor because the Great Successor's word is law, his commands are obeyed without question, and his people's love is unconditional. Most of all, he envies our society, which he knows is free of hostile bourgeois institutions, internal enemies, factionalists, and counterrevolutionaries."

Kim Yo-jong's eyes flared as she considered this.

She said, "Trump is ignorant and rude. It may not be fitting or appropriate for my brother to meet such a person."

"Trump is unpredictable, certainly, and he is coarse, but there is a remarkable consistency to his hunger for power and praise. It is a character flaw that our Great Successor could easily turn to our advantage."

Kim Yo-jong stood up and walked toward him, her thin arms folded, her heels clacking on the wooden floor.

"Trump really confides in you?"

"He does, Respected Comrade."

"What has he said to you, in private?"

"He said that he'd be honored to sit down with our Great Successor over a *hamburger*. Those were his words."

"*Hamburger?*'"

"Double-bun-with-meat."

She started to pace along the edges of the room. Eric remained still, his head still lowered, his bladder now sounding the siren for DEFCON 1.

From behind him she said, "What concession would Trump demand in return for a meeting?" She was a diminutive woman, her footsteps as light as a bird's, but in her presence he felt like a tiny, wayward child. A child who badly needed to pee. "He should know that we would rather eat dirt than give him what he wants," she continued. "The Hwasong missiles are the treasured swords of the Revolution. No one barters their destiny for a meeting."

"President Trump is not interested in details or results," Eric said. "He is interested in personal chemistry. A deal he makes with us does not even need to be real. What is important to him is something he can *present* as real. This is the art of the *bullshitting*."

Kim Yo-jong continued to pace. Eric dared not turn to her, but he had a dawning sense that he was getting through to her.

She said, "The South Koreans will object."

"Respectfully, the South Korean lackeys will agree to the meeting. They know that Trump is impatient with them. He is tired of shouldering the costs of protecting them. They will not dare to interfere."

She continued for a while without speaking. "If what you're saying is true, this is an opportunity that merits serious consideration. This man may not be in office for long . . ."

"It is an historic opportunity, Respected Comrade. To extract concessions from the Yankee bastards while we have the chance."

"But we cannot let down our guard."

Eric lowered his head further. "Of course not."

"The Yankees are an ever-present threat. They have 28,500 troops stationed just a hundred and fifty miles away in the South, along with the THAAD anti-ballistic missile system, pointing at us from just over the border."

"It is my belief that the jackal Trump will withdraw all Yankee forces from South Korea, if the Great Successor will agree to meet him."

Kim Yo-jong stopped pacing. Her shock was palpable. "He would agree to that? Is it not *bull-shitt-ing*?"

"In return for our Great Successor's high opinion of him, yes, he will do it. President Trump has a grave weakness for flattery and praise."

"My brother will wish to take my counsel and think deeply on this matter. Then we will see who wins this contest of wills." She stopped in front of Eric and tilted her head back with an imperious pride. "My dear departed father was a genius at *bullshitting*. My revered grandfather was the greatest master of *bullshitting* the world has ever known. We are a dynasty that is respected in every country for our power to shape events through *bullshitting*."

For one terrifying instant Eric thought he was going to laugh. His throat seemed to catch it just in time. All the pistons of his brain were now diverting their remaining energy to stopping his bladder from exploding.

Please let me go now. Please let me pee.

Kim Yo-jong stared out at the floodlit lawns, thinking. "Now. To the reason we have called you here."

Eric grimaced. *What?*

She looked at him with a bleak disappointment, as if he was a student for whom she'd once held great hopes. "My brother does not tolerate failure, Eric Rahn. If it weren't for your position in the White House, you would have been recalled last year and condemned to the Yodok Concentration Camp. Do you understand how fortunate you are right now, to be standing here talking to me?"

Oh God.

An icy jet of raw terror sluiced through his veins. His ankles weakened; his bladder was lapping at the overflow pipe.

"Respected Comrade," he mumbled, "if I have failed you in any way—"

"You have failed me. Do you even know what I'm talking about?"

Eric had no idea.

Her voice rose sharply. "You had orders to find Ha-jun, the son of the woman named Soo-min Williams. We have studied your reports, and your lack of progress has been noted at the level of the politburo. My brother is gravely disappointed in you."

Eric felt his face flame red hot. His breathing became shallow and his speech rapid.

"Forgive me. P-please forgive me. I exhausted every p-possible avenue of search. If this boy has been deliberately hidden from us, it is almost im-p-possible to trace him in a country of 340 million people. I have tried everything. But I will redouble my efforts! I will—"

She slapped him hard across his face.

Eric reeled. The shock was so great that his heart seemed to leap from his chest and bounce off the insides of his skull. The room began to spin around him.

He fell again to his knees in fear and appalled surprise, and crouched over, his forehead pressed to the floor at her feet, his whole body trembling uncontrollably and his pulse thumping wildly in his throat. His cheek was stinging and hot.

She stood over him like a dark avenging angel, the black hem of her skirt brushing his head. Her tone was low and poisonous. "So much devotion and time and effort were put into creating you. So much love. So much money. To make you into an elite fighter. To carry the vanguard of our struggle to the heart of imperialist beast. And this is how you repay our love. With pathetic *excuses*."

She pressed her foot onto the top of his head, jamming the side of his face to the floor.

"Who fed you when you were hungry?"

Eric groaned in shame and pain. "Your respected father."

"Who enlightened you when you lived in darkness?"

"Your respected father. Please."

"Who gave your life a cause when you had none?"

"Your respected father. Please, please." He was sobbing freely now, his face wet with tears and sweat. "I swore an oath," he said through clenched teeth. "I serve only our Great Successor. I am no other's to command. My life is his."

She pressed her shoe down harder, twisting it on Eric's ear, flattening his left eyeball to the floor until he screamed and the dam burst. A great gush of warm piss flowed freely.

She took a step backward in disgust. "You're an animal."

"I'm an animal," he wailed.

"I am tempted, Eric Rahn. I am tempted to send you to Yodok right now."

He was a sobbing, shaking wretch on the floor.

Then something landed silently next to his face. It was a photograph, which quickly curled in the spreading pool of his urine.

She said, "We believe this is the boy. We had to do your job for you and find this ourselves. But you were right. He is very hard to find."

Eric was too paralyzed with humiliation to raise his head.

"Track him down and eliminate him. We don't care how you do it."

"I will do it. I will coordinate with the network and the RGB. I'll need a hit squad and a—"

"It was the Reconnaissance General Bureau who tracked down this photo, Eric. But this is far too sensitive a matter to be handled by a team. We can't send a hit squad to the United States like we could to Kuala Lumpur Airport. That's why we entrusted it to *you*. You handle this—alone." She walked briskly away. "No more excuses." The door closed behind her.

Moments later Eric was being marched back to the car by guards holding both his arms. He thought he was going to faint. He was mortified with fear and ignominy. He was still crying, and the pants of his suit were glistening wet.

They bundled him into the backseat and drove him at speed back to the airport in the dark.

Only once the plane was in the air, and he was certain that he was departing North Korean airspace and leaving behind the great mushroom cloud of shame and humiliation that towered over Ryongsong Residence, did he finally take out the photo Kim Yo-jong had given him. His hands were still trembling. The paper had dried, but it retained a yellow tide mark from where it had fallen into his piss, and a faint whiff of ammonia.

It was a picture that had been swiped from the Facebook page of someone called Alyssa Jane Wright. A group of teens posing for a photo on a beach. The girl holding the camera on a selfie stick—red hair, freckles, teeth covered in braces—was Alyssa Jane perhaps.

Five others were crowded into the frame, all high-school age. Two girls, three boys. One blond dude making a peace sign; one African American guy with his hair in cornrows; and, at the back of the group, one kid who was East Asian in appearance.

A tiny "x" had been drawn in marker pen above his head. He was the only one not pulling a face of jokey, exaggerated mirth. Spiky black hair, surprised, worried eyes. His smile was provisional, reluctant, as if he hadn't wanted to be in the photo. Black overcoat and black T-shirt. No other details.

This could have been taken anywhere . . .

Behind them was a bay, with land just visible on the far side of the water, and there, on the right and far in the distance, was the blurred upper part of a tall reddish structure. The tower of a suspension bridge?

The Golden Gate Bridge?

The photo had been taken in the late afternoon, by the look of it. The light was at a low angle, and the boy's face was partly in shadow, as if Death's hand was already upon him, and partly obscured by the hair of the blond girl in front of him.

By the time Eric arrived back in his room at the Mandarin Oriental in Hong Kong it was midmorning on Sunday. The hysteria had left him, and he felt calmer, more focused; the aftershocks of the fright Kim Yo-jong had given him were starting to abate and become less intense.

For a long time, he sat in his room, watching the glittering harbor with its ships and tour barges, and the towers of distant Kowloon.

Something was seriously off about Kim Yo-jong's orders to murder this boy, whoever he was. *Why* had she insisted that he act alone, without the aid of the Reconnaissance General Bureau?

We can't send a hit squad to the United States like we could to Kuala Lumpur Airport . . .

Eric doubted this was true. The RGB could assassinate people anywhere . . .

A blindingly obvious thought jumped to the front of his mind and startled him, making him sit up in his chair.

Find him and eliminate him.

Eric's original order from Center had been to *find* Ha-jun, not kill him.

He'd always considered it a hopeless missing person's search—no more than that. Now, finding Ha-jun was not only a priority, but he was also to be bumped off as a matter of urgency.

An alarming, apostatical thought edged its way into his brain: that this order to *kill*, which he'd heard for the first time today from Kim Yo-jong, had been issued to him under a secret, personal charter of her own . . . And the RGB didn't know about it.

Why? Was she freelancing? Going behind someone's back?

Her brother's back?

A morbid chill spread through him as the hair-raising danger of this thought became apparent to him. A thought he did not dare harbor let alone explore. Any knowledge of the private machinations of the Family was strictly forbidden to ordinary mortals like him. The kind of knowledge that could cost him his life. In a conscious act of doublethink, he blanked it from his mind. He knew nothing about it.

But he did know that Kim Yo-jong had him in the palm of her hand. If he wanted to live, if he wanted his life to continue in anything like the way he'd hoped, he had no choice but to fulfil her command. If he failed, the result would be too disastrous and terrifying to consider.

He took out the photo again, and touched his finger to the face of the boy, Ha-jun.

I don't know why I'm searching for you, and I don't care. But I will find you. And by your death shall I be redeemed.

35

CIA Headquarters
Langley, Virginia
Monday morning

Jenna replayed the RT footage of the funeral and froze the frame on a young man with long blond hair standing next to his mother at the graveside. The moment at which he crossed his hands in front of him.

"OPUS's only child," she said. "Name is Alexei Dmitryevich Kuznetsov, according to the *Moscow Times*. The techies pulled his school reports and social media feeds. Twenty-one years old. Final-year law student at Moscow State University. Decent grades. College ice hockey team goalie. A pretty regular kid until—"

"This the only visual?" Warren Allen said, standing in front of the screen with his hands on his hips. Allen had a strange body shape, Jenna thought: top-heavy, all chest and gut. He gave the impression that he might topple forward, as if he was on the verge of losing his balance. His eyes were baggy and watery, as if he hadn't slept. "Could be any damned cufflinks."

Jenna had convened them in the Russia House senior common room. Mira Kowalski had cut short her nine o'clock with the chairman of the House Committee on Foreign Affairs. Warren Allen had made his excuses to the House Intelligence Committee. Bill Cheney had been retrieved from a dentist's chair.

She opened her folder. "These were taken by an AP photographer covering the funeral. All high-res. I've had them enlarged." She passed them to Mira.

Two of the photos had captured a semi-oblique view of the left cufflink on the young man's shirt. The double-headed eagle was just about discernable on the gold of the disk.

Jenna said, "They're the same cufflinks we issued to OPUS. They must have been returned to the family with his personal effects. It would be natural for his son to wish to wear them at his father's funeral." She passed across the photo of the cufflink spy gear taken from OPUS's file.

Mira compared the photos side by side.

"They do *look* similar," she said dubiously. She passed the photos to Bill Cheney.

He, too, took a long time before answering. "Hm," he said, stroking his goatee. "Still . . ."

Jenna looked from one to the other. *It's totally fricking obvious they're the exact same ones!*

Warren Allen also took his time studying them. The Three Wise Ones of Russia House were thoughtful. Something secret was pinging between them.

"Let's watch the rest of that report," Allen said.

Jenna pressed play. Foreign Minister Sergey Lavrov, trailed by bodyguards, respectful in a black overcoat and homburg hat, speaking a few words to the widow, and completely cutting dead the son. He departs. Vadim Giorgadze enters the frame.

"Well, lookee here," Bill Cheney said. "He's taken the afternoon off from the torture chamber."

They had a rear view of Vadim Giorgadze's bald head, half hidden by his upturned collar, offering condolences to the widow, touching her shoulder, and then moving on to the son and saying something into his ear.

"What's that snake up to . . . ?" Mira murmured.

The footage cut back to the studio, but the expression on the young man's face, visible for just a half second, had shown a very clear reaction to Giorgadze's words. Outrage, disgust, despair.

"What happened there . . . ?" Bill Cheney said.

"This is just my gut," Jenna said, "but it may be related to this."

She played them the next video, of the young man's appearance on *Direct Line with Vladimir Putin.*

"It aired just over a week ago, and this clip went viral. More than fifteen million views as of today." They watched it twice. The question. Putin's anger. The audience laughing.

"Brave boy," Mira said, visibly impressed. "Dictators fear laughter more than an assassin's bullet."

"Embarrassing Pooty on live TV?" Allen said. "Yeah, that would get Giorgadze's attention. The kid's being warned."

"Or he's being coerced," Cheney croaked, his head wobbling as he spoke. "That just adds to my unease about those cufflinks, I'm afraid. It's just . . . too easy."

"In what way?" Jenna said.

"OPUS was about to give us dynamite intel stored on spy gear. OPUS is murdered. Spy gear disappears. The Russians show it on TV, telling us where it is and who's got it. It stinks like a bear trap. They'll wait for us to approach the kid. Then we get shit-canned out of Russia. The kid goes to a penal colony for treason. Revenge. Putin always serves it cold."

Mira had been twirling her pencil, but now she placed it on the table.

"But if it's *not* a trap? If it's just old-fashioned incompetence and bureaucracy that returned our spy gear to the family, that young fellow might be wearing everything we need on his goddamn shirt. Names and IDs of every Russian Seed-Bearing operative in the US ... *Priceless* intel. Something we'd pay a billion dollars for. Risky or not, it's all we've got."

Bill Cheney sighed and rubbed his eyes. Another tense silence around the table. "All right. Moscow Rules. We assume it is a trap and plan on that basis."

"Assuming it is a trap," Allen said, "any approach to this kid in Moscow, any contact at all, will be extremely dangerous. They'll have eyes on him from behind every tree. Static surveillance on every street near his home and his route to college. His phone and emails monitored. Ground units following him in multiple layers. They'll spritz his shoes and clothing with *metka* that will brush against any hand he shakes, any document he touches, leaving a fluorescent trail ..."

"Oh, Warren," Mira said, rolling her eyes. "When did your fire go out? I hear 'extremely dangerous' and I think: we'll develop an ops plan that has a fighting chance. We're all retiring soon. Let's go to our gardens in glory."

They were a curious trio, Jenna thought. Three old spooks who'd spent their entire careers in the Game. Each a combination of chess grand master, psychologist, outlaw, illusionist.

Toward the end of the day they reconvened, in the same room.

The techies' trawl of the young man's VKontakte and Instagram caches revealed that he'd deleted his profiles the day after his appearance on *Direct Line*. It wasn't hard to see why. A wave of congratulation had been followed by what looked like an orchestrated and exceptionally vicious Kremlin trolling campaign. It also must have been the same day he learned that his father had died.

"We checked for any new, private accounts linked to his email," Jenna said. "Nothing. The kid's gone dark on social media. But his emails yielded something interesting. He's been shooting off applications to dozens of European and US law firms. According to his résumé he speaks excellent English and possesses all the usual LinkedIn shit about motivation and goals. Looks like he's desperate to get out of Russia. And how about this? Ten days from now, a blue-chip DC law firm named Harley, Feinstein & Hawley will be holding an open day at the Moscow State University careers fair, with an RSVP drinks reception later at the Hotel Metropol. Our guy has registered his interest to attend."

The three were silent for a moment. Then Warren Allen said, "Jackpot."

"He's received an invitation?" Mira said.

"Not yet."

"Let's make sure he gets one."

Allen started pacing. For a heavy man he was surprisingly light on his feet. "Could this law firm be persuaded to move its drinks reception to our Moscow embassy? If our guy's under opposition control, it would be safer."

"No," Mira said, twirling her pencil again. "The FSB will smell a rat. Moscow Rules. Blend in, go with the flow. Ten days doesn't give us much time to prepare, but that's our opportunity to meet our young man. Drinks reception at the Hotel Metropol."

By the next morning the mood among the Wise Ones was somber. Something had changed. Jenna sensed it the moment she walked in. The collegiate atmosphere had gone. The hierarchies had re-asserted themselves.

Mira linked her fingers on the table. Her tone was one of cool pragmatism. "Jenna, I'll come straight to it. The officer we send to Moscow for this op must be one who is not known to the opposition. Someone with intuition, courage, and judgment. And, of course, someone who is trained in denied-area operations. We would like to consider you for this assignment. If you accept, you'll be given additional training over the next nine days to operate securely under intense hostile pressure on the Moscow streets. A dip cover won't work—the FSB has routine surveillance on anyone working out of the embassy. You'll be sent under non-official cover, as a civilian, which means we'll deny all knowledge of you if you're caught, and you will deny any connection to your own government. It's important to be clear about that from the start. Charles Fisk can keep an eye on you from Moscow Station, but he can't offer you any active support. You'll have no immunity, no diplomatic protection. If they catch you, you're looking at ten to eighteen years in a Siberian penal colony. Your only hope for an earlier release is a spy swap, and, I have to tell you, they don't happen every week."

Three sets of eyes were watching her closely, evaluating her reaction.

Jenna had gone very still. "A civilian?"

"A NOC operating in a denied-access country needs a rock-solid cover, one that attracts the least suspicion from the FSB, and in a paranoid police-state like Russia that is no simple matter. This esteemed DC law firm of Harley, Feinstein & Hawley is a godsend for us. You'll be an employee of the firm traveling to Moscow on a business visa from DC. Passport and cover name to be confirmed."

"I'm posing as a lawyer?" Somehow, that seemed a bigger ask than deceiving a ferocious hostile security force.

"No. Recruitment officer. It's a large firm. The lawyers traveling to Moscow won't give a shit that you've only just joined. They'll just want you to do the job."

"I can do the job?"

"You will *appear* to do the job," Warren Allen said, touching the tips of his fingers together. "There are a number of large DC firms and corporations with a presence in Russia. Occasionally they cooperate with us. This firm is one of them. Sid Hawley, the firm's senior partner, will be informed that you're joining the trip under a special charter related to national security."

She tried to stall. "Won't I stand out in Russia?"

Mira gave her an almost motherly smile, which made her think that this woman had been made a similar offer, thirty-five, forty years ago, perhaps in this very room, and had felt the same tingling of fear and destiny. "Moscow is the capital of a sprawling multiracial empire stretching from the Baltic to the Pacific, from the Arctic to the Central Asian steppe. Every third person you'll pass in the street will be a Chechen, a Kazakh, a Mongolian, a Chinese Russian, a Korean from the Russian Far East. Many do not even speak Russian. Moscow's universities enroll thousands of students from Africa and India. Greeks, Vietnamese, Armenians run popular restaurants. Georgians and Azeris owned convenience stores and bakeries. No one will give your ethnicity a second thought."

Jenna had a vision of a dark path opening before her. There was no light to guide her, no hand to hold. If she wasn't going to take it, now was the moment to say so and leave the room. But if she didn't take it . . . what would she do?

They were asking her to make contact with an unsuspecting kid in possession of some intel—stored on, of all things, a cufflink. All she had to do was reel him in, arrange a re-meet with him, if necessary; take possession of the intel, and get the hell out of there. She'd faced way more difficult scenarios before, and she'd always pulled it off.

The expectations—the responsibility—were suddenly crowding in on her.

Life has a way of ambushing us, she thought. *And when it does, a person stands up, or she doesn't.*

Afterward, she didn't remember saying yes, but she must have said something, because all three had gotten to their feet with a sudden air of purpose, a collaborative determination. A light had turned green. They could start drawing their plans.

"We'll begin this evening," Allen said.

36

Washington, DC
Monday

Eric had arrived back in DC in a vile mood. He'd made *eight* separate flights, totaling almost forty-four hours in the air. He'd barely slept since Thursday. The boiling terror of his few hours in Pyongyang had given way to simmering black wrath.

Within an hour of getting home from the airport in the small hours of Monday he had opened his laptop and gotten down to work.

His starting point was the Facebook page of Alyssa Jane Wright—the source for the single photo Kim Yo-jong had given him, which he now placed on the desk next to his laptop. The image of the boy he'd been ordered to murder.

Alyssa Jane Wright, he found, was a seventeen-year-old, junior-year high-school student in Marin County, California. Her account was not private. With a depressing inevitability it revealed that she was partial to blueberry muffins, rock-climbing, K-pop, and the novels of Stephanie Meyer.

Eric selected one of the several fake profiles he'd assembled over the years—this time that of a sixteen-year-old girl called McKenzie—and sent Alyssa a friend request. He started following Alyssa's Instagram.

The group photo of friends taken near the Golden Gate Bridge was from early January, almost two months ago. He found it already buried quite far down Alyssa's prodigious feed.

Straight away he had the names of four of the friends in Alyssa's photo. They were Tyler McCabe, Tammy Halloran, Kyle Mason, and Honoré Jones, all of them fellow students at Tamalpais High School, Marin County.

But the sixth friend, the Asian guy at the back of the photo, above whose head a tiny *x* had been marked, the boy he had been told was Ha-jun . . . He was not tagged or named anywhere.

Eric sent friend requests to Tyler, Tammy, Kyle, and Honoré.

Only Tyler's account was not private. Among the thousands of Facebook friends in his account, and Alyssa's, Eric found no one resembling the mystery boy.

What name do you go by, Ha-jun?

It was a start. If the boy attended the same school or lived in the same area (by no means a given), Eric did at least have a location to search.

Most of these kids, he could see, lived in Marin County's Mill Valley, an affluent corner of the state across the Golden Gate Bridge from San Francisco Bay. Their parents, from what he could gather from the photos, drove high-end cars and owned boats and jet skis moored in the bay.

But after hours and hours of scrolling through thousands of cretinous pool parties, birthdays, grandparents, sports days, restaurant desserts, and dumb, dumb group photos, *nowhere* did he find another image of the boy.

He searched the websites of a dozen public high schools in the neighboring counties and in the San Francisco Bay Area, then he moved on to the private schools. He examined hundreds of faces at graduation events, school year books, proms, football games, trips to museums and theaters, until he had a raging headache and his eyes felt peeled and raw.

After hours of solid trawling, Eric still had only the one single image of the boy.

Whoever this kid was, he was deliberately keeping out of sight. Eric doubted he could do that alone. He must have foster parents or guardians. Or someone who was helping him.

Why? Who the fuck was this kid? What kind of person that age doesn't have their face online?

At 1 a.m. on Tuesday morning Eric slammed his laptop shut and messaged his dealer, drinking whiskey after whiskey until the man finally arrived with two bags of coke. In a few hours' time he was due at work in the West Wing, but he didn't give a damn. He snorted a line big enough for four people and began pacing the apartment, breathing like an enraged bison. By now, his mood was homicidal.

Five people—the five in Alyssa Jane Wright's photo taken that day near the Golden Gate Bridge—were acquainted with this kid, somehow, even if only slightly. *They knew him.* They had *included* him in their photo. They were the only ones who might know his current name and where to find him. And if Eric had to twist it out of them, one by one, then that's what he'd do. With a shearing knife if he had to. For however long it took . . .

On his desk was a stupid glass paperweight he'd been given after the nomination in Cleveland. It was the weight and shape of a brick, with engraved letters.

BUILD THE WALL

ONE BRICK AT A TIME

Suddenly he grabbed it and pitched it with full force at the door. *Thunk.* It had made a deep crater in the wood.

An hour later, when he was drunk and high, he had chilled a little.

He returned to the Tamalpais High School website. Alyssa, it seemed, was an aspiring news reporter and an editor for the *Tamalpais Gazette*, the student newspaper. She was also the vice president of pol-soc, the school politics society.

Interesting . . .

He started scrolling through online back issues of the *Gazette*, and an idea came to him, a small, hopeful possibility of an opening, an approach. Alyssa was ambitious. On an impulse, he checked LinkedIn, and holy fuck there she was, dolled up in shoulder pads like a congressional nominee.

Alyssa would be his key to finding Mystery Boy. The boy who was Soo-min's son and had been born with the name Ha-jun. The boy who had been missing for years. The boy he had been ordered to kill.

Just hours later, Eric arrived for work in the West Wing. He was now severely hungover and crazed from jet lag, which caused his mood to grow fouler still. The work that had piled up in his in tray was overwhelming, as was his schedule of meetings for the week and the calls and emails he had to return. A few aides stopped by to inquire after his imaginary mother, but, mercifully, most people left him alone in his office. The president was hunkered down in the cabinet room to prepare for his first address to the joint session of Congress, and had not asked for him. It was February 28. Tomorrow, it would be March already. Once again, he had that sense of time slipping away from him, vanishing.

He couldn't concentrate on even the simplest task. His brain was a foundry of anvils, hammers, and flames. He wanted to poke his own eyes out with a biro.

The scale and horror of his predicament was becoming clear. He, who prided himself on achieving the impossible, had been taken at his word and given the impossible to achieve.

His job in this administration was his life. It used up all his time, temporally and psychologically. He had to be available for the president at any time of the day or night and could never turn off his phone. He had to drop everything to be at the president's side and have every fact at his fingertips.

And he somehow had to find a way to juggle all that and travel to California by himself to commit murder.

Eric dropped his head into his hands.

Why had this been dumped on him? Did Pyongyang have no appreciation of his true talents? No gratitude? Wasn't he at the epicenter of world events? Didn't he *direct* those events? Hadn't he the ear of the president of the United States? He was a sublime strategist. A master of perception. An architect of reality. He was the eye of the storm. This was his mission. Not chasing ghosts. Not assassination. Not *wet work*.

By midafternoon, he had settled to a brooding, weepy kind of wretchedness. He was a dog on a leash. It was pointless to bite the hand that had fed him. He had been conditioned from birth to obey, submit, act without hesitation. None of this was his fault. When you're born with a destiny you can never escape it, no matter what you achieve, no matter where in the world you go.

All the same, he was feeling a malevolent impulse to blame someone, make someone the target of his rage, and the more he obsessed over it in his mind the more he settled on one person in particular.

GINKGO.

She was the root of all this. Ha-jun was her son. It was because of her that he'd had to crawl in his own piss. *Soo-min.* Such privileges she'd enjoyed at Paekhwawon, and this was how she repaid them all? This was how she treated a comrade? Silent, crazy, disloyal *bitch.*

He bit deep into his knuckle to prevent himself from smashing up his office.

Even he was conscious of becoming unhinged, dangerously unstable. He tried to soothe himself, as he often did at such moments, with thoughts of violence. Slow, patient, exquisite violence.

When, at the end of the day, a couple of aides stopped by and said, "Hey Eric. Drink at the Hawk 'n' Dove? Take your mind off things?" he thought, *Fuck it.*

In the lounge bar of the Hawk 'n' Dove, he drank two highballs in quick succession in the company of some RNC aides and a congressional staffer he'd thought was a lesbian but who kept giving him come-hither looks. He bumped into Marcia, Alex, and Hunter who somehow persuaded him to join them for dinner at Café Milano, where Marcia was hosting some sleazeball campaign consultants. The place was very crowded and noisy. Eric drank several glasses of a mediocre Malbec. Don Jr. stopped by their table, accompanied by a ravishing blonde. He couldn't hear a word the guy said. More wine was poured. Dessert was ordered. Someone pushed a bag of coke into Eric's hand. He snorted two huge bumps off the corner of his Amex in the men's washroom cubicle. (Who had given him the coke? Not Don Jr., surely . . .) And then, high off his ass again, he ordered three bottles of Veuve Clicquot for the table.

The evening really should have ended there, but the WhatsApp messages he'd been ignoring from Bannon's boys inviting him for a late one had by that point become a bearable proposition, and he ended up in a titty bar near Dupont Circle with some borderline personalities from Breitbart News. *Ugh.* Beer served in two-pint glasses. He hated beer, hated the way it made his skin flush, hated the fact they knew that, which was why they had bought him beer.

By one in the morning, bored by the drunken alt-reich talk, bored by the strippers dressed as cowgirls, he called it a night and staggered out onto the sidewalk feeling his emotional state sink deeper into the abyssal trench. The floor of hell was opening to him.

He was drunk, drunk, drunk.

The mood-plunge from the coke, the waste-of-life pointlessness of the evening, the bullshit he'd listened to—the bullshit he'd spoken—was making his disordered self feel anarchically evil.

He took an Uber home to his apartment on Beecher Street, and as he fumbled for the tangle of keys in his coat pocket, he must have squeezed his car fob because he heard his Audi beep and unlock on the sidewalk behind him. Slowly he turned toward it.

Too drunk to drive anywhere. Way, way over the limit.

Before he knew it, he was getting into the car and setting the Satnav for Annandale.

Traffic was sparse. It had rained earlier in the evening and the roads were glossy and black. He drove the eleven-mile distance with the ostentatious caution of a drunk.

Slowly he turned into the quiet residential street of clapboard houses and parked about a hundred yards from Soo-min's house. He turned off the engine and listened. The place was silent. Not a soul about, the houses curtained and sleeping. Lines of parked cars.

What a shitty, shitty neighborhood you live in, Soo-min.

From the glove compartment he retrieved a charged burner phone. It took him several attempts to tap in the number.

It rang.

Come on, GINKGO. I know you sleep all day. You're awake, aren't you? You're thinking about your son . . .

"Hello?"

The voice was so tiny, so faint, that he'd never have believed she was only yards away from him.

"Don't hang up, Soo-min," he said softly in Korean. "If you do, I'll come into the house and up the stairs. I'm outside."

Silence. Breathing.

"Don't you want to wave hello to an old, old friend?"

A high-pitch whine sounded on the line, the sound of her crying.

"Don't believe me? Go to the window, Soo-min. Open the curtain."

He waited, and in the light of the streetlamps he thought he saw the curtain of a second-floor window move just a crack. He flashed his lights once. Among the crappy budget cars parked along the street, his gleaming black Audi must have stood out.

"So, they've given you back your phone," he said silkily. "That sounds like progress."

Her breathing became frantic with fear.

"I am your darkest nightmare, Soo-min. You'll do anything to be rid of me, I know. That's why I'm making you another offer. I'll leave you alone. I really will. In return for one small secret from that locked-up brain of yours. What do you say?"

Her breathing became more agitated.

"Who is the father of your son?" The question seemed to fill the entire night sky.

The breathing stopped. A long silence on the line.

The voice that finally spoke was trembling but clear. "Do you dare to ask me that, Eric Rahn? Do you have that authority?" The next words sounded choked and thick, but whether from fear or suppressed laughter he couldn't tell. "You are nothing but a slave, as I was a slave. Is the slave sure he wants to know the answer to his question? Does he know what will happen to him if he knows?"

37

Undisclosed locations
Washington, DC

Jenna's surveillance instructor was a laconic, shaven-headed man introduced as Martin, who, Mira said, had operated under intense hostile pressure on the streets of Beijing. He didn't look much older than thirty. He spoke hardly at all, yet he carried such an air of authority that Jenna was in awe of him from day one. His technique was not to answer any of her questions, rather to allow her to squirm in frustration, until the answer presented itself to her, like revealed truth. He sent Jenna onto the streets of Washington, DC, for twelve hours a day.

Martin sent squadrons of five, ten cars after her. She was instructed to identify all of them and memorize their license plate numbers. She was tailed by surveillance teams of up to thirty people across the city, around parks, through shopping malls, museums, memorials, and basement parking lots. She had to recall individual faces. Here, she could make mistakes. In Moscow, she couldn't make one.

Jenna had been an ops officer for seven years. She had operated in North Korea under conditions of extreme danger. But nothing had prepared her for this. She was learning to *feel* the street, to be synapse-alert the moment the hairs prickled on the back of her neck, to know when her sixth sense was activated, telling her when she had coverage, even before she spotted it. She counted the cars, watched for doubles, took mental snapshots of faces, noticed anomalies, noted details. *Shoes!* Her watchers could alter their appearance quickly with a disguise, but they never changed their shoes. She switched direction once she was out of sight, losing her watchers before they realized they'd lost her. Martin sometimes appeared ahead of her on a motorcycle. He was observing the way she approached drop sites, her inventiveness in using disguise—wigs, glasses, clothing. Slowly, with each passing day, she felt, almost imperceptibly at first, that she was rising to a new level of skill, one more subtle and less conscious. She began getting inside the teams' heads, acquiring a feel for what they'd do before they did it.

At the end of each long session, Martin would meet her near one of DC's parks or in the vast, anonymous parking lot next to IKEA. He'd appraise her performance, list the vehicles and watchers she had missed, the slips that had given her away. He'd be sitting on his motorcycle, and she'd be slumped against the door of her car exhausted and hungry. On the first three nights, she'd been annoyed with herself, annoyed with Martin for laying out her shortcomings, and desperate to get home. But by the fourth night, as her skill noticeably improved, something shifted and she started looking forward to these appraisals, keen to know if her hunches and instincts had been right. The winter nights were starting to get warmer, unseasonably warm for the end of February, so that she often ended the day drenched in sweat and found Martin waiting for her wearing a T-shirt.

There was something very mysterious about Martin, she thought—with his head shaved daily like a monk's, always calmly waiting for her with his arms folded across his chest, and a prominent vein down each bicep. His body had that economy of movement she'd seen in people skilled in martial arts. She wondered why he never seemed to perspire, how he remained so *present* and undistracted. It had been years since anyone had spent this much time with her when she was feeling vulnerable, frustrated, frightened of failure. She knew he would be reporting everything to Mira, but he said nothing when she occasionally howled in exasperation at her mistakes. It was as if he saw beyond them to other qualities in her, the ones that mattered. His manner was focused, anchoring. It had a remarkably calming effect. She had no idea what was going through his mind when he regarded her with that cool, steady gaze.

Since she had moved into one of Fisk's spare bedrooms in Alexandria, she'd barely had a chance to enjoy the house. After the first full day's training, she had arrived back there delirious with exhaustion. She'd just wanted to drop into bed. Perhaps that's why her guard was down when she'd unlocked the front door, thrown her keys on the hall table, and turned on the kitchen lights, only to stop dead in her tracks.

Seated at the kitchen table had been a neat, rosy-cheeked woman of about fifty.

"You must be Jenna. Good evening. I'm Natasha, your Russian tutor."

"How did you get in?"

The woman had given a small, apologetic smile, and started placing flash cards on the table, as if she were a fortune teller. So Jenna had dropped her bag to the floor and slumped into a kitchen chair.

"We'd better start." Natasha had said, glancing at the kitchen clock.

She'd opened the lesson with the Cyrillic alphabet. The following night, with Jenna again almost speechless from fatigue, and desperate for a large JD on the rocks, dinner, shower, and bed, in that order, Natasha had been there again. This time they'd moved on to basic verb conjugations. By the third night they were practicing simple dialogue. "Where is your suitcase?" "Here it is." "It's so heavy!"

She'd found the lessons hard going, a reminder that rapid language-learning was best done in youth. But after four days she had a very rudimentary, very unsteady grasp of noun declensions, and a sparse, eclectic vocabulary. Like Martin, Natasha was patient, relentless, uncompromising. They did two-and-a-half-hour lessons, seven nights in a row. At the end of each lesson, Natasha would give her grammar exercises and lists of new words to learn, and Jenna, by that hour of the night feeling wired and unhinged on caffeine, would use these more informal minutes to ask Natasha questions about Russian culture and custom, about food, art, music, superstition. Natasha explained that Russian names had diminutive forms used by friends and family. So the diminutive of Vladimir, for example, (a name that meant "one who rules the world") could be Volodya, Vovochka, or the even cuter, and much more familiar, Vova.

"Who the hell calls Putin 'Vova'?" Jenna said.

"Many women," Natasha replied with some distaste. "You'd be surprised."

"What's yours? Your diminutive." It seemed a personal question, but this woman had broken into the house after all. Natasha was coy suddenly, and said she'd preferred not to use her diminutive since coming to live in the US.

"The diminutive of Natasha is Nastya." It was the only time they had laughed together.

On the final evening of her training, Jenna got out of her car near Rock Creek Park, close to her old home in Georgetown. It had been a long day, and her T-shirt was steam-ironed to her back in the warmth. Martin was standing next to his motorcycle talking to an elderly lady with short white hair who was holding a small, caffè latte-colored dog on a lead. It was a simple disguise, but Jenna did not recognize her at all until she spoke with Mira's voice.

"A JD on the rocks?" she said with surprising cheer. "That's your preferred beverage, isn't it? You've earned it. I'm happy to tell you that your performance has been satisfactory. Now, Martin said he'd like to invite you for a drink, didn't you, Martin?" Martin lowered his head solemnly, as if to say, *it would be an honor,* and without another word Mira walked off into the dark between the pools of light from the streetlamps, allowing the dog to pull her along, and leaving Jenna and Martin facing each other, surprisingly embarrassed.

He took her to a quiet bar in Kalorama. She got her JD on the rocks. Martin ordered a small bottle of craft beer which he sniffed suspiciously and hardly touched. The convivial atmosphere—low lighting, Nina Simone playing softly in the background—didn't make him any more forthcoming. Their conversation was stilted and confined to things they'd already discussed at each day's appraisal. The silences between their remarks grew longer, more awkward, and at the same time . . . she was becoming aware of a strange tension between them. Small, evanescent signals—stolen glances, skin flushing, the pulse in the vein of his wrist visibly quickening; small, covert smiles; both of them shifting very slightly in their seats; signals sent and received. She felt a shiver go through her.

His apartment was a tiny, white-walled garret on 20th Street NW. It revealed nothing of its occupant, no framed photos, no books, none of the detritus of a personal life, which made her wonder whether he lived there at all. They took turns in the shower, then met in the middle of the darkened living room, wrapped in towels. He was lithe, smooth, absurdly fit. She cupped his shaved head in her hands and began to kiss him. Moments later they were on the bed. He was unhurried and almost timid at first, but quickly began to exhibit an uncanny hyperacuity for her sweet spots, taking his cues from her, synchronizing with her, holding back for her, and then . . . *Jesus Christ.* All the tension and frustration of the last week released in one shuddering clench.

She could count the number of men she'd slept with on two

hands. Sex had never obsessed her in the way it did many people she knew. But she was certainly aware of the times when she *needed* sex, that deep, carnal urge to sate.

Later, she could not help wondering whether Mira had foreseen and permitted everything that had happened this evening.

38

Moscow State University
Moscow
First week of March

As the lecture wrapped up, Lyosha slid his notepad into his bag and shrugged on his jacket. He was sitting with Anya in the back tier of a vast colonnaded auditorium in the Faculty of Law. Behind the lectern the big hand of a giant, Soviet-era clock had completed its crawl toward ten o'clock. He had barely listened to a word, even though his mid-term examination was tomorrow morning.

The bell rang. Two hundred students began to move. Anya was in a hurry. She had been organizing small demonstrations to take place in Bolotnaya Square every day this week and she was going to be late.

"Before you go . . ."

Professor Mishkin had some announcements. "Alexei Kuznetsov: please see the university security advisor . . ."

Lyosha and Anya exchanged glances.

The university security advisor, a position Lyosha had never heard of, turned out to be a forty-something man named Maxim Fyodorovich Yegorov. He was speaking on the phone when Lyosha entered his office. The desk was a model of bureaucratic order.

Folders, stapler, telephone, in tray were all symmetrically aligned. Nothing unfiled, nothing pending. He wore a white shirt and black tie. His hair was a gray buzz cut. He ended the call and turned to Lyosha with a look of blank hostility, and Lyosha knew at once that this man reported to the FSB, not the university.

"Let us use the informal pronoun with each other," he said, without smiling. "This is a friendly conversation."

He offered Lyosha a seat. The office was bare of any books or personal touches, unless you included the framed portrait photograph on the wall—quite an old image of the president, from a time when his face looked normal.

The man leaned back in his seat and regarded Lyosha thoughtfully.

"You've called a lot of attention to yourself over the past two weeks, young man." He opened the file and Lyosha saw his own student ID photo, upside down. "Tell me . . . are you feeling restless?"

"I don't know what you mean."

"Have you been troubled?" His pale, steady eyes were fixed on Lyosha. "Politically disaffected, in need of psychological help, that kind of thing? Or are you . . ." He gestured vaguely with his hand, trying to avoid saying something distasteful. ". . . a member of a sexual minority, perhaps?"

Lyosha was suddenly feeling very hot beneath his clothes and shifted in his seat. "I just lost my father."

Maxim Fyodorovich gave a solemn nod. "Of course." He stretched his fingers, pulling them back until they cracked. "A lot of people think that your question to our president, on live television, was unpatriotic and impertinent. My first concern is for your welfare, Alexei, and for the security of the students."

"Have I broken a law?"

"Good question," Maxim Fyodorovich smiled thinly. "You're a law student, aren't you, so you know better than me. I think you've broken a very serious law. But whether any action is taken really depends on your conduct from now on."

Lyosha stared cynically at him. He'd just been given the classic Kremlin offer. *Conform . . . or face the law. Which law? There are many. We'll pick one.*

"You speak English, I see." Maxim Fyodorovich turned a page in the file. "You grew up in a home with languages, books, music . . . a wonderful privilege. Do you have any contacts in Russia who are Westerners? Anyone who has tried to befriend you . . ."

"I'm not a foreign agent."

Maxim Fyodorovich gave a small, noncommittal smile, as if to say, *We'll see.*

"You're a bright student, Alexei. Take my advice, and don't do anything else to ruin your future. We know you're applying to Western law firms . . ."

So, you're reading my emails.

"Why not Russian law firms, mm? I'm sure that's what your father would have wished."

Lyosha's anger was starting to simmer. He could feel its heat. But a voice in his ear was urging caution. "The standards in Russia are too high," he mumbled. "I wouldn't be accepted."

The man acknowledged this matter-of-factly, oblivious to the note of irony. "I'll say this as simply as I can, Alexei. Once the FSB starts to think of you as an extremist . . ."

Extremist!

". . . it will be very hard for you to leave the country. They won't let you go unless you can show yourself to be the best of Russia, someone who has demonstrated true loyalty. However . . ." He opened his hands, and his voice struck a more conciliatory note. "That isn't to say the FSB can't overlook this problem if you can make amends. Can you do that, Alexei?"

"Do what?"

"You will be given an opportunity. Very soon, I believe. And you must take it."

"What opportunity?"

He gave a sour, contemptuous smile. "If you have a shred of decency left in you, you'll do the right thing."

Lyosha did not trust himself to say another word. He left the office before his anger made him say something irreparable.

How dare that bastard presume to know what his father had wanted for him? His father hadn't even encouraged him to choose a career in law! Nor had he known that Lyosha had chosen law as his ticket out of Russia. What his father had actually said to him was ... Lyosha slowed his furious pace along the corridor and stopped. Suddenly his heart swelled. What his father had actually said was, "You must do whatever makes you happy."

He leaned against the wall, then slid to the floor and sat there, for how long he didn't know. When Professor Rykov passed him and said, "Young man, are you all right?" he was sitting against the wall with his arms around his knees. He saw that he'd torn his lecture notes into tiny pieces which lay like blossom around him.

As he headed home, and his mind became clearer, he thought over his exchange with 'University Security Advisor' Maxim Fyodorovich Yegorov. The suspicion that some kind of trap was being laid for him only intensified when he listened to a voicemail from Coach Golubev telling him to be on time for tomorrow's 4 p.m. friendly at the CSKA Arena.

A game at 4 p.m. *tomorrow!*? A game that included him?

Last time they'd spoken Golubev had told him to stay away until the YouTube furor had blown over. Lyosha had been left with the definite impression that he'd been dropped. He hadn't attended a team training session since. And they wanted him to play tomorrow afternoon?

He messaged the team's Telegram group chat to find out if this game was a surprise for them too, but no one responded ...

39

CIA Headquarters
Langley, Virginia

While Jenna spent her days evading surveillance on the streets and her evenings learning a new language, Russia Division had been crafting the legend for her cover. She was a recruitment officer named Sarah Hong. LinkedIn profile, family history, high school, names and birth dates of parents, social security number, IRS returns, bank accounts—it was all there. Everything had been carefully stitched into the complex tapestry of an American citizen. A passport was issued by the CIA via the State Department, with Sarah Hong's photograph and date of birth. Jenna memorized it all. Her social media, if anyone troubled to look, was a humdrum feed of elderly relatives, cute animals, unfiltered selfies, quotes from self-help books, and a half-assed practice of yoga. A few fleeting and unserious romances with some dull-looking men. A small circle of girlfriends—smiling in groups, wine glasses raised. A lot of workplace social events and awards evenings. No children. No independent income. A regular jogging habit, for which she often posted her Strava mileage. It was a solid, plausible cover. It felt right. Considerable imagination and flair had gone into the creation of a person so elusive to memory . . .

At the same time, Mira's team had been investigating the status of the twenty-one-year-old target, Alexei Dmitryevich Kuznetsov, now encrypted with the codename PROPHET.

The license plate of his car, a Lada Riva, had been identified. It was registered to a student apartment-share in the Barrikadnaya district of Moscow. A hacked feed from Moscow's traffic cameras revealed his car journeys. His lecture timetable was pulled; so was his ice hockey training schedule. His cellphone call records were produced.

"How did you get those?" Jenna said.

Mira shrugged. She was turning the pages of the fast-expanding file compiled on this kid, PROPHET. "Russia can appear so opaque that you can't see your hand in front of your face. But scratch the surface, and it's the most open society in the world, if you know what you're looking for. In Moscow, kids hanging out at traffic lights will sell you a disk for five bucks. They're a goldmine, an info-bazaar. Ask around, and one of them will have the city's entire license plate register. Tax records. Incorporation certificates. Drivers' licenses. Workplace IDs. Company accounts. Flight records." She stopped at a photograph of a middle-aged woman with wispy blond hair. No makeup. No collagen. A woman with her own gracefully ageing face. "That's interesting . . . OPUS's wife is a psychotherapist . . . with her own practice."

Very quickly a picture of PROPHET's family situation was emerging. His mother was Marina Vladimirovna. Her practice was just off the Old Arbat in Moscow. Her home address was a glitzy newbuild called Victory Palace on the embankment of the Moskva River. The family also owned an enormous new dacha in the Khimki Forest.

Alexei . . . a privileged life you've got, Jenna thought, as she mulled it over that evening.

In his student ID photo, he wore a small black ear stud she hadn't seen in other photos. She was struck again by the resemblance to his father. The same polar-blue eyes. Deep, honest, defiant.

Why did your father risk it all?

Humming with adrenaline from the final day's training and too nervous to sleep ahead of the looming journey to Russia, she sat up in bed and opened her laptop.

"Alexei Kuznetsov" was one of the most common names in Russia, Mira had said—but there he was at the top of the Cyrillic search list on YouTube. The thirteen-second clip of him on *Direct Line with Vladimir Putin* now had sixteen million views.

His face on the giant studio LED screens.

"*We have a lot of young people in the audience today. Let's have a question from one of them . . .*"

He was seated among Russian youths in a studio audience. Pale, visibly nervous, his hand trembling, voice unsteady.

"*Hello, Mr. President . . .*"

In the full, four-hour recording of the show—Jenna watched it all—the studio camera had captured him several times in the audience, looking edgy and apart. He had the loneliness of a person who was guarding the truth like a small flame in a gale, while all around him had surrendered to darkness. He did not join in the full-throttle applause with everyone else there.

"*You read your question. Did you write it yourself or did someone put you up to it?*"

The incident had been a public humiliation for Vladimir Putin—that much was clear from the reaction online. The internet was still free and uncensored in Russia, perhaps because it carried so much pro-Kremlin bile. She watched the clip over and over.

"*Life prepared me for this question.*"

That had taken real courage . . .

"What is the diminutive of Alexei?" she'd asked Natasha during one of her home-break-in tutoring sessions.

"The diminutive of Alexei is Lyosha."

Lyosha.

PART THREE
Moscow

You know, different people tend to "sink" into different things: some through tobacco, some through drugs, some through money. Some say that the biggest dependence is on power. I never felt it. I have never been addicted to anything.

V. V. Putin, April 2006

40

Aeroflot 105, IAD to SVO
Wednesday morning

Jenna boarded the plane from Washington Dulles to Moscow Sheremetyevo in the company of her new colleagues, the lawyers of the DC law firm Harley, Feinstein & Hawley. In the short time that had been available to her, she'd learned as much as she could about the firm. She knew that it did lucrative business in Russia, most of its clients being private banks, high net-worth individuals, and state-owned energy giants. The lawyers themselves—the usual mix of awkward-friendly and pompous asshole—had little time for a non-fee-earning employee like Sarah Hong and had paid her scant attention in the business-class departure lounge before boarding.

She spent the first few hours of the flight trying to study the résumés of every student who had registered their interest to meet the firm at tomorrow's careers fair at Moscow State University. Most of the same students had also accepted the invitation to the drinks reception later at the Metropol, which she could see from her info pack was a grand, art-nouveau establishment located just a stone's throw from Red Square. Among those who had RSVP'd was Lyosha, now codenamed PROPHET.

But her concentration was constantly broken by a colleague in the next seat. Not many people rubbed Jenna up the wrong way, but if circumstance had contrived to seat her next to one of the few who did, it had succeeded. Bethany Hollis was a senior corporate lawyer at the firm. Late forties, whippet-thin, and all sharp angles—beaklike nose, pointed elbows, hair dyed red and styled into a rigid, crash-helmet bob, and a voice that could strip paint from twenty yards.

"First time in Russia?"

"First time!" Sarah Hong said with a nervy gaiety.

"You're in for a treat. The *men*! Especially the young guys from Siberia. I swear to God they're made in some Soviet supermodel factory. They appreciate the mature woman, I can tell you. You married?"

"No, I—"

"Let's get us a couple of real Russian shots, eh?"

"Oh, no, I—"

"Excuse me!" Bethany was waving a thin arm at the steward, a rather sculpted young man with white-blond hair. "See what I mean?" she breathed, jabbing Jenna in the arm. "What's the best vodka you have?"

"We have a Stolichnaya premium label. It's distilled in Kaliningrad in—"

"Sure. Two of those."

Fortunately, the shot, followed by two more, sent Bethany into an open-mouthed sleep. Jenna gently moved the woman's elbow and shoulder blade out of her personal space and gazed out of the window.

America had fallen away beneath her. So little of her real life remained in America that she might almost never have lived there. For the next two days, she was Sarah Hong and Sarah Hong could put up with Bethany. Her passport was stamped with a forty-eight-hour business visa. She was entering a hostile country as a private citizen. She'd done this a hundred times before, but the stress of it never went away. Different passports, crossing borders, struggling to keep an endless list of lies straight in her head knowing that one wrong answer could cost her her life.

The last nine days had been filled so exhaustively with her training and preparation for this op that she'd barely had time to eat or sleep, let alone to dwell on the fact that the mystery she was leaving behind remained unsolved, and had more or less been taken out of her hands. The retired ops officers in Annandale were keeping an eye on Soo-min for her, and as far as she knew the CIA had not yet involved the FBI in the hunt for the North Korean Seed-Bearing operative. When she'd asked Fisk about it, he'd had nothing yet to report. When she asked about Adam, the nurse from the Mount Vernon Hospital, she'd learned that he had never returned to work and that his friends had reported him missing to local law enforcement. Jenna had tried to resist the natural human impulse to join the dots into a compelling narrative—something she'd always been cautioned against in analysis work—but it was hard not to suspect that the lone North Korean had had a hand in the nurse's disappearance. If he had visited Soo-min that day at the hospital, then there might be only two witnesses: Soo-min, who would never talk, and the nurse, who had now vanished . . .

She made herself comfortable and settled into her blanket. High over the Atlantic she watched brief, fiery rays of glory as the sun passed in the opposite direction. Soon, she had drifted off to sleep. She dreamed that she was walking along the ridge of an ancient, rocky promontory that was leading her out into an endless dark sea. She saw herself grow ever smaller and in ever greater danger of being swept away by the towering waves. She was searching for Soo-min, but what hope was there of finding her when Soo-min was lost in the deep? And the waves were very strange. Viscous and reddish. She scooped water into her hand and felt thousands of tiny cells swarming, metastasizing and coagulating in her palm, forming horrible seed-like shapes.

She awoke with a start. The cabin was dimmed and slumbering

to the hum of the aircraft. For the first time, she was afraid, afraid in a pit-of-the-stomach, end-of-the-world kind of way.

She was glad that Fisk was in Moscow. Even if it was too risky to meet him, she was comforted to know he was there, her lighthouse in the dark.

She drifted in and out of uneasy dreams, until a female Russian voice announced the plane's descent. Minutes later, head pressed to the window, she had a clear view of Moscow at night: a spiderweb of concentric ring roads sparkling with the lights of luxury stores and limousines. And there, in the center, the Kremlin. Only thirty years ago, she thought, it had glowed a dim, dirty yellow, a dying ember on the dark fringe of Europe. Now it was a bright, cold neutron star, radiating arcs of malign power.

The wheels lowered for landing with a hydraulic whine.

41

Moscow State University
Sparrow Hills, Moscow

It was almost 2 a.m. by the time the lawyers checked in to the Hotel Metropol and went straight to bed. At ten the next morning, on a bright March day with cold blue skies, they traveled by minibus to the Sparrow Hills district of the city, which was dominated by the fantastical Stalinist skyscraper that was Moscow State University.

The building was a monster—an unembarrassed statement of power and domination, for which the tiny human figures on the ground were required only for the purposes of scale. Its ornate spire held a vast pointed star. To the tower's left and right the wings rose in tiers adorned with clocks, statues of heroic labor, carved wheat sheaves, and Soviet crests. She wanted to hate it. And yet, she was awed by the integrity of its brutality. Russia's premier university, home to forty thousand undergraduates.

If the exterior of MGU was naked power, the inside was flaking wood, weeping concrete, dusty marble. In the vast colonnaded hall used for career fairs, the law firm set up its stand among dozens of rival US and European firms. The marble amplified the noise, and Bethany Hollis's voice. She was wearing a lime-green business suit, which Jenna thought unforgiving on a woman with dyed red hair.

Sarah Hong chatted brightly to dozens of undergraduates. An interpreter was on hand, but most of them spoke eager, excellent English. She explained the firm's areas of interest, trainee application process, visa requirements, answering questions as best she could. But by 2 p.m. she was feeling decidedly uneasy. Harley, Feinstein & Hawley had been a major draw for MGU's senior year law students, but she had seen no sign of PROPHET.

By 4 p.m. the lawyers were back at the Hotel Metropol. That gave her three free hours before the evening drinks reception.

She had hoped her contingency plan would not be necessary, but she was left with no choice. PROPHET's no-show this morning had already complicated her mission.

To prepare, she meditated for a while in her room, counting her breaths, stilling her mind until she'd accessed that calm, alert space she needed before a risky action. Then she got changed, texted the lawyers to say she was going for a run, tied her hair back, and left the hotel in Lycra, running shoes, wraparound Oakleys, and ear pods. The receptionist asked if she needed a map. She held up her phone, saying she'd programmed a route.

She set off at a slow, steady pace, past the gloomy monument to Karl Marx, past the Lubyanka, the notorious secret-police headquarters, toward the Boulevard Ring, with the mechanized voice in her ear pods telling her where to make a left or right. The thrill she felt at being out on the streets of Moscow almost ruffled her calm completely. Moscow was beautiful, romantic, huge in its scale. Streets were eight lanes wide, built for tanks and rocket launchers rather than cars. Here, the state, not the people, was almighty. The domed spires of the Kremlin churches flashed gold in the glowing, late-afternoon sky. Boxy green Soviet-era Zhigulis trailed oily fumes amid the gleaming Bentleys and Mercedes with darkened windows. And police, the police were everywhere. Pedestrians gave them a wide berth.

She crossed the eight lanes at an underpass and emerged in a park that ran along the center of the Boulevard ring. If the FSB had eyes on her, a good run would stretch their surveillance, create opportunities for her to detect watchers. When she was out of sight she changed direction, making them guess wrong, watching for any repeat vehicles or pedestrians, any hats, coats, she'd seen before. She was *feeling the street*. But after twenty minutes running almost at a sprint, so that steam was rising off her in the frosty air, she'd seen nothing suspicious. That didn't mean they weren't watching, of course, just that they were very good. That jogger stopping to tie his laces near the fountain. The babushka in the lottery-ticket kiosk. It took a special level of training to spot the tiny signs that they might be professionals. The danger with all this, she thought, was that it made you hyperaware. You started seeing ghosts—watchers where there were none.

She continued her jog along the tree-lined park at the center of the Sretensky Boulevard, past the monument to Comrade Engineer Shukhov, then she took a sudden left, re-crossing the boulevard at the lights, and selected a route that circled back, via the lanes leading off Kostiansky. Then she slipped into a dim courtyard of an old building with a façade of cracked pastel. A few high-end BMWs and SUVs were parked in the arches where liverymen would once have attended to horses. In the left-hand corner of the courtyard, she pressed a vintage intercom buzzer for apartment 43. There was a pause and then a crackly buzz before a woman's voice said in Russian, "Come up." The door clicked open, and Jenna climbed a stained marble staircase to the third floor.

On the landing an elderly Georgian woman was holding her apartment door open. Short, spry, with unruly, wavy gray hair and friendly, twinkling eyes. In her mid- to late seventies, Jenna guessed.

"Come in, dear." The woman cast a quick glance left and right into the landing before closing the door behind Jenna. She switched to English. "We've been looking forward to meeting you. Some tea?"

"Water, please," Jenna said, breathing hard.

"Of course, you've been running!"

She scuttled off down a narrow hallway, exuding an air of energy and zest. "You're surprised I'm so old?" she called back to Jenna. Jenna took off her sneakers and followed her. "At seventy, Georgian women are in their prime. They climb mountains, eat fruit, and chase men. You know who said that? Josef Vissarionovich Stalin!" She laughed gaily from the kitchen.

Jenna knew the woman only by her cover name, Elene. She wore tan stockings and lace-up boots and a worn, brown woolen cardigan that told Jenna straight away that none of the luxury cars in the courtyard belonged to this apartment. She was welcomed into a spacious sitting room with a view out onto a small park where the ice rink doubled as a pond in summer. The flooring was of polished parquet. While Elene was getting ice out of the freezer, Jenna looked around at the shelves creaking with decaying encyclopedias, volumes of Pushkin, Tolstoy; at the enormous, Khrushchev-era radio, the framed photographs on the wall. In one, a much younger Elene was posing in a bathing costume on a beach with an athletic young man, their hair swept back and both laughing. Beneath it in pencil was written *Sochi, 1968*.

She returned with Jenna's water, rattling with ice cubes, which she gratefully drank down.

"You have a lovely home."

"The apartment was given to Volodymyr's father for services to the Soviet Union. He was a physicist at the Radium Institute in Kiev. Of course, a space like this is worth a fortune now . . ." She looked doubtfully around the room. "One of the reasons we've stayed."

"Is Volodymyr home?" She'd been expecting to meet husband and wife.

"You didn't think we'd let you walk in here without cover, did you, dear?" Elene said, laughing again as she poured herself tea.

"What terrible hosts we'd be. He's outside, making sure no one followed you."

A key rattled in the door.

"Talk of the devil."

A tall, slender man with a white mustache walked in, and hung up his hat and coat. He smiled warmly and shook Jenna's hand with an iron grip. Jenna recognized the man from the photo, long since aged and retired, and still handsome.

"You didn't see me?" he said.

"No . . ." Jenna hesitated. She can't have missed him. She'd run every street in this neighborhood and doubled back on herself to make sure she was clean. She rewound the last few blocks in her mind "Wait. Bus stop on the corner of Rybnikov. Newspaper and walking stick."

"That was me. Welcome to Moscow."

She could easily have missed that.

Elene and Volodymyr, married for forty years, had been CIA Moscow Station's star surveillance team for decades. Jenna had read their file. Their services were so valued that elaborate precautions had been taken to protect them. No one from the embassy or Station ever contacted them directly. Both were retired schoolteachers of Russian literature and had lived in Moscow all their lives, but neither of them was Russian. Volodymyr had grown up in Kiev, Ukraine; Elene in Tbilisi, Georgia. They had six grandchildren, in Ukraine and in Georgia, and made visits to them several times a year. The CIA only ever briefed them outside Russia. They knew Moscow intimately, every metro exit and alleyway. They had an old-school talent for changing their appearances—a well-heeled couple dressed for the ballet one day, a pair of down-and-outs the next. They used prop umbrellas, wigs, glasses, vodka bottles. It was that doggedness, the operational patience to watch a target for weeks, months, that allowed them to stay under the radar. Everything about them, and the apartment she was sitting in, told Jenna that this man and woman had a deep love for Russia, and were heartbroken by what was happening to it. They had decided long ago that open dissent was futile. Their resistance to the regime was personal, very dangerous, and much more effective.

Elene made tea the Russian way, pouring super-strong black shots from a teapot, and topping it up with steaming water from a samovar. Then she went into the kitchen and returned with a tray laden with the kind of Russian hospitality spread Bethany Hollis had warned her about on the plane, all sweating pickles, jellied pieces of meat, and preserved fish.

They sipped the tea in silence for a moment. The hot drink had the effect of cooling Jenna down.

Then Volodymyr said, "Who is this poor rabbit Mr. Fisk has given us, young lady?" He sighed, and Jenna sensed a sadness between them, a disappointment, a sense they'd been given a target that was beneath their abilities. "He's an innocent. He has no idea he's in the Game. Needless to say, he does not suspect surveillance."

"You've seen coverage on him?"

"It's none of our business," Elene said carefully, "and we do not expect you to tell us, but if you're planning to meet with this young man, we must urge extreme caution. We detected a very high level of surveillance on him. They're watching him from the moment he leaves his apartment until the moment he gets home. An inner team and another one at the margins, working in shifts. They've got him wrapped up in onion skins. He trains alone, not with his team, at the CSKA Ice Palace in the early morning or in the evening, after class. He picks up dinner from Teremok, a kind of Russian knock-off of McDonald's on Tverskaya, and he's been staying at his mother's apartment on the embankment since his father's funeral. The only person he meets is a student called Anya Antonovna, who is also on the FSB's radar. She's involved in opposition politics and she's also being watched. He never goes back to her place, and she's been to his only once. I think she's his girlfriend. Volodymyr disagrees with me. He's been skipping most of his lectures, but he attended class yesterday and was in this morning."

"Alexei was at Moscow State this morning?" Jenna said, dismayed.

"Nine o'clock law examination until eleven. He left the campus at 11:30 and went straight home. At least . . ."

Jenna hoped to God he hadn't changed his mind about this evening's reception.

"We're pretty sure he went home. We avoid trailing him to the door of his mother's apartment. Too many watchers."

"That's not the only reason," Volodymyr said, frowning. "One of the recent visitors to his mother's apartment was Vadim Ivanovich Giorgadze . . . That's not a person we get too close to. He's, ah, very senior in Russian counterintelligence."

"Another Georgian," Elene said, trying to keep her tone light, but Jenna saw nervousness in her eyes.

"I know who he is," Jenna said. *The spy-catcher.*

"One more word of caution," Elene said. "Everyone recognizes this poor boy. He's famous suddenly, so it's hard for him to go anywhere without people trying to stop him and take pictures. It's quite a problem for him. You don't want to get yourself snapped on someone's phone."

"If I may say so," Volodymyr said kindly, "if this kid's caught up in the fallout from something big, it would be a shame."

"He seems like a nice person," Elene said, "and he's troubled and lonely."

"I think he's gay," Volodymyr said, sipping his tea.

"No, I don't think so," Elene said with a tut. "That girl seems to really care for him."

42

CSKA Ice Palace
Moscow

Lyosha saw at once that something was up. He had arrived early at the CSKA Arena. FSB vans and police wagons were parked in the forecourt, and multiple buses were disgorging hundreds of people, all of them young and wearing the red, white and blue tricolors of the national flag. The buses had out-of-town license plates.

Who were they? Fans? A week-day college friendly was lucky to attract a crowd of fifty.

Inside the arena lobby, uniformed FSB were everywhere with sniffer dogs. His ID was checked; his bag emptied and searched. He had to pass through a metal detector.

On the rink, the ice resurfacing machine was humming in slow, decreasing circles, smoothing out the ruts and slashes made by skates, spraying water to make fresh, glassy ice.

Lyosha felt a growing unease. He was the first in the locker room and got changed into his yellow jersey. One by one his teammates began to arrive. He raised his hand to high-five them, but all of them avoided his eyes.

"Why are there so many cops?" one said.

Another shrugged. "Fucking bomb threats."

"Where's that crowd from?"

"They must've got the wrong date."

The locker room continued to fill. The lads, conscious of Lyosha's presence, were talking with an exaggerated boisterousness that didn't include him. All of them were pointedly giving him space. The last of the players arrived, making the narrow room cluttered and noisy. Morale-boosting yowls and pre-game banter. The sweat-spore, all-male smell of a team revved up, pumped with adrenaline, and ready to play like hell—but all of it excluded Lyosha. He knew that most of them were patriots with a disdain for liberals. If they were trying to shame him for *Direct Line*, it was working. He felt chilled by hurt. He turned his back on them, to save them the effort of shunning him. They must have heard that his father had died, too. Not one of them offered their condolences.

They fell quiet when Coach Golubev entered, red-faced and out of breath, with two of the refs in their striped jerseys. He climbed stiffly up onto the bench.

Golubev was an old-school Soviet type who had a habit of yelling at them as if addressing a regiment. So Lyosha was surprised when spoke in a low, anxious voice.

"Right lads. Change of plan. Moscow Mules have canceled. They've all got the shits."

"*Whaaat? Nooo!*"

"I know, I know . . .", Golubev raised his palms, waiting for the commotion to die down. "However . . . *however*, the game will go ahead. We've got a substitute opposition. The Night Hockey League have agreed to play our friendly. They're getting changed now."

The team were stunned, Lyosha included.

"The Night Hockey League. Is this a joke?"

"The retired guys?"

"Now, obviously, they don't play at our level. They're older players. They're slower. They play for sport. I want you all to show them some respect out there. *Sportsmanship*. This evening is pure entertainment, guys. We'll play a good game, but it's all for fun. Winning's not important."

Winning's not important?!

Was he drunk? Golubev usually threatened them with castration and the branding of their asses with red-hot irons if they even missed a pass.

"All right. Get your gear on. They're waiting for us. We'll play a twenty-minute warm-up before the game. Let's hit the ice in five minutes."

The mood in the room deflated. A few were laughing. *The Night Hockey League!*

No one was taking the game seriously now. Lyosha strapped on his massive, padded pants with tail-bone protector that made his legs look like giant Lego bricks.

They filed out of the locker room, carrying their helmets and skates. Lyosha was last in the line.

Golubev grabbed him by the elbow and fixed him with a strange look, full of warning. "*Sportsmanship*, Kuznetsov," he hissed. "Understand?"

If he hadn't known Golubev so well, he'd have said the man seemed afraid.

And in that moment, Lyosha knew—that whatever was going on here this evening, it was because of him. He was at the center of this, but he didn't understand how.

He should have seen it coming.

In the tunnel that led to the arena he sat on the floor to pull on his skates, and a shadow fell over him, a figure blocking the light. He looked up to see an FSB man in a gray ushanka.

"Alexei Kuznetsov? Your phone's ringing."

The man was holding out Lyosha's *own phone*, taken from his bag in his locker, which he had just locked.

He took the phone. It was Anya. Her voice sounded strained.

"Hey. Guess where I am."

She didn't need to explain. "Which station?"

"Petrovka, I think. They all look the same. Can you call my lawyer and let my mother know?"

"What's the charge?"

"Nothing yet. You know they like to keep me guessing." She was trying to sound casual about it, but Lyosha could hear the panic in her voice.

"All right, stay calm. We'll get you out of there."

"I will, but can you send Bazurov over here right now? They've been really rough with me this time. It's like they singled me out. No one else was arrested." He heard raised men's voices in the background. "Hey, my time's up. I love you, OK?" The line went dead.

The FSB man was still standing over him, listening to the call. Then he snatched the phone out of Lyosha's hand before Lyosha could make any calls of his own, "I will return it to your locker for you."

The trap was revealing itself.

"Don't forget your gloves," the man said, handing them to Lyosha.

From the arena at the end of the tunnel, the music started up.

BOM—BOM—BOM...ANOTHER ONE BITES THE DUST!

He turned his head toward the reverberating sound. A hard ball of dread was forming in his chest. Echoing up the tunnel was the sound of a truly enormous crowd, cheering and stamping their feet to the beat.

AND ANOTHER ONE DOWN, AND ANOTHER ONE DOWN...

Lyosha rose slowly from the floor and put on his helmet. He could hear his own breathing, as if he had water in his ear. He could hear the railroad beat of his heart. His face was cold and tingling. Everything around him, his teammates, the noise of the arena, had become surreal. A hallucination. A waking nightmare. If he closed his eyes and refused to play, maybe it would all vanish. Maybe nothing bad would happen to him, but he no longer cared what happened to him. If he didn't play, Anya would be doomed.

Lyosha glided slowly into the rink feeling like a man who had been fatally marked.

He'd never seen a crowd this size for a college friendly. But this was no ordinary game, he knew that now. Lyosha's team entered the rink for the warm-up. The seats were still filling.

The noise was tremendous. The music. The applause. The crowd sparkled with cellphone flashes. Drummers on each side of the rink thundered out a deafening rhythm. Cheerleaders waved tinsel pom-poms above their heads in the aisles. Spotlights and lasers formed kaleidoscope patterns on the ice.

In they came. The Night Hockey League entered to an earth-tremor of applause. Red jerseys, white helmets. All of them oldies, retired FSB men, bodyguards, and former army officers, gliding stiffly past Lyosha's team, bumping their gloved fists along the line in greeting. The crowd began to chant.

"RUSS-IA! RUSS-IA! RUSS-IA!"

Suddenly the cheer rose to a frenzy. In came the famous number 11 jersey.

He was bareheaded, so that the people could look upon him. In gear and pads he appeared *tiny*, Lyosha thought. A tiny cartoon superhero. Mighty Mouse. Spongebob.

Little Putin . . . Lilliputin . . .

He skated along the lines of players—his own team's and the opponents—bumping fists a little stiffly, Lyosha's included. Lyosha did not look at him.

Tension ran along the line of his team. A few of them gasped. The amazement. The honor. The joy.

Sportsmanship . . . Now they understood what old Golubev was on about. Of *course* they would show sportsmanship!

Once both teams were facing each other in two orderly lines, the stadium's audio played the first note of the national anthem and like an army the crowd stood as one.

"*Russia is our sacred state,*

Russia is our beloved land . . ."

It ended in another ground-shaking eruption of applause. The whistle blew.

Lyosha's own team's defensemen opened up a wide space around the president.

He had seen Putin play in gala games on TV, and had been forced to admit that he exhibited some above-average skill for a sixty-something amateur, although of course they edited out his embarrassing misses, and the occasions when he tumbled flat on his face on the ice. Lyosha was also pretty sure that they sped up the video when he aimed one of his shots, which were laughably slow and—a miracle!—always hit the back of the net.

Putin's teammates also moved aside to clear a path for him, skating away from him in wide, cautious arcs. Lyosha could see they were experienced players, but they were slow, stiff. They left the neutral zone wide open so Putin could move unopposed.

No one tackled him. No one went anywhere near him.

Watching this Lyosha was reminded of one of those pretend, wish-come-true games for a kid with leukemia. He'd seen more speed in an under-elevens game.

Putin aimed a first shot at Lyosha's net.

Missed!

It hit the Perspex wall like a gunshot. And just for a moment Lyosha felt the exhilaration of a reprieve.

The crowd breathed a good-natured, "*Ohhhh.*"

The reprieve did not last. Four minutes later, the president was moving in for another wide-open shot. This time he slowed right down, steadied the puck with his stick, and putted it weakly toward the net.

Time seemed to thicken and slow. Lyosha watched it travel across the ice toward him. The feeling of unreality was acute now. He was a supporting actor, a sidekick, and the director was counting on him for laughs. Lyosha made a lame pretense of saving the goal, moving as if he were underwater. The shot hit the back of the net. The crowd went wild, and they were laughing.

Laughing at Lyosha.

Two minutes later, the president scored again. Lyosha had seen the shot coming a mile off. He let it fly into the net.

The next hour was pure misery for him. The game was a farce. It had none of the momentum that usually thrilled a crowd—when a forward, crouching and sprinting, surrounded by his wingers, became a miracle of speed and the whole team moved like a swarm of attacking bees. But the crowd didn't seem to mind. They were here to watch the president of the Russian Federation and he could do no wrong. In fact, he could do anything in the world. Fly fighter jets. Paraglide with snow geese. Ride horses bareback.

A black belt in judo! A champion marksman!

The Night Hockey League played an old-fashioned game. Collective, Soviet. Every player in the five-man unit passed the puck a dozen times in a tic-tac-toe before shooting. The referees ignored all their fouls.

What a joke. He was part of the joke.

It occurred to Lyosha then that if he was going to make Putin's game look real, he had to stop at least one of the shots.

So he did—*clack*—and passed the puck to Yuri, his teammate. But Yuri let it fly by, a gift with ribbons to the Night Hockey defensemen.

At the first interval, Golubev again pulled him aside.

"Hey, fuck face. Remember what I said: this is for *fun*! Show some fucking sportsmanship or I'll have your *balls on toast*."

The Night Hockey League won the game 14–7. Top scorer: Vladimir Vladimirovich Putin. The man of the match.

The great man gave a short speech in front of a mic on the ice, helmet in hand. TV, news cameras and press crowded around him at the side of the rink.

"Friends, sports fans, spectators, athletes!" He was flushed from the exercise and giving a rare smile of pleasure. "I congratulate you all. Thank you for inspiring millions of people to get involved in sports. I saw the so-called amateurs play—they were simply impressive. It is not easy for our star students to play against us—particularly as I represent you on the team . . ."

Knowing laughter from the audience.

"Next week, the Ice Hockey World Championship starts. Russia will play against Finland, a strong team. Let us wish them every success. Glory to Russia!"

The crowd applauded generously.

The president posed for a group photo with both teams and signed everyone's jersey with a Sharpie pen. Lyosha watched him write *V. V. Putin* on his yellow jersey, which he resolved to throw in the garbage later.

Finally, the moment arrived. The true purpose of this elaborate public-relations sham: the photograph of Lyosha and the president. Lyosha removed his gloves.

"*Smile!*" someone spat in his ear.

Putin's pale pudding-face turned toward him only for a second, the contemptuous gray eyes meeting his for the brief camera flash that captured the grin and grip. Their hands locked. They turned their heads to another bank of cameras. Another barrage of flashes.

The president and Russia's most famous YouTube star were friends again! All was forgiven. Youth had spoken, and the president had listened. Lyosha's role was done.

In the locker room, he found his phone, which had been returned to his bag. The first message on Telegram was from Anya.

Hey. They let me go!!!

What was that game??? It's all over YouTube.

Call me?

His spirits went into free fall. He checked the news channels, feeling his heart become buttery and faint.

It was worse than he could ever have imagined.

A quote purportedly from him, in words written by the Kremlin, accompanied a smiling photo of his face next to Putin's.

> *One emotional MGU player, Alexei Kuznetsov, who is the son of war hero Dmitry Stepanovich Kuznetsov, had this to say:*
>
> *"I'm insanely grateful to the president. He knows me better than I know myself. Before the game he offered me his condolences because I've just lost my father. To be honest, it made me really ashamed of my antics on YouTube. He knew I'd been duped by the West to stir up trouble. He said he understood that young people get confused sometimes and told me not to feel embarrassed. The president is wise. He is really wise. He sees far beyond what we can possibly see. He does what he must to defend Russia. And did you see him play tonight? I'm no match for a talent like that."*

Dissidents, as everyone knew, were the saddest kind of martyr. Lonely, unglamorous, outcast. What he hadn't known was that there was a further fall. In the lowest deep, a lower deep now was opening wide, about to devour him whole. After *dissident* came a status that was beneath all contempt. The *sell-out*.

The backlash online had already started.

Hero to zero. Dissident to worse-than-scum. Puppet, fraud, laughingstock.

Lyosha changed as fast as he could and left the arena without a word to the others. Coach Golubev tried to detain him again, but Lyosha shoved past him. Outside he pulled his beanie down low and turned up the collar of his coat.

He was too ashamed to call Anya, because Anya—brave, principled, stubborn-headed Anya—would have told him *not to do it*.

She would have gone to prison rather than see him humiliated like that, by a man she despised.

He started walking. He had a confused idea that he should go to his mother at the Victory Palace apartment. She would be worried about him. He would have to take a taxi. He couldn't risk the metro.

Suddenly he stopped and leaned his forehead against a wall, breathing hard. He wanted to scream and howl in despair at the world. He wanted to crawl away somewhere and die alone.

In a street just off Yakimanka he found a small Armenian bar with low amber lighting and walls decorated with old records.

He asked for a bottle of Kursk and sat at a corner table with his back to the room, which had only a handful of drinkers. The sound system was playing "Vladimirsky Tsentral," the gangster ballad heard in every wedding, restaurant, taxicab. A gravelly voice sang about ice melting on prison bars, and missing mother. The music nudged him closer to the looming depression. He could feel it inviting him in, as if through a dark cellar door. On the soundless TV in the corner of the room, a blind girl was asking Putin if she could touch his face.

Everything had slipped through his fingers and was lost. His dignity, his personal safety, his privacy, his college life, his self-esteem. His ice hockey. His father.

What had gone wrong between him and Papa? Why had they fallen out?

He swallowed a large gulp of beer and felt its effect dull his brain.

If that light switch on the wall in front of him could end his life for him in an instant, would he get up and press it?

He thought of the women in his life, Anya and his mother. Lyosha had introduced them last year over lunch at the GUM department store, an occasion that had only invited embarrassing questions for him. His mother had kept grinning at him in that telling way of hers. "Well! She's very pretty, isn't she?" she said afterward. "Is she your girlfriend?"

"She's not my girlfriend." He hadn't liked the question because lurking behind it were the other questions he found more difficult to answer, but which he'd asked himself many times. *What kind of girls do you like? Are you gay?* This last question had been asked—actually spoken aloud—by a teammate on a drunken night after training, and the others had jumped to Lyosha's defense with supposed evidence of his heterosexuality. He wished he could simply have said, "No, I am straight," or "Yes, I am gay." But the truth was, he did not know the answer himself. He was twenty-one years old, and he was the only person he knew who had never experienced any real sexual intimacy. Anya, with the antenna for such things that women possess more than men, sensed the confusion, and did not press him.

He was contemplating another Kursk when the ice hockey game came on the TV. It was the sports item at the end of the seven o'clock Channel One News. He dared not look around.

Its highlights showed three of Putin's shots, and Lyosha's lamentable attempts at stopping the puck. Then he saw his own face, a calcified mask of smile and dread, shaking hands with the Vozhd . . .

A voice behind him in the corner said, "It's him! I told you it was him."

In the periphery of his vision, he clocked two young men at the table near the door. Normally his defenses would have shot up. Perhaps it was the beer, but he was feeling a numb indifference. In fact, there was a part of him that almost welcomed some drama. Perhaps he had been inviting disaster by coming here.

The next thing he knew one of them was standing over him. "It's you, right?"

A young man, perhaps no older than twenty, was leering at him with a full lower set of gold teeth. He wore a cheap black leather jacket.

Lyosha sighed. "Can I help you?"

"I'm Mitya. This is Seryozha."

Then a second man was at the table, an enormous blond bear of a man, this one in a shell suit and gold chains around his neck. "You're famous, right? Can we buy you a drink?"

"Guys . . ."

"Just one. Come on."

Shell Suit had his phone out and was talking. ". . . I swear to God. We're talking to him right now . . ."

"Guys, listen," Lyosha said. "I just need to be alone for a bit. Then I'll come over and have a drink with you. OK?"

"You promise?" Gold Teeth said.

They went back to their table and Lyosha closed his eyes.

Moments later he heard another man enter the bar. "See? There he is. It's like he's got no friends."

Now there were three of them. Lyosha risked a quick glance.

"We're waiting for you!" one of them called.

The new guy was wearing a tartan golf cap. These were *shpana*, Lyosha thought, scum. Men who used to be at the margins of life, but whose behavior was now copied by everyone, including the president. They wore the same cynical smirk, the smile of men who see everything.

Lyosha got up.

"Hey, where are you going?"

"To get cigarettes. I'll be back."

"Leave your bag here." He was still carrying his huge sports bag with three hockey sticks.

He pushed through the bar's door and out into the alley, which was now much darker. The street was poorly lit. The door opened again behind him, and they caught up with him at once. Three of them.

"We were going to have a drink! Hey!"

"Group photo," Shell Suit said, "Group photo." They were laughing now, an ominous hilarity. Their breath was stale with beer.

Shell Suit turned on the flashlight on his phone. It was blinding in Lyosha's eyes. Gold Teeth locked his arm around Lyosha's shoulders for the photo.

"He's prettier in real life, isn't he? I bet you don't have to go into the army, eh?" He forced his fingers over the edges of Lyosha's mouth. "Come on—*smile*."

Lyosha pushed the guy's hand away and shoved him hard backward. "That's enough."

The mood darkened.

Gold Teeth barred his way, opened his leather jacket and showed Lyosha a gun. "Look. See?"

Lyosha pushed him out of the way and started to walk. Shell Suit yanked him back by the grip on his bag. "Too good for us, eh?"

The first punch to his head made his vision go blank. Then they were all at it. Knuckles pounding his face. He fell hard on the wet sidewalk and they started kicking his ribs, his legs. His testicles.

"*Stuck-up . . . elitny . . . cunt!*"

Lyosha curled up to protect himself from the blows. He put up no resistance.

When they stopped and turned him over, blood was pouring from his lip, his ear, his forehead. His face was swelling fast, and on fire, his ribs were exploded landmines of pain.

Gold Teeth pointed the gun at his forehead. "You think I don't have the guts?"

Lyosha heard a roaring wind that seemed to come from far away, and felt a strange stillness in his heart. He looked calmly into their faces, and their smiles faded.

Something in his eyes had spooked them. They saw not terror, or desperation, or drunkenness, but a total indifference.

"Man . . . just messing with you."

From some distance, a man's voice yelled "Police!"

Behind the tinnitus in his ears, he heard his attackers running away into the dark.

He groaned and got shakingly up onto his elbows, grimacing from the pain. Through his watering eyes he thought he saw the lone figure of an old man with a walking stick watching him from the end of the street. Then the man disappeared.

Lyosha touched his lip.

It was starting to rain. He took out his phone to call Anya. The screen was cracked. It showed a calendar notification reminder.

Drinks reception. Harley, Feinstein & Hawley. Hotel Metropol. 19:00.

The event had started a few minutes ago.

43

Hotel Metropol
Moscow

About eighty students from the MGU faculty of law, among them some of the brightest kids in Moscow, were standing about in groups, talking to the lawyers of Harley, Feinstein & Hawley. The room was magnificent: a blaze of gold and green damask; doors gilded with laurel wreaths; glittering samovars in each corner were reflected in the mirrors. It reminded Jenna of the ballroom scenes in *War and Peace*. She declined a glass of champagne, quelled her nerves, and got to work. Sarah Hong, she reminded herself, was a people person! Fun, social, sunny, helpful. Years ago, at the Farm, she had endured evenings similar to this one: training for black-tie embassy social events, where instructors had role-played obnoxious ambassadors or disgruntled nuclear scientists, and the trainees were required to use clever cocktail repartee to elicit snippets of intel or signals that someone was open to corruption by the CIA. She circled clockwise around the outer edges of the room, scouting for PROPHET. No sign of him yet.

Staff were serving drinks and American-themed canapés—corny, she thought, especially the mac 'n' cheese sliders. Jenna introduced herself to the students, remembered names, recalled details from their résumés, asked questions. Most of them spoke the textbook English of a first-rate education. "How do you do. It's my pleasure to meet you." Young people the world over were the same, she thought: some mute with shyness, some aping confidence. All the same, she was struck by the impression these kids made. Courteous, well-informed, well-presented. In Russia, an evening out meant dressing to the nines—boys in dark suits and polished shoes; girls with hair up and heavy on the eyeliner.

She was trying to avoid glancing at the doors each time more guests arrived.

It was now 8 p.m. The event ended in an hour. *Where are you, PROPHET?*

Even if he'd arrived on time, she had a worryingly small window to establish any kind of bond with him, build trust. She was certain someone in this room would be watching him. And then there was the question of how he would react to Sarah Hong.

Butterflies were somersaulting in her stomach; she headed to the ladies' washroom. She'd opted for a simple midnight-blue dress with a gold necklace and her hair tied loosely back. Plain, businesslike. Nothing sexy. She stared at her reflection and steadied her breathing.

Everything she'd learned about PROPHET told her only so much. Assumptions she'd made about his character, state of mind, beliefs, motivations, were just those—*assumptions*. She would have to judge the situation very quickly because she had *one shot* at securing a second meeting with him, which would have to be tomorrow. The second meeting would also be a high-stakes gamble. If she couldn't persuade him to produce the cufflinks tomorrow, she would have to direct him to a drop site: a coffee shop near his shared apartment in Barrikadnaya where he could leave them in the pot used for customer tips. But there was no guarantee that he'd surrender the cufflinks to a stranger. They might be precious to him, a poignant memento of his father. If he refused, she'd be forced to play her ace: she would tell him the biggest thing he never knew about his father. She could *not* fail. There was too much on the line.

Panic again. *Fight it. You're a trained CIA case officer. Assess the target. Elicit information. Manipulate his vulnerabilities. Retrieve the intelligence.*

A toilet flushed in a cubicle behind her, and Bethany Hollis emerged from behind a cloud of vape smoke. "Oh, Sarah, how're you getting on?" Her voice seemed to make the mirror vibrate.

She joined Jenna at the washbasins, looking rectangular and severe in a black pin-striped smoking jacket and stilettos.

"They're impressive, really impressive," Sarah Hong said, nodding.

"Yeah," Bethany drawled, reapplying her lipstick with an exaggerated leer. "I've got my eye on one or two." She gave Jenna a lascivious wink in the reflection.

More guests had arrived, including an older, strongly built forty-something man with a gray buzz cut and an ill-fitting gray suit. Jenna had an instant bad feeling about him. He looked like a nightclub bouncer. He was years older than the students, who seemed unsettled by his arrival in the room. His vibe was heavy, oppressive. Everything about him screamed security services. The students began inching away from him the moment Jenna approached.

"Mr. . . . Yegorov?" she said, reading his name tag. "I'm the recruitment officer, Sarah Hong." She offered her hand.

"Maxim Fyodorovich Yegorov," he said without smiling. His grip was crushing.

Not a name on my list. "You're a doctoral student?"

"Student? No." He was regarding her with a mix of curiosity and aversion, as if he'd come face to face with a type he'd heard nothing good about. "I am a chaperone, you could say."

"The students need a chaperone?"

He moved his head from side to side in that Russian yes-and-no gesture. "We want to make sure you Americans get a nice impression of us."

Jenna smiled. *Every regime depends on people like you,* she thought. *A creature who is bred over decades by subservience, and who is rewarded with small amounts of power.* She was about to disengage herself, when his expression turned suddenly hostile.

He was looking over her shoulder.

She turned and saw PROPHET outside the door. He seemed to be having an altercation with a staff member who was telling him he had to check in his bag, which was enormous and had hockey sticks protruding from it.

"As you can see," Maxim Fyodorovich said, "not all our students know how to conduct themselves."

"Excuse me, please." Jenna headed straight to the door.

PROPHET, now parted from his bag, looked hesitant, bewildered. He was in clothes that looked as if he'd been wearing them all day: jeans, lace-up boots, and a thick red brush-cotton shirt. More surprising was the livid gash above his left eye and the swelling of his lower lip, which was fat with blood. His hair was wet and combed, as if he'd washed in a public bathroom; his face was mushroom pale.

"Hello, Alexei," she said calmly, making a show of reading the name tag that had been pinned to his shirt. "What happened to you? Are you all right?"

"Yeah, sorry. I, er, had a mishap on my way here."

"Oh. Well, you probably need a drink," she said with a small laugh. "I'm Sarah Hong. I think we spoke via email."

He entered the room limping. He was in an even worse state than she had supposed—he was grimacing with pain and struggling to stand straight.

His entrance had drawn the eyes of everyone in the room. Some of the students were glaring at him, embarrassed. Others turned their backs. She saw blood on her palm where she had shaken his hand. His hair was longer than she'd seen in photos of him, and he had grown a wispy blond beard. As she led him into the gilded room and as the dark-attired guests parted to either side, she felt like a secondary figure in a history painting. *Jesus in the Temple.*

"I received your résumé..." Jenna said, conscious of the eyes on them. "Let me get you some water."

PROPHET looked about like a hunted animal. No one had greeted him, no one moved toward him, even though he must have known many of the people here.

He drank down the water, and suddenly his body jolted forward in surprise, causing him to spill some on the floor. Someone had just touched his butt. Then a pale woman's arm appeared like a tentacle and touched his wrist, and a dyed-red bobbed hairdo appeared at his shoulder.

Oh God, no.

"Hello there. I'm Bethany Hollis."

Bethany was holding her champagne glass at shoulder height like a flapper. "I'm the senior corporate law partner at Harley, Feinstein & Hawley. And you are...?" There was an ominously drunken familiarity to her friendliness, and it was turned up way too high. PROPHET recoiled slightly, as if from a venomous plant.

"Alexei Kuznetsov," he said, reddening. He looked to Jenna for help.

Bethany offered him her business card, but her eyes didn't leave his.

"I don't have a card," he murmured.

"Alexei has expressed an interest in structured finance," Jenna said quickly, hoping to snap Bethany into some professionalism before she suggested interviewing him in her room.

"Oh, I *see*," Bethany sighed, moving closer to his face. "You'd like to do some mergers and acquisitions..."

"Uh. That's right. I've been... studying the federal regulations on..." PROPHET's voice trailed off.

The tombstone figure of Maxim Fyodorovich Yegorov had joined them, uninvited. Jenna felt she was losing all control over the situation. Yegorov glowered at PROPHET and muttered a few terse words in Russian.

A bright spark of anger flashed in PROPHET's eyes.

"My apologies," he said, quickly putting down his glass. "This was a mistake. I shouldn't have come."

He was limping out the door before Jenna could stop him. Yegorov followed him to make sure he left. There was nothing she could do to intervene without risking her cover as Sarah Hong.

The final half hour was pure torture for Jenna. The lawyers gave out business cards and shook hands as the students started to leave. Her smile had remained so fixed and strained she wondered how much longer she could sustain it. She continued to answer questions, all the time feeling her mission collapsing in smoking ruins.

"I think that went pretty well, don't you?" Bethany said. "I need another drink."

"That's debatable," Jenna said.

Bethany's glass was being topped up again by a server who was giving her a decidedly wary look. "Who was the wounded soldier? He was a piece of something, right? Say, wanna join me for dinner at—"

"No," Jenna said with more emphasis than she'd meant. "I'm going to hit the sack. I'm whacked. Goodnight."

"Suit yourself."

Jenna crossed the lobby toward the elevators. Security cameras everywhere. A suspicious number of people sitting about, studying maps, looking at their phones, idling next to the enormous brass urns and marble columns.

As she stood waiting for the elevator, a thought came to her, planted by Bethany saying *dinner*. Elene and Volodymyr had told her where PROPHET picked up his dinner most evenings.

Teremok, a kind of Russian knock-off of McDonald's on Tverskaya.

A dangerous, insane idea—they had eyes all over him. But she was shit out of options now.

Slowly she turned and headed toward the reception desk, feeling eyes on her back. The desk assistant's name was Denis. He looked up with a smile that was half sneer.

"Hey there." Sarah Hong turned on her folksiest smile. "I'm kinda in the mood for some fast food. Is there somewhere near here?"

Denis's nostrils flared very slightly. He took out a tourist map and circled in biro the closest outlets. "We hyev McDonald's, Wendy's, and Teremok. That's like a Russian Burger King—"

"Perfect! Thank you."

She swiped the map and headed out of the revolving door and into Moscow.

44

G20 Summit
Hamburg, Germany
Earlier that week

> **Donald J. Trump** @realDonaldTrump
> I look forward to all meetings today with world leaders, including my meeting with Vladimir Putin. Much to discuss.

The Boss had bounced toward Putin like a dog with two tails. It was his first face-to-face with the Russian president, and the handshake, Eric thought, was telling. He'd pumped the man's hand for longer than was comfortable and used his other hand to grab Putin's forearm. Putin had raised his free hand to point a jokey finger at Trump—an extremely rude gesture where Eric came from. The body-language equivalent of pulling a gun. But for one long handshake, two bonfires of vanity had blazed as one.

The handshake over, the two leaders stood and left for their meeting to a battery of shouted questions from reporters. "Mr. President! Will you be talking about how Russia rigged the US election? Sir?"

Then Eric saw her—Sofia Ali, dressed in a dun-colored dress

suit with an Hermès belt. Sofia Ali, Russian speaker, mystery operator, *femme fatale* and ice-queen bitch "colleague" from the White House. She was following the leaders into the conference room.

She was their interpreter . . . ? At their first meeting?

He did not see her again until the summit's pre-dinner cocktails at the Elbphilharmonie, a gigantic new concert hall on the banks of the Elbe River where the evening's banquet was taking place. Eric was on hand to translate, in case the Boss wished to speak with Moon Jae-in, the South Korean president. The Boss showed no inclination to do so, even though Moon was circulating the room, making himself conspicuously visible and available.

Eric was fighting a deadening wave of jet lag that disorientated him like the feeling of being suddenly woken from a deep sleep. He watched this elite club of power players in their finery, musing on the absurdity of his life. He moved in the highest circles of state. He traveled on Air Force One. He was the president's interpreter in a summit that had convened the world's most powerful people. And his mind was devoted entirely to the question of how he was plausibly going to travel alone to California to assassinate a seventeen-year-old kid.

He was standing discreetly to the side of the room with the other interpreters, his back to the wall. He dared not leave his post, even though he could see Sofia Ali tantalizingly in view, making chit-chat with the First Daughter and the eunuch. It wasn't hard to see why Sofia had drifted so easily into the Imperial Family's social orbit. She looked stunning. Manolo Blahnik heels. Slim-fitting black trouser suit. A large, ostentatious platinum chain necklace that drew the eye to her long, slender neck. Dark kohl around green eyes. Hair swept back into a barrette. She looked, in fact, *Russian*. Not ordinary Russian, but super-rich, oligarch-wife, shopping-in-Paris Russian.

A moment of panic grabbed Eric as he realized he'd taken his eye off the Boss, but Trump was busy lavishing public compliments on the French president's much older wife. "You're looking great. No, really. Isn't she looking great?"

He risked another glance in the direction of Sofia Ali. She'd disappeared! The First Daughter and the eunuch were now standing alone with no one to talk to, drinks clutched in their hands like shields, smiles fixed, and a panicky embarrassment in their eyes as they scanned the room for targets. Theresa May, the British prime minister, glided past in a cloud of frosted air, and made no effort to rescue them.

Eric's eyes flitted frantically about.

Suddenly, there, in the far corner of the room, he saw a door closing and the back of Sofia Ali's head going through it.

A bell sounded, followed by an announcement. All guests were respectfully invited to begin making their way into the banquet hall.

Eric weaved through the throng in pursuit of her.

The door she'd gone through led to a service corridor. Large foil-covered ducts. Humming ventilation. Kitchen noises. A chef yelling orders.

He followed it to the end, past the open kitchen doors, turned a corner, and instantly jumped back out of sight. Sofia was about ten meters away, with her back toward him. She was talking to a tall, patrician-looking gentleman with silver, floppy hair. A security lanyard hung from his neck. Whatever she was saying to him, he did not look pleased. In the split second in which Eric had seen his face he'd understood that this man was being threatened.

The clanging and shouting from the kitchens were amplified by the bare corridor. He couldn't hear a word the two were saying.

Next thing he knew, a security guard with radio earphones had panted up to him. "Hey. Excuse me, sir! This is a restricted area."

"Sorry. I was looking for somewhere to smoke."

The guard escorted him back into the reception hall and closed the door behind him. Eric resumed his post deep in thought. Trump was slapping the French president on the back, a little harder than was friendly, and making a show of pronouncing his name with a French accent, which came out sounding like *Macaroon*.

About ten seconds later, Sofia Ali re-emerged, cool and disciplined as if nothing had happened. She was followed, after a discreet interval, by the man with the floppy silver hair.

Eric tapped the shoulder of a young man standing in front of him, one of the German chancellor's aides, and turned on the charm.

"Say, that gentleman over there," he said, gesturing to the man with floppy silver hair. "Who is he?"

"That's Hans-Peter Garmisch. He's from the AA."

Eric stared at the aide in wonder. "Alcoholics Anonymous?"

The aide seemed to find this *amusing* in the most irritatingly German way. "I'm sorry—that's just so funny. No, the Auswärtiges Amt, the German Foreign Office. Garmisch is the director of protocol."

Eric's puzzlement grew. "Protocol . . . ?"

It was coming to him. It was fluttering like a moth near the edge of his comprehension, beguiling him, like the solution to a crossword clue that was on the tip of his tongue.

"You have the seating plan?" Eric said abruptly.

"Of course." The man opened his folder. "Tomorrow morning's conference on climate protection—"

"For tonight's banquet, you jerk."

The man looked as if he'd been stung on the nose. He retrieved a page slowly and with dignity. "There you are."

Eric scanned the names, but he could see nothing out of the ordinary. President Trump was seated between Akie Abe, wife of the Japanese prime minister, and Juliana Awada, first lady of Argentina.

President Putin was seated between Chancellor Merkel and the . . . whatever you call the partner of the president of Estonia.

Eric watched the leaders and their spouses walking in pairs to the banqueting hall, a large, rather sterile place normally used for concerts.

When the last of them had gone in Eric joined the large assemblage of interpreters that followed them. They had been allocated seats several meters behind the leaders in case translation services were required.

And as he entered the hall, he witnessed a small drama taking place near the door. The host, Chancellor Merkel, who was sporting the kind of loose pants one might wear for an afternoon in front of TV soaps, was pointing at the seating plan and speaking in urgent German to a group of security men and diplomats, which included the floppy-haired director of protocol. What was his name? Garbage?

"*OK, egal,*" the chancellor said, clearly annoyed. She had no time to argue.

The leaders and their spouses took their places along a white-cloth banqueting table resplendent with candles in golden cups, flowers, and silverware for four courses.

Trump was seated as per the seating plan.

Putin took his seat next to . . .

Oh.

A last-minute change had been made. The places for Melania Trump and Chancellor Merkel had been swapped. The First Lady now found herself next to Vladimir Putin . . .

Putin, already seated, looked up at her with a show of being pleasantly surprised. If Melania felt any consternation by the change of place, she didn't show it. Her beautiful, caged-bird face was calm behind its frosted mask.

Eric couldn't grasp the logic of this at first, not in words.

But he *felt* it—intuitively. The *effect* this sight would have on her husband, who was seated two-thirds of the way down the opposite side of the table. His reaction. The agitation he would feel at seeing *his wife* seated next to his please-be-my-buddy hero. The jealousy of one who knew that nothing and no one was worth possessing unless they were coveted by others. Someone had just played a deft psychological trick.

Sure enough, Donald Trump could focus on nothing but the fact that his wife had just been seated next to Vladimir Putin. He started making weird hip-hop-type hand gestures to them across the table. A kind of *Ha-ha, you horndog! You're sitting next to my wife! Hey, let's talk!*

The first course was served. Bayerischer Wurstsalat.

The Boss barely spoke a word to poor Mrs. Abe, even though a Japanese interpreter was perched behind them ready to translate any inanity that left his lips.

At the end of the main course—Jägerschnitzel with creamed potato and sauerkraut—Trump could bear it no longer. He tossed aside his napkin, left his seat, walked around to the opposite side of the table, pulled up a chair, and joined the conversation with Putin and Melania.

Within seconds the First Lady had been frozen out, and then the two most powerful men in the world were speaking alone. No third parties present. No state department. No foreign policy, defense, or security advisors. Just the two of them. A private meeting in plain sight. No note-takers. No record. No one knew what they were discussing, what they were agreeing.

Eric knew that Putin spoke better English than he let on, but Eric doubted they'd manage to talk for long without an interpreter.

And then, with balletic timing, Sofia Ali glided toward them from the wings, notepad in hand. It seemed so graceful, so natural. No one would guess what she'd just achieved.

The two men spoke for nearly two hours with Sofia Ali interpreting. They continued talking after all the other guests had left. Donald Trump was the last head of state to leave the venue, at 23:54.

Outside the banqueting hall, Eric waited with the Secret Service agents and the few remaining White House aides. He continued waiting after the Boss had left, and Sofia Ali finally emerged. Her composure betrayed nothing of the triumph that must have been parading through her head like May Day in Moscow.

Her eyes narrowed when she saw Eric.

"Oh. You again," she said, about to breeze past him. "What are you doing here?"

"Same as you, Sofia. We're doing the same job."

"I doubt that very much."

He caught her by the elbow.

"Don't you dare touch me."

"How did you engineer that, mm? A change to the seating plan? Got some juicy *kompromat* on Herr Garbage from AA?"

"I've no idea what you're talking about." But a distinct look of alarm had just flared in her eyes.

"I know what you're doing." Eric moved closer to her, breathing in her perfume, and whispered into her ear. "I *know*. And I want to tell you that I admire your work." She had gone very still suddenly. He could see her pulse throbbing in her neck. "We both share the same aim, Sofia. Let's respect each other and agree not to work against each other. Can we do that?"

Donald J. Trump @realDonaldTrump
Fake News story of secret dinner with Putin is "sick." All G20 leaders, and spouses, were invited by the Chancellor of Germany. Press knew!

45

Tverskaya
Moscow
Thursday, 9 p.m.

On Tverskaya, Lyosha pulled his beanie down low, tucked his hair away, and went into his usual branch of Teremok. Fast food joints were the only eateries he'd risk. Order, pay, eat, leave. He no longer dared go to a real restaurant. He was conscious of his enormous bag drawing attention, with the three hockey sticks poking out of it.

The place was busy. Grandparents with kids. Cab drivers. Nightshift workers. Smells of frying fat and chemical forest. Shouts as orders were placed on the counter. A canned voice was crooning "My Way" in Chechen.

He scanned the gaudy red illuminated menu, even though he ordered the same thing every time: mushroom melt blini with a Teremok Caesar salad and a medium kvass.

He paid and took his tray to a tiny corner table, keeping his back to the room. The wounds on his face were throbbing painfully and starting to bleed again. His ribs were sensitive to the touch and, as he saw when he lifted his shirt, turning a deep plum-and-avocado color. He found a couple of aspirins in his bag, swallowed them with the kvass, closed his eyes for a moment and just breathed. Each time the door opened a blast of freezing air came in and he could hear the babushka on the sidewalk outside playing "Kalinka Malinka" on her accordion. The meal was awful, not even warm. He pushed it away, unable to finish it. He knew he should get out of there quickly before anyone recognized him, but now that he was slumped in the cramped plastic seat, he found that he couldn't move a muscle. All the hurt and despair were catching up with him again, overwhelming him with lethargy and inertia. He stared at the uneaten debris on his tray and just wanted to weep.

A day that had started with a disappointment seemed to have gone into a downward tailspin and had ended in humiliation and disaster. This morning's law examination was one he could have passed but he'd almost certainly flunked it. His mind had been elsewhere for days. Then he'd suffered spectacular ignominy on the ice rink, followed by a vicious unprovoked assault outside a bar where he'd simply gone for a quiet beer. And then: the law firm's drinks reception, which had been ruined for him, ruined by him. What had he been thinking? Turning up there scruffy and bleeding, looking like a freak. But it hadn't been his fault. Hadn't been his fault that that red-haired Baba Yaga had groped him and embarrassed him; hadn't been his fault that Maxim Fyodorovich Yegorov had chased him out, humiliating him in front of the faculty students; not his fault either that his father . . .

Lyosha's face reddened. His teeth were bared and the tears began to flow.

Not his fault that his father had died suddenly, in a foreign land, without a chance for him to say goodbye.

Lyosha's life, which only days ago had been teeming with opportunities and a multiverse of bright futures, was over. Finished. His future had been canceled.

Where does it go from here? Where does it end?

Once again, he had that image of himself skating in slow, decreasing circles around a black hole in a frozen lake. It had come to him often in the last few days—unbidden and yet familiar, like a dark, recurring motif in a Wagner opera. A death motif.

No, he couldn't. He couldn't be so selfish. His mother would die of grief.

And he saw then that there remained one small but significant role available to him, one he might embrace with love and humility, however diminished he now felt now: to care for his mother and comfort her. He wasn't the only one who was suffering. And today was her birthday, too!

He was finally about to take his tray to the service stack and leave when he heard a commotion in the line of customers.

A foreign woman was querying her order in broken Russian. He turned in his seat. Some misunderstanding about an order of Rossi blini. No, she'd ordered the Cherry Varenye blini. She hadn't wanted anything savory. And she'd ordered a Diet Coke, not kvass.

The server was looking at her in exasperation. The manager came over and showed the server how to cancel the order. "Sorry," he said. "This is trainee . . . No, we don't take Amex."

"Oh, shit. I *think* I have cash," she said in English. "Um. How much is it again?"

It was the woman Lyosha had just met at the Metropol. Sarah something.

He left his seat and went to the service counter. "Can I help?"

The woman turned suddenly, wide-eyed. "Oh! Uh, Alexei, right? Sorry, let me deal with this first. I'm holding up the line."

"Please. Allow me," he said. He took out his wallet and paid.

"That's embarrassing. *Thank you.* You didn't have to do that."

"It's OK. It's not exactly the Ritz."

The unsmiling server pushed Sarah's revised order toward her on a tray. Lyosha carried it for her and placed it on the corner table he had just vacated.

"Won't you join me?" she said. "You left the event so suddenly we didn't really get a chance to meet properly."

"Yeah, I don't think the university wanted me there."

"Well, it can't be because of your grades. They're good."

He gave that most Russian of gestures, a high shrug of his shoulders, a weary, self-deprecating smile. "This is Russia. Say the wrong thing and you can find yourself with all kinds of problems . . ." He picked up his sports bag and heaved it onto his shoulder. "I've got to go home. It's my mother's birthday."

"Oh, you don't want to be late for that."

"We're celebrating tomorrow. The Bolshoi. She likes the ballet . . ."

"In that case, are you sure you have to rush off . . . ?"

He was distracted suddenly by snickering from the next table. A group of three teenagers was staring at him and whispering behind their hands. One of them pointed a camera phone at him. He nodded to Sarah. "Goodbye."

Jenna watched him hobble out, his massive bag bobbing on his back. She took her time over the food and pretended to check emails on her phone. In the corner safety mirror above her she saw an elderly man in the green overalls of a street cleaner sipping coffee and reading a newspaper through a pair of reading glasses. Volodymyr. The door opened again, and she heard accordion music.

The ballet? There'd been nothing about that in his emails.

She deposited her tray and left the restaurant. The babushka was sitting cross-legged on the sidewalk. Her head was swaddled in scarves and her back leaned forlornly against a lamppost as she squeezed an instrument that must have dated from World War II. Jenna crouched down to push a few dollar bills into her hand and the woman clasped it with both her hands.

"I need a ticket for the Bolshoi tomorrow night," Jenna murmured.

Elene nodded and continued playing.

By now, she was sure the watchers tailing PROPHET would be reporting his "chance" encounter with her in Teremok. She just hoped that's all they would think it was—chance.

She made a leisurely walk back to the Metropol, as if she were enjoying the chill spring night. She stopped to photograph the grim statue of Karl Marx, and the Bolshoi Theater lit up so that it resembled a wedding cake. But all the while, her brain was in turmoil. She glanced at her watch. 10 p.m. Today was Thursday. She'd secured one more shot at PROPHET. But how the hell was she going to have a conversation with him during a performance at the ballet?

46

Victory Palace Apartments
Moskva Embankment, Moscow

Lyosha opened the door to his parents' place and, for a second, he thought he'd walked into the wrong apartment. Papers were thrown all over the floor. The hall cupboards hung open and had been ransacked. In the sitting room, chairs were overturned. The sofa and cushions had been slashed and the stuffing pulled out. He dropped his bag to the floor.

His mother was sitting alone at the dining table, her thin figure hunched over a cup of tea and a cigarette poised shakingly between her fingers.

"What happened?" He rushed to her.

Marina jumped. She hadn't heard him come in. "Oh, Lyosha. My love." Her voice sounded drowsy, faded. She'd taken a sedative, he could tell. When she saw his face, she clasped her hand to her mouth.

"It's nothing, Mama. Just a tumble in the locker room."

"Oh." She turned back to her tea. "I didn't know you were playing."

"Who did this?" He gazed about at the broken plates on the floor.

Marina took a deep drag on the cigarette. The words came out with the smoke. "Vadim Giorgadze was here," she said, stubbing it out in the ashtray.

"*What?*"

"With some men from the SVR. He said they needed to make sure Dmitry didn't have any classified material at the time of his death. I told them they were welcome to look. I didn't know they'd wreck the place. Then Giorgadze sat down and started to ask me all these questions . . ."

A morbid dread crept over Lyosha's heart. "Questions?"

"He wanted to know about your father's life in New York." She shook her head slowly, as if she'd refused some outrageous request. "I said, 'What life in New York? He went there for work.' I had nothing to tell him. But these questions . . . they went on and on. Did Dmitry have any friends in New York, American friends? Did he ever drop out of touch for periods of time? Was he under any great stress? Were his finances in order? Did he owe money? Had he ever said anything disloyal about the president or the motherland? Then he asked if I knew of any affairs he'd had with other women. That made me really angry with him, but . . ." She frowned as she thought about it. "It was very odd. He could see he was upsetting me, but he was smiling. Dmitry was his friend, but it was almost like . . . he *hated* Dmitry . . ."

Lyosha wrapped his arms around his mother from behind and pressed his cheek to hers. Her body was as fragile as a bird's.

"And on your birthday, too," he said.

She gave a small huff. "I'd completely forgotten that."

Her head turned to the windows. A light seemed to go out inside his mother. For a few minutes it was as if she forgot Lyosha was there.

Eventually she squeezed his hand. "Make sure you've got a clean shirt for tomorrow. I'm looking forward to the Bolshoi. It'll take my mind off all this." She got up and Lyosha held her hand as she stepped gingerly through the minefield of broken wine glasses. He put her to bed as if she were a child. "Eat the pelmeni," she said, smiling weakly as if nothing had happened. "They're still warm in the pan."

For the next two hours Lyosha tried to restore some order to the devastated apartment, his mind working furiously.

Only days ago, Vadim Giorgadze had paid his respects at his father's funeral. Why had he just turned over their home as if Dmitry had been some common criminal? How could he behave like that to a bereaved widow? Perhaps it was, in fact, the completion of Lyosha's own punishment. First the public humiliation; then a private, more personal one. The message was clear: there was no facet of his life, no space—not even inside his head—that the state couldn't fuck with.

Exhausted, he lay on his bed with his hands behind his head, watching the glow of the city reflected on the clouds through his window.

A memory fell open just then. Of something his father had said to him, on the final occasion Lyosha had seen him.

It was Lyosha's first and only visit to the new dacha in the Khimki Forest. Marina had asked him to drive out there because Dmitry was working there for a few days. She'd wanted to send him clean clothes and containers of home-cooked food. Lyosha had been extremely reluctant to go. He was still disgusted with Dmitry for buying that place, and they still weren't speaking.

For miles the narrow road had undulated through dense, ancient woodland. It was only an hour's drive from Moscow, but it was as if he'd traveled back in time to a slower, older Russia—a hinterland of epic skies and dark, mythic forests. Pines had drunk in all the light of day and silver birches strobed white in the car's headlights. The air smelled of woodsmoke and resin.

When he arrived, just after sundown—at the very spot where he and Anya had gone to demonstrate against the felling of the trees—he'd seen a huge enclosure fence with a new gatehouse. A guard with a submachine gun had stopped the car.

"This is a Lada-free zone, asshole. Turn around. Quick."

They'd argued for a minute until Lyosha had convinced the man that he was the son of Dmitry Stepanovich Kuznetsov.

Then the gate had opened, and he'd entered the closed world of Moscow's super-rich. Modern houses that were more fortified mansions than dachas were nestled far back from the road behind security cameras, infrared sensors, laser alarms.

He found the house. The place looked as dull as a barn until the security lights blinked on, blinding, and he saw a building that was massive and new. The ground floor was of monumental white stone; the upper floor was of dark wood and broad eaves. Surrounding lawns were a lurid green under the lights.

He punched in the code for the front door and was again in a deep, shuttered darkness. The house smelled of fresh paint, new sealant, varnished wood. He began feeling the walls for a light switch, and then he heard music.

Someone was playing a piano on the other side of the house. As his eyes adjusted to the dark, he could vaguely make out the huge dimensions of the place. A broad, curved staircase led up to the first floor. At the far end of the hall were two large double doors of polished wood. He recognized the melody. *Barcarolle*, by Tchaikovsky. An impossibly sad, tender piece. Lyosha hadn't heard his father play in years.

He stopped before the doors. The piece had a sequence of three chords that had the power to rend the heart with love, loss, regret. Years ago, before the war in Afghanistan, hadn't his father dreamed of a career in music? He'd forgotten that fact about him. The war had changed him, his mother had said.

The piece ended, and Lyosha heard a page being turned. He opened the doors, and as he did so a draft of warm, night air swept through the house, ruffling his hair, and cooling the tears on his face.

This room, too, was unlit. Dmitry was hidden behind the upright lid of a small grand piano. A chair scraped. His silhouette stood straight up. "Lyosha?"

"Papa."

"I wasn't expecting you."

Lyosha gazed about at the large, unfamiliar room and saw why his father had been playing without light. The moonlight lay in long pale beams across the carpet. The windows gave a view onto a copse of poplar trees, one of which held the evening star like a diamond in its leaves.

Dmitry switched on a table lamp and the two looked at each other as if they hadn't met in years. Lyosha was still under the music's spell. For a few moments it had dissolved all his hurt, all his bitterness and resentment. Without a word they came together in the middle of the room and embraced, thoughtlessly, warmly, until their deep habitual awkwardness overcame them, and they were each embarrassed and unsure what to say. His father was much the same: his hair was still groomed like an old movie actor's and his eyes were searching and clear. But he looked different, somehow. Kinder, more present.

Lyosha sensed that a channel had opened between them and if either of them said the wrong words, it would close, maybe forever.

"I didn't know you still played."

Dmitry gave a sad smile. "They're giving me a routine polygraph test tomorrow. The music calms my mind."

"Diplomats take polygraphs?"

"Sometimes. To make sure we haven't been seduced by the wicked West."

Their eyes met and did not blink. The channel was holding.

But then Lyosha looked again at the room—at the ornate furniture inlaid with gold; the painting over the fireplace that looked like a real Jackson Pollock; the obscene luxury. He compressed his lips, but the urge to judge, to accuse, became too great.

"How can you have . . . this."

Dmitry drew a long, patient breath and exhaled.

"I work with men who've turned their power into wealth and their wealth into even more power. I have to play their game if I'm to play my own. Believe me, Lyosha, if my money was outside Russia, I'd have moved you and your mother to New York long ago."

But before Lyosha could absorb the import of what Dmitry had just said, the words *wealth* and *power* had tripped an explosion of his anger.

"What do you care about Russia!"

And in less than a second, the old dynamic of their relationship had reset itself, powerfully. Dmitry lost his temper. Lyosha shouted back. Dmitry told him to get out. Lyosha stormed through the front door without bothering to close it.

They never saw each other again.

Now Lyosha thought long on that exchange, and he felt a burning shame. If he hadn't been so damned self-righteous, so quick to condemn, he might have taken stock of what his father had been trying to tell him. It was almost as if he'd taken off a mask.

I have to play their game if I'm to play my own.

Everyone in Russia knew how to compartmentalize their lives, he thought. Him, his mother and father, his grandparents, too—they were all people in disguise. They had grown up around secrets that could never be shared . . . And his father's disguise? What had been behind it?

Perhaps Lyosha had always known, but he hadn't known that he'd known. All the signs had been there. Dmitry's secrecy, the long absences, the dearth of anything meaningful to talk about, the heavy air of words unsaid. The strain of a secret. Part of Lyosha had made the diagnosis but had never acknowledged it.

He began to sense then that there may have been more to his father than he had ever known. All Lyosha had seen was the lighthouse and some rather forbidding rocks, but behind them . . . had there been some large, undiscovered continent, a life, a world, that his father had never revealed?

Finally, he forced himself to get up and sort through the dirty clothes in his laundry basket. As he carried them to the washing machine, he noticed that the shirt he'd worn at the funeral was among them.

Where had Anya put those gold cufflinks?

47

Hotel Metropol
Moscow

As Jenna rode the elevator up to her room it stopped one floor below hers, on the third. The doors opened and Charles Fisk stepped in.

Neither acknowledged the other and he turned his back toward her the instant the doors closed, but she could have thrown her arms around him and screamed for joy. The elevator continued to the fourth floor. Just before the doors opened again, he murmured, "Roof in ten minutes." Then he exited and turned left. She turned right toward her room.

She found the service stairs at the end of the corridor. The hotel had long been refurbished to international standards, but these service stairs, unseen by guests, retained the old iron filigree of the *belle époque*. The door to the roof, off-limits to all but staff, had been unlocked. She stepped onto what looked like a darkened stage surrounded by the glowing metropolis. Fisk was waiting for her on the other side of the hotel's grand, barrel-vaulted glass roof, his hands in his pockets. He was gazing at the view.

"Hello, Pilgrim," he said, as she joined him.

"This is a nice surprise."

In front of them the great rampart walls of the Kremlin rose massive and ancient. The stars atop its towers shone a dull ruby red. Searchlights crisscrossed the clouds over Red Square.

He glanced at his watch. "We're good for ten minutes. Took me hours to lose my tails. You OK?"

"Should I be?"

A crunch of marching feet was coming from somewhere off to the left, followed by an echoing cry of *"Urrah!"* They watched as armored vehicles bearing regimental banners rumbled slowly into the square followed by hundreds of troops marching in tight formation, all following white lines marked on the cobblestones.

"Rehearsals for another military parade," he said. "Seems to be one every week now." He folded his arms and sighed. "In 1991, Mira Kowalski and I were staying in this very hotel. A tipping point had been reached. No one, not the people nor the leaders, believed in communism anymore. The Soviet Union had turned out to be an optical illusion. For a brief period, people were happy. There was hope for the future. Now, here I am again. Another tipping point is coming. The people are remembering that there's no future in Russia. Only a mirror to the past. And the past always repeats."

The troops were assembling into a dark legion facing the president's podium.

"Urrah!"

"Feels like we're standing in front of an avalanche with a bucket and spade," Jenna said.

"Well done for developing the target. Tomorrow night at the Bolshoi, you're in the stalls, seat L53. The target's in a private box with his mother, seats B12 and B11, on the third level. To make your visit less conspicuous, we've procured five additional seats for your firm of lawyers. Think you can tempt some of them? Tickets for this thing are like gold dust. It sold out months ago."

Jenna pulled a doubtful face. "Maybe." None of the lawyers had struck her as especially cultured types, but she had an awful feeling that Bethany Hollis would jump at the chance.

"I gotta level with you, Jenna. The Wise Ones in Russia House took a vote. Allen and Cheney think you should abort the op. Mira's still in favor."

"Abort, why?"

"He's trending again. This time, it's attention he really doesn't want."

"What do you mean?"

"He played a 'college friendly' this afternoon at the CSKA Arena. Whole thing looked like a setup. He spent most of the game pretending not to save goals scored by guess-who. It's all over social media."

"What?"

"Yep. Putin made a surprise appearance on ice, and won the game. There is nothing that man won't do for revenge. But the point is: the target must have been coerced, somehow. He may be compromised."

Jenna considered this and shook her head slowly. "That game was this afternoon? I must have met him, what, just a few hours later. He was defiant and angry. He showed up at our drinks even though he was injured and in no fit state. If he's under their control . . . I didn't get that impression at all. I don't believe it."

Charles Fisk rubbed his doughball nose. He looked tired, exhausted by a lifetime in the Game. "Maybe not, but they've reminded him who's master. The kid must be terrified."

"We're not giving up now. My cover's not blown. They don't know who I am. He doesn't know who I am."

"I'm just saying. This has gotten a lot riskier. Elene and Volodymyr are still seeing surveillance on him. It just adds to my bad feeling about this. Even if the Russians don't know about the cufflinks—a big if—they know something's fishy. They're onto him. They're suspicious."

"They're suspicious of *everything*, Charles," she said, frustrated. "They live in a *world* of paranoia, a labyrinth of mirrors. We can't let that deter us. If anything's worth the risk—it's this. We've no other options now."

"Forget the cufflinks, Jenna," he said with heat in his voice. "Forget directing him to a drop site. It's too late. This level of surveillance on him means they're building a case before arresting him, and that could happen any moment. Only thing you can do now? Tell him to get out of Russia—fast. We'll help him. We owe that to OPUS. This comes from Mira."

Jenna went quiet as she took this in. She was trying to ignore the howls of protest in her mind. Once she had committed to a course of action, she hated being thwarted. From the direction of Red Square an order was cried out, booming across the vast space, and a thousand AK-74s presented.

She said, "What's the exfil plan?"

"Same plan we had in place for OPUS. Tell him to show up at Belorussky Station first thing Saturday. Tell him to buy a return ticket to Minsk and board the 07:05 express train. We'll find him onboard and give him new documents. If his mother comes with him, we're ready for that, too."

"Makes the stakes kinda high, doesn't it?" she said quietly.

"At the Bolshoi tomorrow: there's a small champagne bar on the third level for the people who've paid top dollar for box seats. Room for about thirty people. After the curtain goes down for the interval at 8:45, that bar will be full. You'll meet him there. It'll be a pleasant coincidence."

"How do I know he'll show?"

"He'll show. One of the other guests in his box will be an acquaintance of his mother's named Luba Ivanovna. She works for us. She'll make sure he shows. It's a gala evening. Brought something to wear?"

Gala evening? "I'll figure it out."

"How're you going to play this?"

"The target knows me as Sarah Hong. He's no reason to be suspicious of me. What I tell him will be simple: the truth."

Fisk rubbed his eyes and gave a small, rather bitter laugh. "The truth . . . that's not a card we play often. Keep it brief. We have no comms or optics in that bar."

"Which way did you vote? Abort?"

Fisk sighed again. "If it were anyone other than you, I'd say we take a chance. But the idea of risking you—"

"Well, you're stuck with me, Charles. There's no one else."

"Mira has faith in you, Jenna, and so do I. Look, if you sense anything that gives you even the vaguest unease—"

"I know. I promise—I will abort."

"And *whatever* happens," he said, sternly, "you'll come straight back to this hotel after the performance, and you'll depart with those lawyers for the airport. Minivan leaves the hotel at 11 p.m."

"Please don't worry. Whatever happens, I'm leaving Russia tomorrow night."

The evening at the Bolshoi, Jenna discovered, was no repertoire event, but the much-anticipated première of a new ballet called *Nureyev*, which celebrated the life and art of the legendary dancer whose defection from the Soviet Union, in Paris, in 1961, had caused a sensation all over the world. Tickets had sold out within hours of going on sale, with many willing to brave the cold in a long line outside the box office, hoping for a few returns. It made her appreciate, with some respect, the hidden powers that had been deployed in procuring the tickets. The sheer swankiness of the event had proved an issue for the lawyers. Only two of the men had brought outfits that could pass as evening wear. Of the women, only Bethany had said yes on the spot.

To Jenna's consternation a TV news crew outside the theater was filming the guests arriving in their finery, and despite taking especial care over her appearance so that she'd blend in without drawing attention—she'd styled her hair as best she could with the hairdryer in her room; spent some time on her makeup, and had found a new black evening dress at the GUM department store that was a rather elegant but not-too-flashy Lagerfeld knock-off—she became quickly aware that she stood out. Here, every face was white. She stood out even more when a spindly arm slipped around her elbow and she saw Bethany decked out in some violet-blue, cape-like number that made her look as if she were attending a themed ball. It was set off by a large ruby broach that resembled a raspberry.

"I'm looking forward to this *show*," she murmured into Jenna's ear as they passed a program poster featuring the moody-looking, near-naked dancer playing Nureyev. "Shame we're not sitting together. I'm two rows behind you."

"Yes, a shame," Jenna said, mindful of the stares.

"Ballet's kinda like figure skating, right? I've never been, believe it or not."

"No, I believe you."

In fact, none of their small party of lawyers was seated together. She didn't know whether this had been the CIA's intention or whether it was because of the extreme dearth of tickets, but it suited her purpose: she could slip off alone and unseen to the third-level champagne bar for the encounter with PROPHET at the interval.

The women, trailing wafts of perfume and wearing white stoles and diamond earrings, mingled in the ornate circular lobby and air-kissed one another. For the Russian super-rich, more was more. Hair was too big, too many jewels were not enough, makeup was applied in spades. Their husbands, in black tie, were shedding coats and bodyguards. The place was filling up quickly with a noisy hubbub of expectant, moneyed conversations, amplified by the marble walls and chandeliers dripping with crystal. Occasionally, a voice rose brilliantly in laughter.

As the audience ascended the grand double staircase, she recognized several other members of the ruling elite. The great and the powerful were here, the boyars of the court of Vladimir the Terrible.

As the throng became denser, she spotted him easily because of his height—PROPHET, looking out of place in black tie. His long blond hair was gelled back. He was stooping to talk affectionately to an older woman in midnight-blue chiffon whom she recognized as his mother. He was about ten meters away from her with at least a hundred people in between them, collectively worth billions of rubles. Luckily, Bethany, who was taking care not to trip over the hem of her cape, did not see him.

The auditorium, ringed by teetering loggia boxes, had been refurbished in the opulence of the new Russia. All the icons of the Bolsheviks had been removed. Tsarist double eagles, emblazoned with gold, clutched drapes of rich red velour. The stage was dominated by an enormous scarlet and gilt theater curtain, and a warm glow emanated from the orchestra pit.

A bell rang. The stalls were filling up quickly now and the place was warm from so many bodies. Jenna looked around at the people fanning themselves with their programs. Tiaras sparkled, and an ambience of cologne, hairspray, and extreme wealth settled over the stalls. Acquaintances greeted each other across rows of seats. For a moment, she felt a thrill of shared luxury, a glimpse into the lives of others, lives unknown and unlived.

She decided to risk a glance up to the left and saw Lyosha take a seat next to his mother. Two others were behind them in the box, a man and a woman. Lyosha's mother seemed pleasantly surprised to see the other woman, a large, older, bejeweled lady. Her son stared at his program.

From her handbag Jenna took out a small compact mirror to check her makeup and used it to scan the faces in the grand circle behind her.

And there, in the imperial box, she saw a coarse face that was hard to miss. Bald head as round as a cannonball, arched eyebrows, Saddam mustache. The SVR's head of counterintelligence, Vadim Giorgadze. The sight of him sent an icy finger slowly down her spine.

Vadim Giorgadze . . . not a personal friend of Putin's, not someone he'd take fishing on Lake Ladoga, but a man deep inside the circle, nonetheless. A Kremlin fixer. Someone the president liked to call in the small hours when his grudges were keeping him awake. Someone he trusted to carry out his wet work without question. Someone with a sixth sense for traitors . . .

Why was he seated in the imperial box? Wasn't it normally reserved for heads of state? As the lights dimmed and the orchestra took their seats, she risked one more glance in the mirror. And she saw that Giorgadze was sharing the box with a guest—a gaunt, pale, unsmiling woman dressed in a black jacket and white blouse.

Jenna had seen the woman's face for less than a second before the auditorium went dark, but she could recognize a North Korean face at any distance. She lowered the mirror quickly as the curtain went up.

Concentrating on the music of the overture was impossible now, because she was fairly certain, no, positive in fact, that the woman seated next to Giorgadze was Kim Yo-jong, sister of Kim Jong-un.

What the fuck was *she* doing here? Kim Yo-jong headed North Korea's propaganda department. She was one of the most powerful figures in the Family, and possibly the most malign. The vile racism that North Korean state media had directed at President Obama had been her doing. Why was she the guest of Vadim Giorgadze, head of SVR operations?

Jenna was so preoccupied with this thought that she'd paid scant attention to what was happening on stage, until she distinctly heard Bethany's voice, two rows behind her, saying, "Oh, wow!" and suddenly there was a naked man.

Snorts and chirrups of laughter rippled across the auditorium. Marina put down her opera glasses and turned with perplexed amusement to Luba Ivanovna and her husband, who, by some strange coincidence, were in the two other seats that made up their box.

"He looks just like him. It's uncanny," Marina had whispered to Lyosha when the dancer playing Nureyev had first appeared. The surprise of the nudity made Lyosha squirm in his seat. He began staring hard at his program. In the program photograph, the principal dancer, Vladislav Lantratov, had sharp, Tartar cheek bones and ferocious eyes. He really did look a lot like the young Rudolf Nureyev. Quite a heavy musculature for a dancer, too. The ballet's theme, Lyosha figured, was unappreciated genius, and how Russia never truly valued its heroes.

The first scene depicted Nureyev's dramatic birth on board a train in Siberia, then his conflict with family (who disapproved of him dancing), his running away, then his swan-like metamorphosis into the Kirov Ballet's greatest star, a talent too immense for his communist masters to contain.

Soon, Lyosha had forgotten his embarrassment. He was transfixed by the magic of the performance. It was entrancing, uplifting, truly original. The dancers had an animal power, he thought; they simply exploded off the floor. He had the impression of witnessing a daring production—radically daring—for the first time.

The act's final scene ended with a sensuous pas de deux between Nureyev and his male lover. It was the most graceful thing Lyosha had ever seen, but the homoerotic touching was too much for this audience. Murmurs of disapproval and disgust were rippling across the stalls. These rich *elitny* had been *provoked*. And in that instant, Lyosha understood the power and the purpose of art.

The curtain fell on Act One to grudging, scattered applause. The house lights came on. Luba Ivanovna was saying, "Marina, dear, we're celebrating your birthday. I'm treating you and Lyosha to a glass of champagne . . . Yes . . . No, I insist . . ."

The scarlet-carpeted corridor outside their box was already crowded with people heading to the bars for interval drinks and outside to smoke. Luba seemed to know where she was going and was leading Marina by the elbow. The voices around them were scandalized and titillated.

"It *was* provocative..."

"Gay propaganda!"

"They should have warned us about the nudity. I mean, the guy's strawberries were flying everywhere..."

"Quite big strawberries, too..."

"Medinsky walked out..."

Luba led the way into a very small bar that served Crimean champagne from silver bottles. It was already quite full. The barman was a surly Tajik who couldn't pour the drinks fast enough, handing out flutes that were more froth than drink. Lyosha was annoyed with Luba. His mother disliked small, noisy spaces.

The champagne bar was a small, exclusive affair, all polished black marble, and it was already noisy and full. People were clutching programs and picking up preordered drinks, talking excitedly. Jenna threaded her way through the silk and taffeta toward the bar and found a preordered glass of champagne with a name on a card in Cyrillic letters: *Sarah Hong.*

She took a sip and looked tentatively about. She was unaccompanied, with no one to talk to, so she channeled Sarah Hong: she sat on a corner barstool, assumed the fish-out-of-water face of a tourist treating herself to something she couldn't afford, and checked her phone. It was the first time she'd logged into Sarah Hong's Facebook account. And Sarah Hong had received a message. She opened it and the breath left her body.

Someone called Smokey Beanz had left a message saying *How's your trip?* It was the fake profile used by one of the retired ops officers in Annandale who'd been keeping an eye on the house in case anyone came looking for Soo-min. The confused-face emoji at the end was the signal that he had information. She then opened an obscure gamers' page on Reddit and scrolled far down on the comments section beneath an equally obscure video and found this:

A0205AUDR8BLKLPCW1694D0225SOMADNXREGDERICRAHNAD4701BEECHRNW

Gibberish to anyone but Jenna.

Arrived: 02:05. Audi R8. Black. License plate: CW 1694. Departed: 02:16. Single occupant. Male, Asian. Did not exit car. Plates registered to: Eric Rahn. Address: 4701 Beecher Street, NW.

The message had been posted on March 1. Nine days ago? Why was she only seeing this now?

Because of a fuck-up.

Fisk had given the retired ops officers Sarah Hong's contact details and Sarah Hong's Facebook account had only gone live the day before she traveled to Moscow . . . An unfamiliar car had parked in the street outside the house for eleven minutes . . . ? Might be nothing.

But it had sufficiently rattled her to make her feel hemmed in and claustrophobic in this bar. She wanted to make calls, which of course she couldn't do. Had her mom and sister seen this car before? What did the ops officer see exactly?

Eric *Rahn*? Not a name she knew. Korean? Variation on Rhan, or Ran, or Nan?

She googled him. A page of meaningless white-guy faces.

She googled *ERIC RAHN KOREAN*. Images came up of President Trump. Dozens of them.

This is bullshit.

She scrolled down, and down. And then:

Fuck . . .

The bar chatter faded to a low rumble. She had the sensation of cold water rising over her head.

She was looking at a page from *GQ* magazine with the heading *Trump's New Korea Move.*

A black-and-white studio photograph showed a relaxed, movie-star-handsome Korean guy with gelled black hair sitting cross-legged in an armchair. He was wearing an open-necked white shirt and a high-end, gleaming silver chronograph watch on his wrist.

> *You get the feeling that Eric Rahn could make the cover of* Vogue Hommes *someday, but he's Donald Trump's new special advisor for East Asia. In a candid conversation, he reveals his personal insights into Trump's leadership style—explaining how the tycoon's outsider status will work to his advantage, how he asserts true American values, and what he's going to do about a nuclear-armed basket case like North Korea . . .*

Within moments she was finding him everywhere, this person, Eric Rahn. Breitbart. The *Washington Post*. Twitter. She found videos of him offering punditry on the primary debates, speaking at CPAC fringe meetings, the Republican National Convention. Most recently: he was standing behind Trump's left shoulder at the G20 summit in Hamburg . . .

This guy's in the White House . . .

The phone was becoming slippery in her hands, or else it was the heat of her body and the sweat that was now pouring off it, making her arms glisten and shine.

Fisk. She had to warn Fisk. She had to—

"Miss Hong?" She looked up from her phone in a daze.

PROPHET was standing in front of her, smiling, puzzled. The mythical creature was speaking to her. His small black ear stud seemed almost anarchic amid so much power and money. He gave a sardonic half-laugh. "Are you following me?"

"No!" She raced to restore her mind to operational mode, but there was nothing she could do to stop the heat rising to her face. "No, I always *dreamed* of coming to the Bol—"

"Miss Hong, this is my mother, Marina . . . Mama . . . ?"

But Marina was being turned away by the large, bejeweled lady in flowing black silk, the woman Jenna had seen behind Marina in the box.

"Oh. Well. That's my mother. Are you enjoying the performance?"

"I am," she said brightly. "More than this audience, I think." She had found Sarah Hong's voice again.

His smile dropped, and a shadow crossed his face. "This audience can't recognize love when they see it. They only understand power. Love is the opposite of power. The two cannot co-exist."

This was such a left-field remark that Jenna found herself at a loss for a response. Mira had warned her that Russians could be deep. You show up for tea with strangers, she'd said, and within minutes you're talking history, art, fate, power, love. Life is not taken lightly. It is treated with consequence.

Rather moronically, she said, "It's, uh, kinda hot in here. Would you mind asking for some water?"

"Of course."

She took a slow breath and fanned her perspiring brow with her program. She felt as if she were trying to sit two examinations at the same time and had just realized that both were far more difficult than she'd imagined. Then she saw him reach into his back pocket for his wallet and glimpsed a gold cufflink on his shirt sleeve. The sight of it caused the static in her brain to discharge in a single electric flash. Her clarity was restored. She felt solid ground beneath her feet.

Lyosha's mother was gesturing toward her son and trying helplessly to disengage herself from the friendly lady. The friendly lady gave a throaty chuckle and insisted on introducing her to more people.

344

Lyosha handed Jenna a glass of iced water and picked up two chilled glasses of champagne.

He pulled an apologetic face. "I'd better rescue my mother. Enjoy the second act." He started moving away. She was losing him again.

Jenna stopped him by the sleeve of his jacket, causing him almost to spill one of the drinks. She had one card left to play. It was now or never. The words came out low and clear. She felt as if she'd been holding them inside her like a bright molten alloy. "Your father was a very brave man. He worked for us for three years."

He stopped in his tracks. Then he half-turned his head back to her.

"What?"

Jenna rotated on her stool to face the bar, away from him, away from the crowd. Her voice was so quiet that he had no choice but to return to his place next to her. "Your father, Dmitry, took an oath to defend Russia from its enemies. He fulfilled that oath. He was protecting Russia from a man with a sick addiction to power: Vladimir Putin."

She risked a quick glance at him. He was staring at her with an appalled intensity. A moment ago, his eyes had been as clear and bright as a June sky. Now they were bleak, frozen tundra.

"Who are you? This is no coincidence, is it? Running into me again."

"I work for the United States government," she said, still directing her words into the middle distance behind the bar. "Your father was supplying us with crucial intelligence that will help us stop Putin spreading anarchy in the West."

"What are you saying? That my father . . . was a *spy*?"

But he'd pronounced the word as if he'd been searching for it for half his life. *Spy*. And then, staring at nothing, he said, "That's not true . . ."

She detected no anger or conviction in his voice. *You knew and you didn't know.*

Encouraged, she said, "Look how they've treated you since the funeral. I think you know it's true."

"My father was a patriot," he said, rallying. "Who are you to say—"

"Yes, he was. A patriot who loved Russia. Your father felt the same way you do about Putin, Lyosha. That man has no love, for anybody. He despises people. You see that. His only desire is for power. His only emotions are hatred and vengeance, which are basically the same. He has to be stopped."

Lyosha put the drinks down on the bar. She recognized the thousand-yard stare of someone in shock.

"What do you want? Why are you telling me this?"

"Your father was about to give us vital intelligence just before he died."

"Intelligence? What intelligence?"

"About a new breed of spy that will destroy our society from the inside. You're in possession of it. That's why I've been trying to meet you."

"*I'm* in possession . . . ?"

An instant change in the atmosphere of the room had caused everyone to tense, lower their voices. She knew who had just appeared even before she looked.

Vadim Giorgadze had walked in, as casual as a cat. He was rubbing his hands, his bull neck straining at his wing collar and black tie. He had spotted Marina at once. The woman's face became a powdered mask. It was too late for her to pretend she hadn't seen him. Instead, she inclined her head coolly toward him, then took a revived interest in the company of the friendly lady who was regaling a small group with some story. Lyosha had seen him, too, and had taken a half step away from Jenna.

She felt the oppression that pervaded this entire country flowing into this tiny airlock of a bar. The black mark was upon her.

Her voice a rapid patter, she said, "You're in danger, Lyosha.

They're watching every move you make. I strongly advise you to get out of Russia. Be at Belorussky Station tomorrow morning, early. Buy a return ticket for the 07:05 to Minsk. We'll find you on the train. Bring those," she said, pointing at the cufflinks without looking at his face, then she turned on the stool and braced herself for the whirling knives that were coming for her.

"These . . . ?" Lyosha stared at the cufflinks as if he'd never looked at them before.

Two other men had appeared behind the bar—thuggish security types, both in plain clothes and wearing radio earphones.

"Lyosha!" Giorgadze said in a rasping voice. He grabbed Lyosha's shoulder with a hand like a plate of ham. "Shall we speak in English for the benefit of your friend?" He had to use so much breath to force out his voiceless voice that he sprayed spittle into the air. "I can't say I'm surprised to find you at an LGBT striptease that celebrates a traitor. I'll be recommending to the FSB that the theater director is arrested, and the ballet is pulled after tonight. The Bolshoi should be ashamed of themselves . . ."

Lyosha glared at him, his hatred burning bright and pure.

"I suppose you see depravity like this all the time where you're from," the sandpaper voice rasped at Jenna. He gave a nasty smile that made his mustache bristle. She could smell something garlicky and beefy on his breath.

"Leave her alone," Lyosha said, dangerously calm.

She noticed that the people in the bar were being shepherded out by more men in plain clothes, including Marina, who gave a panicked glance over her shoulder at her son.

"Since no one's going to introduce us," Giorgadze said, "Allow me. I'm Vadim Giorgadze. An old comrade of Lyosha's father, Dmitry. I fought with him in Afghanistan in the eighties. I'd have died for that man. But, you know, old Chekists like me understand better than anyone that you can never truly know another person. You can be a man's best friend for thirty years and not realize that he's an enemy, a *traitor*, a degenerate . . ." His face was flushing a deep rose, and tiny beads of sweat were forming on his bald head. "It runs in families, too, eh, Lyosha? Like heart disease, or schizophrenia. And you are . . . ?"

"Sarah Hong," she said nervously, glancing to Lyosha for help. "I'm just a tourist tonight. Well, I'm in Moscow on business, actually. From Washington, DC."

Giorgadze's hand was still gripping Lyosha's shoulder. A signet ring on the man's small finger was like a tight rubber band around a sausage.

"Well, *Sarah Hong*," he said, releasing Lyosha and signaling to the men behind the bar. "It's been a pleasure talking to you. I'd like to get to know you better. In fact, I'd like to know your *real* name."

She reached quickly for her handbag. "Sorry, you've lost me there. It was nice to meet you."

He leaned in closer, so that she could feel his breath. *Goulash.* He'd been eating goulash. "We just have a few questions. It won't take long." He stepped back and made a gesture with his arm as if he had opened a door for her.

She said, "I'm going back to my seat."

"You're coming with us."

Some vestige of Sarah Hong cast a desperate look at Lyosha, at the barman, who had found some glasses he urgently wanted to polish.

The bell rang for the end of the interval. The circular corridor they walked along was almost empty but for a few stragglers.

"Wait," Sarah cried. "Where are you taking me? My co-workers are waiting for me. I'm an American citizen! Get your hands off me! Oh God . . ."

They escorted her to the elevator. Two in front, two behind, just outside her line of sight. Giorgadze had stayed behind. They kept the same formation inside the elevator car, as a golden button was pressed for the basement. An air of unreality came over her, a numbness. They passed along an underground corridor lined with mobile clothes racks and large pieces of prop and scenery, and up a concrete ramp toward a waiting vehicle with its engine idling. It was an unmarked GAZ sedan, with blacked-out rear windows.

She heard Sarah Hong's voice speaking as if it were on a tape recording. "There's been some mistake . . ."

Two of them got in on either side of her on the backseat.

She took out her phone. "I'm calling my employer. I work for an American law firm! You're making a big mist—"

One of them plucked the phone out of her hand and turned it off.

"Hey! Oh my God, oh my God . . ."

She had a tunnel vision through the front windshield as they headed into the Moscow traffic. All her thoughts and emotions had been paused. It was as if she wasn't there at all. This was happening to someone else. She was thinking of the flash cables she needed to send to Headquarters without a moment's delay.

URGENT: c/o advises immediate suspension of White House security clearance for staffer ERIC RAHN.
URGENT: c/o has just been arrested!

She pictured the cufflinks on PROPHET's shirt and thought of the Seed-Bearing Program that had ignited inside America like the fire in the hold of a ship, black and red in the darkness, coming to light in acrid wisps of smoke, too deep to contain.

She thought of Soo-min awake in her bedroom at night, terrified of the wolf that was watching the house.

"Where are we going?" she whimpered.

No one spoke. She could smell the fabric conditioner in the men's shirts, their shaving gel, a vinegar undertone of sweat. The driver glanced in the mirror, eyes cold and impassive. Shaved heads, grim faces. The car turned into Teatralny Prospekt, and one of the men spoke into his radio mic. Jenna's most primal fears stirred and came sharply alive.

48

Moscow

On the gridlocked streets outside the Bolshoi, traffic moved forward a few meters, then snarled up again. Lyosha had nervously smoked two cigarettes already and now flicked the butt of the second out of the car window, watching it trail orange sparks. They were at a standstill outside a throbbing club called Forbes near Lubyanka Square. A cortège of bulletproof Maybachs and Bentleys was inching toward the canopy entrance where limousines were quadruple parked. Along the sidewalk hundreds of stilettos clacked and shuffled. His hands slid off the steering wheel and onto his lap and he was staring once again at the cufflinks.

Your father was supplying us with crucial intelligence . . .

Lyosha's mother, next to him in the passenger seat, was talking about the ballet. She was still so animated by the great chatter that had risen up spontaneously in the audience at the final curtain—as it often did after performances in which excitement had run high—that she had not yet picked up on Lyosha's tension.

What Sarah Hong had told him during the interval had shocked him, utterly confused him. And yet . . . it had finally solved the central riddle of his father's life.

You're in danger, Lyosha. They're watching every move you make . . .

Why? Because of *Direct Line*? He wasn't a trouble-maker. He wasn't even online. He met no one; he spoke to no one, except Anya. This didn't make sense.

Take my advice and get out of Russia. Be at Belorussky Station tomorrow morning, early...

Tomorrow morning?!

That was ridiculous, hysterical. He would do no such thing. He couldn't simply flee the country on a few hours' notice.

But as he'd returned to his seat after the interval, and before he'd even had a moment to process what she'd told him, he'd received another shock. A text message from one of his roommates in Barrikadnaya had told him that the FSB had just raided their apartment with a search warrant, and had "fucking ransacked the place."

He'd sat through the second act of the ballet in an unresponsive stupor, not moving, not seeing, not hearing anything.

Bring those, she'd said.

His cufflinks? What were they if they weren't cufflinks?

No, no. He barely knew Sarah Hong. She could be anyone. Why would he trust her? For all he knew, she was paranoid, a crazy person full of conspiracies.

But was his gut telling him anything different from what she'd told him? From the moment his father had died he'd known that something wasn't right...

"Who was that woman you were talking to?" Marina said, frowning at the line of women in too-short skirts outside Forbes. "In the bar at the interval."

The car radio was playing a rather beautiful Bach partita, which added a surreal backdrop to the storms blowing inside Lyosha's head.

It was a struggle to speak normally. "She's from one of the American law firms I applied to. I met her at the Metropol."

"I hope Giorgadze wasn't rude to her. When I saw him walk in, it nearly ruined my night. I've never been so grateful for Luba's company. That woman's impossible to interrupt..."

Sarah Hong is an American spy. She had as good as told him. *My father spied for the Americans.* Giorgadze had practically confirmed it. In his rush to arrest her, the black drape of secrecy had swayed open a crack. He had called Dmitry a *traitor.*

But a traitor wouldn't have been given a funeral with full military honors . . .

. . . unless it was a charade, a cover-up. They didn't want anyone knowing that one of their own had betrayed them!

His father . . . a spy.

That is what Papa had been trying to tell him, that night in the dacha last summer. Now Lyosha was certain of it. His father had wanted to give him the gift of a secret, because the act of doing so was also a gift, and one that was much harder for Dmitry to speak, but which he must have felt deeply and with great force.

Every person has their own way of showing their love . . .

Papa. So much they could have shared! The realization that he could have told his father everything made him gulp. *All this time they could have been friends.*

Traitor. Putin made no distinction between Russia and his own person. "*Without Putin there is no Russia!*" But Lyosha knew that his father was not a traitor in any true sense of the word, because he was a man who had loved his country deeply. Russia's literature, its history, its music were all Lyosha's parents had talked about at the kitchen table when he was growing up. They were woven deep into the fabric of his parents' lives, as they were into Lyosha's, nourished by a thousand roots below the level of consciousness, so that when Lyosha spoke for himself, he quite unconsciously spoke for all Russians. That's what had given him the courage—no, the right—to challenge Putin on TV. And Putin had comprehended it and was humiliated. Humiliated first by Dmitry, then by his son.

Putin was not a forgiving man. He had said many times that treachery was the one sin he would never forgive. *Traitors will die in the gutter.* Dmitry had risen high in the regime. He had been a good and faithful servant. Putin had promoted him, trusted him. How personal this betrayal must have been to Vladimir Vladimirovich. How betrayed, too, how disgusted, Papa must have felt to take the fateful step of spying for the Americans.

Papa's act of resistance had been much more dangerous than Lyosha's own. It must have taken bravery Lyosha could not even imagine. He thought about this, and he was utterly amazed. It made his father's memory glow and dance like a flame beneath ice.

And in that instant, immediately and without a doubt, Lyosha knew that Putin had murdered his father.

Father and son, traitors both. In Putin's bleak, cynical mind, father and son would have been in cahoots.

The car was still stationary in traffic. Lyosha removed one of the cufflinks and studied it. *This is what they're looking for. This is what connects father and son.* Suddenly the danger of possessing them seemed acutely real, as if he held in the palm of his hand something so lethal that he should fling open the car door and throw them into the gutter right now.

"Do you ever remember Papa wearing these?" he said.

"Don't think I'd ever seen them before," Marina said, taking the cufflink from him and examining it. "They look like antiques. He must have bought them in New York." She handed it back to him.

"This flashy Chinese guy . . ." she said, referring to Lang Lang, the pianist playing the Bach partita. "He slips in notes that aren't in the score."

"Mama . . ." Lyosha said calmly.

"Mm . . . ?"

"I think I want to make a trip to the West soon. I think you should come with me."

"The West? Where? I'm not one for shopping."

"I mean a one-way trip. Tomorrow morning, perhaps."

"What on earth are you talking about?"

She had caught the grave note in his voice and a look of alarm flared behind her eyes. But then her features softened with some motherly understanding. She touched his cheek. "Lyosha, my love. Is there something you want to tell me? You know, if you're not interested in girls, I figured that out long ago. I don't care. Honestly, I don't. Papa said the same. He just wanted you to be happy. I know it's not easy in this country—"

"No, Mama," he said, agitated. "It's because of . . . Papa's work."

The air in the car became very still. Marina stared straight ahead. *You knew, didn't you, Mama? Or you suspected.*

"Papa's work?" she murmured.

"I think Papa's work in New York may have . . . upset the authorities here."

The expression on her face was one he'd seen before on people of her generation when the state did something to make them afraid.

The car came to a standstill again behind an ancient red Moskvitch 2140 with a taillight that flickered like an electric candle and a rear bumper that was hanging off. He'd noticed it earlier behind them. Then it had disappeared. Now, somehow, it was in front of them.

The traffic had narrowed to a single lane because of the endless roadworks. Cars inched forward again, but then the Moskvitch came to a shuddering halt. Moments later its hazard lights flashed on. There were still a lot of these Soviet clunkers on the roads, and they broke down regularly.

"I'll go see what's wrong," Lyosha said.

"No!" Marina grabbed his arm. "Stay in the car. They might be carjackers."

Fumes were pouring from the Moskvitch's rusted exhaust, creating a noxious white fog through which only its blinking lights were visible.

"Someone's getting out," Marina said, putting her hand to her mouth.

The silhouette of a figure in a black hoodie was approaching them through the fumes like the grim reaper.

"Oh, God . . ." Marina gasped.

Only when the figure passed in front of their car headlights, did Lyosha recognize Anya.

He lowered the window.

Relieved, he said, "What are you doing here? Whose car is—"

Anya put her head through the window. Her voice was tense and urgent.

"Ditch your car. Come with us. Right now. There are men in your apartment waiting to arrest you."

49

The Lubyanka
Moscow

Jenna's journey had lasted barely five minutes. The car had glided past an incongruous row of boutique showrooms for Western luxury brands. But in the new Russia, the old one was never far away. Looming before them was a gigantic building painted a dark yellow. Ornate, colonnaded, eight stories high.

The gates opened inward with a groan and the car came to a halt in a dim, cobblestoned courtyard of the headquarters of the FSB, successors to the KGB. The Lubyanka.

Now she could no longer keep her feelings suspended. Her face, she was sure, was still play-acting at Sarah Hong. Going through the motions. Frightened, mascara streaming down her face, convinced of some terrible misunderstanding. But it betrayed nothing of her deeper knowledge, of the genuine, desperate urgency that was now spreading inside her like a blaze inside a locked house, raging and all-consuming.

The three men in suits left. Two armed and uniformed FSB officers pulled her out of the car and propelled her into the building and straight down the gloomy stone stairs. One level, then down to another, past rows and rows of reinforced steel doors, with an officer's fist held in the small of her back. The place smelled of disinfectant and distilled urine; the steps were worn smooth by so many unsteady feet entering this enormous, hidden world for the first time. Doors slammed; locks turned; boots clacked on the stone floors. How ridiculous that she was still in evening wear and heels.

The cell was so narrow she could reach out her hands and touch both concrete walls. An electric light hummed behind a wire mesh. High on the wall was a rectangular, barred widow of thick glass. No blanket, just a rusty bed with a thin mattress covered by a disposable, synthetic sheet, which sparked with static when she touched it. A red light blinking in the ceiling corner was a security camera. The enamel bucket in the corner was the lavatory. The door closed behind her with a submarine clang.

She sat on the bed and dropped her face into her hands.

She thought of her colleagues, the lawyers of Harley, Feinstein & Hawley, settled into their seats for the second act of the ballet; she thought, with an unexpected fondness, of Bethany, who must be wondering where she'd got to during the interval. She reflected on how anyone embarking upon a profession will harbor a secret terror about that career's dark side, its worst-case scenario, the one thing they will try their hardest never to think about. For an airline pilot it might be sudden mechanical failure. For a structural engineer, an error in the calculation of load bearing. For a doctor, a misdiagnosis leading to a preventable death. And for an intelligence officer operating under non-official cover, it was being captured and brought to this place.

No one in the world could help her now.

50

Belorussky Station
Moscow
Saturday morning

Just before 7 a.m., the taxi was pulling into the station forecourt, past the fantastical tsarist turrets that Lyosha had thought so magical when he was a boy and would now forevermore be associated with nightmare. The driver was a tight-lipped Pole with a Virgin Mary hanging from his mirror. "I can't stop here," he said, seeing them gather up their belongings. "There's no stopping . . ."

"We're jumping out," Anya said, putting on her sunglasses.

The three of them, Anya, Lyosha, and Marina walked quickly and purposefully into the ticket hall. The air was cold but still fresh; the sky above them had not yet turned metallic with snow clouds and traffic fumes.

Anyone observing them might have supposed them to be an average, down-at-heel family returning to their village after taking their mother to visit family in Moscow. Lyosha and Anya wore faded hoodies that covered their hair and sneakers that were falling apart. Marina carried a large burlap carryall and had thrown a babushka's shawl over her head.

The station was crowded even at this hour, and gloomy.

Passengers were disembarking from sleeper trains—journeys from half a world away in the east that had lasted days. Koreans, Chinese, and indigenous Siberians with children looked about bleary-eyed, dragging huge, wheeled cases. Drunks were still asleep on the station floor. A couple of werewolves in uniform were shaking down some unlucky Tajik who didn't have documents.

The three kept walking, walking, past the mosaics celebrating Soviet labor, paying no attention to anything but the immediate distance in front of their eyes.

"*Passenger announcement. The 07:05 express train to Minsk will depart from platform three . . .*"

The plan had been to arrive with no time to spare so that they wouldn't have to wait about and draw the eyes of anyone who might be looking for them. Their tickets had been pre-purchased and were in their hands.

Lyosha's heart went into overdrive when he saw the barriers. His pulse and breath were rapid and out of sync. The sweat was pouring down his back despite the cold.

This was the moment of greatest danger. If they were caught, it would be at the barrier.

Lyosha held tightly onto his mother's arm. God knew what was going through her mind right now. She'd said nothing in the taxi.

They turned a corner toward platform 3 and saw a long line of people passing slowly through the ticket barrier. Only a couple of station guards were on duty, talking, not even looking at the passengers. No FSB. They had no choice but to join the end of the line, in full view of the cameras and patrolling station police.

Lyosha had never given much thought to asylum-seekers on the news, until now. This is what it felt like to be a fugitive crossing borders. This is what it was like to experience existential angst—it weakened the spine and petrified the mind so that anything you said, if caught, would come out sounding like a lie. Desperate people with nothing to their names. Now here he was himself—with nothing. Nothing but some cash he'd had on him last night at the Bolshoi and the donated clothes he was wearing. And the cufflinks, of course. The cufflinks he'd wrapped in tissue paper and hidden in the small, riveted pocket of his jeans.

Even Anya, usually so fearless and brazen, was looking about in quick, pigeon-like movements, her pixie-pink hair hidden beneath the hoodie, her knuckles clenched and white. A digital clock counted down the minutes till the train departed. Two minutes fifty-five seconds to go. Marina, wrapped in the shawl, stared up at it as if it were an omen in the sky.

The line inched forward. Only a single gate was in operation. A passenger let his wheeled baggage cart coast into Lyosha's shin. Lyosha wanted to yelp in pain but made no sound.

Most of the trains were *elektrichkas*, suburban services with overhead cables, but others would travel thousands of miles to destinations across desert and tundra. To distract himself he began counting the carriages of the express train departing from platform 4. Halfway across the field of rails the carriages entered a forest of semaphores and signals, then disappeared.

Last night they'd barely slept. If it had been anyone other than Anya who'd appeared in that traffic jam as they left the Bolshoi, they would never have gotten into a strange car. But Lyosha trusted her absolutely. She would gladly suffer hell for him if police were involved, and he would do the same for her. Now the traffic jam and the quadruple parking outside the Forbes nightclub seemed a stroke of good fortune: Marina's abandoned Merc wouldn't have drawn attention for hours.

Marina allowed herself to be led by Lyosha, as if she were a child who had been implored by a frightened adult to stay quiet and do as she was told. Her face had that passive, shutting-down look again that made him fear for her mental state.

The Moskvitch they'd got into had reeked of moldy leather and diesel oil, and, to their surprise, was being driven by an elderly man with a Ukrainian accent. His wife was in the front seat. "Put this on, dear," she'd said to Marina, offering her an old shawl to cover her head.

"It was a devil to find you in this traffic!" the man said with a chuckle.

The pair had spoken little after that, and Anya had put her fingers to her lips. *Talk later,* she mouthed.

There was an unspoken feeling among all of them that events too serious for them to comprehend were fast overtaking them, that they had just burned a bridge and there could be no going back. If Lyosha and Marina did not yet feel like fugitives from the state, that perception began taking form half an hour later when they were ushered up the stained marble stairs of a grand building just off Sretensky, one of the rich merchant's houses that had been carved up into tiny apartments after the Revolution.

The apartment was unchanged in time since the 1960s. Shelves filled with the Encyclopedia Sovietica. Dense collections of symphonies on old LPs. A rotary dial telephone with a frayed cord. The meager comforts of a planned economy.

As soon as they'd arrived, the elderly couple wished them goodnight and retired to a bedroom.

"Who are *they*?" Lyosha whispered, once the door had closed.

"That man and woman," Anya said, making tea with steaming water from the samovar, "are your guardian angels." She'd removed her hood to reveal hair that was freshly dyed a pixie pink. "They told me they've been watching you for weeks. They knew you wouldn't get into the car unless they enlisted me. They acted as soon as they saw Giorgadze's men turn up at Victory Palace this evening."

"Why are they helping us?"

"The less you know, the better you sleep."

"If Lyosha's in trouble," Marina said plaintively, "it can be fixed, can't it?" By which she meant they simply had to find a lawyer who knew who to bribe. "We shouldn't be doing this."

"You can't fix this," Anya said to her, matter-of-factly. "Not if they decide to charge you."

"Charge me?" Marina said, affronted. "What have I done?"

"I told you, Mama," Lyosha said. "Because of Papa's work."

"If your husband's done something that has really angered Putin," Anya said, blowing on her tea, "do you think he'll allow the widow to live on in comfort and the son to leave Russia? He'll take *all* your husband's wealth and property. There'll be charges of embezzlement, tax evasion, corruption. Lyosha will have no career. He'll be drafted into the army as a conscript. This is just the start of the process . . ."

Lyosha had become even more concerned for his mother then. The light in her eyes was dimming. She was retreating into one of her internal exiles.

Then Anya had dropped her bombshell.

"We leave Russia early in the morning. Elene and Volodymyr have bought the tickets for us. We're catching the 07:05 to Minsk."

"Leave Russia?" Marina was aghast.

The helplessness Lyosha had been feeling since being bundled away in the Moskvitch suddenly disappeared. With a sudden clarity he saw that the mysterious elderly couple and Sarah Hong were in this together. This was one and the same plan.

We'll find you on the train . . .

"What happens in Minsk?" Marina said.

If we even get to Minsk, Lyosha thought.

"I don't know yet," Anya said. "Our guardians . . ." She nodded toward the bedroom and lowered her voice. ". . . are urging us to get on the first train. That's all I know. It's too dangerous here."

"Do you trust them?"

"That woman was arrested with me once. We spent hours in the same cell. I remembered her. Elene, I think her name is. Yes, I trust them."

Marina was in a trance. She wasn't taking this in, but Lyosha knew that a door was opening for them, and if they didn't rush through, it would slam shut in their faces.

Anya had taken complete charge: foam mattresses were laid on the floor; towels and new toothbrushes and second-hand clothes had been provided, almost as if their predicament had been planned for.

They changed into the clothes. As they lay on their backs on the foam mattresses, fully dressed, wide awake in the dark and staring at the ceiling, Anya murmured, "Russia without Putin."

About an hour before dawn, Lyosha had gotten up to use the bathroom. Under the lamp over the mirror, he again examined the gold cufflinks that had belonged to his father, holding them at an oblique angle to the light and turning them over in his hands.

A new breed of spy that will destroy our society from the inside.

These cufflinks contained secret intelligence?

You're in possession of it...

They were next in line at the ticket barrier. The guard scanned their tickets without even a glance at their faces. He was joking with another guard.

They were through!

Glory to Russian incompetence! Lyosha thought, as he breathed free air and they broke into a run for the train. *Long live inefficient police bureaucracy!*

Their carriage was halfway along the very long platform. The train was shiny red and new and operated by Belarusian Railways. It wasn't even a Russian train! Not that Belarus was any safer than

Russia. It had an ogre-like dictator of its own, who did anything Putin asked, but Belarus was an enormous step closer to the West, to freedom.

Their seats were in the standard-class section of the train. Most of the passengers were families with children, parents yawning and in need of a coffee.

A whistle blew, long and shrill.

"Welcome aboard the 07:05 from Moscow Belorussky to Minsk Station. This train is about to depart..."

The train's forward motion was almost imperceptible at first, but moments later the platform was gliding swiftly by. The three of them exhaled all at the same time and finally looked at each other. Anya began to giggle. Marina dropped her head back on the seat in exhaustion. The expression on her face was a complicated one, as if she was unsure whether this was an adventure or an ordeal, a terrific prank or a dangerous emergency.

The carriage was clean and air-conditioned. Moscow in all its melting-snow filth was rolling away from them. The eight-lane boulevards; the featureless poverty of the miles of Khrushchev-era apartment blocks. The train picked up speed. People began hanging up their jackets and heading to the buffet car to pick up some breakfast. But it wasn't long before the three of them were back in worry mode.

We'll find you on the train...

Lyosha had said nothing to his mother or Anya of what Sarah Hong had told him, partly to avoid giving them knowledge that would be dangerous to possess in the event they were caught, partly because he wasn't that sure that he believed her. But something needed to happen. They had no documents!

Passports weren't needed for Belarus, but they could not travel on to the European Union without passports.

Within half an hour they had left the capital behind. Fields flashed by, tiny villages, wooden and forlorn, dachas and allotments shrouded in mist, and then forest, endless forest, pine and silver birch, for hours and hours.

No one approached them, except to inspect tickets. The train stopped at Smolensk for ten minutes, which the three of them spent with their hearts in their mouths, counting down the seconds until it moved again. Hundreds of people got on, so that every seat was now taken, then it set off again.

As they approached the border with Belarus the meltwater anxiety returned to Lyosha's stomach. The three of them sat bolt upright in their seats like wooden toys. He had been so laser-focused on immediate danger that it only occurred to him now that the border itself could be a massive trap. Giorgadze's men would have time to put out an alert by now. Now would be the moment to snare them in the net.

What happened next was so smooth and natural that none of the passengers around them seemed to notice. A group of people heading toward the restaurant car passed down the aisle. The last in line was a nondescript middle-aged gentleman, who turned to Lyosha and spoke in Russian: "Excuse me. I think you dropped this on the floor back there." And then he was gone.

He'd slipped a brown manila envelope into Lyosha's hand. Lyosha opened it in his lap, just below the table. Inside it were two new American passports, for himself and for Marina. The photos were their own faces, but the temporary, unfamiliar names he couldn't take in. He closed them without further study and whisked them into his jacket pocket. Two passports, not three. There wasn't one for Anya . . . The Americans couldn't have anticipated that she'd come too.

"What was that?" Anya said.

"Tell you later," he said, tight-lipped and breathing hard, trying to mask the riot of euphoria and uncertainty in his brain.

The train cruised across the border, stopping only to change catering staff, and continued humming along the rails so that they only realized they were in Belarus when the train stopped at Orsha, and they saw cars with Belarusian license plates and heard passengers embarking who spoke Russian in unfamiliar dialects.

They were out of Russia! This time their relief overcame them like the all-clear after a cancer scan. Marina got up to stretch her legs. Anya went to fetch small bottles of wine and plastic cups from the buffet car. None of them dared check their phones. They'd left them switched off. Lyosha got up and intercepted Anya before she'd returned to her seat with the wine. In the narrow, unsteady passage between the carriages he showed her the strange blue passports. She was instantly overjoyed with excitement and relief. "You're home and dry!" she said, trying awkwardly to hug him with two cups of wine in her hands.

Lyosha knew that he would love this woman for the rest of his life. "Come with us," he said. "To the West."

"Without documents?" she laughed.

"We'll figure it out. Claim asylum. At a Western embassy in Minsk."

A look of destiny and sadness came over her then, an aloneness. "No, Lyosha. No, no." She shook her head with a kind of emphatic gratitude. "You have your mother with you. My parents are still at home. I can't leave them. I'll have to return."

Back in his seat, Lyosha turned to the sea of flat brown fields that stretched far into the horizon.

"Well," Anya said with a brave smile. "What will you do when you get to Minsk?"

"Not sure," he said, still thinking.

We go to the American embassy. The Americans need these...

He touched the cufflinks in their hiding place in his jeans.

They were silent for a while. Marina's eyes were closed. Anya stared out of the window. She, too, was lost in thought. Out of the fog of fear and uncertainty, Lyosha was seeing sparkling glimpses of a future. Whatever lay in store for him, he was young, he could navigate it. He would survive and thrive. In Russia, men were lucky to live beyond sixty. People died before their time because they had no hope for the future. They simply gave up. But Fortune had thrown him a lifeline. She had shown him a path out of the forest. He was among the blessed and he felt emotional with gratitude.

About twenty minutes before the train arrived in Minsk Station, a very elegant stewardess in the red uniform of Belarusian Railways came pushing a cart along the carriage. She was distributing hot towels to the passengers as if they were traveling first class on an airline.

"Oh, how nice," Marina said, gratefully accepting a steaming towel from the proffered tongs and wiping her hands.

Anya took one and used it to rub the back of her neck. The stewardess opened a fresh packet of towels. Lyosha took one and covered his face with it. It smelled of citrus and eucalyptus and ocean spray and freedom. The steam opened his pores and he felt cleansed.

Then he rubbed his eyes with it and cleaned his ears.

"This train will shortly be arriving in Minsk Station . . ."

He wondered how far the American embassy was from the station and whether they could walk there. He thought of Sarah Hong's arrest and wondered where she was now, but he wasn't overly worried about her. She was an American citizen and that status was a powerful talisman. They wouldn't dare harm her. He tried to imagine what his father would think of him now . . .

That was his final thought before the world started to whirl in nauseatingly quickening circles, draining all the strength from his muscles, the blood from his heart, and the saliva from his mouth.

Dimly, he heard his mother gasp his name and the sound of his head hitting the window with a thump as oblivion covered him like a black velvet hood.

51

The Lubyanka
Moscow
Friday night

Jenna hammered on the door with the heel of her shoe and yelled for a while, just to get something out of her.

She could vaguely guess the time from a faint change in the noise from the window—distant car radios playing music, the city winding down for the night. Strange to think she was only a few hundred yards away from the Kremlin and the Bolshoi Theater, from which the audience would now be spilling into the streets after the ballet. Bolshoi—Kremlin—Lubyanka. The multiple personality disorder of the Russian state. In less than an hour her lawyer colleagues would be leaving for the airport, and boarding the plane. The plane she was supposed to be on. A few hours after that, her business visa would expire.

She thought of her poor mom, Han. Soo-min had gone missing for twelve and a half years and had returned damaged beyond repair. And her other daughter, where was she? Lost in the labyrinth of the Russian penal justice system.

Accept it. That was the secret of survival. *Wait.* Let the wheels of the system turn. Let the process play out.

She tried to meditate for a while, sitting cross-legged against the door, but the cell was too chilly to sit still. She wondered how long they'd let her stew before the interrogations began, and what she would say. But it would make no difference what she said. Reality was whatever they decided it was.

Perhaps she had known, in her heart, that it would come to this.

Some hours later—she guessed it was two or three in the morning because she could hear sirens as police cars raced about, arresting drunks—the lock rattled, a bolt was pulled back, and the heavy door opened, flooding the room with harsh, magnesium-bright light.

"Get up."

Two officers in brown uniforms handcuffed her and led her upstairs and along a long corridor lined with doors. In one room she glimpsed a seated old man whose face was gray with terror as the door closed.

She was hungry. She hadn't slept. Her hair was a mess. She was still wearing the black evening dress she'd had on last night. The room she was led into was windowless and lit only by anemic strip lighting. Its furniture was a wooden table and two plastic chairs.

A heavy-set, gray-haired man in his mid-forties was seated at the table, arranging papers into separate piles. His tie was loose, and a pen in his shirt pocket had leaked a circle of dark blue into his shirt. His face was pale and unwholesome from lack of sunlight, but his eyes had a wired, caffeinated dance to them. He had a long, gray mustache that gave a civilized first impression. He might have been a university professor, if not for his enormous, pinkish fists. He rubbed his eyes, which became suddenly level and cool, and gestured for her to sit.

"Call me Petrov, if you like." He smiled courteously. "It's a made-up name. Like yours."

Jenna's voice wobbled as if she had a severe case of stage fright. "I'm a citizen of the United States . . ."

"All right." He threaded his huge hands behind his head. "That's a start."

". . . and I demand to see a representative from my embassy."

He pressed his lips tightly together, and nodded, as if she'd said something amusing or wise.

"Sarah Hong. Let's use that name for now. Do you know why you're here?" He spoke slowly and evenly so that she would understand his accented English.

"No." Her voice was a terrified whisper.

For a while, in the cell, Jenna had parted company with Sarah Hong. It was as if she had left her outside the gates, afraid of the trauma this ordeal would have on a vulnerable, innocent woman from upstate New York. But now it was time to drop her into the snake pit, and Jenna channeled her mercilessly. Her eyes became wild and pleading. "Please. There's been some mistake . . ."

"You have been arrested on suspicion of activities contrary to Chapter 29, Article 275 of the criminal code of the Russian Federation."

"I don't understand."

"You're a spy."

Her lip quivered as Sarah's world began buckling before her eyes. "What?"

She looked like a woman on the verge of being driven insane from trying and failing to square the logic of her situation. The nightmare absurdity of it.

He lifted a briefcase onto his lap and retrieved a document.

"This states the reason for your arrest. Please sign it to indicate that you've understood." He slid it across the desk.

The tears were streaming now. "But what have I done?"

He puffed his cheeks and made a vague gesture with his hands, as if to say that all remained to be seen. "I need to know *exactly* what you're doing in Russia. You will answer my questions, and if you try to mislead me, this experience will not go well for you."

He held out a pen. The wheels could not turn without a signature.

Bewildered, she signed, and felt herself entering a vast, impersonal system that one intuitively knew to be evil, but which had a crazy transcendental logic on its side. This man, she saw, was a creature of that system, and within its parameters he was a rational actor, like a sane, blind person who knew his way around a pitch-dark room.

He stroked his mustache. "Let's start at the beginning . . ."

They went through it once. Then they went through it all over again. All her visa application information was in front of him. Her sudden appointment as the recruitment officer to the Washington law firm of Harley, Feinstein & Hawley. Her last-minute inclusion on a business trip to a careers fair at Moscow State University. Her background in recruitment (Sarah Hong had a long, stodgy résumé for this). The reason she had met the university student Alexei Dmitryevich Kuznetsov, not once, but *three times*.

For the first hour or so, Jenna was on solid ground. She could plausibly account for all three meetings. The first, at the Metropol, had been a work drinks reception to which Alexei had been invited by email. The second, soon afterward, in a nearby fast-food eatery close to the Metropol, had been pure chance because she'd gone looking for somewhere to get dinner. The hotel receptionist would back her up. The third, at the Bolshoi, really was a coincidence. She had never been to Moscow before, and the Bolshoi had been the highlight of her trip.

"Coincidence," Petrov said, nodding philosophically. He drew an expansive breath and stared at her. His eyes had acquired an unnerving directness. "There are no coincidences like that, Sarah Hong. Either you have a taste for much younger men, or you needed to meet him for another reason . . ."

Sarah Hong's mouth fell dumbly open.

"Let's start with the first theory. Do you prefer younger men, Sarah Hong? Did you find this twenty-one-year-old attractive? He's quite a looker, isn't he? He plays competitive ice hockey. Did he tell you that?"

"No. And no, he didn't. I would never do anything so unprofessional as—"

"Do you know who his father was?"

This knocked her off balance, as he had intended. Sarah Hong picked herself up again, starting to feel exhausted. "Why would I know that? Lyosha never mentioned his father."

"Oh, *Lyosha*, is it," Petrov said with a smutty grin.

Sarah Hong colored. The thought that she had just helped confirm his suspicions began to take hold of her in the form of an odd symptom—a sensation of pins and needles in her hands. She had the feeling she had come into this room with an opening score of a hundred points, and could only lose them one by one. She could never gain any.

Back to the beginning. They went over every step she'd taken since arriving in Moscow. Where she'd eaten, which routes she'd taken, including the afternoon jog she'd been on the day after she arrived. For that, she had to trust to Elene and Volodymyr's talents: they'd made sure no one had tailed her.

Only when they touched upon her meeting with Lyosha at the Bolshoi, she noticed, did Petrov open the notebook that had remained untouched on the table.

Two or three times over the hours he pressed a buzzer on the desk and called for more coffee and sugar and asked if she wanted any. She declined. She did not relish a Nescafé with two teaspoons of polonium-210. What she badly wanted was water, but she didn't dare drink anything from an unsealed bottle. She watched him blow on his coffee to cool it, and then gulp it down. It seemed to revive him, and his face acquired a fresh resolve, like a runner wearily finding his second wind. Two or three times he left her alone for a few minutes and returned trailing a potent fug of cigarettes. Caffeine and nicotine. The secret policeman's diet.

He plowed on, for how long she couldn't have said. Three hours. Four. Five.

"So, then you saw him again in the champagne bar at the Bolshoi, which was on the third level, but your seat number was L53 in the stalls. How did you even know about that bar?"

"All the other bars were full. I just wanted somewhere to sit. And to get away from my co-workers."

"I see. So you sat, and then—what a coincidence!—in he walks."

"Yes."

"What did you say to him?"

"I've told you." Sarah started sobbing again. "Not much. I don't recall. It was only a few seconds."

"Think, Sarah Hong, think. I advise you to think very carefully." He leaned toward her. "I've warned you what will happen if you mislead me."

This was the moment he kept coming back to. Those few seconds in the champagne bar. This was the clearing in the forest where all the trails connected. He was extremely suspicious about this incident. Something had happened, but he didn't know what. He didn't know about the cufflinks.

The paradox of interrogations was that they could often reveal more information to the prisoner than to the one asking the questions.

The FSB did not know her real identity. They could accept one coincidence but not a second. They suspected that the reason she met Lyosha had something to do with his father's treachery.

"You are not who you say you are, Sarah Hong. You are going to *tell* me who you are, and why you needed to meet this young man."

"Oh, God. This is insane," Sarah moaned.

He opened a laptop and turned it to her. "This is from the champagne bar's security camera." She saw a pinkish-gray video of her head from above. People in evening wear, milling about. The camera was in the corner ceiling. "There you are—seated on a bar stool, staring at your phone. You're doing a lot of scrolling . . . Something interesting?"

Jenna's mind lit up like a Christmas tree. Could the camera see what she'd found on her screen? The images of the man who'd been watching her house? *Eric Rahn.* This line of questioning was veering dangerously close to a heavily mined area: her sister. She felt even more panic as she remembered that the matters were linked. Eric Rahn. The Seed-Bearing Program. The memory card on the cufflinks.

But the screen of her phone, what could be seen of it on the video, was a pale-blue blur.

"It was just Facebook. I was killing time during the interval—"

"Now here's our leading man."

Lyosha was in the frame. And here, she really had looked up in a daze. Her surprise appeared genuine.

"He was just . . . there," Sarah said, wiping tears from her sleeve. "I asked him to get me some water because I don't speak Russian."

Lyosha turned toward the bar, then he handed her a glass of water.

"See?" she said, desperate to be believed.

"Wait." Petrov held up a hand. "Here's the interesting bit."

Lyosha turned away. She made a grab for his sleeve. Petrov froze the frame.

"Why did you do that?"

"To thank him."

Petrov said nothing. And for the first time, Jenna felt a modest swell of optimism. The footage showed nothing.

She almost dared to hope that it was over, but then he said, "I had hoped things would go easier for you, Miss Hong. But that was really up to you."

He put the cap on his leaking pen and closed his notebook. It may have been a signal, because the next moment the door flew open and hit the wall with a bang, and four guards entered the room. One of them pulled her up from the chair. Another cuffed her hands behind her back. She was bundled out of the room with her head forced down in a stress position.

In the courtyard Jenna saw a waiting *avtozak* police van with blacked-out windows, its engine idling. From the length of the shadows and the aroma of borscht, she guessed it was about noon. She looked up and saw a square of marbled gray sky. Even in daylight the walls of Lubyanka courtyard gave a feeling of doom. The cuffs were reattached inside the *avtozak* and looped by a chain to a rail above her head.

They drove for about an hour eastward into the drab industrial outskirts of the city. Power stations puffed tall plumes of white smoke into the spring sky. Grim housing blocks surrounded concrete children's playgrounds.

She smelled the prison before she saw it. A smell of damp and cigarettes and unwashed clothes. The *avtozak* passed through three sets of iron gates. Giant bolts turned. And dogs, many dogs, barked and scratched against the vehicle.

52

Minsk, Belarus
Meanwhile

Lyosha regained consciousness a few times, but only briefly. He felt like a wounded diver struggling upward from some oceanic abyss. The first time he surfaced, he was on his back in the train aisle. His mother and Anya, sitting in adjacent seats either side of him, were talking across each other in desperate, urgent voices. Another woman he couldn't see (a passenger?) was leaning over from behind him checking his pulse. The train had stopped. From outside he could hear passenger announcements. They were in Minsk? Mouths were moving but he could make no sense of their words. He was desperately thirsty but couldn't remember the word "water." Worst of all was his searing headache and a smell of vomit, which he knew was his own. He managed a groan, and his mother and Anya looked down.

"Lyosha, my boy, stay with us, stay with us . . ."

Why was it so hot? He was burning up so badly his clothes were soaked, but no one else was sweating. His sweat smelled strong and strange, like rotting fruit.

He felt unbelievably terrible, but apart from the raging headache there was no real pain. Just a terminal feeling of life leaving his body.

All he knew for certain was that he was dying.

"Lyosha?" said the lady he couldn't see. "I'm going to look into your eyes with the light on my phone; then I'm going to check your reflexes . . ."

A blinding light sent orange stars through his brain, then he again sank beneath the surface of consciousness.

When he came to again, the scene was the same, but the cast was changing.

"Paramedics are here." A sudden commotion as the women disappeared and concerned, serious people in green uniforms examined him again.

"He's been poisoned!" Anya shrieked.

That voice . . . it could de-ice airplanes in the Arctic Circle. It could unblock industrial drains.

"What was the last thing he ate?" one of the paramedics said.

"Nothing for hours. Breakfast in Moscow." His mother's voice.

Anti-life, Lyosha thought. *I've eaten anti-life.*

"Does he suffer from low blood sugar?" one of the men said. "Any metabolic disorders? Alcoholism?"

"No, no, nothing like that."

"He's the healthiest guy in Moscow!" Anya's shout was really something. "He plays hockey! Look how fit he is."

"Atropine," one of the medics said to the other. "Two milliliters."

Another one was making a call. "Yes—we need a critical-care ambulance . . ."

Then his world returned to primordial void.

53

SIZO No. 6 Women's Prison
Moscow
Mid-March 2017

The lighting in the strip-search room had been merciless. In the corner there had been a small cage where they conducted the examination. The guards were all women now.

"Face the wall! Take off your clothes. All of them. Shoes off! Panties off!" The room had been freezing. "Now do ten squats."

"Oh God," Sarah Hong had murmured. "Oh God. Why?"

"So we can make sure you don't have anything hidden *there*."

She'd squatted ten times.

"Now bend over."

In all the scrapes she'd gotten into in the past, this had never happened to her before.

Nothing prepares a person for a humiliation like this.

She was issued with a scratchy gray prison smock, a blanket, which had been fumigated (she could smell the chemicals) but not cleaned, and a blue-and-white-striped mattress that had lost almost all its stuffing. It was a relief to get out of the evening dress. The registration process took so long—forms, photograph; a medical in which she sat naked on a hospital trolley—that by the time she was shown to her cell and given a meal served on a steel tray through a hatch in the door, it was time for 9 p.m. lights out. She was so bone-tired by now that she fell into an instant deep sleep.

In her dream she was trying to make an urgent phone call, but no one would pick up. It just rang and rang. Later, she would learn that this was a very common dream in the first week in prison.

She awoke to a violent hammering on the door, fist against metal, and to the jolting horror of her new reality. A woman's voice yelling in Russian. Jenna couldn't understand. Soon, after hearing the same phrases repeated every time she was too slow to get up, she would learn that the woman was saying, "You think this is a fucking resort? Or are you deaf? Get out of bed now, scum!"

That first morning she had slept right through the morning siren. The sky outside was still dark. She could hear distant trains passing and a wash of traffic. She guessed it was about 5 a.m.

Although she could hear women everywhere, shouting, cursing, laughing, the only women she saw were the guards. On the way to the showers, she asked one of them where she was.

"SIZO No. 6."

SIZO No. 6, she would learn, was a women's detention center for dangerous criminals.

The showers were filthy. Cracked yellow tiles and puddles of gray scum. The water changed from meltwater cold to volcanic hot with nothing in between.

The guard, whose malice she would get to know well, was a heavy woman called Irina. Her uniform looked like the lagging pulled tightly around a boiler. She watched Jenna try to wash using steam. Jenna's vagina still hurt where they'd searched her without using medical instruments, just rough fingers in latex gloves. She could feel the woman's eyes on her and something inside her flared.

She turned, back straight, chest out, and faced the guard. She did not cover her nipples or her pubic area. *Go on, have a good look.* She stared the woman down and flexed the strength in her legs. Water trickled over her breasts, and down her sodden black hair.

"Think you're special, don't you?" Irina folded her arms and slowly shook her head.

By the next day, it had become clear that she was not being allowed near the other prisoners. She showered after them, and exercised in the yard when they were all back in their cells. They were going to keep her apart, and in solitary.

The toilet in her cell was a reeking hole in the floor of a small, raised platform. Food appeared twice a day in a bowl placed on the floor. Watery vegetable soup with stringy pieces of sinew and tendon. Crumbling bread baked from the poorest quality flour. Her window, too high to see out of, faced west, and let in the sun full blast, making the afternoons so hot it turned the cell into a baking tin, but at night a frigid air seeped in. She noticed that the cracks between the wall and the window had been plugged with hundreds of tiny balls of dough and sanitary pads to keep out the cold. Winter in this place would be a long, drawn-out torture.

Irina was her dedicated guard, the only one of these gorgons in uniform responsible for her. The woman's heavy tread followed three paces behind her in the exercise yard, which had a ceiling mesh of rusted metal lattices. She accompanied Jenna to the shower—surely the highlight of Irina's day, the period when she was most attentive in her duties—and on occasional visits to the doctor. Twice a week Jenna was allowed to watch TV in a room that smelled of warm bodies and cigarettes from the women who had just vacated it. Since she understood little Russian, she went along with Irina's favorite reality show, which was about women who stay in relationships with violent boyfriends.

On each of these brief journeys she sensed the gaze of other prisoners watching her from the windows. The special prisoner. The American. Rumors about her must be swirling.

On her second night the cell was so cold that she had to fold the mattress in half and lie in the middle like a filling in a fajita. She rarely slept for long. The hours of darkness were almost as noisy as the day. Klaxons blared at regular intervals as transits of new prisoners arrived like shoals of Atlantic herring, passing through the prison on their way to the gulags in the east.

Irina's eye peeped in through the judas hole at unexpected times. "Hands outside the blankets!"

On the third day, Irina cuffed Jenna's hands behind her back and took her to a windowless basement chamber lit by blinding overhead lights. She was ordered to sit in a tiny wooden chair. It was like a child's schoolroom chair, except that it had leather restraining straps to bind her arms to the seat rests.

A doctor in a grubby white coat entered, wheeling a gas cannister. He was followed by a uniformed woman stenographer who took up position at a desk in the corner. Finally, an officer entered wearing the petroleum-blue uniform of the SVR.

So, there had been a power struggle over her. The FSB was responsible for internal security, so in theory a spy caught on home turf was theirs. But a *foreign* spy was of intense interest to the spooks in the SVR, responsible for foreign intelligence. Perhaps an appeal had been made to the man at the top.

Sarah Hong's eyes were popping out of her head like bird's eggs. She looked petrified, ready to scream, but inwardly, Jenna had already decided she was going to have fun with the stenographer.

"Oh God, oh no, please . . . Pleeeeeease," Sarah Hong pleaded, and started to blubber. The stenographer was already tapping away at her portable machine.

"Miss Hong, you're here to answer our questions," the officer said, in slow, accented English. "It is futile to resist. Your operation here has been foiled. If you cooperate, we can avoid any unpleasantness and you will have the possibility of an early release."

"I've done nothing wrong," Sarah whined, wilting under her tears. "I've got to get home. My dog needs me. Will I ever see my dog again?"

"That depends on you."

"My poor dog. He's called Mr. Schneebles."

The stenographer paused her typing.

"Shall I spell that for you?"

The officer backhanded Jenna hard across the face, and the instant Jenna felt the sting of the blow and the blood heating her cheek she grew stronger. They would never get her that way.

The officer nodded to the doctor, who clamped a rubber ventilator mask over her mouth. It was attached by a tube to the cannister. She just had time to note the smell before she lost consciousness. *Nitrous oxide,* the same used by dentists. Laughing gas.

When she came to, she was still strapped to the chair. This was the danger moment, she knew. The ecstasy that accompanied the rising to the surface after a deep dive—that's when she was at most risk of blurting out the answer to anything they asked.

"Why did you come to Moscow?"

Mirth rippled deep in her chest.

"What is your name?"

Then she started shaking silently, laughing until she had a cramp in her stomach and her cheeks were wet with tears.

The next day, she was taken to a bright, spartan room where the sun shone through reinforced glass. It gave a view onto a bleak courtyard of stained pipes and cracked walls. The man waiting for her shook her hand warmly. "I'm Colonel Anton Nikolayev," he said. He was in his forties. His blond hair was neatly parted, his nails were clean, his cheeks rosy and wholesome, his uniform new and sporting a line of ribbons and gold shoulder tabs. He reminded her of a Nazi from the movies, the cultured type with a doctorate and a passion for Bach.

Colonel Nikolayev asked her if there was anything she needed.

"An extra blanket and a bottle of Jack Daniel's."

His smile was one of amused regret. "The first of those items shall be furnished forthwith. The second is beyond even my power, I fear."

His English was excellent and his manner so mild and understanding that Jenna was instantly on her guard. This man, she suspected, was a specialist, and she would have to hold onto Sarah Hong like a lifebuoy, with all her strength, and never let her go, no matter how long this took.

His opening question confirmed her suspicion. "Why don't you start by telling me why you became a spy?"

"I'm not a spy, sir. I'm a recruitment officer."

He continued in his gentle, probing manner, as if he hadn't heard her. "Were you recruited at university? Or later?" He knitted his hands together on the table and leaned toward her, still smiling, as if she were some student prodigy whom he was thrilled to meet. "What was your *motivation*?"

The questions were all in this vein, always starting with the premise of her guilt—that she had committed espionage—and building on it. Did she have an especial hatred for Russia? What had she been hoping to achieve? Couldn't she see that the organization she served, the CIA, had let her down? Then he would sigh and talk about life's regrets and disappointments, and how he admired courageous people like herself, and how it was only natural—part of the human condition, wasn't it?—that we suffer delusions, but there was a cure for those delusions, if she was ready to make a simple effort of will.

"I want to see someone from the US embassy."

54

Clinical Emergency Hospital
Minsk, Belarus
A few days earlier

When Lyosha next emerged, he was in a bright room with a tube squeezed into his throat and a drip in his arm. A monitor was beeping softly. His arms and legs were dead and unfeeling. He couldn't move his eyes.

Two Belarusian medics were speaking in hushed voices.

"... this is a very specific field. There are only two hospitals that can handle a case as serious as this, and they're in Strasbourg and Berlin. He must be evacuated to Europe ..."

"... which is a very dangerous substance. Everyone in here should be wearing personal protective gear ..."

Later, he didn't know how much later, he could hear but only partially see.

His mother again. "We demand that you release him so he can be treated in an independent hospital we can trust! He's in a very bad condition. We do not trust a hospital in Belarus ..."

Some kind of negotiation was going on around him, but it was very confusing and unclear. The doctors were losing the floor. Two men in gray suits (Belarusian security services?) were now present in the room and they seemed to have taken control of the diagnosis. One of them said, "Severe alcohol poisoning."

"That's BULLSHIT!" Anya's voice could raise the dead from their graves and send them flying. "If it's just alcohol poisoning, why won't you release him for transfer? STOP LYING!"

"The doctors need to keep him stable. They can't allow his transfer in this condition..."

Later: his mother's voice, outside the room in the corridor. "Three days!? Why? So you can wait for the poison to leave his system? You can see how serious this is. His body is a *crime scene*..."

Sometime in the evening, he heard Anya say, "They're keeping him here so he'll die without anyone knowing how they killed him. We've got to do something. You heard how those toads are already changing the story. We're in an information war."

"We need outside help," Marina said, frantic.

"Lyosha's a YouTube star, isn't he? If he's going to have a chance, we've got to get ahead of this now."

There was a pause as she did something with her phone.

"What are you doing?" Marina said. "You want the whole world to see him like this?"

"Sorry, Lyosha, my darling," Anya said. "I know I'm doing this without your consent." She was pointing her phone camera at him. Then she pressed record and started narrating: "Hello, everyone. To our friends in Russia. To our friends in Europe and America. We are in the ICU of the City Clinical Emergency Hospital in Minsk. The person you're looking at is on life support. He is Alexei Dmitryevich Kuznetsov, the young guy who had the balls to call out Putin on live TV. You all know the clip. Well, this is what happens to anyone who crosses the tsar. This morning Lyosha was traveling by train from Moscow to Minsk. He fell sick onboard with a case of severe poisoning. Now he's on life support in—"

The monitor's tone changed to a flat, continuous sound.

Anya and his mother ran to the bedside as Lyosha's eyes rolled back and he sank into a coma. The recording on Anya's phone was still rolling.

55

SIZO No. 6 Women's Prison
Moscow

The evening after her first interview with Colonel Nikolayev, Jenna was back in the basement with interrogator number one. Same doctor, same stenographer. This time, the doctor had brought a black medic's bag filled with a neat row of syringes. For the first time Jenna felt a jolt of genuine alarm.

Years ago, at the Farm, she'd been taught techniques for resisting psychotropic drugs, but it had all sounded like theory. She'd never had to put the theory to the test.

Focus obsessively on a single object, they'd told her. If there's no object, then a thought or a person. Do that, and the mind can counteract the effect of interrogation drugs. She remembered that the drugs spiked only briefly in potency before dissipating.

"Just relax," the doctor said, as the doctor injected her arm with the first of three drugs.

"The first injection is an amobarbital," he said. "The second is scopolamine. The third is ethanol. It's our house cocktail. We're going on a pleasant trip."

That, Jenna soon found, was a gross lie. She felt sick to her stomach suddenly, and then an overwhelming sense of vertigo sent her brain into a nauseating, confused spin as the drugs invaded one lobe, then the next, forcing her conscious self into a chaotic retreat. Her body felt unstable on the hard chair.

"Tell me your name." The voice was quiet, soothing.

Keep breathing. Who was the first boy you ever kissed? John Moloney. Keep breathing. Where was the first place you ever flew on an airplane? Jackson, Mississippi. Keep breathing. What was the gift you loved so much on your sixth birthday? A pair of ruby-red Mary-Janes.

"Tell me your name."

Keep breathing. "You are stronger than any of them," said Fisk's voice inside her head. *The point of focus—find one and stay on it.*

The room was bare, and now she knew why—there *was* no point to focus on. But above the interrogator's head she noticed that a small flake of plaster had fallen from the wall leaving a shape that roughly resembled the state of Florida. She locked onto that ruthlessly. That, and nothing else. She would never talk, she told herself—not until Florida iced over, and that would never happen. *The drugs won't work because I'm not here, I'm in Palm Beach, Florida.*

She held onto that point on the wall for dear life, even as her field of vision began to shrink. All around her, she became aware of dark hallucinatory tendrils like black seaweed, flowing and rippling underwater. The tendrils brushed closer and closer to the Florida shore. How long this went on—five minutes? Five hours?—she had no idea. She kept breathing, kept focusing, until the fog in her brain began to evaporate, giving her an ebullient rush of adrenaline. She was out of the dark cave system, and her eyesight became hyper-clear. She could discern particles of grime on the doctor's coat. She could see the chip in the pink nail varnish on the stenographer's fingers. The drug was dissipating as quickly as it had come on. The doctor looked to the interrogator and shook his head.

The next morning, Colonel Nikolayev's attitude was more pressing, more enthusiastic, as if his line of attack had grown in importance after the failure of the drugs. He never seemed to tire.

The next day, and the day after were the same. Same questions, same answers.

Each evening, she returned to the rancid cell. She slept in her clothes. She ate the rank soup and she chewed the powdery, dry bread, which stuck to the roof of her mouth.

A week went by, then another. She awoke to Irina yelling abuse and hammering on the door at 5:15 a.m. Jenna was learning the Russian words for *cunt, scum, worthless lay-about*. She showered under Irina's gaze, which betrayed a nasty mix of lust and envy on some days; contempt and prejudice on others.

Slowly, Jenna's repeated denials to Colonel Nikolayev began to exhaust her. With the drugs they'd hoped for instant results, but his was a longer, much more patient game, and he was confident of his method. She had only to accept the truth, he said, and she would find liberation. By the end of each session with him, truth, logic, make-believe, deception, were blurring in her mind to the point where she was moving closer and closer to the reality Nikolayev was painting, and she had to admit it was taking on a powerful appeal. This man was an artist at work. Gradually, always with concern for her feelings, he was casting a massive psychological dragnet around her, no matter in which direction she swam. He was reeling her in, slyly twitching and tugging her toward the dark door, and once she went through it, she would never come out. They both knew that if she betrayed even one tiny aspect of herself, if Sarah Hong stumbled once, she would not be able to stop.

"It's easy, really," Nikolayev said, as if he were instructing her in basic logic. "We simply need to establish *why* you came to Moscow, what your *objectives* were, and then we're done." She almost reached for his hand.

At certain points, her brain braised and shredded from exhaustion, and her guts in uproar from the watery soup, she felt herself slipping toward him like a cold, hungry person seeing the light of a warm kitchen hearth. Then she would force herself to focus on her mom, and on Soo-min, and her childhood bedroom in Annandale, the wings of her mind flying high over the streets and yards they'd played in as children.

One morning Jenna entered the room to find not Colonel Nikolayev, but a man in a suit and tie she vaguely recognized. He leapt up when he saw her.

"Sarah, oh boy." He smiled and looked at her sideways, as if he were about to offer something she was desperate to receive. "Can I give you a hug?"

The American ambassador.

He had the well-tanned look of someone who spent time on the tennis court. His teeth were game-show white. His hair was moussed and silver-gray. It gave him the air of a model in an ad for luxury senior-citizen cruise vacations.

"We're doing everything we can, Sarah, everything."

"That's good to know, sir."

"The president has been briefed."

"President Trump knows I'm here?"

"Absolutely. One hundred percent. And he's raising it with Putin this week. I'm very hopeful."

I'm cooked, she thought.

56

Moscow Central Court

The next day Jenna was taken to Moscow City Court for her bail hearing. They left her to wait in a basement holding area for three hours, handcuffed to a bench.

Ten minutes before the hearing, a pudgy man with frizzy ginger hair introduced himself as Markov. He told her that bail was unlikely to be granted in view of the evidence against her.

"What evidence?"

"I have not been permitted to view it, but I'm assured it's substantial."

This unimpressive person, appointed by the court, was her lawyer.

Jenna said nothing, but she was interested to see that the defendant's name on the application documents (all in Russian) was still Sarah Hong.

They don't know. They've got nothing.

Markov rode with her in the elevator to the courtroom, standing so close to her she could smell pickles on his breath. A group of FSB officers stood about with Alsatians in muzzles. They stared at her as if she was a famous serial killer. She was led through a door and found herself in a steel cage inside the courtroom.

The judge's chair was beneath the double-headed eagle of the

Russian Federation. The public chairs were empty except for the US ambassador and his aide. He projected a theatrical look toward her and formed his hands into a heart symbol. She smiled weakly. So, no cameras, no press, no public. *A closed hearing.*

"Defendant, please stand." Someone was interpreting for her, the voice on audio inside the cage.

The judge entered in black robes, a grandmotherly figure with thick glasses and her hair tied back in a bun.

"Well?" she said.

Markov said, "My client is innocent of the charges. She has exhibited exemplary behavior in custody and poses no flight risk. She is without a passport and will be supported by the embassy of the United States."

"Defendant?"

"Your honor, I don't understand the charge," Jenna said in a quavering voice channeling Sarah Hong again. "I've done nothing wrong." She began to sob, at the sheer absurdity of it all, at the world that was buckling before her eyes. And not all the tears were Sarah Hong's, she realized. They were Jenna's too.

To her surprise the judge yelled at her. "What don't you understand?"

"Everything."

The prosecutor remained on his feet. "Sarah Hong is a dangerous American spy. The authorities have not yet completed their investigation, and evidence is still being gathered."

The judge nodded and closed the folder in front of her. "Bail denied. Defendant will be remanded in custody until trial."

She was led from the cage and saw Markov waiting for her like a rangy alley cat on the other side of the door. He began to say something to her, but she cut him off.

"You're fired."

Jenna had never been under any illusion that her situation was not serious. But she'd been in bad, bad corners before and, whether through chance or skill, had always found a way out. Now, handcuffed in the *avtozak*, riding back to the prison through the vast, gloomy city, she saw that a part of her mind had been holding onto a wholly irrational belief, a folly—that however dire things might be right now, they would resolve, somehow. A chance would present itself, some high-level negotiation would take place, and she would emerge from her predicament.

But what if she never emerged? Had she truly considered that, in all its bleak finality? What if this was her life now, what was left of it? Prison and deprivation, stretching for years into the future . . . endless days, and every one of them the same.

She was thousands of miles from home, locked in a freezing cell, and denied all contact with the world. Like a captured chess piece, she thought. Removed from the board, irrelevant, no role left to play.

The prison gates loomed, she caught the frowzy, unwashed smell, heard the dogs barking and scratching at the vehicle, and the full horror of her reality began properly to sink in.

I'm never getting out.

PART FOUR
California

It's an odd thing, but anyone who disappears is said to be seen in San Francisco.

Oscar Wilde

57

Marin County, California
April 2017

Alyssa Jane Wright double-checked that she had everything with her—her notes, which she'd memorized and rehearsed, her makeup (her forehead tended to shine when she got nervous), and the packed lunch Maria had left for her in the refrigerator. She hung her school blazer on the backseat, slipped on her Ray-Bans, and started her BMW coupé (a seventeenth birthday present from Mom). The sound system instantly pumped out Snap's "The Power" and she turned it up. This morning she didn't give a hoot about the neighbors.

Traffic on Miller Avenue was already sluggish, which set off another spasm of nerves, but then she was through the lights at the intersection and hitting the gas.

I got the Power.

She felt keyed-up, expectant, bobbing her head to the beat. Ahead of her, Mount Tamalpais rose above the pines like a scene from the Old Testament. The air was still cool along the narrow, wooded canyons, and when she reached the coastal road on Richardson Bay, fog was rolling magically down the mountainside to the sea.

I got the Power.

Resilience—that's what she had. She'd expected the spring semester of junior year to be a struggle, but her GPA had recovered from its nosedive in January, and her most recent SAT score had been a pleasant surprise to her parents. This time four months ago she'd been at rock bottom. Weight gain from too many unsupervised milkshakes and waffles during her parents' divorce, antidepressants, and a humiliating breakup with Kyle that had caused her grades to tank.

She gave an impatient little shake of her head. Whatever. She was over it.

She'd lost the weight, her dental braces had finally come off, and most importantly, she was on track to get into UC Berkeley.

I got the Power.

She pulled into the school parking lot and turned off the music, closed her eyes, and breathed in. She could do this. Then she nearly jumped out of her skin. A boy was pressing his face against the driver's window so that his cheeks looked like a butt crack.

"Stop it, Tyler," she said, pushing him away as she opened the door. "I need your support today."

"Why? 'Cause you've invited a fascist?"

"OK. Fuck off."

The school building was Mission Revival with arches, courtyards, bell-gables, and huge, shady sycamores. She had about half an hour before assembly—enough time to make sure everything was in order. She turned on the projector, tested the mics, and adjusted the volume. She made sure chairs were in neat rows and the men's washroom was spotless, in case her guest needed to use it. Cars started to arrive. She heard the students larking about near the courtyard fountain before they started shambling slowly into the assembly hall in twos and threes as the bell rang.

Her nerves were jangling wildly. *Oh Jesus.* Her guest had just texted to say he was two minutes away.

I can do this.

"You'll be fine, Alyssa." It was the school principal, Dr. Helmsley, smiling at her with a very un-Californian set of teeth.

"Thank you, sir. Just a little nervous," she said, using her notes to fan her face, which she hoped hadn't begun to shine.

Her phone buzzed again. *He's here.*

She straightened her skirt, adjusted her hair, plastered on a smile, and headed out of the main door of the school to the forecourt.

A man was getting out of a luxurious Mercedes hire car. He sauntered toward her, taking his time, his tie loosened and his suit jacket hung over his arm as he beeped a key fob and the car lights winked. He was effortlessly casual and debonair, as if he'd stepped from the pages of a fashion magazine, which was in fact where she'd first seen him. He took off his aviators and gave her a smile that dimpled his cheeks. She was trying not to look at him in awe.

"Alyssa. So great to meet you at last. Hope I'm not late."

"No, you've arrived exactly when you said you would." She inclined her head in what she thought was a professional manner and offered her hand. "Welcome to Tamalpais High School." She repressed the urge to say, "How ARE you??" because this was a *professional* interaction. And, as she professionally escorted him into the school building, she explained, in words she had already prepped, how many students were majoring in what, the speaker's format—forty minutes, max—and Tamalpais' proud history of inviting diverse and distinguished speakers.

He leaned in close to her as she spoke, nodding, brow furrowed, as if she were an esteemed colleague. He smelled gorgeous, she noticed, of cedar and sandalwood. Everything about him projected success: the car, the shiny black hair (beautifully cut), the polished black shoes, the elegant navy suit with a burgundy silk lining in the jacket. She couldn't believe this person had accepted her invitation. Well—actually, she *hadn't* invited him. He'd simply *offered* to come, and she'd leapt at the chance. It had started when he'd "liked" her tweet about the federal budget. The next thing she knew they were swapping witty public remarks about press conference etiquette. Then she'd asked him what it was like to work in the White House, and he'd said why don't I come to your school and tell you, and now—*OH my God*—here he was walking alongside her toward the assembly hall of *her* school.

Alyssa was vice president of the school's politics society, and the idea, at first, had been a modest one: that her invitee would be the guest speaker at a pol-soc event. But as soon as the faculty advisor got wind of it, the teaching staff were suddenly on board and before she knew it Dr. Helmsley was suggesting that he address the student body at the assembly. The teachers were visibly impressed with her initiative. This was a real boost for her résumé.

While the students gave the pledge of allegiance and mumbled their way through the Tamalpais prayer she waited with her guest to the right of the stage. The lights had been lowered in the wings, making the dial of his Rolex luminesce, but she sensed that his eyes were gazing at her, and he was standing so close it was almost like he was scenting her skin, breathing her in. It was unsettling and confused her utterly for a moment, as if an animal had crept up on her in the dark.

Dr. Helmsley was concluding his announcements.

This is it—I'm on.

She took another deep breath and strode across to the lectern, her posture straight, her manner bright and confident, as if she did this every day. She positioned herself in front of the mic, feeling her knees turning to paper, her smile going into spasm at the edges of her lips as she waited for the hubbub of voices to subside.

Every seat was taken. A sea of red blazers. The staff were standing at the back of the hall and along the aisles. Tyler, Honoré, and Tammy were in the front row. She'd resolved not to look at them at all but couldn't resist. They were beaming at her and juggling their thumbs up and down.

"Ladies and gentlemen . . ." Her notes were trembling violently in her hand. "Our speaker today was born to a poor family in Korea. He arrived in the United States when he was eighteen years old with barely a dollar to his name. But he'd studied hard and he'd won a scholarship to Harvard and from there to the Kennedy School of Government . . ." Scattered whoops and murmurs of respect from the audience. "That, to me, embodies the American dream." After those words in her notes, she had written *Look up. Smile.* "But he was only getting started. In 2015, he demonstrated exceptional political acumen by volunteering to work on the campaign of a presidential candidate whom no one believed stood a chance. I know I sure didn't!" *Pause for laughter.* "But his belief in the candidate never wavered, and neither did the candidate's confidence in him. Today, our speaker is a White House *special advisor* and a *trusted confidant* to the forty-fifth president of the United States . . ." The applause began to rise like the sea before her. "Ladies and gentlemen, please give a warm Tamalpais welcome to Mr. ERIC RAHN."

Eric Rahn walked onto the stage rather shyly, she thought. You'd swear he was a movie star from the students' reaction to him, but rather than lap it up like some egomaniac, he appeared honored, surprised even, by the reception. He put his hand to his heart and bowed, mouthing *thank you* as the clapping continued. Then he shook Alyssa's hand again, making her feel as if she'd just introduced the president himself, and took a page of notes from his breast pocket, which he unfolded and placed on the lectern. They were just a few printed bullet points for the themes of his speech, at the top of which he'd written . . .

Did she just imagine that?

Alyssa left the stage as the applause subsided and took her own seat in the front row, which she'd had the foresight to reserve with a card bearing her name.

"Good morning, Tamalpais. That was a heck of a welcome. I guess you've heard I've got the kind of boss who gets jealous about things like that . . ." Audience laughter.

No, she hadn't imagined it.

"I'd like to thank Alyssa for inviting me here today..."

Eric Rahn glanced down at her in the front row, and she could have sworn she now saw another face entirely behind the smile.

Next to his bullet points, Eric Rahn had scribbled a list of five names in pencil.

She'd seen it only for a split second, long enough to see they were the names of her three closest friends, who were sitting right next to her in the front row... plus her ex-boyfriend, Kyle.

58

The Charité hospital
Berlin, Germany
Meanwhile

Lyosha could hear again before he could see. Hearing was the first of his senses to stir and rouse itself from the sediment. The sounds made no sense to him, except for the noise of his own breathing, but there was something weird and artificial about that, as if it were a machine moving and not his lungs. Voices were speaking in German. He couldn't understand a word. But he could detect varying tones of optimism, excitement, doubt, caution. Occasionally someone translated the words into Russian, and he heard his mother's voice speaking in a low, hushed nervousness, as if she were waiting for news of an especially difficult birth in which no one was sure if mother or baby were going to make it. His eyesight was the next sense to be reborn, and this slow, coming-online of his vision sent exclamations of joy through the voices in the room. Bright lights were shone into his pupils, but he couldn't close his eyelids against the glare.

"They're dilating," said a man's voice in translation. "He's responding to visual stimuli."

"Oh, thank God," Marina gasped. Next, his mother was over him, her face lowering to his as if she were emerging from white clouds. Her lips buckled and her tears fell onto his face. He did not feel their wetness. His body still had no sensation. But his own tears pooled freely in his eyes.

Soon after that, his sense of smell returned. The comforting scent of his mama's skin, and the tang of new equipment and unfamiliar disinfectants.

Lyosha's brain remained in a thick fog. Data from outside his body reached him intermittently. It was like watching a car's headlights approach from a distance across dark, hilly lanes. Occasionally, he heard his father's voice nearby, as clearly as if he were reading him a bedtime story, and he realized he was hallucinating. Sometimes he heard the deathly strains of that ogre Giorgadze; sometimes, a friendly voice, urgent, pleading, appeasing. American.

Sarah Hong.

It was Sarah Hong's voice that triggered in him the kind of anxious agitation he often experienced after bad dreams, when he had something of great import to remember but he'd forgotten what it was and his forgetting of it had let everyone down, including himself.

Over the next few days, his progress was slow, but it was progress. By the third day, he could move his fingers and toes very slightly and with great effort, as if they were wardrobes or safe boxes. He still could not speak. Marina did not leave his bedside. She slept in a chair next to him. When he dozed or closed his eyes against the afternoon light from the windows, he could feel her presence, her love. He drew comfort from it. He never saw her eat.

No sight or sound of Anya. That voice that could split the atom.

Even after he was able to sit up in bed and the mechanical ventilator and the tube and the drip were removed, he simply stared straight ahead, unable to say anything or focus for long on anyone. His voice would be the last of his functions to join the reunion.

Snatches of meaning made it through the fog and brushed lightly over his mind, before slipping away again. He remembered little of what anyone said.

"... been in a coma for almost a month ..."

"... The Charité. That's where you are. Berlin ..."

"... Anya made a YouTube clip of you in the hospital in Minsk and the Germans saw it. They kicked up a diplomatic fuss and got you transferred here by train ..."

"... poisoning. Without knowing which poison to test for it's difficult for the toxicologists to determine ..."

"... possibly one of a group of nerve agents called cholinesterase inhibitors ..."

"... Anya's thrilled to know you're sitting up ... look, she's sent you a video message ..."

"... Recovery is going to be slow ..."

"... A lot of physiotherapy ..."

"... Back on the ice rink next season, Lyosha ..."

"... the German foreign minister's been here! You've been all over social media, again ..."

Soon after he started regaining movement in his limbs his hallucinations got much worse. A hardcore Russian rap group called Kasta, which he'd always hated for the dreary profanity of their lyrics, started riffing inside his brain, so loud and so unbearably vivid it was as if he had his head inside the speakers at a gig. His hands started shaking uncontrollably. That was a good sign, the German doctor said.

He could tell from the professional caution and concern in their faces that they thought his recovery was touch and go.

The doctor who'd said "a good sign" looked like some hospital high-up, a consultant. Under his white coat he wore business attire. A tie and a blue-striped shirt with cuffs. Cuffs with cufflinks.

I had cufflinks. Gold ones. I put them in my ...

"Mama, where're my clothes?"

It was the moment Lyosha finally spoke, and everyone in the room exhibited the histrionic relief of seeing someone safely returned form a very dangerous place.

Marina clapped her hands together and laughed and kissed him on his forehead. The nurses, a man and a woman, high-fived. The consultant smiled.

"I've bought you *new* clothes," his mother said, as if it were Christmas morning.

"My jeans," he mumbled, "My jeans." His eyes rolled in such distress that he sent them all straight back into worry mode. "Where're my jeans?"

The consultant told the nurse to give him an injection of propofol, a sedative, which gave him the sensation of falling onto a feather bed in a soundproofed room. It was a relief after listening to Kasta.

The next day, the aural hallucinations were still plaguing him, but they had retreated to the cellars of his brain. He could eat some solid food and think a little more clearly, if only for brief spells. His speech was still labored, as if his tongue was not his own.

"My jeans . . . Mama. Where are they?"

"I don't know where they are." Marina's voice was full of loving patience, as if he were a little boy again. "Those KGB men in Minsk must have taken them when we were in that hospital. Why are you so attached to those old things?"

KGB men? Yes . . . yes. The security forces in Belarus were still called the KGB . . .

The knowledge returned to him with a shock as violent as if he'd been covered in hot ash. He dropped his head back on the pillow.

"Lyosha, my love, what's wrong?"

Spies . . . His father had been a patriot who loved Russia. His father had taken an oath to defend Russia against its enemies. His father had been about to give vital intelligence to the United States just before he died . . .

That American woman, Sarah Hong, had come to Russia to retrieve the intelligence. It was stored in the CUFFLINKS.

For a few minutes he felt a real anger toward Sarah Hong, a person he barely knew. But when he puzzled over why he'd reacted like that he realized that his mind was trying to shield him from pain. It was displacing his emotions, disguising them, casting them over decoys. It was not real anger but guilt, and the source of his guilt was his father. Whatever was in those cufflinks was so important that his father had died for it. And now they were lost.

"Oh, my love. What's the matter?"

That evening a junior minister from the German Foreign Office visited him with a personal message from Chancellor Merkel. She wanted him to know that if he and Marina wished to claim asylum in Germany, the government would view their application favorably.

Lyosha managed to say, "Where's Anya?"

Marina's face became serious. "Anya's gone back to Moscow, my love. She decided to risk it. She wants to sit her exams and she said she can't leave her parents."

59

Marin County, California

Eric's eyes roved across the sea of faces before him in the assembly hall. Rich kids. Entitled. Kids who felt they not only mattered but were important. Kids destined for USC (the University of Spoilt Children).

"My theme today is one I know many of you have studied: *revolution*. Dr. Helmsley, I've been told, is a scholar of the American Revolution. So it is with some humility that I offer a few thoughts of my own on its relevance to our present time . . ."

Three of the kids who were with Alyssa in the Golden Gate Bridge photo were seated in the front row. He'd recognized them instantly: the peroxide-haired, too-cool-for-school guy was Tyler McCabe, the homecoming queen with the skirt near the top of her thighs was Tammy Halloran, the Black kid with the cornbraids was Honoré Jones.

Oh, Facebook, you banisher of privacy, you revealer of lives.

"What is a revolution? It is a violent overthrow of a government or social order in favor of a new system. A revolution almost never draws its disruptive power from inside society's Establishment. Often, it takes an outsider, someone untainted by the culture of the ruling elite, to enact a truly radical political change. It is my belief that President Trump is such an outsider . . ."

A few snorts of ridicule rose from the assembly and an unmistakable hissing sound rolled in from the juniors and seniors in the back. Members of staff were frowning, arms folded, wondering where this was going. Dr. Helmsley shushed them angrily.

"No, sir. That's OK," Eric said, with a benign smile. "I know I'm in California, not Texas. But you're all smart kids—with inquiring minds." He opened his hands benevolently. "Would it *hurt* if you listened to an opinion that you're not familiar with? Would it *upset* you to know how folks see things elsewhere?"

The students shifted in their seats, chastened. None of them wished to be considered assholes by the people they considered assholes.

"Actually, let's talk about those folks for a moment. Let's do the simple thought experiment of putting ourselves in others' shoes. Wouldn't you be angry if the government ignored you? Wouldn't you feel aggrieved if the benefits promised to you were snatched away by forces larger and more powerful than you? People in every state grew up believing that they were heirs to a great promise—the American dream. But what if that promise has become an impossible fantasy for the very people who were supposed to inherit it? Donald Trump is the first president who listened—truly listened—to the people who have come to feel like strangers in their own land . . ."

As he spoke, Eric continued to scan the rows of seats, noticing that the students had become alert, serious. He was connecting to each of these young, undefended souls. *I may disagree with you,* their eyes were saying, *but you respectfully have my attention.*

His real target, Ha-jun, was not a student at this school, he was fairly sure of that now.

But four of the kids in that photo are sitting just yards away from me . . . He squinted into the rear of the hall. *And there's the fifth!* Back row. Corner of the room.

A dark-haired, handsome boy was regarding him with naked skepticism.

Kyle Mason. Ex-boyfriend of Alyssa Jane Wright. All five of you in one room. And one of you is going to give me my prize.

"Donald Trump is the ordinary citizen who, in times of crisis, uses his common sense to save others. The revolutionary, the *hero*, is, by definition, an anti-politician. Yes, a revolutionary breaks things, but sometimes they're things that need breaking. I'm thinking of our self-appointed, meritless intelligentsia. Our entrenched, herd-like media. The globalized big money that values profit over local jobs . . ."

The atmosphere in the assembly was no longer relaxed, but becoming pressured, straining like the hull of a submersible going too deep for comfort. Here and there across the hall, he could see students visibly suppressing their disagreement. They were getting riled, keyed-up, restless for the Q&A at the end. Hands were already being raised in question. Teachers were glancing at each other, wondering if they should cancel Eric mid-speech.

"Sure, the deep state will fight like hell against its own destruction, but destruction is also creative, and can massively increase the quotient of individual freedom . . ."

Eric had come here intending to make some bland, standard remarks, but faced with this sea of privilege, he couldn't resist fucking with them, and the dark signature of his own views was overwriting everything he'd prepared.

"What we're seeing today is a national community rising like a phoenix from the years of decadence that have all but destroyed it. What have liberals ever achieved for us but the elevation of the mediocre and the weak at the expense of the authentic and the principled? Why should ordinary people suffer the bonds of political correctness by showing respect toward those they do not respect? Why should they stand idly by when criminal migrants flood across our borders to poison our lifeblood and degrade the values our nation holds dear?"

"Fascism!" someone shouted.

"No, no," Eric said, speaking through the groans of protest now stirring across the hall. He held up a finger. "Not fascism. Not any ideology. But a *reset*. An overdue correction."

Alyssa's smile, he saw, was pinned tightly in place, her eyes moving left and right in alarm.

"If people's fears go unaddressed . . . if they become convinced that the system no longer works for them, society is ready to explode. Americans are forced to work multiple jobs just to survive. We are starved of purpose, meaning, identity at a time in our national history when the things that used to fill our lives—faith, patriotism, hard work, family—have disappeared. And what has taken their place? What has filled the void? Wokeism. LGBTQ. Climate hysteria. Globalism. Depression. Anxiety. Opioids. Suicide."

A perfect silence fell. Eric could feel his charisma crackling around him, he could feel it in the heat of his hands. Its energy was growing as he continued to speak. He was starting small fires inside each mind and who knew where those fires would spread? Now, when he lowered his voice, he knew that every word he spoke was being heard.

"In such times, something's got to give. We are approaching our 1776 moment. And a politician is not the answer."

A small sprinkling of applause landed on the general hostility of the room, germinating new areas of support.

"Vladimir Lenin wrote, 'A revolution is not a dinner party.' Revolutions are not fun to live through," Eric said, clasping both sides of the lectern. He was really warming up now. "They bring pain, suffering, upheaval. All the freedoms you enjoy right now are the result of past revolutions. But the very laws and systems that have set you free have fossilized and corrupted. Over time, they have fallen so far behind people's cultural consciousness that a revolution is the only way to catch up . . ."

Eric glanced at his watch. What a shame he only had forty minutes! A little longer and he could give them all PTSD.

He concluded by saying, "Students of Tamalpais High, the Trump Revolution is the realization of America's historic founding majority. As such, Donald Trump is ushering in the next stage of the American Revolution. Donald Trump is the heir of George Washington. Thank you."

The assembly hall was an instant tumult of applause and loud, unrestrained booing. Several students had jumped to their feet, yelling. Arguments were breaking out among groups of friends.

Dr. Helmsley dashed to the stage to speak into the mic before the situation descended into chaos. "All right. All right. Remain in your seats. All right. I'm sure we'd all like to, ah, *thank* Mr. Rahn for that, ah, provocative and *stimulating* speech. I think we can say we've just heard from a true *drummer* of the MAGA movement. Now, we're going to take some questions . . ." At least a hundred hands shot straight up. "Mr. Rahn, if you could keep your answers brief, we'll try to fit in as many as we can."

Eric returned to the mic smiling as if he were accepting a Grammy. He cupped his hand to his ear as the first question was called.

"Sir, my question is: how can we respect a man who lies? Donald Trump lies all the time! He doesn't care what's true or not."

Eric pursed his lips and nodded solemnly. "Everyone's truth is subjective to a degree. But no one can say that President Trump's *emotions* aren't true. That's why he was the only candidate who came across as authentic. He's a man who speaks from the heart. The MAGA movement makes more sense if you see it as essentially an emotional movement."

Someone else was waving their hand urgently from left to right.

"Yes." Eric shaded his eyes against the mid-morning sun now flooding the right side of the room.

"Seriously? You're comparing *Donald Trump* with Lenin and George Washington?"

"Yes," Eric said without irony. "But if you want a more accurate historical analogy, I think Trump is closer to Mao in wanting to smash a deep state that holds onto old ways of doing things and resists change. Next question . . ."

"Do you think it's OK for the American president to be a con man and a misogynist? Why won't he publish his tax returns? What's he got to hide?"

"I'd say that's just the kind of sneering and condescending attitude toward President Trump that prevents you from understanding the reasons behind his shocking political success."

The questions and answers continued in this vein, way beyond the allotted ten minutes. After nearly half an hour, and after he had fielded some twenty questions, with many more hands still in the air, Dr. Helmsley called an end to the session as the bell rang for the first break.

"Well, Mr. Rahn, I can honestly say that, ah, no speaker we've invited here before has engaged the student body quite like you have today. I have never seen everyone so switched on and eager to participate . . . Please, let's give Mr. Rahn another round of applause."

And with those words, Alyssa breathed an inward sigh of relief, more so when she heard the reaction from the students, a mix of reserved applause and exclamations of horrified respect. For the past forty minutes, her emotions had veered from proud and aspirational, to alarm, to a crushing feeling of doom, to a mortifying sense of public humiliation for inviting this person, to a dawning notion that the situation might be salvaging itself, and finally to a quiet elation and triumph for successfully pulling off a major event at Tamalpais. Whatever the students here thought of Eric Rahn's views, they had not sat here in bored resentment. They had been triggered. And they had been entertained.

"*Thank* you, Eric," she said, finding him alone in the wings of the stage.

"Was it OK?" he said. A note of concern.

"Ah, *yes*. Oh my God. They'll be talking about you for months. Oh, do you need to rush? I'll show you out."

"No, I've got a minute. I was thinking I could stop here for lunch? Baring my soul like that has made me kinda hungry."

"Um . . . Sure!" Alyssa's mind scrambled to deal with this development. "Lunch break isn't for another hour and a quarter . . ."

"It's cool," Eric said, putting a hand on her arm. "Just a coffee is fine."

That, too, sent her thoughts into a near panic. The only coffee machine was in the staff room. "I'll get you one. Uh, we usually sit outside on the benches at first break. Let me show you."

Alyssa felt herself erupting in a hot flush. She'd prepped so much, even the handshake, but this had caught her off guard. As she led Eric out onto the lawns, feeling two hundred sets of eyes turning toward her from the fixed tables and benches that were now crowded with students on first break, her brain began frantically shuffling her talking points. Every table was full. She had no choice but to steer him toward the center table, the one she and her friends always sat at.

Tammy, Honoré, and Tyler were there, engrossed in their phones, but looked up as she approached, all of them realizing at the same moment that it was too late to escape.

"Guys," Alyssa said, breezily. "Mr. Rahn is just stopping for a coffee. Would you look after him while I go get him one?"

"Sure," Tyler said, after an uncomfortably long pause.

"Eric, these are my closest friends: Tammy, Honoré, and Tyler."

"Great to meet Alyssa's friends," Eric said.

Honoré looked frozen with embarrassment and returned to his

phone. Tammy gazed at Eric with her usual dreamy numbness, her blond hair in bunched buns on either side of her head. Only Tyler seemed unperturbed and shifted along the bench to make room for Eric, whom Alyssa now couldn't help thinking was a deeply ambivalent presence sitting among her friends, a persona shuttered behind dark sunglasses and an expensive suit.

"Whassup, man," Tyler said by way of greeting.

"Back in a minute," Alyssa said, and rushed to the staff room to get Eric's coffee. Three minutes later, when she was returning to the table with a spilling cup, Eric was talking. Her three friends were looking perplexed at something he was showing them on his phone.

"Maybe Alyssa knows?" Tammy said, relieved to see Alyssa.

"Know what?" she said with a forced brightness.

"Who's this guy?" Eric said, showing her a photo on his phone. "I saw it on your Facebook page. I'm just curious. He looks a lot like someone I know. I think he might be a cousin of mine."

Alyssa shaded the screen from the sun and peered at it. It was a group photo she'd taken with her selfie stick sometime in January in Golden Gate Park. She thought she'd deleted it because Kyle was in it. She and Kyle had been dating at the time. Eric's fingernail was pointing to a boy at the back of the group, an East Asian guy with spiky hair whose face was partly obscured in the photo by Tammy's hair.

"I ... don't know who that is," Alyssa said, confused. "He's someone my ex-boyfriend knew. We just ran into him on the beach that day."

"Your ex-boyfriend ... Kyle Mason?" Eric said encouragingly. "That guy next to you?"

Alyssa was starting to feel her day spinning out of all control. Her face reddened. But then something switched inside her and turned her cold, and she looked from the phone to Eric's face, seeing her suspicion in the reflection of his sunglasses.

"How do you know that's Kyle?"

"You tagged him in this photo. But there's no tag for this fellow at the back."

"This is *weird*, man." Tyler was shaking his head.

"Why are you so interested?" Tammy said, in the scratchy, Valley-girl voice she'd been cultivating this year.

Eric's shoulders fell. "So, just to be clear, your ex-boyfriend Kyle knows who this Korean boy is, but none of you do. Right?"

"How d'you know he's even Korean?" Honoré said, looking up from his phone.

"I'd know a Korean anywhere," Eric said, getting up. He glanced around at the crowd of students at the various tables. "I saw Kyle at the back of the assembly hall. Can we ask him? Is he here somewhere?"

"What the fuck . . ." Tyler said incredulously.

"What's going on?" Tammy said, clearly spooked.

Alyssa, feeling responsible for the situation, said, "Kyle and I haven't really spoken since we broke up."

Eric turned his head slowly toward her and she again saw her reflection in his sunglasses. She looked tiny, a prehistoric fly preserved in ice.

"Well. Thanks for inviting me," he said. His tone had changed utterly, as if he'd said: *this has been a complete fucking waste of my time.* Then he walked away quickly, fishing his car keys out of his pocket. His coffee remained untouched on the table.

60

Marin County, California

From his corner seat at the back of the assembly hall Kyle Mason knew something was wrong with the tenor of the day. He'd sensed it the moment this month's guest speaker was introduced on the stage.

The guy was a thirty-something up-his-own-ass special advisor from the White House who'd spouted what had sounded, to Kyle's mind, something not unlike fascism. But in Tamalpais High's perverse tradition of inviting all sorts—the nutty, the boring, the worthy, and the downright offensive—the speaker was judged a success, and that had earned some kudos for Alyssa, who'd invited the guy.

Kyle was happy for her.

After that, he'd used first break to "study" in the library for his SAT retake. Then he'd given up completely and sneaked off to play hooky for the rest of the day, watching TV and swimming in the bay near the jetty at the back of his parents' house on Belvedere.

When he climbed out of the water and went dripping up the steps into the kitchen to retrieve his phone, he saw that he had multiple missed calls and voice notes.

Not from the principal's office about skipping classes ... but from *Alyssa*.

"Kyle . . . ? I know we haven't spoken in a while. Um. Something weird happened with that speaker this morning that you need to know about. Call me?"

"Me again. You weren't in American Lit. Listen, that speaker this morning . . . he wanted to ask you about this guy in a photo? I'm sending you the photo."

"OK, where are you? This is freaking us out."

He opened the photo she'd sent and the world around him receded. The kitchen, the ocean, his body. They were drained of weight and substance. Everything was hollow.

Emotional pain—his on–off companion for the last year—had struck home again with reinforcements.

He remembered it: the group photo taken at the beginning of the year on the beach in Golden Gate Park with Honoré, Tammy, Alyssa, Tyler, and himself—when he was still part of that clique.

It had been a bright January afternoon, but with a chill breeze off the bay. He and Alyssa had been holding hands. Tammy's hair had kept blowing across her face. Tyler and Honoré had been having some dumb argument about Minecraft.

Then, just before they'd reached the bridge—what were the chances?—they'd run into the very person Kyle hadn't been able to stop thinking about for weeks.

The beach had been dotted with Sunday strollers. Kyle hadn't noticed Stephen approach, nor had Stephen noticed him in the group, until it was too late.

Stephen's eyes had registered a brief alarm, then he'd inclined his head, smiled, and looked away as he passed by.

Kyle had given him a curt, "Hey," and continued walking.

"Someone you know?" Alyssa had said in a complicit tone that had made him want to pull his hair out by the roots.

"Uh. Maybe. Can't remember his name."

"He was kinda hot. One for you, Tammy."

The girls put on their sunglasses, and both turned around to get another look at Stephen. At the same moment Stephen had turned to glance back at them. Alyssa beamed at him. "Hello," she said, as if addressing an animal at the zoo. "Who are you?"

Stephen went still, his body in dark outline with the sun behind him, his black hair ruffling in the breeze off the bay. "Stephen," he said, sounding a friendly note.

Only Kyle knew what reluctance lay behind Stephen's decision to speak his own name. Then to Kyle's mortification Alyssa had drawn Stephen into the group. They were standing in an awkward circle on the sand as she attempted to divine Stephen's place in San Francisco's social ranks. "You live in the Bay Area? Which school are you at? How do you know Kyle?"

Kyle could not meet his eyes. He felt that if he did, he'd slip into some awful locker-room persona. Regular bro-jock-with-girlfriend, man.

"I think we met at Coffee Shack?" Stephen said. "I asked to borrow his charger."

That was true.

"Oh! Yeah," Kyle said, with a show of disinterest. He was already half turning to get away.

Stephen's vague responses about school and neighborhood were not satisfying Alyssa.

"Group photo!" she said brightly, which Kyle knew was her signal for wrapping up any social situation she had tired of, while at the same time gratifying her habit of collecting selfies with hot guys. She took the picture so quickly that Stephen had no chance to demur or step away.

In the three weeks since Kyle had met him, Stephen had not allowed him to take a single photo of him. There *were* no photos of Stephen Lee—anywhere. Kyle knew because he'd searched.

"Good to meet you guys," Stephen said, and left, picking up his pace.

Moments later, as they continued their stroll, Kyle's friends had

419

already forgotten Stephen. Alyssa took hold of Kyle's hand again and squeezed it, oblivious to the violent revolution that was now stirring inside his head.

For the first time in his life, Kyle needed courage—real courage, of the kind required to overcome an acute fear of death or exile.

The next day after school, he drove to Alyssa's house in Almonte and ended their relationship. Before she could start crying and demanding to know why, he said, "I'm gay."

She had stared at him in silence for several seconds with a look on her face that he had not expected—one of hard pragmatism.

"Who have you told?"

"No one. Only you."

"Maybe keep it to yourself?" she said, rather coldly. "I mean. This is my junior year. Next year's my senior. If everyone finds out, it'll be ruined for me. People will be laughing." Kyle tried to give her a hug, but she pushed him away angrily. "You've made a fool out of me."

For a few weeks after the breakup, Tyler, Honoré, and Tammy had gamely tried to maintain their friendship with Kyle, but since Alyssa lapsed into a frosted silence whenever he came near them, Kyle decided to spare them. He dropped out of their clique and started eating his lunch at the nerds' table.

He hadn't heard from Alyssa in months ... And now she was leaving weird messages about a photo of Stephen, a person Kyle was certain she had completely forgotten.

That speaker today was asking about Stephen?

This didn't surprise Kyle as much as it might have done. Stephen had gone to extraordinary lengths to make himself invisible to the world. It must have been for a reason. But Kyle didn't want to think about that anymore. And he sure as hell didn't want to return Alyssa's calls.

It was only in the last week or so that he'd felt the page beginning to turn on Stephen, but even now the pain was still raw, especially when his memory was jolted unexpectedly, as it had been a moment ago.

For reasons that Kyle had never fathomed, Stephen lived his life behind maze-like walls of privacy. *Extreme* privacy, as in no social media, no photos, no identifiable usernames. He regularly changed his phone number. Even after they'd cooked meals together at Kyle's house on Belvedere Avenue on the many weekends when his parents were absent, and they'd made out and dived off the jetty afterward, even after they'd cuddled in bed for hours—the first real intimacy Kyle had ever experienced—Stephen had been no more forthcoming about his life. When Kyle asked him about his family, he said he had none. He lived in Richmond with his foster parents, he said, who were good people. This turned out to be the only meaningful biographical information Stephen ever gave him.

Stephen's ethnicity was also a riddle. Kyle wondered if he was Japanese—there were many Japanese in San Francisco. But his surname, Lee, was common in many countries. It was another thing Kyle felt he couldn't ask. The name was also conveniently untraceable. He'd try googling "Stephen Lee" and he'd get tens of thousands of results, none of them for his Stephen.

At first, he'd assumed that Stephen's elaborate reclusion was borne of some fear about people finding out he was gay. But when Kyle tried to tease him about this, he'd looked at Kyle as if he were an innocent child and said, "Privacy is freedom."

He'd said that so openly that Kyle understood in that instant that Stephen was a good person. Not fearful or mistrusting or deceptive, but profoundly guarded because, for some important reason of his own, he had to be. Rather than hide inside a funnel-web of lies, which he could so easily have done, he'd chosen to say nothing, and Kyle understood that he should accept that silence as a gift of honesty and trust. This was communicated to Kyle wordlessly in myriad different ways—when they'd looked far into each other's eyes with their heads on the same pillow; when Stephen smiled serenely if Kyle asked him a question that would be totally normal to ask anyone else ("When's your birthday?") but which, with Stephen, seemed probing and unfair. In all their time together they went out only once: to an old dive on Castro called XXL Bar. Stephen seemed to like the place, perhaps because it was so dark and anonymous. Kyle had the distinct impression that Stephen had been there before.

Kyle knew he was falling in love with someone who did not quite seem real. But he was discovering that there was more than one way to truly know another person. There was a kind of cognitive level, which always needed facts, details, words, and a hundred other signifiers that fed positive or negative impressions. And there was another level, deeper, more spiritual, which was only gained through insight and feeling. A person could shine with love and trust that was impossible to fake, and yet reveal very little about themselves.

During the first flush of romance, the sheer mystery of Stephen was the driver of Kyle's love for him.

However, as the weeks went on, the superficial level of knowing—the cognitive level—slowly rebooted inside Kyle's mind. Suspicion sprouted small roots that could only begin to grow.

When Kyle had sneaked a look inside Stephen's wallet (Stephen was in the shower), he felt grubby for doing it. He knew he was crossing a line. But he'd found no driver's license, no library ID, nothing with a date of birth or a home address. Just a few dollars in cash.

The disastrous decision to follow Stephen home hadn't been premeditated.

It was at the end of another blissful Sunday in the house on Belvedere. As usual, he'd watched Stephen depart by cab—never an Uber; always a taxi service that had to be booked with a phone call. He'd waved goodbye, and stood forlornly on the drive with his hands in the pockets of his jeans, listening to the hissing of the lawn sprinklers, and feeling very alone again. As he turned back to the house, he realized he was holding his car keys in his hand.

Kyle had watched enough movies to know that he should hang back some distance if he wasn't going to make it obvious that he was following. For most of the drive along the 131 toward Belle Aire he made sure there were two or three cars between his own and the yellow taxicab.

But soon he was getting so lost in paranoid fantasies that he became unaware of how close he was getting to the yellow cab, and as it turned off Britton Avenue and onto the Golden Gate Bridge, he was barely five meters behind it, making himself obvious.

If Stephen turned around in his seat, he would recognize Kyle's car, a distinctive dark brown Mercedes, immediately.

Kyle was on a kind of autopilot, thrumming with suspicion and unease.

Was his name even Stephen?

He snapped out of it as the road merged onto the 101 North and he allowed a decent interval of space to open between them. The cab took the exit toward San Quentin and Drake and kept right toward Richmond. Another two miles and they hit the slow Sunday evening traffic approaching San Pablo and MacDonald. Then the cab turned left into a neighborhood of low-rise public housing, a small area Kyle vaguely knew was one to avoid. Some windows were boarded up. The garbage hadn't been collected.

Is this what Stephen had been hiding? Poverty?

Cars were fewer here, and the Mercedes was conspicuous. It was dark now and the cab had slowed as it reached the corner of the block, its taillights glowing. Without warning, it stopped and Kyle had to brake hard. He pulled over and turned off the engine.

The cab's interior lights came on. He saw Stephen pay the driver and get out, but instead of walking toward a nearby house he very deliberately turned and stared at Kyle.

Kyle couldn't see his face, just the top of his hair glinting in the street light overhead.

But he knew. There was a look of terrible betrayal on Stephen's face.

Then Stephen's shoulders sagged, and he walked quickly down an alley between the houses and disappeared. Already Kyle knew that to follow him on foot, try to speak to him, apologize, would be useless.

On the drive home, Kyle understood, with a sadness that was almost tidal, that their relationship was over. There could be no coming back from a betrayal like that. Stephen would have felt violated by the boy he loved.

For a brief period after the breakup with Alyssa, Kyle had felt as if he had jumped from a burning ship and was swimming toward a lifeboat. But the closer he got to the lifeboat, the further into the mist it had drifted, and now it had vanished altogether. The new beginning he'd imagined had been nothing but an illusion borne of desperation and hope, or rather hope's dreary cousin, wishful thinking.

He had broken Stephen's heart and in the act of doing so had also broken his own.

Stephen never contacted him again.

Kyle barely noticed his surroundings anymore. The teachers mistook this for rebellion or punk attitude, but the truth was he just wanted to get away and never come back. He stopped hanging out with anyone. He never went anywhere.

He took one last look at the photo Alyssa had sent him, the only photo he had ever seen of Stephen, and deleted it from his phone.

Then he entered his running route into Strava and set off for a long hard run to shake the day from his head. Running eased the pain. Running needed no thinking, no people, no permission.

The month after Eric Rahn's visit, after Kyle's parents had attended a meeting in the principal's office to discuss his grades, the teenager was removed from the school at his own request. His parents reluctantly agreed that his chances of a good college would be improved by sending him to summer school and then enrolling him in a private school in Tiburon for his senior year.

Kyle could not have imagined that a moment would come, twelve months later, when he'd see how ill-fated his decision had been to play hooky from school that day Eric Rahn had been the guest speaker at assembly. If he'd been present at first break when the man had questioned his friends, if he'd talked to them before dropping out of school and disappearing, he might have picked up on the same evil fricking vibe coming off him that Alyssa had noticed. Then he might have gotten a sense that the little knowledge he had of Stephen—just about the only knowledge anyone had of Stephen—had placed him, Kyle, in mortal danger.

61

National Assembly
Seoul, South Korea
November 2017

"Since my election exactly one year ago today, I celebrate with you. I celebrate the Korean miracle..."

President Trump was on his feet delivering a rousing speech to the packed-out South Korean National Assembly, the highlight of his state visit. He was praising South Korea's wealth and democracy—reminding his audience in no subtle terms that they had the United States to thank for that.

Eric, seated to the rear of the auditorium, had never seen him on such superb form. The man was on fire.

The president then began to paint the darkest imaginable picture of his audience's cousins just across the border in the North.

"The Korean miracle extends exactly as far as the armies of free nations advanced in 1953—twenty-four miles to the north. There, it stops; it all comes to an end. Dead stop. The flourishing ends, and the prison state of North Korea sadly begins..."

The speech was heavy with Eric's own redrafts, edits, and ideas. He knew the Boss so well that the Boss hadn't even needed to tell him what to write: turn up the pressure to the max and let Kim Jong-un sweat. Drive him crazy with a public shaming... then wait.

The Boss switched to his sad, sing-song voice. "An estimated hundred thousand North Koreans suffer in gulags, toiling in forced labor, and enduring torture, starvation, rape, and murder on a constant basis..."

Then he paused, index finger and thumb pressed together in the air.

"I have come here to deliver a message directly to the leader of the North Korean dictatorship: the weapons you are acquiring are not making you safer. Every step you take down this dark path increases the peril you face..."

The applause started in smatters from the edges of the hall.

Now, let's really turn up the heat.

"North Korea is not the paradise your grandfather envisioned. It is a hell that no person deserves. Yet, despite every crime you have committed against God and man... we will offer a path to a much better future..."

The applause was quicker now, accompanied by shouts and exclamations of support.

"The destiny of the Korean people is not to suffer in the bondage of oppression, but to thrive in the glory of freedom..."

Two or three members were on their feet. The applause crested and began to roll. The Boss's finger was pointing toward heaven, captured on the giant screens to his left and right.

"Together, we dream of a Korea that is free, a peninsula that is safe... Our eyes are fixed to the North, and our hearts praying for the day when all Koreans can live in freedom!"

The ovation cascaded across the hall like a Mexican wave. Eric rose to his feet along with everyone else.

If that won't do the trick...

"Thank you... Thank you..."

North Korea's response to the speech was explosive.

On November 29, the country tested the Hwasong 15 missile, the most powerful yet. It reached an altitude of nearly five thousand kilometers and flew for fifty-three minutes before re-entering the atmosphere over the Sea of Japan.

Eric saw it all on screen from his position at the back of the White House Situation Room, sitting behind the joint chiefs of staff. The launch took place on the runway of Pyongyang International Airport and was watched through binoculars by the Great Successor himself, seated in an armchair on a hastily built observation platform. He had ordered the test only at eight that morning, and the 1st Red Flag Hero Company of the Missile General Bureau had undertaken an intense revolutionary struggle-session to get the missile ready for blast-off at three.

US military satellites monitoring the missile's trajectory calculated that it had a downrange of about thirteen thousand kilometers, which would bring Washington, DC easily within strike range of a North Korean nuclear attack.

To the watching world, the two countries had never come so close to war.

But then: the mood music from Pyongyang changed.

It began to lighten. No longer bellicose and unhinged, but reasonable, conciliatory. The Great Successor made a televised announcement: "We have completed our rocket program." It was now time to improve the lives of his citizens, he said.

That was the signal, Eric knew. Kim had amassed his chips. Now he was ready to deal. It was happening! Happening so fast it sent Eric into a paroxysm of ecstasy and nerves.

The wheels are turning. The pieces are in motion.

62

Tannenhof
Baden-Württemberg, Germany
Fall 2017

On the day Lyosha had been discharged, Anya had wanted him to livestream the moment—leaving the hospital, punching the air, alive, healthy, and on two feet. "It'll be a great *fuck you* to the crook in the Kremlin," she'd said to him on the phone from Moscow. But Lyosha had said no. He was done with all that. He'd never wanted to be famous. He wanted to live his life freely, and that meant a life unobserved. He was also concerned for Anya: he didn't want her drawing any more attention to herself than she already had.

It was a shock to be outside. The air smelled nut-clean, even though he was in the center of a capital city. Sounds—traffic, birds, music from car radios—seemed bright, as if polished to a high shine.

In truth, he was quite far from feeling fully recovered. The key stages of the journey—breathing, speech, appetite, movement, memory—had all been passed, but he still had months of physical therapy ahead of him. Most of the time he walked with the aid of a frame. He became exhausted very quickly.

Throughout his stay at the Charité, Anya had maintained a regular blog on his progress. It had generated massive publicity, in

Russia and in Germany. Berlin was treating him as a *cause célèbre*, a political enemy of Putin's, which, he was forced to admit, was what he had become. The Germans offered him and Marina a resettlement package and a temporary place to live. He was warned to be wary of Russian well-wishers in Berlin.

For the next eight months, Lyosha and his mother were settled into a comfortable house in a village called Tannenhof, although it might have been called Silent Night, or Nothing Happens Here. It was situated in the southern part of the Black Forest in southwest Germany, close to where the Rhine formed the border with Switzerland. Here, he would have the space and fresh air he needed to get his body back to strength. To that end, the place was perfect. Rolling green meadows were dotted with herds of dairy cattle, like an image from a chocolate box. The pastures gave way to a horizon serrated with beech trees and firs, and beyond them was the epic sweep of the Alps, brilliant in the crystalline air. The buildings of the village were part house, part barn, all of them solid and prosperous, with gently sloping chalet roofs and broad eaves. Lyosha could wander all morning and not see a soul, apart from the cows, who would shamble up to the fence to say hello. He gave each one of them names.

With every passing week he was feeling stronger. Energy was flowing back into his limbs, charging him, giving him new life.

Fall came early in southern Germany that year. On the morning when the first frost appeared, as he was completing his first proper run—a modest, three-kilometer circuit along the lanes around the village—he knew that he and Marina would soon run out of reasons for being here. All his mother's energy had been devoted to his recovery. The busyness had been good for her; it distracted her from her own grief. But Lyosha knew that she was starting to feel isolated, and her sense of mourning and exile would soon become unbearable. Nor was she ready to retire.

She missed Russia; she even missed the things she'd always

complained about: the fatalism, the borscht, the Napoleonic temperatures. And Moscow, of course. The city seemed to have a hold over the soul in a way few other places did. She missed the view from her apartment: of the Moskva, not yet frozen, curling mysteriously through the savage city, and the dim ruby stars of the Kremlin's spires.

"Freedom," she'd said vaguely. "Earthquakes, wars, we don't fear. But freedom? Russians don't know what to do with it. We are afraid of it."

His lungs began to heave as he tackled the slope that led through the woods above the village. Oak trees sparkled with hoar frost. Spiderwebs hung like white lace. As he followed a curve in the lane, he saw a gleaming black car stationary in the middle of the road. Its engine was idling, sending up a great cloud of white exhaust vapor in the still air. It had German government plates. The driver's door opened, and a German policeman got out and waved to him. Lyosha felt a spike of fear and suspicion. For a split second he wanted to turn and run. But then the rear passenger door opened, and an elderly lady got out. She was small and muffled against the cold in a stylish black padded coat and an ancient fur hat.

"Hello! Lyosha!" she called.

Lyosha slowed as he approached, panting. Steam was rising from his hair as the morning sun slanted through the trees and melted the frost.

"Do I know you?"

The woman must have been about eighty. Her face was friendly, but her honey-colored eyes were like molten steel when they caught the light.

She spoke in English. "Would you sit with me in the car for a minute? It's freezing out here." She saw his hesitation, then turned to the driver and policeman and said, "Give us a moment, please." They zipped up their coats and walked away from the car. "It's all right, young man," she said. "You're quite safe with me." Her accent was strange—American, but with a husky underbrush of Eastern Europe.

He got inside the car, which was warm and smelled new. When she removed her fur hat, he saw that her hair was dyed auburn—rather amateurishly. It displayed a centimeter of gray roots. "I didn't speak to you in Russian just now," she said, "because I didn't want to alarm you. Now, then. How are you? On the road to recovery, I see."

"You haven't told me who you are."

"My name's Kowalski." Her hand was a small avian claw with a remarkable grip. "I've come from Washington to ask for your help."

"My help?"

"I'm very worried about a dear friend of mine who is in prison in Moscow. I believe you may have met her: Sarah Hong."

Lyosha regarded her carefully then. He had the sensation of being drawn into another complicated game where none of the rules were known. "Do all Sarah Hong's 'dear friends' have armed police protection?"

"No," the woman said. "Maybe only the ones who work for the government."

"You're CIA."

The woman gave him an intelligent smile that left him in no doubt that she was a person of great influence and importance.

"We're on the same side, Lyosha. Let's keep this brief, or your mother will wonder where you are. Did you meet Sarah Hong?"

"Yes. Three times, in fact. Briefly. Once at drinks in the Hotel Metropol. The two other times I bumped into her in public, but that may not have been by chance, I think."

"No, they weren't accidental meetings. She was working for me."

"You want to know if I have the cufflinks."

The woman's eyes remained clear and unblinking. "First tell me what happened to Sarah."

Lyosha recounted the evening at the Bolshoi, his encounter with

Sarah in the third-floor champagne bar, her public arrest by Vadim Giorgadze.

"Tricky place to get your attention," she said. "A crowded bar."

"She got my attention, all right. She told me that my father had been passing secrets to the USA."

For the first time the woman betrayed some emotion. His words seemed to pierce her armored exterior. He thought he saw pain in her eyes.

"So, you know about that," she said faintly. "I wasn't sure." She drew a deep breath. "Lyosha, I want to tell you that I view Dmitry's death as one of the biggest personal and professional failures of my life. He was on US soil, and we didn't protect him. I take responsibility. He wasn't just an agent, he was a friend, a good man in evil times. I won't insult your grief by saying sorry, because sorry doesn't nearly cover it."

They were silent for a moment. The driver and the policeman were standing in the road, smoking cigarettes, stomping their feet against the cold.

"I failed him, too," Lyosha said, staring into space. "The cufflinks. They're lost. The security men in Minsk kept my clothes. I'd hidden them in my jeans. That was stupid."

The woman said nothing but turned her gaze toward the frosted wonderland outside, which reflected in her eyes. The steel seemed to have gone out of her. Then she inhaled slowly and gave a smile that was both sad and gracious, as if she'd loved and lost and nothing more was to be done.

"We had people waiting to meet you at Minsk Station. But by then, of course, Putin had poisoned you . . ."

They were silent again for a moment, listening to the sparrows chirping in the undergrowth.

"Why?" Lyosha said, quietly. "Why did he want to kill me? Because of my father? Because of the fuss on YouTube? . . . Because of whatever was in those *cufflinks*?"

Mira shook her head vaguely, then she took his hand in her gloved fingers and squeezed it.

"Maybe all those reasons, Lyosha, and maybe others too dark for us to fathom. There's no point asking why. It'll drive you mad, and you may never know the answer. But . . ." She stopped, then let out a sigh, as if pondering the wisdom of what she was about to say. "I can offer you the humble theory of an old woman. You have a free mind, Lyosha, and a free, natural spirit. You have your father's integrity, decency, his sense of justice. And you have true courage. Putin witnessed all that when you spoke to him on *Direct Line*. You're everything that a man like that isn't. And the whole world saw it. He loathes you for that. He'd have made your life a long-drawn-out misery if you'd stayed in Russia—because of *Direct Line*, because your father had been spying for us—but I don't think he'd have killed you . . . It was your act of defection that did it. Because then you were truly free and no longer in his power. Then he could never force you to submit. The idea was intolerable to him in a deeply hateful, personal way. That's nothing you should feel bad about. In time, I hope, you'll take great pride in it."

She opened her handbag and retrieved a card. "This is a private number. You can call it any time if you ever want to talk to me, or if you need my help. You'd better go now."

When he got back the house was filled with a wonderful aroma. His mother was fed up with German bread and was making her own. He put his arms around her from behind as she was preparing lunch and hugged her.

"Mama, the only people I love in the world are you and Anya."

63

SIZO No. 6 Women's Prison
Moscow
December 2017

It had snowed heavily overnight, and the prisoners' hour in the yard was canceled.

Jenna sensed her interrogators didn't know what to do with her. Threats and intimidation hadn't worked, neither had the drugs. They'd beaten up prisoners at night and made sure she heard; they'd turned the heat off in her cell. But still she'd endured. Colonel Nikolayev had come the closest to breaking her, but she sensed that even he was at his wits' end. She had triumphed. She was stronger than any of these bastards. The weeks dragged, but the months flew. She had been arrested in March, and now it was December already.

One afternoon Colonel Nikolayev entered the interrogation room wearing an enormous military greatcoat like an officer in a war movie, home on leave. "I stopped on the way to get you this," he said, placing a liquor store bag on the table. "*Merry* Christmas."

Jenna opened it and found a bottle of Jack Daniel's.

It was such a thoughtful act of kindness. She wanted to laugh, but she felt sudden tears in her eyes. "Thank you."

"It's against all the rules . . ." He fished two small shot glasses out of his pocket and plonked them conspiratorially on the table. "So, we've got to be quick."

He poured them each a glass, keeping the bottle hidden in the paper bag.

"Happy holiday," she said, raising her glass, and knocked it back.

She closed her eyes. The heat of the spirit warmed her at once, like a log fire on an icy night. JD, she reflected, was one of her true pleasures. The remedy to all stress and a reminder of home, no matter where she was. Nikolayev knocked his back.

"Nicer than vodka? One more quick one."

He poured her another, and she drank that, too, and savored it.

When she put her glass down and opened her eyes Nikolayev's expression had changed utterly. It was as if she were in a room with a stranger. He was regarding with a kind of disgusted triumph, as if he'd avenged himself on some ancestral enemy.

With shocking suddenness, Jenna felt her reality lurch. She was giddy and nauseated. Before she knew it, she was slipping heavily into a hallucinatory dream world in which she seemed to be observing herself, only half-conscious, from far away, through a lens that kept refracting and warping. She began sweating freely as she fought a miasma of fear. She had to grip the sides of the plastic chair. She knew what was happening, but now her mind was an exploding box of fireworks.

"That's it, Sarah," Nikolayev said in a voice that was both intimate and far away. His mouth had turned into a sunken black hole. His back had sprouted two huge wings ending in claws. "Go with it. Perhaps you should lie down." He walked around the table and shoved her roughly to the floor.

Jenna groaned. Her mind was tumbling open like a wardrobe full of junk. She couldn't close it. What was secret and what wasn't— she didn't know. The core of her being was melting beneath lavafalls of chaos. Neurons were misfiring. Synapses snapping. The ceiling was moving into a sickening, accelerating spin.

Nikolayev kneeled next to her and lowered his face to hers. His features had become transparent. She could see his skull. His hair was a wreath of flames. She tried to take deep breaths to oxygenate.

"Your drink was a psychotropic drug called SP-117, a sodium thiopental. It has no smell, taste, or color. We mixed it with quinuclidinyl benzilate and some LSD. Quite a blend. To be honest, we've never tried it before." The sparks were pouring from his mouth and landing on her. She tried to brush them away, but they turned into ants that began crawling all over her arms. "It's amazing how fast it works. How uninhibited you'll feel." His eyes glowed a uranium green. "Really, you can forget that technique they taught you."

The drug was completely swallowing her head. The room became black-and-white like an old silent movie, and Nikolayev began flickering in and out of reality, his movements, jerky and unnatural.

"Now then. Your name."

She could see nothing real to focus on, so she held her hand in front of her face and in her palm and fingers she saw the nighttime half of the world, as if from a satellite, total blackness with glowing clusters of city lights and towns.

"Your name."

"My name . . ."

And then the roof blew off the building and she was sucked into the night, past the stars and out into pure darkness where nothing was real except annihilation. The shrinking capsule of her intelligence began to disintegrate. She could feel the hull burning up. And when the capsule blew apart and the fragments separated into atoms, there was nothing left of her but the atoms themselves. In the dimension she had entered there was no space for a human mind.

He began to ask questions, and Jenna heard a distant voice answering. It was like hearing a conversation upstairs in a house with all the doors closed. Now and then one of the atoms became self-aware and tried to resist the onslaught, but it was useless. She was nothing but particles being shot around a hadron collider and smashing into a much stronger force.

She would never know what happened over the next few hours. After falling to the floor, she recalled only fragments, like half-developed Polaroids of some horrific crime scene, left scattered after the pharmacological explosion in her head: sudden vivid moments, snatches of words and faces. Faces, yes. At some point she had awoken not on the floor but in a bed, with her arms strapped tightly to the metal rails on either side.

Another man had joined Nikolayev in asking questions.

She thought she'd met him before, but she wasn't sure of anything anymore. A brute of a man with a bald head with arched eyebrows and a heavy mustache who never raised his voice above a whisper. But he, too, was blinking in and out of reality, like a quantum particle.

64

Washington, DC
February 2018

The positive vibes from Pyongyang continued during the weeks leading up to the Winter Olympic Games, which were held in Pyeongchang, South Korea, a little-known town that many commentators confused with Pyongyang. Eric was following it all on the news channels.

Sensing the pleasing change in the diplomatic wind, the South Korean president invited North Korea to participate in the Games, the first time in two years the two countries had even said a word to each other. The North accepted: it would send a delegation of athletes.

And then the Great Successor played a move no one saw coming: he would not attend the Olympics in person, he said, but his sister would represent him.

Sister?

Even the keenest North Korea-watchers knew little of the thirty-year-old Kim Yo-jong except that she was the head of the Workers' Party Propaganda and Agitation Department. Most of the world had never heard of her.

Straight away, the international media was abuzz with chatter and anticipation. A North Korean princess? The Supreme Sister? What did she look like?

Whatever type of figure they were expecting—a person of high fashion? Sunglasses and bling?—it was not the woman who descended the steps from the Ilyushin Il-62, her brother's personal jet, after it landed at Incheon International Airport in Seoul. The media got a better view of her as she entered the airport's VIP lounge surrounded by athletic North Korean bodyguards in black suits and sunglasses.

This powerful red princess, this descendent of the sacred revolutionary bloodline of Mount Paektu, was dressed in plain functionary's clothes. No makeup. Unpierced ears. No jewelry, except for a pin displaying the faces of her father and grandfather over her heart. Her hair was pulled back in the no-nonsense style of a factory worker.

When she saw the South Korean officials waiting to greet her in the lounge, she smiled faintly but her eyes did not linger on anything. She betrayed no nerves, no excitement, no interest. Her much-tweeted-about comportment was gracious and erect. She kept her neck straight and her head still. She was demure when spoken to, but otherwise she said almost nothing at all. Later, at a meeting with President Moon, TV news cameras captured her deferring respectfully to the older members of her own delegation, urging them to be seated ahead of her. Such polite humility made a very favorable impression on the watching public.

"Look at that posture!" gushed a commentator on KBS, South Korea's main news channel. "Bolt upright. And her smile! An enigma. So pretty, so polite. Like a lady from a folktale . . ."

Overnight this "down-to-earth princess" became an object of global fascination. The next day's press was calling her the Ivanka Trump of North Korea.

"You have become a star in South Korea," President Moon told her. She smiled glacially.

At the opening ceremony of the Games, Kim Yo-jong was seated directly behind US Vice President Mike Pence in the VIP box. Pence decided to ignore her grandly and didn't even turn his head in her direction.

That made him look petty, petty, petty, Eric thought. The Boss would never have done that. He'd have greeted her warmly, told her she was looking fantastic. He'd have asked her how she stayed so skinny when her brother was so damned fat.

The next day, she was driven to the Blue House, South Korea's presidential palace, carrying a personal letter from her brother asking if President Moon would like to meet him.

The ice was really melting now. The vessels were coming loose and beginning to float. Events were moving in a very positive direction. She was clearing the diplomatic waters for a meeting between her brother and the forty-fifth president of the United States.

But no one was seeing what Eric was seeing.

Where the public saw respect and humility in Kim Yo-jong's aspect, Eric saw an imperious arrogance. She had been raised to dominate and oppress, not to be modest. He noticed it again when she declined to take off her coat for the press photos with President Moon. The South Koreans were her inferiors. This visit was a sufferance for her. She was just dropping by. Her propaganda department had only recently called Moon a "Yankee parrot" and a "political dwarf." (It could have been worse: it had called his female predecessor, President Park, a "crafty old prostitute.") Only one eagle-eyed viewer had called in to a South Korean TV breakfast show to point out a detail that suggested Kim Yo-jong was not quite as "down to earth" as she appeared: the discreet black handbag she carried was alligator skin and retailed at eighteen thousand dollars.

Eric, of course, had direct, personal experience of Kim Yo-jong.

He knew that this calm, enigmatic woman was a sadistic despot. Like father, like daughter. And her presence at these Olympics, representing her brother, suggested that her power had grown dramatically, inside the Family and politically inside the regime.

And as he pondered this, a fresh anxiety of the most morbid kind stirred his heart. Unless he acted quickly, he was going to pay a heavy price for this hoped-for summit. Because in none of his plots and schemes had he foreseen that this woman, Kim Yo-jong, would be at her brother's side during the events to come.

A week after the Olympics, things gathered pace at an alarming speed. South Korean diplomats traveled to the White House with a message they had received from North Korea: Kim Jong-un was eager to meet President Trump.

Trump said yes on the spot.

"Why don't you," he said, pointing at the bemused South Korean diplomats, "go outside and announce it."

"Now?"

"Now."

The Boss was elated, as if Kim had just proposed marriage to him and he wanted the whole world to share in his joy.

The Boss's tremendous mood continued when he saw the American coverage. *Audacious! A breathtaking gamble! Another day of swirling drama! Trump's improvisational style leads to historic breakthrough!*

He drew plenty of flak, too, and the pile-on was intense. Just like that, the Boss had granted the world's last totalitarian communist tyranny something it had craved since the day it was founded—*respect*.

"Big fucking deal," he said, throwing the New York Times across the Resolute desk. "It's just a meeting. A meeting! It's two days. I'm not giving him anything."

An intense flurry of diplomatic energy was unleashed as the groundwork for the summit was prepared. The secretary of state was dispatched to Pyongyang to meet Kim Jong-un in private. Official declarations were made by both sides expressing great optimism for the summit's success. Kim jong-un and his wife traveled to Beijing to secure the Chinese president's blessing for the summit. The royal couple were given the red-carpet treatment and were shown lavish courtesy.

But every time Kim appeared now, the Sister was always somewhere behind him, often standing alone, drawing no attention to herself, the mysterious half smile on her face. *She is the shadow that follows him,* Eric thought.

Expectations were rising. The venue was chosen: Singapore, for its location, security, and neutrality. Trump and Kim began to exchange letters of rhapsodic flattery, which Trump showed to Eric.

"Dear Excellency," Kim had written. "I'm prepared to cooperate with you in sincerity and dedication to accomplish a great feat that no one in the past has been able to achieve and that is unexpected by the whole world."

"You see that?" Trump said, grinning. "He calls me 'Excellency.'"

During these weeks Eric lived in his office. He was proactive in every meeting with the State Department, the Defense Intelligence Agency. He took every conference call. He drafted press releases, fielded questions from reporters, wrote speeches and briefing notes, and coordinated with all the involved foreign parties, including China and Japan. He was crazed with work. He ate dinner at his desk, if he had time. Time became unreal, something that vanished. He was strung out on caffeine during the day; doped up on Xanax and whiskey at night. The Boss would call him in for long sessions of happy talk. He wanted to know about camera angles, lighting, where the handshake with Kim would be staged, the hotels, the menus, the seating plans, which tie he should wear.

Everything Eric had hoped for was coming to pass. His dreams were coming true before his eyes. But far from reaping the dividend, allowing himself feelings of victory and all the energy and glow that went with it, he was barely holding himself together. His responses were flat and automatic, his actions lethargic. He was not stepping up to the leadership role that even the bottom-feeders in the West Wing now thought was his due. He was exhausted and edging deeper into a full burnout. Most terrifying of all for him, he could feel the void that was ever-present inside him starting to acquire mass, gravity, a depression.

As the Boss's closest advisor in the preparations for the summit, Eric would naturally be making the trip with him to Singapore—and that meant he would be coming face to face with his tormentor again, the Supreme Sister. And Kim Yo-jong would not suffer his failure a second time.

Time was running out.

It had been more than a year now since Eric had made that trip to California to track down the faces in the Golden Gate Park photo. He was *no closer* to finding Ha-jun, but not from want of trying. The only one of those kids who knew Ha-jun's current identity—who may even have known his whereabouts—was Alyssa's ex-boyfriend, Kyle Mason. And Kyle was the only one Eric had failed to meet that day he'd visited Tamalpais High School.

But Kyle, too, had disappeared!

He'd been removed from the school register; he'd gone dark on social media. Why? Was the boy depressed? In rehab? Had he run away?

What the fuck was the deal with these disappearing kids?

Eric was almost back to square one—almost.

It had taken him weeks of late-night trawling to discover that Kyle had enrolled at a new school, a private one in Tiburon, for his senior year. And then, finally, on one of that school's students' feeds, he'd found a recent photo of Kyle in singlet and shorts, snapped as he ran cross-country, puffing away on a half-marathon event organized by the school's running club. Also in the same feed was a screenshot from the student's Strava app, showing the half-marathon's route and the runtime.

He had less luck finding Kyle's address.

He'd searched for anyone and everyone with the surname Mason who lived in the vicinity of Mill Valley, and he *had* found a Mrs. Lynda Mason, an interior designer with her own website which displayed tasteful pictures of her well-appointed home. The house was on Belvedere Avenue, about six miles from Kyle's new school. But was it Kyle's house? He had no way of knowing for sure.

That was all he had. Nothing else.

He'd tried to put a spin on things in his reports to Center, suggesting that this meager lead was in fact a promising breakthrough, which he was busy investigating. But Center was increasingly impatient with him. They had repeatedly demanded to know when he would be returning to California.

Of course, he'd known all along that he would have to return, but his workload was so crushing now that he had no free weekends, no time even to eat or sleep. He had *no time*. But also, if he was honest with himself, he'd been feeling that deep inertia that tended to overcome anyone facing a difficult, unfinished task that offered no clue as to how it could be completed—and the temptation that comes with such a feeling to keep putting it off, just for a little longer, until it becomes a full-blown crisis.

What would he even do when got to California? Sit outside that house in a hire car? Blag his way inside, posing as a potential client of Mrs. Mason's, expressing an interest in her signature earth-tones, and creepily inquiring after her teenaged son?

This was verging on the surreal, the absurd. The humiliation of it enraged him.

On an evening in early June, with the summit just days away, he'd fallen asleep in the back of the government Lexus driving him home from the White House, and almost tumbled out onto the sidewalk in front of his apartment. He was half-heartedly climbing the steps to his apartment when he realized that he didn't want to go inside. He couldn't face the empty refrigerator, or the sheets he'd had no time to change, or the silence that spoke to him every night of his failure to find Ha-jun, of time trickling away. So he delayed the moment by walking to the twenty-four-hour liquor store at the end of the block.

Was he really going back to California? Did he have to? He was so exhausted.

Eric stopped walking and leaned against the wall next to the liquor store's recycling dumpster. A light rain was beginning to fall, making his jacket damp and the darkened sidewalk glisten in the streetlights. He felt overwhelmed with exhaustion and pity for himself. He wanted to cry.

Why, why was this happening to him?

He pulled himself together, wiped his face with the palm of his hand, went into the store, and bought a bottle of Macallan.

As he was leaving, a skinny hooded white guy came out of nowhere toward him with a beseeching kind of slouch, his dirty hands cupped in front of him.

"Excuse me, sir? Spare a few bucks for the shelter?"

"Fuck off," Eric said, and walked briskly away.

Fucking bums. It's getting as bad as San Francisco.

But then a more consolatory thought made him slow his pace, stop, and turn around. The guy was already accosting another customer leaving the store, who had ignored him.

"The shelter?" Eric said, kindly.

The guy trotted back to him like a starving dog. "Yes, sir, on Lincoln Street."

"Aren't the homeless shelters in the District of Columbia free of charge?"

The guy's face went blank. His young eyes were addled and dead in the streetlight. His skin was awful, like diseased fish scales. "I'm hungry."

"So, you want money for food, not the shelter? Doesn't the Department of Human Services provide free meals?"

The guy said nothing.

"What about meth? Would you like money for meth?"

"Please. Just a few bucks, if you can—"

"You fucking *stink*, do you know that? You stink of poverty and *piss*."

Inside his coat pocket he had looped his key ring over the middle finger of his right hand so that the keys formed an improvised knuckleduster.

"Hey, *fuck* you, man!" The guy squared his shoulders and rose up on his toes, suddenly menacing. "Some people have real problems, you know . . ."

"Oh, so do I, buddy."

"*Fuck* you! You live round here, asshole? Do ya? 'Cause I'll remember your face, you know. You see me? You run."

Eric pretended to turn away as the guy took another step toward him, but then he swung around and smashed his right fist into the guy's mouth, his latchkeys crunching against enamel, lacerating his lips. The guy flopped to the sidewalk like a damp twig, clutching his bloodied mouth and moaning.

And the rage that had been building inside Eric for weeks released in one ecstatic, savage charge. He kicked the guy hard in the ribs, and again and again, until he heard a dull crack, and the guy was bleating like a lost lamb.

Eric turned away, walking fast, panting, euphoric, suddenly feeling much more like himself. He started to laugh. He was flooded with endorphins from sated rage.

He was almost back at his apartment door when a thought came to him. It made him go freeze-frame still, with his key poised in the air in front of the lock.

You see me? You run.

Then he hurried inside and went straight to his laptop and flipped it open.

Eric had long ago written off Alyssa, Kyle's ex-girlfriend. She was no longer of use to him because she'd clearly had no idea who Hajun was when he'd shown her that Golden Gate Park photo. But

Alyssa's online world was an open book. He'd even guessed her email password (Seriously? Dog's name plus year of her birth?). Now he accessed her email, initiated a password reset, and took control of the account. For the first time in months, excitement churned in his chest. He used the new password to obtain an Apple one-time security code and then he accessed her iCloud. And there he found a hoard of treasure: her stored payment methods, all her dumb music and videos, and hundreds of cached photos from the time she was dating Kyle, which she probably didn't even realize she still had, including dozens and dozens of screenshots he'd sent her from his Strava running app, showing his heat maps, his mileage, his routes.

Why did he send you all those, Alyssa? Did you demand them—as proof that he wasn't cheating on you? Or was he unconsciously trying to tell you something? That he was running, running, running away from you?

Kyle, *bless him*, was a creature of habit. He would set off from home—Bingo! The house on Belvedere Avenue—and run a loop around the coastal road, sometimes even along the trails of Mount Tamalpais. And always at the same time, in the cooling evenings, after rush hour, when the light was perfect and the air fragrant with pine and ocean spray and eucalyptus.

Eric laughed with joy. He poured himself a generous glass of the Macallan and put on some music.

What the fuck had been the matter with him? What kind of pussy had he become lately? Letting things get on top of him. This was his life! This is what gave him meaning. Who was he to complain about an order from the Supreme Sister? It was like complaining about the weather. You get the order you get. Now he knew *exactly* where and when to find Kyle, and he would do whatever it took to make him give up Ha-jun. With electrodes attached to his balls, if necessary. Or with acid squirted in his eyes.

All was not lost, not lost at all.

65

Marin County, California
June 2018

The sky was fading to a deep purple and a sliver of a crescent moon, as sharp as a sickle, was rising over the bay. The hillsides were dark, except for the glow from houses situated in the forested canyons and the headlights of an occasional car cruising up the avenue.

Kyle was running at a slowish pace along the edges of the lit tennis courts and darkened golf courses. He was warming up, breathing in the cool air and the scent of the eucalyptus and jacaranda trees.

He checked his watch. At twenty-one minutes into his run he was rounding a broad curve in the road and the Pacific slowly opened wide in all its black expanse. He picked up his pace, starting to sprint along the ocean side of the sidewalk, his calves working, all spark plugs and pistons, reveling in strength. He would maintain this speed for a full twelve minutes before slowing down for the incline on the loop back home.

Traffic was sparse. No one was about.

The road unrolled before him as if suspended in the beams of the streetlights. Mountain and forest to his right, ocean crashing against the rocks to his left.

He was approaching the turning for the access road that led up to the trails and campsites on Mount Tamalpais, when, far off, he saw another lone runner coming toward him.

Like Kyle, the man was running on the ocean side of the road. He was wearing a black singlet and black running shorts, the phone strapped to his biceps aglow as he moved.

A rolling boom sounded as a big wave hit the rocks to his left, sending spray high into the air.

Kyle kept his eyes on the lone runner as they drew closer and closer to each other . . . And then something ignited in Kyle's heart.

For a few electrifying seconds he was convinced that the figure running toward him was Stephen. He was a beautiful, East Asian man. Slender, with an athlete's legs, shining black hair.

Kyle gave an involuntary exhalation of joy and lengthened his stride, sprinting to reach full steam, the engines of his lungs working fast.

But as the two runners drew closer and as the man passed beneath a streetlight and the features of his face resolved into eyes, nose, mouth, Kyle saw that it was not Stephen.

It was, however, someone Kyle thought he recognized.

The man was approaching at a fast, graceful pace, arms working, hands stiff and fingers extended, white AirPods in his ears, face blank with concentration. He gave no sign that he was even going to acknowledge Kyle as they passed.

And then, with barely ten meters remaining between them, the man's knee gave way. He came skipping painfully to a halt, his face contorted in pain, teeth bared.

The man stopped and bent over, panting heavily, clutching his knee.

Kyle, too, slowed down and stopped. He pulled out his AirPods.

"You OK, man?"

"Yeah," the man said, still bent over, grasping his knee. He was shining with sweat. "Oh, boy." He was still catching his breath. "This route's a killer on the knees."

He straightened up and tried to rest his weight on the knee, wincing in pain again.

"D'you need to call for a ride?" Kyle said, trying to get a better look at him. The man's head was bent over his knee.

"My car's just over there, thank God," the man said, nodding toward the access road that led to the campsites. He tried to take another step and flinched again.

"Here, give me your arm."

The man looked at Kyle then and his expression seemed strange in the streetlight. In fact, it was as if he had two faces—one of an injured runner, and another behind it, cold, calculating, and utterly ruthless.

And in that moment Kyle knew who he was. *What the fuck?*

The speaker who'd come to Tamalpais last year.

What happened next was so fast that Kyle had no time to move away or raise his arm in defense. With shocking violence the man's fist struck a massive blow against the side of Kyle's neck. Only later, and only briefly, would Kyle understand that there had been a syringe in that fist.

"Hello, Kyle," Eric said.

66

Novo-Ogaryevo
Moscow
June 2018

To Jenna's surprise, conditions in SIZO No. 6 Women's Prison had improved dramatically for her. Meals had started arriving with fresh vegetables and real bread. She'd been given longer in the exercise yard each day, although always at separate times from the other women. She'd been allowed to visit the gym, which had some rusty free weights and an ancient standing bag hung from a gruesome chain, which she kicked and punched ferociously to regain muscle and strength, while her guard, Irina—always a baleful presence outside the cell—seemed less vigilant. Books in English had been procured for her—dogeared paperback romances by Judith Krantz, published forty years ago. She even practiced her Russian conversation with Irina, whom, she discovered, was human after all. The woman became almost chummy at times, complaining of verrucae, her husband's drinking, her wayward son doing military service who was always asking her for money.

The interrogations had stopped. No one from the SVR had visited since that pharmacological torture session, which had left her curled up on her mattress for days. She knew that the defensive walls of her brain had been breached and her mind had been ransacked. There was a black hole in her memory, a hole in time. Her meditation practice, which for years had helped her find peace, became arduous. Drifting into a state of alert consciousness came to feel like a mental probing of the black hole, and although she never saw what was inside, it would nevertheless release the demons, leaving her in a bleak, defeated mood for days at a time.

She had no recall of what she'd told them. Either they knew the truth, or they didn't, or—perhaps—she'd given them some mashed-up version of it. The technique for resisting truth drugs seemed farcical now. Everything in her mind had been blown away by a chemical hurricane. No human could have withstood it.

She'd now been a prisoner for well over a year. No trial date had been scheduled. The prison had become her universe. She read. She slept. Through her high, barred window, she'd watched the light change with the seasons. In late spring, the icicles along the prison's eaves had begun to glisten and drip.

In the exercise yard she'd smelled the thaw in the air just days before summer came on full blast.

Not a night had gone by without her dreaming of her mom and Soo-min. She would fantasize endlessly about taking Soo-min somewhere far away. A fresh start to get her sister clear of all the fresh starts she'd made before.

Today, something was afoot, because she'd been summoned to see the governor.

In his office she stood on the worn white cross marked on the floor, arms at her side, eyes up front. By now, her Russian was rudimentary but usable, the dividends of her conversations with Irina. She was not permitted to look directly at him, but from the lower rim of her vision, she could see a harassed, balding fellow with thick glasses crouched over his desk. He barely glanced at her, which made for an oddly disjointed exchange.

A file was open in front of him. She waited for him to inform her of the date of the next pre-trial hearing. Instead, he said, "Are you in good health?"

"Yes, sir."

"No infections of any sort?"

"No, sir."

"Do you have a temperature, or a cough?"

"No, sir."

"Any stomach problems? Diarrhea?"

Since the food had improved, the violent insurrection in her guts had calmed.

"No, sir."

"What about lice? Have you had any parasites or insect bites?"

What the hell? "No, sir."

There was an odd uncertainty in his voice, as if he was as bewildered as she was by these questions and why he was having to ask them.

"All the same . . ." He closed the file and studied her through his lenses as if she were a distant dot on a far horizon. "We should get you checked out." He called Irina into the room. "Take the prisoner to the infirmary."

Jenna was led away confused. Since when did anyone here care about a prisoner's health?

The medic examined her with a sensitivity that was quite unlike his treatment of her when she'd arrived. He took blood and urine samples for tests, put a thermometer into her mouth, and asked about her medical history. "What about vaccinations? Measles? Polio?"

Her puzzlement mounted when she returned to her cell to find a new mattress laid out with fresh sheets folded on top. And next to those: a set of clean, new clothes. Jeans, underwear, a padded coat from Zara, new trainers that fitted.

And suddenly she felt an almighty rush of hope: that this

bizarre concern for her welfare was the signal of an impending release.

They don't want the Americans saying I've been poorly treated.

That evening the meal on her tray was chicken basted in butter and herbs and served with white rice and asparagus—the type of meal she'd often cooked for herself. Good food and a soft mattress gave her a sound night's sleep. In the morning, her hopes surged again when her porridge arrived with fresh blueberries and a cup of hot coffee. *Coffee.* It was instant and smelled rank, but she savored it as if it were a luxurious hot chocolate. She hadn't tasted coffee in months.

That day she was kept in her cell. No exercise outside. No sign at all of Irina. The suspense was driving her crazy. It was in the air, an expectancy, a tension. She couldn't sit still, let alone meditate. She kept trying to tamp down the excitement, her burgeoning hope and desperation to be free. But her emotions kept slipping their reins and defied all her efforts to manage them. The yearning was bursting from her heart and flooding her body with tingling sensations.

As day turned to evening, the sky behind the bars faded to deep blue then to a duck-egg green. The days were getting longer. She smelled pollen and saw bees buzzing past her window. New life. *Hope.* As the light was fading altogether, she heard footsteps outside the cell.

She was ready for them. She had dressed in her new clothes that still smelled of factory and outlet store. Four large men wearing olive green flying jackets and garrison caps entered the cell. All had "FSB" on their backs in large yellow Cyrillic letters. One of them put her in handcuffs, locking her hands in front of her, not behind her back. Another spoke into a lapel radio, then guided her out of the door with one hand on her shoulder. She was escorted out of the main prison building and into a waiting prisoner transport van with blacked-out windows. She was the sole prisoner. Two guards sat in front. Another two followed the van in a car. She knew that prisoners were sometimes taken to court in the middle of the night, confused and disoriented, but this felt different. This was out of the ordinary. She could see it in the men's faces: a kind of heightened diligence, an added caution in executing an order.

Nothing could be seen through the windows, but she started listening intently for clues. She was fairly sure they were headed into Moscow. Traffic sounds grew denser, as did music from passing car radios and the occasional chatter of pedestrians when they stopped at lights. But after an hour or so the van began to pick up speed. They were traveling on open freeway, but in which direction she had no idea. By her vague reckoning of time, they had driven for about three hours before the van turned off the freeway and slowed. It was stopping at a checkpoint. A window was lowered. Papers were exchanged. Voices spoke via two-way radio. Then a second checkpoint. A longer wait this time, and when the driver again lowered his window, Jenna smelled not city and traffic but pines and crisp, clean air. They had passed through Moscow and had emerged . . . where?

Moments later, the van turned onto a long gravel drive and about five minutes after that it came to a halt. The rear door opened, and she was ordered out. It was night. She emerged, dazed, into some kind of stable yard. She could smell horses, hear them stamping and snorting; she could hear trees sighing in the wind. Then she turned to see a very large house—like a mansion in a Tolstoy novel, all white stucco and cornices, apricot walls, and ornamental trees to either side of a grand pillared portico.

The US ambassador's residence?

Something didn't feel right.

Heavy raindrops were hitting the gravel in sparse single grenades, followed moments later by a downpour. A cool wind picked up, sending the trees into a frenzy. She shivered.

An officer with gold shoulder tabs emerged from the huge doors, prompting her four guards to salute. He ordered them to remove the handcuffs and Jenna rubbed her wrists. Now she was being escorted around the house to a side entrance. This led through a mews arch built of enormous limestone blocks. They emerged in a large stone courtyard and entered the house itself, where she was shown into a small, very warm waiting room with paneled walls. The officer told her that some refreshments would be brought to her shortly.

"Can I ask where I am?" she said.

He ignored her and left, locking the door behind him.

The room was curtained with dense velvet drapes. She parted them an inch. The windows were old, with glass thickened to withstand the Russian winter. Outside, the wide stone courtyard was deserted and lit by flickering gas lamps hung beneath the arches. On one side of the room an ornate marble fireplace appeared disused; the heat was coming off the radiators. *Heat on in summer?* Above the fireplace, a rather garishly gilded mantel clock told her that it was almost midnight.

The small threads of anxiety that had been unspooling all around her since she'd arrived in this place began to coalesce in the air of this stifling room. When she peered closer at the clock, she saw that it was not an antique as she had supposed, but new—it made no ticking sound—and it had been engraved in small italic letters in English.

Presented to
President V. V. Putin
Shanghai Cooperation Organization Summit
June 2012

The realization happened so fast it was electric. And when the door suddenly unlocked, and Vadim Giorgadze entered the room in full uniform, and regarded her with a strange look—part disdain, part respect—she felt no surprise. She had already figured it out.

"You again," he said, holding open the door as if she were a disgraced child being let out of detention to see the headmaster. "Medic check you out? No temperature? No coughs or sneezes?"

67

Marin County, California

Eric pulled up a collapsible camping chair to sit beside Kyle, whose eyelids were beginning to flutter as he regained consciousness.

He was lying on a fold-down sofa and was zipped into a sleeping bag with the ropes tied around the outside to ensure that no marks would appear on his body.

A remarkable thing, the interior space in an RV, Eric thought. Room for six people. And the privacy. It made for a very convenient mobile torture chamber. Park it in any remote beauty spot and no one would give it a second glance.

Finally, Kyle opened his eyes, drowsily at first and then wide in shock as he took in the horror of his situation.

Eric had hung a small battery-powered LED lantern above the sofa. The moths outside were flicking softly against the window, trying to reach the light.

"Some people radiate vulnerability, Kyle. The look on your face right now says, 'I am afraid of you.' Faces like yours simply invite abuse. You expect to be hurt, so you kind of encourage it, did you know that . . . ?"

"Oh God." Kyle had started to whimper. "Oh God." His body undulated like a caterpillar in the sleeping bag, straining against the ropes.

"Help!" he screamed suddenly, his neck muscles training. "Help!"

"Yeah, this campsite's closed to visitors. There's no one out here. Parks Department is fixing the trails, apparently. Been a lot of rockfalls lately."

"Oh God . . . Oh God . . ."

Eric sighed. "Right. I'm sure you want to get this over with as quickly as I do . . ." He got up and opened the RV's small closet where a black rubber apron was hanging up. He looped it over his head and fastened it at the waist, then donned a clear Perspex face screen. Then he sat back down and lifted a toolbox onto his lap.

"Question one, Kyle. Ready?" He opened the toolbox and took out a printout of a photograph, the one Alyssa took in Golden Gate Park. "The Asian guy standing at the back of this photo. This guy here. Do you know him?"

"Please . . . please . . ."

Eric rolled his eyes and put on a pair of blue surgical gloves. Then he took out a small electric power drill and squeezed the trigger, giving a few high-pitched revs.

"Yes!" Kyle yelled and started crying. "His name's Stephen. Stephen Lee."

A shiver of excitement spread upward through Eric's body.

Stephen Lee.

Kyle said, "B-but I don't even know if that's his real name . . . He's very private."

"And he's very wise," Eric said, reasonably. "Because he's very hard to find. Question two: How do you know him?"

"He was my boyfriend."

Eric was so surprised that he pulled off the face mask and stared shrewdly at Kyle. This intimate angle had never occurred to him.

"How did you meet him?"

Kyle let out a cry like a wounded goat, and Eric revved the power drill again.

"Coffee Shack," Kyle said quickly. "The one near Union Square. He asked to borrow my charger. I swear to God . . . that's what happened . . . I swear to God."

Tears began to flow freely down his face.

"It's all right," Eric said softly. "Thank you for sharing that, Kyle."

Eric paused for a moment, thinking. He was immensely relieved to have finally found a source of real intel and the relief was making him generous. He almost wanted to spare Kyle more suffering. Perhaps he would let him go when this was done . . . It was an intriguing thought to entertain, but it was only a thought. Kyle had seen Eric's face this evening, and there could be no witnesses. Kyle wasn't going to see tomorrow.

"Are you still in touch with . . . Stephen?"

"No. He broke up with me."

"Why?"

"B-b-because I followed him home one time . . ." Kyle's voice rose to a screech as he spoke through his tears. "I wanted to see where he lived."

"You followed him home? He didn't like that?"

"No, he was *private*. Really private."

"And where is his home, Kyle? Where will I find him?"

Some defensive fortification suddenly activated inside Kyle. Eric could see it in his eyes. Some storm barrier was going up.

Kyle clenched his teeth and shook his head.

Eric pulled down the clear plastic mask and picked up the drill again. Suddenly, he threw the toolbox aside and grabbed Kyle's throat, holding his head in place while the drill was poised over his forehead, whining as it spun, a horrible sound like enamel being scraped off teeth.

Kyle screamed. The drill pierced his skin, making a tiny, round, cherry-red mark.

"Stop, stop, stop, please . . ."

"The next one goes through bone," Eric said soothingly.

"He lives in public housing near San Pablo and MacDonald," Kyle said in a rush. "I don't know where exactly. That's his neighborhood. Richmond. I don't know the address."

"Who does he live with?"

"Um. Foster parents? He lives with foster parents . . . That's all I know, I swear. I don't know anything else. He would never tell me . . . Please let me go."

Eric eased the pressure of his grip on Kyle's throat. "Does he ever go out? He can't stay indoors all day, can he?"

"I don't know. I don't know. I swear."

"Think, Kyle, think." Eric revved the drill again.

"Um . . . He'll definitely go out on Gay Pride. He said he liked it 'cause no one knew who he was in a crowd."

"*Gay Pride?*" Eric pulled a face as if he'd just smelled the worst smell in the world.

"He might be in XXL Bar on Saturday night."

"How do you know?"

"It's where we liked to go . . . I was planning to be there, too."

"Because you're hoping to see him again?"

Kyle's body was convulsed with sobs. "Yes."

"XXL Bar . . . Gay Pride is this weekend?"

Kyle nodded. His nose and lips were swollen from crying. "Please let me go now . . . I've told you everything."

"This bar . . . is it like a rave?"

Kyle shook his head. "Just an old-school dive. Leather guys. Stephen thought it was ironic-cool."

Eric released his throat and sat back down, deep in thought. After a while he said, "You've been a real help, Kyle. I mean it."

Then he picked up the flat rock he'd been hiding under the fold-down sofa and brought it down on Kyle's forehead with a heavy crack. The force of the second blow broke his cheekbone. The third crushed the orbital bone around his eye, sending linear spatters of blood across the RV's laminated panels.

He felt exhausted suddenly, almost too tired even to check the pulse in Kyle's neck as it faded and died. He just wanted to lie down and sleep.

With an enormous effort of will he untied the ropes—tricky, with his hands in gloves—and unzipped the sleeping bag. Kyle's eyes remained open and unseeing.

It was hard going heaving Kyle's heavy, athlete's body over his shoulder and out of the RV, but he didn't have far to go. Just a few yards to where a rockfall had covered the opening to the nearest trail, spilling scree and boulders into the forested ravine below.

Eric tilted gently and Kyle's body rolled off his shoulder, tumbling almost soundlessly into the dark. Then he smashed Kyle's phone under the heel of his boot and kicked it into the ravine after him.

"Very dangerous," Eric said, wiping the sweat from his forehead, then resting his hands on his hips. "Running alone along mountain trails."

Across the bay the lights of San Francisco glittered and danced on the inky water.

Ha-jun. Stephen Lee. Are we finally going to meet?

68

Novo-Ogaryevo
Moscow

Jenna followed Giorgadze through the vast house, with four armed guards of the Presidential Protection Service trailing behind her. Giorgadze's gait was hasty, boot heels clacking on black-and-white tiles. He glanced at his watch more than once, and seemed sweaty and uncomfortable in his uniform, which was not surprising since the heat was on in every room. They were headed toward the rear of the house, she guessed. Soon, the gilded hallways and chandeliers gave way to a modern annex of smooth, pale-gray concrete walls, thick beige carpets, and recessed lighting. The air seemed different, too. Filtered and purified. An armed sentry stood at every ten meters or so. Giorgadze was clearly expected, since each of them nodded him through, their gazes following Jenna with a stony curiosity.

She felt like a courtesan being led along secret passages under the knowing eyes of the servants. Eventually they reached a small office area manned by a young desk officer who regarded them with a brisk indifference. Giorgadze straightened his tunic and showed some form of ID, which was inspected. An entry was made into a computer. The officer picked up a telephone, punched in a one-digit number, and lowered his head to speak into the receiver. Then he said, "The Vozhd is working. He may call you in or he may not. He says you're to wait. Leave your briefcase here. Take out everything you need and hold it in your hand. If you're called in, do not reach into your inside pocket for anything."

Giorgadze gave an anxious smile.

Jenna followed him down a narrow stone stairway. The guards' boots began to thump down the steps after them, but then Jenna heard the officer say, "Not you." The guards retreated, and she found herself alone with Giorgadze in some kind of antechamber furnished with black velvet couches and wall lamps set into elegant gold brackets. Large, epic Russian landscapes hung spotlit on each of the walls, which were also black. The tiny red lights of cameras blinked from each corner. The room was so dim that she almost didn't notice the ominous steel door at the far end of the room. Giorgadze turned to her and whispered, "Sit there. Don't make a sound." His ears were aflame, but his face was as pale as a candle. His hands had a slight tremor to them.

This man's ambition has carried him too far, she thought. *Once you make it into Putin's inner circle there's no way back.*

He removed his officer's cap to wipe his bald head with a handkerchief. A bead of sweat trickled down his arrow nose and onto his revolting mustache. The room was windowless, and infernally hot.

Minutes ticked by, then half an hour. The sight of Giorgadze's unease had the effect of making Jenna feel less afraid for herself. Whatever was about to happen, it was out of her hands. There was nothing she could do except to stay alert and stay calm. But the situation was very strange. She was alone in a closed room with the head of SVR operations, without handcuffs and unguarded.

A soft chime sounded from a silver panel near the door, and the light of its button changed from blue to green.

Giorgadze stood up, rather too quickly, and replaced his cap.

"Do you understand how privileged you are to meet him?" he hissed.

Jenna said nothing.

"You are not to go near him or try to touch him. Understand?"

The steel door slid open with a hum of hidden machinery.

The room she entered was long and narrow, and it had a private, intimate feel. Low ceiling. Long bookshelves crammed with volumes of history. Sofas and armchairs. A large antique globe. At the far end was an enormous hearth, where a fire of pine logs was just starting to catch and crack as if it were deep midwinter, not a mild night in summer. The fire provided almost the only illumination apart from a few table lamps that cast pools of amber light.

Giorgadze waited respectfully near the door, placing Jenna just in front of him where he could keep an eye on her.

Seated at a large escritoire on the right side of the room was the man who was master of one sixth of the world. He was speaking on the telephone, the back of his chair turned toward them. His workspace was covered in leather-bound report binders and an array of telephones. The beam of a desk lamp on the papers cast the back of his head in dark silhouette.

Jenna looked slowly around the room. Above the mantel was a sinister assortment of hunting rifles, glinting swords, and gold-plated handguns. The other side was all floor-to-ceiling windows of double-paned glass, which gave a view onto a gloomy orangery lit by small spotlights set into the gravel. Among the shadows of the trees were what appeared to be four or five statues, until one of them moved and turned on a pencil flashlight, and she glimpsed helmets, combat fatigues, submachine guns.

She had the feeling she'd entered a little boy's den, to which only the closest of friends were admitted, even though she suspected that the room's occupant had no real friends. The whole scene was ambiguous, confusing.

Putin continued to talk on the phone. A log tumbled in the fire, sending golden embers cascading onto the hearth stone. The atmosphere was stifling and heavy.

Putin, Fisk had once told her, abided by Stalin's working hours, which kept everyone on their toes. He rose at about eleven, did a workout with his personal trainers, a few laps in the pool, chaired a couple of meetings, had his lunch at four, dinner at nine, then worked late into the night. In the daylight hours, he was the Manager-in-Chief, the thuggish, no-nonsense, ex-KGB officer beloved by ex-cons and babushkas, whose face gazed from a million fridge magnets. He would make sarcastic quips about the opposition, fire people, and interrupt ministers during televised cabinet meetings to correct them on points of fact. He would open another new church, award medals to Olympians banned for doping, and keep world leaders waiting for hours in super-heated anterooms.

But by night, he had another kind of power: the power of dream and myth. He was the all-powerful Father of the Nation, Vladimir the Great, scourge of the West and defender of Orthodox Christianity. He became conflated with Peter the Great and Ivan the Terrible, with whose spirits he communed. In these hours, she imagined, working in his private man cave, his mind was a wasps' nest of grudges and paranoia, his energy became darker, more creative. He'd pore over maps, redraw borders, found new provinces, and abolish old ones. His resentments would open their claws as he thought of novel and better ways to reverse the country's shrinking birthrate. The banning of same-sex marriage! Medals for mothers of large families! He would pencil amendments to the constitution to award people the freedom to elect him as their president for life, if they so desired, and even if they didn't. He'd pace about, seething over the depravity of Westerners, their hypocrisy about human rights, and their pro-pedophile political parties. (He knew there were no such things as pro-pedophile parties, but it suited him to throw gays, trans people, and sex offenders into one disgusting pot.) He'd lose himself in reveries, remembering long-ago conversations with his enemies, especially the ones he'd had poisoned, driven to suicide, or pushed out of tenth-floor windows.

Finally, Putin ended the call, and swiveled around in his chair. The face was puffy and doll-like, but his eyes were flint arrowheads. He nodded grimly in the direction of a couch and two chairs and Giorgadze gave a small exclamation of delight.

Putin made no acknowledgment of Jenna. He looked small and tired and older than he appeared in photographs. Despite his immense power, he was, after all, only a garden-variety dictator. A gnome. Pedantic and uncharismatic. A bureaucrat who'd permafrosted himself deep into the organs of state, impossible to remove.

Jenna was watching intently, hardly breathing. Giorgadze hitched his trouser legs and perched on the edge of the couch, which was a mistake, since it was disadvantageously low and deep.

"Respected Vladimir Vladimirovich, you ordered me to bring you the American spy Jenna Williams. Here she is."

Putin turned to look at her with no apparent interest.

"Welcome, Jenna Williams," he said in English. "Sit down, please." He'd pronounced her name *Jyenna*.

Jenna's heart sank with shame. She'd let down the Agency, and Fisk, even though Fisk had been the first to tell her, years ago at the Farm, that everyone gave up their name in the end.

Giorgadze forced his face into another pained smile. "Mr. President, I would be failing in my duty if I did not insist that your personal security detail be brought into this room to—"

"Actually, you can go," Putin said irritably.

Giorgadze looked as if he'd bitten on glass. He inclined his head and heaved himself up with some difficulty.

After he'd gone, Putin watched Jenna as she sat down—in an upright chair, not the couch. The fire was blazing now, sending bright sparks up the chimney and a rippling glow across the ceiling of the room. She was sweating uncontrollably.

The dictator closed the report binders on his desk and crossed the room to settle into an armchair opposite her. He was dressed informally in black: expensive-looking casual jacket, polo shirt undone at the collar, jeans, and slip-on Pradas. The impression was less that of a powerful crime boss than an aging heavy-metal talent manager.

An off-the-books meeting, she thought. *A meeting that isn't happening...*

He leaned toward her, his elbows on his knees. He wasn't sweating at all. It was as if he needed this greenhouse heat, like a newborn tarantula.

"It's an honor to meet you, Jee-min," he said in Russian. "That is your Korean name, I believe."

Jenna said nothing.

"You are—I think it's no exaggeration for me to say this—something of a legend. Not to the public. But in the secret world—*our* world—you're famous. It's true. Don't be embarrassed." He said this with only a trace of a smirk.

What was this? Professional vanity? A meeting of *colleagues*? Whatever he was getting at, he was savoring it.

"I don't understand," she said in Russian, feeling the engines of her brain come online, drawing on all her reserves of energy as she realized that this whole conversation was going to be in Russian.

"I have made my heart a sunless place, Jenna Williams, and so have you. There is no forgiveness, or love, or inner peace for people like us. Whatever game the CIA was playing by sending you here to meet up with some dead traitor's son, they have lost. But you and I are both, I suspect, cynics. We accept the consequences of failure."

She could only follow the odd word of this. "Why am I here?"

Putin had not taken his eyes off hers. The light of the flames was casting a Mephistophelian effect onto his small round head, his cruel half smile. "I make it a rule always to look a person in the eye before I make an important decision about them. I need to determine what to do with you, CIA operations officer Jenna Williams."

"I thought you had. I'm facing trial and years in prison."

"Not anymore," he said, reclining into the chair. "Seeing you in the flesh has helped me to decide. I'm letting you go."

This conversational swerve caught her completely off guard. She pressed her lips together as a warning to herself not to speak. Anything she said now would be playing into his game.

He arched his fingers and said, "You see, there is someone else who wants you much more than I do, 'Most Wanted Person Number One'. Once you're in his hands, believe me, an eighteen-year stretch in Siberia will seem like a wonderful vacation you missed." Putin had a quiet, snorty snicker of a laugh. "You're a wanted person, Jenna Williams. A terrorist. An assassin. The North Koreans have spent years searching for you, and here you are. That's worth something to me."

For the first time since entering this room, she felt a sheet of dread drape over her. She went ice cold despite the suffocating heat.

"You're giving me to the North Koreans?"

Putin leaned further back in his chair, enjoying himself. Everything about this bizarre piece of theater was starting to make sense. Something else he had in common with Stalin: *sadism*. Nothing was sweeter to this man, more satisfying, than to see his enemies abased, humiliated, utterly vanquished.

"I wish it were that simple," he said, still spinning his yarn, using every spare inch of thread to make it last. "Kim Jong-un has two obsessions: eliminating all threats to his legitimacy . . . and finding the person who killed his father."

"You think I killed his father?"

"That's not for me to say. You probably have some explaining to do. But, forgive me, I do not think that Kim Jong-un will be very interested in your explanation. He's less patient than I am. The fact is: you were the only other person present inside that train carriage when his father suffered a fatal heart attack on a December night in 2011."

Jenna was on the edge of her seat now. The fire was combusting into a bright blaze, casting the room in a theatrical light. Heat like this would make any visitor suffer, but it only now occurred to her that it was simply more sadism.

"Kim Jong-il was frail from a stroke and suffered from a weak heart. I did not kill him."

"All the same, perhaps you can begin to see the reasoning behind my decision. On the one hand you're a CIA officer who entered Russia illegally, and that is a matter that should be dealt with harshly under the law. The United States may raise objections, but somehow, I don't think Mr. Trump will care one way or the other what happens to you. On the other hand, Kim Jong-un is an important ally of Russia's, and he wants your blood."

"Some friends you have."

"Unfortunately, I cannot simply *give* you to Kim Jong-un as a gift. He's too proud a man for that. And this matter is very sensitive for him personally. He would lose face. No, the North Koreans need to *find* you themselves. And it is my intention of making sure they have a high chance of success. If for some reason they are unsuccessful, well, then you stay in Russia to serve an appropriate sentence determined by the courts."

She felt oddly calm now, as if she were watching someone else's trial.

Putin stood up.

She was almost within striking distance of the vagus nerve on the side of his neck. One hammer strike from her hand and she could cut the blood-pressure signals to his brain, disrupt his heart rate. She could crush his windpipe, pull his eyes out with two fingers.

He seemed to read her mind, because he was looking down at her with a cold disdain, and a faint, knowing irony around his lips.

"I've enjoyed our meeting. Good luck."

He glanced in the direction of the door and nodded. Without her hearing anything, two masked Spetsnaz troopers had entered the room and were aiming pistols at her with both hands.

69

Castro Street
San Francisco
June 2018

The flow of human traffic along Castro was intense. Gay Pride, the holiest day in the city's calendar. Sound systems in every store were pumping out a cacophony of deep-cheese club anthems. The air was a heady admixture of amyl nitrate and incense, crotch and armpit. Eric felt like a visitor to an alien civilization. Boys pretending to be boys. Sleazy old daddies. I-won't-be-ignored drag queens who looked like cartoons. Everyone faking it to be real.

It was crowded and chaotic and noisy, and yet . . . he'd never experienced an atmosphere that felt quite so *alive*, that offered such a limitless license for fun.

He had no difficulty finding a store called Mr. Leather. He bought some suitable apparel and headed back to the RV as fast as he could. He'd arrived just as the day was ending in a soft white haze, but now a chill damp air had rolled in from the bay and the city was twinkling forlornly in the fog.

He'd walked past XXL Bar twice and the augurs were good: blacked-out windows, dark interior, strobing lights, a body-vibrating techno bass, no metal detector. A run-down place, probably with a dated security cam setup, if any. Through the open door he'd seen that the bar and dance floor were almost empty. He figured it would get going later tonight. He was counting on a busy night. A humid crush of bodies, darkness, noise, confusion, everyone drunk and high off their ass. That would be his cover for murder.

At ten, he started getting ready. He stripped down to his Calvins, flattened his hair with gel, and inspected his muscle definition in the RV's small closet mirror. He'd been working out his abdominal obliques and was pleased to see those elusive defining lines, the signifiers of male physical perfection. His lats and biceps looked excellent. Smooth and hairless.

When he finally emerged, he was wearing a black leather harness—four studded straps that met in a silver ring in the center of his bare chest—along with tight, low-waist jeans, heavy lace-up boots, and black leather gauntlets over his forearms. He'd never worn anything so dumb in his life, but he had to admit he kind of liked the vibe. On his head was a plain black baseball cap to shade his face from cameras. He completed the look with his reflective aviators.

Masc-presenting Asian dom top. No fems. Kind of your type, Stephen?

Castro was still heaving, and now the bars were in full swing.

To his dismay he saw that XXL Bar was already packed, and an edgy-looking line of clubbers, mostly men, many of them half naked, was waiting outside on the street. An unseemly altercation was taking place at the front of the line, where some cosplaying hetero had been rumbled and was being turned away.

Eric walked along the line, inspecting it, unsure of what to do, but then something magical happened.

Heads turned toward him. Those who hadn't seen him were nudged by their friends. Dozens of stares crisscrossed his body like laser sights. The door-whore, a large, ruddy bear of a man in a white vest said, "Right this way, sugar." The voice was both matronly and thuggish. Eric went straight in.

Inside was tacky and hellish and electrifying.

The bar area was so crowded that no one could move. Everyone was simply buffered about by collisions. Many of the guys were younger than him, stylish, muscular, and bratty, and had removed their T-shirts. Only the older guys wore leather. Getting a drink would involve storming a barricade of bare flesh.

But again, Eric felt that enchantment enveloping him like a force field.

Face after face began noticing him, and the bodies parted like the blades of a scissors. Renewed strength flowed into his body, along with power.

"Heyyy, Daddy," someone said in his ear.

To Eric's eyes, these people looked like extras catching their first sight of the star.

The bar was backlit by purple lights that looked like bug-zappers. To his left, deeper into the club, he could see a small, crowded dance floor. Fists pumped the air in silhouette. A miasma of dry ice and falling glitter. Beams of colored lights rotated on the walls.

He asked for sparkling water, practically yelling his order over the noise. Everyone around him seemed intoxicated, but he was clear-headed, and feeling a cold singularity of purpose. He was beginning to sense, from the carnivorous stares he was attracting, that his looks had a downside. But it was his physique they were seeing, not his face. Someone touched his ass. Eric turned and glared so coldly that the boy shrunk away, spooked.

He'd spotted only one camera, which was facing the bar. He turned his head and moved, pushing his way toward the dance floor. One boy, off his face, tried to kiss him. Eric swatted him aside roughly. He was searching for a spot on the periphery where he would be inconspicuous, where he could lean against the wall and wait.

As he approached the forest of dancing forms, ghostly in the light, he noticed an exit off to the side that led to a pitch-dark room, a portal into pure unlight. A stream of furtive traffic was shuffling in and out, those emerging zipping up their flies and smirking. Eric turned away feeling such disgust that he thought he might vomit.

The DJ's playlist was following an arc that seemed to build slowly, swell, peak, and then release to a great cheer. The dance floor again filled with hissing dry ice.

It was getting harder and harder to discern individual faces in the grayscale light and bright flashes, but he wasn't going to remove his cap or aviators. Dancers appeared as brief snapshots and blurred as they moved, like old video. For some reason, Eric had thought that finding Stephen in a bar would be as easy as finding someone in a pool hall, standing along a wall, or leaning over the brightly lit baize of the table. Finding him here was going to be much harder.

The clientele was getting sketchy—drunk, shouty, loose. Bare torsos cold with sweat slid against him like slime. The place smelled of hair gel and the sour odor of spilled beer. He didn't think he could stand much more of this.

After about half an hour he spotted a short, shirtless muscle boy whose chest was crisscrossed by bandoliers full of plastic shot glasses. Pride rainbows were painted onto both his cheeks. He was circling the dance floor, handing out free tequilas. Eric watched him smile and slosh out booze, apparently drunk himself. Then he offered one to the boy standing in front of Eric, but briskly withdrew it before the boy could touch it. "Sorry, honey. Didn't see your wrist. You can get a free soda at the bar."

"Uh. Sure."

The kid had been given a green wristband at the door, meaning that he was under twenty-one. Eric's wristband was red.

Eric craned his head to get a sideways look at his face.

Blessed be the fruit.

Stephen Lee, the boy himself. Standing right in front of him, just inches from his face.

Eric went very still. He was feeling a great inner torsion, as if he were a big cat with prey in its sights.

And the prey seemed to be alone, and not particularly enjoying himself. He was wearing a baggy black T-shirt that made him utterly nondescript. His body was as bony as an alley cat's. Eric could see the angles of his shoulder blades, his spine beneath the smooth skin of his neck.

Eric moved his head closer so that his nose was almost touching Stephen's hair.

All that loneliness and watchfulness. But you let it all out, occasionally, don't you? Somewhere crowded and anonymous. You don't dare thumb through a hookup app . . . It would leave a trail. You're condemned to come to places like this . . .

Stephen's clothing smelled fresh and laundered. He wasn't damp and disheveled like almost everyone there. Eric caught the scent of his skin, his antiperspirant, his fabric conditioner. Perhaps he'd only just arrived. He clearly hadn't been dancing.

Poor kid. Lost in your attempt to lose yourself. But you're not lost anymore.

"Want me to get you a real drink?" Eric said over the noise.

Stephen turned to face him, as if surprised to be spoken to.

And in that moment Eric beheld a sight so arresting, so surprising, that his resolve momentarily faltered. Stephen's small face was a few strokes short of real beauty. His features were fine and sharp. He had Soo-min's lovely mouth and lips. But in his other attributes, the delicate nose that ended in a fine tip, the slightly broad forehead, the unruly black hair—Eric discerned, clearly and alarmingly, the features of Stephen's *father*. None of this had been apparent in that Golden Gate Park photo, where half of Stephen's face had been in shade, and partly obscured by Tammy's hair. But here, right now in close-up, it was as plain to Eric as daylight.

Had he already known?

It *had* crossed his mind—that night in DC when he'd been

drunk and he'd driven to Soo-min's house. He had asked her who the father was. But he'd erased the thought in a deliberate act of doublethink. It had been a drunken heresy, too dangerous to harbor, and he'd forgotten about it until now.

But there was no denying the evidence of his eyes.

He knew who Stephen was. And now he knew why the Sister wanted him dead.

Stephen was regarding him warily, this man who was staring at him as if bewitched. He was taking in the dimpled half-smile, the muscles, the harness, the boots, the face opaque beneath aviators and cap.

"Oh, um. Sure, why not. Thanks."

Eric's mind honed into killer mode. He was calculating whether he could do it right here, in the crowd and confusion at the edge of the dance floor. He hadn't spotted any more cameras, but he wasn't going to risk it. There could be one he missed, a concealed globe with an infrared head. No, he would get the kid into the bathroom. Or into that horror-filled dark room, which was barely three meters away. The knife in his right boot was suddenly hot against his calf.

The drink!

Eric leaned over and just managed to catch Tequila Boy, grabbing him by the strap of his bandoliers before he disappeared into another cumulus of dry ice. He held up his wrist with the red band and yelled over the noise for two shots. "They're both for me."

Tequila Boy gave him a naughty smirk and sloshed out the shots.

Eric was aware of Stephen just behind him in the crowd like an item of great value left unattended and in danger of being swiped.

Finally, the drinks. Eric turned back to Stephen and put the small plastic glass into Stephen's hand. Even just inches in front of Eric's eyes, Stephen's black T-shirt threatened to dissolve and vanish into the darkness of the dance floor.

Your last drink.

"Cheers," Eric said, and downed the shot, feeling the delicious burn of the alcohol glowing in his chest. His murder engines moved up a gear.

"Cheers." Stephen gave it a doubtful sniff and took a small sip. "You're Korean?" he said over the deafening beat.

"Ah. Yeah," Eric yelled, grinning. "Just here for the weekend. You?"

"I'm . . . kinda from all over."

"I'm Eric."

Stephen dropped a dry hand into his. "James."

James, now, is it?

The dance floor was starting to thin out as people moved on to other bars, but the dark-room commuters were more numerous, shuffling inside, emerging with a drugged-up, zombified look. A hellhole for the damned.

"Oh, I *love* this one," Eric said suddenly, gyrating his hips sexily to the opening whump of some track he'd never heard before. Cheers rose from the dance floor.

For a few minutes the two of them danced side by side, close, hands and hips brushing. Eric sensed Stephen's awkwardness, his hesitation. He could see the uncertainty on his face as it flickered in and out of the strobing lights, as if he wasn't sure how to have fun.

But Eric was having fun. His heart was thrumming with adrenaline, his body tense and tingling, like a high-jumper just before he makes the leap of his life. He smiled at Stephen, and it was a smile of exquisite malice.

I know who you are, boy foundling.

What he did next felt like the most natural thing in the world. He slipped his arm around Stephen's small waist and kissed him lightly on his cheek.

Stephen did not push him away, but he stopped dancing and his body went still.

A bloodlust was rising in Eric, and he knew it was showing in his face, in the way his lips pulled back to reveal his teeth. The ecstatic look of someone about to cum, or kill, or be delivered and redeemed. It didn't matter now. He was so close.

Stephen turned to him and yelled into his ear over the noise.

"Actually, I ... think maybe I should go," he said, and without waiting for a response moved to get around Eric, but Eric stood in front of him and blocked his retreat. All the warmth had left his face. His expression had changed to something colder, all pretense gone, and Stephen saw it.

He was trapped. Suddenly his eyes were bright with knowledge, and he looked afraid, very afraid.

You knew it would come to this. You—

Then Stephen did something Eric did not anticipate. He darted away to the left—straight toward the dark room.

Eric lunged after him and caught the back of his T-shirt. He felt it pull and tear. Stephen whipped his thin arms over his head, and the T-shirt came free in Eric's hands.

The pale, slim boy was wriggling past the gruesome dark-room trade, into a chamber of horrors, the mangrove swamp of bodies.

In one smooth movement Eric stooped to slip the knife out of his boot and held it with the point downward at his side as he heaved his way into the inferno of writhing, sweat-soaked bodies of men having sex. The air inside was heavy with moisture. It reeked of semen and lubricants and mold. The music became muffled, distant. No one could see a damned thing. But the slim, shirtless boy was barely visible in front of him. Eric grabbed him from behind by the waist and slit his throat—fast, left-to-right, deep and clean—and turned his own body sideways to avoid the blood.

A horrible, bubbling scream went up, causing the movement in the room to still.

Someone turned on a flashlight on their phone. In the strange, chiaroscuro scene between a shadowed forest of legs, the young man falling to his knees was clutching his spurting throat.

Cries of "Oh my God, oh my God" became infectious. Eric moved ahead of the desperate flood of people surging for the room's exit. He surreptitiously wiped the blade with Stephen's T-shirt and slipped the knife back into his boot.

All hell was breaking loose. The music stopped. Bright lights came on. People screamed and called for help. Drinks were dropped. Bar stools knocked over. People fell and were trampled upon as everyone stampeded from the building in terror.

Eric left the bar with everyone else, a great crowd disgorging onto the street, feeling utterly anonymous.

He was invisible now, a bystander, and a victim himself.

The young man he'd just seen in the flashlights in the dark room, the young man whose throat he'd slit, had been blond, and definitely not Stephen.

He hung around for a minute or two, watching the crowd of traumatized people, some of them in tears, or making calls to tell people they were safe. No sign of Stephen. Before the night was out, Eric was quite sure he would have skipped town, taken another new name, vanished again.

He walked away down Castro, possessed by the sad serenity of one who had just been given the date for his own execution.

He had failed. He'd come *so* close . . . and he'd failed.

He realized just then that he was still holding Stephen's T-shirt in his hand. He scrunched it into a ball and dropped it in a trashcan, and the instant he did so, he spotted the street camera pointing right at him.

PART FIVE
Siberia

If you are afraid of wolves, stay out of the forest.

J. V. Stalin

70

Amur Oblast
Eastern Siberia

Jenna was seated in the windowless cargo hold of a gigantic military transport plane. She seemed to be the only cargo.

At Kubinka, an airbase west of Moscow, she'd caught a brief glimpse of the aircraft at sunset before a hood was thrown over her head. Its turbines were beginning to whir. It was a monster, an Ilyushin Il-72—too large for a hangar. The hood wasn't removed until the plane was airborne. Her hands were cuffed in front of her, rather than behind her back, so that she could be seated for the flight and get up to use the bathroom. Her guards were two bored-looking conscripts in army fatigues who sat in one of the long rows of hard, plastic fold-down seats used by troops. There must have been room for three hundred men and their equipment.

For the first few hours she kept her eyes closed and focused on her breathing, trying to make peace with the fact that she was flying into the unknown, literally. This only partially assuaged the roiling sea of anxiety in her stomach.

Eventually her meditations turned, as they always did, to Soo-min. She imagined them both as twin stars in the constellations above, the two of them always in each other's orbit, no matter how distant their ellipse.

In the months in which Jenna had languished in SIZO No. 6, as good as dead to the world, she'd sometimes hoped that the North Koreans *had* learned what had happened to her—that they knew she'd been captured and neutralized—because then she'd have the peace of knowing that they'd never again harass Soo-min in a bid to find her.

But with no news of her family, no means of contacting them without admitting that she was not Sarah Hong, her fears for Soo-min's safety had run riot.

In hindsight, she saw that she'd made one serious mistake. The US ambassador had visited her in prison a couple of weeks after her arrest. That had been her one chance to raise the alarm about Eric Rahn, Soo-min's stalker. Eric Rahn, a North Korean agent *operating inside the White House* . . . but she'd been so committed to not blowing her cover that she'd said nothing. All she could hope for was that the retired ops officer who'd seen Rahn's car outside the house had been suspicious enough to follow it up.

What vanity, what fool's courage had deluded her? *Everyone gives their name in the end!* The SVR had pumped her with drugs, ripped the lid off her identity, and her one chance to buy security for her sibling had gone.

The guards opposite her took turns to watch her: one on duty, one dozing. One of them wore a wristwatch on which she could occasionally see the time, and once they had been flying for four hours, she tried again to figure out Putin's game.

I cannot simply give you to Kim Jong-un as a gift . . . The North Koreans have to find you themselves.

The more she thought about it, the more convinced she became that her destination was China. Moscow would inform the Chinese authorities that an assassin named on North Korea's Most Wanted List was at large in China. The Chinese would tip off the North Koreans, who would launch a manhunt for her. She knew that agents of the North Korean secret police, the Bowibu, were permitted to operate freely in China to hunt down defectors and criminals.

Wherever she was going, Putin wouldn't be taking any chances. He knew she was trained to evade capture. He'd make sure she was being sent into a net with no possibility of her giving anyone the slip.

If for some reason they fail, well, then you stay in Russia to serve an appropriate sentence determined by the courts . . .

What did *that* mean? *Stay in Russia.* Perhaps she was headed somewhere in Russia . . . But how would the North Koreans find her in Russia? The two countries were friendly, but to her knowledge Kim Jong-un had no reach or presence inside Russia.

The worst flight of Jenna's life lasted eight hours. The hood went back over her head. A wall of heat and humidity hit her as she was led down the plane's ramp. The voices of the ground crew were Russian, and so were those of the new guards who took charge of her. She was led across the runway to another transport van.

Her meal on the flight had consisted of two slabs of black Russian bread with salty white cheese and a liter bottle of Svyatoy Istochnik mineral water. Now, in the transport van, she was given the same meal again and told to eat it under the cloth hood over her head.

The journey in the van lasted only a few minutes and she guessed they'd driven to a different section of the airbase. When it came to a halt, she was kept handcuffed to her seat for about an hour. Then she heard the whine of rotor engines starting up. Very quickly she was bundled out of the van with someone pushing her head down clear of a helicopter's spinning blades. This time the hood remained on her head. Another military aircraft, she guessed, but much smaller and more uncomfortable, flying at low altitude, and rocked by winds. The noise was so loud her ears screamed. No one had given her hearing protection. The tiny cabin had the hot-wire smell of banks of electronics.

The helicopter landed after about two hours, but the rotors did not stop. Her handcuffs were removed, and she was shoved, still hooded and blind, out of the door.

The ground that hit her body was soft and wet. Something else landed next to her head with a thud, sending a spatter of mud across her neck. The whooshing downdraft from the rotors was deafening. She remained still for a minute, wondering if anyone else would get off the aircraft, but it was impossible to tell over the roar. Then the helicopter was in the air again and soon its noise had receded to a distant flapping.

With a groan she turned over and pulled off the hood, squinting into bright sunlight. She was in a peat bog and surrounded by tufts of dead yellow grass. All she could see above the foliage was a high blue sky. The sun's heat was strong on her skin. It must have been about forty degrees. No breeze stirred the grass. The humid air was filled with the stench of rotting mulch and an ambient humming of flies. The unsuitable city clothes they'd given her were instantly itchy and uncomfortable.

She had a sensation of vastness in every direction, an expanse unimaginable to anyone who lived in a developed country. A space without limit. The helicopter was still visible, just a black dot low on the horizon and heading . . . northward, she guessed, from the position of the sun. And then it was gone. Already she was attracting the clouds of mosquitoes and midges that swarmed over the mud. She crawled toward the object that had been thrown out of the helicopter after her. It was a dark-green military backpack. Inside it she found more packets of black bread, a block of cheese in greaseproof paper, an army blanket, a large demijohn of water, a blister pack of water purification tablets, and . . . she pulled everything out and rummaged in the bottom of the sack and the pockets . . . *Nothing else.*

No compass, no map, no tent, no knife. Nothing that would aid her, except to keep her alive long enough for her to be caught.

She felt weighed down suddenly by exhaustion and mud. She

had been thrumming with anxiety and anticipation in the helicopter, but now that her true situation had revealed itself in all its desolation, she just wanted to curl up in the warm filth. Go to sleep and never wake up. But she was a hunted animal now.

Start moving or die.

She hauled herself up by the tussocks of yellow grass and slowly turned a full 360 degrees. Just as she'd thought: an infinity of flat wilderness. Sky met earth in one stark vista with nothing else in between the two. The absolute ass-end of nowhere. She'd had no sense of crossing any kind of border: the transport plane had landed in a Russian airbase, so she was pretty sure that she was still in Russia, which hardly narrowed things down.

The only topographical feature she could discern across the endless bog was a distant tree line, rippling in the heat, maybe two or three miles away. Trees were cover. That was her direction.

She hoisted the backpack and tried to walk, but her feet squelched deeper into the mud with every tread. She found it more arduous and tiring than anything she remembered from her training. The new shoes they'd given her in SIZO No. 6 were laughably inadequate. She still had the hood, which she fashioned into a headscarf to keep the mosquitoes away from her head, but soon it became so soaked with her sweat that she stuffed it into the backpack and took her chances with the bugs. After an hour of slow, slow walking, her T-shirt, too, clung to her body like a hot flannel, and she took that off as well, walking in her bra. Nearly a quarter of her water was already drunk, but at least it made her load lighter.

After struggling for what seemed like hours, when she was finally within a quarter mile of the trees, a buzzing sound made her stop and listen. A large hornet, perhaps. She continued her trudge then stopped again, still hearing it, but louder now. Not a hornet. She looked up.

A drone.

A wave of dread washed over her. Running was impossible, and there was nowhere to hide unless she could reach the trees. She looked at it again. It was a small one, a quadcopter, high up and stationary, watching her. Then it buzzed away northward. How long did the batteries in those things last? No more than two hours. It couldn't follow her for long . . .

The fir trees, when she reached them, provided a sublime shade. Finally, she was on firmer ground, and the air was a little cooler. A deep primeval stillness pervaded the place. Almost at once she fell into a deep sleep on the soft forest floor.

It was evening when she woke up. She touched her cheek, which was sore and crisscrossed where it had rested against pine needles. Her arms and legs were covered in insect bites, which would soon become scabrous and infected if she scratched them. Rest here for the night or keep moving? The setting sun was casting rays of citrus-red light into the trees. Her stomach was growling. She rationed herself to one slab of the black bread and a chunk of the cheese.

The last light penetrated the forest to its depth, suffusing the trunks of the pines with a red glow. Stars were already visible. In a few minutes she wouldn't be able to see her hand in front of her face.

A flashlight. The other thing they'd "forgotten" to give her.

She was returning the food to the backpack when an unholy sound made her body tense. She heard it again, with a second howl overlapping it.

Wolves.

Some potent mix of fear and adrenaline gave her a strength beyond the human. She leapt up the nearest pine, legs and arms pulling herself up in bursts of energy. Branches lashed and cut her face. Rough bark lacerated her hands. When she was about six meters up, she found she could jam herself between the trunk and the smaller branches, with a sturdy enough support to spend the night. It was only then that she realized that the backpack was still on the ground for anyone to find.

The unearthly howls continued for hours, impossible to tell whether they were near or far. Atonal, banshee-like cries. Something primal in her had been triggered, some fairytale fear of the forest.

She managed only an hour or so of light, fretful sleep. When the stars began to fade one by one, and the sky turned a neon blue, she again tried to take stock. But without knowing where she was, her thoughts ran into a dead end. To the east, forest stretched to the limit of the horizon, for as far as the eye could see. To the west was the endless yellow tundra of grass and bog.

This wasn't the first time Jenna had had to fend for herself in a forest. Years ago, during her training at the Farm, her team had been abandoned in the pines near Williamsburg for days. They'd had to figure out for themselves how to survive . . .

And suddenly a memory came back to her—an arcane piece of knowledge she'd never imagined needing. She looked up. The brightest star—Polaris, the North Star—was still visible. She stretched out her hand to the horizon and made a fist. If the width of her fist represented 10 degrees, then she figured that Polaris was about 55 degrees above the horizon. That gave her a latitude position. Calculating her longitude was tricker, but she knew that her flight from Moscow had lasted eight hours. It had been sunset when she'd left and the sun had been high in the sky when she'd landed here. So the flight would have carried her, she guessed, about six time zones to the east. If she was six hours ahead of Moscow, then she was eight hours ahead of Greenwich Mean Time. The earth rotated 15 degrees of longitude each hour. Fifteen multiplied by eight was 120. At a rough estimate, then—very rough, because she had no idea in which direction the helicopter had flown for two hours—she was 55 degrees north and about 120 degrees east. That would place her . . . where?

She racked her brain to visualize the maps of Russia she'd studied in preparation for the op, with all their rivers and mountain ranges. She dredged up the courses on geopolitics she'd taught at Georgetown years ago, on border conflicts and international treaties.

By her estimation she was somewhere between the very southern part of a vast region called Yakutia and the northern part of the Amur Oblast. So she was deep in eastern Siberia, which was practically in Asia. Which meant she couldn't be far, relatively speaking, from the Pacific Ocean, which was hundreds—rather than thousands—of miles to the east. She felt a small surge of confidence.

East. Her route was east into the forest. The direction of the dawn.

She landed on her hands and knees and found the backpack undisturbed.

Again, the question returned. Why here? Why the Amur Oblast? Even if North Korean agents were crossing into Russia right now to hunt for her, she would be a needle in a haystack out here. There were no roads. The nearest town might be hundreds of miles away. There were no other humans who might see her. And drones wouldn't spot her in the forest.

She pondered this as she made a path through the undergrowth, using her bare hands. It was easier going than the bog, but without a machete or gloves, it was still an ordeal that would have tested the toughest explorer. Here and there she found a narrow animal track to follow, but mostly she battled dense thickets of spruce and bramble. Occasionally she came upon small clearings in the trees, but she skirted around them, afraid the drone would spot her in the open.

After about three hours, and already wrung of all strength, she rested on a flaking boulder near the edge of a clearing. Lunch was another rationed slab of bread, chewed slowly to make it last. Her demijohn of water was now two-thirds empty. No wind stirred the trees. The heat was already unbearable, even in the shade. She would need to find food soon, berries or edible roots. And water . . .

Siberia . . . hell in winter; hell in summer.

The skin on the back of her neck prickled suddenly. She spun around to see a pair of yellow eyes watching her through the grass. The animal scampered off, then turned to look back at her. A red fox. She released her breath. She broke off a crumb of the cheese and flicked it toward the fox. The offering was sniffed at, then eaten in one bite.

There had to be *some* settlements in this region, even if they were scattered and sparse. But even if she found a village, what then? A half Korean, half African American face would draw instant curiosity. They'd turn her in faster than she could say *help*.

Or would they? Indigenous Siberians—like the Evenks—were Mongol or East Asian in appearance rather than Slavic. Would she look so uncommon to them?

She was about to continue walking when she heard the drone again.

It was buzzing high above the clearing, motionless, surveilling, even though she was concealed by the trees.

How the hell had it found her? She was miles from where it had last seen her.

Then a thought came to her.

She emptied out the backpack to look for a tracker: feeling carefully along the canvas lining, and in the pads of its shoulder straps. Nothing. She did the same for her clothing, only guessing where it was hidden when she re-tied her shoelaces. *The trainers.*

Using a shard of rock, she hacked open the rubber heel of the first trainer. Nothing inside. Then she tore off the entire sole. Nothing. She did the same with the other trainer and there, embedded in the hollow space of the heel, she found a black oval-shaped object, about the size of a dental-floss container.

Fuck.

She was about to hurl it as high as she could over the treetops when she had a better idea. She broke off a large chunk of the cheese, pressed the tracker into it and left it on the ground for Mr. Fox.

Her trek was renewed at a frantic pace now, crashing onward through undergrowth and low branches. The forest had afforded her no cover, and now they could figure out her direction. And without shoes, with nothing but prison socks on her feet, her determination was beginning to flag. The sky had clouded over, trapping the heat close to the ground. She had no sun to guide her now.

After another hour of forging through virgin forest, she was a wild woman. Mud-covered, reeking of sweat, shoeless, very hungry, hunted, afraid. She had become an animal of the forest. Her hair was matted with twigs and dirt. Her hands were bleeding and would soon begin to swell. Mosquitoes followed her in relentless swarms.

Her pace slowed until the moment came when she could go no further.

She lay down on her back, dog tired, and tried to think. Her situation was dire, but a thought was quietly opening in her mind, tempting her to explore it further: that her capture would be a relief. That she would soon start to welcome it.

She was still lying motionless, watching the clouds through the branches, when she heard the soft snap of a twig.

All her instincts stirred sharply to life. Another twig snapped. A tread too heavy for a fox. Carefully, silently, she inched her body beneath a branch of pine that was almost brushing the ground, and dragged the backpack slowly after her.

She wasn't breathing now, just watching wide-eyed from behind a curtain of filthy hair.

Someone was approaching by stealth. Another footstep—in the grass further to the right. More than one person.

Then, a combat boot moved slowly into her line of sight.

The man was in camouflage fatigues, his face hidden by camouflage paint and the shade of a bush hat, also camouflaged. He was holding a telescopic sight to his eye and aiming a gun, so that it inched slowly ahead of him. The barrel was unusually long and thin. Sniper rifle?

Tranquilizer gun.

A second rifle, an M24, was slung across his back. The sidearm in his holster looked like an old Soviet Type 74.

Any thought she'd had of submitting to her own capture vanished.

She had clicked into operational mode as instantly as a room going dark at the touch of a switch. She felt no fear, just a calm, trip-wire alertness, a charged kind of presence that was also weirdly detached, as if she wasn't fully there.

That sharp rock she'd used to break open her trainers ... she wished she'd kept it.

The man took another step forward, then another, then lowered the gun to retrieve a small monitor device from his pocket. He was following the tracker.

He continued into the undergrowth until he was out of sight.

She did not dare move a muscle until she was certain her pursuers were no longer nearby. Then slowly she climbed the tree, hauling the backpack through the foliage, and waited there for hours, hidden from view. But she saw no one else. She heard nothing, just the rustling and whistling of the pines. The men did not return by the same route.

When the sky turned an ominous red as the sun started to set, she climbed down to the ground and ate more of the bread. It was fast running out. She had enough food left for the day ahead. After that, the forest would have to provide.

She had never experienced a darkness so complete in the outdoors. Movement was impossible, which was just as well. The tension of staying still for so long had given her acute pins and needles in her already sore feet. But after a couple of hours, the cloud cleared, and the forest was black against a night sky that was deeper beyond imagining. She watched the stars arc their course above the treetops, their constellations sharp and wild. Polaris shone brightly above her, as if encouraging her. Eventually, the moon rose, piercing the trees with rays of pale light. Nocturnal creatures were at work all around her, spinning webs, echolocating, scurrying, hunting.

Steadily, one tired foot in front of the other, she continued her trek.

Just before dawn she saw the first sign of civilization: a dirt road. From the depth of its ruts, she guessed it was used by heavy machinery. She decided to rest awhile and wait to see what passed, and eventually, as the sun came up on her third day in the wilderness, she heard the clatter of an approaching truck.

She was positioned at a bend in the road, so she got a clear view of it as it changed to a low gear and slowed. The thing was an ancient open-topped jeep loaded with red gas cannisters. The driver was not young, and he had coppery, weathered skin.

An Evenk.

Hide or show herself? She had two seconds to decide.

She stepped onto the road and waved him down. His face registered enormous surprise. He braked suddenly, sending up a hail of dust and gravel.

The man was about fifty. She saw his surprise morph into suspicion and then concern.

"Can you give me a ride?" she said in broken Russian.

"Where have you come from?" the man said, revealing a flash of steel teeth. "Are you Russian?"

Jenna shook her head. "Daur. From Mongolia. I am a scientist. I am lost."

He frowned, taking in her filthy clothes, her bare feet.

"I . . . was attacked by wild animals," she said, not knowing the Russian for wolves. "I need a doctor."

He nodded, and then gave an astonished smile. "You're Daur? Really?" He opened the passenger door for her. "Get in."

Jenna was so grateful she could have kissed him. She threw the backpack next to the canisters and hopped in next to him, seeing his nostrils inflate at the aroma coming off her. He restarted the engine and pointed to a jerrycan on the floor in front of the passenger seat. She opened it, took several long gulps, then washed the dried blood from her hands. The jeep shook so violently the water sloshed over her lap.

"This road." Jenna shouted over the noise. "Goes where?"

"Camp," the man said.

"Army camp?"

The man shook his head. "No Russians here. Foreigners."

Suddenly he swerved to pull over as a gargantuan articulated truck rumbled past in the opposite direction, straining in first gear. As it passed, peppering the jeep with loose chippings, she saw that it was stacked with logs secured with chains. Its red paintwork was covered in mud. The clouds of beige-colored dust that trailed behind it were so dense that the Evenk had to turn on his windshield wipers. He made a sawing motion with his hand and a buzz-cutting noise.

Logging camp.

"Big camp?" she said.

"Very big," he said laughing.

Now she could hear distant chainsawing on either side of the road. The air smelled of fresh-cut lumber.

"Foreigners . . . from where?" she said.

He turned to Jenna, pointing at the huge wooden gates and chain-link fence coming quickly toward them. "Camp. You get help in camp."

Before she had time to assess this sudden environment they were through the gates. The jeep bumped and lurched into a vast lumber yard. On one side was a vehicle pen with rows of giant trucks like the one that had just passed them on the road. Heavy, Soviet-era, eighteen-wheelers. Tatras and Urals used for transporting timber.

A few battered SUVs. Rough lumber stacked everywhere like giant cigars.

"Railroad near here?" she said.

"Yes, yes, railroad for timber."

"How far?"

The Evenk moved his head from side to side. "About fifty kilometers."

He steered to the right and entered a canyon cleared between mountains of junk. Wire coiled in heaps, old truck tires, oil drums, piles of rusted, broken shovels. They pulled up inside a ramshackle garage built from corrugated iron. It was filthy and smelled powerfully of diesel fuel. She could hardly breathe from the fumes.

"I take you," the man said, getting out. "Administration building. Don't walk here. Floor's bad." He lifted a pair of old lace-up work boots from the back of the jeep and gave them to her. They were at least three sizes too large.

The old Evenk was a delivery man, she guessed. An outsider. He lifted out her backpack for her and offered his arm as support. She was limping quite badly now.

Something wasn't right with this place.

Her senses were sending up a multitude of small red flags, too fast for her to process. A familiar aroma in the smoke drifting from an open-air grill. An empty brown bottle that looked a lot like a liter bottle of Taedonggang beer. The sound of an army chorus blaring from a distant loudspeaker. A smell of coal bricks and kerosene.

"Administration building," the Evenk said, pointing, as they emerged from the avalanches of garbage.

It was a long, squat single-story office building.

Above the windows a slogan was painted in a bright red Korean script that spanned the entire length of the structure:

LET US GLORIFY THE GREAT ERA OF COMRADE KIM JONG-UN!

The building's front door flew open and three rail-thin Koreans in indigo workers' overalls came running toward them, yelling.

Jenna took an involuntary step backward, her feet lost in the boots. Only one other "road" led out of the junkyard toward the main gates.

And it was blocked by another jeep careening toward her at a dangerous speed, carrying three men in bush hats and camouflage fatigues. The same men she had seen in the forest. One driving; two riding on the sides of the vehicle, one of them aiming a gun. The jeep swerved and almost lost control as it braked.

The dart hit her in the chest, just below her left collarbone.

71

Washington, DC

When Eric returned to Washington his mood was veering dangerously between rage and a kind of blank non-presence that he found impossible to hide.

The summit in Singapore was on Tuesday next week. The events he himself had seeded and set in motion were coming to a spectacular fruition. Through him, Pyongyang had an all but direct line to the president of the United States. He had manipulated Trump into a radical change of policy toward North Korea, agreed by no one at all in the White House or the State Department or the intelligence services.

But somewhere along the way, and he didn't really understand how, things had gone badly awry for him. He felt as if he were pulling off a legendary, once-in-a-lifetime, sell-out stadium event that would be watched live on TV by more people around the world than any other news event in history, only for him to understand, too late, that the climax to the show would be his own execution.

There was nothing he could do to stop it now.

The world's media was already descending on Singapore. On the TV news the city was taking on a carnival atmosphere. Commentary was at a fever pitch of excitement, even in the fake-news media, and the president's tweets were doing nothing to manage expectations. Fox News showed two Trump–Kim lookalikes shaking hands on the city's waterfront. The guy pretending to be Trump had plastered his face with a burnt orange foundation and wore a MAGA cap with his baggy suit. He pursed his lips and scowled for the cameras, a mannerism that captured the Boss's vanity and almost comical lack of dignity.

Salesman, showman, conman, clown.

Eric was filled with a restless, formless dread. He'd be safe in Singapore, wouldn't he? As safe as anyone could possibly be. He'd be at the Boss's side wherever he went, inside the toughest security bubble in the world, and surrounded by CIA and Secret Service. But he knew he was grasping at straws. Once he went near the Supreme Sister's orbit, he would be at the mercy of forces capricious, lawless, unseen.

The night before he flew to Singapore, Eric went for dinner at Le DeSales, which was just a stone's throw from the White House, with Marcia, Hunter, and Alex.

"Think you'll get to meet Kim?" Marcia said, after she'd twice asked for them to be reseated.

"I should think so," Eric said, distracted, playing with the silverware. "The president wants me to be his official interpreter. State Department's gone apeshit . . ."

Not many things made Marcia look up from her phone. *"Eric."*

"Wow, like, wow, man, wow," Hunter said, cretinously, and started clicking his fingers to get the waiter's attention.

Eric's friends were squeezing his shoulder and ordering a bottle of something expensive and raising their glasses. He managed a few play-along remarks, but his alarmingly dissociative state was rendering him incapable of following any but the simplest stage directions. *Order. Eat. Go home.* The restaurant was raucous and very busy, but he himself was deep inside a private isolation ward of his own. He was studying the pores of his skin in the reflection of the butter knife. He was flesh and bone; he was real, he occupied a physical space in the universe. He had the characteristics of a human being. But he wondered if he was simply imitating reality, simply resembling a human. His depersonalization was so complete that he doubted he'd ever really been a real person, except perhaps as a baby.

"Eric?"

"Yeah. Sorry. I'm just . . . really tired."

Conversation was directed at him, over him, in streams of sound and meaning that bypassed his ears. He pushed away the steak-frites he couldn't finish, ordered a whiskey soda, downed it immediately, and waved for another.

There was something else on his endless to-do list and he suddenly remembered what it was. He took out his phone and googled Kyle's name. A grid of images appeared: yearbook portrait photos, selfies, shots of Kyle in his running gear, crossing the finishing line of the San Francisco marathon. Candle emojis. Prayer emojis. Someone had composed a poem.

Kyle Mason, 18, a final year student at Tiburon School has died in a tragic fall while running in Mount Tamalpais National Park on Thursday evening . . .

Then he googled XXL Bar in Castro.

Suspected homophobic knife attack during SF Gay Pride. Police are looking for this man seen leaving the bar at 12:30 a.m. . . .

There was a grainy pink-yellow security-camera screenshot of Eric in his leathers looking at the street camera just as he was dropping Stephen's T-shirt into the garbage can, but his face was mostly obscured by the shadow cast by his cap, and his aviators. He scrolled down a few times but didn't bother finishing the article.

"Would you care to see the dessert menu? Sir?"

He felt nothing at all. There was no real Eric, he mused. Just an abstraction. All the chaos he had caused, the evil he had done, it meant nothing to him. His indifference was both flat and infinite. He had wanted power and glory for himself and no one else, but instead his efforts had earned him nothing but rage, which endlessly crested and rolled, and a dull, always-present pain. He wanted everyone in the world to feel his rage, feel his pain, and to inflict it upon them forever. But even his perception of this truth about himself meant nothing to him.

As he was leaving Le DeSales to go home, he received a link to a video.

From the long list of urgent matters to worry about, the only item the Boss had engaged in with anything like real work was the making of a four-minute movie trailer that he wanted to show to Kim Jong-un. "North Korea has fantastic beaches," he'd said in the Oval Office earlier, holding up photos of Wonsan on North Korea's east coast. "Look at that view! They could have the finest luxury hotels in the world right there."

Idiot. You fucking clueless idiot, sir.

He'd been tempted to inform Trump in front of everyone there that the Kim family spent every summer on that beach. That they *already* enjoyed a home there that was more luxurious than anything even Trump would have seen in his life. That their favorite private palace—one of seventeen—was the one at Wonsan, that its facilities were of a class that would put the crown prince of Saudi Arabia to shame. That they didn't give rat's fuck if their starving population had no condos or hotels to enjoy. That they'd strongly prefer *not* to attract pernicious foreign vacationers who would corrupt their unspoiled land with seedy, capitalist behavior.

He would have laughed off the video as a bad meme if the experience of watching it right there on the sidewalk outside Le DeSales hadn't been such a personal torture for him. The kitschy visuals, the corny special effects, the tired-looking stock shots—they were raping his eyes.

"Featuring President Donald Trump and Chairman Kim Jong-un," boomed the blockbuster voice-over. "In a meeting to remake history. To shine in the sun. One moment. One choice..."

Kill me now.

"Will this leader choose to advance his country and be part of a new world? Will he shake the hand of peace and enjoy prosperity like he's never seen? What will he choose? To show vision and leadership—or *not*?"

Jesus Christ.

And in that instant Eric knew that he was ashamed of the Boss, hotly ashamed. That Trump should think this high-school-production-standard video was worth one second of the attention of Comrade Great Successor Kim Jong-un, the third in the dynasty of his name, the heir to the sacred revolutionary bloodline of Mount Paektu. That he'd give up *nuclear weapons* for the disgrace of accepting American money. *Nuclear weapons in exchange for a fucking McDonald's franchise?*

Power, Mr. President. Power means power for life. Power means every word you speak is law. Power is not just ruling your country but owning it. The power you think you have is an illusion. Your reality is term limits and swing states. Power means extreme wealth, which the Kim family has in abundance, wealth magnitudes greater than your few dozen millions that you pretend are billions. How much are you really, personally worth, Mr. President? Four hundred million? A little less? A pathetic worth. A paltry sum. A lottery win shared between nineteen postal workers.

Next week, in Singapore, you will shake the hand of a man who wields true power, power in its purest form, power free of check and balance. Unlimited, untrammeled, elemental power.

And you're going to show him this home-made cartoon?

72

Amur Oblast
Eastern Siberia

Jenna opened her eyes to a ceiling stained yellow by nicotine. The room stank of stale ashtrays. She was lying on her back on a linoleum floor. Male voices around her were speaking in North Korean dialect. Strong accents.

"Are you awake?" someone said in broken Russian. She was prodded roughly in the arm. "Hey!"

She murmured and tried to turn over on her side. A sharp kick to her calf.

"Hey! Wake up!"

She must have been out for an hour or longer because her back felt stiff and painful against the floor. When she opened her eyes, she saw a Korean man of about forty standing over her. His face was hard and dented, like an old copper boiler. He grimaced at her, revealing the bridgework on his teeth. "Here." He dropped what felt like a wet flannel onto her hands. "Clean your face. I need to take a photo."

Jenna slapped the flannel onto her eyes with both hands, feeling as if she had a monster hangover. When she removed it from her face the man was pointing an old digital camera directly down at her. "OK," he said, checking the photo and taking a drag of his cigarette. "One more."

She was in a small, grimy office. Cork boards pinned with work schedules. Lists of work teams. Calendars in Korean. A yellow hard hat on top of a filing cabinet. Everything smeared in oil. No one else was present.

The man took a seat in front of a boxy old Microsoft desk computer and connected the digital camera to it with a lead. Then he started to type with two fingers, bashing out an email, the cigarette hanging from his lip. He was wearing moleskin pants, engineer's boots, and a hi-vis orange jacket.

The wall behind the desk displayed the Father–Son portraits that hung in every North Korean home and workplace. Their distant, air-brushed faces gazed down at her with a look of triumph.

The man stubbed out the cigarette and hit send. "Right." Then he picked up a plastic chair and kicked it across the floor toward her. "Sit."

Jenna heaved herself up, feeling nauseated and groggy—the effects of the tranquilizer, dehydration, and a lack of food.

"I am Director Ri. I don't know who you are, and—"

"You can speak in Korean," Jenna said, brushing her hair from her eyes. "It will save us both time."

"You're Korean?" The man sat up straight, the sides of his mouth turned down in astonishment. And then: "But you're Black."

Jenna sighed. She'd forgotten how racist North Koreans could be. The country had long ago ditched its commitment to world communism and had reinvented itself as an ultra-nationalist state of pure-race Koreans, untainted by foreign blood or foreign culture.

"Well observed, director."

"I was saying, I don't know who you are and I'm not going to ask. It's not my place to question orders from Pyongyang, even if they ask me to find a mystery woman in the forest and bring her here by force if necessary . . ."

Putin had tipped off the North Koreans so that they could capture her themselves ... What she hadn't known, but was now beginning to figure out, was that there was an area of eastern Siberia operated by a North Korean logging concession, one of the many that were spreading across the interior like alopecia, slowly denuding the landscape of trees. This camp must be a lost speck in a region larger than the Amazon.

A logging camp. With a workforce of ... North Korean laborers? Most of them probably slaves. But with minimal security ... No guards or soldiers, just thugs and foremen and hunters ... No walls. No fences. None needed. The limitless forest is more effective than any wall ...

"... but I *do* want to know how you got here. We are thousands of kilometers from anywhere. We do not welcome visitors or prying eyes. The camp's security is my responsibility."

"I'm your guest," she said, wearily. An aroma of barbequed pork had begun to waft through the small, open window. She was suddenly acutely hungry. "Show me some hospitality."

Director Ri was older than her, and according to Korean custom should be spoken to with respect. But far from being offended, he seemed decidedly wary of her. He lit another cigarette and took a deep drag. Two flutes of smoke blew out of his nose.

"How did you get here? You didn't just fall out of the sky."

"Actually, I did. The Russians dropped me by helicopter."

"Why?"

"I won a vacation on a game show."

Director Ri stared at her through the cigarette smoke. She could almost see the cogs and rotors of his mind turning. *How should I treat this woman? ... Pyongyang wouldn't have ordered me to capture her if she wasn't important ... What if she's* really *important? ... Perhaps this is some state secret ... and I shouldn't be speaking to her at all ...*

He went to the window and yelled at someone outside to bring in lunch.

The food was simple but surprisingly tasty. Grilled pork with white rice, kimchi, and pickles. How quickly the nourishment turned to energy inside her.

Director Ri leaned forward in his seat, the fingertips of his hands touching.

"Better?" His tone was cautious now. She could tell he had a dozen questions on his lips but didn't want to risk knowing something he shouldn't.

She hated being watched while she ate.

"Look," she said, chewing. "You just emailed my photo to Pyongyang, didn't you? They want confirmation that I am who they hope I am. When they see it's me, they'll give you a medal."

Director Ri scratched his head and got up to check his email.

"They've replied . . ."

While his back was turned, she glanced at the door. The brass bolt was turned. He'd locked it. Through a small, frosted window to the side of the door she could see people coming and going. The building seemed busy. The open window next to his desk was too small to escape through . . .

Director Ri turned slowly away from the computer after reading the message. His face had turned the color of sour cream. Without meeting her eyes, he pressed a button on his desk telephone that lit up red and picked up the receiver.

A hail of static sounded from loudspeakers near and far.

"Camp announcement! All available men to the director's office immediately—"

Jenna leapt to her feet.

In one stride she'd reached his desk. She grabbed the receiver's coiled cable and tried to yank the handset out of Director Ri's hand.

"Security situation! Help—"

She pulled again, causing him to crash chest-first onto the desk.

Then she smacked her hand down onto the red button, turning off the intercom. Director Ri slid backward off the desk, fell into his chair, and started frantically pulling open drawers, looking for a weapon.

For a few seconds Jenna watched him vainly throwing out pens and old batteries, but the damage was done.

The entire camp had heard the struggle.

She felt the rumbling of many boots thumping across the linoleum floor as every man in the building descended on the room. The door cracked and splintered as someone kicked it down.

Director Ri was now holding a screwdriver in two shaking hands as if it were a samurai sword. His big rough face looked like a crying baby's. At least six men had entered the office.

"Throw her in the tank! . . . Maximum security! . . . Open the gun safe . . . Kang's got the key . . ."

Outside, a crowd of men had gathered, including the hunters with the bush hats. A great scrum of them surrounded her as she was frog-marched across the lumber yard, her arms held behind her back in a stress position, her feet loose and clumsy inside the worker's boots the Evenk had given her.

To her right she noticed the vehicle compound behind a padlocked, chain-link fence, and a massive articulated diesel tanker truck with the logo RRT Global. A refueling truck. Beyond that, she spotted rows of wretched *bantong* huts—old wooden railroad cars that she guessed were the housing for the workers.

Someone was yelling, "The hatch! Quickly. Open the hatch!"

She was being pushed up some cinderblock steps and onto a rough concrete roof. A circular black hole opened in front of her. Before she knew it, she was being dropped inside, feet first, by the men holding her arms. The hatch slammed shut after her with an echoing clang.

73

Schöneberg
Berlin, Germany
Summer 2018

Lyosha awoke to a message on his phone from Anya that transformed the low mood that had dogged him for months. It made him leap out of his duvet with so much joy that he decided to take his mother breakfast in bed.

He had been in a state of limbo since Christmas. His recovery was complete, but he felt he was wasting it. Of course, he was grateful for being in Germany, which had welcomed him and sheltered him, but he missed his ice hockey, he had no friends here, and the abandonment of his law degree at Moscow State had affected his pride more than he liked to admit. Who was he now? How would he describe himself to anyone he met? "Refugee" wasn't a career. "Defector" sounded faded and sad.

"This is what it must have felt like after 1917," Marina had said. "All those titles and estates, gone. Former grand duchesses drifting around Europe, pawning jewelry, surviving as house guests . . ."

They had left Tannenhof in the New Year and were settled in a small apartment located in a leafy street in Schöneberg in west Berlin, courtesy of the government. Lyosha was enrolled in a beginner's course in German at the Goethe-Institut, but his heart wasn't in it. Marina had found work as a Russian-language tour guide at the Alte Nationalgalerie. They both received a modest stipend from the state, but Lyosha would have to find work, and soon. The thought of it exerted a low-level stress upon him that made him listless and uncommunicative. Marina worried about him. He worried about her.

Anya's message blew away his feelings of gloom. It was like waking up on one of those crystal-clear mornings in early spring that fills one with a sense of renewal, and hope. Normally, she phoned him with gossip, news of friends, long descriptions of the demonstrations she'd been on, updates on the preposterous charges she faced after her inevitable arrests, which seemed to be getting more and more frequent.

It was a text message on Telegram to tell him that she had finally decided to leave Russia. The crackdowns on the opposition had gotten much worse since Putin's re-election in March, she said. More and more of her friends were being charged with "extremism"—a handy, catch-all crime that could include liking a Facebook post. She had planned to come to Berlin for his birthday in May, and had bought a ticket, but then couldn't make it because the FSB had thrown her in fifteen-day detention. The final straw had been her arrest and custody at Brateyevo police station. This time, they'd thrown a plastic bag over her head so that she couldn't breathe and told her they would smash her head in with their boots if she didn't talk. "There are no laws here," they'd said to her. "You are not men!" she'd screamed. "That's right," one of them replied. "We are beasts."

She'd had enough, and now she was afraid.

"*Budushchego net.*" She'd been saying that for months. *There is no future.* It was an expression people in Russia used when their hopes had died. For a brief time, after the collapse of the Soviet Union, the future was exhilarating beyond imagination. It had exploded into a vast, wide-open space. But slowly, year by year, under Putin,

Vladimir Vladimirovich, the Soviet-era vision of the future had been restored. Marina said she pictured it as a long, dimly lit corridor that gradually got narrower and narrower.

Anya's news had the effect of bringing home a powerful truth for Lyosha: that Russia's future was no longer his. It was like having his vision suddenly corrected by a pair of lenses. It made him see that he had options. He had freedom to choose. His life was his own. What had he been waiting for? He didn't know. Perhaps this is what had been weighing upon him. His mother had been right. *Freedom—Russians don't know what to do with it.*

Whatever lay in store for him—the future that was his—it had not yet revealed itself. Anya was arriving in Berlin in a few days. Somehow, and he couldn't have explained why, he knew that it was Anya who would show him the way.

74

Logging Camp 32
Amur Oblast
Eastern Siberia

The drop from the hatch to the floor of the "tank" was about three meters. She landed painfully on her ankle on the hard floor. She was in perfect darkness. Not a single photon of light. No sense of the room's dimension.

Her adrenaline was still surging from her struggle with Director Ri, the neurons still firing in her brain, which the sudden dark turned to hallucinatory embers before her eyes. She leaned her back against the cool cinderblock wall and sank to her knees, but before she had a chance to think, something inside the cell moved.

A dragging movement, just a few meters away.

A moment of pure horror grabbed her.

"Who's there?"

She listened. No sound, only her own breathing. And then a fumbling noise. She got back on her feet again and pressed her body to the wall.

A scraping flick, flick of a lighter. Then a small flame appeared, illuminating a hard, care-worn face, surrounded by dark. The man was sitting on his haunches, peasant-style. He was regarding her with that dead-eyed look of one for whom hope, despair, and curiosity had been abandoned long ago.

The tank. A punishment cell for workers who break the rules.

The flame extinguished and the darkness returned complete. He wanted to preserve the lighter.

"Who are you?" he said at last.

"I lost my way in the forest," Jenna said.

"You're an outsider?"

"A scientist. From Mongolia."

"Never seen a woman here before. You must be the first."

A deep, resigned silence returned to the tank. He asked no more questions.

Eventually, she said, "Why are you here?"

She heard a long inhalation of breath, which he let out in a sigh. "Failure to care for the machinery . . . The chain saws here are ancient. The thing was falling apart in my hands. Fucked beyond repair."

Jenna allowed the silence to gather again, not wanting to rush her main question. From his accent she guessed that he was from Ryanggang Province near the border with China, one of the poorest regions of North Korea.

"Don't worry," he said, taking her silence for despair. "No one spends more than a day or two in the tank."

"Been in the camp long?"

"About a year. Two more to go. Three-year contract."

This was a surprise. "You *volunteered*?"

Another silence, and she sensed that she'd offended him. "Don't make me feel more of a fool than I already am, lady. They offered three hundred dollars a month. Hard currency. That's a lot of money where I'm from. Enough for all my family to get by."

"Have you ever seen the money?" she said carefully.

Long silence. "They're paying it direct to our families," he said softly. "I mean, I hope they're paying it to our families . . ."

Jenna's heart melted for him. In a criminal scam it was often the victims themselves who were the last to acknowledge the truth. These men had been enslaved. The timber trade was a lucrative foreign currency earner for the Kim regime. The workers got nothing.

"Two years will fly by," she said consolingly. "Then you can go home."

The man gave a short laugh through his nostrils, which turned into a wheezing cough.

"Most of the men I arrived with are dead already. Some in accidents, which happen every day here. Some from infections, frostbite. Others from sheer despair. We work seven days a week in all weathers. They give us two days off a year . . . So, no," he said wanly, "I don't think I'll be going home. My wife and daughters won't see me again."

"Has anyone escaped?"

He lit the lighter again for a few seconds, his face surprised and suspicious now, as if he wanted to check whether she was being serious. The light went out. "A few have walked off into the forest. Usually they come back, half dead. There's no way out. We have no papers. Where would anyone go? We're thousands of kilometers from anywhere."

"There's a railroad, isn't there? To transport the timber."

"A branch line about fifty kilometers south. A small station called Tutaul. Connects to the Baikal–Amur Mainline."

"And from there to Vladivostok?"

"Vladivostok and the Pacific to the east, Moscow and Europe to the west. Congratulations. You're at the center of the world." The man sighed again. In an exhausted voice, he said, "Look, lady. Whatever you're thinking, do yourself a favor and forget it. No one gets out."

Anger rose like a bruise in her chest. Even in this far outpost, North Korea maintained a slave state. The tank was a prison inside a prison. Darkness within darkness. And this man had accepted it. He had been born to accept it.

She said, "Is there a network signal out here?"

"Of course not." The man laughed quietly. "The foremen use two-way radios. There's not even a landline."

"How does the camp communicate with Pyongyang?"

"I don't know, lady . . ." His voice drifted off. "I really don't know."

Satellite link. Director Ri must have used a satellite link to send her photo to Pyongyang. Had she seen a satellite dish on top of the administration building? She couldn't remember . . .

Now her mind began to work. Pyongyang would be sending an armed mission to retrieve her and take her to North Korea. Perhaps they were already in the air. That meant that she didn't have much time. And she needed to act before the tank made her lose all sense of time.

To escape she knew that she might have to kill. But she was feeling no dread, no empathy, nothing. The men who ran this camp were brutal slavedrivers. The idea that the slavedrivers, too, were victims of a murderous regime that made them act as they did—did not make her feel pity for them.

She said, "You say no one spends more than a day or two in the tank. When will they release you?"

"Tonight, probably. They need my labor tomorrow. If the team's short, the quota is short. Even Director Ri gets into trouble for that."

So, the hatch will open soon, in the next few hours . . .

She divided her problem into parts.

First, she had to get out of the tank. Second, she had to steal a vehicle. Third, she had to knock out the camp's communication. Fourth, she had to make sure no one pursued her.

Considered like that, the challenge seemed near damned impossible. Then she imagined Mira's voice saying, *I hear "impossible," and I think: when did your fire go out?*

She combed back through her memory, going over every detail she'd seen in the lumber yard. The articulated Tatras and Urals were parked behind the chain-link fence of the vehicle yard. But she'd also seen SUVs in there. They were guarded by someone who sat in a wooden hut inside of the fence. That hut was probably also where the vehicle keys were kept. The giant sixteen-wheel trucks that transported the timber used a lot of fuel. She guessed that the Russian diesel truck she'd seen was itself the fuel tank for the vehicles. When it ran low, it drove off and another one arrived . . .

A rudimentary plan took shape in her mind. It was a long shot. It was insanely dangerous. But it was a plan.

An escape would only succeed if it happened at night, and she needed to know *when* it was night. She also wanted to spare her companion in the tank any more punishment. She would not confide in him.

She allowed a few hours to go by before initiating the first part of the plan.

"I don't feel too good," she said, her voice a whimper.

"You're sick?"

"Epilepsy. I need my medication."

Silence.

"I can't stay here much longer," she said, close to frantic. "My brain's getting seizure signals."

"If you can hold on," the man said, "I'll tell them when they open the hatch."

"Thank y—"

"Hey?" The lighter flicked on. And the man saw her suffering a violent seizure on the tank's floor.

In a couple of leaps, he bounded up the horizontal bars set into the cinderblock wall—the ladder out of the tank—and banged his fist on the heavy iron hatch.

No one came for at least another hour.

When the hatch finally opened, a cool night air flowed down into the tank. A sweet smell of pine resin. She heard no noise from the lumber yard. No chainsawing. No rumbling of truck engines. Work for the day had ended.

"Chun Myeoung-bo!" a voice said. "Out you get."

The man, Chun, climbed out.

"The woman in there is in a very bad way," she heard him say.

"Why, what have you done to her?"

"Says she needs her medication."

"All right," the voice said without interest. "Go back to your *bantong*. I'll deal with it."

She heard Chun walk away across the roof of the tank. Then she heard the guard swearing, and a grunt as he lowered himself to his knees at the mouth of the hole. A flashlight came on. "Hey!"

Jenna lay prostrate, twitching in the glare of the beam. He lowered his head inside. "Are you sick?"

Silence. For the past hour she had been easing herself into kill mode: hyperconscious, hostile intent, no emotion, no thought.

The guard swore again as he prepared to descend into the tank, heavily lowering himself down, one step at time, the flashlight held awkwardly in his hand.

When he reached the bottom and again focused his beam, Jenna was nowhere to be seen. "What—?"

Her bootlaces, formed into a loop, dropped silently over his head from behind.

Jenna pulled with all her strength. The laces dug deep into the man's neck, compressing his throat. He tried to cry out but the only sound that came was a strangulated gargle and the desperate flailing of his hands as he struggled to loosen the garotte, but it was too deeply buried into his flesh. His fingers could get no grip. His windpipe was being squeezed and crushed.

Jenna pulled tighter, harder, cutting off the blood flow to his brain, the oxygen to his lungs. He dropped heavily to his knees. He tried to grab Jenna behind him, but she easily dodged his hands. Then he passed out and became a dead weight. Without releasing tension in the garotte, Jenna lowered him to the floor and put a knee in his back, strangling him for another two minutes to be sure of death. When he was no longer moving, she pulled the laces from his throat, leapt up the horizontal bars of the ladder, and into a sky blazing with stars. Quietly, she closed the heavy iron hatch behind her.

The oversized worker's boots were difficult to walk in. More so without laces. But once she was off the roof of the tank, she touched the ground and found that it was dry and covered in soft wood chippings. She decided to risk moving in her stockinged feet, holding the boots and laces in her hand.

The camp was eerily silent. Beyond the pyramids of stacked lumber, the yard was lit by security lights, which were brightest around the vehicle pen. Slowly she skirted the chaotic edge of the yard, the heaps of tires and rusted junk, where the lights did not penetrate.

She crept as close to the vehicle pen as she could get without stepping into the light.

She could clearly see the wooden guards' hut on the inside of the chain-link fence. Where was the guard? Inside it?

Suddenly a splashing sound made her shrink further into the shadows and compress her body as small as it would go. About five meters away a stick-thin man was urinating. He was silhouetted by the security lights. He must have been standing there a while trying to pee because she'd heard nothing to warn her of his presence. He looked like one of the workers. She waited until the flow ended. When he'd finished and zipped up, he took out a cigarette from behind his ear and struck a lighter.

Cigarettes, lighters. The workers' only solace.

The flame lit up the shadows and in that moment his eyes connected with Jenna's. The man froze. Jenna raised a finger to her mouth. Then he turned and ran. Next to his frothing puddle of piss she saw that he'd dropped both cigarette and lighter.

Would he raise the alarm? *No, he wouldn't.* North Koreans knew that it was safer not to see and not to know.

She pocketed the lighter and took another peep at the vehicle pen. There was no way of reaching it without stepping into the lights. Still no sign of that guard.

It's now or never.

She left the shadows of the junk and made a dash for it—into the lights of the lumber yard, toward the high fence of the vehicle pen.

Her life was on the line, but she had no choice, and when she had no choice, she could contain her fear. It was when she was risking others' lives—that's when she had a problem with panic.

Almost there. The lights were blinding. No one was about. No one to challenge her. Above the administration building, she saw, a dedicated electric light was illuminating the painted red slogan: LET US GLORIFY THE GREAT ERA OF COMRADE KIM JONG-UN!

And above the sign, she could see the rim of a satellite dish.

She reached the fence, her blood singing in her ears, her heart going into hyperdrive.

Let us Glorify . . .

She tied the boots together by the laces.

. . . the Great Era . . .

She looked for a place to throw them.

. . . of Comrade . . .

The boots had to land somewhere where they'd make no noise and where she could retrieve them on the other side.

. . . Kim . . .

She spotted a narrow alley between two closely parked lanes of sixteen-wheeled Tatras.

. . . Jong . . .

She leaned her body back like a javelin-thrower and took aim . . .

. . . UN!

Over they went. High across the top of the fence. Her aim was good. They landed silently between two of the trucks.

Without hesitating, she scrambled up the wire mesh and jumped over the top. She landed on both feet and then lay flat on the ground, listening for a sound, waiting for a cry of surprise, a shout, a challenge.

Silence.

Cautiously she raised her head. Still no sign of the guard.

Wherever he was ... she had to silence him, or all hell would break loose.

A wan bulb glowed from inside the guards' hut, which resembled a gardening shed. Its door was closed but it had a window that faced the trucks, which meant that he would see her coming. There was no chance of sneaking up on him. But as Jenna approached, hiding in the shadows between the vehicles, she saw no one inside the hut. She doubled back, collected the boots and laces, and approached the hut again along a different alley between the trucks so that she had a centered view into the hut's window.

Yes ...

There was the key rack! The keys to every truck and SUV, labeled and organized in rows on the wall. On a small plastic table inside, she could see a folded newspaper, *Rodong Sinmun*, North Korea's national daily, probably months out of date, and the guard's gun, an old Type 88 assault rifle.

The camp was still dead quiet. If the hut's door was locked, she would have to force it and risk making a noise. She tried the handle. It was not locked.

A fume of alcohol hit her. And then she froze.

The guard was lying flat on his back, his head toward the left-hand corner. Next to him was an empty bottle of soju.

She didn't dare move a muscle.

The keys were about two meters in front of her on the wall on the other side of the table. She could almost lean over and touch them. But which one was the gate key?

A congested snore rose from the guard.

She inched slowly around the table, taking extreme care not to tread on the guard, but as she got closer to the keys and reached out her hand, the change of balance in her body made the floor creak.

Again, she froze, her arm extended in mid-air.

The guard's breathing stopped. She looked down. His eyes had opened. He was staring right at her.

"Hey!" he said heaving himself upright. "What're you doing?"

She thought quickly. She couldn't garotte him from the front. But could she strangle him?

"You been drinking on the job?" she said, turning to block his view of the rifle on the table. "Director Ri wants a car—now."

"Director Ri . . . a car?" The man scrambled to his feet. He was struggling to break the surface of his drunkenness and confusion. "Who the fuck are you? You can't be in here."

"Don't you dare speak to me like that. I'm Director Ri's girlfriend. We're heading out."

"At this hour?"

Jenna closed her eyes disdainfully and raised her shoulders in a show of impatience. "Yes, at this hour. He wants to show me the meteor shower. Why am I talking to you, asshole? Get a move on. Director Ri's waiting."

The man blinked at her, unbelieving, trying to sober up. Then he unhooked the two-way radio from his belt. And the instant he took his eyes off her, she rammed her knee with full force into his groin.

The man doubled over and groaned through gritted teeth. Then she brought her knee up again and cracked his nose and teeth. The man was reeling, shocked, not knowing whether to hold his groin or his face. Before he had a chance to cry for help, she'd grabbed the rifle from the table.

"Look at me," she said, gripping the rifle as if it were a spear.

He looked up in agony, and she lunged the barrel of the gun deep into the socket of his right eye, causing his head to hit the wall with a thump.

He keeled over to the floor. His body twitched once. The blood oozed black from his ruined eye. And now he was still.

She listened. The camp was silent.

Next: she examined the key rack. Every one was labeled with a license plate number, except for the one helpfully marked "gate."

Still keeping to the shadows between the trucks she crossed the vehicle yard to the gate. The administration building was directly in front of her across the lumber yard. She undid the padlock, then removed the chain as gingerly and quietly as she could. She was in full view here, under the lights.

Then she returned to look at the vehicles. There were three SUVs, all battered and covered in beige mud, but only one was parked in a position where it could be easily moved. The others were boxed in behind. She checked the license plate, then returned to the hut to take its key, which she spotted immediately with its Toyota logo fob and the label matching the license plate of the car. As she left, she tore a page from the guard's newspaper and scrunched it into her pocket.

The place was still very quiet. No one had yet found the guard inside the tank. No one had heard the commotion inside the hut.

She got into the Toyota SUV. The interior light came on, illuminating her for anyone to see. She closed the door quickly so that she was again in darkness, and started the engine. Nothing she could do about the noise it would make in the dead of night, but hopefully there were no other guards outside the perimeter. If this were a camp inside North Korea, there'd be guards patrolling in pairs everywhere. Dogs too.

She checked the fuel gauge. *Almost empty.*

She smacked the steering wheel. *Damn.* This meant she would have to drive the car to the side of the vehicle pen where the Global RRT diesel fuel truck was parked and fill up. Slowly, she moved the car, circulating around the back of the vehicle yard so that she wouldn't be seen from the administration building. When she was alongside the tanker truck she was back on stage, bright under the lights again.

She ran her finger along the dashboard switches and found the one that opened the filler cap. Then she jumped out as quietly as she could.

The tanker was fitted with a heavy hose and nozzle. She put the nozzle into the filler pipe of the car and squeezed the handle.

Pump machinery whirred, and the fuel flowed.

She looked around as she filled up, as alert as a bird, listening for the sound of voices. Any second now she expected to hear shouts.

And as she looked about, she noticed a second, smaller refueling tanker truck parked behind the RRT Global truck. The second truck held *gasoline*, which was much, much more flammable than diesel ... Of course—it was gasoline that powered the camp's chain saws and machinery.

The tank filled to the top and the pump clicked off.

Quietly, she replaced the filler cap, slowly drove the car to the unlocked gate, and turned off the engine. Again, she listened.

Silence.

Then she got out, returned to the smaller gasoline truck, and took down its nozzle. She squeezed; the pump whirred and gasoline gushed to the ground.

She watched it flow beneath the trucks and SUVs, spreading in a widening lake. The fumes were overpowering. She felt dizzy. It wouldn't take long for someone to smell them. But she had to be certain, really certain, that no one would follow her into the wilderness. Then she lifted the hose up high and began to douse the trucks as if she were watering a large garden, splashing the windows, wheels, cabins, and high up onto the roofs of the sixteen-wheelers. Then she sprayed the gasoline tanker itself and finally the giant Global RRT diesel tanker.

The gasoline had now spread out of the gates and was flooding in small wavelets into the lumber yard. She was about to return to the SUV, when a man's voice shouted.

"Kang! What's going on? Kang? Where are you? You've got a fucking fuel leak! KANG!"

Director Ri was plodding quickly toward the gate. He had clearly been awoken by the fumes and was still in his nightwear—a dirty white vest, and large, flapping shorts. His shoes were a pair of rubber sandals.

"What's this car doing out? KANG!"

Jenna took out the scrunched page of newspaper and dipped it in the gasoline on the floor. Then she took out the plastic lighter, held the paper over it, and flicked, flicked, flicked. *Nothing.*

The gate gave a ferrous screech as Director Ri opened it. "Kang . . . ? Hey!"

Director Ri saw her, saw what she was doing, and started yelling.

She flicked again. Nothing. The lighter was empty.

Shit, shit, shit.

And then Director Ri miscalculated. Rather than run to raise the alarm, he ran toward her.

Unwise, Jenna thought.

Unlike in the hut, she had plenty of space this time. She sprinted toward him, her arms working, gaining the momentum to spin kick him, and the kick hit him like a mule at the top of his fat belly. He landed with a thud on the soaked floor, sending a splash of gasoline onto her clothes.

Then he let out a roar. She jumped on his chest with both feet, her full weight knocking the wind from him, then she fell on top of him and started grappling in the pockets of his filthy shorts.

Every North Korean man she'd ever met smoked cigarettes. Kim Jong-un himself was never without a smoke, lighting up whether he was inspecting a fireworks factory or a post-natal care unit for sick babies. Often, his sister held the ashtray for him. In North Korea, heavy smoking was the mark of a worker, a real man.

She found Ri's packet of cigarettes. Ruyi, North Korea's most popular brand.

But where is your lighter?

Director Ri was a strong man. While she fumbled in his pockets, he'd gotten his rough hands around her throat.

Her fingers touched a small box, made soggy by the gasoline.

His thumbs squeezed her windpipe and she saw orange stars in her eyes.

But she was still on top of him. With a massive summoning of her strength, she got one knee onto his chest and smacked it hard into his chin, knocking out the bridgework of his teeth. Then she rolled off him and pushed herself backward by her hands and feet through the slush of gasoline. Ri was disoriented, and struggling to heave himself to his feet.

She had his box of matches. Her hands were shaking violently now. She struck one. *Nothing.* Another. *Nothing, nothing.* They were damp. Then the fourth one caught. She used it to set fire to the remaining matches in the box and tossed it into the lake of gasoline.

It flared up suddenly, shockingly, with a soft *whumpf.* Flames of blue and fuchsia, gold and amber spread instantly across the floor and up the sides of the vehicles

Director Ri had gotten to his feet, but the sea of fire reached him before he could take another step. His skin and hair were soaked with gasoline and ignited instantly. He screamed in terror as his body twisted into a human steak flambé.

Jenna ran to the SUV at the gate before the flames could reach it. The heat on her back was so intense she feared she'd have no time to escape the blaze.

Ri was still screaming. Then the camp's alarm started blaring from every loudspeaker. Long dashes of deafening sound. Men started to appear in the lumber yard, confused from sleep, all in vests. She'd lost the element of surprise. She was out of time.

She put the car in gear and jammed the gas pedal to the floor.

Sparks flew as the SUV smashed through the unlocked gates. Men dived out the way.

As she turned out of the camp and onto the road heading south, she looked in the rear-view mirror. A bright conflagration rose above the pines. Steel was melting; rubber was burning and sending up black smoke licked with tongues of red flame.

After a mile or so bumping down the dirt road, she already felt far from the camp. Her headlights picked out the gravel and the ruts, the bends and turns between two endless seas of forest.

And then a deep boom sounded as the gasoline tanker exploded, pouring a great pillar of orange flames high up into the night, illuminating the forest for miles. In the mirror she saw swirling clouds of fire with bright projectiles flying from it in all directions like pyroclasts.

"Absolutely beautiful," she murmured, and returned her eyes to the road.

She needn't have worried about knocking out the satellite dish. She must have torched the entire camp.

75

Shangri-La Hotel
Singapore
June 2018

Donald J. Trump @realDonaldTrump
I am on my way to Singapore where we have a chance to achieve a truly wonderful result for North Korea and the World. It will certainly be an exciting day . . .

Air Force One touched down at the Paya Lebar Airbase about thirty-six hours before the summit started. The Boss seemed unfazed by the melting humidity. He was wearing a dark-blue suit of light fabric; his signature hair flick was kept sharp and rigid by styling products.

"I feel really great," he said to the dignitaries greeting him at the bottom of the steps. He towered over all of them. "We're going to have a great discussion and, I think, tremendous success. It will be tremendously successful."

He had command presence, Eric thought. He was full of dazzling confidence and vigor. He had no hesitation about how he would handle himself, even though he understood nothing at all about nuclear proliferation, and had done no preparation whatsoever, even on the plane.

On the flight over, a team of aides had tried to brief him and restrain him. (Could he even point to North Korea on a map? No one was sure.) There had been no detail—not military, not political, not historical—that Trump had seemed to grasp. He rebuffed anyone seeking to counsel him. "I went to an Ivy League School. I'm highly educated. I know words. I have the best words." He was a very diligent student, however, when it came to what played well at home.

"You're making history, sir," Eric told him. "We're getting reports that there'll be five thousand news cameras covering the handshake at the Capella Hotel . . ."

"Five thousand, huh? Make sure that's reported. Obama never got that many . . ."

In the quieter stretches of the flight, the Boss had used Eric as a sounding board for the things he wished to say to Kim, and Eric took advantage of those precious minutes to continue telling him exactly what he wanted to hear.

"Even if you don't budge on sanctions, sir, withdrawing our ground forces from South Korea could be the dealmaker . . . It's costing us *five point six billion dollars a year* to keep them there. Our military presence in the region makes the North Koreans very jumpy . . . the annual joint exercises alone cost us hundreds of millions of dollars . . ."

His words were crude oil gushing into the tankers of the Boss's mind, so that, when the moment came for him to make a decision—by the seat of his pants as always—he would have all the fuel he needed.

Eric was walking right up to the line now. He could see suspicion of him in the faces of everyone around the president. But what did he have to lose? Even if he was exposed, arrested, and tried for his crimes, it would be a walk in the park compared with the seven hells he would suffer at the hands of Supreme Sister Kim Yo-jong. So why not go all out? Why not burn it all down? He was holding onto this small, thin hope, he realized. That if he got Trump to agree to the impossible, she might yet spare him.

As he returned to his seat just before landing, someone grabbed his elbow roughly and shoved him hard into a small service area where canapés were prepared. Trays rattled; cutlery clattered to the floor.

"What are you whispering to him about?" John Bolton, the new national security advisor, was baring his teeth in Eric's face. His gruesome floor-brush mustache was bristling like an old-timer's from the *Simpsons*.

"Get your fucking hand off me."

"Did I just overhear you urging him to *withdraw US ground forces—American hard power!*—from the Korean peninsula? *Tell* me I didn't hear that."

"I don't know what you're talking about."

"You snake. What's your game?"

"What's my game?" Eric's rage projected upward like a hot geyser. "My game is to give the president exactly what he wants— the best show on earth! What's *your* game, you boring old fool? World peace? Getting him to walk away? Telling him he can't make a deal with the commies? You know what this summit's about, right? It's about *him, him, him*! Nothing else." He pushed the man aside. "Don't spoil his day."

The hotel could have been one of the Boss's own. A private, brushed-gold-effect elevator connected to the presidential suite. Artworks of gold leaf. Rosewood furniture with gilt trim and gold brocade. Panoramic views over lit palm gardens and illuminated pools.

The Boss couldn't stop pacing the enormous suite, picking up knickknacks and putting them down, cracking open Diet Cokes, and tweeting.

"When does Kim get here?"

"He's already here, sir," the press secretary said, opening her schedule on her lap. "His party arrived at the—"

Donald J. Trump @realDonaldTrump
Great to be in Singapore, excitement in the air!

"—St. Regis Hotel about an hour ago, I believe."
"Where's that?"
"Less than half a mile from here, sir."
"What are we waiting for? Let's meet him now!"
"Um. Your first meeting is with Prime Minister Lee Hsien Loong, sir, followed by—"

Donald J. Trump @realDonaldTrump
The fact that I am having a meeting is a major loss for the U.S. say the haters & losers.

"Who?"
"The prime minister of Singapore, sir, and his cabinet, followed by a working lunch—"
"Cancel it. I wanna meet Kim now."
Eric jumped in. "Mr. President, you're meeting Kim at 9 a.m. the day after tomorrow. Back home that's evening prime time. Wouldn't you prefer to be on prime time, sir?"
The president did prefer. Another protocol crisis was averted.
The press secretary mouthed *Thank you* to Eric.

Eric had been checked into a smallish third-floor room on the same corridor as the other staffers. Once he was alone, he put the chain on the door and the "Do not disturb" sign on the handle.
The streets around the hotel had been declared a "special event area" for the duration of the summit, meaning that heavy security was in place and normal traffic and access to the public was

suspended. He was inside a tight bubble of protection, but he couldn't shake the feeling that he was vulnerable, exposed.

He kicked off his shoes, flopped onto the bed, and turned on the TV.

The preparations for the summit were on every channel. The BBC was playing footage from earlier of Kim's private jet taxiing to a stop at Changi Airport and the North Korean delegation filing off the aircraft and down the steps. All of them *men*—diplomats, army generals in uniform, bodyguards, aides.

She wasn't on the plane!

Eric felt a small fizzle of hope. But before he had time to process it, a sensational breaking news event was crawling across the bottom of the screen.

KIM JONG-UN GOES ON WALKABOUT

Eric sat straight up on the edge of the bed.

The Comrade Great Successor was taking an impromptu evening stroll along the city's glittering waterfront, surrounded by a dense phalanx of black-clad Supreme Guard Command bodyguards. Surprised shoppers and tourists were holding up their phones to photograph him. The bodyguards were keeping them back. Moments later every channel was covering it, live. The city was abuzz as the news spread. People in the streets, ordinary Singaporeans, were calling out his name and applauding him. Kim waved to them.

In the sweltering heat he was sporting his five-button black Mao suit, the camera flashes lighting up his smiling face. His glasses were steaming up. The Guard Command surrounded him like a priesthood, but in their midst was a cameraman walking backward as he filmed, its spotlight trained on Kim. Korean Central Television? Of course, it was recording his every word and gesture for the Party's annals. The Singaporean foreign minister was his tour guide, pointing out the city's architectural wonders. Minutes later they were ascending to the Sky Park, an open-air bar on the fifty-third floor of the Marina Bay Sands Hotel. By now, huge crowds of local well-wishers had gathered outside the hotel. The footage showed his entourage walking past startled bathers in the infinity pool on the roof, past astonished diners in the C'est la Vie restaurant. A living god was walking among them. Revolution made flesh. News helicopters were flapping overhead, catching him in their searchlights.

Traffic on the bridges seemed to have stopped. It was as if the whole city, sparkling with a million lights, was saluting him, opening for him like a lotus flower. Eric was entranced. He gave his head a rough shake and scrunched his eyes. Had he fallen asleep on the bed? Was this a dream?

How had this happened? How had the Brilliant Comrade been so transformed? The world was seeing him as Eric saw him.

I did this.

The great man appeared a little travel-worn, Eric thought. His breathing was labored, his gait heavy from the excessive strain of one who had devoted his life to the people's cause.

Was Korea Central Television broadcasting this *in North Korea?* Were the people being permitted a view of all this luxury, the clean and orderly streets, the beautiful cars and gardens and well-dressed people?

Now he was posing for a selfie with the Singaporean foreign minister—*a selfie!*

Then he spoke: "Singapore is clean and beautiful, and every building is stylish. We have much to learn from the good knowledge and experience of Singapore."

How gracious. How magnanimous.

The Brilliant Comrade was returning to his waiting motorcade. His car was a gleaming custom-built Mercedes-Maybach saloon. It was gigantic. As big as the Boss's Beast. The hundreds of Guard

Command bodyguards spread outward around the car in a great protective ring as he climbed in, and then a trickle of ice pooled in Eric's stomach. A dreadful foreboding washed over him as the dream dissolved into nightmare before his eyes.

There, for a half-second, he saw a young woman waiting for Kim in the back of the car, illuminated by the interior lights. Not Kim's wife. Not an interpreter.

She's here.

A black jacket over a pure white blouse, smiling her mysterious closed-lip smile, her hair lank in the heat.

She is the shadow that walks here, Eric thought. *My own angel of death.*

76

Amur Oblast
Eastern Siberia
The previous day

The SUV may have had four-wheel drive, but Jenna's progress was not as swift as she'd have liked. The road's surface was a morass of deep furrows and loose stones—too rough for speed. The front wheels hit one rut with such violence that the vehicle's left headlight was knocked out. She had only a single beam to light her way.

She knew that Tutaul, a small logging colony, was about fifty kilometers to the south. From there, a railroad branch line connected with the Baikal–Amur Mainline, one of the two railroad lines that spanned the entire expanse of the Russian Federation, the other being the Trans-Siberian. If she could get onto one of the mainlines heading east, it would carry her to Vladivostok—a large port city on the Pacific—where there was a US consulate. There, she would be safe. She would obtain new documents, and get the hell out of Russia, if she made it that far. She'd had no contact with anyone from home since the US ambassador had visited her at SIZO No. 6 last year.

She reached Tutaul at dawn and saw the railroad straight away. It was a small siding surrounded by a goods yard, some wooden shacks emitting smoke from thin flues, and commercial warehouses. Timber was loaded onto flatcars by rusted yellow derricks. She abandoned the SUV in the trees at the side of the road before anyone recognized it. Then she got out and walked, as nonchalantly as she could, toward the goods yard.

News of her escape wouldn't have got out yet, but soon it would. She couldn't linger here.

A train was waiting, its diesel engine running. Workers in hard hats were standing about, smoking, drinking tea from flasks, waiting for the day's first convoy of trucks to deliver lumber from the logging camp. She could see no Slavic Russian or North Korean faces. The men looked like Evenks or other indigenous Eastern Siberians...

And they had families with them. Women and children were sitting on huge sacks of wares that they were perhaps hoping to sell in the nearest market, wherever that was. A few weathered, stoic faces glanced in her direction. Her hair was wild, her face coarsened by her time in the forest, and her clothes were rags. But the Evenks appeared incurious. She could pass for a nobody from Central Asia.

Poverty. Nobody notices the poor.

It took her a moment to realize that she had a very obvious problem. The train wasn't going to depart unloaded. It was waiting for the timber from the camp...

She was contemplating returning to the SUV and taking her chances on the road when she had a mighty stroke of luck.

The workers turned their heads in the direction of a growling vehicle engine. A small jeep appeared, bumping down the road she had just come from. It was the old Evenk who'd given her a ride to the camp yesterday. She turned her head so that he wouldn't spot her, but she heard him stop the jeep and speak to the workers who manned the derricks. "Nothing today," he said in Russian. "Forest fire."

The men gave a groan and shrugged. This would cost them a day's wage. Then they ambled away. Forest fires happened every summer. That was life. Two of them went off to confer with the train driver. A decision was made.

Just minutes later a whistle blew, and the women and children dashed across the yard toward the flatcars and clambered on. Jenna followed them. The men stayed behind. After another agonizing wait while the train took on water, with the engine vibrating the iron floor of the flatcar, she felt a sudden forward lurch. Iron screeched on iron. Couplings banged together. Slowly the train began to grind its way southward beneath a cobalt dawn sky, moving to the steady beat of the tracks.

Where was this train going? Would it stop to pick up timber from another camp?

Jenna had been so keyed-up with adrenaline that she was only now noticing the hunger pains in her stomach. She had nothing to barter with these Evenk women who had barely looked at her; she had no money to offer them for the white dumplings they were passing around among themselves. Eventually she noticed an ancient pair of eyes watching her. The old woman's face was dark from years of sun and campfire smoke. She gave Jenna a smile that crinkled her whole face and offered her a hunk of black bread and some dried, salted meat Jenna thought might be reindeer. She felt humbled with gratitude.

Everyone hopped off the flatcar as the train slowed for the approach to the first stop, a major town called Shimanovsk. Once again, Jenna was watchful and alert. She had no ticket, no documents, no money for bribes.

But her luck continued to hold. As the train pulled into a weed-strewn siding situated about a hundred yards from a very picturesque yellow station, she saw scenes of chaos.

Hundreds of people with voluminous baggage were trying to board a train that had just arrived at the main platform—a passenger service on the Baikal–Amur Mainline heading eastward, its end destination . . . *Vladivostok.*

She was already inside the station enclosure. She had no ticket barrier to contend with. All she needed to do was cross the tracks . . .

Moments later she was amid the writhing scrum of passengers. She heard languages she didn't recognize, and guessed she was among migrant workers from all over Central Asia. Only one blue-uniformed guard appeared to be on duty, leaning lazily against the wall in his shirtsleeves, smiling at the scene. From the blood vessels around his nose and his glassed-over eyes, it looked like he'd made an early start on the vodka.

The carriage was ancient—wooden, from the Soviet era. Every seat was taken. There was standing room only in the aisles and around the toilets, body pressed against body. No inspector was going to fight their way through a mass of people as dense as this. No one would trouble her for the documents she didn't have. With each stop eastward, the languages and ethnicities of the passengers became more East Asian. Chinese and Koreans who lived in the Russian Far East. The landscape grew flatter and sparser, the clearings between forests now running for several miles across fields of grazing brown cattle. Wooden villages and churches dotted the shores of deep, crystal-clear lakes that reflected sky and cloud. But the train was slow, creaking to a lengthy stop at every small town.

By the time it reached Belogorsk, she had been standing in the carriage for three hours. Unless she could change to a faster train, this journey was going to take days. She didn't have that kind of time. News of her escape could reach the authorities any moment now. The alert would go out, and then every policeman in Russia would be hunting for her.

Despite the absence of police or ticket inspectors the carriage was not without danger. She carefully kept her back turned toward the tattooed Slavic Russians drinking vodka, young men whose moods turned nasty if anyone declined to join them in a toast. The train, already crowded, became dangerously full after Belogorsk, and tempers began to fray. People started ignoring the "No Smoking" sign. Babies cried. Toddlers screamed. The noise and the heat and the frowsy odor of bodies and fried food was becoming an ordeal for everyone on board.

It was almost dark when the train screeched to a halt at Khabarovsk. Jenna had now been traveling for many hours. She had eaten nothing since dawn when that old Evenk woman had given her a snack on the flatcar. She looked out of the window for the platform's digital departures board and immediately saw an opportunity.

The train standing on the opposite platform was an express service that would speed through all the small towns, stopping only three times between here and Vladivostok. *And it was about to depart.* She squeezed and cleaved her way out through the scrimmage of bodies and dashed across the platform just before the express train's doors closed with an automated hiss.

Straight away she knew that she'd made a big mistake.

This was a sleek, air-conditioned, high-speed sleeper train. No one was standing in the aisles. Everyone in standard class was settled into a comfortable, pre-booked, numbered seat for the overnight journey. And she was a ragged, pungent, ticketless vagrant. But it was too late. The service was already gliding out of the station.

"*Welcome on board the 22:45 express service from Khabarovsk to Vladivostok,*" a soft, female mechanized voice announced in Russian. "*This train will be stopping at Ussuriysk, Artem, and Vladivostok . . .*"

She found a table seat that had just been vacated by a family with children, and surreptitiously helped herself to a bag of abandoned, half-eaten pelmeni, feeling a dome of anxiety rising in her stomach. She was a sitting duck—easy prey for police and ticket inspectors and FSB informers, and she was already drawing suspicious glances from passengers. She'd been on the run for at least twenty-two hours. The alarm must have been raised by now. She pictured thousands of FSB officers receiving an alert on their phones with her photo.

Escaped American Spy
DANGEROUS!

Once again, her instincts defaulted to operational mode. A feeling that was like ice-cold water spreading over her chest.

A stewardess was walking past, smiling at passengers. She was dressed in an immaculate navy skirt suit and a white blouse with an enameled pin with the Trans-Siberian logo on her lapel. Her hair was pinned back in a neat bun beneath a navy flight cap. Jenna shrank into her seat and turned to the window to avoid her attention. Luckily, the carriage lights had been dimmed. Passengers around her were already starting to doze off.

With some sustenance inside her from the pelmeni, she tried to foster a feeling of calm. She had almost made it, she told herself. Just a few more hours to go . . . She simply had to hold her nerve.

When the inevitable happened, she was ready. A uniformed ticket inspector appeared at the far end of the carriage. Passengers started reaching for jackets and wallets for their tickets.

Calmly, she left her seat and went to the bathroom that was located behind her at the end of the carriage. She closed the door, but did not lock it, so that the green "vacant" sign remained on. She waited, holding her breath, willing the seconds and minutes to tick by, projecting a kind of Jedi mind trick that she hoped would repel anyone from coming near in the next few minutes. She stood still in front of the open toilet bowl, which was clean and smelled of chemical roses. If anyone came in, she would pretend she'd been taken ill with sudden nausea. And then she caught sight of something that gave her such a shock that she momentarily forgot all danger. It was her first proper look at herself in many months.

There'd been no glass mirrors in SIZO No. 6. She barely recognized her own face. In a year and a half she had aged three years. Face scratched and filthy; cheeks bony and drawn; hair frizzing and showing gray for the first time; lips cracked and thinner. She pumped generous dollops of liquid soap into her hand and began to scrub vigorously, up her arms, over her face, inside her ears, in between her nails, seeing the water in the small steel sink turn black with the dirt of the forest, the grime of the logging camp. She dried herself with paper towels. Nothing she could do about her ragged clothes, which still reeked of gasoline, or the ridiculous oversized boots.

After about ten minutes, she judged that the danger had passed. No one had disturbed her in the bathroom. She returned to her seat. No one looked at her; everyone was slumbering. And gradually, as the train sped smoothly through the endless Siberian dark, she felt her nervous energy give way to exhaustion. She closed her eyes, thinking she'd meditate for a while. Before she knew it she had fallen into a deep sleep.

When she woke up a man was seated opposite her.

Where had he come from?

She had an instant bad feeling about him. He was a Slavic Russian, in his forties, heavily built, blond hair combed over to hide his baldness. He was wearing an open-necked shirt and a cheap casual jacket—a standard plainclothes on-duty look. The carriage was dim. Most people were asleep, but he was engrossed in his phone, which illuminated his face. Or rather his eyes were on his phone, but she had an uneasy feeling that all his attention was on her.

How long had he been there?

She cupped her hand to the window. The sky was beginning to lighten with a pre-dawn glow. She must have been asleep for hours! Darkness was lifting to reveal flat, murky fields flying past. She kept her head turned and her eyes on the view, but now she could feel the man's gaze upon her like heat. Perhaps he hadn't been able to get a good look at her with the lights dimmed, but the carriage was about to fill with daylight.

She felt the frozen panic of one who has just stepped on a landmine and doesn't dare move.

But she had to move. All her instincts were telling her to get away from this man. Where on earth was she going to hide?

Passengers started to stir and yawn when the first rays of the sun burnished the undersides of the clouds. A few of them got up sleepily and began heading to the restaurant car for coffee and breakfast. The man opposite was again staring at his phone. She got up casually, as if to get breakfast. Her heart was feeling buttery and faint. She didn't know what to do.

She went through the automated door to the next carriage, only to see the stewardess again, returning down the length of the train.

She turned around and went back into the bathroom, again not locking the door so that the green "vacant" sign remained on.

Her luck, she sensed, was about to run out. Dramatically.

Suddenly, the bathroom handle turned, and the door started to open. She stopped it with her foot. She caught a glimpse of the man, his brute face, his comb-over.

"Oh, Excyuse me," he said in accented English. She slammed her full weight against the door and flipped the lock.

Then she pressed her head against it to listen, feeling her heart pounding violently. The man was talking in a low, urgent voice into his phone. She could understand only the odd word of his Russian. "Confirmed . . . target identified . . . Requesting backup . . . Vladivostok Station . . . All units . . ."

Well, Jenna. You've done it this time. Out of a hole and into a corner.

In the mirror's reflection she looked like an animal caught in a hunter's snare. Deer-eyed, frightened, with a desperate, compressed energy coiled inside her.

When you make a mistake, boy, you make a big one. Give yourself up. There's no way out.

The man knocked on the door. "Excyuse me, Jyenna. We know who you are. You heff to come out now."

She listened again. She could sense him doing the same on the other side of the door. No one else seemed to be with him. Not yet.

His phone rang. He answered it. "*Da . . . OK . . . spasiba . . .*"

She looked back to the mirror and inhaled. And then from somewhere, in the back of her mind, a voice that sounded a lot like Fisk's piped up.

There's always a way out, isn't there?

She braced herself, then she opened the door very quickly, aiming to gain the advantage of a split second.

The man's face registered surprise. His hand was still holding the phone. As his free hand reached for something inside his jacket pocket, she grabbed his arm and pulled him into the tiny space. He was even bulkier than she'd realized. In the confined room, combat options were limited. Next thing she knew, both of them were grappling violently, neck muscles straining, hands and nails squeezing and gouging. He brought his knee up into her stomach with extreme force, winding her, and again tried to reach into his jacket. Her hands went for his eyes. She dug her thumbnails deep into the corners between tear ducts and eyeballs. He screamed. Then she grabbed his ears, pulling his face toward hers as if to kiss him, and sank her teeth into his nose. He cried out again and fell backward against the door, a string of flesh and cartilage dangling bloodily from the tip of his nose. He was flailing now, blinded, desperate to get out of there, but she again flipped the lock on the door so that there was no escape. Then she managed to get her arm around him in a headlock. With all her strength she rammed his head downward onto the protruding chrome faucet below the mirror, caving his forehead against the metal. His body slumped heavily to the floor next to the toilet, his comb-over splayed over her boot.

Her lungs heaving, she placed her feet on either side of him and stood over him. She was about to untie her bootlaces to garotte him, when she saw his body convulse twice. She felt his neck for a pulse. Nothing.

She'd killed him.

Inside his weekend-wear jacket she found a holster with an MP-443 Grach, a standard FSB sidearm, and handcuffs. She weighed the gun's heft in her palm and pocketed it.

A metallic scream rose as the train careened into a long tunnel. The weak daylight outside the small bathroom window disappeared. Then she saw something glowing on the floor.

His phone.

It had been kicked about during the struggle.

She picked it up as if she'd found a holy relic. Her hands were shaking. The glass was cracked . . . but the movement must have kept the screen awake. It was still unlocked.

Without hesitating she called a number that had been hardwired into her memory. A number only to be used in the direst emergency.

She heard a soft ringing tone and then a series of odd clicks and beeps as the call was rerouted through multiple darknets. Would anyone answer? It was late at night in Moscow.

Please pick up, please pick up . . .

On the tenth ring, it was answered. An elderly Georgian lady spoke in English. "I'm listening."

"This is Sarah Hong," Jenna said, her voice tremulous, "requesting emergency assistance." A three-second pause filled the line. "Hello?"

"What is your location?" The voice was dead calm.

Jenna lost the signal for a few seconds as the train thundered into another tunnel. The compressed noise made her ears pop.

"Um. Somewhere between Artem and Vladivostok? I think? I'm on the 22:45 express from Khabarovsk. Situation extremely hostile. I need to get off the train before it arrives in Vladivostok Station. The FSB is waiting for me."

A crackle-filled pause on the other end. She pictured the cool concentration on the face of the speaker, Elene. Perhaps Volodymyr was right next to her, sitting up in bed in their pleasant apartment off Sretensky Boulevard. Jenna knew they had a long-cultivated network of sympathetic contacts. In Soviet times, that network would have extended along the Trans-Siberian, the main transport route across Russia. Did they still know people? Someone who could stop the train?

The percussion of rail on track seemed as loud as the heart thumping in her ears.

She heard the tapping of a computer keyboard.

"Got it. Train arrives in Vladivostok Station in sixteen minutes... Can we call you back on this number?"

"Uh. Yes. But please hurry."

"One minute."

Jenna remained in the bathroom with the body, hoping, willing, praying, that this man's superiors weren't about to call him for an update.

"*Passenger announcement. The restaurant car will be closing in five minutes...*"

The phone rang again displaying a withheld number. Jenna answered.

"All right. Stay calm, Sarah." Volodymyr's voice. "I can see your location. We have no one in the network we can reach at such short notice. This is my advice: in just under five minutes the train will pass through Morgorodok, a small commuter line station, without stopping. You'll know when you're approaching it because you'll cross a series of three short bridges. I recommend you alight from the train at Morgorodok."

"Alight from the train? How?"

"My dear girl—pull the emergency cord."

Jenna ended the call and turned off the phone, her mind reeling. The train began to rattle as it reduced speed to take in a bend in the track.

Morgorodok.

How could she walk off the train unnoticed at an unscheduled emergency stop? She looked like a vagrant from *Les Misérables*! Every passenger on board would see her. They all had camera phones. The FSB would find her within minutes, seconds.

No, she would have to change her appearance...

Extreme situation. Extreme measures.

She carefully lifted the dead man's leg below the knee and exited the bathroom before the leg and shoe fell back against the door, making it difficult for anyone to push it open from the outside. Directly in front of her she saw a floor-to-ceiling luggage rack holding some heavy suitcases. One of them was broken and had been secured with yellow and black hazard tape, which had been wound around the case several times. She unpeeled a strip of the tape and stuck it across the toilet door. To the incurious, she hoped, hazard tape was a subliminal message. *Bathroom out of order.*

Then she turned to face the door to the carriage that separated her from the restaurant car in the rear of the train. Sunlight was now slanting through the windows. Every seat was occupied. People were awake, chatting, checking their phones, all of them oblivious to the bloodbath that had just taken place in the washroom.

If she passed through this carriage every pair of eyes would clock her. Her clothes were filthy and wild. Her fingernails were laced with gore.

"This train will arrive at Vladivostok Station, our final destination, in fourteen minutes..."

But then she saw every passenger in the carriage turn their heads in unison toward the windows. The train was crossing a long sea bridge and a sudden, stupendous sight—an infinite expanse of dark-blue ocean dotted with vast container ships—had taken their attention. The view stretched so far one could almost see the curvature of the earth.

A voice in her head said: *GO!*

She darted quickly through the carriage doors and down the aisle. The train shuddered violently as it crossed a railroad switch, causing her to almost lose her balance and fall into someone's lap. But no one's eyes met hers.

Halfway across . . . Two-thirds the way across . . .

She felt like an illusionist, pulling off an impossible optical trick. She reached the door to the restaurant car and the boozy atmosphere hit her like a solid wall. The car was heavy with male laughter and raised male voices.

Earlier, she had vaguely wondered why no one was drinking on this long rail journey. Now she knew why. The consumption of alcohol was only permitted in the restaurant car. Drunken men had been carousing here all night. No one seemed to notice her.

Behind the bar, an immaculate young stewardess in the navy uniform of the Trans-Siberian was regarding her customers with a long-suffering air. Jenna watched as a man teetered toward her to buy another drink. The woman glanced at her watch, then briskly told him that the restaurant car was now closed. Before he could say a word, she had pulled a rattling shutter down from the ceiling to the counter and locked it.

Jenna moved to the service counter at the side of the bar.

"We're closed," the woman said without looking at her, and began to wipe spilled beer from the counter with a cloth.

Jenna did not move.

The woman turned to her. "I said we're—" Her eyes bulged in shock. "Oh my God!" she gasped, recoiling from Jenna as if from a violent beggar, clutching her hands to her chest.

Jenna held up her palms to show she meant no harm and gave a smile she hoped was disarming. "Don't be scared," she said in halting Russian. "And please don't scream."

For several seconds the two women's eyes locked. The restaurant manager was not Russian, Jenna saw. The name on her tag was Gulmira. A migrant worker?

From behind the shutter, Jenna could hear the restaurant car's door repeatedly open and close as the men returned to their seats, loud voices passing out of earshot.

"What do you want?" Gulmira whimpered, glancing at the cash register.

"I don't want money," Jenna said calmly. "I just need your uniform."

Gulmira stared at her more intently then, surprised, and Jenna thought she saw a distinct re-evaluation take place behind the woman's eyes.

"My *uniform*?"

"Yes. I'm sorry. Please take it off."

Jenna's hand returned to her pocket and gripped the MP-443 Grach. Had she checked whether it was loaded? She couldn't remember.

The woman continued to stare, perplexed, taking in Jenna's fearful appearance, the matted hair, the dirty clothes, the bloodstains.

"There's no need," she said breathlessly. "I have a spare."

The woman opened a narrow closet next to the bar and took out a hanger holding a navy-blue skirt suit with the enameled pin of the Trans-Siberian logo on the lapel. There was a pressed white blouse underneath.

Jenna took it from her and nodded her head in thanks. "I'm getting off this train at Morgorodok."

"We're not stopping at Morgorodok."

"You don't understand. There's a man on this train who tried to kill me just now. I must get off. It's my only chance."

"Kill you?" Gulmira's eyes opened wide.

"I'm going to pull the emergency cord."

"What?" Gulmira was aghast. "Don't do that. I'll call the police for you."

"If you call the police, they'll just give me to him."

The woman continued to stare, her evaluation of Jenna evolving again and the expression on her face changing to one more knowing, sympathetic, angry.

"All right," the woman said solemnly. "I will stop the train."

"How?"

The woman glanced through the slatted shutter. All the customers had left the restaurant car apart from one enormous bearded man who was passed out drunk and snoring with his head on the table.

"I'll call the emergency services for that man and inform the driver. The train will be forced to stop at Morgorodok." She glanced at her watch again. "But you'd better hurry. We're almost there."

She lifted up the counter and directed Jenna into the narrow kitchen area of stainless-steel surfaces and microwave ovens.

The train was beginning to reduce speed as it approached the urban outskirts of Vladivostok.

Without a word, the woman handed Jenna a boar-bristle brush from a handbag on a shelf. "Tie your hair back. Oh—your *shoes*. Oh dear. Here, take mine." She slipped off her black heels. "They might fit. And here's my makeup. No time for your eyebrows, but there's everything you need in there . . . I'm making the call now."

Jenna changed into the uniform in the kitchen and threw her dirty clothes into a trash can. She quickly rinsed her hands in the steel basin, wet her hair, and brushed the knots out of it as best she could. She tied it back in a bun to hide the matted strands. The woman's compact contained a small mirror. Jenna had never worn much makeup and applied it inexpertly. Her hands were still shaking, and the train juddered again as it crossed a series of double railroad switches.

The woman had been speaking on the phone.

Then: "I've called an ambulance and informed the driver. The train is stopping." Her eyebrows shot up. "Oh, my God, your makeup. Here, let me." The woman brushed her cheeks with a feathery brush, trimmed her eyebrows with tiny nail scissors, and applied eyeshadow. Then she squeezed some cream hair mask into her hands and flattened Jenna's hair so that it was shiny and sleek. "Better. Do you have any money?"

"None."

The woman rummaged in her purse, found nothing, then opened the cash register and counted out ten thousand-ruble notes. "Here," she said, pushing the money into Jenna's hand.

The train had slowed to a crawl. A sign for "Morgorodok" slid slowly past the window. Jenna took a deep breath and put on the uniform's flight cap.

"Ladies and gentlemen. This train will be stopping here for a few minutes due to a passenger emergency."

The woman opened the platform-side door and stepped down to the platform to wait for the paramedics.

"Good luck," she murmured, as Jenna descended the steps.

"Thank you, Gulmira," Jenna said.

"Wait—" Gulmira went back inside and retrieved a small black cabin bag with wheels. "You'd better take this. We never leave the train without one. Take the exit over the walkway bridge and no one will see you. Don't walk along the platform."

Jenna squeezed the woman's hand in gratitude and strode away with as much poise as she could muster in the heels, pulling her carry-on bag behind her. Made-up, confident, elegant, unavailable, cold. A career woman in Putin's Russia.

Outside the station she walked calmly past a pair of traffic cops and felt their stares. Her hand was in her jacket pocket, gripping the MP-443 Grach. She approached the nearest cab in the rank and told the driver to take her to Pushkinskaya Street in central Vladivostok. The United States had three consulates in Russia in addition to the embassy in Moscow. As part of her preparation for the op last year, she'd memorized the addresses of each of them.

The driver gave her a curious glance in the mirror, but Jenna gazed coolly out the window, as if she'd made this trip a hundred times.

On the backseat of the cab, she could feel her excitement rising like bubbles in her chest. The particles of the air seemed charged with freedom. The city looked modern and European with brightly lit chain stores and clean streets. Streetcars whirred past, and buses and new cars. She was back in the civilized world.

When the cab crested the brow of a hill, she got a view through the front windshield of the gateway to the world. The sky had clouded over, but here and there sharp rays made fields of light on the dark ocean. A forest of gantries and derricks served a vast array of supertankers, giant container ships, and smaller tramp ships. She heard the distant thump of the shipyards' heavy forges pounding the air.

After twenty minutes, the cab turned into Pushkinskaya Street. She passed elegant neo-classical offices and grand houses built in tsarist times. She could see the US consulate building, tall and red-bricked. She could see the Stars and Stripes waving from a flagpole that stuck out horizontally from its third-floor balcony.

The cab stopped in front of a news kiosk selling newspapers in a dozen different languages.

As she was getting out, she saw something that made her reality split in two. She was so confused that she wondered whether she had escaped into an altogether different universe.

On the banner headline of the *International Herald Tribune* were the words:

TRUMP MEETS KIM IN HISTORIC SUMMIT

77

US Consulate
Vladivostok

Jenna walked into the consulate expecting to have to explain herself. She was wearing the uniform of a stewardess of the Trans-Siberian Railway and was still wheeling the carry-on Gulmira had given her. She had no form of identification. She imagined a long process as calls were made and verification was sought from Langley.

But to her surprise one of the desk officers jumped up the moment he saw her. He held up his finger to her, indicating for her to wait a second while he turned his back to make a hurried call.

"Yes, she just walked in . . . Yes, sir."

On the desk was an upside-down copy of the same newspaper she'd just seen in the kiosk outside.

"May I?" she said, picking it up as she was whisked up the stairs.

The consul had been waiting for her in a state of nervous agitation. He was a pleasant, tweedy man called Evan Patterson, who looked like he might once have taught philology at Yale and had somehow been dragooned into a world of cloak-and-dagger.

"No time for a welcome, Jenna. Unless you want to be holed up here for years like Julian Assange." He lifted a large canvas kit bag from under his desk and pressed it into her arms before she'd had a chance to say a word. "Change into these—fast. Every cop in

Russia is waiting for you at Vladivostok Station. It'll take them no time to figure out where you are now." He directed her into a small bathroom just off his office. "Two minutes? A driver's waiting to take you."

"Take me where?"

He closed the door. Jenna's mind went into a spin. Langley must have picked up Russian police signals traffic and alerted the consulate.

The clothes in the bag flummoxed her: a shabby, well-worn chef's outfit, a grimy white cap, and a pair of white, half-length rubber boots. She emerged from the bathroom feeling faintly foolish.

"Good to go?" Mr. Patterson had been pacing outside the door. "This is for you." He handed her a clear plastic folder. "Passport, shore pass, and port authority documentation to enter the goods yard."

"Goods yard?"

"We'll explain in the car. This way. Hurry."

Jenna was rushed down three flights of stairs ahead of Mr. Patterson.

Moments later they were in a basement parking lot where the orange car waiting for her looked like a cab from the city's taxi fleet. Before she knew it, she was bundled inside with the enormous kit bag on her lap, the engine was starting, and Evan Patterson was saying, "Good luck," and rapping his knuckle on the car's roof.

A young copper-haired man was already seated in the back next to her. Rosy, corn-fed cheeks, oversized teeth. Fresh out of college.

"It's an honor to meet you, Jenna. I'm the vice consul? Greg Sanderson?" He gave a boyish laugh. "Jeez, this is exciting. I've never done anything like this before—"

Jenna glanced at the driver. The car was turning left into traffic on Pushkinskaya Street.

"Oh, it's OK. Yuri's one of us. Believe it or not, he's from Coney Island. His parents came from—"

"The plan, Greg."

"Yep. We got to get you out of Russia right now. You're departing on the South Korean container ship *Hanjin*. The vessel is undocking as we speak and is sailing at 10:00."

Jenna glanced at the car's clock.

"That's . . . in eighteen minutes."

"I know, right?" Greg balled his fists and mimed a little shadow fight, clearly enjoying himself. "They're expecting you on board. You're a contract worker. A member of the kitchen crew. Don't worry. No kitchen work required. They'll hide you below until you're in international waters. The ship's first stop is Busan, South Korea, which is where you'll disembark. Our guys will meet you at the port. Then we'll fly you home from Seoul. I guess you could use a vacation—"

"My cover is a chef?"

"Yes. If you would look at your documents . . ."

Jenna opened the kit bag and took out the plastic folder.

The passport was South Korean. It belonged to a woman called Sung Gil-soon who was about Jenna's age but who looked nothing like her. It was stamped with a crew visa. A slip of paper stapled inside was her shore pass.

"Yeah, better not ask me how we got that," Greg said, tapping the side of his nose. "And don't freak out about the photo. The shore leave pass and the seafarer's ID are the only things they check at the barrier."

Poor Sung Gil-soon. Attached to the passport with a rubber band was everything the woman needed to get back on a ship—paybook, seafarer's ID, vaccination records, a letter confirming her employment with the Pan Ocean Line (South Korea), and a document listing every ship she'd served on.

There was zero chance of memorizing all this in a few minutes.

"The *Hanjin* is sailing from berth number fifteen. You might be able to see it from here . . ."

The driver, Yuri, was careful to stop at every light, and was constantly checking his side mirrors. Ahead of them the port area was floodlit as the clouds became darker. Massive red derricks and gantries towered above the portside buildings, and at the end of each street they passed she could glimpse supertankers, unloaded container ships, and vast container yards lit by arc lights.

"Any questions?"

Events were overtaking her so fast she was in danger of missing a chance here. A big chance. She took out the crumpled newspaper she'd lifted from the consulate's reception desk. Until she saw it at the top of the page, she'd had no idea what the date was.

Today was Sunday, June 10, 2018. The summit in Singapore was on Tuesday, June 12, the day after tomorrow.

"First stop is Busan, you say? How long is the voyage?"

"Well now . . ." Greg was like an annoyingly bright, over-prepped college quiz contestant. "Assuming a speed of twenty-five knots and no bad weather, about twenty hours."

So, she'd get to Busan early tomorrow. *Monday.* Which would give her time to get to . . . First things first: she had to warn Fisk about Eric Rahn.

"Will I have access to secure comms on board?"

"Nope. Nada. Radio silence for the whole voyage.."

"OK, Greg. Can you do something important for me?"

"Sure!"

"I need you to get a secure message to Charles Fisk at our Moscow embassy—"

At that instant a police car overtook them, red-and-blue lights flashing, siren blaring. Then another, racing in the direction of the port.

Greg looked panicked suddenly.

"Did you hear me? Send a secure message to Charles Fisk at our embassy in Moscow: tell him I've identified an agent of the opposition whose name is Eric Rahn. *R-A-H-N.* Got that? Repeat it back to me."

The car stopped at a red light. A police car was directly in front of them. Yuri's eyes met Greg's in the mirror and Greg nodded.

"Got it. Eliot Rahm."

"Eric Rahn!"

"This is where I leave you, ma'am. Port is straight ahead. Good luck." He threw the door open, and he was gone.

Traffic was much busier around the port. Streets were clogged with hooting trucks. Signage buzzed with neon. Raucous beat music was coming from the open doors of sailors' bars called Blue Angel and Cutty Sark. Flashing signs in Cyrillic and Korean. The sidewalks looked damp and slippery from a salty drizzle that had begun to fall. The air smelled of diesel fuel off the ocean.

Yuri joined a line of cars in front of the port entry barrier, and she felt her heart rattle so hard it threatened to come loose in her chest. But her shore pass was the only document she was asked for. The official in the booth scanned it and waved them through.

The car turned into the port itself and along a long straight road until they reached berth number 15. The wharf was a city in its own right. Giant coils of hoses for refueling the ships, forklift trucks, straddle carriers with huge, gantry-like legs, and container carrier trucks. Everywhere men in red hard hats. Everything lit up like a movie set.

There it was, the *Hanjin*, its name in massive white letters across its stern. The ship was huge and black, as big as an apartment block. And it looked like it was getting underway. Mooring lines were being cast off. Shoresmen were shouting and giving hand signals. The engines had started in a cloud of noxious diesel smoke.

Yuri half turned his head to her.

"Run."

PART SIX
Singapore

"Getting a good picture, everybody? So we look nice and handsome and thin? Perfect."

Donald J. Trump, June 18, 2018

78

Singapore
Next day

When he wasn't in meetings, Eric was spending the day hiding in his room at the Shangri-La, even while some other aides slipped out to enjoy the gardens and spa.

The Boss had grudgingly gone to his "waste of time" meeting at the Istana, the official residence of the prime minister of Singapore, and would be staying for a working lunch—even the Boss had seen the need to show some courtesy when he'd understood that Singapore was footing the fifteen-million-dollar bill for the summit, including the hotel costs for him and Kim, and all the heightened security.

Other staff had already gone to the Capella Hotel on Sentosa Island, the venue for tomorrow's summit, to ensure that everything was going to plan—that there were no security blind spots inside the building, that the coast and airspace had been closed to all traffic, that the walk between every room had been timed and scheduled, that the menus had been double-checked and the ingredients analyzed. Secret Service and Diplomatic Security agents had conducted a building sweep, including the elevators, kitchens, toilet seats, and gardens. The North Koreans were running all the same checks, with the addition of Kim Jong-un's personal food taster, to whom the hotel's chef had taken offense. Eric could reasonably and plausibly have gone to the Capella Hotel today and witnessed for himself the bizarre scenes of Americans and North Koreans cooperating in an atmosphere of real optimism.

But he did not dare. *When the news is bad, play for time.*

If he was to have any chance of departing Singapore on Air Force One tomorrow evening, rather than drugged and handcuffed in the cargo hold of an aircraft heading to Pyongyang, he needed to delay his encounter with the Supreme Sister for as long as possible. But encounter her he would. He was quite sure there was no avoiding that.

Over the last few months, Eric had watched the rise of Kim Yo-jong with mounting fascination and dread. She was featuring more and more prominently on North Korean state television and in the Party newspapers. State media still had not mentioned her by name, nor did the North Korean public even know that the Great Successor had a sister—the branches of the Family's tree were always kept opaque and mysterious—but Eric, like all North Koreans, was adept at reading the signs and symbols.

This woman is important. We are gradually introducing her to you, the people.

In nearly every one of her brother's recent official appearances—in his nicotine-growl addresses to the Supreme People's Assembly, in his on-the-spot guidance tours of kindergartens, fish-canning plants, and missile-engine factories—she was in the background, often standing alone, sometimes holding the Montblanc pen he used to sign documents; sometimes relieving him of bouquets of flowers presented to him by saluting Young Pioneers in red neckerchiefs; always dressed in her dark functionary's clothes.

Since her last appearance on the world stage at the Winter Olympics, she'd been appointed to the Politburo of the Workers' Party, a position of real power, with her own authority to decide who was monitored, fired, promoted, or executed in a stadium before thousands of onlookers. With power like that, no one would dare cross her or annoy her, or—God forbid—disagree with her.

Something else Eric had noticed from watching the footage: there was a marked change in the behavior of the people surrounding her. Male officials twice her age covered their mouths with their hand when they spoke to her; they avoided her eyes and kept their heads lowered. Ordinary mortals were not permitted to look upon the face of the goddess-princess. Some visibly trembled with nerves. Even more astonishing was her behavior around her brother. She laughed, she swung her arms when she walked. On one occasion she even left the room while he was speaking—an unheard-of crime for anyone else. A firing offense, literally: as in firing squad.

But one event in particular convinced Eric beyond all doubt that she was now her brother's chosen successor. It had taken place in February just after the Winter Olympics. The Great Successor had been filmed riding his steed at a gallop to the summit of Mount Paektu, the cradle of the Revolution. To a background of heroic music, the propaganda narration was histrionic. "His unsurpassed greatness shakes heaven and earth!" It was powerful, iconic imagery for the Family's mythology: sacred mountain, dazzling snow, the sky a sharp blue, and the great man rearing up the horse's front legs for the cameras. The West had seen it quite differently, of course, and the overwhelming reaction had been ridicule. ("That poor horse.")

It seemed that no one except Eric had noted the significance of *his sister accompanying him.*

Riding behind him through soft snow, like a scene in a Christmas card, the Supreme Sister had been dressed in the cloth cap and uniform of the Worker-Peasant Red Guards. Most telling of all, the horse she rode was adorned with a shining, five-pointed silver star on its headstall, the dynasty's regal insignia. No other member of the Family had been accorded an honor like that. To display it there, on hallowed Mount Paektu, had a revolutionary import that Eric had immediately grasped.

It was an anointment.

As her brother continued to chain-smoke and pile on the pounds, as he was treated for diabetes and heart disease and gout, her new prominence on the world stage began to make complete sense. Her brother was positioning her to act as regent in the event of his early demise, and until his own children came of age. But would a person like her ever give up absolute power?

Later, while eating a TV dinner alone in his room and flipping between endless news channels, he'd also gotten his answer as to why she hadn't been on the Great Successor's plane when it landed in Singapore yesterday. She'd flown separately, like a member of the British royal family, not wanting to risk the succession if something happened to one of them.

Now that the picture was clear to him, it was not so surprising that she had dealt so mercilessly with the Great Successor's half-brother at Kuala Lumpur Airport—Eric was quite sure, now, that the assassination was her doing, not her brother's. Nor that she was so eager to murder Soo-min's son.

No one was seeing this coming. Kim Jong-un's children were still infants. The man himself was a heart attack waiting to happen, and when it did, the next absolute dictator of patriarchal North Korea would be a woman. If the transition was to succeed, there could be no male rivals with a prior claim to the succession. Nothing, and no one, was going to block her path to power.

79

Singapore
Tuesday, June 12, 2018

Eric rose at five the next morning. In the presidential suite the Boss was restless and excited. He'd eaten little of the lavish breakfast buffet brought up to him. He was energized, Diet-Coked-up, and possessed of an absolute conviction that he was about to make one of the greatest deals in history.

Eric slipped through the door just as National Security Advisor Bolton was making a last-minute bid to restrain the Boss from giving away the store. The Boss was gazing at the panoramic views, pacing, tweeting, and didn't seem to be listening. Bolton pulled his stink-in-the-room face when he saw Eric, then turned his back on him.

Eric would be at the Boss's side all day, translating the Boss's every word into Korean. The Boss was his protection. If he made it through the day and onto Air Force One unscathed this evening, then perhaps, *perhaps* there was hope for him . . .

At eight thirty the president's eighteen-car motorcade crossed the land bridge to Sentosa Island. Kim, out of respect for Trump's senior age, had arrived at the venue first—an arrival so cinematic that it threatened to upstage the Boss: his Mercedes-Maybach saloon had been surrounded by forty suited and jogging members of the

Supreme Guard Command, as if he were an emperor arriving on a curtained litter. The jogging bodyguards had already become an internet sensation.

Both leaders were now in the building. And at the stroke of nine history was made. Eric saw it all on a live feed in the delegates' hall.

On a terrace of colonial-era white stucco, lined, incongruously, with the Stars and Stripes and the North Korean red star, the two men walked toward each other, smiling in recognition like long-separated cousins. Kim's dark Mao suit was of such a generous cut that the pants flapped about like pajamas. His curious black shoes had a suggestion of Cuban heel. The Boss was the seasoned TV star he'd always been, relaxed, basking in the attention, finally about to collect his Emmy.

The handshake lasted twelve seconds. In one momentary lapse of focus the Great Successor gaped at Trump with his mouth open, but quickly recovered. Thousands of camera flashes lit up in crackling fusillades.

This was the first time—ever—that the North Korean watching public had set eyes on a president of the Yankee jackals. And what a vision he was for them: seven inches taller than the Brilliant Comrade, his hair an elaborate nest of spun gold. He was older, much older, and yet, in some ineffable way that was also very apparent, not a grown-up.

The Great Successor spoke no English, but, as lip readers later reported, he'd learned the words to say, "Nice to meet you, Mr. President."

Now the two men were walking together back into the hotel, where Eric was standing with the waiting delegates. Kim was nodding away agreeably to whatever incomprehensible English blather the Boss was speaking into his ear. The droves of press and cameramen followed them inside.

A brief press conference now took place with the two great men seated in armchairs.

"We're gonna have a great discussion and, I think, tremendous success," the Boss said to the cameras.

Eric had never seen the Comrade Great Successor in the flesh before. How strongly he resembled his father, more so than in photographs. And as with the father, whom Eric had met many times during his boyhood days in Paekhwawon, Eric felt as if he was standing next to the sun. More than anything he was struck by Kim Jong-un's easy and genial manner. He was gracious. He smiled and joked. He even took an unscripted question from a foreign reporter—an absolute first.

"Chairman Kim, are you confident about a deal?"

"Well, it's too early to tell," he said through his interpreter, "but I wouldn't say that I am pessimistic."

In fact, he betrayed no signs of nerves at all, which was astonishing given what was at stake, not to mention the pressure of knowing that a billion people around the globe must be watching him live right now. He was absolutely the Boss's equal.

The short press conference was wrapping up.

Still no sign of *her*.

"Holy shit," the Boss murmured to Eric as they left the room. "Did you see that wall of cameras? Biggest I've seen in my life. More than the Academy Awards . . ."

The next, much-anticipated private meeting took place in a shuttered, bug-swept conference room. The atmosphere was convivial from the start. This was the moment the Boss had been looking forward to: the getting-to-know-you, sizing-you-up personal rapport that had worked so well for him in his Manhattan real-estate days. Nothing of what would be said in this conclave would be divulged—the world could only guess. Eric was privy to a secret moment of history. There were only four people present: Kim, the Boss, Eric as the Boss's interpreter, and Kim's female interpreter.

Eric had expected the Boss to make happy talk—the Boss loved happy talk. But even he was blindsided by Donald J. Trump's opening remark to Kim Jong-un.

"Tic Tac?" The Boss was offering him a mint. Kim seemed uncertain how to react.

"Breath mint," the Boss said, and dramatically blew into the air. "Breath mint."

Perhaps fearing an attempt to poison him, Kim shook his head.

The Boss's next words lurched further into the surreal. "Have you heard of Elton John?"

Eric translated. The Great Successor looked baffled.

"El-tong-jun?"

"I brought you a gift," Trump said, and handed Kim a CD from his suit side pocket. It was *Honky Château*, the 1972 album featuring the hit song "Rocket Man."

Kim accepted it with both hands, smiling, in utter confusion.

No matter. The Great Successor had a gift for the Boss: a rare, solid-gold pin displaying the smiling faces of his father and grandfather.

"Wow," the Boss said. "I will treasure this next to my heart."

The parties sat down. There was no agenda for this meeting, but Eric knew what was coming next.

"I wanna show you a small movie, Mr. Chairman. It's called, 'A Story of Opportunity.' I think you're gonna like it very much."

Eric handed the Boss an iPad. The president hit play, and the preposterous four-minute movie he'd had specially made, showing the idyllic, leisurely future that lay in store if Kim gave up his nukes and built condos started to roll. Eric watched it reflected in Kim's glasses. At the sound of the blockbuster soundtrack, he felt his face redden.

"*Two men. Two leaders. One destiny . . .*"

It was like having a front-row seat for the opening night of a very bad two-man play.

When the video ended Kim nodded vigorously and looked to his interpreter for help.

"The Comrade Great Successor says it's like a science fiction movie."

"I knew you'd love it."

For the next twenty minutes the two men enjoyed a relaxed back-and-forth as they swapped dictator tips on personal security.

"You wanna take a look at the Beast? I'll show you the Beast. It's got night vision, smoke screen devices, the whole works."

Kim confided he'd got the idea of the running bodyguards from a favorite Clint Eastwood film: *In the Line of Fire*.

The only words of real substance came toward the end of the forty-five minutes of allotted time. Kim started dropping hints about his price for signing the joint declaration.

Everyone in the US delegation—except, apparently, Trump—knew that Kim would rather eat grass than surrender his nukes. It was simply never going to happen. But they also feared that Kim would happily sign any piece of crap if the Boss agreed to one very sensitive North Korean demand. And the Boss was in grave danger of conceding it because Eric had been pushing all his buttons on this matter for months. The Boss had been primed to do it. When the moment came, he would not be able to restrain himself. The United States maintained 28,500 troops on the ground in South Korea, along with extensive US-run military camps and airbases. These protected South Korea against a North Korean invasion, and projected American hard power throughout the region. Every year these troops conducted joint military exercises with South Korean forces to maintain combat readiness. And every year, the North Koreans went apeshit. They felt provoked. Kim wanted an end to it.

The North Korean term for the joint exercises was "war games."

The Boss leaned forward in his seat with the tips of his fingers touching, looking, Eric thought, like a giant shrimp. "I'm gonna cancel the war games," he said, using the North Koreans' term without missing a beat. "There's no need for them. They're expensive, and it'll make you happy." When Eric translated these words for Kim, he made sure he repeated "war games" rather than "joint exercises."

To North Korean sensibilities, this was like a first line of coke. The Great Successor was beaming although he was visibly trying to keep a solemn face. It was as if a large thorn had just been removed from his ample side. And it was only now that Eric saw that Kim might have been holding in a great deal of concealed tension. The men shook hands and stood.

"Give me your notes," the Boss whispered, and confiscated Eric's interpreter's notes.

The reporters were waiting for them outside the room.

"Mr. President, how was the private meeting, sir?"

"VERY good."

"What did you discuss, sir? Did you keep a note of the meeting?"

"I don't have to keep notes because I have one of the greatest memories of all time."

The next, bilateral meeting, at which both sides were joined by their delegations, including John Bolton, took place down the corridor in the Cassia restaurant, which had been converted into a conference room for the occasion. This was the summit proper, although Eric knew that neither side would be doing much negotiating. Rather, their purpose was simply to frame some vaguely goodwilled wording for the joint declaration, which would be little more than a mashup of previous, vaguely goodwilled declarations—all of them pans of loose stool water with nothing you could point to that was solid. But the Boss didn't care. All he needed was a piece of paper that he could sign this afternoon in front of thousands of cameras; then he could proclaim to the world that history had been made.

In this meeting the Boss did not say a word about the secret deal he had just struck with Kim Jong-un: stopping the "war games" with its implicit offer to withdraw all US forces. Apart from Eric, whom the Boss trusted, no one on the US team knew about it—for now. By the end of the bilateral session, Bolton looked relieved. As far as he was concerned, nothing had been given away.

Still no sign of her.

Then, just as the meeting was winding up amid more handshakes and pleasantries and the talk was turning to lunch and the afternoon's signing ceremony, Eric watched a US Diplomatic Security officer enter the room and place a note under Bolton's nose. Bolton had been seated at the very end of the table—in the least distinguished position—as a signal to the North Koreans that the Boss wasn't going to allow this old buzzard to mar the event.

Bolton looked slowly up from the note and stared at Eric. Not in shock, but with a cold fury, a kind of: *I knew it!*

Had Bolton just found out about the secret deal? *How? How had he found out?* And as the man continued to stare at him, Eric stared straight back, his face full of defiance and contempt.

You're not getting in my way now, you Cold War cuck.

No phones had been allowed inside the room, and now he could see Bolton itching to get out of there, urgently wanting to talk to whoever had sent in that note. The instant the parties stood up, Bolton dashed for the door without waiting to shake hands. North Korean heads turned.

"Just ignore him, folks," the Boss breezily. "He's pissed off that we've made a great deal."

Eric translated, his voice sounding flat and robotic. His mind was already in pursuit of Bolton. Where had Bolton gone? Who was he talking to?

Eric felt his reality suddenly warp and slide. The secret deal was the *only* thing he'd achieved that might appease the Sister—that might get him off the hook. He had to find Bolton. He couldn't let that old war hawk ruin the only hope he had left.

80

Capella Hotel
Singapore

Jenna was waiting in the manager's office behind the main reception desk of the Capella Hotel. She was with the local CIA station chief and two other ops officers she'd never met before. The atmosphere in the windowless room was stuffy and tense. Her journey over the last few days had been one of such relentless speed and momentum that she was now finding it physically difficult to sit on the edge of a desk, be still, and wait.

She had no idea whether her note would be read in that meeting, or what would happen if it was. But the president of the United States and the national security advisor were at this very moment sitting in a room with a foreign agent who for months might have been whispering poison into the president's ear and who was now in a prime position to influence the outcome of a high-stakes summit in favor of a hostile state.

> *CIA suspects that Eric Rahn is an active North Korean operative. Recommend his immediate removal from the vicinity of the president. Jenna Williams. Operations Officer.*

She was lucky to have made it here in time. When the *Hanjin* had docked at Busan, two junior diplomats from the US embassy in Seoul had been there to meet her, a man and a woman. They'd brought her US passport, a bag of goodies including chocolate-chip cookies, new clothes, and a secure phone she could use to call her family to tell them she was alive. The plan had been to drive her to Seoul in comfort, get her checked out by doctors, and fly her home. So they were more than surprised to see her running toward them along the wharf in Busan dressed as a chef, yelling at them to tell her where they'd parked, and demanding that they drive her immediately to Gumhae International Airport on the other side of Busan. On the way there, she'd asked the diplomat who wasn't driving to book her onto a direct flight to Singapore.

She had caught the afternoon flight by a whisker. It was a Monday, and the plane wasn't full. Once she'd boarded and was fastened into her seat she called Charles Fisk on the secure phone, just as the cabin crew were asking passengers to turn off all personal electronic devices.

No time for a greeting. "You got my message?" She knew Fisk would have acted immediately on a word from her. He'd never doubted her.

"Jenna?"

"*Ladies and gentlemen, welcome on board Singapore Airlines Flight SA12 . . .*"

"You're on a plane?"

"What's the situation?"

"Which one?"

"Goddamnit, Charles. The Eric Rahn situation!"

"Who?"

Oh, God. Jenna screwed her eyes shut and pinched the bridge of her nose. Her message hadn't made it to him. Langley had just lost a whole day in which they could have stopped this sociopath before the summit started.

She dropped her head between her knees and struggled to keep her voice down. "We have an operative of the North Korean Seed-Bearing Program *on the president's staff*. Name: Eric Rahn. *R-A-H-N*. He's Trump's special advisor on East Asia . . ."

"Jesus Christ." She heard a chair scrape as Fisk leapt to his feet. "How do you know this?"

"No time to explain. He's *with the president in Singapore* right now, Charles. The same guy who traced me to Langkawi where the North Koreans tried to smoke me."

A steward was leaning over her with an impatient smile. "Excuse me, madam, could you turn off your phone please?"

Jenna held up a beseeching finger. *Two seconds, please.*

"He's got to be apprehended before the summit."

"OK. I'm on it . . ." Fisk said. "Er, where are you flying to?"

"Where do you think! Singapore!"

"Madam, your phone—"

"What?!" She felt Fisk's shock like an explosion underwater. "Are you out of your mind? Do NOT go to Singapore, Jenna. The place is swarming with North Korean spooks right now. It's too dangerous for you, do you hear me? Hey! Are you listening—"

The aircraft had completed its taxiing to the runway. The engines were starting to roar and seats beginning to shake.

"Sorry, Charles. Plane's taking off."

When she landed at Changi Airport five hours later, she called Fisk again. While she'd been in the air, Fisk had seen some unrelated information about Eric Rahn—and from a surprising source. There were online rumors about him. Twitter sleuths had noticed his resemblance to a grainy photo released by the San Francisco Police Department appealing for information about a suspect involved in a gruesome stabbing in a bar on Castro Street during Pride weekend.

Rahn had made two return trips to California in recent months, Fisk said, once as the invited speaker at a high-school event in

Marin County, the other for reasons not yet clear, but he'd flown back to DC from San Francisco the day after the stabbing occurred on Castro. The screenshots captured from CCTV outside the bar in Castro Street were not conclusive, but the suspect bore an undeniable resemblance to Rahn. San Francisco Police Department declined to comment on the rumors.

What was he doing in California?

By the time Jenna had arrived in Singapore, the chief of Station had been ordered to offer her whatever assistance she required to remove Eric Rahn from the summit and return him to the US for questioning. It was decided that National Security Advisor Bolton should be the one to break the news to the president.

Jenna jumped to her feet when Bolton entered the room, looking like an angry old judge from *The Muppet Show*.

"What the hell is this?" he said, holding up the note.

"Sir," Jenna said. "We have reason to suspect that—"

"You're Jenna Williams?"

"Yes, sir. We have reason—"

"Jeez . . ." he said, peering at her through his rimless glasses. "It is you. How did you get out of Russia?" He glanced at his watch. "Never mind—"

"Sir, I have strong reason to suspect that the president's special advisor and interpreter at this summit is an active operative of an espionage offensive known as—"

"The Seed-Bearing Program?" Bolton said. He folded his arms thoughtfully. "Yes, I know about that. Mira Kowalski briefed me. What makes you so sure?"

Jenna hesitated. "I'm ninety-nine percent sure, sir, that Eric Rahn concealed his background on the SSB1 and the vetting process. He's Korean but he's not from South Korea. I also believe he betrayed my location to the North Koreans during a covert op on Langkawi last year. His car was seen outside my family home shortly after that."

"So, no smoking gun. Just a few circumstantial anomalies and the rest gut feeling and suspicion?"

Jenna felt heat rise to her face.

"It's all right," he said, seeing her discomfort. "You're not the only one with suspicions."

Much as she found Bolton almost comically unlikeable, she knew that he was one of the best-informed figures in the administration, and ferociously intelligent. He left work at the White House at five every afternoon, giving strict instructions that no one was to call him later than eight. Then he was back in his office at five thirty in the morning, which gave him five undisturbed hours to work before the president descended from the residence at the end of watching his morning talk shows. She also knew that he was the only advisor close to the president who had a clear-eyed understanding of Kim Jong-un.

Bolton opened the door and spoke to the men of his own security detail. "Go get Eric Rahn. Tell him there's an urgent phone call for him in this office. Don't make a scene. Do it quietly. Then handcuff the motherfucker to a chair."

A voice outside the door said, "Sir, the president's asking where you are."

An idea had started gathering in Bolton's mind. Jenna could see it in his eyes as he turned back to her. "Let's catch him before he sits down to lunch with his new bestie, Kim."

"The president?"

"Yes, I think you should meet him."

Jenna's eyes opened wide in alarm. "Sir—I can't go in there. I have a, uh, *history* with the North Koreans. What if they figure out who I am?"

"I'm aware of that. They know you were on that train when Kim Jong-il died."

Exactly, so why would you ask me to—

"You know the real reason North Korea has nukes?" he said, his blue eyes drilling into hers. "Not to keep the country safe—nukes are of no benefit whatsoever to the North Korean people. The nukes are there to keep the Kim family in power. Nukes make them unremovable. That *family* is our problem, Jenna, not the people . . ." His voice lowered to a whisper. Bolton was really quite ruthless, she thought. "I think we can provide a little scare that only the Family will understand."

"What do you mean, sir?"

"You. You're the scare."

"Sir, I'm not sure what you have in mind, but it's not a good idea for me to—"

"Follow me. You'll be quite safe here. More security in one damn building today than anywhere else in the world."

81

Capella Hotel
Singapore

Eric was the last to file out of the conference room. The delegates were headed toward the banqueting room for lunch while the joint declaration was drafted and printed. The Boss's triumph was almost in the bag. A small crowd of North Korean aides and American staff waiting in the corridor were applauding, and the Boss raised his fist. He looked radiant, victorious, a caesar about to proclaim his own divinity.

Outside the banqueting room, Americans and North Koreans were mingling, actually mingling. The Boss had walked ahead of everyone, his flaxen head towering above the throng. Both sides were making small talk and laughing with all the relief and benevolence of old enemies reconciled. An incipient celebration was in the air.

Eric looked about for Bolton but couldn't see him anywhere.

Where was the Boss? He needed to stay close to the Boss. He felt himself spinning into a panic.

The room was filling up with more Korean bodyguards in black suits, the unit of the Guard Command accompanying—

The temperature in the room seemed to drop as she walked in. In Eric's ears the hubbub of voices faded to background noise.

She was wearing a black headband to hold back her hair, and the light makeup she had applied gave her smile an almost ethereal softness. On the lapel of her signature black jacket, she wore the small silver emblem of the Workers' Party, but otherwise she had eschewed all adornment. Her blouse was white and slightly frilled at the collar. It was a display of cold, revolutionary virtue. Her posture was elegant, bolt upright. She walked in heels but had taken care that they did not make her taller than her brother.

Eric fixed his eyes on an arrangement of roses and lilies in a vase. His breathing had become shallow. His heart felt as if it were being squeezed by an iron hand. He wanted to hide. He wanted to be anywhere but in this room, but the Boss needed him. Any second now the Boss would call him over. And Bolton—if Bolton reappeared, he somehow had to stop him from confronting the Boss about the secret deal and ruining everything.

Both delegations were socializing freely. Waiters in white gloves were circulating with trays of aperitifs. From the periphery of his vision, he saw the dark blur of her figure approach him like a shadow from a tomb. No one seemed to notice. No one would see anything unusual in her exchanging a few words with him, a member of the US delegation. Eric could not look at her face. His eyeballs would not move in her direction. His fingers and toes had become as cold as frostbite. He started to shiver.

"Well?" she said softly.

Eric barely had the breath to speak. "I . . . I need . . ."

"You've failed, haven't you?"

". . . more time . . . Failed? No. Trump has agreed to stop the w-war games . . ." He was trying to keep his voice low, but it was coming out in a compressed screech. "He will announce it at the p-press conference after the signing ceremony. He will—"

"I gave you an order, Eric Rahn." The stillness of her voice annihilated him.

Finally, he forced himself to look at her. So pretty-plain, so normal, so terrible to behold. She was gazing in the direction of her brother, whose back was toward her, his severe haircut exposing the roll of flesh around his neck. Her profile looked as if it was sculpted from a fine alabaster. Expressionless, except for a slight puckering of her lower eyelids. Inwardly, Eric knew, she had already passed sentence upon him.

"I gave you an order."

She walked away from him, leaving a very faint trace in the air of Chanel Number 5.

He had run out of road. There was no further move he could make; nothing left for him to say. He was flailing, falling. The only way was down.

And he had sounded pathetic. A condemned man. A dead man. A *loser*.

Eric was struggling to breathe now. He felt his knees dissolving and his guts turn to water. His face was breaking out in cold sweat for everyone to see.

The Boss. Where was the Boss? He had to stay near the Boss.

"Mr. Rahn?"

"Yes."

Two suited gorillas of the NSA's security detail were suddenly on either side of him.

"Urgent call for you."

"A call?"

"You can take it in the hotel manager's office."

Jenna was taken in haste toward the banqueting room, with Bolton leading the way. Everything was unfolding in such a rush, and in such an unexpected twist, that she was utterly unprepared for the sight that greeted her as they turned the corner into the lounge where canapés and aperitifs had been served.

Walking toward her was the man with the model-handsome face she'd first seen on her phone in Moscow. The *GQ* magazine cover. "Trump's New Korea Move."

Eric Rahn.

She saw him before he saw her, because his attention had been drawn by the sight of Bolton, whom he glared at with a look of pure loathing. Two grim-faced members of the NSA's security detail were walking very closely to either side of him, so he must have guessed that his removal from the room was a ruse. But did he understand that the game was well and truly up?

Jenna's instinct was to lower her head, hide behind Bolton, not to meet the man's eyes, but she found herself unable not to look at him, this bastard, this sociopath who had haunted Soo-min, who had almost gotten her, Jenna, blown to shreds on Langkawi, who had inveigled himself into the personal confidence of the president of the United States.

Then their eyes met, just for a half-second as they passed, and his face exhibited an immense shock. They both glanced back again at each other as they were led in opposite directions. She saw him mouth *Jenna*. She saw his body recover from its defeated slouch. He seemed electrified, euphoric, as if someone had just given him simultaneous shots of atropine, adrenaline, and cocaine.

The cameras were permitted into the banqueting room for two minutes. Trump stood behind his exalted center seat at the long white table of luxurious silverware and displays of tropical flowers. Kim Jong-un took his place at the center of the opposite side.

Bolton walked straight up to Trump and spoke in a low voice into his ear. "Mr. President, Eric Rahn is indisposed."

"Whaddya mean? Get him in here. I need him now."

"Ms. Williams here will be your interpreter until he returns." Bolton stood aside to reveal Jenna standing behind him.

"It's an honor, Mr. President," she said.

Trump glowered angrily at her, but this was no place to make a scene. The delegates were finding their places to the left and right of the leaders. Jenna took her place just behind the president.

Kim Jong-un smiled at Bolton and addressed him like an old frenemy. "You're famous in my country!" Jenna translated. Bolton, who had been called "human scum" and "bloodsucker" in North Korean state media, smiled as if he'd been paid a marvelous compliment. "Would you like a photo with me?" Kim added. "It might improve your image."

Then Kim Jong-un's sister entered, walking confidently past the men, each of whom turned deferentially toward her. Her aura of power was almost palpable. She was the only other woman present. Kim Jong-un smiled at her and took her arm. The pair, brother and sister, whose father Jenna had watched die onboard a blazing train seven years ago—she had *willed* him to die—were turning toward her. For one appalling instant Jenna feared they were about to speak to her, but Kim Jong-un merely wished to present his sister to Trump.

"Mr. President. My sister, Kim Yo-jong."

Donald Trump was capable of great charm when the occasion demanded, as it did now. He smiled broadly as he took her proffered hand. "It's so great to meet you. Really great. Your brother and I have a great relationship. I saw you at the Winter Olympics, by the way. You looked fantastic."

Jenna translated, keeping her gaze on a middle distance and her head lowered. The Sister gave a small laugh of pleasure, which made Jenna think of rattling ice cubes. And then they took their seats.

Lunch was beef ribs, sweet-and-sour crispy pork, and soy braised cod. Conversation was light, with much talk about basketball and cars. There were no awkward silences because Trump flooded the zone with talk. It was a lot to translate, a constant patter of inanities, repetitions, non-sequiturs and bizarre boasts, but quantity had a quality of its own and the North Koreans were enjoying it. Toasts were proposed; glasses raised. Trump did not drink alcohol and he only pretended to take a sip, she noticed, but the Great Successor, of whom Jenna had a clear view across the table, was already getting rather merry and had undone the top button of his Mao suit. The Sister ate and drank very little; she laid her chopsticks down after every bite and dabbed at her mouth with a napkin.

The North Koreans looked repeatedly toward Jenna—they could hardly *not* look at her, since she had so much of the president's verbiage to translate—but they did not seem to *see* her. She was a nobody. Beneath them. The provider of a service. The fact that she was also African American and a woman made her less than nothing to them, an inconvenient necessity. But still, weren't they curious? A Black woman, speaking Korean . . .

The president jumped from one unrelated topic to another, seemingly at random.

"Chairman Kim," he said, "did you see our friend Dennis Rodman showed up in Singapore yesterday?" Kim, who was basketball crazy, had twice hosted the star player in North Korea. "He was weeping on live TV 'cause he's so happy that you and I are here talking today. So happy for the two of us. I like the guy. Of course, I had to fire him on *Celebrity Apprentice*. When he misspelled Melania's name on an ad campaign, I said: that's it. You're fired. Plus, the thing about Rodman is, you never know when he's gonna fall off the wagon . . ."

Jenna's mind was speeding to interpret this intelligibly for the North Koreans. How could she approximate "fall off the wagon?" With no time to think, she opted for a colloquial expression in North Korean dialect along the lines of "fall down drunk."

The instant the words were out she knew that she'd taken a bad step.

The North Koreans looked at her and this time their eyes stayed on her. For the first time they were *seeing* her.

The Sister was the first to speak. "Mr. President, your staff are most impressive. Today you have given us not one, but two interpreters who are fluent in the Korean dialect of the North. It's most unusual. Even when I visited Seoul, I met no one who spoke our dialect."

"Hey, no one has better staff than I do, right?"

The president continued to talk and talk. Jenna translated.

But the Sister's eyes did not leave her now. It took a great mustering of Jenna's powers of concentration to continue translating the president's bombast into coherent and comprehensible Korean while the focus of the Sister's attention was upon her like a magnifying glass concentrating the sun into a death ray onto an ant. Outwardly, Kim Yo-jong's face remained placid and glacial. Only Jenna, and perhaps Bolton, were sensitive to the wild truth of the situation and might have noticed, had they dared to look directly at her, the progression of emotions unfolding behind the mask.

Uncertainty. Confusion. Recollection. Recognition. Surprise. Shock. Rage.

The only signals of this turmoil were a slight pushing away of her plate, to indicate that she would eat no more, and an infinitesimally mild change in the color of her cheeks, from pale to a faint rose color. Then she turned her head to the man on her right, speaking into his ear at an oblique angle in the manner of the Secret Service, so that her lips could not be read.

The man she had spoken to was about seventy and his hair was dyed jet black. He was a high official of the regime, but Jenna couldn't immediately place him. Then he, too, turned his eyes on Jenna with a look of extreme hostility—and then she recognized him. He was Kim Yong-chol, director of the Reconnaissance General Bureau, North Korea's chief spymaster and one of the most brutal operators in the regime.

Jenna kept her eyes fixed on the president's back. She was desperate to get out of there. For this to wrap up. As far as she was concerned, her job here was done. Eric Rahn had been removed and neutralized. Why was she playing the dupe in some spur-of-the-moment psych-op that Bolton had just dreamed up?

A dark chocolate ganache was being served for dessert. In half an hour the leaders would adjourn to the ballroom for the signing ceremony in front of thousands of reporters and cameras.

The sibylline half-smile had disappeared from the Sister's face. She was now regarding Jenna with unalloyed hatred, and she was reaching for her brother's arm. She was about to whisper into his ear when the Great Successor was asked a question by Trump.

"Want me to show you the Beast? I can show Chairman Kim the Beast, right?" The second question was directed at his Secret Service men standing near the door, who were giving him tight, frantic head-shake signals. *No way.*

Lunch was over. Jenna followed the president toward the door.

Suddenly the seventy-year-old spymaster was at her elbow.

"I hope you don't think me impertinent, young lady, but we think we recognize you. You have been to our country, perhaps. May I know your name?"

Before Jenna could say a word, he had grabbed the security lanyard hanging from her neck and turned it so that he could read her printed name. He stopped walking, causing the ribbon around her neck to pull tight. The man appeared shocked to the core, as if he'd just seen an evil spirit, a devil of the seven hells incarnated as a lowly interpreter. The color leached from his face, making his dyed hair even blacker and wig-like. In the same moment Bolton joined them.

"This is an outrage," the man breathed. He was shaking with anger and fear. "What are you playing at? How *dare* you bring this human scum before Comrade Kim Jong-un." Unfortunately, he had no choice of interpreter. Kim's had left the room with him. Jenna translated. "Do you expect us to sign the joint declaration after this? You have gravely insulted us."

Bolton bared his teeth beneath the floor-brush mustache. His voice came out in a cold, compressed anger.

"Oh, the Great Comrade is going to sign, all right." He gave a mock-friendly squeeze to the spymaster's elbow. "President Trump can be very, ah, *unpredictable* when he doesn't get what he wants."

The Sister was watching all this. She turned imperiously on her heels when Jenna looked at her and followed the rest of the delegation out of the room, her neck straight, head held high, in that much-remarked-upon comportment and grace.

Outside the hotel's main doors Trump was showing off the Beast to Kim. For one crazy moment Jenna wondered if they were going to drive off somewhere together, but the Boss's Secret Service agents intervened. *No North Koreans near the presidential car.* Instead, the two leaders opted for a stroll in the grounds—just the two of them, for the cameras, as if they'd announced their engagement.

Jenna was not needed for the next few minutes. She crossed the lobby to the manager's office. She was determined finally to confront the man who had wreaked so much havoc on her own life and Soo-min's. She had questions of her own for him, before the investigators laid into him.

But as she approached the office door she stopped.

It was ajar. The lock had been forced, splintering the wood. She nudged it open slowly with the tip of her shoe and saw the detritus of a massive struggle. Chair overturned, papers over the floor, telephones off the hook, framed certificates knocked from the walls and smashed. The two men who had been assigned to guard Eric Rahn lay semiconscious on the floor, both clutching head wounds. One of them groaned.

Jenna ran back into the lobby, which was now crowded with diplomats, aides, press, and security waiting for the signing ceremony. She shoved people out of the way until she saw the nearest Secret Service man standing watch. "Two officers down in there. Call a medic."

Where the hell had he gone? There was nowhere he could go!

82

Capella Hotel
Singapore

Eric held up his security lanyard and walked calmly out through the front door of the hotel.

"Sir, if you leave now, we can't let you back in."

"Sure."

He removed his tie and saw that his shirt was torn, his buttons lost. The knuckles of his right hand were sore and starting to swell painfully from pummeling those men's heads. The glare of the afternoon light was intense. He felt in his pocket for his sunglasses, but he must have lost them in the struggle.

He guessed that the decision to arrest him was not general knowledge. The Americans would try to keep it quiet. But soon, the alert would go out and they would come after him. The window of opportunity he had made for himself was small, but it was a window.

How had they found him out?

Her, of course.

He started laughing quietly to himself with all the release of a man who was finally free. In fact, he was feeling vibrant, elated. He was feeling galvanized and revivified. Violence was such a thrilling restorative. A tonic. A shot in the arm. A pure high.

For one uncanny moment he'd thought it was Soo-min passing him in that corridor.

Identical, and yet different. The same, and not the same. Amazing.

So, she's here. Jenna Williams is here. Most Wanted Person Number One. On this tiny island. Fortune has thrown me one last chance and I'm not going to waste it.

That the Yankees would be so brazen, so vile and shameless, as to allow *that woman* anywhere near to the Great Successor . . . well, it was astonishing to him. It *disgusted* him, outraged him. He had to do something.

Where would he wait for her? Where could he go so that she might follow? She might not follow him at all, of course, but his instinct told him that she would. The two of them had just set eyes on each other for the first time and it had electrified him—electrified them both. He'd seen it in her face. What were the chances of them seeing each other just now, on this day, in this place? There were no coincidences like that. Fortune was contriving to join their paths . . . and neither of them was done with the other yet.

One of us is going to die, Jenna—and it's not going to be me.

A short distance to the right of the portico he spotted a small, secluded garden for the use of the hotel's guests, off-limits to everyone else. In its center was a decorative copse of lush tropical trees—rain trees and tembusu trees—with a circular stone path around its perimeter providing a shaded walk. He headed toward it.

It was cooler beneath the trees. The sultry light filtered through the leaves, which were such a lurid lime green that they seemed almost artificial. Branches creaked in the breeze. Mynah birds called.

But Eric didn't notice the beauty of the garden. He was possessed by a single thought. It was stark, simple, and binary.

Kill Jenna, and all will be forgiven. Avenge the Great Successor's father, whose miraculous life ended at that she-devil's hands, and all past failures will be forgotten, all sins washed away.

Kill, or be killed.

He slowed his pace as he looked for a place where he could hide in ambush. Why was everything so manicured and neat and clean? He detested the orderliness of this country. He yearned for chaos, disorder, entropy . . .

Some corner of Eric's heart knew that he was under the effect of a grand delusion, insanity. Some quiet voice in the back of his head was warning him that he should have stayed in that locked office, in American custody, because his *only* chance of survival was to leave with the Americans, even if it meant spending the rest of his life in a supermax penitentiary. The Supreme Sister was not going to allow him to live, even if he killed Jenna for her. Even, for that matter, if he'd succeeded in murdering Ha-jun. In a cooler, less unhinged frame of mind, he might have understood that the Sister was never going to risk letting him spill her secret—that she had gone rogue behind her brother's back, that she had been pruning the family tree of all heirs and successors to clear her own path toward absolute power . . .

Yes, a part of him knew the truth. But he didn't care anymore. His delusion was a comforting one, and it was momentarily keeping at bay that fathomless black void that had always been inside him and would soon engulf him for good.

Kill, or be killed.

Jenna ran through the hotel door and into the humid afternoon light. Beyond the portico was a view of the broad, downward-sloping lawn and the grand driveway. It was guarded by dozens of police and Secret Service agents standing at regular intervals along the driveway's edge. To the left, a large crowd of news cameramen and reporters, hundreds of them, were being kept behind a cordon until the joint declaration was signed and the leaders emerged.

But off to the right she spotted a stone path leading into a small, private garden. An arboretum of tropical trees.

He must have gone in there. There was no other place he could have gone.

"Sir," she said to the nearest Secret Service agent. "I'm concerned about a male individual who may have gone into that garden. I need you to come with me."

"No, ma'am, that was Mr. Rahn. He's on the president's staff."

"Mr. Rahn's clearance has been revoked. We need to apprehend him."

He turned to her, expressionless behind his Oakleys, his protocols kicking in. In an unconvinced, deadpan voice he said, "I'll radio for backup, ma'am, but I can't leave my post."

Jenna wasn't going to wait for backup. She couldn't.

The North Koreans could easily spirit him away from here. What if Soo-min's tormentor escaped? What if the man who'd almost blown her to bits on Langkawi got away scot-free?

The injustice of it, the rising panic that he was about to slip the net, was disabling her instincts, making her ignore the red warning lights that were starting to flash all over her mind.

She entered the garden.

Peacocks trailed long blue feathers. Sparrows launched off the grass in one chirruping flock as she approached.

The atmosphere was strangely private and still, considering it was surrounded by multiple rings of security, and watched over by a thousand news cameras, dozens of helicopters, and the secret services of the two nations congregated in the building behind her.

She stepped off the path and into the copse. The canopy of the trees cast a lovely shade. She stopped and listened. Nothing but the drone of insects and the squawking of parakeets.

She advanced slowly, soundlessly.

And there, on the peaty ground between the lush green ferns she saw Eric's security lanyard, with his name and photo ID, and a pair of black shoes. His shoes?

The light darkened suddenly. Instinct made her look up.

She had a split-second impression of an enormous beast falling from the tree before Eric's body slammed onto her and knocked her instantly to the ground, his full weight on top of her. She was winded, disorientated. Before she knew what was happening, he'd slid his tie around her neck. His head was next to hers. She could feel the heat of his breath in her ear.

"Jenna."

For a few seconds they writhed violently, intimately, in the dirt, straining and grappling—Jenna trying to free her arms from under her to break his hold, Eric struggling to find purchase for the noose.

Before he could maneuver his knees either side of her to sit upright and start choking her, she head-butted him hard with the back of her head.

He cried out in pain. The garotte loosened.

Then with all the power in her arms and legs she pushed herself up onto all fours, so that he rolled off her onto the ground.

Her lungs were heaving from the exertion. He scrambled to his feet, his back to a tree trunk. He touched his ruined nose and examined the blood on his hand, and she saw the sting of outraged vanity in his eyes.

He launched himself at her again and shot out his leg to kick her head. She ducked, spun around, and back-kicked him hard with the ball of her foot—right in the liver. He doubled over.

From somewhere beyond the trees, off to the right, they heard Secret Service agents speaking into two-way radios.

"You're out of practice, Eric."

A subdued commotion was coming from the direction of the hotel, making them both turn their heads. Security personnel were entering the garden and fanning out cautiously left and right along the stone path surrounding the copse, their black suits visible between the trees. Some were holding—not firearms; none were permitted on the island for the duration of the summit—but what looked like Tasers.

"It's over," she said, panting. "You're surrounded."

Between the trees they had a glimpse of more men moving along the paths: to the right were North Korean bodyguards of the Supreme Guard Command; to the left were American Secret Service agents. There must have been forty in all.

Eric gave a bloody smile. "So are you."

Then he lunged at her with all the ferocity of a cornered bear.

Jenna's reaction was reflexive and lighting fast. She stepped toward him, pivoted her body sideways and launched a massive turning kick to his neck with her right foot, using the swing momentum of her hips. It unbalanced him, sent him staggering sideways. She aimed a second kick with her left leg. He ducked it and swung a hard punch to the side of her head.

The two of them separated, fists raised, feet apart, inching around each other in a sparring posture. The side of her head was stinging with pain.

"This is an interesting situation, Jenna," he said, starting to laugh. "Yankees behind me. Comrades behind you. Who's going to claim who?"

"I guess the odds are even."

If she hadn't been so flared up with tension and adrenaline Jenna might have admitted that she was intrigued by the man in front of her. Eric's shirt was now dirt-stained and soaked with sweat and blood. His hair had come loose. But he was outwardly a very beautiful creature, a trick of nature that fools humans into seeing meaning only on the surface. And she could discern an unnerving madness in his eyes—something bestial that had shaken free inside him, but which was usually well concealed. He was the Seed-Bearing Program made flesh, a pure-bred psychopath, a sabotage machine.

"Crazy, isn't it?" he said. "Meeting like this today, after all this time."

Say nothing. This guy is not going to get inside my head.

"Here we are brawling like drunks in a bar when we could've used this precious time to talk about your sister's son . . ."

And just like that he got inside her head.

Jenna stayed silent, but the surprise in her eyes must have betrayed her, and the power seemed to drain from her limbs, starting with her fists.

"That's right," he said. "Your nephew. Ha-jun. Took me *years* to find him."

"You found him?" she breathed.

"Nice guy, actually. Takes after his mother. A little lacking in confidence, perhaps."

Some synapse in her brain was sparking and connecting. She was jumping to a conclusion, but she knew with the force of revelation that it was the right one.

"That's why you were in San Francisco."

Eric took a step toward her. She moved back a step.

He said, "Soo-min never told you who the father was, did she?"

The father?

Ha-jun's father had been a young man named Jae-hoon—her sister's boyfriend, who had been abducted with her in 1998. That's what Soo-min told her, and Soo-min would never have lied about that. So why was she feeling a weakness overcoming her like a virus, a sense that malware was installing in her brain, disarming her from the inside?

"Jae-hoon," she said with a quiet defiance. "Ha-jun's father was Jae-hoon."

"No," Eric said pityingly, and started to laugh again. "I'm talking about his real, biological father, although . . . the kid certainly doesn't take after *him*. I saw no greatness in Ha-jun . . ."

A swooshing noise ended in a dull thunk.

Both of them turned to see a feathered dart embedded in the trunk of a tree that stood halfway between them to her left. It had been shot from the direction of the Guard Command. Through the trees to the right, she saw a North Korean bodyguard down on one knee and aiming a long-barreled gun like the one she'd seen in Siberia.

"Who?" Jenna said, unable to help herself. "Who is the father?"

Eric's laugh was silent and manic.

"Oh, you're going to be mad when you hear this . . ."

Behind Eric's head, Jenna could see the foliage moving—American Secret Service agents were entering the trees at a crouch, aiming Tasers.

And the instant she took her eyes off him, he grabbed her neck with both hands and shoved her hard, forcing her to a gap between the trees where the North Korean bodyguard had a clear line of sight.

The swooshing sound came again.

"You're part of the F—"

The world went silent and still. Time stopped.

The dart was bedded deep into the side of Eric's neck. His throat gurgled with pain and laughter. He managed to pull it out and throw it aside.

". . . the Family."

Then he dropped to his knees in front of her, and fell heavily, face-first, to the ground.

Without pausing to think or look behind her, Jenna scrambled through the ferns toward the Americans, to safety.

What the hell just happened?

The North Koreans couldn't have missed her.

They had deliberately shot Eric Rahn.

From the direction of the hotel came the rising swell of applause. The joint declaration had been signed.

By the time she found Bolton, standing at the back of the ballroom, behind the press and cameras, the North Korean delegation had already departed. Trump's press conference was wrapping up and he was now inviting "respectful" questions from the press. Her clothes were dirty; she was in a state of utter confusion, and her ear was ringing with pain.

Bolton did not take his eyes off the president as Jenna spoke into his ear.

"The North Koreans took Eric Rahn, sir."

He turned to look at her, stupefied. "He escaped?"

"Yes, go ahead . . ."

"Not exactly."

"*Yeah, we will be stopping the war games. I think they're very provocative . . .*"

Bolton's head shot back toward the president.

"*They're inappropriate. So, number one: we save money—a LOT . . .*"

"What the hell . . ."

"*And number two: I think it's something they really appreciate . . .*"

Bolton looked as if he were about to have a brain aneurysm. She could see the blood pumping in the veins of his neck. "We did *not* agree this . . ."

"Did North Korea give you anything in return, sir?"

"*Well, we've gotten, you know, I've heard that. Some people are saying the president agreed to meet, he has given up so much. I gave up nothing. I'm here. I haven't slept in twenty-five hours, but I thought it was appropriate to do, because we have been negotiating for literally around the clock with them . . .*"

Bolton had turned puce in the face. He was shaking with anger. "This man."

83

Wannsee
Berlin, Germany
Summer 2018

It was a perfect afternoon for a picnic on the Strandbad, the lakeside beach in the leafy Wannsee district of west Berlin. The air was so still and warm that sounds carried clearly across the dark-blue water, even from the far shore. This had the odd effect of causing everyone to keep their voices low. The beach, although crowded with sunbathers, was placid and subdued. Even the wavelets around the small white sailing boats seemed to splash more quietly than usual.

Lyosha had been so overjoyed to see Anya that he couldn't stop embracing her and telling her how well she looked. This was partly to conceal his alarm at the change in her appearance. Her hair was no longer the pixie pink of last year in Moscow, but Bible black, which made her skin appear very pale, and she'd lost a lot of weight, as if the fight had gone out of her. He had been at the Ostbahnhof earlier to meet her off a sleeper train that had come via Warsaw. The journey had tired her, naturally, but she also seemed dazed and frightened as her momentous new reality began to bite.

She had left Russia. She had no idea if she would ever return.

Lyosha and Marina tried to entertain her with a ceaseless stream of upbeat chatter until Lyosha realized it was exhausting her. She was sitting quietly at the edge of the picnic rug, smiling for form's sake, raking the warm sand with her fingers. Her face was hard to read behind the enormous sunglasses. She seemed to rally a little when Marina laid out the picnic, producing a frosted bottle of vodka from the cooler, and a tiny jar of caviar she'd bought in Berözka, the Russian delicatessen, along with some smoked kolbasa sausages to eat with rye bread. Lyosha passed around the small *stopka* glasses.

"Well, we tried," Anya said, raising her glass. "To Putin! Down with him."

"To the future," Lyosha said, gently.

"To love," Marina said, unexpectedly, and to Lyosha's shock he saw his mother begin to cry. He dropped his glass and hugged her, and Anya, seeing Marina's distress, seemed to forget all thoughts of herself. She took Marina's hand. For a few minutes they were an emotional trio. Lyosha put his strong arms around them both, which to a casual observer might have resembled a sacred composition: Christ with his mother and Mary Magdalene.

Marina dried her tears and gave an apologetic laugh, which reset the mood of the occasion like the sun after rain. All three of them felt their individual strains and doubts suddenly lift. In Anya, this was apparent the moment she spoke again: the timbre and volume of her voice was restored.

"I nearly forgot!" she cried. "I brought you something for you from Moscow." She rummaged in her bag and retrieved two small packages wrapped in tissue paper. Marina's contained a snow globe showing the Kremlin and the Moskva river. "To remind you of the view from your apartment," she said. It was just a silly piece of tourist tat, but Marina loved it.

Lyosha's contained a tiny box tied with a ribbon.

"What's this?" he said. "A ring?"

He undid the ribbon and opened the lid.

Later, that moment would remind him of a notion Freud had

called *unheimlich*, or the "uncanny": that feeling you have in dreams and occasionally in reality when something is not only mysterious but frightening in an oddly familiar way.

Inside the box, on a bed of cotton wool, were his gold cufflinks.

"I guess you'll never wear them, but I knew you'd want them back," Anya said. "They were your father's."

Lyosha looked up at her, his face a huge question mark.

Anya shrugged. "I saw those KGB men in Minsk stealing your stuff. So I stole it back from the trunk of their shitty-ass Lada parked outside the hospital. Oh, here—I got your wallet too."

84

Singapore

Amid all the action and drama of the last few days, Jenna had had no mental space to call home and tell her family that she was alive and well. The phone she'd been given when the *Hanjin* had docked in Busan had already been lost—smashed and broken during the struggle with Eric Rahn in the garden. When the press conference in Singapore ended, a brisk and rather striking young woman on John Bolton's staff gave Jenna a phone so that she could finally call her family.

But when she'd started keying in her mother's number, a thought gave her pause.

How would she account for her long absence (the first thing Han would ask)? Her silence? Had the government, or anyone, given her family some explanation? The op in Russia had been classified. As far as her mother was concerned, she'd been in Kuala Lumpur. Could she now reveal where she'd been? That she'd suffered fifteen months in a Russian prison? Amid all the action and drama of the last twenty-four hours she hadn't thought to ask anyone about the official line. She tried calling Fisk again, but he was on a flight to Moscow. Mira was incommunicado but had sent her a brief message via Singapore Station to express her immense relief that Jenna was back in safe hands, and to say that she was looking forward to seeing her in the next few days, if she was feeling strong enough.

While Jenna pondered this, she used the phone to log into the security cameras surrounding her house in Annandale—for the first time since she'd gone to Russia, more than a year ago.

Her biggest fear was that Soo-min's condition had worsened while she'd been away. In the past, if anything had been wrong at home, Jenna could usually tell simply by looking at the house. During Soo-min's relatively good spells, the house and garden were neat and maintained. When Soo-min was suffering one of her episodes, and all her mother's time and energy were devoted to her care, the house was neglected and went into a noticeable decline.

But when she saw it, in the camera app's live-feed, freshly painted and glowing in the summer morning light, she felt her vision swimming. The lawn had been mowed. The windows were sparkling and clean. Flower beds had been weeded. Mom's car was parked in its usual spot. Soo-min's bedroom window was open, as were the curtains. Nothing was amiss. All the signs were good.

Again, she started to call her mother's number . . . but then she had a much better idea.

She would turn up on the doorstep and give them an amazing surprise. A homecoming to remember.

She found the young woman who had lent her the phone and gave it back to her.

"Oh, that's OK," the young woman said, with a cool smile. "You can keep it. It's an office secure phone. One of the spares."

"You sure? Thanks, I appreciate it. What's your name?"

"Sofia Ali. John's executive assistant."

Jenna was beyond exhausted. It was going to take her a long time to recover her fitness, physically and mentally. She hadn't even begun to process and make sense of all that had happened in Singapore. She certainly didn't yet have the psychological stamina she'd need to disarm and dismantle the depth charges Eric Rahn had dropped inside her head.

Was anything he'd said actually true? Had he really found Hajun? Or had he been playing some psychopath's mind-game? These questions had the power to unhinge her—and Rahn had known it.

By the time she arrived at the airport for the long flight home, she had convinced herself that it was the latter: Rahn had been deliberately fucking with her.

Of course he had. It was obvious.

Lie, manipulate, gaslight. Debase, coerce, control.

That was his skillset. That was his MO. He hadn't simply wanted to kill her in that garden. He'd wanted to abase her and destroy her sanity—and then kill her.

She'd met a very similar type in Vladimir Putin . . .

She wondered where Rahn was now. Back in Pyongyang, probably. Feeling groggy and nauseous as he came round from the tranquilizer. Maybe he was even strapped to a hard, upright chair, facing bright lights and an interrogator, or tied to a stretcher, feeling the electrodes being pinched onto to his sensitive parts. She'd probably never know the reason they'd attacked him and not her. The machinations of the Kim cult were mysterious and opaque, even to its initiates.

She was just settling into her seat, getting comfortable before takeoff; she had her ear plugs in and the blanket over her, and was looking forward to a good sleep, when the phone buzzed. The borrowed phone Bolton's assistant had given her.

She took it out and looked at it. It had one percent battery. She had no names or numbers stored in this phone, and she couldn't even guess who was sending her a link for an article in today's *Korea JoongAng Daily*, a Korean-language newspaper widely read by the community in Annandale, or even know if the message was intended for her.

She opened it, and in almost the same instant the screen died.

In the split second before the battery gave out, she'd seen a photograph of an unsmiling, strangely familiar-looking youth with a shock of unruly black hair—familiar-looking . . . because he'd had an uncanny resemblance to herself and Soo-min.

Beneath the photo she'd seen a caption:

YOUNG DEFECTOR CLAIMS HE IS THE LOST SON OF KIM JONG-IL

PART SEVEN
Virginia

Donald J. Trump @realdonaldtrump
Our relationship with Russia has NEVER been worse thanks to many years of U.S. foolishness and stupidity and now the Rigged Witch Hunt!

Ministry of Foreign Affairs, Russia @mfa_russia
We agree

85

Annandale, Virginia
One day later

Jenna gave the front door a tentative knock and stood back to wait on the step.

This was the moment she'd fantasized about for more than a year, the scene that had come to her in dreams almost every night in her freezing Russian cell.

"Hey! It's Jenna!" she called, and knocked again. "I'm home!"

But she was not feeling the relief of a homecoming. The very real excitement she was experiencing right now—for the imminent, joyous reunion with Soo-min and her mom—was marred by an ominous unease, a residual horror from the news she'd glimpsed in that link before the phone died on the plane.

There was no answer at the door, even though she thought she'd heard movement inside the house, so she went to look for the spare latchkey that her mother had always kept hidden beneath a pot behind the garage.

She had spent the entire flight from Singapore sitting upright and hyper-awake. Sleep had been out of the question. She could not still her mind or her feet or her hands, so great was the shock of knowing the truth about Ha-jun's father.

Eric Rahn *had* been telling her the truth—torturing her with the truth. What a sadistic satisfaction he must have taken in it. She was quite sure that he had revealed a deep and sensitive secret that she was never meant to know, but he hadn't seemed to care. There had been a madness, a desperation in him. His final act had been to make damn sure she knew that the joke was on her, and that the ridiculous irony of her life was exposed—that the dynasty whose power she'd spent years working against was her own kin. She was related by blood to the Family, a family of monsters. She had been biologically compromised by her enemies in the most personal way imaginable. They owned her. Her own family was theirs. One and the same.

For the first few hours after the cabin lights had dimmed, she'd felt as if she was on a bad trip, literally—as if she'd ingested some malignant psychedelic that was peeling away her mind, splitting into fractals her most cherished beliefs about her sister, herself.

How could Soo-min not have told her? How could she have lied to her own twin about something like that? Someone with her sister's genes now carried the Kims' genes! Their family had been poisoned!

But as the first waves of revulsion had subsided, she'd felt deeply ashamed of these thoughts. Soo-min had been a victim. She'd had no choices. She'd been abused and exploited in a manner more profound, more complete than Jenna could ever have imagined. Soon, her disgust had given way to anger, and compassion. She felt enraged on Soo-min's behalf; her heart bled for her, and for Ha-jun. The son was innocent of the crime done to his mother, and his mother had loved him and cared for him desperately. Ha-jun had Soo-min's blood, and she his. The sins of the father would not be visited upon the child.

She thought back to that fateful day she'd rescued her sister, which now, with the passage of time, seemed to have become imbued with the dreamlike haziness of a legend.

Soo-min had been a member of Kim Jong-il's personal entourage. She'd been present on board his private armored train, in attendance upon him, made-up, and dressed in a silken *hanbok* dress. Soo-min had never explained why she'd been on that train. Now, it was all too easy to understand. She had been a favorite, someone whom Kim Jong-il liked to keep near him, a woman he had perhaps been abusing for years.

A woman with whom he'd had a child. A son.

Soo-min had had no control over her fate in North Korea. No agency, no free will. So why, after she'd been brought home, was she never able to recover . . .

Another piece of the jigsaw dropped into place.

The abuse didn't end.

It had *continued*—in Virginia, when Eric Rahn started showing up, playing his mind games on her, lying to her, controlling her.

At first, in the six months after her return, Soo-min's condition had seemed to improve. Back then, she was still full of optimism that Ha-jun would be found. As time went on, and the search became hopeless, she'd slid into a mental and physical hole from which she'd never really emerged. Jenna had always believed it was because of Ha-jun—that she began to despair as she lost hope that he was ever going to be found.

But maybe there'd been another reason. Soo-min had never mentioned Rahn. Why?

Because he'd threatened her, or threatened harm to Ha-jun if she didn't cooperate.

Why?

Because she was his only link to me. To finding me. "Most Wanted Person Number One." The only witness to Kim Jong-il's death.

Piece by piece, over the course of that interminable flight, the caverns and tunnels of this mystery were being illuminated. Its shadows were receding.

But there were still questions. *Why* had Ha-jun been sent to the United States when he was eight years old, apparently with the intention that he should never be found?

Once again, an answer presented itself, as revealing as a moonbeam falling on a hidden door. She was stunned that she had not seen it sooner.

Ha-jun was a threat.

In the sacred revolutionary bloodline of Mount Paektu, Kim Jong-un was not the dynasty's rightful successor. He was Kim Jong-il's third son, the youngest. PANDA, the first son, was the true heir, followed by PANDA's twenty-one-year-old son, Yong-won. Both had been murdered, one after the other. Kim Jong-un had been shearing off branches of the Family to make sure that his own legitimacy was never challenged by any of his brothers or their sons.

And the father, Kim Jong-il, must have *known this would happen* when he anointed the ruthless young Jong-un as his successor . . .

Is that why Kim Jong-il sent Ha-jun away while he was still only a boy? So that the son he'd sired with a favorite concubine would not be harmed?

He'd picked the right destination to send him. The Main Enemy America would have been a difficult place for North Korean agents to launch a manhunt.

Took me years to find him, Rahn had said.

By the time Jenna had landed in DC, unrested, strung-out, her mind a smoldering landscape of smoke and ash, she felt as if she'd been through the five stages of grief. Denial, anger, bargaining, depression, acceptance. And with acceptance she felt a distinct sensation that the great spell that had kept her twin a prisoner in her own mind, that had made her opaque and mysterious to the normal world, was now starting to break.

She had found the latchkey. She was about to let herself into the house.

Did Soo-min know about yesterday's article in the *Korea Joong-Ang Daily*? Surely her mom knew. Someone would have called to tell her. Fisk would have called!

She closed the front door quietly behind her. The aromas of

baking and furniture polish were more positive signs. The place looked as spic and span as she'd ever seen it.

"Hello?"

Laundry had been folded into a neat stack on the stairs, ready to be put away. Surfaces gleamed. An arrangement of fresh flowers stood in the mock-celadon vase on the windowsill.

"Anyone home?"

She walked through to the dining room and stopped dead in her tracks.

Soo-min was sitting at the dining-room table with her back toward Jenna. She was wearing an enormous pair of headphones and gently moving her head to some inaudible beat. A laptop was open in front of her.

Jenna did a slow blink. Her sister wasn't wearing a bathrobe, nor was she lying in bed, or staring into space. She was sitting up, dressed in jeans and a white linen shirt. And she appeared preoccupied with what looked like an actual activity. Her hair had a healthy sheen and was loosely tied back in a ponytail. A blue raincoat, which Jenna had bought for her a few years ago and had never seen her wear, was draped over one of the dining chairs as if she had just been out or was about to go out. Jenna didn't dare move or blink again. She was afraid the vision before her might vanish as suddenly as a rainbow.

Soo-min glanced at her watch. *When had she started wearing a watch?* Then she pulled off the headphones and tilted her head toward the ceiling.

"Mom! It's two o'clock. If you want me to drive you to Mrs. Choi's, let's go now. Do you want me to put the cake in a box?"

Jenna, still motionless in the doorway, gave an involuntary exhalation of breath.

Soo-min's shoulders tensed at the sound and she half-turned, startled. For the tiniest moment her face was full of dread, but then her eyes popped wide in amazement.

"Oh!"

She stood up from her chair, and for a few moments neither of them moved. They both stared, taking each other in. It was as if some vast synchronization was taking place—too large to be instant. And then, a tremendous kinetic force seemed to pass simultaneously from twin to twin.

"It's you," Soo-min whispered, and started to laugh. They embraced in the center of the room. "It's you."

"Soo-min," Jenna gasped, pressing her cheek to her sister's and holding her so tightly she could barely breathe. Her twin was still bone-thin. Whatever transformation had taken place it had happened recently. Their tears flowed silently at first, their bodies shaking. Her sister's hair smelled of jasmine and freesias. Her skin was clear and healthy. "What happened?"

Soo-min could not speak through her laughter, tears, a bodily shaking. It was almost as if she was having a seizure. Her nostrils had turned pink from crying. "Where have you been?" she managed at last. "We thought you'd gone forever."

Their reunion was interrupted by Han's footsteps coming stiffly down the stairs. Jenna could see her mother's slippered feet appear through the banisters.

"I'm not taking the cake," she was saying in Korean. "Last time I went to the trouble Choi had the nerve to tell me she was on a diet, although you'd never know from looking at her—"

Han froze on the bottom step when she saw the scene in the living room: the complete twin set of her daughters, standing arm in arm, hand in hand, facing her. A spooked, fearful look crossed her face like a shadow, as if she had seen a spirit of the dead.

"Omma," Jenna said and reached for her hand.

Han was so overcome that she flopped down on the bottom step in a semi-faint. For the next few minutes mother and daughter were breathless from tears of heartbreak and relief until Han finally managed to pull herself together and shout, "Where on *earth* have you been!" in a tone so familiar that Jenna could have exploded with joy.

The household in Annandale had come alive again and was full of sound, like a hedgerow in spring after a long punishing winter.

So intense and helpless were their emotions and so difficult was it for any of them to speak at all—or when they did, they talked across each other—that when Jenna managed to say, "The news—about Ha-jun!" and Soo-min said at the same time, "We've had news about Ha-jun!" they both came to a momentary halt, and then spoke across each other again:

"You know he's been found?"

"He's made contact with me."

Jenna's hands went to her cheeks. "What? How? When?"

Soo-min clapped her hands, tipped her head back, and laughed. Then she fetched the *Korea JoongAng Daily* from the table and showed Jenna the full article.

This is what had transformed her sister—pulled her clear out of her depression as dramatically as if a rescue helicopter had scooped her up from the basin of a flooded valley.

> *Stephen Lee, an eighteen-year-old high-school student from San Francisco, claims he is the fourth son of North Korea's late leader Kim Jong-il and the half-brother of the present leader Kim Jong-un.*
>
> *Lee, who came to the US aged eight, says he was raised by his American mother in North Korea before being sent away to live with Korean foster parents . . .*

In the center of the page was a color photograph of a shy-looking young man sitting at a café table. He was holding up an expired North Korean passport opened at the photo page. Clearly visible was his name, Kim Ha-jun. Place of birth: Pyongyang. Date of birth: January 10, 2000.

"We got a call last week from the *San Francisco Chronicle*," Han said. "A reporter asked if I was Soo-min's mother. I knew something was going on, because no one asks me that these days . . ."

Over the next hour, Soo-min and Han told Jenna what information they knew, which, it turned out, was still quite sketchy.

There had been some kind of knife attack in a crowded gay bar in San Francisco during Pride weekend. Someone had died in the attack. Ha-jun, or Stephen as he wanted to be known, had presented himself to the police as a witness to the attack. The police found Stephen's DNA, and the victim's blood, on a T-shirt that had been thrown into a trashcan by the suspect, a screenshot of whom had been captured from CCTV. When the police questioned Stephen again, he told them that he had been the intended victim. Then the whole story came out. The cops dismissed it as fantasy, but a reporter got wind of it.

The monochrome passport photo that Stephen was holding up to the camera showed a po-faced eight-year-old who could have been anyone, which perhaps explained the crazy-if-true tone of the article. The reporter seemed to be hedging, reserving judgment in case this boy turned out to be delusional.

> *I ask Stephen why he thinks he's Kim's son. "Because I met him many times," he says, candidly. "He treated me differently from the other kids. He'd visit the compound where I lived with my mom. He'd bring me gifts, like candies and video games. My mom told me he was my father. That's one of my first memories from North Korea."*

Jenna stopped reading and reached for Soo-min's hand. The joy in the room seemed to fade to sadness tinged with pain and shame. Han looked away, but Soo-min met her eyes, and in them Jenna saw a soul that had passed beyond all suffering and torment and now thirsted only for knowledge and love.

"I survived," she said, gently. "And so did Ha-jun."

We're sitting in Coffee Shack, just off San Francisco's Union Square. "This is the first time I've shared this story with anyone," Stephen says. He admits that he's nervous, and no wonder. The story he tells me sounds like a Greek tragedy with a spy thriller twist.

"My mom was from Virginia. I was never told how she ended up in North Korea, but I'm pretty sure she was one of the abduction victims..."

Stephen explained that his father, Kim Jong-il, had suffered a serious stroke in the summer of 2008, and wasn't seen in public for months. The dictator knew he didn't have long to live and was in a hurry to name a successor. He must have understood his chosen successor's character pretty well, because that's why he decided to send Stephen somewhere where he could not be reached or found. He was being protected from his own half-brother, Kim Jong-un.

Stephen was entrusted to Korean foster parents for his protection. The article mentioned nothing at all about how he'd arrived in the US, under what documentation, or where he'd been living.

Asked why he'd decided to come out of hiding, he said that the tragedy in the bar on Castro had been the final straw for him. "Someone died because of me. An innocent person died because the killer thought he was me. I had to come forward. I couldn't handle the guilt. I owed the truth to the victim, and his family."

But he was also deeply unsettled, he said, by the recent friendliness in Singapore between President Trump and Kim Jong-un. "I was afraid that if Kim Jong-un asked Trump to give me up, Trump might say yes. Hiding's not an option for me anymore. They've already found me once. I figured it would be harder to send me back if the world knows me. I don't feel comfortable with it. Generally speaking, I'm a very private person..."

"The reporter thought Soo-min was still a missing person," Han said. "He was stunned when I told him that she's sitting right next to me."

It was the reporter who had broken the news to Stephen that his mother was alive and living in Virginia. A phone call with Stephen was arranged, from the *Chronicle*'s office in San Francisco.

"He didn't say much," Soo-min said simply. "He asked me a few questions that only I would know the answers to, but of course I knew the answers. He went quiet after that. The call lasted only a few minutes. And he would only speak in English. I think he has doubts . . ."

"Of course he's suspicious!" Han said. "Who can blame him, after all he's been through?"

"That's why we called Charles Fisk," Soo-min said. "To ask his advice about a visit."

"When?"

"Soon, I hope," Soo-min said. "In the next few weeks. Mr. Fisk wants to speak to Stephen to put his mind at ease. To tell him that he knows us. That we're his real family and that we can't wait to meet him."

It was Fisk who had sent Jenna the link.

Jenna thought of Eric Rahn just then. She wondered if now was a good moment to talk about that. But she didn't know if her mother had been told about him. It was possible that Soo-min had kept the horrible nightmare of knowing Eric Rahn from her.

Just as she was thinking this, she received another link from Charles Fisk. She'd managed to partially charge the phone in the cab ride from Dulles. This time it was to an archived news article from April 2017: Missing nurse's body recovered from Potomac.

At home in Annandale, Jenna slept for much of the next three weeks. Han's home-cooking—meals Jenna had taken utterly for granted when she was growing up—made her feel so much humility and gratitude after the months of prison gruel, that she would find her eyes tearing up when her mother, smiling at her lovingly, placed various childhood favorites in front of her. Fisk said that he had been in contact with Stephen about a meeting, and the family had gotten the impression that some kind of negotiation was underway, about which Fisk was tight-lipped. Mira had sent baskets of fruit and chocolates, and a fresh display of flowers each Monday, with cards wishing her a speedy recovery. Jenna sensed some imperative, some urgency, behind all this solicitude from Mira: Russia House was anxious for her debriefing. Soo-min was a constant companion, a renewed source of joy and wonder to Jenna. Her sister's life had finally been unpaused. She would sit on Jenna's bed and talk about everything and anything, in a way she hadn't done for years. She laughed, she made plans for the two of them, she reconnected with old friends who hadn't heard from her in twenty years. But behind it all, Jenna saw, there was a nerviness, a fear of what was coming next. How would her son react to her when they finally met again? How would she explain her own guilt over all that had happened?

In July, her government phone, the one given to her in Singapore, which had remained silent next to her for weeks, lit up. It was Fisk.

"Jenna, are you well enough to come to Headquarters today?"

"What's happened?"

The audio changed as he put his phone on speaker.

"We got 'em." It was Mira, joining the call. "All of them. The complete list. Every name and face."

Jenna had no idea what they were talking about.

"The goddamn cufflinks turned up!" Mira said. "Lyosha came through."

86

CIA Headquarters
Langley, Virginia
An hour later, second week of July 2018

The data stored on the mock-tsarist-era cufflinks was staggering. A gold mine buried in tiny gold disks. Two hundred and sixty-one names, with passport photos and contact details. That was just for starters.

Two hundred and sixty-one individuals were quickly found to be linked to two hundred and sixty-one LinkedIn profiles, which had been printed out and laid in careful rows across the enormous conference table in the Russia House senior common room. The Russian Seed-Bearing Program's scale and depth of penetration was laid bare—and the Wise Ones of Russia House were shaken.

A discovery of this scale would by now be setting alarms ringing across the Agency, the FBI, and Homeland Security, but Mira was adamant that nothing was to leave this room until she said so. The smallest leak might tip off any of the targets, allowing them to crash their network and run, or—the apocalypse scenario—trip them into bringing forward their goals. Mira was steely and unflappable as usual, but she looked unwell, Jenna thought—sallow and tired. She'd lost weight, too.

"Some of these devils are only a handshake away from a cabinet member . . ." Fisk said as he walked Jenna around the table. "Don't be fooled. Every one of them is a Russian."

He started pointing out profiles at random.

"Sara Perlman, born in Tel Aviv, became a US citizen in 2013, now head of programming at Comcast . . . Axel Noel Krueger, born in Johannesburg, became a US citizen in 2012, now chief coding engineer at Lockheed Martin . . . Karl Gustav Schultz, born in Hamburg, became a US citizen in 2014, vice chairman of the Federal Election Commission . . . Jamal al-Saleh, born in Damascus, became a US citizen in 2011, deputy chief economist at the Federal Reserve . . . William Suk, born in Bangkok, became a US citizen in 2012, chief Cloud engineer at Apple . . . Zahra Rahimi, born in Tehran, became a US citizen in 2011, professor of strategic studies at Brown and a regular pundit on RT and Fox . . . Viktor Nagy, born in Budapest, head of policy at the Hoover Institute . . . Ignacio Roberto Ruiz, born in Bogota, specialist in the mechanisms for exchange-traded funds at the New York Stock Exchange . . . On and on it goes. Energy companies. The Treasury. Biotech. Satellite systems. Merrill Lynch, Verizon . . ."

Young, clear-eyed, smiling faces, basking in their success and expertise, rising up the corporate ladders of private hedge funds, the Department of Health, Department of Defense, NASA, lobbying firms, philanthropic foundations, big pharma, air traffic control, Ivy League universities, right-wing think tanks, left-wing think tanks . . .

"Jesus," Jenna murmured.

"Oh, it gets better," Warren Allen said with a sour chuckle. "A superficial trawl of their social media feeds has revealed that an unusual number of them are in romantic relationships with much older partners . . ."

"Some things do not change," Fisk said.

"So far, we have a Democrat congressman who chairs the House foreign relations committee, an elderly Republican senator who sits on the House intelligence committee, a two-star NATO general, a US undersecretary at the UN, and the CEO of a semiconductor start-up . . ."

"Men are such fucking idiots," Bill Cheney said.

"The general's a woman," Mira said, vaguely.

The elation of the discovery was already fading. Fisk rubbed his face. He was looking haggard and exhausted suddenly. The three Wise Ones were seated on far-separated chairs along different walls of the room, lost in their individual thoughts.

It felt as if the whole country had been infected by a deadly pathogen, and it was spreading to the heart. Its symptoms were still hidden and festering, but soon, and without warning, it would make the whole body politic sick. Then the stock markets would free-fall, the internet would go dark, planes would drop out of the sky; no one would have a clue what was true, what was false. Disorder, panic, riots, looting. A complete societal breakdown. That Putin now wielded such an insidious, catastrophic power over the United States was horrifying, astonishing.

The second cufflink contained equally sensational data. The use of both cufflinks suggested that OPUS had downloaded this intel from a different server at the *rezidentura* in the Russian mission in New York and hadn't wanted the second server to "see" what was on the first cufflink.

This provided the actual "paroles" for each of these individuals. These were the unique codenames and codewords known only to the operative and to Moscow Center. The parole allowed both parties to authenticate their identities if they needed to communicate. It opened a tantalizing possibility: of entrapping them by posing undercover as someone from Moscow Center.

"Russian illegals will obey an order only if the correct parole is used," Mira said, pouring more coffee for Jenna from a flask. "Get it wrong and it's an emergency signal to run. The problem is that these paroles are more than a year old. We don't know how often they're changed. If I were a wily old spider like Vadim Giorgadze, I'd be changing them every month. Every week! I wouldn't risk a compromise."

"And we don't know if these individuals communicate with each other," Fisk said. "Freak one of them out and it may trip an emergency signal to all of them."

"Forget the paroles," Warren Allen said, glumly. "They're worthless. We need something else if we're gonna snare them."

There was so much paper covering the table that they adjourned to the small conference table in Bill Cheney's office to eat their lunch, where he had to shift boxes of files and dusty manuals out of the way for them to sit. His shelves were groaning with forty-year-old books on the Cold War.

Once seated, they said nothing for a few moments. The fan on Cheney's desk turned slowly, ruffling Mira's hair. She'd given up dying it.

Fisk was the first to break the silence.

"No one got any ideas?"

Mira let out a sigh. "I'd like to lock up every darn one of them tomorrow, but we don't have a case, do we? They're bona fide US citizens with fourth amendment protections. We don't know if they've even committed a crime. We'll need search warrants, surveillance teams—"

"Too many of them," Allen said, scratching furiously at the scaling skin on his forearms and sending a small snowfall onto the tabletop. "We'd have to entrap them all simultaneously, and arrest them simultaneously, and they're in states all over the country."

"We use the Patriot Act," Bill Cheney said. "Arrest the fuckers and *then* build our case."

"And if there's no case?" Mira said, dropping her head back on her seat. "Even with the Patriot Act they can't be detained indefinitely without evidence. Sooner or later, they'll have to be brought before a judge. What if they protest? They may say they're innocent of any crime, and they may be right. Put yourself in their shoes. They'll be keeping their hands clean until the moment comes to strike..."

"We don't have *time* for due process!" Allen said, moving his scratching from his arms to his neck. "These are ticking fucking time bombs who could crash the country at any moment. They've got to be apprehended *now*. One of them's about to accompany the president to Helsinki on Monday, for Chrissakes. She'll be on Air Force One!"

"Talk about bad timing," Cheney said. "Trump won't want anything to ruin his day with Putin..."

"*What?*" Jenna said, appalled. "Who? A staffer from the White House?"

"An interpreter. Works for the NSA."

Another tense silence hung between them for a minute.

Jenna turned her gaze to the shimmering acres of parking lot, and the forests of Virginia beyond, dark and dusty in the summer heat.

"So we do it the blunt way," Cheney said, his head wobbling. "Get the FBI to tell each of them they're busted, then deport them."

"On what grounds?" Mira raised her hands, exasperated.

"Violation of immigration law."

"The evidence, Bill. We won't find it unless we dig deep into their pasts. That could take months."

"Failing to register as agents of a foreign power," Allen said.

"The evidence, the evidence—"

"Forget evidence," Jenna said, still staring out the window. "The situation's too critical. Our priority is to get rid of them as fast as we can, right? Not convict them of felonies. We can do that without evidence... We might even be able to turn this to our advantage..."

"How, Jenna?" Cheney said. "By shooting them? This isn't Belarus."

"The president's meeting the Russians in Helsinki on Monday, you say? He can tell Putin, in confidence, that his two hundred and sixty-one Seed-Bearing Program operatives are busted and under surveillance. Then he could make him an offer: recall them to Moscow, quietly. No arrests, no announcement, no humiliation, no rubbing anyone's nose in the dirt, no drama. Putin'll have no choice. He won't want a public scandal that'll make him look weak and defeated. He doesn't know we've got no evidence. For all he knows we've been watching these operatives for years. And it will put President Trump in a strong negotiating position."

The energy in the room seemed to revive and stir.

"A pretty neat bluff," Mira said, thinking. "Get the Russians to remove them for us."

"If I know Trump," Fisk said, "he won't want anything to spoil his personal chemistry with that man. What if he refuses to do it? We'll be back to square one."

"Only one way to find out," Mira said. "It's time to send this up the chain."

"Oh boy," Cheney said, stroking his beard. "This is going to be special."

"When does the president leave?" Mira said.

"Tomorrow," Fisk said. "NATO summit in Brussels, state visit to the United Kingdom, then summit with Putin in Helsinki on Monday."

"This can't wait another hour," Mira said. "We schedule an emergency meeting with the president this afternoon."

"He's in Mar-a-Lago," Fisk said.

"Then I guess that's where we're going."

"Florida in July," Allen said. "Ugh."

"And if he won't listen?" Cheney said. "Russian interference is a sore subject with him."

"He's the president of the United States!" Mira said, slamming the table with both hands. "He cannot go into a meeting with

Vladimir Putin not knowing we've just found two hundred and sixty-one Russian spies on US soil."

"This is only going to work, Mira, if we take Putin by surprise," Fisk said calmly. "If anything leaks before the summit, if any of these operatives are tipped off, we lose our advantage. We lose control over what they might do."

They filed out of Cheney's office in silence and back into the common room with its stacked sets of LinkedIn profiles.

Mira said, "I want every one of these names compiled into an alphabetical list with a face photo of each. A list that the president can take out of his jacket pocket and hand to Putin."

Jenna stared at the table covered in printouts and walked along it, studying the names, the bright, earnest faces. Then something made her slow and stop in her tracks.

"The interpreter accompanying the president to Helsinki," she said. "Which one are they?"

Fisk reached over and picked up the LinkedIn profile of a young woman with soft, glossy brown hair and cool, sea-green eyes.

Jenna recognized her instantly. She was unusually beautiful, in a classical, Hellenic kind of way. The kind of face you'd see in ads for expensive perfumes. Not a face one might easily forget.

"Sofia Rima Ali," Fisk said, "born in Beirut, naturalized in 2014. Translator and executive assistant to National Security Adv—"

"I've met her," Jenna said abruptly. "Three weeks ago in Singapore . . . She gave me a—" She froze and stared at the table. "She gave me a phone . . . so I could call home . . ."

The phone on which Fisk had called her this morning in Annandale. The phone on which Mira had said, "We've got 'em. The complete list. Every name and face."

Jenna turned slowly around to face Fisk, feeling the blood drain from her face.

"Shit."

87

Mar-a-Lago
Palm Beach, Florida
That afternoon

"You know how I know this is bad news?" the president said, handing his golf gloves to a Secret Service man. "'Cause every time I see you guys it's bad news." He had greeted them next to a row of sun loungers at the side of the illuminated pool. The air was moist and very warm, but a breeze had picked up. The palm trees surrounding the pool rustled and thrashed. Stately, oyster-gray clouds were blowing in from the sea, carrying a smell of rain. The president was wearing beige golf slacks and a white polo shirt, with a blue trucker's cap emblazoned with the number 45. If he'd been doing any work at all to prepare for his NATO summit, his state visit, and his meeting with Vladimir Putin, they saw no evidence of it. No advisors were with him, no State Department diplomats or NATO chiefs. No briefing folders.

"Take a seat."

"Mr. President," Mira said, "this one's for the SCIF."

Mar-a-Lago, the president's 1920s Spanish Revival resort on Palm Beach, was not a suitable venue to hold a meeting involving sensitive intelligence. Part of the complex was open to paying club members and the public. For this reason, one of the ground-floor rooms had been fitted with a sensitive compartmented information facility.

"I don't wanna use the SCIF," Trump said irritably. "It's too small for five people. I'll be able to smell what you had for lunch. We can talk here."

Reluctantly, Mira, Fisk, Cheney and Allen pulled up chairs to sit around a poolside table.

In a steady, patient voice Mira explained that they'd come to brief him on a classified matter of extreme sensitivity and urgency. She showed him the list of the two hundred and sixty-one Russian operatives currently working in prominent organizations all over the United States. Then she started outlining the scale of the threat and the danger to the country, even as the president started rolling his eyes and glancing at his watch.

"You tell me this list came from a Russian source? Why would you trust someone who betrays their country?"

"A highly reliable source who was working for *us*, Mr. President," Fisk said. "A source whose intelligence we can't discount—"

"It's the stupidest thing I ever heard. Your intelligence is not intelligent. It's low-IQ intelligence. You come here telling me it's all source and no evidence? Gimme a break. That's because it's another fucking *hoax*. You want me to throw hundreds of so-called Russians out of the country *the weekend before I meet Putin?*"

"No, sir," Mira said with epic forbearance. "We propose a solution that would allow President Putin to save face, and which would greatly strengthen your negotiating position with Russia. But allow me to be clear, sir. These individuals cannot remain in the country. If the Russians don't remove them, we will—and that could cause considerable embarrassm—"

"Putin's not my enemy."

Mira closed her eyes as she was interrupted.

"Someday he'll be my friend. It'll happen, but you—" he pointed his finger, moving it so it took in all of them "—don't want it to happen. You're all the same people who said Saddam Hussein had WMD. I'm not buying it. I don't need you. I can get better intelligence on my own. You're dupes, you're losers. You're always sabotaging and interfering. It's the reason I'm keeping everyone outta the room."

Mira glared at him for a beat as this sank in. "Excuse me, sir . . . you mean you're intending to meet with President Putin *alone?*"

"No one else in the room!"

A strong gust of wind released a spatter of rain across the terrace and blew the president's cap from his head.

The meeting ended abruptly.

The five of them rushed to gather their flapping papers. As they left, Fisk turned to see the president chasing after his cap. His hair was waving about his head like the fronds of a sea anemone, exposing a baldness no one was permitted to see.

"That went well," Cheney muttered after they'd climbed into the SUV to head back to the airbase.

"It's time to bring in the big guns," Mira said, calling a number on her phone.

"Is that wise, Mira? We've got to keep the club on this one small, otherwise—"

"It's too late. Trump's saying no. We need reinforcements . . . yes, get me the director of the FBI, please . . ."

The following morning Trump found himself ambushed by an emergency meeting in the White House Situation Room, this time attended by the intelligence services top brass, including the director of national intelligence, the director of the FBI, the joint chiefs, and the attorney general, all of whom had now been read into the secret and shown the list. This had greatly increased the danger of a leak, but all of them immediately swung their support behind Mira.

Jenna was not present. The scene was relayed to her later by Fisk.

Every one of them had tried to impress upon the president the need to be tough with Putin and show him the list.

"Don't box me in!" he'd yelled, throwing papers across the table. "I'm not threatening Putin with a list of so-called spies. I need to be open. And I wanna talk to him in private."

"Mr. President," Fisk had said calmly, "you cannot go into that room alone with Vladimir Putin. At least take the secretary of state in with you."

"No! No one else in the room. I'm afraid of leaks, leakers. Why the fuck are you all looking at me like that? You think Putin's got dirt on me, is that it? You think he's got a tape of me with prostitoots? Do I look like the kind of guy who uses prostitoots?"

But as the morning went on the pressure had started to get to the president. A group of senior House Republicans had just urged him not to meet Putin one-to-one in private.

In the end, just as Air Force One was about to leave for Brussels, and with a furious, petulant reluctance, the president had agreed to a compromise: no one could talk him out of his private one-to-one with the Russian president, but he would give the list of Russian Seed-Bearing Program operatives to Putin, tell him they've been busted, and invite him to recall them to Moscow on the quiet. The whole matter would be handled with the utmost discretion and secrecy.

"But shove the list in his face and look strong doing it," Mira had said.

A solemn atmosphere had pervaded the backseat of Mira's car as she and Fisk were driven back to Langley.

"Think he's going to do it?" Fisk said.

"I don't know . . ."

88

West End
Washington, DC
Thursday, July 12, 2018

When Sofia Ali arrived home from work, she immediately closed the blinds and curtains of her small apartment, even though it was still bright outside, then she poured herself a glass of Sauvignon Blanc, closed her eyes, and exhaled slowly.

All day she'd felt an incoming tide of panic that had threatened to breach her chill composure, shatter her inner calm.

The wine bottle was pretty much the only item in the refrigerator. She hated buying groceries and ate very little, surviving on a diet of canapés. Tonight, she was the plus-one for a Texan satcom tycoon, a major donor to the First Lady's Be Best initiative, which was holding a gala fundraiser at the Mayflower Hotel. Her job working for the NSA gave her control over Bolton's diary and meetings schedule, which naturally was of keen interest to Moscow. Her true value, however, was in the access she enjoyed to DC's elite. Society was her specialism, the habitat in which her charming guile was most useful. The best spies might know all the tradecraft in the book, but how many of them could do what she did—persuade powerful men to talk, effortlessly introduce them to each other, turn them against each other, become the nexus of their DC social lives, their complex personal networks of power?

And yet it was tradecraft that had pitched her into the crisis she was in right now.

It had been a simple trick, handing Jenna Williams that phone in Singapore.

The malware in it had connected to Sofia's special laptop, so she knew that the phone had been used five times. Once to log into the security cameras surrounding a rather low-class-looking suburban home; once to open a link to an article in the *Korea JoongAng Daily*; once to open another link about the discovery of a nurse's body, and twice to receive phone calls from withheld caller IDs, the recordings of which she'd listened to several times. It was the call from the second withheld caller ID that had set Sofia's emergency alarm bells ringing.

We got 'em. All of them. The complete list. Every name and face. The goddamn cufflinks turned up! Lyosha came through.

Again, she felt the suffocating dread of a net closing in on her.

The words could mean anything. Or they could mean what they said. A complete list of every name and face, from a source called "Lyosha."

Today was Thursday, so it was decision time. If she was going to inform Moscow, she had to do it now.

Every Thursday evening, at the same time, a car from the Russian embassy on Wisconsin Avenue drove along K Street and passed within fifty yards of her apartment, which was located in West End, near the St. Gregory Hotel. This provided her with a brief, weekly window in which to contact Moscow Center, if she needed to. It was accomplished by a neat technological trick—a temporary private wireless network in which two laptops could pair with each other using each other's unique MAC, or media access control address. Any data transmitting between Sofia's laptop and the laptop in the car thus avoided flowing over the internet, where it might be hoovered up.

The window was just minutes away. She took another gulp of wine, then hurried to retrieve the special laptop from its hiding place in a panel behind her dressing-room mirror. The sequence of passwords alone could take several minutes before she was ready to transmit.

With just seconds to spare she was live. Her laptop was searching for the unique address nearby as the embassy car passed below in the street.

The laptops paired. Center gave the parole codeword.

Sofia stared at it in panic. *It was out of date!* But only slightly ... Should she risk it?

She didn't know what to do. She risked it.

She tapped out a rapid, high-priority message stating that the attached audio file had been recovered from the phone she'd given to Jenna Williams.

It was done.

Her hands were shaking from fear and nerves. She knew that Moscow prized good news over the truth, but if the network was about to go down in flames, she needed orders. Whatever she did next, it was now Moscow's call, not hers.

The laptop in the car outside sent an automatic acknowledgment. Transmission received.

She waited.

Five minutes went by, then ten. The laptops were still paired, so she couldn't log off. It was dangerous to pair for longer than a minute or two. The car in the street must have pulled over and stopped, otherwise it would be out of range by now. This had never happened before.

Again, she was gripped by dread and paranoia, a fear that her world was shrinking fast and the walls closing in.

And then: a response.

MEET ST. GREGORY HOTEL TEN MINUTES ROOM 512.

Sofia froze, electrified. Then she logged off, slipped on her heels, and grabbed her handbag and keys. Moments later she was out on the sidewalk and heading toward the St. Gregory Hotel. Her overwhelming feeling was relief: the waiting had been unbearable; now she had a course of action to follow, a purpose.

If her world hadn't just gone into such a spin, she might have paused to ask herself why Moscow Center was calling her to a meeting at such short notice that it gave her no time for reconnaissance or surveillance detection; that they'd never, in fact, made such a demand on her before, because any personal meetings with Center were extremely risky and might be noticed by the FBI. But the message seemed to confirm what she'd already sensed: that she was in the midst of a full-blown emergency—that if she didn't act exactly as they demanded she'd have no time to save her own skin.

She rode the elevator to the fifth floor of the hotel in a paroxysm of nerves. She'd had no time to refresh her makeup, to prepare herself psychologically for whatever scenario she was about to enter.

Room 512 was at the far end of a long, carpeted corridor. The distance gave her a moment to recover her poise, compose her face, slow her breathing. She walked with her neck straight and her head up. She was a professional! She would do whatever had to be done. Her heart began to pound and hammer again. She was unafraid!

She raised her hand and knocked. She heard movement inside the room, a moment's silence as an eye observed her from the peephole in the door. Then it opened.

A short, spry gentleman of about seventy was smiling at her. He greeted her in Russian.

"Come in, Sofia," he said, turning back into the room. "I'm sorry my response to your message took a few minutes."

He had a trim white goatee and his head wobbled somewhat, as if he had Parkinson's. His age surprised her.

Sofia followed him warily into the room, where the lamps emitted a dim glow.

She said, "Sir, may I ask you to identify yourself?"

The old man hitched his trouser legs up and sat carefully down on a chair at the room's table. "Yes, of course. Forgive me. My name's Bill Cheney."

The name meant nothing to her. "Directorate S sent you?"

"Alas, no. The CIA sent me." He was looking over Sofia's shoulder. "Ah! I think you've met Jenna?"

Sofia spun around in alarm. Jenna Williams was standing in the door.

Jenna smiled pleasantly at her. "Hey."

Behind her in the corridor were a group of three men and three women wearing flying jackets emblazoned with "FBI." Jenna stood aside for them to enter.

"Sofia Rima Ali, you're under arrest on suspicion of espionage."

89

Lynchburg, Virginia
July 16, 2018

It was an odd gathering of people for a weekend in the country. A handful of elderly spooks, plus Jenna, her mother, and Soo-min. They had been invited to Fisk's weekend place in the woods of Bedford County, near Lynchburg, an old ramshackle house set amid ancient oaks and a large wildflower garden that sloped down to the shores of Smith Mountain Lake. Beyond the water, the Blue Ridge Mountains rolled soft and hazy in the afternoon light.

When Jenna's car turned onto the gravel drive, she saw Bill Cheney and Warren Allen changing out of waders on the porch steps. They'd spent the morning fishing. They waved to her.

On the journey from Annandale, Soo-min and Han had chatted excitedly for the first hour, listening to hits from the nineties on the radio, but as the Satnav guided them from freeway to minor road, to country lane, closer and closer to their destination, Soo-min had become subdued, and stared out the windows, her expression hidden behind her sunglasses. Her dream was finally about to become real, and she was nervous. Her nerves affected Jenna, too.

Stephen was waiting for them in the house. Charles Fisk had arranged it and had flown him from San Francisco at his own expense. Fisk had become a kind of godfather to the family, Jenna thought. Stephen had insisted on a private reunion, and Jenna and Han had concurred. After all they'd been through, she didn't think any of them could handle news cameras and reporters.

It had been ten and a half years since Soo-min had last seen her son. He would no longer be the small boy she remembered. He was no longer Ha-jun; he was Stephen. And she was no longer the mother he'd last known in North Korea. She'd been ill for so long, she said, that she felt as if she was rebuilding her whole persona from scratch. (Jenna felt that she'd simply recovered her old self, but it was taking some getting used to.)

Soo-min's fears were real, and not irrational. She was afraid that her son would no longer know her, would not know how to accept her into his life again. She was afraid that he carried so much damage and hurt that his heart had turned cold toward her.

Fisk opened the front door and greeted them warmly. Behind him they could hear other voices and the sound of children playing.

He embraced Jenna, then he bowed to Han. He was about to bow to Soo-min, when she unexpectedly hugged him.

"Thank you, sir," she said. "For doing this."

"Come in, come in. You must be hungry after that drive. Lunch won't be long. Sorry if it's all a little chaotic. My son and daughter are here with their children. Still getting used to being a grandfather . . . No, no, don't bother taking off your shoes . . ."

Fisk, too, seemed nervous. No one was sure what to expect.

They followed him into the lovely cool house. Old quilts and stitched samplers decorated the walls, and the furniture was dark and simple. The floorboards creaked as they walked through the living room toward a sunlit veranda at the back where Fisk's family was seated.

"It's like a house in a movie," Han whispered to Jenna.

"English, please, Omma."

On the veranda a long table had been laid for dinner. Four

adults, two men and two women, rose to their feet. Introductions were made. Children were told not to be shy and to shake hands. In the first few seconds of happy, awkward social commotion Jenna did not notice the slender young man dressed in shapeless black clothes who was seated apart from the children. But Soo-min had seen him.

The sight of him seemed to turn her to stone.

He rose slowly from his seat, and the rest of the company fell quiet.

Neither son nor mother smiled. Neither one said anything. They simply gazed at each other across the table, as if across the expanse of a decade.

And then Soo-min moved slowly toward him and, shockingly, got down on her knees and put her forehead to the wooden floor. She stayed there motionless.

The children looked uncomfortable, turning to the adults for an explanation.

"My son," Soo-min said in Korean. "Please forgive me."

For several seconds no one moved.

Then Stephen put his hands to her shoulders and lifted her up to her feet. "For what, Mother?" he said. "There's nothing to forgive."

Then mother and son embraced tightly and with great emotion.

The company around the table sighed, and began clapping, but the atmosphere was tinged with a sense of loss and heartbreak.

"Well, I'd better check on the ribs," Fisk said, his voice altered and quavering, and headed off to the barbecue.

Wine was poured. Bread was passed around.

Soo-min was overcome, and Stephen continued to hold her arm tightly, saying in Korean, "It's all right, Omma. It's all right. We've been through so much. But here we are."

When she finally collected herself a little, she said, "This is your grandmother, Han. And this is your aunt, Jenna."

Stephen seemed dazed with happiness. He clasped both Jenna's hands and hugged her. "I never knew I had any family," he said, "apart from my mother."

And your father, Jenna thought. *You knew about your father.*

A small chill spread over her just then. This was something she still had not processed, let alone accepted. In all the years she'd spent trying to guess the secret Soo-min had kept locked deep in her mind, never, even in the wildest flights of her imagination, had Jenna supposed that the Kim family might be her family, too—that she was related by blood to someone who was himself a branch on the cruel, sacred tree.

Now she understood her twin's trauma and fear. Her son was no civilian. He was the heir to a throne. His bloodline was so rare and royal that its legitimacy, its *authenticity*, posed a mortal threat to his own life, as it had to PANDA, and to DIAMOND. Someday, when everything had settled down, she would talk to Stephen about them, his uncle and his cousin, and make sure he knew that they had been good people. Secrecy would prevent her from elaborating too much on her own role in their lives.

She tried to put all that out of her mind for now. Nothing was going to spoil this day.

Stephen took his mother for a walk through the garden, holding her hand. *What a fine line there is between sadness and joy,* Jenna thought.

She found the scene so distracting, so heartbreakingly happy, that polite conversation with the other guests proved a struggle for her, until Han told her she was being rude.

Just as lunch was about to be served, they heard another car rumble up the gravel drive.

"More guests," Fisk called from the barbecue. "Someone get the door, please."

Jenna went to the front porch and waved to Mira as she was helped out of the car by her driver. The sight of her looking so frail, and moving with such difficulty, distracted her for a moment from the other person getting out of the back of the car, and then she was astounded to see Lyosha. He seemed a little travel-worn and disoriented, his hair long and tucked behind his ears, and he was sporting a pair of wire-frame glasses that failed to disguise his good looks.

Lyosha laughed loudly when he saw her on the steps and smacked his forehead. "Oh, no! This time, I'm following *you*."

The CIA had brought Lyosha to the US to be thanked in person by the director and to receive a posthumous citation awarded to his father.

Jenna changed her mind about the hand she had proffered for him to shake and hugged him instead.

"Welcome to America. I guess you can call me Jenna now."

The afternoon light grew brighter as lunch ended.

They were enjoying the magical sight of sunlight dancing on the lake when Fisk received an alert on his phone.

"Helsinki. It's wrapping up."

Cheney, Allen, Jenna, and Mira repaired to Fisk's upstairs study to watch the live news coverage.

"Think he showed Putin our list?" Jenna said.

"We'll know when we see their faces . . ." Mira said.

In the bright, chandeliered ballroom of the presidential palace in Helsinki the press was seated in packed rows facing the podium where two bulletproof lecterns with mics awaited the presidents of the United States and the Russian Federation. Behind the lecterns was a theatrical backdrop of red, white, and blue—the Stars and Stripes and the Russian tricolor. The leaders' private one-to-one meeting was about to finish. Camera lights were turned on. The hubbub of voices fell to a low murmur.

The instant Trump emerged from a door to the right Jenna knew that something had gone wrong.

His body language was unrecognizable. All that fuck-you

swagger had gone out of him. He walked slowly. His jacket flapped open. His shoulders sagged. He climbed listlessly onto the podium and kept his eyes on the floor.

"What the hell . . ." Warren Allen said.

"He looks like a beaten dog," Cheney said, moving his head closer.

All five of them were standing in a semicircle around Fisk's desk, eyes fixed on the screen.

Putin followed him into the room, and the contrast between the two men was extraordinary. The Russian president practically bounced up to the lectern, looking self-assured, cheerful even, and gave the Russian reporters in the room a winner's smirk. Though by far the larger man, Trump seemed to have diminished in stature next to him, like a kid who'd been given a massive dressing down by a teacher he'd idolized.

"He's been judo-slammed," Jenna murmured.

"We warned him," Mira said, softly.

Putin gave a prepared statement. Trump gave a prepared statement. Then they invited questions from the floor.

"Sir, just now President Putin denied having anything to do with the election interference in 2016. Every US intelligence agency concluded that Russia did. Would you now, with the whole world watching, tell President Putin—would you denounce what happened in 2016 and would you warn him never to do it again?"

Trump pursed his lips and nodded.

This was his chance, Jenna thought, to stand tall and manifest the immense power of the United States, a chance any US president would grab with both hands. To tell this two-bit tyrant next to him that he had made a grave and foolhardy mistake. That the Russians were playing with fire. That if they ever pulled a stunt like that again, there'd be a shock-and-awe response from the world's mightiest nation.

But each of the five viewers in Fisk's study could already see that he wasn't going to do it. What Jenna had not expected, and which stunned all of them in the room, was that he would do the opposite.

"*All I can do is ask the question. I have President Putin. He just said it's not Russia. I will say this: I don't see any reason why it would be . . .*"

Fisk's mouth dropped open. Mira covered her face with her hands. Bill Cheney said, "Oh, Lord. I'm gonna sit down."

For a few seconds the reporters in the hall continued scribbling and typing. Then, as the magnitude of his words sank in, they simply stopped, looked up, and stared at him.

The commander-in-chief had just sided with a hostile power over the unanimous advice of the intelligence agencies of his own country, which had told him that Russia had attacked American democracy.

Then all at once the reporters continued tapping away in frenzy.

"*. . . but I will tell you that President Putin was extremely strong and powerful in his denial today. And he made an incredible offer. He offered to have the people working on the case come and work with Russian investigators. I think that's an incredible offer.*"

"Putin's lied to you, you chump!" Allen said.

President Trump then embarked on a meandering, nonsensical riff about the FBI not investigating the Democratic Party servers and Hillary Clinton's missing emails.

"What's he even talking about?" Allen yelled. "Somebody put a stop to this. He's just digging himself in deeper. Somebody stop the conference!"

A reporter had a question for the Russian president.

"*President Putin, does the Russian government have any compromising material on President Trump or his family?*"

"*Yes, I have heard these rumors. Well, distinguished colleague, when Mr. Trump visited Moscow in the past, I didn't know he was in Moscow. Back then he was just a businessman . . .*"

The five of them in the study let out a gasp. Just a businessman!

Not a powerful tycoon, or a reality-TV star, or a real-estate mogul. Just a businessman!

Behind his lectern, Trump visibly wilted.

"Thousands of American businessmen visit Russia each year. Do you think we collect compromising material on every one of them? Please disregard this rumor. It's hard to imagine such nonsense."

Trump leaned into the mic with a lame, final remark.

"And I have to say that if they had it, it would have come out a long time ago. This is a disgrace to the FBI. A disgrace to our country. And a total witch hunt."

Fisk turned off the screen. For a few seconds the silence in the room felt like the aftermath of an explosion. No one had any words for what had just happened. No one could articulate the humiliation of such a disgrace.

Jenna glanced at her phone.

Twitter was already lighting up. "National embarrassment . . ." "Open TREASON . . ." and these posts were from his own supporters. "What does Putin have on Trump that he's so afraid?" the former Speaker of the House mused to her millions of followers.

"I've never seen him like that before," Fisk said gravely. "That wasn't the Trump I know. He was obsequious, *servile*. What the hell happened in that room?"

"He'll never tell us," Cheney said. "You can be sure of that."

"Oh, the Russians," Allen said, scratching furiously at his scalp, "*they* know what happened in there. But we're in the dark about what he agreed, what he promised, what he gave away. We don't know what our own policy position is . . ."

The window of Fisk's study gave a sweeping view of the lake and the mountains now casting shadows as the sun moved into the west.

That meeting is a black box, Jenna thought. *We can only see the inputs and the outputs. But whatever happened inside is a mystery.*

At the far end of the garden, she could see Stephen and Lyosha walking slowly together toward the shore.

Those two seem to be hitting it off . . .

"Trump went into the room unprepared," Fisk was saying. "And he got snookered. By something devastating and, I'm guessing, extremely unpleasant."

"This is a major fucking crisis," Allen said. "Seriously—what's Putin got on him?"

They were silent again for a moment, thinking hard. On the veranda outside they could hear the children playing with Soo-min.

Jenna folded her arms, and turned from the window. How had they gotten to him?

Trump was a man so shameless that he'd become a single-word celebrity, like Beyoncé or Ronaldo, his name ALL-CAPS and gold plated on the sides of airplanes and skyscrapers. What was a man like that afraid of?

Mira said, "The Russians have been studying Donald Trump for a long time, Charles. They know him better than we do. They've had a file on him ever since he visited Moscow in 1987 with an Eastern European wife on his arm . . ."

Allen and Cheney started rattling through a list of possibilities.

"The 2013 Miss Universe pageant in Moscow," Cheney said. "They taped him misbehaving with girls in his hotel room."

"Nah," Fisk said, rubbing his eyes. "No way. If such a thing even existed, he'd flat-out deny that the guy in the video is him. 'Fake!' he'd say. 'Not me!'"

"Proof that Russian money bailed him out after his bankruptcies?" Allen ventured.

Fisk shook his head and sat heavily into an armchair. "No one would give a shit. Wouldn't faze him in the slightest."

"Some *kompromat* involving his family?" Jenna said. "His eldest sons?"

"Are you kidding? He has nothing but contempt for his sons. It's something else, something we don't know about . . ."

The study had taken on the grim atmosphere of a war cabinet after a shocking battlefield defeat. How had the enemy pulled off such a sleight of hand? How had they secretly compromised an American head of state?

The discussion went on in this vein for hours, but none of them could think of anything in the lurid treasure trove of this man's abuses and disgraces that seemed to stick. Everything he'd done—sexual, financial, political—was public knowledge. Trump lived his life openly, scandalously. He had no private persona, no hidden hinterland, no secret life of the self. What you saw was what you got. He'd breezed his way through embarrassments and exposures that would have atomized any normal politician, caused most people to crawl into a hole and die of shame.

After they'd talked themselves out, Cheney said, "Well, I think we can assume he didn't show Putin our list. Where does this leave our two hundred and sixty-one Russian guests?"

"They're not going anywhere," Mira said quietly. "For now."

She had remained silent throughout the discussion, her gaze lost on some distant mountain through the window.

"You OK, Mira?" Jenna said, concerned. Mira's face was drawn and gray. Her blouse was hanging off her.

She sighed and gave Jenna a rather formal smile. "I have cancer. I was going to tell you all next week."

An expression of pain spread across the faces in the room. Fisk was about to speak first, but Mira held up her hand to stop him.

"No. Please. Spare me that. I can't stand the sympathy. The mistake people make is fighting it. No one can fight it. All one can do is keep an eye on it . . . and accept it. Accept it as part of oneself . . . like these damned spies. So, let's be realistic. They're here to stay, at least while this president's in office. But we watch them, like the sparrows watch a cat. We'll spend the time building our case, digging up their pasts, finding their complete biographies."

"If they find out we've got Sofia Ali in custody, it could make 'em very jumpy," Allen said.

"We'll figure that out tomorrow."

The veranda outside was quieter. Only the adults were talking. Jenna guessed that the children had been put to bed. As the sky faded from blue to gold, they began lighting incense coils to keep away the bugs and small lanterns along the garden path that led down to the lake.

Lyosha and Stephen were sitting on the jetty at the end of the garden, talking and playing music. She could see the glow of their phones. Fisk, Allen, and Cheney went to join the others for a glass of wine on the veranda. Soo-min was telling them, quite openly and without bitterness, about her experiences in North Korea. The transformation Jenna had thought would never happen was remarkable, astonishing, and in it, Jenna recognized her own old self, the person she'd been before trauma had upended her life and launched her into a career in the secret world.

"The air's so clean here," Mira murmured in Jenna's ear. "The skies—so vast and clear. Almost makes me forget I'm sick."

"Do you need to lie down?"

"No. I'm tired of course, but I don't sleep much at all. Will you take my arm? I'd like a short stroll down to the lake." The moon was rising above the mountains and the first stars were beginning to twinkle. On the far shore, the lights of other houses glowed warmly in the advancing darkness.

Jenna guided her along the garden path lit by lanterns, but the walk proved too ambitious for Mira, so they sat down in the fragrant grass, amid the orchestra of cicadas, and admired the beauty of the evening. When they looked up, the constellations appeared as spray on their faces.

They were silent for a while, then Mira said, out of nowhere, "My sister-in-law, Greta, was a nice woman. Her parents had adopted her when she was an infant. But very few people knew that fact about her because she would do anything to keep it a secret."

"Why?"

"We don't know. No one in the world would have thought any the less of her for knowing she was adopted. But it was a source of acute shame and fear for her. Something she worked all her life to keep hidden at any cost . . . I'm telling you this for a reason: everyone, in their own way, is a mystery to others, even if you've known them all your life."

Jenna mumbled her agreement, even if she wasn't sure where this was going.

"Trump was outclassed by a master today," Mira went on. "By walking into that room alone with Putin he made himself the victim of a clever psychological op. The Russians *understand* something. Something that causes him terrible anguish and shame. And here's the thing: it doesn't need to be big. It could be a very, very minor thing. The kind of thing you and I would think nothing of, but to him—it's kryptonite, psychological death. Something so personal to him that he'll do anything in his power to keep it a secret. That's the kind of hook the Russians are so skilled at finding. Odd, small vulnerabilities none of us here would even consider."

"But you've got some idea?"

Mira shook her head slowly, staring at the lights on the far shore.

"Donald's whole life has been an effort to avoid humiliation. And yet, he comes close to it all the time. One could even say that he's drawn to it . . . tempts it. His father, Fred, taught him that there could only ever be one winner. That everyone else had to lose. And to be a loser was worse than humiliation: it was annihilation. That to be the best at everything, the most successful, in business, in bed, he had to be smarter than anyone else. Know more than anyone else about everything . . .

"We'll probably never know what happened in that meeting . . . but I've been studying Putin for years, so here's my one guess: Putin deliberately made him feel stupid today."

Jenna waited for her to say more, but when she didn't, she said, "That all?" She felt like laughing and groaning at the same time. "That's ridiculous."

"Of course, it is," Mira said, dead serious. "It's nothing . . . and yet it's everything. I think Putin would have had some evidence, something to show Trump, to prove that he knew the truth behind the charade."

"Such as what?!"

Mira shrugged. "His college grade transcripts? His *IQ number?*"

"That's insane."

"Yes, well. On such things the fates of nations turn. You saw how frightened he looked today. That wasn't the fear of someone who'd been threatened. That looked like the fear of someone who'd been *found out*. Whatever it was, Donald would have offered anything to keep it quiet: denied election interference, given Russia a free hand in Ukraine, pulled out of NATO . . . Anything.

"But, as I said, I'm guessing. Could have been something else. Could have been anything at all . . . Oh, look," she said, suddenly cheerful. "Oh, that's cute. That's made my day. They don't know we can see them . . ."

Jenna turned her head.

A few yards away on the jetty, Lyosha and Stephen were lying on their backs, pointing out stars, still deep in conversation. Low-fi music was playing quietly on one of their phones. Train's "Drops of Jupiter."

"Think they'll fall in love?" Mira said.

Jenna gave a surprised laugh. "They've only just met!"

"Well, they should hurry up about it," she said, reaching for Jenna's arm and getting up with difficulty. "World's going to shit. And youth is wasted on the young."

Soo-min was coming along the path toward them. She appeared so content and relaxed that Jenna wanted to cry. She took her twin's hand.

"I thought I'd talk to Lyosha," Soo-min said. "I haven't really gotten to know him yet."

"You'll like him very much," Jenna said. "He's over there with Stephen."

"Two nuclear powers tried to murder them," Mira said, "but here they are, in a wildflower garden in Virginia."

They watched the youths for a moment, and Soo-min seemed to pick up on something unspoken in the air.

"Well, let's leave them for a while. They seem happy where they are."

Soo-min took Mira's arm and led her back toward the house. Jenna followed, then turned again to take in the scene, because she wanted to remember it forever.

Dusk was darkening to a deep, velvet-blue night. The stars reached down to the mountains and reflected in the softly lapping water. She could hear the boys' voices clearly on the still air, now getting a little chilly.

"What is the opposite of power?" she heard Lyosha say.

"Hm. Weakness, I guess," Stephen said.

"The opposite of power is love . . ."

Jenna turned back to the house, smiling. *The world turns and turns and gets nowhere,* she thought. *The only things that matter are moments like these.*

Author's Note

I have always been fascinated by autocrats. Not because of the respect they command or the fear they spread, but because their vanity and their delusions tend to make them faintly ridiculous figures.

Unlike the dictators of the twentieth century, today's strongmen present themselves as commonsense tough guys. They are virile, their language is coarse, and their antics are entertaining. They are willing to break norms and taboos that no traditional politician would break. They seek to shock, disrupt, and divide. But the tricks of their trade are little changed since ancient times. The repression, cronyism, lies, and corruption; the abuses of power and the othering of minorities—all of this would have been familiar to the citizens of ancient Greece and Rome. And behind the cults of personality that may surround them, they are usually quite fearful and paranoid individuals.

With the rise of demagogues everywhere, even in previously uneventful democracies, we are once again living in an age of autocracy. But for the first time in history, we have an elected president of the United States—the leader of the free world—who makes no secret of his admiration for those who rule through fear, or of his desire to emulate them.

This is what made me wonder if I could write a story that encompassed the most celebrated autocrats' bromance of our time. The members-only club that includes the mutually admiring Vladimir Putin, Kim Jong-un, and Donald Trump.

Although this story is based around real events that took place during Trump's first eighteen months in office in 2017–18, readers are reminded that this is purely a work of fiction. It is my own imagination, and nothing else, that has filled in two notable blanks in the record of that time, namely Trump's private one-to-one meeting with Kim Jong-un at the Singapore summit in June 2018, and his private one-to-one with Vladimir Putin at the Helsinki summit in July 2018.

No one knows what was discussed in those meetings, or what was agreed, or promised. There are no transcripts, or even any notes. (Trump confiscated his interpreter's notes.) They remain black boxes. The private meeting with Putin caused a national outcry in the United States because of Trump's behavior at the leaders' press conference immediately afterward, at which he appeared uncharacteristically browbeaten and subdued. (Putin, standing next to him, was in a buoyant mood.) It was at this press conference that Trump publicly accepted Putin's word that Russia had not interfered in the 2016 US election, and disavowed the evidence of his own FBI, which insisted that Russia had indeed interfered. Even voices in Trump's own party wondered if the Russians were in possession of some personal and embarrassing *kompromat* on him.

Tempting as it is to believe this, the truth is probably much more mundane, as it often is. Trump went into that meeting wholly unprepared, and Putin probably used the opportunity to give him the full bingo card of Russian grievances: the treachery of NATO, the hypocrisy of the West, and so on. In the past, he has done much the same thing to presidents Obama and George W. Bush, hectoring them at great length.

The spur to start writing, however, was an incident that occurred on Russian television's Channel One. The program was 2017's *Direct*

Line, the annual live telethon in which Vladimir Putin answers questions from the public by phone and video link. (The scene in the novel in which Lyosha confronts Putin on live TV is based directly on it.)

This tedious, self-serving show was in its fourth hour when the studio mic was handed to a member of the audience, a sixteen-year-old boy named Danila Prilepa. Danila's question was a brave one: he wanted to know what the president was going to do about corruption, because prosecuting the odd corrupt official "for show" wasn't solving the problem.

This touched a nerve with Putin, whose own personal corruption is a don't-go-there subject in Russia. Putin's response was sarcastic and cold. He asked Danila if this was his own question, or if someone had told him to ask it. Danila was unfazed. "Life prepared me for this question," he said. Then, with epic innocence, he looked directly at the cameras and smiled. The audience laughed and gave him a round of applause. Putin the all-powerful suddenly looked rather shifty and small. He forced a smile. "Nicely done," he said. (A partial clip of the incident can still be viewed on Meduza, an online Russian news outlet that has since been banned in Russia: https://meduza.io/en/news/2017/06/16/the-teenager-who-asked-putin-about-corruption-says-the-president-s-response-was-unsatisfying.)

In those four hours of praise for Vladimir Putin, this was the only moment that had seemed unscripted and real. It was a minor incident, but a revealing one.

The autocrat is invariably a bully, and the marks of a bully are cruelty and cowardice. It's important to know that the autocrat is secretly very afraid of people who are honest, principled, and brave. Such people tend to hold dangerous beliefs when it comes to democracy, human rights, transparency, accountability, and the rule of law, all of which are as fatal to the autocrat as sunlight is to a vampire.

It wasn't just the subject of Danila's question—corruption—that gave Putin an uncomfortable moment on live TV. It was also, I believe, Danila's innocence (which is the opposite of corruption) and lack of fear. Added to this was the alarming fact that the audience laughed. The autocrat cannot bear to be laughed at because when people laugh, they lose their fear of him.

In his quarter century in power, Putin has only truly been frightened of one opponent: Alexei Navalny, whose honesty and almost supernatural lack of fear made him a mortal threat. Navalny's anti-corruption campaigns shone a very bright spotlight on Putin, a creature who operates in darkness and secrecy. This is why Putin twice attempted to poison him and finally imprisoned him in an Arctic penal colony where he died in suspicious circumstances in 2024. Navalny's simple message to his followers was "Do not be afraid," because without fear, an autocrat's power is revealed to be an optical illusion.

I wanted to give Lyosha some of Navalny's qualities, and Danila's, and for Putin to deal with him as Putin would have done, by publicly smearing him, undermining him, then trying to kill him.

I've mentioned that this novel is based around real events, but loosely so, because I've taken liberties with some of the dates for the purposes of the story. For example, Trump's candlelit evening at Mar-a-Lago with Japanese prime minister Shinzo Abe took place in May 2017, not February; Vladimir Putin's annual TV show *Direct Line* is usually aired in June each year, not February; the 2017 G20 summit happened in September, not March (and some of the national leaders mentioned in the story weren't in power until later that year); San Francisco's 2018 Pride weekend took place in July 2018, not June, and so on.

What follows is factual information relevant to the events in the novel.

The Murder of Kim Jong-nam

On February 13, 2017, Kim Jong-nam, the elder half-brother of Kim Jong-un, was assassinated in the departures hall of Kuala Lumpur International Airport. He'd just spent five nights at a resort hotel on the Malaysian island of Langkawi and was checking in for his flight home to Macau, where he'd been living for the last ten years.

The attack was captured on CCTV. His attackers were two young women who had crept up behind him and smeared what looked like baby oil over his face before running off to wash their hands. (One of them was wearing a T-shirt with the letters LOL.)

Minutes later, Jong-nam was in the airport's clinic, complaining of being in terrible pain. The "baby oil" was in fact VX, one of the deadliest nerve agents in the world. He collapsed to the floor in front of panicked medics, and died in agony.

Throughout this grim scene, several North Korean agents were watching nearby to make sure the assassination went to plan. When they saw that it had succeeded, they passed quickly through the departure gates and returned to North Korea.

It was a gruesome end for someone who had once been the heir to the North Korean throne.

As a child, Kim Jong-nam had lived the life of a crown prince. His father, Kim Jong-il had doted on him. He received a first-rate education in Moscow and Switzerland to prepare him for his role as the future supreme leader. But while Jong-nam had been in school abroad, his father had started a new family with his third wife, and it seems that the father's love and affection had been transferred to a new son, Kim Jong-un.

Jong-nam took this loss of favor badly. He started to embarrass his father by acting out, drinking heavily, and womanizing. Eventually, his father allowed him to leave the country and live in exile in Macau, China. There, he led a louche life in the company of gangsters and gamblers. He did maintain close ties with North Korea, however. He ran errands for the regime, and probably used his gambling businesses as money-laundering fronts for North Korea.

But when his father died suddenly in 2011, and his half-brother, Kim Jong-un, came to power, Jong-nam's position as an exiled prince started to look precarious. He became increasingly afraid of assassination.

There were good reasons why Kim Jong-un might have wanted his brother dead.

First, Jong-nam's claim to the succession was much stronger than Kim Jong-un's. He was the first son, and according to Confucian tradition the power and title should have passed to him. Kim Jong-un was only the third son. As long as Jong-nam was alive, therefore, he remained a threat to Kim Jong-un's legitimacy.

Second, Jong-nam was loose-mouthed and indiscreet. He often gave interviews to foreign journalists and was fond of posting photos of his playboy lifestyle on Facebook. Kim Jong-un must have resented his brother for this, for the fun he was having, for his freedom and lifestyle, while he, Kim Jong-un, was condemned for life to play the role of an austere communist dictator in a buttoned-up Mao suit.

Still, there are several mysteries surrounding the death at the airport.

When the police opened Jong-nam's small backpack, they found four North Korean passports in the name "Kim Chol," one hundred and twenty thousand dollars in cash, and, astonishingly, a selection of antidotes for munitions-grade nerve agents, including VX.

Why hadn't he used one of these antidotes in the fifteen minutes he had between the attack and his death? Surely he must have guessed that he'd been poisoned. Probably, he was in too much of a blind panic to think straight.

Why had he been carrying so much cash? And what exactly had he been doing in Langkawi? In her excellent book *The Great Successor* (John Murray, 2019), Anna Fifield has credibly argued that Jong-nam was a CIA source. Had he been meeting a CIA contact on Langkawi, a contact who paid him in cash?

If the North Koreans had suspected him of talking to the Main Enemy, America, it would have been another powerful motive to kill him.

The assassination didn't go entirely to plan: it is likely that the North Koreans wanted the incident to look as if an ordinary middle-aged fellow had suffered a tragic heart attack in the departures hall. Unfortunately for them, when the police found the North Korean passports in the backpack, they called the South Korean authorities by mistake. As a result, there was no chance of the event passing unnoticed. The South Koreans leaked the story, and the death became a global news sensation.

The Seed-Bearing Program

So much about North Korea is stranger than fiction. Readers might find it hard to believe that for many years the North Korean state ran a criminal conspiracy to kidnap hundreds of randomly chosen foreign civilians. Most were snatched from remote beaches in Japan and South Korea and taken to North Korea in vessels disguised as fishing boats. For decades, no one knew what had happened to them. It was as if they had vanished from the face of the earth.

The victims were housed in isolated compounds known as "invitation-only zones." A few of them were put to work teaching language skills to North Korea's spies; some of them had their identities stolen. But it seems that the main idea was to brainwash them, then send them home as spies for North Korea. The project was the brainchild of Kim Jong-il. When it failed—probably because the victims resisted all efforts to "re-educate" them in the regime's ideology—the whole scheme needed a rethink.

This was the genesis of the Seed-Bearing Program, which came to light thanks to Jang Jin-sung's remarkable memoir *Dear Leader* (Rider, 2014). Before his escape from North Korea, Jang was a regime insider with privileged knowledge of some of the Kim family's deepest secrets. He has described how North Korea had been sending attractive female agents abroad with the aim of being impregnated by men of other races—men with white, black, or brown skin. Their half-Korean babies were then born in Pyongyang. The children would be North Korean born and bred—but they would look foreign. The idea was to raise loyal, thoroughly indoctrinated agents for the North Korean state. These children were kept in isolation from the rest of the North Korean population and their needs were attended to by Section 915 of the party's Organization and Guidance Department. Whether this program remains active and current under Kim Jong-un is not known.

Poisons and Nerve Agents

Murder by poison has been a specialism of the Russian secret services since tsarist times. But in the 1990s, the Kremlin's military scientists started developing a sinister new range of chemical and biological weapons intended for highly targeted assassinations. These new nerve agents, deadly germs, and radioactive poisons were designed to kill without leaving a trace. They could be slipped into food and drink, injected, sprayed onto skin, or inhaled as a vapor, resulting in death by a sudden heart attack or multiple organ failure. To the unsuspecting, it would look as if the victim had died of natural causes. The scientists didn't stop there: they also studied the biomolecular structure of ordinary prescription medicines to figure out which combinations of these could become lethal cocktails. They even refined a new generation of psychotropic drugs intended to destabilize the mood of the target, for example by plunging them into such despair that they'd take their own lives.

Most famously, Alexander Litvinenko, a former FSB officer who had defected to Britain, was poisoned in the bar of the Millennium Hotel in Mayfair, London, after he'd been poured a cup of green tea by some Russian acquaintances. The tea contained radioactive polonium. It took Litvinenko three weeks to die an agonizing death from radiation poisoning, long enough for him to work with the police to solve his own murder. The Kremlin may have hoped that murder by polonium would be untraceable, since it emits almost no gamma radiation, and no radiation was detected using Geiger counters. Only hours before Litvinenko's death did investigators finally discover the presence of alpha particles in his body, the hard-to-detect signature of polonium-210.

Then in 2018, another former Russian intelligence officer, Sergei Skripal, together with his visiting daughter, were poisoned by a nerve agent smeared onto the door handle of Skripal's house in Salisbury, England. The substance had been contained inside an expensive perfume bottle, which the assassins then discarded in a dumpster as they hastened back to Russia. The Skripals survived the attack, but tragically, the perfume bottle was discovered by a local man who gave it to his girlfriend as a gift. It was a cruel twist of fate that an innocent local woman, who had no quarrel with Putin, should become the victim of a Russian attack. The perfume bottle contained enough nerve agent to potentially kill thousands of people.

The weapon used on the Skripals might also have gone undetected. However, after the Litvinenko incident, the British authorities knew that they were dealing with something sophisticated and soon identified the weapon as an extremely rare nerve agent called Novichok.

Putin may not have cared too much that the weapons in both these attacks were identified, since they sent a powerful message to anyone thinking of betraying Russia's secrets. He'd stated several times that traitors deserved to "die in the gutter."

Trump's Disclosures of Classified Information

Throughout his first term in office, President Trump exhibited an insouciant attitude to classified documents. On dozens of occasions his aides saw him shredding or tearing up papers in the White House and on Air Force One, even flushing them down toilets. (Aides would attempt to retrieve and reconstruct them.) His former press secretary, Stephanie Grisham, witnessed him showing documents to guests at Mar-a-Lago. After leaving office in 2020, he took numerous boxes of top-secret government documents (including nuclear secrets) to Mar-a-Lago, where they were insecurely stored, including, at one point, in a bathroom and on a ballroom stage.

On May 10, 2017, in an Oval Office meeting with Russian foreign minister Lavrov and Russian ambassador Kislyak, Trump spontaneously disclosed highly sensitive intelligence that had been shared with the United States by Israel, which concerned an ISIS plot to smuggle bombs hidden inside laptops onto airplanes. He seemed oblivious to the possibility that Russia might pass this intel on to Israel's enemy, Iran. The White House initially denied that anything sensitive had been leaked, but Trump later defended himself, saying it was his "absolute right" to share the information. The US intelligence agencies were sufficiently alarmed by Trump's conduct that they decided to extract a high-level Kremlin source, who had been passing secrets to the US for years, out of fears for his safety.

On August 30, 2019, Trump tweeted an exceptionally high-resolution image showing damage to an Iranian spaceport following an explosion. It had been taken by USA-224, a highly classified US spy satellite. The image's quality would have been of great interest to Russia, Iran, and China, since it revealed the US's most advanced surveillance capabilities. Again, he said he had an "absolute right" to share the image.

North Korean Logging Camps in Russia

For decades, North Korea has been sending workers abroad to earn foreign currency for the regime. The Siberian logging camp in the story is just one example. Workers have also been sent to construction sites in the Middle East, to restaurants in China, fisheries in Russia, and to shipyards in eastern Europe.

The workers sent to Siberia endure extremely harsh working conditions. They live communally and are closely monitored by North Korean security forces to make sure they don't defect. The logging camp is effectively a state within a state. Any infraction of the rules is punished severely. The workers receive two days off a year (probably on the two biggest national holidays, the birthdays of Kim Jong-un's father and grandfather). The US State Department has described this migrant labor as "slavery." In fact, the truth is more nuanced.

In the early days, the workers comprised criminals and political prisoners. Today, however, the workers can expect to earn $150 to $300 a month, after the cut taken by the North Korean state. Although this is a scandalously poor wage for such heavy labor, it is nevertheless serious money in North Korea. It says much about living conditions at home that most of the workers volunteer for these jobs and are even willing to pay a bribe to secure one. By the end of their contract (usually two to three years), they may have earned as much as $6,000, enough to start a small business and improve their families' social status in North Korea.

Further Reading

I could never have written this book without the numerous memoirs, histories, and pieces of journalism I read during my research, by authors whose expertise and insight I came to know well and admire greatly. The following is a small selection. I should say that any inaccuracies in the novel, or any liberties taken with the truth, are mine alone.

Masha Gessen's *The Future is History* (Riverhead Books, 2017) is a superb study of the subtle ways in which the totalitarian mindset has crept back into Russian life. By following the lives of four individuals from the fall of the Soviet Union to the nadir of the Putin era, she shows how the dismal hand of the state has regained its grip, creating a fatalistic sense that there is never a future in Russia, only a mirror to the past. I'm indebted to Masha Gessen for details about the growing, state-sponsored homophobia in Russia.

The Sister by Sung-yoon Lee (Macmillan, 2023) is an eye-opening read that warns of the rise of Kim Yo-jong, younger sister to Kim Jong-un and the most powerful woman in North Korea today. It is highly unusual for a woman to rise to prominence in such a patriarchal society, but as a woman Kim Yo-jong is no threat to her brother's legitimacy. She has also exhibited competence in government and ruthlessness, showing no qualms about showering foreign leaders with outrageous foul-mouthed insults. Lee argues that Kim Jong-un may be grooming her as a potential regent in the event of his early demise, or even as his successor.

Too Much and Never Enough by Mary L. Trump (Simon & Schuster, 2020) is the best psychological insight I've read into the personality of Donald Trump, written by a professional psychologist who also happens to be his niece. Much about Donald's obsession with winning at any cost can be explained by his upbringing in Queens and the baleful influence of Fred, Donald's father, whose love for his children was highly conditional.

We Need to Talk About Putin by Mark Galeotti (Ebury, 2019), my absolute favorite commentator on Russia, is filled with many insights and observations about Putin, delivered in Galeotti's usual wry and humorous style. He reminds us that Russia is not Mordor (I thought it was).

Everything Trump Touches Dies by Rick Wilson (Free Press, 2018) is a hilarious takedown of Trump's first term in office. Wilson is a Republican strategist who holds true to traditional Republican values and has no truck with Trump's relentless lies, narcissism, profound ignorance, cruelty, pettiness, and incompetence.

Siege by Michael Wolff (Little Brown, 2019) is a gripping work of reportage; it was written at speed as the second half of Trump's first term unfolded. Wolff's sources are a surprising number of White House insiders, even Trump loyalists, who found themselves at the ends of their tethers with Trump. I'm indebted to Michael Wolff for the final scenes in the novel surrounding the scandal of the Helsinki summit.

Russians Among Us by Gordon Corera (William Collins, 2020) is by far the best account of the tragicomic careers of Russian spies in the US ("illegals"), some of whom lived quiet, suburban lives for decades and started families. Imagine growing up as an American teenager and being told out of the blue one day that Mom and Dad are, in fact, Kremlin agents and that the whole family is being deported to Russia.

Riot Days by Maria Alyokhina (Allen Lane, 2017) is a harrowing account of the Russian state's persecution of the all-girl punk band Pussy Riot, written by one of its members. I'm indebted to this book for scenes in the novel that are set in a Russian women's prison.

I cannot recommend these books highly enough.

Acknowledgments

I'm extremely grateful to my agent, Antony Topping, who always had words of encouragement for me during the very long time it took to write this book, and to my editors at Vintage, Katie Ellis-Brown, Mikaela Pedlow, and Sam Matthews, who are professionals without peer. This novel would never have been finished without the love and support I've received from my parents, and from my friends, especially Jamal, Claudia, Philippe, and Martin. I have no words sufficient to thank you.

Credits

Vintage would like to thank everyone who worked on the publication of *RED STAR DOWN*

Agent
Antony Topping

Editor
Katie Ellis-Brown

Editorial
Anouska Levy

Copy-editor
Sam Matthews

Proofreader
Hugh Davis

Managing Editorial
Sam Stocker

Contracts
Gemma Avery
Ceri Cooper
Rebecca Smith
Humayra Ahmed
Kiran Halaith
Anne Porter
Hayley Morgan
Harry Sargent

Design
Dan Mogford

Digital
Anna Baggaley
Claire Dolan
Brydie Scott
Charlotte Ridsdale

Zaheerah Khalik

Inventory
Rebecca Evans

Publicity
Mia Quibell-Smith
Amrit Bhullar

Finance
Ed Grande
Aya Daghem
Samuel Uwague

Marketing
Ellie Pilcher
Mairéad Zielinski

Production
Konrad Kirkham
Polly Dorner

Sales
Nathaniel Breakwell
Malissa Mistry
Justin Ward-Turner
Ben Taplan
Lewis Cain
Nick Cordingly
Kate Gunn
Sophie Dwyer

Maiya Grant
Danielle Appleton
Phoebe Edwards
Amber Blundell
Rachel Cram
David Atkinson
Amanda Dean
Andy Taylor
Dan Higgins

Rights
Lucy Beresford-Knox
Celia Long

Beth Wood
Annamika Singh
Agnes Watters
Lucie Deacon
Liv Diomedes
Jake Dickson

Audio
Nile Faure-Bryan
Hannah Cawse

Thank you to our group companies and our sales teams around the world

About the Author

D. B. John has lived in South Korea and is one of the few Westerners to have visited North Korea. He co-authored *The Girl with Seven Names*, Hyeonseo Lee's *New York Times*-bestselling memoir about her escape from North Korea.